Spirits' Desire

The Legend of Draconis

Draconis Calls the Heart

in

Book II

By

Janet Taylor-Perry

Spirits' Desire
The Legend of Draconis
Draconis Calls the Heart
In
Book II

Dragon Breath Press, LLC
Ridgeland, MS

ISBN-13: 978-0999069202
ISBN-10: 0999069209

Other Books by Janet Taylor-Perry

The Raiford Chronicles:

Lucky Thirteen
http://amzn.to/1ld8grm
Heartless
http://amzn.to/1iWuYmP
Broken
http://goo.gl/6YTwyz
Whatever It Takes
http://goo.gl/1eLv66

The Legend of Draconis:

King Satin's Realm
http://goo.gl/wf7UbM

April Chastain Intrigues:

Wilted Magnolias
https://goo.gl/2oJOjc

Disclaimer

All entities in the following story are fictional. Any resemblance to any person living or dead is coincidence. Historical places and names are strictly for determining time setting.

Dedication

For Uncle Bill and Aunt Ruth (Ishee) for their abiding love. You showed me what it truly means to love. It is a gift from Heaven and should be cherished and nurtured. Thank you for being open vessels to the working of God. I love you from the deepest part of my soul. I know you now have your spirits' desires by being together in the presence of our Lord.

Also, for Bruce and Diane Perry, my *former* in-laws, but another shining example of true and enduring love.

Acknowledgements

I would like to extend a very special word of thanks to my friend, Sarai Storment, who translated all the passages that needed to be translated into Spanish, and then to Nidia Hernandez who made sure they were European Spanish rather than Mexican Spanish.

Thanks to my thenextbigwriter.com friends who stuck with this to the end, Nicholas Andrews and Rebecca Vaughn

To my two editors, Lottie Boggan and Christopher Stowe, I'd be lost without you.

Red Dog Writers, small group from Mississippi Writers Guild, and Mississippi Writers Guild, Central Mississippi Chapter, Mississippi Gulf Coast Writers, I appreciate your support more than words can say.

More appreciation goes to my daughter, Mary Catherine Perry and Nidia Hernandez for reading this in its infancy; and to Aunt Ruth for allowing me to read this over the phone to her many moons ago. Also to my other beta readers, Megan Fox, my proofreaders, Lottie Boggan, Mary Catherine Perry, and Rob Finney, and my ARC reader, Suzanne Hatch, merci beaucoups.

My family and friends, you give me strength and make me believe I can do this.

More thanks to:

William Shakespeare

Don Francisco for singing a song that inspired Morgan's dedication to her husband ("I Don't Care Where You've Been Sleeping").

French translations courtesy of freetranslation.com

Scripture passages from the King James Bible.

And once again, gracias, merci, danke, to my awesome cover man, Christopher Jurod Chambers. You can find him at juroddesigns.com.

Delight thyself also in the Lord: and He shall give thee the desires of thine heart.

Psalm 37:4

Contents

Part Four
Going Home

Prologue

The glistening gray dragon gently set the boat on the beach and wrapped his wings around the human that sat in it. The dragon smothered the man in his embrace and undying love. "Rennin! You are home! You are in truth home!"

"Smoke, I cannot breathe."

Smoke loosened his hold. "Rennin Drake O'Rourke, I'm so happy to see you. Welcome home. I knew you would come back, but where is everyone else? Morgan said you were coming."

"What do you mean she said I was coming?" Rennin caressed the shining brass urn. "Morgan has gone to her real Home, Smoke. I brought her ashes to scatter in our meadow. Of all the majestic places we saw, that simple meadow remained her favorite spot in all the world."

"Morgan came here some months back. She only stayed a day. She said she had finished her walk among the living."

Rennin smiled at the thought. "She would think to stop here." He heaved a great sigh, and answered the rest of Smoke's question. "Donovan and Cameron are living their own lives. I doubt they will ever come back here, but maybe someday, one of my descendents will make his way to this wonderful, mystical place.

"Smoke, tell me, by some miracle are my father and mother yet alive? What about Kieran? I feel him strongly still. And Ricardo? Does he live yet? Did his father arrive here safely?"

Smoke chuckled. "There are many still alive who will rejoice to see you and to hear all you have done and seen. The messengers told us much, but to hear your own words…I'm sorry, Rennin, but nobody here was able to send messages. We tried. Only Draco seems to be able to reach beyond this realm, at least at this time, and that directly to someone's mind."

"Then Draco *did* speak to Morgan and me. I have much to tell, but, Smoke, are Mam and Daidí still alive?"

"Yes, they and your uncle Colin and aunt Mary Kate and Ricardo and Danielle. We have lost only Alexander, Duncan, Priscilla, Elizabeth, and Pablo who did spend his last days with Ricardo, though they were few. Elizabeth died only last year. She became a powerful sorceress with longevity that accompanies such a gift. Ricardo has taken over all her duties, including training Seamus and Ginny, who married Seamus. There is also a very special lady here that you sent to us years ago. She has waited for you all these years."

Inaudible to all ears but a dragon's, Rennin barely whispered, "Kiandria. (Key-ahn-dree-ah)"

"Yes, Rennin."

With misty eyes, the tall distinguished gentleman that Rennin O'Rourke had become climbed onto the dragon's back. "Smoke, I only have a few items to carry. Right now, I want to go home. I want to hug my father and have my mother stroke my hair. Tomorrow I will scatter Morgan's ashes with all her loved ones present." He stroked the urn again.

"Do you think it would be wrong for me to love again? It would not be the same as my love for Morgan. Nothing can ever compare to that, but it would be a comfort in my old age."

As they flew, Smoke said, "No, it would not be wrong. Kiandria has had no other all these years."

"I told her not to wait for me, but to marry and have children. It's a shame that she wasted her youth and beauty on a fantasy."

"She has a son, Rennin. You know his father very well. I'm the only one on Draconis who knows who his father is. She has never confided in anyone else but me. Colin would be most displeased."

He slapped a hand over his mouth and spoke choked words through his fingers. "Smoke, I swear I never knew. There were very extenuating circumstances. Kiandria left immediately after we were together that one time."

"She has told me, but Colin isn't as lenient as I am. Tell me, Rennin—did Morgan know?"

"I never lied to Morgan. She knew everything and loved me in spite of myself. In all our years together, that was the only thing that I was ever ashamed of, Smoke. Even *that* Morgan understood. She and I had two more sons and one daughter, Duncan, Colin, and Rachel. What is my other son's name?"

"Kiandria named him Matthew, for she said he was truly a gift of God. He carries the last name of Oded."

"That is something I shall correct, but I do hope Uncle Colin is too feeble to give me another black eye. At this moment, though, I want Daidí to see his wild child has come home to settle down permanently."

Part One

Strange New Worlds

1
What's in a Name?

As the man with the wavy, sable locks and jade eyes stirred beans and fried salt pork, his two traveling companions roared into camp. Behind them, they dragged a tall, thin, yet well-endowed, mousy-brown-haired woman. She wore a buckskin dress, moccasins, and a feather woven into her hair. The braid indicated she was married; the feather showed who had won her favor.

The man preparing dinner calmly interrogated the other two. "What exactly is going on here?" He eyed the woman who thrashed and attempted to pull her wrists free. His eyes narrowed in recognition, for he had seen the woman once before. Instantly, his hand flew to the six-shooter by his side, and he asked a more urgent question. "Do you two fools have any idea who this woman is?"

The Rumpelstilskin-like Pierre Boudreaux triumphantly acknowledged, "Oui. We done and gote us Black Cloud's squaw!" He laughed menacingly.

The green-eyed man bellowed, "Are you crazy? Do you want to get all of us killed? Black Cloud will have your scalp!"

Pierre laughed again. "Naw! I gote heese!" He brandished a mop of long black hair that still dripped blood. "And now I will haf heese woman agin!"

Pierre planted a slobbery kiss on the woman even as the man who had been arguing with him rose to his full height of six and half feet. He held his back erect and displayed an expansive chest and massive arms. In a commanding voice, he spoke. "Pierre, take your hands off that woman. You are an *animal*. What do you mean 'again'?"

Bart Mercier, the other partner, restrained the man. "O'Rourke, let him be. Me an' him boff done had her tonight. We brung her to share wif you. She ain't nothin' but an Injun whore. I plan to have me some more of her, too, afore Pierre slices dat purty neck."

"Over my dead body." O'Rourke glared at Bart, and, with long deliberate strides, he reached Pierre and yanked him by the collar, throwing him several yards.

Angered, Pierre pulled a long knife from its sheath. "O'Rourke, are you really willin' ta die fer a piece of used Injun meat?"

O'Rourke gently pushed the woman's hair from her face and lifted her chin. Her lip was caked with dried blood and a big black bruise appeared on her cheek. Rage seeping from his tone, he addressed Pierre and Bart. "You idiots! This woman isn't Indian at all. Even if she were, she's a human being and deserves to be treated with dignity. You will *not* harm her." He looked kindly into two frightened, but soft, dove-gray eyes.

Bart laughed. "You're probly one of dem abolitionists, too. You don't thank niggers should be slaves."

O'Rourke spoke softly. "Slavery is inhumane treatment of one created in God's image."

Pierre was still angry. "O'Rourke if'n ya don't want none, mind yer own beezness an' let us haf some fun."

Continuing to look into the eyes of the terrified woman, O'Rourke said, "This *is* my business. You made it so. My God, Bart! How could you? She's not a day over sixteen."

"She's done been Black Cloud's squaw for nigh on a year. She ain't no blushin' virgin."

Pierre had had enough of what he considered O'Rourke's meddling. As he passed his knife from hand to hand, the air around him turned cold. He lunged at O'Rourke's back with his knife held high. The woman shrieked in warning.

Pierre's blade grazed O'Rourke's left shoulder. The two men struggled over the knife. For a man who was only five-feet and five-inches, Pierre was as strong as a bull elephant. O'Rourke had a fight on his hands, especially with the wounded shoulder. Pierre fought dirtier by throwing sand into O'Rourke's eyes. O'Rourke stood near the woman trying to clear his vision. Pierre lunged again with his knife, but, unexpectedly, the woman stuck her foot out and tripped him. Dropping his knife in the subsequent fall, Pierre reached into his boot for his Derringer. By then, O'Rourke had cleared enough sand from his eyes to see Pierre's intention. O'Rourke fired quickly from the hip, striking his target squarely in the chest.

O'Rourke growled, "Bart, do you want to be a part of this, too?"

Bart shook his head. "Jest gimme my horse, an' I'll be gone."

O'Rourke untied the rope from Bart's horse and sent him on his way. Bart slung over his shoulder, "O'Rourke, ridin' alone out here is real dangerous. You never know what kind of varmint will happen up."

"I'll keep that in mind, Bart. You had best remember how lightly I sleep."

"Don't fret, O'Rourke. I ain't plannin' to tangle wif da likes of you."

Bart rode off at a high gallop. O'Rourke turned to the woman and removed her fetters. As he massaged her hands gently to restore the circulation, he spoke compassionately. "You're safe now. I won't hurt you."

O'Rourke poured water from his canteen and carefully washed the dirt and dried blood from the woman's face. He talked soothingly as he worked. "What's your name? Mine is Rennin O'Rourke. Crude men call me O'Rourke, but my friends call me Rennin. You may call me Rennin."

The woman did not speak. Rennin thought perhaps she had lived with the Pawnee so long she did not understand him, yet he talked softly, gently, unthreateningly. "Tomorrow, I shall take you back to your village. I considered Black Cloud a friend, no, a brother." Rennin looked at the scar across his palm. He had mixed his blood with Black Cloud's many years before. "I'm sorry for your loss."

Gray eyes dropped toward the ground. Something akin to a sob escaped her throat. Almost inaudibly she said, "Rennin O'Rourke, I cannot return to my village. I would be an outcast for what has happened to me. Black Cloud is no longer there to protect me. Sleeping Fawn's family will no longer want me. I would become precisely what Pierre called me."

Rennin realized the seriousness of the situation. This woman would be demeaned among her tribe. She would be treated as if what Pierre and Bart did was her fault, and, perhaps, even be accused of being complicit in Black Cloud's death. In an attempt of kindness, Rennin said, "Then, tomorrow I shall take you to Ft. Laramie. Perhaps, you can find your family."

She laughed bitterly. "Rennin O'Rourke, I cannot live with white men either. You have seen how they will treat me. I thank you for your kindness, but it would be best if you simply leave me here to die for I have no people. I ceased to be Rebekah Sinclair ten years ago, and now I cannot be Eyes of a Dove either. I am no one, and I have nowhere to go."

Rennin's heart broke for the plight of this young woman. "Don't be silly. I shan't leave you here to die."

"Then, what am I to do, Rennin O'Rourke?"

The woman's plea for help did not go unheard by the man's kind heart, but he responded, "We'll think of something tomorrow, but right now let's eat something. I made supper for three. There is more than enough for two."

When he lifted the ladle, Rennin realized how deeply wounded his shoulder was, and he winced, dropping the ladle back into the pot. Suddenly, he felt gentle hands unbuttoning his shirt. The woman slipped the cloth from his shoulder. As he had done to her, she carefully washed his wound. She commented, "It is not very deep. You need some healing herbs, or you will get a fever. I will gather moss near the river. Rest until I return."

"It's already dark, Rebekah."

The woman smiled softly. "You may call me Rebekah, Rennin O'Rourke. Rennin is such an unusual name. How did you get it?"

He leaned against a boulder. "I'll tell you about it sometime, but right now, I think I'll rest. Take my gun to the river with you. Bart could be lurking around."

Rebekah gathered the moss she needed and bandaged Rennin's shoulder with a clean kerchief. She served them both a plate of beans and salt pork and a cup of coffee. "Now, Rennin O'Rourke, tell me about your name."

He laughed. "It's not an unusual name in my family. There have been many men named Rennin in my family, my grandfather for one, and several before him. Would you like to hear about the first Rennin O'Rourke? I actually have his exploits written in a book. I can read them to you."

"Yes, I would like that, Rennin O'Rourke."

"Please, just Rennin."

Rebekah smiled. "Yes, Rennin, I would like that."

2
A Traveling Companion

Rennin pulled a leather-bound book from his saddlebag. In the flickering firelight, he read about a mystical land where men and dragons were friends. The story told how an evil sorceress, Quazel, had come to the land; and how she had turned all the people into talking animals and tried to destroy all the dragons. Then, Rennin told the story of how Alexander O'Rourke, a wizard and a very distant ancestor of Rennin, had escaped to the mountains with a few gestating dragon eggs and how he had protected them for a new generation of dragons to be born. Rennin read how Alexander had battled wits with Quazel to protect the inhabitants of Draconis. He recited a prophecy that told of a tall man with green eyes, who was left handed and related to Alexander, who would come to deliver the land.

Pointing at his bandaged arm, Rebekah sat up very straight and gasped. "Rennin, you are tall and have green eyes, and you are left handed."

He laughed loudly. "No, Rebekah. I'm not the one the prophet meant. His story is in the book, too."

He placed a small slip of paper in the manuscript and closed it. Showing disappointment, she said, "You are stopping?"

He nodded. "We must get some sleep. I'll read more tomorrow night. We have several days to travel."

Chin jutted, lips firm, Rebekah said, "I will not go to the fort or back to the Pawnee."

He puffed out his cheeks and acknowledged her. "I understand. Perhaps the mission, but we will discuss it in the morning."

Rennin untied his bedroll, and Rebekah lay on the ground. He shook his head hard. "You're not sleeping in the dirt."

She questioned, "Do you wish me to share your blanket?"

"No," he said.

"You do not find me desirable?"

Flustered, Rennin said, "No. Yes. No, that's not it." He rubbed a hand down his face. "Rebekah, you are not my wife. It would be wrong."

She tilted her head to the side. "Why? Is it white man's law? I owe you my life, Rennin O'Rourke. The least I can do is give you myself."

"No, it's God's law. There's another book I'll read to you as we travel, too. Perhaps it will help you understand. Rebekah, you're a beautiful woman. I'll need to be strong in my convictions not to give in to temptation, but rules by which I govern my life tell me to be with anyone other than my wife is wrong. Do you understand?"

"Yes, I do. You are a man of honor. I am grateful."

Rennin took Pierre's bedroll from his horse. "I'll use Pierre's bedroll. He has no need of it now. I'll bury the lowlife tomorrow morning if the coyotes don't eat him. Use my bedroll. It's a bit cleaner. Get some sleep. Good night." He dragged the body to the edge of the firelight and threw a blanket over it.

Rebekah slipped under the blanket. For a long time she watched Rennin's back on the other side of the fire. She could tell he slept from his slow, even breathing. As she drifted to sleep she thought: *All of the men I have known, save Black Cloud who had also mentioned God's law, both white and Indian, would have taken advantage of me; but not this one. I will not leave him.*

Rennin awoke to the smell of frying salt pork and brewing coffee. For a moment, he was startled to see a woman kneeling by the fire until in an instant the events of the night before flooded his mind. He remembered that he had a body to bury, but not on an empty stomach.

It was early. The dew still lay on the ground, but the inviting smell made Rennin roll from his covers. He slipped on his boots noiselessly and approached the fire.

"Good morning, Rennin O'Rourke, Friend of Dragons."

He laughed heartily. "Rebekah, I've never seen a dragon except in my dreams and occasional flights of fancy. I don't even know if these stories are true. Perhaps, they were made up by someone with a lively imagination to entertain people."

"Oh, no," she said as she shook her head. "They are *true*, and I am sure that if you ever go to this land called Draconis, you will be welcome there because your forefathers protected the land and saved it from certain doom. They left you a legacy."

This woman's reasoning amused Rennin. "Perhaps you're correct. It's an interesting thought. What's for breakfast? Rebekah, are those eggs? Where did you get eggs?"

"Some settlers must have lost their chickens. I know where they roost. Rennin, or I think I will give you an Indian name in case you ever need one. You will be called Friend of Dragons. We should leave soon before the Pawnee look for Black Cloud and his murderers."

Rennin ate eggs, salt pork, and biscuits Rebekah had made. He said to her, "We'll leave as soon as I bury Pierre."

She grunted. "I say let the buzzards have a good meal."

He looked at her. "I understand how you feel, but that would be wrong."

Rennin buried Pierre in a shallow grave.

When he returned to camp, the mule was packed, and the horses were ready except for their saddles. Rebekah informed him, "I do not know how to saddle a horse. I have never used a saddle."

He said, "I'll teach you." He did.

When they had mounted their horses, Rebekah said, "Rennin, I have made a decision about where I am to go."

"Where is that?"

"I will go with you."

His jaw dropping, he exclaimed, "Rebekah! You have no idea where I'm going. You can't go with me."

She furrowed her brow and said, "Do not try to stop me. I will follow you if I must, but I will go with you."

He dismounted and held his hands up to the obstinate woman. "Get off the horse, Rebekah."

"Why? Are you going to tie me up and leave me here?"

"No. Get off the horse, Rebekah."

Knowing after the previous night, Rennin would not hurt her, she did as she was asked. He put his hands on her shoulders and stared at her stubbornly. She stared back defiantly.

Sensing he would not win the argument, he said, "The first thing we're going to do is get you out of that buckskin."

Rebekah looked at him with wide eyes. He became flustered again. "That's not what I had in mind!" He pulled a pair of pants and a shirt from Pierre's bag. He said, "Put on these. They might be a little big, but that will help to disguise you."

When Rebekah had changed clothes, Rennin twisted her hair and put it under Pierre's hat. Then he surveyed his handiwork. He sighed. "From a distance you might pass for a man; but if anyone gets close, they will see just how pretty you are. But it's the best we can do."

He stuffed the buckskin dress into Pierre's saddlebag, and the two rode west.

Each night when they made camp, Rennin read from the book his namesake had written. He related how Duncan O'Rourke had gone to Draconis and mistakenly thought he was the prophesied one, only to be changed into a panther who became King Satin.

Rebekah leaned toward him. "An actual panther? Not a Spirit Guide?"

"That's what the books says."

He read how Seamus O'Donnell had pretended to be Satin when Duncan needed to be himself and about the Draconian civil war.

"Oh, my!" Rebekah exclaimed. "Quazel was simply evil to want to enslave every one."

Rennin told how Diggory Danaher had been the only one of Duncan's crew to return to their home of Stonebridge, Ireland, and how Diggory had befriended Duncan's only son when he thought his mother had died.

Rennin presented the voyage that had taken Aidan O'Rourke and his wife Caitlin, along with their family and friends, Colin and Mary Kate Fitzpatrick and Diggory and Elizabeth Danaher and a little white cat called P.C. who turned out to be Pricilla O'Rourke, Aidan's mother, to Draconis. He retold the magic Elizabeth performed in order to save Mary Kate and Caitlin.

"She was more powerful than any medicine man," Rebekah whispered reverently.

He smiled at her enthusiasm and read about the kidnapping of Mary Kate's daughter and the family connections.

Rennin read about the pirate, Ricardo Morales and the change in his life. The story related how Ricardo helped to defeat his own blood relative—Quazel.

Rebekah applauded when Rennin read how Aidan had finally killed the wicked sorceress. She was spellbound when Rennin told how the demons that had inhabited Quazel had moved into Aidan and Ricardo. She clasped her hands in fright over her face as Rennin recounted the exorcism. She laughed and cried when Rennin read how the first Rennin had fallen in love with his cousin, Morgan, and how they had joined their lives. She was enthralled with the stories of Kieran and Miranda and Ricardo and Danielle. She said wistfully, "Maybe someday someone will consider me to be heart of his heart, though I cannot imagine a love so powerful."

This cold night by the fire, she anxiously awaited what would happen next after Rennin and Morgan left Draconis to conquer new worlds, but Rennin closed the book. Rebekah exclaimed, "They came to America! Or at least their children did. Do we have to stop? The words are so beautiful."

Rennin said, "I can teach you to read them for yourself."

"That would be nice, but I love to hear you read. I know my letters and can read a little. Teach me to read the other book. It's good, too. My father used to read from that book."

"All right, Rebekah, we shall have reading lessons."

Next morning was cold. Rebekah asked, "Rennin, where do you plan to winter?"

"What do you mean?" he asked. "I'm going to San Francisco."

With a knowing look and half-smirk, she asked, "Have you traveled this land this far west before?"

"No."

"Then listen to someone who has wintered ten times with the Pawnee. You cannot cross the mountains in winter. You must find shelter and wait until spring. We have, perhaps, one moon until the snows come. There is a deserted trapper's lodge about two days' journey north. They say it's haunted, but it's warm, and we can winter there. Rennin, the winters here are harsh and deadly."

"All right, Rebekah. We'll go to the lodge for the winter. I'll listen to you for you know this land better than I."

3
Refuge

The trapper's lodge was filthy and in need of repairs. For two days Rennin mended chinks in the logs and patched the roof while Rebekah cleaned and scrubbed. Thinking the place was finally livable, he built a fire in the fireplace. Within minutes, smoke billowed into the room. Rennin quickly put out the fire, and he and Rebekah ran out the door for air.

He lay on the ground, laughing. "I can't believe I forgot the chimney." He looked at Rebekah. She was covered in soot. He laughed harder. "Do I look as badly as you?"

Rebekah gave Rennin her hand to help him up, but he pulled her down instead. She landed on top of him. He wiped smudges from her cheeks. In that instant, Rennin realized his heart was pounding. He fought an overwhelming urge to kiss this woman. Rather, he fingered her feather, hesitant and unsure of himself as he had never felt this way before.

Rebekah broke the spell. "Rennin, I think we could use a bath." She took her cleaned buckskin dress and walked to the nearby spring.

Rennin sat up and put his chin on his knee. *Oh, God, give me strength. She's so beautiful. She's a widow. Are You trying to tell me something? How am I to spend a whole winter alone with her? I've spent almost two months with her as it is.*

The next few days Rennin hunted game and preserved it with the salt that had been left in the lodge and tanned the hides for furs and skins for clothing. Rebekah gathered berries and other wild fruits and dried them in the sun.

One evening in early November, Rennin came back with a large buck across his shoulders. Something was disquieting about the cabin. Rebekah usually came out to meet him, but there was no sign of her. He dropped the buck on the porch and kicked the door open.

Rebekah sat on one of the low stools in the cabin. A burly, bearded, barrel-chested man rubbed greasy hands across her hair.

Rennin aimed his long rifle, ready to fire. He commanded, "Take your hands off my wife."

The grizzled mountain man growled, "Your wife? You ain't Pawnee, boy. This gal has been with the Pawnee." He lifted Rebekah's feather. "I could swear this here feather has Black Cloud's markings. You ain't Black Cloud."

Rennin held his aim. "Eyes of a Dove *was* once Black Cloud's woman. Black Cloud is dead. She now belongs to Friend of Dragons. You may tell whomever you meet that she is mine. Now, take your hands off her before I shoot them off." He pulled the hammer back.

The trapper lifted his hands off Rebekah and picked up his belongings. "I have wintered in this cabin many a time. I can see that I will not be here this winter. I had hoped for a little extra warmth and comfort." He stalked from the cabin.

Rennin closed the door and dropped the latch into its hole. Rebekah ran to him and threw her arms around his neck. She buried her face in his chest and cried tears of fear and relief.

He soothed her hair and kissed the top of her head. "Did he hurt you, Rebekah?"

She checked her tears. "No, but I was so frightened."

Rennin held her hand, and they sat by the fire. He took her marriage feather in his hand. "Rebekah, I think it is time to get rid of this. You are no longer Black Cloud's wife. The feather only betrays you to some who would harm you."

She walked away from his piercing green eyes. "Rennin, why did you tell that man I was your wife?"

Feeling guilty, he stared at the floor. "I thought he would be more afraid of a jealous husband than a traveling companion."

"I see," said Rebekah with a hint of disappointment. "Rennin, I must tell you something. I am Black Cloud's widow, and I will wear his token unless I have another husband. I have been degraded enough. Rennin O'Rourke, I am with child."

"Oh," he groaned. His brows almost obscured his eyes when he drew them into a deep scowl. He whispered, "Rebekah."

"Rennin, I can only pray the child belongs to Black Cloud." She turned to face the man who had risen. "I am so afraid Bart or Pierre could be the father. What am I to do?" Her tears fell unbidden.

He pulled her into his arms. "Oh, Rebekah." He could feel his heart racing again and could stand it no longer. He held the woman's face in both his hands and turned her to look at his face. "Rebekah, remove Black Cloud's marriage token. Let me be your husband. Let me be this baby's father." He kissed her passionately. She responded without hesitation.

With trembling fingers, Rennin removed the feather from Rebekah's hair. She slipped from her buckskin dress and stood before him. Taking his hand, she placed it on her breasts and whispered, "Touch me, Rennin. I want to be your wife."

He ran his fingers across her breasts and pulled her to him, kissing her hungrily. He tore himself from her and breathlessly said, "Rebekah, please get dressed. I cannot lie with you until you are legally my wife."

Gentle hands touched taut shoulders. "By Pawnee custom, a man and woman need only agree to be bound before the girl's family. I have no family. You believe God governs your life. I agree before God now to be bound to you."

Rennin clenched the table in front of him. "Rebekah, I am not Pawnee. Oh, that I were! But if anyone asks, you are Rebekah O'Rourke. As God is my witness, you will be as soon as I can make it so."

4
A Winter's Tale

With dawn came winter's first snow. Rennin's feet crunched through a thin white blanket as he skinned and dressed the buck from the night before. He knew they had a great deal of preserved venison, squirrel, and rabbit; and he could cut through ice and fish after the spring froze. He would have to melt ice for fresh drinking water anyway, but still he worried about Rebekah. *She needs to eat well. She needs fruits and vegetables and milk. What about when spring comes? What business does a pregnant woman have traipsing over the mountains?*

Rennin hung the venison from hooks on the porch. They would eat this deer first because the weather was not quite cold enough to keep it from spoiling. Anything shot in the dead of winter would keep thanks to the bitter cold.

When he went inside, Rebekah handed him a steaming cup of coffee and massaged his frozen fingers. He sat at the small table and slipped his arms around her waist. He laid his head on her chest. She stroked his hair. Breathing deeply, he said, "Rebekah, you make this hard for me. Having your arms around me feels so good that it frightens me."

She planted a kiss on his head. "Rennin, may I tell you something?"

"Of course."

"I have never wanted a man until you. Not even Black Cloud, but I resigned myself to being his woman. At least he was good and kind to me. He never treated me as I saw some of the tsápaat being treated. He never treated me like property, and he never hit me. I am certain Sleeping Fawn's mother would have put him in his place if he had. Still, I did not love him like a wife should love her husband. Rennin, I love you."

He pulled her onto his lap. She laid her head on his shoulder. He caressed her cheek and kissed her gently. "I love you, too, Rebekah."

For a long time, they sat holding each other until Rennin asked, "Rebekah, tell me how you came to live with the Pawnee."

A shudder ran through her, and he held her tighter. "I was seven. By the way, I'm seventeen, not sixteen. We were traveling west. A Blackfoot raiding party attacked us. They killed my mother and father and my three older brothers. I hid." She shrugged. "I suppose they never knew I was there. I remember sitting alone for two days until a single Indian rode up. It was Black Cloud. He buried my family and even put crosses on their graves. I was surprised he spoke English so well. He must have been about fifteen. He took me back with him, and I went to live with Sleeping Fawn's family. He never took a wife until I was old enough. Then, he courted me. I suppose he loved me. I will confess I was very fond of him, and I would have been true to him. How did you know Black Cloud?"

"He came to the mission, where my father taught, to learn English." Rennin grinned at memories. "He was only three years older than I was. Since I was the only boy of seven children and youngest, we were drawn to each other. We became friends." Rennin held up his scarred hand. "We became blood brothers."

Rebekah touched his palm. "He told me he was blood brothers with a white man. I remember his scar."

Rennin laughed. "We used to get into such trouble. We would sneak off and go fishing or rock climbing. Father had a conniption when we came in with our hands dripping blood from the ritual. He lectured us about the foolishness of such a barbaric custom and the danger of infection. Trust me, a ten-year-old boy and a thirteen-year-old boy did not care. We were proud of our friendship."

He rubbed his cheek across Rebekah's shoulder. "Black Cloud must have been returning home from the mission when he found you. I saw you once when I came to visit Black Cloud. He pointed you out to me and told me he was taking you for his wife. Rebekah, even then I thought you were the most beautiful woman I had ever seen. I left thinking Black Cloud was a lucky man indeed."

"I remember." She nodded. "Black Cloud never told me who you were, but I could tell he thought highly of you. I only remember two other white men being welcome in his tent. One of them looked a lot like you, but he was older."

"That was my father, Rowan."

"I would like to meet him."

"He died last year. My mother died when I was born, and all my sisters are married. That's why I came west. Father always said I had the wanderlust just like my ancestors."

"Rennin, will you read to me now? We have not read in days."

"Get the book."

Through the long, cold winter, months, Rennin read most nights about the first Rennin.

Early before daybreak, the sloop carrying the family of four docked in Barcelona. Wearily, Rennin O'Rourke securely tied the line. Their journey had been long and treacherous, but treachery would become a familiar term to Rennin.

Rennin rested for a few hours before the businesses opened. He had a daunting task ahead of him. He had promised to claim the successful business ventures of Ricardo Morales for himself.

After Morgan O'Rourke fed her husband and two sons, Donovan and Cameron, Rennin left the boat to investigate the status of seven businesses Ricardo had deeded him. He returned several hours later full of excitement.

"Morgan, these businesses are worth millions. You should see the villa where Victor Jordan, Charlotte's father, lives. 'Tis next door to the Morales villa, but 'tis twice as grand. I understand why Ricardo was so angry. That man stole everything from Ricardo—his love, his fortune, his freedom, his honor, his dignity! I would like to strangle him myself."

Morgan put both her hands on Rennin's arms. "Honey, calm down. You cannot run into this without preparation. First, you need new clothes. You must look like a gentleman. Then, you must inform Ricardo's family of his safety and happiness. After that, I think it would be wise to seek advice from someone with legal expertise. This man is cold and ruthless. Remember what he did to Ricardo."

Rennin kissed his wife. "I knew I loved you for some reason. What would I do without you?"

For two days, Rennin had clothes made for his family. Then, they went to the Morales villa where Pablo Morales resided. Ricardo had given Rennin a letter to deliver to his father, which explained all that had befallen him. Rennin pulled the velvet cord by the door, and bells chimed resoundingly. A maid wearing a cap and apron opened the door.

In Spanish Rennin said, "Soy Rennin O'Rourke. He venido a ver Señor Pablo Morales a favor de su hijo, Ricardo." ("I am Rennin O'Rourke. I have come to see Mister Pablo Morales on behalf of his son, Ricardo.")

The maid showed the family into the foyer and went to deliver the message. She returned in short time. "Señor Morales te vera' en la biblioteca. Venga esta manera." ("Mister Morales will see you in the library. Come this way.")

She showed the O'Rourke family into a room that had three walls covered with books. Rennin stood in awe as he whispered, "This must be a little piece of Heaven."

A voice at the door said, "Ellos son solo libros escritos solomente por manos mortales." ("They are only books penned by mortal hands.") An elderly man leaning on an ivory-handled cane entered the library and summarily sent the maid to bring refreshments for his guests.

Pablo Morales extended his hand and in a heavily Spanish-accented English said, "Mr. O'Rourke, welcome to my home." He turned to Morgan. "Mrs. O'Rourke." He kissed Morgan's hand and bowed.

Rennin said, "Please, call me Rennin. This is my wife, Morgan, and our sons, Donovan and Cameron."

The maid returned with fresh baked cookies, bread and jam, spiced wine, and milk. Pablo closed the door behind her and turned eagerly toward Rennin. "You have news of my son? Is he alive and well?"

Rennin quickly allayed the old man's fears. "Yes, sir, he is quite well. Indeed, he is happy."

Pablo indicated chairs to his visitors. He poured wine for adults and milk for the boys. He showed the two children an area filled with wooden puzzles and left them to eat cookies, drink milk, and play. Then he joined Rennin and Morgan. "Please tell me about my son. Please tell me he is not cruel and wicked as I have been led to believe. He is wanted for murder both here in Barcelona and in Gibraltar. Rennin, you do not appear the sort that would associate with thieves and murderers. Please tell me you are my son's friend."

Rennin set down his cup. "Señor Morales, your son is my good friend and mentor. He has taught me many things. His language is only one example." He sipped the spiced wine.

"Sir, there was a time when Ricardo lived as a pirate. Barbarism was his way of life. However, all that has changed. Ricardo now lives on an island called Draconis. He plans never to return to Spain. He is very happy there.

"As you must know, many years ago, Ricardo was in love with Charlotte Jordan. Charlotte's father and the man she married conspired to have Ricardo sold as a galley slave, but before he was spirited away, he fathered a child. You knew her as Miranda Montgomery. She, too, is alive and well with her true father. She does not wish to return here either and asks that you never reveal her location.

"Ricardo has also married a wonderful woman, the former Danielle Martin. They have four children, Seamus, Richard, Leila, and Charlotte." He lowered his voice. "Ricardo is currently apprenticing in wizardry with my great-grandfather."

"Wizardry!" Pablo said in horror. "Please tell me he is not following in the footsteps of his Aunt Quazel, though you may know nothing of *her*."

"On the contrary," said Rennin, "I know her too well. Morgan is her great-granddaughter. Quazel is dead, and her evil is gone with her. Ricardo had a hand in vanquishing that evil. No, Señor Morales, Ricardo has become a good man."

Pablo leaned back in his chair and closed his eyes. "Then I may die in peace."

Rennin spoke kindly. "Sir, I would appreciate if you would stay alive a bit longer." He retrieved the letter and deeds from his coat pocket. "Ricardo asked me to deliver this letter to you, and he deeded all his business ventures to me. Might I impose upon you to help me find a barrister to see that they are properly and legally made mine?"

Pablo took the letter and put it inside his coat to read in private. Then, he looked over all legal papers Rennin had brought. "Rennin, I wish for you and your family to join me for dinner. I shall have my solicitor join us. I will insist that he see these franchises be turned over to you immediately. In all honesty, I would love to see Victor on the street with an alms cup in his hand."

That evening the O'Rourke family dined in high style with roasted pheasant, Spanish rice, asparagus with Hollandaise sauce, and chocolate mousse. After dinner, Pablo sent the children to the stables with his groomsman to see the horses. Meanwhile, he had his lawyer review documents Rennin had brought.

Juan Santiago, the lawyer, was a young man who had taken over his father's clients. He said that the papers were perfectly legal. All he needed to do was to file them with the magistrate. "¿Usted se da cuenta de que esto pelará a Victor Jordania de todo su riqueza y el poder, Señor Morales?" ("You do realize that this will strip Victor Jordan of all his wealth and power, Mister Morales?") he warned, unaware Rennin spoke Spanish fluently, and Morgan enough to survive.

Pablo replied, "Absolutamente. Será así como hizo a mi hijo. ¿Ahora, hay acción legal que puede ser traída contra Victor para reclamar falsamente qué no fue su y para poner a mi hijo por años del infierno?" ("Absolutely. It will be just as he did my son. Now, is there any legal action that can be brought against Victor for falsely claiming what was not his and for putting my son through years of hell?)

Thoughtfully, Juan said, "Supongo que podría ser acusado del secuestro; sin embargo, desde que ambos sus cómplices están muertos, no hay evidencia que corrobora menos la palabra de este hombre, un extranjero total". ("I suppose he could be charged with kidnapping; however, since both his accomplices are dead, there is no corroborating evidence except the word of this man, a total stranger.")

"Que tal carta de Ricardo?" ("What about Ricardo's letter?") asked Pablo.

Santiago addressed the elder man. "Podría discutir que la carta es una falsificación. Las Señor Morales, traten con un problema a la vez. Primero, veamos a transferir propiedades del negocio de Ricardo al del Señor O'Rourke." ("He could argue the letter is a forgery. Mister Morales, let us deal with one problem at a time. First, let us see to transferring Ricardo's business holdings to Mister O'Rourke.")

The lawyer spoke to Rennin in a condescending tone. "If you will give me the papers, I will file them in the morning, Mr. O'Rourke."

As Rennin started to hand documents to Santiago, Morgan softly touched his hand and shook her head. Rennin raised an eyebrow at her in question. Morgan spoke softly, but decisively. "Señor Santiago, my husband and I will meet you tomorrow morning at the magistrate's office. My cousin did not deed all of his holdings to my husband for him to hand the documents to anyone."

Taken aback by the woman's candor, Santiago said, "Do I sense some distrust on your part, Mrs. O'Rourke? Should I be the one detecting secrecy? I did not realize you were related to Ricardo Morales."

"Yes," said Pablo, "Morgan is my cousin. Do not be offended, Juan, but she is right. Those documents must not leave Rennin's hands until they are properly filed."

Stiffly, Santiago agreed. "Very well. Mr. and Mrs. O'Rourke, I shall meet you at nine o'clock. Señor Morales, I shall take my leave of you this evening. Thank you for a lovely meal."

Juan Santiago left the house and climbed into his coach. He fumed at "la impertinencia de esa mujer" ("that woman's impertinence."). As he passed the driveway to Victor Jordan's house, Santiago shouted to his driver, "Gire aquí dentro. Necesito hablar con el Señor Jordan." ("Turn in here. I need to speak to Mister Jordan.")

Meanwhile, Rennin asked Morgan, "What was that?"

Morgan looked at both men. "Frankly, I do not trust him. He treated you contemptuously, as if you were a bug that needed to be squashed. Were you not listening to what he said to Pablo? It was as if he were trying to convince Pablo of your dishonesty."

Pablo defended his attorney. "His father has handled my legal affairs for over thirty years!"

"Exactly!" reaffirmed Morgan. "His father, not he."

Rennin closed the book. Agitated, Rebekah said, "I do not trust him either. Why is he visiting the enemy? Rennin, don't stop!"

Rennin laughed. "Rebekah, it's after midnight! I'm sleepy."

He put his arm around her. She pouted, "I shan't be able to sleep. I'll worry about what underhanded scheme that Santiago is planning."

Rennin kissed the top of Rebekah's head. "Yes, you will. You'll close your eyes and dream of flying on dragons."

She sighed. "No. If I sleep, I shall dream of you. Always, I dream of you."

"Truly?" Rennin laughed naughtily. "What do I do in your dreams?"

She giggled. "I do not think I shall tell you, for then, *you* will not be able to sleep."

"Rebekah! Am I that bad in your dreams?"

Rebekah grinned slyly as she moved to her own blankets. "No, Rennin. You are quite good in my dreams. Good night. Sleep well."

He banked the fire, blew out the lantern, and climbed under his blankets to sleep, but he tossed and turned. He could not stop imagining what Rebekah might dream, and he longed to make her dream reality.

Finally, as dreaminess overcame him, he whispered, "I love you, Rebekah. I truly love you."

5
Surprises

Rennin was a light sleeper. Trickling water woke him. In the corner Rebekah was taking a spit bath because the spring had already begun to freeze, and there was no tub. She had stoked the fire to a blaze. Still, she shivered in early morning cold. Despite his intentions, Rennin could not tear his eyes from her. He studied every inch of her body, her every movement in predawn light. He closed his eyes tightly and prayed silently. *Oh, God, please help me. Please, give me a way to make this right. God, I'm only a man. I don't know how much more I can withstand. I love her, Lord, with all my heart. Please show me a way.*

Rebekah put on her borrowed pants and shirt, carefully cleaned her buckskin dress, and hung it over the back of a rickety chair. As if by a sixth sense, she turned toward Rennin. "How long have you been awake?"

He could not lie to her. "A while. I'm sorry. Forgive me, but I couldn't take my eyes off you. You are so beautiful."

Living as she had for the last ten years, Rebekah was used to lack of privacy, but she sensed it made Rennin uncomfortable. She sat beside him. "I will be sure to bathe when you're out since it distresses you, but soon you won't find me appealing as this child grows within me."

Involuntarily, Rennin placed his hand on Rebekah's abdomen. "How are the two of you feeling? You haven't been sick?"

She shook her head. "Only queasy, especially when I smell onions."

He chuckled. "Don't cook onions, and don't mind me. Bathe whenever you like. I'll learn to control myself."

Rebekah took a deep breath. "Rennin." She stroked his face. "I'm frustrated, too. I love you so. Perhaps soon your God will provide a way for us to be together, one that will pacify your conscience. If that happens before winter is over,

I shall believe He is real again. I used to believe when I was very young. I would like to believe as you believe."

He kissed her fingertips. "It will happen before winter is out. I have faith."

"Rennin, would it be wrong for me to lie in your arms for a while?"

"No. I would like to hold you forever."

Rebekah snuggled under Rennin's blanket and cuddled into his arms. He kissed her softly. She laughed lightly. "Are you growing a beard?"

"Should I?"

"It would keep you warmer, but it would hide your wonderful face. No, wear a scarf. I like your face, but not your bristly stubble."

He laughed and tickled Rebekah's neck with his chin. She squealed. Rennin teased, "I might keep my whiskers right where they are so I can tickle you."

"No! Please shave!"

He kissed her again. "I'll shave later. Right now, I'm busy holding the woman I love."

Rebekah laid her head onto Rennin's chest, and they were quiet. Before either of them realized what happened, they fell back to sleep.

Rebekah awoke with a start. "Rennin, where are you?" He was not beside her. She smelled coffee. Obviously, he was awake. "Rennin!" He was not in the cabin. The nightmare that had awakened Rebekah sent her into panic. She sprang from the pallet and burst through the door. "Rennin! Rennin!" Her voice was choked by tears.

Rennin emerged from the ramshackle barn. Barefoot and coatless, Rebekah raced through snow into his arms and sobbed. "Rebekah, what's wrong?" he questioned, embracing the nearly hysterical woman.

"Nothing now. You're safe."

41

Totally befuddled, Rennin said, "Of course, I'm safe. Why would you think otherwise? I only came out to feed the horses."

She shivered. Rennin scolded her. "Rebekah, you're freezing. Let's get out of the cold." Teeth chattering, she started into the barn. "No, lady. You may not go in there," he said as he blocked her way.

Suddenly, he realized she was barefoot. He picked her up in his arms and swiftly carried her to the fire. "Rebekah, are you crazy? You will catch pneumonia. What could have possessed you to run outside barefoot?"

"You weren't here when I awoke. I was so scared."

"Why?"

"I had a nightmare. You were lying in a puddle of blood with an arrow in your chest. You did not move."

Rennin held Rebekah close. "Oh, my love, it was only a dream. I'm just fine."

After a time, Rebekah relaxed and asked, "Why would you not let me into the barn?"

"It's a surprise. You know what happens next month, so don't be nosy."

Rebekah creased her brow. "What happens next month?"

"Christmas, silly."

"Christmas." Rebekah laughed. "I had forgotten Christmas. The last time I celebrated Christmas, I was seven years old."

"Well, we will celebrate Christmas, and St. Nicholas himself has commissioned me to make your gift."

"Rennin, I do not believe in Santa Claus."

"What? Shame on you! I guess you'll see."

From that day on, Rennin would not let Rebekah anywhere near the barn. Every night he returned with frozen fingers, so Rebekah started a little surprise of her own.

As Rennin came in from the barn, he had a hard time shutting the door against blustering wind. "It's colder than a witch's ti...It's cold out there. The wind has really kicked up."

Rebekah massaged his fingers as she chastised him. "Rennin, your fingers are frozen. Whatever you're doing out there cannot be worth losing your fingers. You nearly have frostbite. You will not go out there tomorrow."

"I have to feed the horses. Besides, I'm almost finished."

Rebekah slipped Rennin's hands inside her shirt. "I am *not* attempting to seduce you. I'm warming your hands."

"That's not all you're warming," he joked.

"Be quiet. I'm trying to save your fingers. Do you not realize how close you are to being frostbitten?"

He laughed. "They have been worse. I'll be fine. Would you like to release my hands now?"

"If I must."

Rennin slowly pulled his hands from her shirt. He took a deep breath. "How about some hot coffee and some time reading by the fire?"

"All right," she sighed as she poured the coffee.

Rennin turned Rebekah around. He kissed her passionately. "Rebekah, please help me get through this winter. I ache to be with you although I know it would be wrong."

She took his face in her hands. "I love you, but I will not allow you to compromise your values. Now, read to me."

Rennin opened the book and continued the story of his ancestors.

Rennin and Morgan, along with the boys, were waiting for Juan Santiago outside the magistrate's office, promptly at nine o'clock as indicated by the sundial in the square. Santiago was late by half an hour. He apologized, "I am sorry to be late. My coach had a loose axle this morning."

Rennin controlled his irritation and the group entered the magistrate's office. Behind a counter sat a stern-looking, gray-haired man. The older man greeted Santiago cordially. Santiago explained Rennin's situation, and the older man examined the documents.

Speaking in stilted Spanish, he said, "Mister O'Rourke, these are very old papers. I am sure I have copies on file, but it might take some time to find them. Come back after lunch, and I should have the matching documents by then." The older man started to the back with Rennin's deeds.

Rennin detained him, speaking the language with ease. "Sir, I would not like to let my copies out of my sight. I do not mean to impugn your character, but the history of these papers warrants caution."

The older man cleared his throat. "I understand. You and Mister Santiago are welcome to help me search for copies, but since it could take a while, perhaps, Mistress O'Rourke and the children would like to do some shopping or study some lessons."

Rennin said, "Go ahead, Morgan. I'll meet you at Señor Morales's for dinner." Morgan took the boys to her cousin's and Rennin entered the back of the magistrate's office with the older man and Juan Santiago.

In the dimly-lit file room, Rennin vaguely made out a man lying unconscious on the floor before he felt a crashing blow to the back of his head and saw nothing but darkness dotted by pinpricks of light.

Rennin awoke to cold and damp and blackness. He was bound hand and foot and gagged, and the silence around him was deafening. He strained all his senses to figure out where he was, and he felt gentle listing of the ocean. *The hold of a ship!* Ricardo's stories flooded Rennin's brain as he struggled against his bindings to no avail.

Hours later, light filled the hold. The magistrate accompanied it. "Mr. O'Rourke, let me introduce myself. I am Victor Jordan. Did you really think you could prance in here and destroy my life? I fear you are about to suffer the same fate as Ricardo Morales. By morning you will be a wanted man because our poor old magistrate was hit a bit too hard. You killed him. In less than half an hour, you will be on your way to the auction block in Algiers. Someone as young and strong as you will bring a tidy sum."

Rennin lashed at Victor with his bound feet as his emerald eyes flashed anger. Victor continued his little speech. "Oh, do not concern yourself about your pretty young wife. Like my daughter, she will move on with her life, probably with a handsome man like Juan Santiago. He finds her fascinating. She will be fine if she keeps her mouth shut, but no one will believe her story. After all, she is the descendant of a witch and the cousin and wife of known murderers. It would be better for her if Pablo spirited her and her two brats away. Now good-bye, Mr. O'Rourke." Victor slammed the hatch, and a few minutes later, Rennin felt the ship lurch as it left dock. His heart sank, yet his mind prayed and his spirit called out to Morgan.

By nightfall Morgan O'Rourke was in panic. Pablo Morales had sent his servants in every direction to search for Rennin. He was nowhere to be found.

Juan Santiago said that he left Rennin at the magistrate's office to go to another appointment, but returned an hour later to discover the magistrate dead and no sign of Rennin. Both copies of the deeds were missing. The constable immediately issued a warrant for Rennin in connection with the death of the magistrate.

When Morgan saw the magistrate's body, she grabbed Pablo's arm. "That was not the man we saw this morning."

"What do you mean?" asked Pablo.

Morgan described the man she had seen that morning.

"Dear God!" exclaimed Pablo. "That was Victor Jordan. Come home with me, Morgan. I fear for your safety. I can protect you under my roof."

Morgan and the boys moved in with Pablo, and they began their own investigation into both Rennin's disappearance and the magistrate's death.

After two days, Morgan took it upon herself to visit Victor Jordan. Victor invited her into his parlor.

"Mrs. O'Rourke, how may I help you?"

She leveled a cold, icy stare at the man. "I want to know what you did with my husband."

"I beg your pardon, Madame. I know neither you nor your husband."

"Mr. Jordan, do *not* play games with me. You know exactly what I mean."

Victor smirked cockily. "Mrs. O'Rourke, you are young and beautiful. I suggest you consider yourself a widow and start a new life. Your husband has gone the way of his friend, Ricardo; but this time my nemesis will *not* return. There is no use in your trying to prove anything, either. It is my word, the word of a respected, wealthy merchant, against yours, the wife of a suspected murderer and the cousin of a known murderer."

Morgan calmly took a step toward Victor and whispered, "Mr. Jordan, do not underestimate me. I may be small and fragile in appearance, but I am far stronger than you realize. Mayhap this is a good time to remind you that I am the great-granddaughter of both a sorceress and a wizard, and that I spent fifteen years of my life training in the black arts. Do not trifle with me." She turned and walked with a measured, steady gait to the door of the parlor. Pausing, she turned. "You have exactly one month to return my husband, or I shall unleash a wrath so great you will be decimated." She left through the front door with a bang. Her heart raced, and she felt her legs to be twine. Still, she kept her pace until she entered the door of the Morales home where she sank to the floor and wept.

Victor stared after Morgan in awe until he could see her no more. *Could this petite quiet woman be that formidable in magic?* He laughed nervously to himself. He dared not report her threat for fear of his own discovery.

Rennin was dragged onto the deck of a ship along with several other strong young men. Obviously, he was about to be auctioned off to the highest bidder. He surveyed his potential buyers, and his eyes alighted on a dark woman who wore a veil and haggled in French about being allowed to bid. He spoke in French. "Laisser l'offre de femme. De vous quels sont craintif? Son or est-il une création d'alchimistes" ("Let the woman bid. What are you afraid of? Is her gold a creation of alchemists?")

The captain of the ship started to strike Rennin, but the woman shouted, "Arret! Je celui-ci acheterai pour un mille denars avant vos debuts d'encheres. Je mets pense avec son attitude de irreverent il prelevera beaucoup sur le bloc d'encheres." ("Stop! I will buy this one for one thousand denars before your auction starts. I do not think with his irreverent attitude he will fetch that much on the auction block.")

The captain was a greedy man. He had hoped for eight hundred for the blond one, but a thousand? Victor Jordan need never know the actual price. "Le faire quinze cent." ("Make it fifteen hundred."), he dickered.

The woman stepped forward and ran her hands over Rennin's hard muscled body. "Est-ce qu'il parle toutes autre langues?" ("Does he speak any other languages?")

Rennin answered for himself in French. "I speak French, Spanish, and English, and I can read Latin."

The woman raised an eyebrow. "What are you doing on a slave's auction block?"

"I shall gladly tell you that at another time if you pay this man's price."

"You have no intention of remaining a slave, do you? How do you intend to repay me what I spend?"

This woman does not play games. I like her. "I am wealthy enough in my own right. I can afford to repay you."

The woman said to the captain, "Je vous donnerai douze cent." ("I'll give you twelve hundred.")

"Treize." ("Thirteen.")

"Douze cinquante." ("Twelve fifty.")

The transaction was made and the captain pushed Rennin toward the woman with his hands still bound. "Untie him" she demanded. "He will not run away. He is a man of honor. I can tell."

The captain removed Rennin's restraints, and Rennin followed the woman through the crowd. When they were clear of the mob, the woman spoke authoritatively. "I am Princess Kiandria Oded. I need a male servant. You will come to my palace where we will discuss terms of your eventual release. What do they call you?"

"Je suis Rennin O'Rourke." ("I am Rennin O'Rourke.")

"Very well, Rennin. I need you at least until I secure my husband. Is it agreed?"

"How long will it be?"

The princess glowered at him. "Hopefully less than a year. Rennin, I am not a harsh mistress, and I shall grant you your freedom once my future is settled. Until then, I own you. You will do my bidding. My father is not so gracious as I am. Do not betray me, or I will sell you to him. Am I clearly understood?"

"Tres!" said Rennin angrily. ("Very!")

"Bon, et ne pas essayer se d'echapper. Etre patient. Je promets je vous libererai. Venir cette facon." ("Good, and do not try to escape. Be patient. I promise I shall free you. Come along.")

Rebekah stomped her foot as Rennin closed the book. "No! I want to know what happened to *that* Rennin. Did Morgan turn Victor into a toad?"

Rennin laughed. "I love you, Rebekah Sinclair. You are extraordinary. We have all winter to read."

6
Misplaced Vengeance

Early winter in the mountains was brutal. Wave after wave of blizzards hit the small cabin. Rennin and Rebekah were snowbound. For a month, he was unable to hunt, forcing them to eat some of the preserved meat they had hoped to save for the spring.

Still, in the severe cold, Rennin spent hours in the barn making Rebekah's surprise. In the afternoons and evenings, he read the first Rennin's story and taught Rebekah to play dominos, chess, and poker, and to read.

Late one afternoon in early December the snow finally stopped and the wind subsided. Rennin burst through the door with a triumphant grin. He sported a string of trout he had caught ice fishing.

"Did you clean them?" Rebekah asked.

"Not yet."

"Please clean them outside." For the first time, Rebekah ran from the cabin and vomited.

Rennin cleaned and cooked the fish. Rebekah gratefully ate what he had prepared. "I'm sorry, Rennin, but the fish smell was worse than onions."

He touched her face. "There is nothing for which to be sorry. You are *not* my slave. You're the woman I love. I enjoy taking care of you."

She stood to clear the table and kissed him.

He held her hand. "Leave the dishes. I'll do them later. Sit with me." Rebekah snuggled by the fire with Rennin. He told her, "I'm going hunting tomorrow if the weather stays clear. I want turkey for Christmas."

"I can cook that."

Wrapping his arms around her, he asked, "Do you want to read?"

Rebekah sighed, "In a minute. This is much nicer."

"Yes, it is, but I thought you would be chomping at the bit to find out what happened to my namesake."

"I'm afraid of what the princess will want Rennin to do. I would scratch out her eyes if she had my Rennin."

He pushed back slightly. "Rebekah, are you the jealous type?"

"Let some other woman touch you and find out."

Rennin chuckled. "I think I like your being jealous. I think I like it a lot."

Rebekah ran her fingers through his hair that now hung to his shoulders. "I have never loved anyone like this before."

They sat for a long time simply listening to each other's heartbeats. On this night, the story could be left on the shelf. Rennin held Rebekah, and he realized she had fallen asleep. Then he gently and lovingly covered her with a blanket and washed the dishes. From his saddlebag, which hung by the door, he pulled a leather-bound journal and began to write. He stopped and smiled toward the sleeping woman. Pensively, he asked, "Rebekah, do you think a hundred years from now our descendents will be as thrilled to read about our lives as you are to read about those of old?"

The morning dawned cold, but clear. Rennin bundled into an extra pair of flannel long-johns, wool socks, and his fleece-lined coat. Rebekah made the heartiest breakfast she could. Using some of the dried apricots, she made a pastry sprinkled with sugar and served it with venison sausage and hot coffee. Rennin left with high hopes after a kiss for luck in the doorway.

Neither of them was aware a pair of eyes watched them. Nor was Rennin aware that a lone man followed him.

Rennin had a successful hunt. He bagged two turkeys and three rabbits. He could taste rabbit dumplings or maybe rabbit stew. With child-like enthusiasm, he triumphantly called as he neared the cabin, "Rebekah! Come see what I got!"

In a clump of evergreens, the solitary figure that had followed Rennin all day nocked an arrow into his bow. As Rebekah opened the door of the cabin, her sharp eye caught the glint of sunlight on the head of the aimed arrow. "Rennin!" she screamed in horror and ran toward him just as the arrow released.

"Rebekah!" Rennin dropped his game as she slumped into his arms, an arrow protruding all the way through her upper left shoulder. "Rebekah...Rebekah...Rebekah."

Weakly, she stammered, "At least my nightmare did not come true."

The next sound Rennin heard was a wild whoop as a lone Indian charged him with a flailing tomahawk. Rennin laid Rebekah down and flipped his assailant over his shoulder. Before his attacker could stand, Rennin grabbed the slightly smaller man and slammed him into the side of the barn. The Indian lay unconscious in the snow.

Rennin carefully lifted Rebekah and carried her inside where he broke the rear of the arrow shaft and lovingly removed the blood stained buckskin dress she wore. Rebekah moaned as pressure was applied to her wound, and her eyes fluttered open. Rennin covered her with a blanket and smoothed her hair as he soothed, "It's all right, Rebekah. I'm going to get the arrow out as soon as I get some hot water."

At that moment the door burst open. There stood Rennin's would-be assassin. Rennin turned his fury on him. "Running Bear! Have you absolutely gone crazy? What were you thinking?"

"I have been tracking my brother's killers for three months. I never thought I would find you, Rennin O'Rourke!" Running Bear snarled through clenched teeth.

Enraged, Rennin pinned Running Bear to the wall with his forearm across the Indian's throat. "You think I killed Black Cloud? You fool!" Rennin released the man and held up his palm. "Black Cloud was my brother, too. I never would have done anything to hurt him. In fact, I killed the man who *did* kill him. But"—He took a steadying breath—"I swear to God, if Rebekah dies, I *will* kill you."

"If you did not kill my brother, what are you doing with his wife?" Running Bear demanded to know.

"I rescued her from the man who killed Black Cloud."

"Then she has been safe with you. Perhaps I misunderstood what I witnessed this morning. I have come in search of Eyes of a Dove to take her into my lodge. Since she was raised Sleeping Fawn's sister, I have the right to take her as my wife also. Black Cloud would want her protected."

"You did not misunderstand. I love Rebekah very much, and I plan to marry her. She does not wish to return to your people. Running Bear, you *cannot* do that to her." He swallowed a lump in his throat. "She is with child. The child may not belong to Black Cloud."

"You have made her your whore?" Running Bear shouted in anger and disbelief.

Rennin ground his teeth. "Don't you ever call her that again! As long as we have known each other, you should know me better than that. I would never lie with Rebekah until she is my wife. The man, who killed Black Cloud, and his friend ravished her. She could not bear the humiliation of going back to your people. She wanted to die." He removed the water from the fire.

"Running Bear, your intentions are honorable, but how could Eyes of a Dove live if this child turns out to be white? She would be viewed as a harlot, although it was not of her doing. You could not love her or her child."

"I *do* love her. I don't care who sired her baby. I will be the child's father. You have not embraced as many of the white man's beliefs and customs as Black Cloud did, but you know we were blood brothers; therefore, let me bring Rebekah into my lodge to be my wife. I will protect her *and* love her. I think Black Cloud would approve."

Running Bear looked compassionately at the semiconscious woman. "What if the child is Pawnee?"

"He will be my child and have my name, but I will gladly tell him of his noble father who died before he was born."

"I did not intend to harm Eyes of a Dove."

"No, I was your target. Running Bear, perhaps you should be sure of your facts before you decide to seek vengeance."

"I am sorry, Rennin O'Rourke, and I am grateful that you have avenged my brother's death. Let me help you care for Eyes...Rebekah. She will make you a fine wife."

Rennin's eyes lit up. "You are forgiven, my friend, and I would be grateful for your help. I will need to cauterize the wound as we remove the shaft. Then, we will have to pray no infection sets in."

Rennin boiled water, and then the two men removed the arrow and cauterized the wound in Rebekah's shoulder with the heated blade of Rennin's hunting knife. Then, Running Bear dressed the game Rennin had shot. He stretched the rabbit skins to dry for the fur would make warm gloves or boot linings.

After that, both men sat by the sleeping woman to await her recovery.

Near dawn Rebekah groaned, "Rennin?" Both men started from a light slumber. Rennin took her hand.

"I'm right here, darling." She clutched his hand.

"Running Bear?" she asked timidly.

"I am here, too, Eyes of a Dove."

Rebekah tightened her grip on Rennin's hand. He comforted her. "It's all right. Running Bear was confused when he came here, but he understands everything clearly now."

"Everything, Rennin?" Rebekah whispered.

Running Bear answered her. "Yes, everything, Eyes...Rebekah."

Rebekah was stunned into silence as she heard Running Bear use her English name.

Running Bear continued to speak softly, without intimidation, to his sister-in-law. "Rennin has discussed with me that he, too, is Black Cloud's brother. We have agreed that in your case, he is the better brother to take you into his lodge to be his wife. I will make it right with Sleeping Fawn's mother. Do not worry. I meant you no ill will when I came. I mean you none now. It is understood Eyes of a Dove died with her husband, and Rebekah Sinclair was reborn. You are free to go with Rennin if that is what you want."

"It is," Rebekah affirmed. "Thank you, Running Bear."

"If the child you carry proves to be Black Cloud's, you will tell him of his father?"

"I will tell him what a great man his father was and what a generous man his uncle is. If he wishes to come to his people when he is old enough, I will not hinder him."

"You are a strong and courageous woman, Rebekah Sinclair. My brother and Rennin O'Rourke are lucky men, indeed."

Rebekah went back to sleep, and Rennin and Running Bear slept soundly for a few hours before the sun rose high in the sky. When Running Bear determined that Rebekah would recover, he prepared to leave, but Rennin asked him to stay. "Running Bear, you no longer have a quest to fulfill. Winter with us. Return to your people in the spring. Besides, you are the answer to my prayers."

Running Bear laughed skeptically. "How can I be the answer to a white man's prayers?"

"Running Bear, Rebekah is a beautiful woman, and even with all my good intentions, I *am* a man. The temptation to lie with her has been strong, especially knowing she would not refuse me. Your presence will help me to keep my virtue. I want to marry Rebekah. In the spring, we can find a minister to marry us."

Running Bear grunted. "By spring, Rebekah will be heavy with child. Your white minister will scoff at your so-called virtue. He will assume you have committed immoral acts. He could even refuse to marry you."

"I will explain that Rebekah is a widow and that the child belongs to her husband."

Running Bear argued, "You would be better off going before Sleeping Fawn's mother and letting me vouch for you."

"Perhaps," Rennin conceded, "but I still believe in miracles. I think my God will give us a way to be married before anyone can tell Rebekah is pregnant. Nonetheless, I still want you to winter with us."

Doubtfully, Running Bear said, "I will stay just to see if you get your miracle. If you do, perhaps, I will believe as Black Cloud believed."

When Rennin told Rebekah that Running Bear was going to winter with them, she replied, "It is a good thing you are not roaming in the blizzards, Running Bear. I would not wish for you to meet Black Cloud so soon. Rennin, Running Bear will also enjoy the stories about your ancestors. Why do you not read to us now? The stew must simmer for several hours."

"Very well," said Rennin. He gave Running Bear a brief synopsis of the story. Running Bear was fascinated, so Rennin began where he had left off.

A month passed, and Morgan awoke early. She dressed in solid black. At breakfast, she asked, "Pablo, are you ready to watch Victor Jordan squirm?"

"Morgan, what do you plan to do?"

"I'm going to get him to tell the truth. Will you trust me?"

Pablo smiled wryly. "I more than trust you. I look forward to watching the man suffer and his eventual demise."

Morgan grinned mischievously. "Let's go, Cousin." She turned to Donovan. "Bring me the vials from my bureau and Nana's black satin cape." Donovan returned with the cape that once belonged to Elizabeth Danaher when she attempted to deceive her own mother, the evil sorceress, Quazel, and a vial containing a white powder and one containing a clear liquid. Then, Morgan, her two sons, and Pablo Morales walked to their neighbor's house.

Morgan rang the bell at Victor Jordan's villa. When the servant answered the door, she said, "Permita por favor que el Victor Jordan sabe que ese Morgan O'Rourke ha venido a preguntar si él está listo para decir la verdad y volver a su marido. Usted lo puede decir que es innecesario para él entretenerme. El necesita sólo contestar mi indagación." ("Please let Victor Jordan know Morgan O'Rourke has come to ask if he is ready to tell the truth and return her husband. You may tell him it is unnecessary for him to entertain me. He needs only to answer my inquiry.")

The butler returned after a short time. "Señora O'Rourke, Señor Jordan desea que mí transmita esto mensaje corto y enigmático a usted. El dice decirle 'Caer muerto.'" ("Señora O'Rourke, Señor Jordan wishes me to convey this short and cryptic message to you. He says to tell you to 'Drop dead.'")

"Gracias," Morgan said. With measured pace, she walked onto Victor's well-manicured lawn where she spread her cape and knelt. She poured the contents of the vial containing the white powder into her hand and held her hands skyward. She spoke loudly. "Dominus mei Deus potentia veritas increbresco." ("O Lord, my God, may truth prevail.") Then, she blew the powder in her hand toward Victor's house.

Victor watched all this from his window, and he quickly shut his drapes.

Morgan and her small entourage started home. When they rounded the hedge out of sight, Morgan sent Cameron through the bushes to the drinking water barrel into which he poured the contents of the second vial.

Pablo cautiously asked, "What was in these vials?"

Morgan handed him the vial that had held the white powder. "You tell me. Smell it."

He sniffed. "Why, this is nothing but talcum powder. What is the other one?"

"Syrup of ipecac."

"Morgan, you have not performed any magic at all," said Pablo, mouth agape.

"Victor doesn't know that, and he and his whole household will be very sick quite soon. He will think I have cast a spell on him. Day after tomorrow, castor oil goes into the water. I do have stronger items I can use if he forces me to, such as opium and ergot. If these do not work, I shall manage to scratch him with curare. Pablo, all this is to prick his conscience. My true power lies in the prayer. I have witnessed the awesome power of God Almighty. I've seen Him return my uncle from the land of the dead. I've seen Him vanquish cursing, screaming demons. I've seen Him melt the heart of stone and change it into the heart of a kind and loving man, Ricardo. Victor Jordan is no match for my God."

By nightfall, every member of Victor Jordan's household had vomited repeatedly. The more water they consumed, the more they vomited. The doctor could not explain the suddenness of the attack or the widespread effect.

Victor lamented, "It was the witch next-door."

Two days later, Morgan made sure Victor saw her in Pablo's garden where she arranged feathers in a pentagram. Silently she prayed, *Lord, if what I'm doing is wrong, forgive me, but I want that man to be afraid, very afraid.* Aloud, she prayed again, "Dominus, punctum conscientia et fervefacio viscus possessio Victor Jordan." ("Oh, Lord, prick the conscience and melt the heart of Victor Jordan.")

While Victor and his servants watched the small, unintimidating woman, Donovan poured castor oil into the water supply. Once again, by nightfall the doctor was called to Jordan's home. The entire household suffered from unexplained diarrhea.

A week later, the doctor returned to see Victor because he experienced severe chest pains. Morgan declared, "I had nothing to do with this, Pablo, unless his heart cannot stand the fear he must be feeling."

Meanwhile, Rennin resided in plush accommodations and ate plenteously. Princess Kiandria was true to her word—she was not a hard mistress. On the contrary, she enlisted Rennin's services to tutor her in both Spanish and English and to teach her to read Latin. In turn, she taught Rennin rudimentary Arabic.

She boasted that she would be invaluable to her future husband if she could speak four languages and read contracts produced in Latin. As a matter of fact, the only manual labor Rennin was required to perform was to walk through the luxurious gardens or ride with his mistress and care for her horses. Rennin waited each day for some other tragedy to befall him. His greatest fear was that the king would decide to force him into permanent servitude and turn him into a eunuch, as many of the servants had told him to expect. The handful of other male servants for Kiandria were eunuchs.

As many months passed, Kiandria often shared her dreams with Rennin, and he told her about Morgan and his sons and Draconis. Most of their conversations took place in French, unless one was testing the other on a different language.

"You love your wife very much, don't you, Rennin?" Kiandria asked one day as they rode across her father's demesne.

"Oui, elle est ma vie." ("Yes, she is my life.")

Kiandria sighed. "Arab men do not always love their wives. Women are often viewed as property. I am lucky. Ammar professes to love me."

"Unfortunately, that can be said of other societies as well. Princess, you are a wonderful woman. I think Ammar is the one who is lucky."

"Vraiment?" ("Really?") questioned the princess. Then, she did something strictly forbidden. She removed her veil. "Rennin, if you were unmarried, could you love me?"

His jaw dropped. He looked at her liquid black eyes, her perfect smile, her glossy raven hair, and her deep brown complexion. He pondered the question for he had never contemplated the thought.

"Rennin, why do you hesitate so long?"

"Kiandria," he addressed her by her first name. "A man that could not love you would be a fool. Not only are you kind and loving, but you are extraordinarily beautiful also."

Suddenly, Rennin found himself knocked from his horse. He was at the mercy of a very large black man, holding an ivory handled janbia to his groin.

Rennin swallowed the rising bile in his throat. *This is it. There goes my manhood. Will Morgan love me anyway?*

Kiandria screamed, "Ammar! L'arreter!" ("Ammar! Stop it!")

The princess's angry and jealous fiancé spat vehemently, "This infidel has seen your face, something that not even I should have seen yet! Allah is displeased."

"Bah, Allah!" defied Kiandria. "You know I prefer the Christian God. You should, too, if you want to compete in the European market. Rather than threatening Rennin's life, you should be thanking him. He has been teaching me Spanish, English, and Latin, making me an invaluable wife."

"Il est un homme, Kiandria!" ("He is a man, Kiandria!")

"A man with a wife and two children, all of which he loves very much. Ammar, you are acting like a jealous fool. Now, let my friend go."

"Your friend? I thought he was your servant."

"Temporarily. When you and I are wed, he is free to go back to his family. It is our agreement."

Ammar pushed Rennin from him. "Kiandria, put your veil back on before someone else sees you." She complied with a tisk and a shake of her head while Ammar commanded, "Rennin, do not refer to the princess in such familiar terms again."

Haughtily, Rennin answered, "Je ne reverais pas de cela, Sheik Ammar." ("I would not dream of it, Sheik Ammar.")

"Prince Ammar." Kiandria's fiancé glared at Rennin, who in turn gave a tight-lipped smile.

He turned to Kiandria. "Princess, the answer to your question is 'yes,'" he responded to the woman in English, just to gall Ammar for he felt sure the prince could not understand what was being said.

Kiandria's eyes danced. "I am glad. Rennin, you may return to the palace. Ammar will ride with me for a while."

The prince scowled at the conversation he had difficulty understanding.

Later that night Rennin knocked softly at the princess's chamber. She answered, without her veil and dressed in bedclothes.

"Rennin, what are you doing here?" Kiandria whispered as she pulled him into her rooms and shut the door. "Ammar is not the only one who would kill you if you were found here. My father would have you beheaded at sunrise. What could be so important?"

"I have brought you something." Rennin handed Kiandria maps showing the way to Draconis. "L'anglais, Kiandria. Parler l'anglais si n'importe qui écouter ne comprendra pas. ("English, Kiandria. Speak English so anyone listening will not understand.") I fear your life with Ammar will not be the fantasy you hope. No, I fear it will be a nightmare. If it becomes too hard, hire a ship and go to Draconis. You will be free there. Men and women are treated equally. There are all races there. None is considered better than another, and the majority of the people have chosen to be Christian. Tell them you are a friend of mine. They will welcome you with open arms."

"Rennin, do you care so much for my happiness?"

"Yes, Kiandria, I care for you. I want you to find the happiness you deserve."

She caressed his cheek. She whispered shyly, "Rennin O'Rourke, first thing tomorrow I will sign the paper granting your freedom, but will you do one thing for me tonight?"

"Of course."

"Kiss me just once. You must know in your heart I have fallen in love with you. I ask only a kiss from you. Then, tomorrow I will give myself to a man that I can never completely love, and you can return to the woman you cannot stop loving."

He touched Kiandria's cheek. Then, he took her in his arms and kissed her, one long-remembered kiss. "Au revoir, Kiandria."

Rennin returned to his quarters and wept. *Morgan, I am so sorry. It was necessary to ensure my freedom. As kind and beautiful as Kiandria is, I'm sure she could be just as vindictive if she felt betrayed. I am sorry, my love. It was only a kiss. My heart belongs to you.*

Kiandria stood with her back to her door and her hand to her lips. She spoke to the zephyr. "Oh, Rennin, je souhaite nous avait recontre dans un autre dendroit et temps. Bien que vous soigné me comme vous fait un cherre amie, votre couer et votre ame est a un autre; et je suis devoir espouser Ammar." ("Oh, Rennin, I wish we had met in another place and time. Though you care for me as you would a dear friend, your heart and your soul belong to another; and I am duty bound to marry Ammar.") She hugged the map to her. Then she opened her bureau and signed the paper that would release Rennin. With great purpose, she walked to her father's chambers and knocked.

Her father opened his door. The interaction took place in Arabic. "What are you doing up at this hour, daughter?"

"I am trying to get all my affairs in order. I shall be far too busy tomorrow to think of some matters." She handed her father Rennin's papers. "I want Rennin released tonight. Ammar is unreasonably jealous of him. I am afraid he might hinder the process. I gave my word, Father."

The king rang a bell, and an old and trusted servant appeared. King Ahmed handed the paper to the servant. "See immediately that my daughter's manservant is set free." The servant bowed and went straightaway to Rennin's chambers. Rennin packed his scanty belongings, which consisted of a few clothes and toiletries Princess Kiandria had bestowed, into a knapsack provided by the servant, and left.

Kiandria talked a moment with her father and showed him the map Rennin had given her as she shared the story of Draconis.

Down the hall, Ammar gave a bag of silver to a snaggle-toothed henchman. "That blond infidel is not to make it out of the Kasbah tomorrow. Am I understood?"

"Yes, Your Highness."

Rennin glanced at his captive audience. "We will read more later. I believe our stew is ready."

7
The Gift

Running Bear went with Rennin to feed the horses. "What is this?" he asked Rennin.

"A Christmas gift for Rebekah."

"Oh, yes. Christmas, the celebration for the birth of the white man's Savior."

"Not just white men, Running Bear. He's the Savior of anyone who believes."

"Humph! I will believe if you get your miracle."

"Fine. Go on back inside. I have something to do out here."

Running Bear went back into the cabin, and Rennin turned his attention to making a new quiver so that Running Bear would also have a Christmas gift.

Rennin came into warm rabbit stew and cornbread with molasses that had been left in the lodge. Immediately after supper, Rebekah started to nag Rennin to read. "I do *not* trust Ammar. He is trying to harm Rennin. Please continue the story." She sat on Rennin's lap and put her arms around his neck. "Please?"

"How can I say 'no' to you?" He kissed her and opened the book.

The sunrise found Rennin at the docks searching for a place on a ship to *anywhere*, Kiandria dutifully preparing for a wedding she did not want, and Ammar raging that Rennin had already left the palace.

Rennin landed a job on *The Morning Star*, a spice carrack, headed for India and China and ultimately Lisbon, its port of origin. He planned to go from Lisbon back to Barcelona and

Morgan. The next morning, when he would ship out, could not come soon enough.

While Kiandria donned the traditional dress for a Muslim wedding, great tears dripped down her cheeks. King Ahmed knocked at his daughter's door. Opening the door, he saw how distraught the princess was. He hugged his only child. "Father, I do not love Ammar, and I truly fear he is only marrying me to inherit your throne," Kiandria confessed.

"Oh, daughter, we cannot terminate our agreement now. If Ammar ever treats you badly, he will meet with an untimely death. *That* I promise you. If I must, I will choose a successor from among the people."

Meanwhile, Ammar fumed and summoned his men. "Find the blond infidel, Rennin O'Rourke. He will not escape what he has done to Kiandria!"

"What has he done, Master?" ventured one servant who knew Rennin.

Jealousy reared its ugly head as Ammar lied. "He has defiled her. If I find she willingly allowed it to happen, she, too, will be punished." An evil plot hatched itself in Ammar's mind. As his henchmen left to find Rennin, Ammar congratulated himself. *I'll have the kingdom and be rid of both the infidel and the whore who would love him. Moreover, not even the king can help them. He will not defy the law.*

A few hours later while Kiandria vowed fidelity to a man she did not love, four lackeys boarded *The Morning Star*, and subduing Rennin after a great struggle, they dragged him, bruised and beaten, before the High Council. For two hours Rennin sat, gagged and bound while no one so much as acknowledged his presence.

During this time in the wedding chamber of the palace, Kiandria shrank from Ammar's touch. "Wife, why do you not come to me? I am your husband. I have rights by law now," Ammar reminded her as he continued his tirade. "Is it that you are afraid I will discover you are not a virgin? Have you defiled yourself with that infidel slave?"

In disbelief, Kiandria gasped, "No, Ammar! How can you say such a thing?"

The haughty prince roughly grabbed Kiandria's arms. "Then, why do you keep yourself from me?"

Kiandria looked away and tried to free herself from Ammar's grasp. He held her all the tighter and growled, "Answer me!"

"I am frightened, but it is because I *am* a virgin. Ammar, you are hurting me."

"I hope so," he hissed. "Tell me, wife: Do you love your Rennin, or do you love your husband?"

"Ammar, you have no reason to be jealous. Rennin is gone. I am married to you."

"Answer the question I asked," he demanded.

In defiance Kiandria spat, "No, Ammar, I do not love you. Yes, I love Rennin, but he is devoted to his wife. In time, if you treat me the way I should be treated, perhaps, I will grow to love you; but right now, you are scaring me and making me very angry."

"Harlot!" Ammar slapped Kiandria across the face repeatedly. He slammed her into the wall with his hands around her throat. She clawed at his hands. Ammar loosened his grip. "I would be within my rights to break your pretty little neck, but I shan't. Whether you actually betrayed me with your body, I care not. Worse is that you betrayed me with your heart and your mind. I will not kill you myself. No, I will let the High Council decide your fate and the fate of your precious slave."

"What do you mean?" gasped Kiandria.

"You will see." Ammar laughed cruelly. "Not even your father can help you."

Ammar dragged Kiandria from the wedding chamber and through the streets until he reached the assembled High Council. Hearing the commotion, King Ahmed peered from his window. He followed his daughter for he knew something was greatly amiss.

Inside the council chamber, Ammar threw Kiandria at Rennin's feet and growled in French, "Voici votre prostituee!"

("Here is your whore!") Then, he turned to the Council and conducted his business in French, unaware that Rennin could have understood Arabic. "Honored lawgivers, this evening I regretfully bring before you a harlot who came to my marriage bed tonight defiled by this"—He pointed at Rennin—"infidel!"

"Liar!" screamed Kiandria.

"Be quiet," commanded the High Judge. "You will be given an opportunity to defend the charges. Please continue, Prince Ammar."

"Most exalted ones, my heart is too broken to bring further charges, but if you will allow me, I would like to pose some questions to both the man and the woman. Their own words will condemn them."

"Please feel free to ask whatever you like, Prince," granted the judge.

Ammar began his inquisition. "Kiandria, did you only yesterday remove your veil in the presence of this man who was your servant?"

Kiandria looked at Rennin. "Yes, but..."

Ammar cut off her explanation. "Has this man ever been alone with you in your bed chamber?"

As if in a nightmare, Kiandria answered, "Briefly once to give me a gift."

"A gift. What kind of gift?"

"One to ensure my future happiness."

As if he were grieved, Ammar covered his face with his hands. "Do servants normally give their mistresses gifts?"

"No, but..."

"Why was this infidel not made a eunuch?"

"I promised to free him when we wed so that he could return to his wife—whole."

Ammar held up his hand to quiet Kiandria. "Has this whole man ever professed to have feelings for you?"

"Only friendship."

Sounding exasperated, Ammar said, "Kiandria, please. Did this man not tell you that he could love you, and that any man who could not love you would be a fool? Did he not tell you that you are extraordinarily beautiful?"

Kiandria looked at the floor. "Oui."

"Do you love him, Kiandria?"

"Ammar, stop this. You know your accusations are false. The only law I have broken is to show my face to someone other than you."

"Answer the question, Princess," ordered the High Judge.

"Oui," Kiandria whispered.

Ammar turned his attentions to Rennin. "Please, remove the infidel's gag so that he can condemn himself." One of the hired henchmen removed Rennin's gag as Ammar questioned him.

"Rennin O'Rourke, have you ever touched this woman in any way other than to help her dismount her horse?"

Boldly, Rennin answered, "Oui."

"Have you ever put your filthy mouth on my wife?"

Rennin glared at Ammar. "No. Never on your wife."

Ammar was momentarily stunned at Rennin's response, but recovered quickly.

"Have you ever referred to the princess in a familiar way?"

"Yes. She's my friend. I call my friends by their names."

"Have you ever encouraged Kiandria to leave me?"

Rennin and Kiandria knew that someone had betrayed them to Ammar. Rennin answered curtly. "Yes. I told her that her life with you would be a nightmare rather than the fantasy she hoped. Apparently, I was correct."

"Were you intimate with Kiandria?"

"I kissed her good-bye. That is the extent of our intimacy."

"Did you tell Kiandria that you could love her?"

"Yes, if my heart did not already belong to another."

Feigning tears, Ammar addressed the court. "Most exalted Council, need I ask any more? Not only have I been betrayed, but Kiandria has betrayed Allah as well. Ask her. Ask her what she believes."

The High Judge addressed the princess. "Princess, have you abandoned your faith?"

"No. I have found faith. Please, Your Excellency, hear me. All my husband's accusations are untrue. Although I may have special feelings for Mr. O'Rourke, I have never been with any man. Ammar is insanely jealous. I am innocent."

Ammar lamented, "Gentlemen, you have heard both Kiandria's and Rennin's words. They have been alone. They have feelings for each other. My wife did not want to come to my bed. I had to force her. It was obvious that she was not innocent."

The High Judge looked at the accused, who were looking at each other as if trying to figure a way out of their situation. The Council whispered among themselves for a moment. Then, the High Judge spoke. "Princess Kiandria Oded, Rennin O'Rourke, it is the finding of this Council that you have broken several laws of this land, discretions that are punishable by death. Tomorrow morning at sunrise you will be executed. You will be beheaded." The judge signaled to a guard. "Take them away."

One guard took hold of Kiandria while two armed guards dragged Rennin toward the door where the bewildered king stood. Kiandria implored, "Father, help us. You know Ammar lied."

King Ahmed spoke. "Most exalted Council, I cannot commute your sentence, but I beg of you to let my daughter spend her last night in her own quarters, not a prison cell. Your guard may stay outside her door."

The High Judge said, "Granted."

The guard and the king walked with the princess. She said, "Pere, Rennin..."

"Do not speak, Kiandria." commanded King Ahmed in his native language. "Not a word."

With Kiandria locked in her room and sobbing, King Ahmed once again sent his old and trusted servant on an errand. The servant arrived at the prison with a royal edict. "Immediately release to the king's custody Rennin O'Rourke as the last and final request of Princess Kiandria Oded before execution."

"The king wants the prisoner?"

"It is the princess's final request to have this night with her lover. Since they are to die tomorrow, what harm can it do?"

"None I guess. Was the princess in truth unfaithful to Prince Ammar?"

"She claims her innocence still. Mayhap, the relationship was platonic and the prince is unreasonably jealous. Rennin O'Rourke always seemed honorable. He talked about his wife incessantly. Mayhap, he was lonely and the princess impressionable. I truly do not know."

"Ah, well. It is a shame her life must end so early. Let me get the prisoner."

When Rennin saw the old servant, he took heart, but the servant was very short. "Do not speak to me. The princess has asked for you as her final request. Her father has seen to it that she has what her spirit desires."

The guard outside Kiandria's door read the king's edict. He untied Rennin's hands as he shoved him through the door and locked it behind him. He figured the two, condemned peopled could not get past him, and to try to escape from the princess's window would be suicide.

Kiandria was staring out the window as Rennin stumbled through her door. She turned with a start and darted to the man she loved. "Rennin!" she cried as she flung her arms around him. "Je suis se desolé. Que est-ce que vous faites ici?" ("I am so sorry. What are you doing here?")

"Anglais. S'il vous plaît? ("English. Please?") "Your father sent for me. The letter said you had asked for me as your final request."

Kiandria sighed. "Father cannot come to me. He must have read my mind. At least he knew my heart."

"Kiandria, is there some way out of here?"

"No. The wall is far too steep to go out the window. It is a sheer drop of at least one hundred feet, though we could jump and save the executioner the trouble," she said bitterly. She shivered at the thought and continued. "Father sent you to me to spend our last few hours together. He must believe we are lovers. I am sorry, Rennin." Kiandria began to cry.

"Please don't cry," begged Rennin. "Why do women always cry? Is it that they know it breaks a man's heart?" He hugged Kiandria close and kissed the top of her head.

"I do not want to break your heart, Rennin. As wrong as it might be, I love you. I always will." She laughed nervously. "I suppose always will be a very short time for me."

They sat on the thick Persian rug and reclined on the plush pillows. He let her lie in his arms. He, too, needed to be comforted.

After a time, Kiandria said, "Rennin , êtes-vous peur de mourir?" ("Rennin, are you afraid to die?")

"Peur? Non. ("Afraid? No.) I just don't want to die like this. I had hoped to grow old and die in my sleep like Diggory did—peacefully and without suffering."

"I do not want to die without ever having been loved." Kiandria stroked Rennin's cheek. "Rennin, make love to me. Give me one moment of my fantasy."

"Kiandria."

She put her finger to his lips. "We are going to die in less than twelve hours. We have been condemned for being lovers. I do not want to die for something I did not do. I spared making you a eunuch. Give me this."

Rennin gently touched Kiandria's black eye and cheek. "What did Ammar do to you?"

"He beat me. We did not have relations. Make love to me. Be the one man who ever touched me. Let me comfort you. I will beg if it will accomplish anything." Tears dripped from her dark sad eyes and traced lines down her cheeks. "Please?"

Rennin softly wiped the tears from her face. "Don't cry, beautiful lady." He tenderly kissed Kiandria's trembling lips. Then, he gathered her in his arms and laid her on her bed. Quietly he laid his clothes to the side and lovingly undressed the forlorn girl. They made love, tenderly and sweetly. Their melancholy souls found temporary comfort.

Despite their impending doom, both Rennin and Kiandria fell asleep, while outside the princess's chamber, a robed monk appeared, his face well-hidden. "King Ahmed has sent me to his daughter to hear her confession. He knows she has rejected Allah and prefers the Christian God. It is our custom for the condemned to be afforded a chance to repent. Please let me pass. It will not take long."

As the guard unlocked the door, from beneath the folds of his robe, the monk raised a club and rendered the guard unconscious. He went into the princess's room.

The creaking door roused the sleeping lovers. As they beheld the monk, he slipped off his hood.

" Père!" gasped Kiandria.

"My precious girl, if you were not guilty earlier, you are now; but I knew this would happen when I sent Rennin to you. Dress quickly. We haven't much time. Pack a quick bag. Bring your map that Rennin gave you. Rennin, your things are still aboard the ship you were on, are they not?"

"Yes, sir. Sir, I swear that we were innocent before."

"I believe you, but it makes no difference. Now, let us go."

Rennin paused by the unconscious guard. "He will live to report that some robed monk helped you escape," said King Ahmed.

The king led them to a black marble sconce. As he pulled it, a panel slid open.

"Father, a secret passage?" asked Kiandria.

King Ahmed chuckled. "Do you know how many kings have escaped assassination through this passage?"

The underground passage wound for miles all the way to the docks. They emerged only three wharves away from *The Morning Star* and directly in front of a barque called *The Fantasy.*

Unaware that Rennin understood him, King Ahmed spoke haltingly in his native tongue, overcome with emotion. "Kiandria, you have always been the light of my life. I want you to know that even as we speak, Ammar is meeting with an untimely death as I promised you he would if he hurt you. Bruises on my daughter's face and neck are reason enough for me to keep that promise, even if you had been guilty of his charges. He will never sit on my throne." The king gathered

Kiandria in his arms. "I know I shall never see you again. Board your ship and go to the wonderful place about which Rennin told you. You will be free there. Your freedom and your life are my gifts to you. I love you, Kiandria."

The king turned to Rennin in French. "I wish my daughter had met you under different circumstances. I would have been honored to have you succeed me to the throne. Alas, it is not to be, Rennin; your ship sails in half an hour. Your captain has been paid well to return you to your family. Go and never return here. I am afraid you will bear the blame for Ammar's death. I am sorry, but that cannot be helped."

Rennin replied, "I only regret that I am not the one seeing to Ammar's demise. I would have taken pleasure in it."

King Ahmed hugged Rennin stiffly. "Say good-bye to my daughter and leave. Your wife is waiting for you. Put from your mind what happened tonight. Consider it your gift to a young woman who will never love another. I will give you five more minutes with her. Then, she, too, must disappear."

Rennin took Kiandria in his arms. "Good-bye, beautiful lady. Draconis will welcome you warmly, and I will never forget you."

"I will wait for you, Rennin, if it takes a lifetime."

"Don't be silly, Kiandria. Fall in love. Get married. Have children."

"I am in love. I want no other. I will wait for you. Someday I think you will be free. If not, so be it." She touched her abdomen. "Who knows? Mayhap I will have children. I will not say good-bye, but I will wish you a good life. I love you, and I always will." Kiandria kissed Rennin, and he returned her kiss. She stroked his cheek. "Go back to Morgan. Think of me as a strange, but ultimately pleasant, dream."

Rennin boarded *The Morning Star* and watched *The Fantasy* pull into the sea. The king in the monk's robe disappeared. *The Morning Star* began its long voyage to China and back.

Rennin closed the book when he saw Rebekah was crying. "Rebekah, what's the matter?"

"I want to be angry with Rennin, and I want to hate Kiandria for what they did to Morgan, but I feel sorry for them. Rennin will probably hate himself, and Kiandria will pine away."

Running Bear laughed. "No. Rennin will get home and tell Morgan the truth. She will forgive him and love him because she is a strong woman. Kiandria will go to Draconis and be happy. Maybe she even carries Rennin's child."

Rennin laughed hard. "Are you two going to fight over the possible outcome of the story? The book tells us what happened to Rennin because he wrote it, but that was the last time he ever saw Kiandria unless he found her on Draconis. The story doesn't go that far, but Rennin's life was far from dull. Remember: We still have Victor Jordan to bring to his knees."

"Then, read," demanded Running Bear, slapping the table top.

"You are as bad as Rebekah. I need a break before I lose my voice, and I'm starving."

The weather grew colder, but the snow held off until Christmas Eve.

"Damn!" said Rennin when he looked outside. "I have to go out for a bit. While I'm out, Rebekah, I want you to use a needle and thread and string this popcorn. Running Bear, you do the same to these dried cranberries. Then, cut out the paper figures I drew this morning. I'll be back as soon as I can. By the way, Rebekah, you might want that turkey brought in to thaw. Tomorrow is Christmas."

Rebekah and Running Bear sat at the table and strung their assigned items. "Rebekah, why are we doing this?" the Native American asked.

"I don't know, Running Bear, but it seems important to Rennin."

Several hours later, Rennin burst through the door, dragging a five-foot cedar sapling with the roots still attached. He leaned the tree against the wall and grabbed the water bucket with the hole in it that had been set outside. While Rebekah and Running Bear watched in amazement, Rennin carefully placed the tree in the bucket. "I started to chop it down, but its shape was so perfect that I thought we could replant it after Christmas."

Running Bear asked honestly, "Rennin, why do you have a tree inside your house?"

Rebekah whispered, "It's a Christmas tree. I have not seen one since I was seven years old."

Rennin said, "Bring the popcorn and the cranberries. You'll see, Running Bear. It's a Christmas tradition, except the roots."

Handing Rennin one end of the popcorn, Rebekah said, "I like the roots. Let's always have a sapling and replant it on New Year's Day. That is still a special day, isn't it?"

"Yes." Rennin smiled broadly. "That's what we'll do. We'll replant the tree on New Year's Day."

Running Bear followed his example, and before long they had wrapped the tree in popcorn and cranberry garland. Rennin picked up the crude paper figures of angels, stars, stockings, candy canes, and trees. "They aren't very pretty."

Rebekah argued, "They're beautiful." She placed them throughout the branches.

"Oh! I have some other things outside on the porch," said Rennin. Outside he had several sprigs of holly berries and one sprig of mistletoe, which he held over Rebekah's head and kissed her. He hung the mistletoe from the rafter with a piece of thread. "Every time you walk under this, I'll have to kiss you. Sorry, Running Bear, this is just for Rebekah and me. I won't kiss you, and you can't kiss my girl."

"You have a deal, Rennin," laughed the Indian who was enjoying this Christmas tradition.

The wind howled and the snow fell in blinding swirls, but the little group was safe and warm inside. After supper, Rennin pulled his Bible from his saddlebag. "Tonight we'll read a very special story. It's the story of the birth of a King, the Savior of mankind." Rennin read the Christmas story with as much passion and feeling as when he read about his ancestors. When he finished, he sang in a perfectly pitched tenor voice, "O, Holy Night."

With a lilt in his voice, even as a child would have, Rennin said, "Let's hang our stockings now." Rebekah used one of the wool socks she had pilfered from her dead assailant. Rennin hung a bright red wool sock. They turned to Running Bear.

"I do not have any stockings."

"Then, we'll use your boot," joked Rennin.

Running Bear cocked his head. "I do not think I should like to poke a hole in my boot."

"Very well," said Rennin. "I'll lend you a stocking, but next year you have to get your own." Rennin forced Running Bear to hang the mate to the bright red sock at the other end of the mantle.

"Why do we hang socks on the fireplace?" asked Running Bear.

"Tomorrow they will have gifts in them," said Rennin.

"Do these gifts magically appear?"

"You could say that. Santa Claus brings them."

"Santa Claus?"

"I'll explain tomorrow. Let's get some sleep."

When he thought that both Rebekah and Running Bear were asleep, Rennin sneaked to his saddlebag and removed their gifts that he had made for their stockings. Into Running Bear's stocking, Rennin stuffed the new quiver, and into Rebekah's stocking, he slipped a comb he had carved from a tortoise shell, and a brush made from a tortoise shell and oak bark. With one eye open, Running Bear watched Rennin. When Rennin was asleep, Running Bear thought about this Santa Claus. He realized that he had no gifts to give his friends and that Rennin's stocking was empty.

Before dawn, Rennin woke Running Bear. "I need your help to bring Rebekah's gift inside," he whispered.

The two men went to the barn and carried the large oval tub, made from bark strips held together with pine tar, to the house. "What is this again, Rennin?"

"A bathtub."

"It is very large. How many people will be bathing in it at once, and how will you take it with you?"

"We'll leave it, but Rebekah can enjoy it for a while; and if I get my miracle, I'll happily join her in the tub."

They eased the tub through the door and put it to the side of the fireplace. Running Bear noticed that Rennin's stocking now bulged. He listened to Rebekah and realized that she only pretended to be asleep. He grinned as both men slipped back under the covers for a couple of hours. *This sneaking to give surprises to the ones you love is fun.*

When Running Bear heard the even breathing of his two friends, he slipped once more to the barn where he unrolled the new blanket he had planned to take back to his wife. Inside were many items he had thought to give Sleeping Fawn. One item was a turquoise pendant hanging on a thin silver chain. It would suit Rebekah much better than Sleeping Fawn. He had three small leather pouches. Why he had them he did not know, but they would be good if Rennin struck gold in California. He carefully rerolled the blanket, a brightly colored shawl, and several trinkets. Quietly, he placed the necklace and the leather pouches into the stockings of his friends. He felt a sense of happiness that he, too, had something to give.

As the sun streaked the sky and reflected a prism of color from the white blanket that covered the ground, the three dozing adults with children's spirits awoke eagerly to see what was stashed in the stockings that hung from the mantle. Rebekah squealed, "Rennin, what is this monstrosity?"

"Monstrosity? It's a bathtub."

She teased the two men. "You two will have to stand outside in the snow while I soak in my bathtub in steamy relaxing water." Her eyes danced mischievously as she laughed blithely.

Rennin looked at Running Bear and shrugged. "I guess we'll be spending time with the horses."

Rebekah hugged Rennin. "You two can face the door. I shan't make you freeze. Open your stockings."

The men took their stockings from the hooks. Running Bear was pleased with his new quiver and the rabbit skin mittens Rebekah had made for him. "Thank you, my friends."

Rennin, then, delved into his stocking. He looked quizzically at the small leather pouches. Running Bear explained. "They are for the gold you will find when you get to California."

"Thank you, Running Bear. I like your optimistic attitude." Then, Rennin pulled out two pairs of gloves, one rabbit lined pair to keep him from "getting frostbite," and one lightweight pair to keep the reins from blistering his hands. Rennin slipped one of each on to see if they fit. "Thank you, Rebekah. Now, my hands won't freeze or get too rough to touch you."

Rennin urged excitedly, "Check your stocking, Rebekah."

"Oh, there shouldn't be anything there. I already have my bathtub." She skipped to the fireplace and took her stocking, removing first the turquoise and silver necklace. "It's beautiful, Rennin."

"Don't look at me. I didn't do it."

"Running Bear?"

"Wear it as a token of my esteem."

"Will you fasten it on me?"

Running Bear fumbled with the clasp. "Ask Rennin to fasten this. I am unfamiliar with the white man's jewelry."

Rennin fastened the necklace and Rebekah pulled the brush and comb from the stocking. "Rennin, did you make these?"

"Yes."

"They're lovely."

Rennin took the brush from her hand. "Sit by me." He bushed her long brown hair until it shone.

Rebekah finally said, "You two try those new gloves and feed the animals. I'll start the turkey roasting." As Running Bear and Rennin left for the barn, Rebekah detained Rennin. She playfully stood under the mistletoe and pointed upward. He gathered her into his arms and kissed her.

"Merry Christmas, Rebekah."

"Merry Christmas, Rennin."

8

Auld Lang Syne

During the week between Christmas and the New Year, Rebekah kept the little sapling's roots packed in snow. On New Year's Eve, she packed the roots once more and caressed the fragrant, verdant needles as if they were a child's hair. Rennin knelt beside her and put his arm around her shoulders. "Rebekah, it's a tree."

"It's more than a tree, Rennin. It is *our* tree. I want to leave the popcorn and the cranberries on it when we plant it, so the birds and squirrels can eat them. Maybe a robin will build its nest in our tree in the spring."

He laughed softly. "Rebekah, you want to make life better for everyone. I'll be glad to leave the food for the critters."

Running Bear came in from the barn. "The snow is falling hard again, and the wind is gusting. I think we are in for another blizzard."

Worried, Rebekah said, "We have to plant our tree tomorrow."

Rennin poured hot coffee and said, "Don't worry about tomorrow. Tomorrow will be a new year. Would you two like to hear about our other Rennin and his Chinese New Year? Rebekah, we might get to see a Chinese New Year celebration. I understand there are a lot of Chinamen in San Francisco.

"Oh, yes. Please, read while the storm rages outside," agreed Rebekah excitedly. "When will Rennin ever get home to Morgan? Will she forgive him?"

Running Bear agreed it would be a good time to read. Rebekah warmed some leftover turkey and simmered it in gravy. She served the meat and gravy over fresh biscuits and sautéed some onions and peppers for the side. That was their lunch for the day. Then they settled in for an afternoon of story time.

Morgan awoke with a start, her spirit deeply grieved. She could feel something was tearing Rennin apart. She came to breakfast with a haggard face. Pablo was exceedingly worried. "Morgan, what is the matter?"

"I don't know. Something has happened to Rennin. He's not hurt or sick, but something is troubling his spirit. I can feel his heartache."

"What do you think it is, Cousin?"

Two big tears splashed onto Morgan's plate. "Another woman. Rennin has been with another woman. I don't know why or how, but now his guilt is eating him alive. Pablo, if I feel Rennin this strongly, do you think I can make him feel me?"

"What do you want him to feel, Morgan?" asked Pablo. "If he has been untrue to you, what do you want him to feel?"

"I want him to know how much I love him. I want him home."

"Then go somewhere quiet and concentrate on your husband. Pray that his spirit will be comforted. I am sure he will feel your love."

Morgan disappeared for several hours in Pablo's garden. Beneath the honeysuckle that Rennin loved so much, she sat and prayed and talked to Rennin as if he were beside her. "Rennin, I don't care where you've been sleeping. I don't care who has made your bed. I would give my life to set you free. There is no sin you could imagine that is stronger than our love. All I want is for you to come home again to me."

Without realizing what she had done, Morgan had held a butterfly in her hands as she spoke the words. When she finished speaking, she released the creature, and it flew east. Feeling a sense of peace, she found her two boys and took them to the candy store before she came back home and went to bed, totally exhausted.

In the crewmen's quarters of *The Morning Star*, Rennin tossed and thrashed in a nightmare. Morgan pulled one arm while Kiandria pulled the other. Behind Morgan stood Donovan and Cameron. As Morgan called, "Rennin, come home. I love you," the boys chanted, " Daidí! Daidí!" At the same time he could hear a baby crying with Kiandria while she screamed, "Rennin, help me! I love you."

The pulling continued until the man was rent in half. At that moment, Rennin heard an evil voice and laugh he had once heard come from his father's mouth in Aidan's darkest hour. "How did it feel, Rennin, to betray your beloved Morgan with such an exotic beauty?"

Rennin sat upright in his bunk and screamed, "No! Stop it! Reverend Devereaux sent you back to the pit of Hell. Leave me alone!"

Rennin's bunkmate, a brawny man with carrot-orange hair and pale-blue eyes, Geoffrey Montague, shook Rennin. "Wake up, chap. You're 'avin' another nightmare."

Rennin woke completely. "Geoffrey, will you, please, give me some water? I can't breathe."

The hefty man, who weighed as much as Rennin but was half a foot shorter, dipped Rennin a cup of water. "Rennin, chap, why don't you tell me what's disturbin' you so? I'm a good listener. Mebbe I can 'elp."

Rennin scrutinized his bunkmate. The big man had a fun-loving streak, but a temper that flared at the drop of a hat. Rennin had seen him take swings at many who riled him and leave many in need of medical attention. He and Rennin got along well, but Rennin kept to himself a lot. A number of the crew knew King Ahmed had paid for Rennin's safe passage. They were either jealous or distrusting of Rennin's being aboard. Geoffrey, however, did not care why Rennin was onboard. He, himself, had spent many nights in jail cells. All he cared was that Rennin did his share of the work. Geoffrey's opinion of the crew was that most of them were a bunch of lowlifes looking for a way to escape their real responsibilities.

Rennin breathed deeply. "Geoffrey, I was unfaithful to my wife with Princess Kiandria. That's why King Ahmed paid for my safe passage. He helped both of us escape execution. It only happened because we both thought we were going to die. I know you've heard the rumors. I swear we were innocent when Prince Ammar brought the charges. We only sinned after we were condemned, but I don't know how I can ever face Morgan. She is heart of my heart and life of my life. How could I ever have betrayed her?"

"Is she gonna meet you with a meat cleaver in 'er 'and?"

Rennin looked at the floor. "'Tis much worse than that, Geoffrey. Morgan will likely greet me with open arms and forgiveness. She will never let me know how much her heart will have been broken."

"Why do you 'ave to tell 'er? She'll never know if you just keep your mouth shut."

"She would know. She would see it in my eyes or hear it in my voice. I could never lie to her."

"You love 'er that much, do you?"

"Yes."

"Then, tell 'er the truth, and take what comes. Now, what about the princess?"

"She has gone away somewhere safe. I will most likely never see her again."

"Then, chap, your biggest dilemma is your own guilt. It sounds like your woman is a rare find. Are you a prayin' man, Rennin?"

"Yes, I pray."

"Then ask God to forgive you and let the guilt go. If you don't you're gonna tear yourself up inside. You won't be no kinda good to your woman then."

"Mayhap you're right. I have to concentrate on getting home to Morgan and my boys."

"Ah! There's somethin' you can look to, 'uggin' your boys. I got a little darlin' girl myself. 'Er name's Emily Claire. Thank the Lord she takes after 'er mother."

Until late in the night Rennin and Geoffrey talked about their families despite the grumbling of several other sailors. Rennin told Geoffrey about the magical world he had left behind, and Geoffrey could not understand why Rennin would have wanted to leave. The two men became good and loyal friends.

The voyage was long and tedious. Many days Rennin thought that they would never reach their destination. At one point, he recognized his surroundings. A small change in direction would take him home to Draconis. He was tempted to steal a dory and go home, but the thought of life without Morgan was more than he could bear. With thoughts of holding his wife and sons, he stayed his course.

Finally, after months of nothing but water and rough sailing around the Cape of Good Hope where Rennin kept a young crewman from drowning, *The Morning Star* docked in the Bay of Bengal, and the crew journeyed overland upriver to Calcutta where they loaded elephants with Indian spices and Indian cotton, as well as woven fabric. The captain gave the crew a weeks' leave in the city before they would go back to the ship and sail for China.

Rennin found himself browsing the kiosks with Geoffrey, looking for a special gift for Morgan and the boys as Geoffrey shopped for Emily Claire and his wife, Nancy. Rennin found an exquisite forest green and honeysuckle print shawl. The sight of the flowers made his senses smell Morgan. He purchased the shawl and bright yellow linen for Morgan to make a dress. He thought how she would look like radiant sunshine. Geoffrey chose a royal-blue for his wife and a light-blue with green sprigs for his daughter.

As the men left the bazaar, a native came screaming from the wooded area. He was covered in blood that was not his own. Closely on his heels charged an enormous Bengal tiger, also covered in blood that was not his own.

Rennin shoved his gifts into his friend's arms and flew between the terrified man and the charging beast. As the locals screamed and hid, the massive tiger stopped abruptly and snarled threateningly. Rennin shook his head at the tiger and slowly laid his hand between the eyes of the creature. The beast's fur was warm and coarse, so much like Rennin's remembered his mother's being when Caitlin had been changed into a tigress. The animal made several snorting sounds before it retreated into the forest, leaving Rennin unharmed.

The witnesses to the incident were awestruck. They were as afraid of Rennin as they were the tiger. Rennin said to Geoffrey, "Let's get back to the ship before these people think I'm a god or have some magical power."

"Just what did you do, chap?"

"I told you my mother was a tigress for most of my young years. A tiger never attacks face-on. The worst thing these villagers can do is run. They must look these creatures in the eye."

Geoffrey laughed nervously. "I wudda run like a scared rabbit."

"Now you know better. Never run. Look him in the eye. Challenge him with your own 'eye of the tiger.'"

As they walked away, Rennin's insides trembled with the power that had surged through him as his thoughts had mingled with the tiger's—visions of its slaughtered mate and captured cubs as he shared memories of his mother, Caitlin, and then Morgan and the boys with the beast. He dared not speak what he felt and knew in his heart—his magic was real.

Several more months went by before *The Morning Star* pulled into the harbor on Hong Kong Island. The ship would go on to Shanghai in a few weeks, but little work was taking place because the Chinese people were preparing to bring in their New Year, the Year of the Dragon.

Rennin was fascinated by the costumes and preparations, but he was most intrigued by the Chinese rendition of a dragon. His eyes danced and he could not keep from doubling over in laughter.

"What is so funny?" asked Geoffrey.

"Dragons don't look anything like that, except for the spectacular colors. Draco looked like mother of pearl; Char was a sleek, glossy black; Brindle was a deep mahogany with tiny flecks of beige; Esmeralda was bright green; Scarlet was dark crimson; Sandy looked like sandstone; but my favorite was Smoke. He was a shimmering gray. He was perfectly camouflaged against the mist and fog. We used to sneak away together or back in from some escapade just before dawn while the mist still shrouded the island because we knew we would be undetected."

"Rennin, you speak as if Smoke were a childhood playmate."

"He was. He was my best friend. We used to talk about meeting the perfect woman. At that time I thought Morgan was a boy." Rennin laughed at the memory. "I still cannot believe I thought she was a boy. She was small, but I told myself she was a runt. Somehow I knew though deep inside because I fell in love with her. I was afraid something was wrong with me. Smoke told me after I married Morgan that he had known she was female all along because she smelled different, sweeter."

"Rennin, why did you leave?"

He shrugged. "Wanderlust, I guess. Granddaddy Duncan told Morgan and me that we would conquer worlds yet unknown."

"You sound so lonely."

"I miss Morgan. I think I shall buy her a silk kimono. Why not buy Nancy one, too? Then, when Morgan and I come to London, they can have something to show each other. We will come once we take care of our business in Barcelona."

Geoffrey bought his wife a black kimono with gold embroidered roses. Rennin bought Morgan a bright red kimono with green and gold embroidered dragons. Then, the two men wandered around until they stumbled upon an artist attempting a mural of a dragon on the wall of his house.

Rennin studied the painting and mused, "This one has real potential."

The young artist had understood Rennin's words. "You rike painting?"

"Do you speak English?" Rennin asked in surprise.

"Speak rittle Engwish."

"This painting looks more like the dragons I've seen. It's quite good." Rennin complimented the man's work.

"You see dwagons?"

"Yes."

"Gwandfodda see dwagons. Said dwagon no rike doze." He waved his hand toward the town. "More rike diss."

"He's right. Do you have paper and pencil? I shall sketch a dragon for you."

The young man invited Rennin into his home where Rennin sketched a portrait of Smoke for the man.

The young artist looked at the drawing. "Rook rike Gwandfodda say. Gwandfodda go to far away isrand as rittle boy. Say men wide dwagon. You see, too?"

"Yes, I saw, too."

"Den, Gwandfodda not die cwazy. Good to know." He nodded fast and hard, just once, in assurance of his grandfather's memory.

The young artist worked diligently to transfer the portrait of Smoke onto his outside wall, but he added a great deal of color to the painting. Rennin thought it was magnificent.

The two friends continued to explore the various shops. They watched an acupuncturist work. They took in a Chinese massage parlor. Both men left rather embarrassed. Finally, they stopped in a Chinese tearoom for a bite to eat. They were served a strong hot tea and a bowl of fried rice, which contained bacon, eggs, small green peas, and onions. They had no forks, only two wooden sticks. Rennin was lost. Geoffrey laughed for this was his second voyage to China. He laughed even louder when he realized how little he remembered about how to use chopsticks; however, both men managed to finish the food. Neither had any compunction about using his fingers.

Rennin snickered. "I see why these people are small. They never get enough food."

As they finished their meal, an old toothless woman and a young boy approached them. The boy spoke enough English to ask the men if his grandmother could tell their fortunes by reading their tea leaves.

Rennin said no, but Geoffrey taunted him, "You don't really believe this stuff, do you? Let's 'ave some fun. This is the old woman's livelihood."

Rennin consented, saying, "I don't know about tea leaves, but I do believe in magic, Geoffrey."

First, the toothless old woman swished Geoffrey's cup around. The young boy translated what his grandmother said. "Gwandmudda see you and son building a house in a stwnage new rand."

Geoffrey laughed, "See, Rennin, chap. I don't 'ave a son."

The boy said, "Gwandmudda say you do now."

It was Rennin's turn to laugh. "Mayhap you have a surprise waiting for you at home."

The old woman took Rennin's cup from his hand and her grandson interpreted. "Gwandmudda say dat your spirit bwoken, but you must take heart. She see beautiful rady wid bwown hair holding her arms out to you. She has two rittle boys wid her and dey are vewy sad. Beautiful rady no care about udda woman."

Dismayed, his eyes wide, Rennin asked, "What does your grandmother see about the other woman? Is she safe?"

"Gwandmudda say all croudy, but no danger, but beautiful rady much danger.

"What kind of danger?"

"Gwandmudda say evil man, but old gentleman shield her. He your gwandfodda?"

"No. He's Morgan's cousin. Pablo is taking care of Morgan and the boys. What else?"

"Gwandmudda say beautiful rady have much magic. Image fade. No more."

"Magic? Morgan?" Rennin said doubtfully. At that moment a butterfly landed on his hand.

The old woman began to screech and chatter. The young boy said, "Gwandmudda say risten to buttafry. It have stwong magical message for golden hair."

Rennin gave the old woman two golden coins and two more to the boy. The boy's eyes grew round as a full moon. The old woman chattered. "Gwandmudda say golden hair vewy genowus man." They left.

Rennin stared at the butterfly. *Morgan, have you found your magic after all? What do you want me to know?*

Suddenly, Rennin's mind was filled with Morgan's words: "Rennin, I don't care where you've been sleeping. I don't care who has made your bed. I would give my life to set you free. There's no sin you could imagine that is stronger than our love. All I want is for you to come home again to me." The butterfly fluttered away.

Geoffrey noticed tears on Rennin's cheeks. "Chap, what 'appened to you just now?"

"I heard Morgan's voice as clear as a bell. It was as if that little butterfly spoke to me. Geoffrey, how long will it take us to get home?"

"With good weather and no stops, a minimum of six months."

"Six more months? I've missed over a year of my sons' lives already, but they're all waiting for me. I can do this, Geoffrey. Hey! You have a new baby at home. At least I didn't miss the birth of another child. I think the first thing I shall do when I get home is make a little girl with Morgan, one with big brown eyes to melt my heart."

Rennin felt a sense of release, and it showed in his demeanor. The brooding vanished, and he returned to the happy-go-lucky boy who had played in the meadow on Isla Linda. Geoffrey liked the change in his friend very much.

The two men continued to explore the shops and bought interesting toys and trinkets for their children. They shared many strange new experiences, such as martial arts, tattoos, and mijiu. They shared a few regrets, such as the hangover after the mijiu.

As evening approached, the Chinese people began their celebration of the New Year. The first thing to herald the merrymaking was hundreds of pigeons with whistles tied to their tails being released from the marketplace. The noise was deafening. The celebration continued with music and parades, which included brightly colored dancing dragons. The revelry culminated in a majestic display of fireworks. Rennin marked the day and celebrated it as special every year.

Finally, after two months in either Hong Kong or Shanghai, *The Morning Star* began its trek home with its precious cargo of spices, cloth, and tea, as well as two men who could hardly wait to see their families.

Rennin closed the book about his ancestors, and Rebekah began her usual discussion. "Was that the same butterfly Morgan released?"

Running Bear interpolated, "Perhaps it was a Spirit Guide. Rennin your religion frowns on such things, but it seems your ancestors believed in and practiced strong magic."

"Yes, they did," mused Rennin. "This was a time when many things defied reason."

Running Bear smirked. "And you, my friend, do you believe in things that defy reason?"

"Some things. Yes, I do."

Running Bear gave him a friendly slap on the back. "Perhaps you have big magic, too, Rennin O'Rourke."

"No," laughed Rennin. "I don't have any magic. Other than Alexander and Rennin all those years ago, it seems to have been only the women who had any magic." Rennin winked at Rebekah. "Maybe someday we will have a daughter who will be magical."

Rebekah sighed. "First we have to get our miracle. That will be powerful magic for me."

Rennin held Rebekah's hand and kissed her fingertips. "We will. I know we will."

Just before supper, the snow and wind stopped. As Rennin and Running Bear took care of the livestock for the evening, they heard a loud clattering. Emerging from the barn, they beheld a covered wagon on sleigh runners. Bundled in furs and blankets, a stern-looking woman and a man with a long, frazzled beard sat up front. Neither Rennin nor Running Bear could believe his eyes.

The man descended from the wagon seat and jovially greeted the two men. "Good Evening! I am Jedediah Franklin, and this is my wife, Keturah. We are on our way to meet a group from the Missionary Society in Cheyenne. We will be planting a church at the gold rush come spring. We saw the smoke and hoped to spend a night inside."

Rennin said, "Planting a church? Missionary? Mr. Franklin, does that mean that you're a minister?"

"It does. Is that a problem for you, young man?"

Rennin said hastily, "No. Can you perform a wedding ceremony?"

"I can." Jedediah looked comically at the two men.

Rennin extended his hand. "Mr. Franklin, welcome. I'm Rennin O'Rourke, and this is my friend Running Bear. Please, come inside. My fiancée has made a pot of rabbit dumplings. You are welcome to dinner and a spot on our floor."

Mrs. Franklin said prudishly, "A woman is staying here with you?"

Rennin was instantly pained by the woman's accusing tone. "Yes, Mrs. Franklin, my brother's widow is with me. She is inside preparing supper." Rennin turned to Running

Bear with squinted eyes. "Running Bear, will you please show Mrs. Franklin in and introduce her to Rebekah while I help Mr. Franklin settle his team?"

Running Bear grunted and stiffly escorted the woman inside where Rebekah innocently and graciously welcomed her.

Meanwhile, Rennin helped Jedediah Franklin settle his two geldings. He talked to Mr. Franklin openly. "Sir, Rebekah was actually the wife of Running Bear's brother, Black Cloud, who was also my blood brother. Black Cloud was murdered about four months ago. The man who murdered Black Cloud would also have murdered Rebekah had I not rescued her. Rebekah is white, but she has lived with Black Cloud's tribe for many years, since the Blackfoot killed her family. She has traveled with me since the day Black Cloud died. During that time, we have fallen in love, and we wish to be married. We had thought we would find a minister in the spring to marry us, but it seems God has sent *you* to us." He draped the harnesses over a rail in the rickety barn.

"Both Rebekah and Running Bear scoffed when I told them God would send us a miracle so that we could be married this winter, but they also indicated an acceptance of faith should I receive that miracle. Mr. Franklin, will you be my miracle? Will you marry Rebekah and me so that we can start a new year as husband and wife? Perhaps, you could also be instrumental in creating faith in two hearts."

Jedediah Franklin stood with his mouth agape. "Keturah said we should wait and not battle the weather, but I told her I thought there was an urgency to go despite the weather that I am not unfamiliar with, being from Maine. Mr. O'Rourke, is there something you're neglecting to tell me?"

Rennin looked at the ground and shuffled his feet. "Rebekah is expecting a child. I had hoped to be married before it became obvious."

"Hmmm. Is the child yours?"

"No!" He held up his hands "I have not touched Rebekah, although the temptation was strong before Running Bear came a few weeks ago. No, the child is not mine by blood, but I will be his father in all the important ways."

"I see," said Jedediah. "Is Rebekah dark enough to pass off an Indian child as one of your own?"

"No, but that might not matter either. The man, who killed her husband, and his cohort raped Rebekah. She doesn't know who the father is. She hopes that it is Black Cloud because at least he was her husband by Pawnee law, but if we are married, the child will be mine by right." He wagged his head.

"Sir, she has suffered tremendously in her short seventeen years. First, she saw her entire family slaughtered. Then, she was taken to be the wife of a man she did not love, although he was a good and compassionate man, a man of faith, which is probably why he took Rebekah to be his wife. After that, she was beaten and ravished by cruel and wicked men and watched her husband's murder. Now, she must have a child that *could* be a reminder of all her pain. I don't want her to suffer anymore. I do love her, and she loves me. So, I ask you again: Will you be the miracle I have prayed for, Rebekah has hoped for, and Running Bear has doubted?"

Jedediah stood, misty-eyed, as he listened to Rennin's plea. "Yes, Rennin, I will marry you immediately after breakfast tomorrow. So, when do I get to meet this child who has had such a hard life?"

Rennin beamed and shook the minister's hand. "Right now, Jedediah. Right now."

9
Happy New Year

Rennin and Jedediah entered the old trapper's lodge, talking as if they had known each other their whole lives. Keturah Franklin sat on one of the stools with her lips pursed while Rebekah stirred the dumplings with her back to the dour woman and talked about planting the little Christmas tree. Running Bear sat on the floor with his arms folded and watched the sour woman.

As the two men came into the dwelling, Keturah spoke shortly. "Jedediah, I will not sleep in this den of iniquity. That woman is living in a house with two men, neither of which is her husband. Moreover, she is obviously with child. God only knows which of the two is its father."

Rebekah let the ladle clatter to the floor as she stood slowly. In her buckskin dress, a little pooch in her abdomen was noticeable. She touched herself protectively and looked at Rennin with eyes that brimmed with tears. He held his arms out to her, and she ran into the haven of his embrace and wept.

Jedediah spoke sharply to his wife. "Be quiet, Keturah! Come outside and help me get blankets for the night."

"I will not!" she snapped, indignantly.

"You will, now!" Jedediah commanded.

While the couple was outside, Running Bear, pointing an angry finger, growled, "I told you how your white ministers would judge you. That woman is a prime example."

Rebekah merely cried softly in Rennin's arms. "Why was she so mean, Rennin? I was nice to her."

"I don't know, honey." Rennin tried to comfort the hurt girl. "Maybe she can't have children, and she's jealous. Don't worry about her. Jedediah will put her in her place. Guess what!" He could not help but show his enthusiasm.

"What?" said Rebekah, taking a deep breath.

"Jedediah is a minister. He has agreed to marry us tomorrow morning. We're getting our miracle, Rebekah. You will be my wife."

She wiped her eyes. "Not if that witch has anything to say about it."

Rennin chuckled as he eyed both Rebekah and Running Bear. "You two have to have faith. You promised."

Just then, Jedediah pushed the door open. Keturah stepped humbly through the door carrying a bundle of clothes. Jedediah stomped his foot. Keturah stammered, "Rebekah, I'm sorry for what I said earlier. I drew wrong conclusions and judged you unfairly. Please forgive me for my harsh words and evil thoughts."

Rennin squeezed Rebekah's hand. She smiled sweetly. "I forgive you. Thank you for understanding my circumstances." She looked up at Rennin, knowing he had explained the situation to the minister.

Rennin was still bursting with excitement. "Well, Mrs. Franklin, Rebekah is to be a bride again in the morning. Perhaps you can help her get ready."

Keturah Franklin smiled with relief. With the sour expression gone from her face, she was quite attractive. "I'd love to help. As a matter of fact, I have several lovely dresses you can choose from, Rebekah."

"Oh!" She put her hand to her throat. "I don't know." She looked up at her fiancé.

He pushed her toward the fire. "Go ahead. Take the dumplings off the fire and put them to the side. We can eat in a little while. We men will make up some beds."

The two women chattered and whispered, and Keturah hid Rebekah as she sorted through several dresses. Rebekah looked longingly at a soft pink linen dress with a white pinafore. She touched it reverently. "Do you like this one, Rebekah?" asked Keturah.

"It's beautiful, but I couldn't use it."

"Nonsense! You may have it. In case you haven't noticed, I don't have any children. I have lost four at the stage you are now. Chances are that I will never have a daughter to wear a beautiful dress for a wedding. Please take this dress if you like it."

"Are you sure?" Rebekah asked tentatively.

"Absolutely."

"Thank you so much. Keturah, pray for a miracle. God might give you a baby. He gave Mr. Franklin to Rennin and me."

Keturah was surprised by the young woman's words. Rebekah smiled shyly. "I promised Rennin I would believe if we got a miracle and were able to be married before the spring. How can I do otherwise? Running Bear said the same. He, too, will keep his word."

The small cabin was full on New Year's Eve. At midnight Rennin made a point of kissing Rebekah. "Happy New Year, heart of my heart, life of my life. You are my reason for breathing, and I will love you until the day I die. This is your last night alone. I will never leave you."

Rebekah had a hard time sleeping. She was excited, but Jedediah Franklin snored louder than a locomotive. She finally sat up and, in the flickering firelight, saw that Rennin, too, was leaning on one elbow. When Rennin saw her, he motioned to her to put on her coat. When they were dressed warmly, Rennin gathered the Christmas tree in his arms, and Rebekah opened the door carefully as they slipped into the clear cold night. Rebekah skipped to get the shovel.

The moon was full and illuminated the ground well. Rennin carried the little tree to the spot where he had found it. He placed the tree in the hole he had dug, and Rebekah patted the icy dirt around its roots. Then, Rennin took out his pocketknife and carved into the bark, **Rennin loves Rebekah forever."**

After the tree was put back in its original home, he put his arms around her and kissed her. "Should we try to get some sleep over the roar in the cabin?"

Rebekah giggled. "Rennin, be nice. Mr. Franklin is our miracle."

"That doesn't mean I want him to sleep near me every night. I don't know how Mrs. Franklin stands it."

"It hasn't bothered Running Bear," Rebekah mused. "Sleeping Fawn snores, too."

Rennin laughed. "Well, at least neither of us snores."

The happy couple walked back to the cabin with their arms around each other and slept a few hours despite the loud reverberations.

Keturah Franklin hung a blanket in the corner where she made Rebekah hide so Rennin could not see her. Keturah made a breakfast of oatmeal and dried fruit. After breakfast, Rennin bathed quickly in Rebekah's tub; shaved, leaving a thin mustache; and changed into a clean shirt and pants. Then the men waited outside so Rebekah could have a bath. Keturah took her behind the blanket and helped her dress. The dress was too big for Rebekah, but Keturah tied the sash on the pinafore tightly and whispered, "You can wear it while you grow."

Then Keturah used Rebekah's brush until the young girl's hair glistened. Finally, Keturah pulled pink ribbon from her things and pinned Rebekah's hair into a bun with the ribbon around it. Keturah patted the girl's cheek. "You are pretty. Mr. O'Rourke is a lucky man."

Rebekah shook her head. "No, I'm the one who's lucky to have found a man like Rennin. He has a big heart to want to love my baby."

"Yes, dear, he does seem to be a good man. Are you ready to become his wife?"

"Oh, yes."

"Then, let's go."

Keturah took down the blanket. Rennin stood mesmerized by the delicate beauty he beheld. Rebekah walked on clouds as she went to his side.

Jedediah spoke clearly as if a crowd were present. "Friends, we are gathered here today to witness the joining of this man and this woman in holy matrimony. If there be any present who can show just cause why these two should not be joined, let him speak now or forever hold his peace."

Hearing no objections, Jedediah continued. "Rennin Aidan O'Rourke, will you take this woman to be your lawfully wedded wife?"

Rennin replied confidently, "I will."

"Rebekah Suzanne Sinclair, will you take this man to be your lawfully wedded husband?"

Softly, but clearly, Rebekah replied, "I will."

"Since the two of you have agreed to be joined as husband and wife and there are no objections, I will ask you to make vows to each other and before God. Please join hands."

Rennin took Rebekah's hands in his.

"Rennin, do you promise to love, honor, and cherish Rebekah in good times and in bad times, in sickness and in health, and forsaking all others, cleave only unto her as long as you both shall live?"

Rennin spoke with tender assurance. "I do."

"Rebekah, do you promise to love, honor, and cherish Rennin in good times and in bad times, in sickness and in health, and forsaking all others, cleave only unto him as long as you both shall live?"

"I do," answered Rebekah with as much confidence as Rennin.

"Rennin and Rebekah, as you have pledged yourselves to each other in the sight of God and these witnesses, I pronounce that you are husband and wife. What God has joined together, let no man put asunder. Rennin, you may kiss your bride."

Rennin held Rebekah's face in his hands and kissed her softly.

Jedediah shook Rennin's hand. "Congratulations, Rennin. You have a beautiful bride." Then he kissed Rebekah on the cheek. "Mrs. O'Rourke, I think you have a fine husband. I wish you all the best."

Jedediah and Keturah prepared to continue their journey. They had only about two days left to meet their party, but what surprised Rennin and Rebekah was that Running Bear was also packed to leave.

Rennin objected, "Running Bear, you can't leave."

Running Bear laughed, "Rennin, newlyweds should be alone."

"But it is the middle of the winter."

"I will be fine, and I will be with my people in a week if the weather holds and I ride hard. Rennin, I, too, am a man. I miss the comfort of my woman. There is a request I have of you, though. Please send me a copy of your Rennin's book and a copy of a Bible to the trading post. I can read the words thanks to your father. I should like to know the outcome of Rennin and Morgan's lives. I should also like to know more about the God you worship."

"Of course, I will send them to you." The two men embraced. "I shall miss you, my friend."

Running Bear's eyes twinkled. "Rennin O'Rourke, we, too, should be brothers," he said as he pulled his hunting knife from its sheath. Running Bear cut a line across his palm and handed the knife to Rennin.

Rennin hesitated only briefly. At ten he had thought this a fantastic custom. At twenty-two he was aware of the danger of infection and the silliness of the ritual, but he would not offend this man. Rennin made a cut across the scar already in his palm and the two men clasped hands. Rebekah was ready with clean strips from flour sacks to bandage both hands.

Running Bear gathered Rebekah in an embrace. "Have a good life and many children with this man." In a manner completely out of character he choked, "I love both of you very much." Then he climbed on his Palomino pony and rode toward where he knew his people would be camped.

Rennin and Rebekah watched Running Bear out of sight. Then Rebekah took Rennin's hand and said, "We need to clean that cut before it becomes infected. I guarantee you Running Bear is washing his even now."

They went inside where Rebekah washed and rebandaged Rennin's palm. She bustled about putting things away until Rennin said, "Rebekah, come here." He put his arm around her waist and set her on his lap. "Relax. The blankets aren't going anywhere and neither are the dishes. We don't have company, and I don't expect any. We're alone, and we're married."

He pushed a stray hair from her face and ran his finger along her jawline. He traced her lips with his fingertip. Then he kissed her lips, barely brushing against them. "I love you, Rebekah. I promise I will never hurt you. I always want to make you happy."

She put her arms around his neck. "I am happy."

Rennin kissed her again, and she responded, pulling her body closer to his. He felt Rebekah's heart racing as he untied the sash on the pinafore and fumbled with the buttons on her dress. She pivoted on his lap so he could see the buttons. Even then, his hands trembled as he unbuttoned Rebekah's wedding dress.

He kissed the back of her neck and moved his fingers down her spine. He slid his hands up her back and slipped the dress from her shoulders. Rebekah turned to face her husband.

He lovingly caressed her breasts. Rebekah stood and the dress slid to the floor. She took Rennin's hand and led him to the straw covered with blankets near the fire. She unbuttoned his shirt and tears welled in her eyes.

Rennin whispered, "What's wrong?"

As the tears dripped down her cheeks, she murmured, "I'm scared. You're a white man. This is different from what I'm used to. I don't know what to do."

Rennin brushed his bride's tears away and kissed her. "Rebekah, I have never made love to a woman, but let me show you how I have imagined it to be. Do you trust me?"

She nodded. He kissed her again, softly and gently; then again with more passion. Rennin slowly removed the ribbon and pins from Rebekah's hair. He kissed her neck and her breasts and her mouth again. Rebekah instinctively ran her hands up Rennin's back as she returned his kisses. He lowered her to the blankets and tenderly made love to his new bride.

The newlyweds lay snuggled beneath the warm blankets as dusk approached. Rennin groaned, "I have to go feed the animals."

Rebekah ran her fingers through his dark-brown waves. "Hurry back. I'll keep your place warm."

Rennin dressed hurriedly in his trousers, boots, and coat. He left his shirt off. As he left the warmth, Rebekah picked up his shirt and smelled his scent. Suddenly realizing that they had not had lunch and it was suppertime, Rebekah crawled from the covers and pulled on Rennin's flannel shirt. She stoked the fire and made coffee. She reached out the door and snatched some venison sausage, dried peppers, onions, and dried tomatoes. She quickly fried the sausage with the onions and tomatoes. She made some rice and mixed it with the meat. This she stuffed into the peppers.

Rennin walked back into savory smells and realized how hungry he was. Rebekah had not heard him come in; and since he barely cracked the door to keep out the cold, she had not felt the draught. Rennin noticed she was wearing only his shirt and smiled at the thought. When she did not turn around as Rennin entered, he quietly removed his coat and boots and sneaked up behind her, slipping his arms around her. Rebekah screamed as she turned around.

"Rennin! You scared the daylights out of me."

"I'm sorry, but you were so tempting."

"Was I, now? How so?" she said twining her arms around her husband's neck.

"Well, there you were, totally unaware of my presence and wearing only my shirt. By the way, what do you have on under there?"

Rebekah blushed all the way to the roots of her hair and sputtered, "Nothing."

"That's what I thought. There you were, wearing *my* shirt. You do understand that is *my* shirt. I was thinking how much I would like to take back *my* shirt." Rennin unbuttoned the top button and kissed Rebekah's throat. "Then I smelled the food, and I realized I was starved and needed nourishment." He nibbled her neck. "Mrs. O'Rourke, you taste delicious, and I am *very* hungry."

Rebekah giggled. "Then maybe you should have supper."

"I'd rather have you."

"That can be arranged." Rebekah reached behind her and scooted the pot off the fire. Then she kissed Rennin. He scooped her into his arms and took her back to bed.

Later as they held each other, Rennin's stomach growled loudly. Rebekah burst into laughter. "What would you rather have now, Mr. O'Rourke?"

He laughed, too, and said, "Food. I'm starving."

Rebekah started to crawl over Rennin. He held on to her a moment. "I might change my mind if you do that. Stay here. I'll bring the food."

Rennin wrapped a blanket around him and verily danced to the coffee pot. He brought two cups, which Rebekah took. Then, he scooped several peppers onto one plate and grabbed two forks. They ate by the fire.

After dinner Rennin reached for the book to read. Rebekah touched his hand. "Not tonight. This is your night. I don't want to hear about any other Rennin. I love this one too much." She kissed her husband and rolled on top of him. "I have other plans for tonight."

Rebekah and Rennin slept until the sun was high in the sky the next day. Rennin dashed out to care for the animals. When he returned, Rebekah still lay under the covers, softly crying. He lay beside her. "Sweetheart, is there something wrong?"

"I don't know, Rennin. I have a very strange sensation. Is there something wrong with the baby?"

"Are you in pain?"

"No."

"Are you bleeding?"

"No."

"Where is this unusual feeling?"

"Here." Rebekah put Rennin's hand on her abdomen. He almost snickered, but realized this young mother-to-be, without any motherly guidance of her own, was genuinely frightened. Instead, he comforted her. "Rebekah, among my six sisters, I have over a dozen nieces and nephews. Nothing is the matter. The baby is kicking. That's all."

"Are you sure?"

"Yes, my love, I'm sure. Don't worry unless you don't feel the baby kick for several days. Now that you have begun to feel him kick, the kick will only get stronger."

Relieved, Rebekah snuggled close to Rennin. "Are you hungry?"

"A little."

"There are some peppers in the pot. They're still good. I'll get them."

"Bring the book, and we'll read for a while. That always takes your mind off your troubles."

Rebekah sighed. "I suppose I'm silly, but I have never had a baby before. Rennin, sometimes I wish I was not having this one because he isn't yours."

"But he *is*. In my heart he's mine because he's a part of you. Rebekah, babies are always gifts from God—*always*." Rennin held Rebekah close and kissed her. "Now, bring me some food and our book, woman," he joked.

She laughed and served two plates while Rennin got the book.

After months at sea and a voyage that took him around the globe and more than two years away from his family, Rennin O'Rourke, aboard *The Morning Star*, pulled into port in Lisbon. He was almost unrecognizable. His already blond hair was bleached platinum by constant exposure to the sun, and he had allowed it to grow to several inches below his shoulders. His skin was deep bronze, and he had grown a full beard and mustache.

Both Rennin and his good friend, Geoffrey Montague, now wore earrings in their left ears and sported dragon tattoos, starting at their left shoulders and going diagonally across their backs, direct results of too many cups of mijiu during the celebration of the Chinese New Year.

Rennin and Geoffrey embraced in a manly fashion. Rennin threw his knapsack over his shoulder as he prepared to board another ship that would dock three weeks hence in Barcelona. "Geoffrey, as soon as I take care of my business in Barcelona, Morgan, the boys, and I will head for London. I cannot wait for you to meet my wife."

"I look forward to it, my friend. Godspeed!" Geoffrey waved jovially as Rennin bounced down the gangplank, eager to see his family.

Another three weeks found *The Dragonfly*, a much smaller ship, dropping anchor in Barcelona just as the sun set on the horizon. Rennin once again threw his knapsack over his shoulder and, dressed in black, walked discreetly down the street. He decided not to let anyone know he was back in Barcelona for fear of reprisal by Victor Jordan. He wanted time to discuss a plan of action with Morgan.

As he sneaked past the Jordan mansion, Rennin noticed the drapes were drawn. He shook off an eerie feeling. Rather than going to Pablo Morales's front door, Rennin climbed the stone fence and jumped the hedge into the garden. Lights were ablaze on the second floor, but downstairs was already dark.

Looking up, Rennin saw the silhouette of a petite woman rising from a sitting position. He watched the figure lean over, apparently tucking someone into bed. The lantern in that room went out. Rennin breathed, "Morgan."

Almost simultaneously, the room beside the boys' room went dark. Rennin surmised that to be Pablo's room. Obviously, the household was going to bed. Rennin watched as light shone in the room on the other side of the boys' room. As he watched the woman's shadow brush her hair, his heart beat wildly. It was all he could do to keep himself from shouting Morgan's name.

Suddenly, the balcony door to Morgan's room opened, and she stepped into the night air. Her honeysuckle scent wafted on the breeze to lure Rennin, but he slid behind a shrub and watched the woman he longed to touch. As she had done every night since she had released the butterfly in the garden, Morgan spoke to the winds. "Rennin, I read a Chinese proverb in one of Pablo's books. It said, 'If you love something set it free. If it comes back, it is yours. If it does not, it was never meant to be.' My love, you are free. I'm waiting here for you to come back to me. I will wait here forever if I must, but my heart tells me you will come. Make it soon, my love."

Morgan went inside and closed the French doors. The light went out. Rennin wept silent tears and whispered, "It will be tonight, heart of my heart."

After Rennin thought the household had had enough time to go to sleep he reverted to his boyhood tactics; however, scaling a stone wall was not as easy as climbing a trellis. Rennin groped in the deep darkness, since the sky was overcast, for footholds and handholds. He slipped several times and once clung precariously to the flimsy ivy on the wall. Finally, he dropped over the balcony rail and laughed softly as he thought, *I'm not sixteen any more.*

Taking a brief respite to catch his breath, Rennin deposited the canvas bag on the balcony and stealthily opened the French doors that led into Morgan's room. He listened to her breathing. She slept.

Cat-like, Rennin crept to Morgan's bedside. The fragrance of honeysuckle all but intoxicated him. Unable to contain himself, he brushed his fingers lightly across her hair and then softly ran his hand over her bare arm to her neck and cheek. His thumb caressed her lips before he came to his senses and pulled his hand back.

Morgan's eyes popped open, but she lay perfectly still, feeling the presence in the room with her. Her hand snaked beneath the pillow where she felt the handle of the dagger she kept there. Something strangely familiar about the presence kept her from thrusting the weapon upward. Almost inaudibly she breathed, "Rennin?"

His heart pounded at the sound of her saying his name. "Yes."

She turned over and reached for the man whose life she shared. He lifted her to him and buried his face in her hair. Morgan reached for his face. "You have a beard. Your hair. Oh, I care not! You're home!" In the dark Morgan found Rennin's mouth and kissed him, pouring all the love and passion and loneliness of two years into one kiss.

Rennin choked, "God, I have missed you!"

Morgan began to shed tears of joy as she stroked his beard. "You're truly here. You've come home again to me."

The very phrase broke Rennin's heart. "Morgan, I have to tell you something."

She put her mouth on his. "I don't care. I don't want to know about her right now. Just tell me you love me."

He panted, "I love you. I love you. You are heart of my heart, life of my life. You are my reason for breathing, and I will love you until the day I die."

Before Rennin could say another word, Morgan ripped the fastenings from his dyed cambric shirt. "Morgan?"

"Don't talk, Rennin. Make love to me."

"Morgan, I have to know."

"What?" she asked as she slipped from her nightgown. "What could be so important?"

"There was a butterfly. It talked to me in your voice. It said, 'Rennin, I don't care where you've been sleeping. I don't care who's made your bed. I would give my life to set you free. There's no sin you could imagine that is stronger than our love. All I want is for you to come home again to me.'"

She whispered, "It found you."

"Morgan, how?"

"I shall tell you later, but not now. Now I want to be with my husband. I need to feel you. I love you so. I have missed you so. Make love to me."

Rennin pulled Morgan's body to his, and they melted into each other. There was no yesterday. There was no tomorrow. There was only the moment, and no one else existed in the world.

As the sun cast its gold and orange rays through Morgan's window, she awoke, thinking she had had the most wonderful dream; but there was Rennin with his head on her chest, sleeping like a baby. Morgan looked at every inch of him—the hair that had lightened so much with the sun's rays and grown so long; the beard that tickled her skin; the dark bronze skin; the diamond in his ear; the strange picture in the skin of his back. Morgan lifted his hand, callused by the hard work of a sailor without gloves, but still wearing the chain loop that symbolized their love and union. Momentarily, Morgan wondered if this was a stranger in her bed.

Rennin opened his eyes. The glistening emeralds left no doubt that this man Morgan held was her one and only love. The distant rumble of thunder made Rennin jump from the bed. He snatched the blanket and wrapped it around him as he cautiously opened the French doors and retrieved his knapsack before large drops of rain began to fall and clouds obscured the brilliant sunrise.

Rennin jumped on the bed with the big gray bag and opened it. "I have some things for you."

Morgan leaned on Rennin's back and kissed his strangely painted shoulder. "What is this?"

"A Chinese rendition of a dragon. Do you like it?"

"It's very colorful, but it looks very little like a dragon. Will it come off?"

"No. It's here to stay. Smoke will laugh when he sees it."

"When, Rennin?"

"Someday, we shall go back—someday," he said thoughtfully.

He became quiet. Morgan slipped her arms around his waist. "You said you had something for me. What is it?"

Rennin shook off his momentary melancholy and pulled the Indian shawl with the honeysuckle print and the yellow linen from the bag.

"Rennin, it's beautiful."

"'Tis not all. The material and shawl are from India, but I went all the way to China and around the world with a stop in the Caribbean. I brought you this from China." Rennin pulled the red silk kimono from the bag. Morgan gasped. "Put it on," whispered Rennin. "I want to see you in it."

Morgan slipped into the kimono. She reverently touched the material. "Rennin, I have never seen anything so beautiful."

"I have."

"What?"

"You." He knelt before her and laid his face against the silk. She lovingly stroked his hair.

"I love you, Rennin. Stand up."

"I am unworthy of your love."

Morgan knelt with her husband. "Tell me about her. Then put it out of your mind. Do you love her?"

When he did not answer, Morgan took his face in her hands. "Look at me. Do you love her?"

"Part of me does. Morgan, she did *not* deserve what happened. If you hate anybody, hate me."

"I could never hate you. Tell me what happened."

Rennin confessed his sin to Morgan and begged her understanding and forgiveness ending with, "I'm surprised you didn't use the dagger under your pillow. I deserve it."

She held him in her arms. "Let it go, my love. You are where you belong. I promise you we will never be apart again until we are separated by death."

He kissed her. "I know only one thing more beautiful than you in that kimono."

"What is that?"

"You without the kimono," he replied with a mischievous grin.

"Oh? Do you mean like this?" Morgan let the red silk slide down her back to the floor.

Rennin breathed, "Exactly like that," as he scooped her into his arms and went back to bed.

Rennin closed the book and grinned at Rebekah. "This gives me ideas."

"What kind of ideas, husband?"

"Maybe I'll buy you a kimono."

"Why?"

"So you can take it off."

Part Two

Starting Over

10
Picking up Pieces

Mid-January brought howling winds, blinding snow, and sub-zero temperatures. Rennin kept a fire burning in a Dutch oven to give the animals warmth. Rebekah commented that she had never seen a winter so harsh. Several times Rennin was forced to tie rope to his waist as he went to the barn just to find his way back inside

On one such evening, he used his whole weight to force the door of the lodge to close against the wind. Once he got the door shut, he sat on the floor out of breath as blood gushed from his head. "Rebekah! I need your help."

"Rennin, what happened?"

"Limbs are falling from the weight of the ice and snow. One caught me."

She washed his injury. There was a gaping gash on his scalp. "Rennin, I need to stitch that up."

"Make it quick. I'm feeling a little lightheaded."

She pushed his long dark hair to one side and touched his odd ears, a small point evident. Trying to relieve the tension, she asked, "Are you sure you didn't cut yourself."

"Yes." Rennin laughed lightly. "Father often told me I had devil horns. Katie has the little imperfection too." His voice sounded wounded.

Rebekah sighed. "Your father missed your halo, no doubt." She worked quickly after that to put seven stitches in Rennin's scalp. "You're going to have a terrible headache," she said.

"I'll live, but I don't think I can read tonight."

"I'll read."

"Really?"

She laughed. "You've taught me to read. If I have trouble with some of the words, I'll ask for help."

"That sounds like a plan."

Rebekah helped Rennin to their straw bed, and he relaxed. She opened the book and continued the story of Rennin and Morgan.

Rennin and Morgan lay wrapped in each other's arms as two boys burst through their mother's bedroom door. Donovan fumed, "Momma, Cameron spilled milk on my new shirt!"

Cameron defended himself. "It was an accident! You had your glass too close to the edge of the table."

Both boys stopped talking as they realized Morgan was not alone. They stared at the blond, bearded man that sat up beside their mother. For a moment they were befuddled. Neither of them recognized their father at first. Then, Rennin put his elbow on his knee and his chin on his hand and cocked one eyebrow as he always did when he was about to playfully scold the boys.

Simultaneously, the boys screamed, "Daidí!" They piled onto the bed with their parents. Rennin pulled his boys into his arms.

"Oh! I missed you two. I love you so much."

As the family reunion took place, Pablo limped to the door on his cane. "Morgan, I am sorry about the mess..." He stopped in mid-sentence. "Rennin!"

"Pablo, I hope you don't mind harboring a fugitive. I've returned, and I plan to bring your old nemesis to his knees."

Pablo laughed. "Morgan has already done that." He looked at the woman. "Have not you told him yet?"

"I've not had time. He sneaked through the window in the middle of the night. We had more important things to discuss," Morgan finished with a smirk.

Pablo surveyed the situation. "Boys, let your mother and father get dressed and come down to breakfast. Rennin can tell us all about his adventure, and Morgan can tell him about mean old Mr. Jordan next door. Scoot!"

The boys scampered out the door with the aged cousin. Rennin laughed out loud and fell back on the soft down pillow.

"Oh, the joys of the lack of privacy! What if they had come in an hour earlier?"

"They would have learned a lot about the facts of life and love very quickly."

"Morgan!" Rennin began to realize this was not the shy, demure woman he left behind two years earlier. He reached out and touched a few strands of solid white hair to the right of her face. "What is this?"

"The gray hair you gave me. After I sent your butterfly, it was there. Rennin, I never knew I had powers of any kind, but I discovered just how strong my powers are in my desperation to get you back." She covered his hand with her small one.

"It all started when I tried to make Victor think I was performing magic. I never imagined when I prayed, God would prick Victor's heart that the old goat would have a heart attack. Then, there was the butterfly. When I released it, I was completely drained of energy for days. I felt your heart breaking. I knew what had happened. You didn't tell me what Kiandria looked like—or even her name. Let me tell *you*." She took a deep breath and continued. "Kiandria was tall, as tall as Aunt Caitlin. Her hair was long, black, and perfectly straight. Her eyes were so brown they seemed black, and her skin was a deep brownish-bronze. She was young, maybe sixteen. How am I doing?"

In awe, Rennin whispered, "Perfectly."

"I saw you. In my dreams, I saw you. I saw you with a man with hair redder than Daidí's. He's your friend."

Rennin nodded. "Geoffrey."

Morgan went on, "I saw you quell a tiger's fury. I saw an old woman who could not speak English give you peace of mind. I saw you pulling huge ropes. You let them go and snagged a young boy who was about to fall overboard during a storm."

Rennin whispered, "And I felt your love and your strength. It was as if all I needed to do was call out your name, and you were there. Morgan, are our spirits bound so strongly?"

"I think so."

"Tell me about Victor."

"Let's go to breakfast before the troops come back. I shall tell you all about it, but, Rennin, you can leave out certain details when you tell the boys about being the slave of a princess."

Rennin and Morgan came to breakfast. Donovan had changed his milk-covered shirt, and the boys and Pablo were waiting eagerly to hear Rennin's story. The boys fidgeted in their chairs as Rennin sipped his coffee and smirked. Finally, unable to contain himself, Donovan shouted, "Come on, Daidí. Finish your coffee already. What happened? Where have you been? What did that mean old goat do to you? We put syrup of ipecac and castor oil in his water."

Rennin choked on his coffee and began to spit and cough. "You did what?"

"Momma told us to."

Rennin gazed at Morgan's innocent-looking face and dipped his left eyebrow. "Mayhap your story is more interesting than mine."

"Daidí, please," Cameron begged as he crawled onto Rennin's lap.

Rennin picked up his younger son and moved to the settee where he set Cameron on his right side. Then, he motioned to Donovan to sit on the other side. With one arm around each boy, he told his story, leaving out a few details.

After several hours of listening, Donovan tried to peer down Rennin's collar. "Show us your tattoo, Daidí. What is mijiu?"

As Rennin removed his shirt, he explained, "Mijiu is like wine made from rice."

Cameron put his hands on his hips. "You were drunk when you got this thing on your back. It's beautiful. When can I get one?"

"Never," said Rennin.

"Why not? You have one."

Morgan giggled. "You brought this on yourself, my love."

Rennin rubbed his knuckles across the boy's head. "I have one because I was very foolish and drunk. It hurt."

"What about this?" asked Donovan, pulling Rennin's ear.

"Ouch! Only sailors who have sailed around the world get that. Have you sailed around the world?"

"Close."

"Yes," mused Rennin. "Close, but have you sailed around the world as a working sailor?"

"No, but I might someday."

Rennin laughed. "Then, *someday*, we will worry about a hole in your ear. It hurt, too."

"Did it bleed?"

"No, but it hurt; and sometimes for some people, it does bleed and gets disgusting and nasty and infected. You might even have to cut off your ear," Rennin teased.

"Not us. We're O'Rourkes," boasted Cameron.

"Yes, well." Rennin was not getting his point across, so he changed the subject. "Boys, do you think I should hear about your time before I give you some presents?"

"No! Presents come first," cried the boys.

"All right. Bring my knapsack downstairs carefully. Some of the things might break."

While the boys were upstairs, Rennin quickly gulped down another cup of coffee and pointed at Morgan. "Don't think you're off the hook. I want to know what you did to Victor Jordan. Did you turn him into a newt?"

"No, silly. I broke his spirit."

"How?"

The boys charged into the room, one on each end of Rennin's knapsack. Donovan complained, "Daidí, this is heavy. What's in here?"

"You'll see. You should try carrying it on your back and scaling Momma's bedroom wall at the same time." Rennin flashed his boyish grin.

"Don't give them any ideas," said Morgan. "They're bad enough as it is."

Rennin winked at Morgan. "Sit down." He opened the bag.

"First, a gift for our host. Thank you, Pablo, for caring for my family." Rennin gave Pablo a bottle of Chinese mijiu and an intricately sculpted golden dragon.

The aged cousin commented, "Exquisite work of art. Rennin, you should not have brought a thing for me."

"Nonsense! You're my dear friend's father and protector of those I love. You deserve far more.

"Now, boys. First, we have Chinese handcuffs for each of you." Rennin handed the small pieces of woven straw to the boys. "Put your fingers in." The boys did as they were told. "Now, take them out."

Rennin roared with laughter as the boys tried to free their fingers. The harder they pulled, the tighter their fingers were held. Rennin returned to the table for more eggs and coffee. "That should keep you occupied while I have something to eat."

Pablo laughed. "Rennin, it is almost time for the noon meal."

"Do you know how long it has been since I had any truly palatable food? I shall eat breakfast and dinner and still be hungry."

The boys squealed and laughed, "Daidí! Help! Get us out of these things."

Rennin slowly ate his eggs and a yeast roll. "Figure it out, boys. You can do it if you think."

Finally, Donovan whooped in victory. "I did it!" He was free.

Rennin said, "Donovan, help your brother."

"Why?"

"Because he's younger than you, and I've not forgotten how to swing a strap."

Donovan grumbled, "Oh, all right. Come here, baby."

"Donovan!"

Donovan helped his younger brother get free before he asked. "Daidí is that all you brought us?"

"Should I have brought you something else?" Rennin teased.

Suddenly, Donovan threw his arms around his father's legs. "I don't care, Daidí. I'm just glad to have you back." The boy sobbed. Cameron joined him as he began to cry, too.

Rennin knelt with them and held them tightly. He cried, too, as he kissed their heads. "Oh, my babies, I swear I will never leave you again. I love you so much. I missed you more than you can ever know. Thinking about this moment kept me from going mad. Now, dry your tears. I did bring you something else, but you cannot cry on them, or you'll ruin them."

The boys settled down, and Rennin pulled silk pants and shirts from the bag. "People in China wear these everywhere, but I think you should use them for sleeping. People around here would laugh if you wore these outside."

The boys touched the shimmering material as if it would melt. Rennin retrieved a couple of toys and a box of fireworks. "The things in this box are dangerous. I'll show these to you on the date of the Chinese New Year. They're pretty and a lot of fun."

Cameron thoughtfully said, "What about Momma?"

Morgan put her arms around the boy and put her chin on his head. "Daidí already gave me gifts last night when he sneaked in the window."

"Show us."

"Yes, show us," echoed Rennin.

"I would love to!" Morgan scampered up the stairs and returned wearing her kimono and carrying the linen and the shawl.

The four males blinked at the vision, but Cameron spoke what was on each one's mind. "Momma, you're pretty."

"Beautiful," agreed Pablo.

"Breathtaking," whispered Rennin. He pulled one more item from his bag, a slender black box. "I have one more gift for you, my love." He handed Morgan the box.

She opened the box. Inside on a gold chain, hung an intricately carved jade dragon. "It's gorgeous. Please fasten it on me."

Morgan lifted her hair as Rennin fastened the necklace around her neck. Then, he kissed her nape. She turned around into his arms and put her arms around his neck. She pulled his face to hers and kissed him. "Welcome home. I love you." Then, she giggled. "Are you planning to keep the facial hair?"

"I am until I know Victor Jordan and Juan Santiago are no longer threats. I only grew it a few weeks ago, purposefully as a disguise. When are you going to tell me what happened? I need to know."

The maid came in to clear the dishes and serve lunch. Startled, she dropped the silver tray she carried.

Pablo teased her. "Que esta'equivocado, Maria? Ha visto usted a un fantasma?" ("What's wrong, Maria? Have you seen a ghost?")

"Es realmente Señor O'Rourke volvio vivo?" ("Is it truly Mister O'Rourke returned alive?")

"Si, Maria es yo," Rennin answered. ("Yes, Maria, it is I.")

"Ah, los Santos sean alabados! Señora O'Rourke nunca se riadio la esperanza. Los Santos sean alabados!" ("Oh, the Saints be praised! Señora O'Rourke never gave up hope. The Saints be praised!")

"Gracias, Maria."

Pablo exclaimed, "Tendremos un partido esta noche! Maria, invita a toda mis amigos. Es tiempo ellos reunieron Rennin." ("We shall have a party tonight! Maria, invite all my friends. It is time they met Rennin.")

"No," said Rennin. "Que tal nuestro enemigos?" ("What about our enemies?")

"Morgan, dice por favor a su esposo scerca de sus enimigos sobre el almuerzo." ("Morgan, please tell your husband about his enemies over lunch.")

Maria prepared a scrumptious meal of sautéed chicken with peppers and onions served with flat bread and blueberry cobbler. Rennin ate until he was stuffed. All the while Morgan told Rennin her story...

Rebekah noticed that her Rennin was nodding off. "Honey, don't go to sleep. You need to stay awake a while longer with a bump like that. I've seen many go to sleep and never wake up."

"I'm so tired, Rebekah. I can't seem to keep my eyes open."

"Perhaps you should step outside for a moment. The cold will wake you up."

Rennin stood, but sank back to the bed. "I can't. I'm too dizzy."

Rebekah put his arm over her shoulders. "I'll help you. I cannot allow you to go to sleep. I cannot lose you. My life would be over without you."

He leaned on Rebekah to the door of the lodge. The blast of frigid air temporarily woke him. The two of them together had a hard time closing the door against the force of the wind. Rebekah said, "I'm sorry, Rennin. I had no idea it was blowing so hard."

"It's all right. I'm awake." He began to laugh. "I remember falling off the barn and from a huge oak tree when I was little. My father told me my head was too hard to get hurt. He asked me if I cracked the ground. I wonder what he would say if he could see me now."

"He would tell you to lie back down and let your wife take care of you."

"Would he?"

"I'm sure he would." Rebekah propped Rennin on her shoulder and took him back to the bed. "Do you feel sick?"

"Not really, just very dizzy."

"I know you want to sleep, but it's safer for you to stay awake."

"I know, but the reading makes me sleepier."

She stretched her eyes wide. "Am I that boring?"

"No. I've read the story many times. I'm finding it hard to concentrate on it."

"I see. Perhaps I can think of another way to keep you awake," Rebekah said with a wink.

"Rebekah! I'm injured."

She laughed. "Only your head."

Rennin's jaw dropped. Rebekah laughed harder. "Rennin, I'm teasing you, but it might keep you awake."

"Indeed!"

She continued, "And it would be a tremendous sacrifice on my part since I would be required to do all the work. You would be eternally beholden to me. You would owe me a great debt."

Rennin's eyes danced as he became fully alert with anticipation. "Yes, I would, and I would gladly repay that debt."

"Would you? You have no idea what I might ask in return."

"I don't care! I'll pay anything! Now, get over here! I am wide-awake, Mrs. O'Rourke. You have succeeded in that." Rennin pulled Rebekah down onto the bed with him.

Sometime later, snuggled under the cozy blankets near the crackling fire, Rebekah ventured, "Rennin, are you asleep?"

"No. I'm trying to stay awake. How long should I fight the need to sleep?"

"I don't know. Are you feeling queasy or dizzy now?"

"No, but I'm lying down. Would you like me to read Morgan's story to you?"

"Do you feel like reading?" She carefully touched the stitches. There was no fresh blood.

Rennin said, "I owe you a great debt as I recall."

"I like the payment I'm currently receiving."

"You can snuggle beside me while we read if you like."

"I like very much, Mr. O'Rourke."

"Okay." He rose carefully in case he became dizzy and walked to the table where the book lay. He wiggled back under the blanket and propped on pillows. Rebekah squeezed under his arm, and he continued the story.

...All the while Morgan told her story.

"Well, Rennin, two days after you were abducted, I paid a visit to Victor and gave him an ultimatum—one month to return you and confess his actions or suffer the consequences of wrath from the great-granddaughter of Quazel and Alexander. At the time, I thought I was truly bluffing about any magical powers." She touched the white strip of hair.

Pablo interjected, "I am exceedingly glad he was afraid of prison himself, or he might have reported Morgan to the authorities for being a witch."

Rennin cocked his head to the side, not understanding.

"Ah," Pablo explained, "many people have been interrogated and tortured, even killed, for practicing witchcraft. Most of them had no powers at all."

Rennin ground his teeth at the thought of Victor possibly causing Morgan pain or even death.

She touched her husband's arm. "One month later, I visited Victor's house. He told me to drop dead, so I blew some talcum powder toward his house, and Cameron put syrup of ipecac in his drinking water."

Cameron nodded with enthusiasm at the role he had played.

Morgan laughed and went on. "I prayed that justice would prevail. Two days after that, Donovan put castor oil in the water."

Donovan grinned broadly.

Morgan's smile grew. "Of course, Victor thought all his ailments were from magic. I prayed that God would prick Victor's heart, and he had a heart attack. That was not my intention, but I confess that I took advantage of the situation." Morgan took a deep breath.

"I went to visit Victor. I told him the truth about what I had done. Then, I told him about the power of God to forgive and to heal. I told him about Ricardo and Uncle Aidan. I also told him that although I believed these things, I had discovered I had the power to make his life a living hell if he did not confess and bring you back."

She clamped her teeth shut, knitted her brow, and growled, "Rennin, Victor Jordan was the most stubborn, evil, selfish son of...that I ever met. He and Quazel would have been a perfect match, albeit a match made in Hell.

"I visited him every day and talked to him about forgiveness and a new life. The man's heart was so cold and hard that he spat curses, obscenities, and profanities at me day in and day out." She released a long sigh.

"One day I was totally fed up with him. There he lay, an invalid, knowing that another heart attack would kill him, yet he was willing to go to his grave and let you remain accused of murder and rot in some distant land. After six months of treating the old goat with compassion and kindness, I was angry, truly angry. I'm afraid I did a very cruel thing."

"You cruel? You don't have a cruel bone in your body," objected Rennin.

"You would be surprised what desperation can do to a person, darling. Do you remember that I dumped *all* of Quazel's headache powder into one glass and knocked her out cold? Well, this time I dipped the tip of a needle in the curare I brought with me. It was hardly enough for the effects to last for one hour, but it put fear into Victor. I pricked his finger, and within the hour, he was unable to move even his eyelids.

"During that hour, I informed him that a prick with more poison would render him in a state of assumed lifelessness for days. I asked him if he were ready to be buried alive and stand before God for judgment.

"I started listing his sins. I talked about Ricardo, the dead magistrate, stolen property, and, of course, you. Under the influence of the drug, he was unable to scream at me. He had no choice but to listen.

"As soon as the curare wore off, he begged for the constable and a priest. He confessed everything, including Santiago's involvement. Santiago is in prison, and Victor is dead!

"He lived a few more weeks and begged for me to sit with him every day. He wanted assurance that God would forgive him. Rennin, I held his hand when he died. He apologized a thousand times and was heartsick for he truly did not know where you were." She waved her hand in the air as if to erase something.

"For me it was harder after Victor died because I had no one left to blame. I had seven businesses to run or find someone to run. Pablo was invaluable with that. I had a huge villa. That is why it's closed. Rennin, we own a large part of this city. What are we going to do with it all?"

"Sell it or give it to Pablo."

Pablo said, "What?"

Rennin explained, "We aren't staying here forever. I have agreed to meet Geoffrey Montague in London."

Exasperated, Morgan exclaimed, "Rennin O'Rourke! How could you make a promise like that without even discussing it with me?"

Rennin stumbled over his words. "I-I-I didn't think you'd mind. You said you would go anywhere with me."

"I will, but I would appreciate being asked."

"I'm sorry."

"What about *Pablo*?" Her voice was heavy with emotion.

Rennin suddenly realized that Morgan had become attached to her cousin. He had provided the only stability in her life other than Rennin.

"I-I don't know. Pablo, what do you want?" Rennin turned to their host.

The old man took a deep breath. "Rennin, my boy, what I would like to do before I die is to put my arms around my son and tell him how much I love him. If you do not want to stay here and become a businessman, then sell the businesses and the properties. Take a great deal of capital and go on your adventures, but guard your money to have for a long time. Turn some into gold and send it with me to your wonderful island for your dragons to rebuild their treasure stores.

"Rennin, I have twelve servants in this house. All have heard about Draconis. Ricardo was my firstborn. His mother died having our second child who did not survive either. He is all I have. I want to spend my last days with him. I want to meet my daughter-in-law and hold my grandchildren.

"Even though you and I are years apart in age, we both have many pieces of our lives to pick up and put back together. I know you understand my heart."

Rennin was quiet and thoughtful. Finally, he said, "Then that is what we will do. We will sell everything. Morgan and I will take some proceeds and continue our travels. You will take some to Draconis and start to build a stronger economy. You can decide exactly what to do after you talk to my grandfather. He's governor of Draconis. Morgan, does my suggestion meet with your approval?"

She looked at Rennin. "You know I will do anything you suggest and go anywhere you go, but it means a lot to me that you asked. I think Ricardo would be pleased to see you, Pablo."

Still a little unconvinced, Rennin asked, "Are you sure I'm cleared of all charges?"

Pablo nodded. "Absolutely. I wish I could say the same for Ricardo; however, he is still a wanted man."

"Not on Draconis," said Rennin.

So it was decided that Pablo Morales would spend his last days with his son, and the O'Rourke family would continue their travels. The decision having been made, Rennin and Pablo put all their holdings up for sale and waited for buyers, but not until Pablo threw one party in honor of his new cousin and friend.

Rennin laid the book aside. "That seems like a good stopping place. My dear, do you think I can possibly sleep now? I think my drowsiness is from fatigue and the lateness of the hour."

Rebekah sighed. "I suppose you can sleep for a while, but you had better wake up in the morning."

Rennin awoke the next morning and many after that. For weeks the storms raged and Rennin battled the ice and snow. Finally, the blizzard broke and he decided to go for fresh game if he could find some. "I can at least get a mess of fish after I feed the animals."

"I'll feed the animals," said Rebekah. "You go before the weather changes its mind."

"All right, but be careful of that crazy mare, and don't lift full buckets."

"Yes, sir," Rebekah responded as she kissed her husband.

Rennin returned late in the afternoon to a sight that terrified him. A trail of blood spots led from the barn to the cabin. He raced through the deep snow and burst through the door in panic. "Rebekah!"

She lay crumpled in a heap upon the straw bed. Rennin knelt beside her and whispered, "Rebekah?"

She grasped his hand. "It hurts. It hurts so much." She groaned and squeezed the man's hand. "Help me, Rennin. I don't want my baby to die."

He gently laid Rebekah on her back. "Honey, I have to see what's happening," he said as he caressed her hair.

After examining her, he sat on the floor and put his head on his knees, releasing a small sob. He took a deep breath to control his emotions and said softly, "Rebekah, push."

"No! It's far too soon, Rennin."

"Rebekah, *push*! It's too late. There's nothing I can do for the baby, but you have to push it out. I don't want to lose you, too."

Rebekah started to cry. "I should have known something was wrong. He hasn't kicked me in days."

Sounding angry, Rennin said, "Rebekah, you can cry later. Right now you have to push."

With Rennin's harsh tone, Rebekah cried harder.

"Damn it!" Rennin snarled.

At Rennin's outburst, Rebekah sobbed.

Rennin stomped out the door. Rebekah heard the big man scream, "Why?"

After a few moments he came back inside. Although he was freezing, he gathered Rebekah in his arms. "Sweetheart, I'm not angry with you. I'm sorry I sounded so gruff. I'm scared. If we wait too long to expel the baby, you can get very sick. I know. My eldest sister almost died after her miscarriage. Please work with me now. Push the baby out. I love you, and I don't want to lose you."

She choked, "Okay. I'm sorry."

"For what, my love? None of this was your fault." Rennin kissed Rebekah softly and went to work on her again.

After a few minutes, he held a tiny lifeless baby girl in his hands. He saw that although the sorrow was great now, God, in His infinite wisdom, had been merciful to Rebekah and the baby for the little angel's skin had not closed over her spine.

"Rennin," Rebekah spoke haltingly. "Is he Indian?"

"It's a girl, Rebekah. Yes, she's Indian."

She began to cry again. He started out the door. She called after him, "Rennin, I want to see her."

"No, you don't, Rebekah."

"Rennin, please?"

Dejectedly, Rennin brought the baby to Rebekah. The heartbroken mother gingerly touched the underdeveloped hands and feet. Rebekah, too, saw the child's malformation. "Oh, Rennin, it's better this way. She could never have survived in our harsh world. We have to name her."

"What would you like to name her, honey?"

"Firelight. She was Indian, and that was the first thing I saw after she was delivered. Black Cloud's child deserves to have an Indian name."

"All right. Firelight O'Rourke. Honey, do you want to hold her while, I make Firelight a coffin?"

"Yes. Rennin let's bury her beside our tree."

"That will be the perfect place." He laid the stillborn baby on Rebekah's breast and kissed his wife's head. "I'll be back in a little while. I love you."

Outside, Rennin split a small log and planed it with his hunting knife before he carved it into a casket. His silent tears stained the wood as he worked. He stopped his work and spoke to his departed friend. "I'm sorry, Black Cloud. I would have been a good father to her, but she's with you. You can be her father after all." Rennin continued his work and shaped a cross on which he carved the words: "Firelight O'Rourke, daughter of Black Cloud and Eyes of a Dove, adopted daughter of Rennin O'Rourke—Resting with her Heavenly Father and her earthly father."

By the cedar sapling, Rennin dug a small grave after clearing two feet of snow. The ground was frozen solid, and it was hard work to dig even the small grave.

Rennin took the little coffin inside where he found Rebekah asleep, cradling her dead baby in her arms. He gently woke her. "Let me take Firelight now. It's already dark, but we need to bury her tonight. The moon is bright. I'll be able to see fine."

He wrapped the baby in a clean flour sack and tenderly laid her in the coffin. When he turned to go, Rebekah leaned against the wall in her coat. "Honey, you need to rest. I can do this," he chided her.

She shook her head. "I have to go, Rennin. She's my baby."

Nodding, he handed Rebekah the miniature casket and scooped her into his arms. "I can walk," she protested.

"No, you can't. If you're going, you're going this way."

"All right. I don't have the energy to argue with you."

Together Rennin and Rebekah laid Firelight in her grave and placed her marker by their tree. Rennin prayed a simple anguished prayer. "Lord, we don't understand why we suffer, but we know You are watching over us. We leave Firelight safe in Your arms and ask that You help us pick up the pieces of our broken hearts and start life afresh. Amen."

They returned to the cabin, and Rennin cleaned their sleeping area while Rebekah bathed herself and washed her soiled clothes. That night, Rennin and Rebekah held each other without words. They needed only to feel each other's hearts beating for love and comfort to radiate between them.

11
Another Journey

One bright, crisp morning in early March, Rennin bounced through the door of the lodge, grinning from ear to ear and holding his hands behind his back.

Rebekah instantly recognized the look of boyish mischief. "What are you up to?" she asked warily.

"Nothing." He handed her a vivid yellow daffodil. "Spring has sprung! We can leave for California."

She took the happy flower and held it to her nose. "Don't be in such a rush. Wait one more month."

"Why?"

"There always seems to be one more blizzard in April. April snows are the worst." She inhaled the faint fragrance. "Don't let this little one fool you. Have you seen a robin yet?"

"No."

"When you see a robin, we can pack to go."

Rennin plopped onto the bed like a disappointed child and sulked. "I'm ready to go now."

Rebekah sat beside her husband and put her arms around his neck and kissed him sensuously. She kissed his lips, his cheek, his neck, and his ear. She whispered, "Let me take your mind off everything."

He held her at arms' length. "Can we? Is it all right? Has it been long enough?"

She smiled seductively as she unbuttoned his shirt. She cooed, "It has been too long."

Easter morning broke clear and cool with crocuses popping up everywhere. Rennin and Rebekah took time to reflect on the day's significance. Rebekah sliced a deer roast thinly and put it between sliced baking-soda biscuits and made apple tarts from rehydrated apples. Then, they spent the day picnicking by their tree and Firelight's grave.

After the day in the woods, Rebekah insisted that they soak together in her tub. Then, they ate a supper of fried rabbit, rice, and gravy.

On the day after Easter, true to Rebekah's prediction, April 1st played a wicked practical joke. By noon, the day, which had dawned cold and clear, turned black and dumped freezing rain and sleet, causing icicles to drape from the trees once more. The nightfall brought howling wind and nine inches of fresh snow.

Struggling back from the barn in the freezing slush, Rennin announced, "I'm a blessed man. God gave me a wise and discerning wife. I would be a block of ice somewhere in the mountains if it were not for you—another debt of love I owe you."

As Rebekah put warm venison steak smothered in gravy, fresh biscuits, and dried cinnamon apples on the table, she quipped, "I'll take a payment right after supper. You can call it an installment. Over the next fifty years, I'll collect often."

Rennin hung his coat on a hook and slipped his arms around her waist. "Why wait until after supper?"

"Because I'm starving tonight. I must have nourishment. I won't have energy for anything else until I eat," She stated matter-of-factly.

He was dismayed by Rebekah's reluctance. Never had she put him off. "Is everything all right? Have I done something to upset you?"

"No. I'm hungry. That's all."

"That's not all. I know you better than that."

She heaved a great sigh and sat down to her plate. Rennin sat down to his dinner, but reached out and took Rebekah's hand. "Tell me what's bothering you. Let me help."

"I'm scared, Rennin."

"What frightens you?"

"We're going to have a baby. I'm afraid something will go wrong again."

"A baby? Are you sure?"

"Pretty sure. I'll give it two more weeks. Then, I'll be positive."

"That's wonderful!" His smile went all the way to his dancing eyes. He stood and came around the table to hug her tightly

She looked up at him. "Aren't you even a little afraid?"

"Nope."

"I keep thinking about Keturah Franklin telling me that she lost four babies at the stage I was. Rennin, what if that happens to me?"

"It won't. We must have faith. You do want to have my children, don't you?"

"How can you ask me that? You know I do."

"Then, be excited. Hope! Plan! I'm extremely excited. Let's think of names. I love you, lady."

Rebekah stood and flung her arms around Rennin. "You're wonderful. I *will* be excited."

They ate supper and talked about baby names and going to California. They decided they would leave two weeks hence.

After the supper dishes were clean, Rennin grabbed the book, and he and Rebekah snuggled near the fire. "Shall we continue the story, Rebekah? You might find you have something in common with Morgan."

She giggled. "I thought I was going to get a payment on your debt."

"You will in a little while, but I want you to relax first. Reading helps you relax." Rennin read.

Many months passed by the time Rennin and Pablo were able to sell all the business holdings and two villas. Rennin sent Geoffrey a letter explaining his delay. Geoffrey responded and told Rennin that he did, indeed, have a son, Ian David Montague.

During the months that it took to liquidate their assets, Morgan, too, gave Rennin another son, Duncan Paul. She commented, "I'm becoming greatly out numbered! Rennin, can we not have one little girl?"

"Maybe next time," he answered, kissing both Morgan and Duncan.

Morgan feigned indignation. "Next time! How much do you think I love you?"

"More than I will ever fathom."

Rennin also displayed the fireworks on the date he had marked as the Chinese New Year. Donovan and Cameron were enthralled.

Finally, after eleven months, Pablo Morales embraced the family he had come to love one last time as he sailed toward Draconis, laden with gold and silver and letters for every family member and friend, both human and dragon. Rennin, Morgan, Donovan, Cameron, and Duncan sailed toward London and more adventures.

During the trip, the O'Rourke family learned how treacherous the Atlantic Ocean could be. Overnight the sea changed from serene and placid to billowing and pounding swells. The wind roared. Morgan left the boys below deck and helped Rennin steady the ship.

Suddenly, Rennin felt someone tug on his pants. He yelled, "Cameron! Get below! Now!"

"Daidí, Donovan fell down. He won't get up. He has blood on his head."

Rennin bellowed over the wind, "Morgan, take care of the boys. I can do this."

She gripped Cameron's hand as they started for the cabins. Just as they reached the stairs, a monstrous wave lunged over the sloop, knocking Morgan, Rennin, and Cameron from their feet. Morgan lost the child's hand. She pulled herself up by the knob on the door and scanned the deck for Cameron. Terrified, she shrieked, "Cameron!"

She made her way to the rail and craned her neck in every direction, desperately searching for her son. In a flash of lightning, she saw him bobbing in the waves, fighting to stay afloat.

"Rennin, help!"

"Why?" he yelled.

"Cameron is overboard!"

Rennin did not wait another second, but left the ship to flounder and came to his wife's aid as quickly as he could. The sloop tossed to and fro and came dangerously close to capsizing. Rennin pulled Morgan off the rail and, without hesitation and with no thought for his own safety, plunged into the churning water.

Morgan was beside herself. She had one child unconscious below deck, a baby that might have been tossed about, and another child and her husband struggling in the sea. A wicked chuckle and voice she had not heard in years screeched above the moaning wind, "You're all going to die." The voice faded away.

She continuously prayed, "Oh, God, help me. I must be imagining things. Quazel is dead."

Without consciously thinking, she went to work. She threw a line to Rennin who had somehow managed to snag Cameron's collar. She pulled with all her might, but Rennin was twice her weight and she fought gargantuan waves. She didn't know which blinded her more, the torrential rain or uncontrolled tears.

After what seemed eons, Rennin, with Cameron holding tightly to his father's neck, fell over the rail onto the deck. Morgan wrapped her arms around her two half-drowned males while Rennin exhaustedly draped his wrist around her neck and Cameron's little fingers rubbed her cheek.

The winds calmed somewhat, and the rain slacked. The three tired O'Rourkes practically crawled to below deck where Donovan and Duncan were. Donovan had regained consciousness and leaned against the wall, holding a screaming baby. Donovan wailed almost as loudly as Duncan. "Please be quiet, Duncan. I cannot feed you. Momma will be here soon."

Drenched to the skin, Morgan merely dropped her wet clothes to the floor. She felt Rennin drape a warm dry blanket around her. She pulled it tightly and mumbled, "Thank you."

Morgan turned to Donovan. "Give me the baby and come sit beside me. Tell me what happened to you."

"Duncan started crying. I went to get him. The ship pitched. I guess I fell and hit my head real hard. When I came to, Duncan was screaming, and Cameron was gone."

"Cameron went swimming."

"Huh?"

Nursing the baby on one side, Morgan put her other arm around Donovan and kissed his head. "Cam fell overboard when he came to get us because you were hurt."

In another corner of the cabin, Rennin dried Cameron and wrapped him in a blanket. Then, he removed his own wet clothes and wrapped himself and Cameron on his lap in a blanket. Cameron still shivered and coughed and gagged seawater.

Rennin held Cameron for a while before he carried him to sit by Morgan. "Sit with Momma so I can tend to Donovan."

Without a word Cameron laid his head on Morgan's lap and continued to shiver.

Morgan said, "Rennin, put another blanket on him."

Rennin covered his second son with another blanket and turned to his eldest son. "How badly did you hit that noggin, mate?" He tried to sound lighthearted.

"I'm all right, Daidí. I guess I might have a scar to give me character, though."

Lighting several more lanterns from the one that hung by the hatch, Rennin examined Donovan in brighter light. "I'll say you'll have a scar!" Across Donovan's right eyebrow gaped a hole. "How brave are you?" Rennin asked. "Daidí needs to clean that up and put a few stitches in it. It'll hurt. Can you handle it?"

Honestly, Donovan said, "I might cry."

Rennin hugged the little boy. "'Tis understandable if you cry; just don't move."

Morgan finished feeding Duncan and laid him in a cradle made from half a barrel. She pulled Cameron into her arms to warm him and carried him to be near Donovan. Morgan held Donovan's hand while Rennin patched him. As the child predicted, he cried, but he tried to stay still.

After a grueling afternoon, all three boys finally fell asleep. Physically and emotionally exhausted, Morgan collapsed into Rennin's arms and wept uncontrollably.

He kept silent and let her cry, for he knew that if he spoke a single word, he would join her in her distress.

When she had spent her fury and frustration and fear, Morgan took a deep breath and laughed lightly. "You once told me I could cry any time I wanted. This is one time that I needed to cry."

Rennin stroked her hair and kissed the top of her head. He huskily whispered, "Me, too."

She touched Rennin's face with the back of her hand. His cheeks were wet. *I can't tell him what I heard. It would be too much.* She whispered, "I'm sorry. I've not thought once about how hard today must have been for you. Forgive me for being so selfish."

"You're not selfish. You're a terrified mother," Rennin soothed as he started to kiss Morgan's palm. "Alack! Your hands are like raw meat."

"I shall be fine."

"Sit down!" Rennin gently washed Morgan's hands and bandaged them after rubbing ointment on them. "The ropes did this. How have you kept working?"

"I had to, but how am I to cook with bandaged hands?"

"I shall cook."

"We shall starve," she teased.

"Very funny. You can stand my cooking for a couple of days."

"I might, but what about the boys?"

"Morgan Fitzpatrick O'Rourke! Stop jesting about my cooking. I make mouth-watering barley cakes." He turned the corners of his mouth down.

"Barley cakes. Yes. Well, I suppose we can survive on barley cakes three times a day for a while."

"Keep this up, and you'll be fasting."

"Would you do that to me?" she asked as she draped her wounded hands over her husband's shoulders.

"You know better," Rennin assured as he cupped Morgan's face in his hands and kissed her.

She scooted inside his blanket. "I can think of something that might help to sustain me if I am forced to eat barley cakes three times a day."

"What might that be?"

"Let me show you." She ran her bangdaged hands across his bare buttocks.

"Morgan! The boys."

"They will *not* wake up."

Rennin closed the book. "That reminds me. I have a payment on my debt due."

Rebekah quipped, "I have never known anyone so eager to pay his debts."

As Rebekah spoke, the wind howled. She snuggled closer. "The weather at sea can be as dangerous as the mountains."

"Yes, it can. I understand the weather in California is almost always warm and sunny."

"That would be pleasant."

"I can think of something more pleasant."

"What?"

"Paying my debt."

The O'Rourkes decided to leave in the middle of April. They had one more picnic near the cedar sapling that had taken good root. They transplanted a few daffodil bulbs to Firelight's grave and bade her good-bye.

After the day in the woods, Rebekah insisted that they soak one more time together in her tub. Then, they ate a supper of fried fish, corn fitters and stewed apples. Finally, Rennin picked up the book to read one last night in the cozy cabin.

With the treacherous sea lapping behind them, Rennin, Morgan, and the boys dropped anchor in London. The next leg of the journey was to be easy. They hired a hansom to take them to the address on the letter Rennin had received from Geoffrey. When Rennin knocked on the door, a tall, dark-haired woman answered.

Rennin looked at the paper in his hand and drew his brow into a deep confused frown. "Excuse me. I might have the wrong address. I'm looking for Geoffrey Montague."

The woman stared accusingly at Rennin. "Who be you?"

"I'm Rennin O'Rourke. I've just arrived from Spain, and I'm supposed to meet my friend, Geoffrey, at this address."

"So, you're the O'Rourke chap." She reached behind her and handed Rennin a scrap of paper. "Geoffrey and Nancy moved. He said if you come lookin' fer 'im to give you this address. I amn't to give it to nobody but you." She shut the door in his face.

Rennin returned to the cab and asked the driver to take them to Geoffrey's new address.

The driver asked, "You sure you wanna go there? You folks look a mite well-to-do to be goin' to tha' neighborhood. Real poor folks live down there. It might not be safe for the likes o' you."

"We shall be fine," Rennin told the driver, but to Morgan he said, "I don't understand. Geoffrey isn't extremely poor. Not rich, but not destitute either. Something must have happened."

When they arrived, Rennin understood the driver's comment, for the Montague home was a small flat in one of the seedier areas. The streets were filthy and smelled rancid.

Morgan said, "Rennin, are you sure this is the address on the paper?"

"Yes. Morgan, you won't judge Geoffrey for being poor, will you?"

"Of course not!" She scowled deeply. "You know I will judge him by his character. You think highly of him, so he must be a good man."

Rennin knocked strongly on the door. A heavyset blonde-haired woman with a jovial round face opened the door. "Mrs. Montague?" he aksed.

"Aye."

"I'm Rennin O'Rourke, Geoffrey's crewmate. He's been expecting us."

"Aye!" replied Nancy Montague. "Come in, come in. Our place ain't much, but you're welcome. Geoffrey's workin' at the wharf, but he'll be mighty glad to know you've come at last." Nancy was friendly and easygoing.

Rennin and the driver unloaded the bags. Inside the flat, the atmosphere was much more pleasant and inviting. Though sparsely furnished, the small two-bedroom apartment was clean and cheerful. There were two lovely paintings hanging on the walls with the signature—

Morgan commented, "Your work is beautiful, Mrs. Montague."

"Please, call me Nancy, but many thanks. I'm afraid I've gotten into a great deal of trouble over a few of my pieces. Some of the more prudish folk found them offensive. I've often wished I could live in Paris where such things are readily accepted."

"You would love Draconis. The people would embrace your talent and encourage you."

"Geoffrey shared the stories Rennin told him. Are they true, Morgan?"

"Oh, yes."

"Then, how could you leave it?"

"Rennin has the wanderlust. I fear we will never settle in one spot, but I shall go wherever he goes. I love him more than Draconis."

"I understand. My Geoffrey is one reason I'll never live in Paris. What we won't sacrifice for our men!"

Rennin came in with the bags. "Did you say you were going to sacrifice your men?" he teased.

The ladies hooted in laughter.

That evening Nancy splurged on the meal. She prepared a pot roast with turnip roots, carrots, celery, and onions; thick slices of fresh-baked bread with butter; and strawberry short cake with whipping cream. Geoffrey was anxious to hear what had become of Victor and Juan. He was thoroughly impressed with Morgan's tenacity once he heard her story.

Rennin became serious, "Geoffrey, when you sent your letter telling me you had moved, you said you had moved up to a larger house. I went to the address on the letter. The house was quite nice. Why so much change? What happened to your small cottage?"

Geoffrey dropped his head. "I'm embarrassed, Rennin, to say I lost our 'ouse with some bad investments. Right now this is the best I can afford."

"Geoffrey, let's take a walk to the tavern. I'm buying."

The two men left the women and children to make their own fun.

Over a few pints of beer, Rennin talked. "Geoffrey, you know if you needed help, you could have asked me. Now that everything is settled with Victor, I've more money than I can *ever* use."

"The time it would've taken to notify you would've been too long, and I was ashamed to admit my gullibility. I invested in a scheme that sounded too good to be true. It was, and I was swindled out o' most o' our savings. Although on the surface the deal looked legal, it was crooked. If I 'ad come forward with a charge, I would've been the one spendin' time in prison. It's better to be poor with my family than to be in prison."

Rennin chuckled thoughtfully. "Maybe we should set Morgan on them."

Geoffrey laughed heartily and raised his stein. "Hear! Hear!"

"Seriously," Rennin continued, "Morgan and I have decided to go to the New World. Why don't you and Nancy join us? I could use a good strong seaman to help me cross the Atlantic."

"The New World?" said Geoffrey in disbelief. "Rennin, that sounds almost too good to be true. If it were any other man but you askin', I'd laugh in 'is face."

Rennin smirked wryly. "I'm sure you're destined to go with me. After all, I believe your fortune included you and your son building a house in a distant land."

"Let me talk to Nancy. I ain't gonna make a decision this big without 'er. That's 'ow I got in trouble before, not consultin' my better 'alf."

"Of course you must talk to your wife, but I don't think she'll be hard to convince."

Rennin was right. Nancy all but insisted they go as soon as possible, so the two families prepared to set sail for The New World in early June.

Rennin closed the book and planted a kiss on his young bride. "Tomorrow we start another leg of our journey. Let's rest. We've many nights to read by our campfire."

She ran her hand across his cheek. "But we've no more nights for a while to have assured privacy."

"What are you saying, Mrs. O'Rourke?"

"You know exactly what I'm saying."

12
Perilous Travel

Rennin and Rebekah began the last leg of their journey on a crisp, clear April morning, but before the week was out, they attempted to travel in driving rain. Finally, Rennin found a cavern big enough for him and Rebekah, as well as the horses and mule. There they spent several days, patiently waiting for the rain to stop.

"There are going to be a multitude of flowers this May," Rennin said sullenly.

"Why will there be more than usual?" asked Rebekah.

He laughed. "You always manage to find a way to change my mood. Don't you remember the old adage: 'April showers bring May flowers'?"

"No, but I suppose it's true."

Rennin stared at Rebekah and worried about her. Sometimes he forgot that although she was white, she had been brought up as an Indian. She was truly naïve and ignorant of white men's customs. Feeling a sudden overwhelming need to protect this woman who had captured his heart, he gathered her in his arms and held her silently, afraid to let go.

"What was that for?" she asked.

"Do I need a reason to hug my wife?"

"No, you may hug me anytime you like." Rebekah slid her arms around Rennin's waist and laid her head on his chest. "I love you."

He smoothed her hair and breathed, "I love you more than words can ever say."

A shattering clap of thunder shook them from their tender moment. The volume of the rumbles agitated the livestock, and Rennin tried to calm them. The mare, which had been Pierre's, continued to stomp. With a blinding flash and a loud *BANG!,* as lightning struck a tree near the entrance of the cave, the mare reared, knocking Rennin from his feet. Her hooves landed squarely on his left arm. He uttered a sharp cry as the bone cracked.

As Rennin rolled away from the spooked creature, Rebekah made sure the mare's tether was tight, being careful to keep her distance. Then she knelt beside her husband.

"It's broken," he acknowledged through clenched teeth. "There are some splints in the medical pack on the mule."

She started for the mule, and Rennin call after her, "Rebekah, you are *not* riding that lunatic mare again. I'll ride her from now on. As soon as we can, we're trading her."

"Don't be silly, Rennin. She's frightened."

"That's the point. She's afraid of her own shadow. She's dangerous. What if she should throw you? Rebekah, think about the baby."

Rebekah touched her abdomen protectively. "All right, Rennin, but right now I'm worrying about you."

She came back to him and carefully splinted his arm, making a sling for it from torn flour sacks. Although his arm ached dreadfully, Rennin leaned against the wall of the cave and fell asleep.

The rain still poured, but the thunder and lightning subsided. Rebekah gently stroked the buttermilk-colored mare's nose. "That horrible man hurt you, too, didn't he? Don't you worry. We'll talk to Rennin. He'll come around. We won't get rid of you. Believe it or not, he's just scared, too." As if in answer, the mare nickered softly and nuzzled Rebekah's cheek.

Rennin stirred at the sound. Rebekah moved away from the horse and sat beside him, lovingly lowering his head into her lap. She caressed his cheek and hair. Soon the lull of the steady rain sang Rebekah to sleep as well.

When Rennin and Rebekah awoke, it was late in the afternoon, and the fire was almost out. Rennin moaned as he sat up. His arm throbbed, but he managed to throw a couple of dry twigs onto the fire to get a blaze. Rebekah set about feeding everyone, including the mare. She filled the feedbags for both horses and the pack mule. Then, she set about making a supper of beans, dried venison and fresh dandelion greens she had gathered early that morning during a brief stop in the rain.

During supper she said very little. Rennin asked, "Rebekah, what's on your mind? You're never this quiet unless there's something on your mind. Tell me what it is."

"I want to keep the mare."

"Rebekah..." he began.

She interrupted, "Oh, Rennin, she has been mistreated. Pierre was obviously cruel to her. She needs a kind hand. She was only afraid of the bright flash and loud noise earlier. Please, can't we love the fear from her?"

Rennin reached his uninjured hand, which he had been awkwardly using to hold his fork, out to take Rebekah's hand. "Your depth of compassion amazes me. She's a horse, yet you want to make her life better."

"Rennin, she's more than a horse. I think you'll find her to be a jewel someday. As a matter of fact, I think I'll name her Jewel. You call your horse Buster, so my mare's name is Jewel."

"Okay, Rebekah. We'll see how she does for a while, but I'm going to ride her just to be safe."

"Agreed."

"Now that we've had our first argument, and you won, do you want to read some more about my namesake's voyage to America?"

"Yes, I'd like to read, but were we arguing?" Rebekah asked with concern.

"Let's say we had a difference of opinion about Jewel. Rebekah, we won't always agree, but that's all right so long as we work it out."

"We'll always work it out. I don't want to argue. So, let's read now."

"Fine. We'll read, but I have an idea. Whoever wins our arguments gets to decide how to spend our evening. Since you won this time, we'll read tonight." Rennin made the arrangement laughingly.

He struggled to hold his ancestor's book while his dominant hand was in a sling, so Rebekah held the book while Rennin read.

The O'Rourke family and the Montague family sailed westward without incident for several days. One dreary morning, Emily Claire awoke with a high fever and a great number of tiny blisters covering her body. Geoffrey came on deck with his face drawn and taut with worry. As Rennin approached his friend, Geoffrey warned, "Stay back, Rennin. We must isolate our families."

"What is it, man?" Rennin asked, horrified by Geoffrey's demeanor.

"The pox. My little angel 'as the smallpox. We're all sure to come down with it. Do you know 'ow deadly this disease is, Rennin?"

"I've heard. Geoffrey, what can we do to help? There must be something. Mayhap some of Morgan's potions or some of the herbs from Draconis can help."

"I cannot let Morgan take that chance, Rennin, but oh, Rennin, I don't want my angel to die." The burly father dissolved into tears.

Despite his warning, Rennin embraced his friend. Through his sobs Geoffrey chastised, "Are you crazy, man? You're exposing yourself to almost certain death."

"I'll take my chances. Do you truly think I would desert you in your time of need? That is not how I was taught to behave. Good and true friends are like family. They support, encourage, and help one another through tough times and rejoice and celebrate through good times. Now, how can we help?"

Geoffrey took courage from Rennin's words. "The fever is the killer. If we can get Emily Claire's fever under control, she can fight."

Rennin said, "I know Aunt Lizzie sent strong herbs for fever. Morgan can brew a tea for Emily Claire; and, Geoffrey, we'll pray fervently for all of us."

Morgan dissolved cinchona bark into tea, and Nancy spooned it to her sick child. Within days the entire Montague family had contracted smallpox. Morgan nursed them tirelessly. By the week's end, every person aboard the sloop except Morgan was stricken with the illness. Her stomach roiled with fear, especially for her infant son.

She found a quiet place, and taking a deep breath, turned to face the four directions, hands outspread. As she made the full three-hundred-sixty-degree circle, the wind wafted her hair in a swirl, and words in a language she did not know flowed freely from her lips. "Cau amdanaf ag amddiffyn. Grymuso mi iachau. Waddoli fi gyda phŵer. Tynnu cysgod angau yn. Cymerwch cystudd hwn, ac yn rhwygo ei assunder." ("Encompass me with protection. Empower me with healing. Endow me with power. Remove death's shadow. Take this affliction, and rend it assunder.") Feeling a supernatural tingle throughout her body and an unexplainable surge of energy, Morgan returned to the sick.

For weeks, she attended the entire crew of *The Rover*, the name Donovan and Cameron had given the ship. Even through his delirium, Rennin fretted about Morgan. His fevered brain dreamed of losing her to either illness or total exhaustion. Still, Morgan worked with the energy of a dozen women.

As Rennin mumbled in his delirium, Morgan stood on deck and spread her hands. Unbeknownst to either of them, they spoke the same words. "Leighis spiorad, Cuimsíonn dúinn. Chosaint chugainn ó dhochar agus Doirt amach beannacht orainn." (Healing spirit, encompass us. Protect us from harm and pour out blessings upon us.") Again, she felt the same feeling as the day she had sought peace and power.

Finally, after weeks of cool cloths, medicines, herb teas, and Morgan's words about God's power to perform miracles, Emily Claire and Geoffrey awoke fever free. Throughout the week, each person who had been afflicted recovered completely, with nothing more than a few scars to show for their suffering. Worn to a frazzle, Morgan collapsed into her bed and slept for two full days. Surprisingly, neither did she contract the disease nor did she lose a single patient. As she drifted into a deep sleep, she whispered, "Thank you, Lord."

After that, they traveled along encountering dolphins and whales. Rennin delighted the children when he took them swimming with the dolphins. At first Emily Claire was frightened, but Donovan teased her mercilessly. "You are such a ninny."

"I am not a ninny. I'm cautious."

"All right, scaredy cat, chicken, coward! Which name do you like best?"

"Emily Claire, thank you," she said haughtily.

Cameron joined his brother in the taunting, "Hey, Donnie, call her Emily Chicken or Emily Coward."

The boys chanted, "Emily Coward, Emily Coward."

"You two are just asses!" shouted Emily Claire.

"Emily Claire!" scolded Nancy.

"Well, they are, Mum. They're mean and hateful and nasty, especially Donovan."

"I am not!" shouted Donovan. "You're a know-it-all bossy-breeches, and nobody likes you."

"I hate you, Donovan O'Rourke!"

"I hate you, too."

Geoffrey put his hand on Emily Claire's shoulder. "Watch saying things like that. You will probably end up marryin' 'im someday." Geoffrey laughed.

"How disgusting, Papa!" Emily Claire grimaced and spoke loudly enough to be heard in the water. "I'd rather marry Cameron. He is cuter and nicer."

"It matters very little to me. They're both my best friend's sons. Right now, I want you to put your dress to the side and go swimmin' with the dolphins and me. They really are 'armless."

Finally, Emily Claire plunged into the water with the creatures and had a good time.

After the excursion, Rennin was quiet and thoughtful as he stared at the ocean. When no one was paying any attention, Morgan walked behind him and slipped her arm around his waist. "Where has your mind wandered?" she whispered.

Rennin pulled her in front of him and held her tightly. "I was remembering how Kieran and I used to frolic in the sea with Danielle while she was still a dolphin. God! I miss my brother."

"Send him a message."

"How?"

"Talk to one of your dolphin friends. I shall help. Remember the butterfly, Rennin."

Once again Rennin swam with the dolphins, but this time Morgan joined him. Together they swam and talked to one of the friendlier animals. As they talked, it made little cackling noises back to them. The sleek creature left carrying a message that all was well, news of the voyage to London and The New World, and greetings of love and longing."

For the children, the voyage seemed endless although every day the three eldest children had chores and lessons. Morgan taught them reading and arithmetic; Rennin taught them science, history, and geography; and Nancy gave them art lessons. Late in the afternoons, Geoffrey taught the children how to fish.

After three months of water, even the adults grew irritable. With the smallpox past, there had been few real challenges. They became lackadaisical in their vigilance of a fickle sea. From breakfast until lunch one bright morning, the temperature dropped twenty degrees, the skies turned pitch black and loosened a deluge of water, and the wind changed from helpful gusts to turbulent, uncontrollable swirls that roared.

Morgan and Nancy took the children below deck. Sternly, Morgan held both Donovan and Cameron by the arm. "Under no circumstances are any of you to come up top. Do *not* walk around. I don't want a repeat performance of our trip to London. Do you understand me?"

Both boys nodded and said sheepishly, "Yes, ma'am."

Morgan hugged and kissed both boys. "I'm not trying to be mean or cruel. I love you two so much. It would kill me to lose you. Donovan, you're the eldest child here. You're in charge while we're on deck. Treat the other children the way you think I would treat you. The rest of you listen to Donovan, even you, Emily Claire. I see your mouth opening to object. I trust Donovan to do what's wise and right. He has had more experience at sea than you. You help keep the little ones busy with something."

Morgan and Nancy sped to assist their husbands. On deck, Geoffrey had lashed himself to the helm. While Rennin worked frantically to secure the sails. The ladies made sure any loose items were fastened down. Rennin then ordered them below with the children.

As hard as Rennin and Geoffrey tried to keep *The Rover* afloat, the wind and waves tried harder to capsize her. When darkness fell, the tempest still raged. Even Rennin's flawless sense of direction could not tell him which way the ship was headed, so many times had the wind spun her that day. The men were satisfied they were not at the bottom of the sea. Then, near midnight, Rennin's heart leapt into his throat as he heard the crunch of wood against rock. *The Rover* moved no more.

Rennin closed the book and whispered, "What do you hear, Rebekah?"

"Crickets."

"Exactly. The rain has finally stopped. We can continue our own journey tomorrow."

"Then, Rennin, my love, we should get some sleep. Dawn will be here far too soon."

She retrieved the bedrolls and put the two together to form a softer bed. Rebekah slept on Rennin's right side rather than his left side in an attempt to protect his broken arm.

The sleeping arrangement made for an awkward night, but both awoke, eager to continue their journey. A brilliant tangerine blaze greeted them. The cool clean air invigorated the animals, and they made up a great deal of lost time, stopping for only two short breaks and a quick lunch before dusk when they made camp under a grove of spruces on soft, tender, young grass shoots near a trickling mountain brook.

Too tired to do anything but have a bit of supper, Rennin and Rebekah slept soundly under a crescent moon and twinkling stars. The crickets' song was their lullaby, and the lark's tune, their alarm.

Several weeks of warming days and pleasant nights came to an abrupt halt when Rennin and Rebekah came to the ford in the river, swollen by previous weeks' rain and melting snow in higher elevations. The current was strong and swift. Rennin rode up and down the bank looking for a safe crossing.

"Rebekah, it will take a lot of effort to cross, so we had better get started."

She suggested, "Rennin, let's ride upstream to where the river becomes more narrow. It might add a few days to our journey, but at least we'll be safe."

Irritably, Rennin snapped, "I'm frustrated with all these delays! Buster can swim this. Let's go."

Calmly, Rebekah dismounted the black stallion. She turned to Rennin. "Buster might have the strength to ford the river here, but Jewel and Jack do not. Please get off my horse. If you want to take Buster across, Jewel, Jack, the baby, and I will meet you on the other side in about a week."

Flabbergasted, Rennin was speechless. For a moment, his mouth opened and closed without sound. "Rebekah, have you lost your mind? You aren't riding upriver alone."

"No, Rennin. I'm being sensible. You're acting childish and irrational. I'll be safer going upriver alone than I will be crossing here, even if I ride Buster. Jewel doesn't have the strength for this current. She cannot take either of us across safely. If Jack tries to swim here, he will either drown or at least lose our supplies. Be reasonable. If we are to find gold in California, it will be there when we get there. If not, then I'll be content to be the wife of a dirt farmer, so long as that farmer is you."

"Damn, woman! Why do you have to be so practical?"

Rebekah smiled mischievously. "Does that mean we're riding upstream?"

In a mocking voice, Rennin said, "Yes, that means we're riding upstream."

She remounted Buster, laughing blithely. She spurred the horse to a quick trot and flung over her shoulder, as Rennin sullenly nudged Jewel to move, "That means I won our argument, and I get to choose how we spend our evening!"

Rebekah urged Buster into a light gallop. Rennin picked up Rebekah's insinuation and called, "Rebekah! Slow down! Wait for me!"

She tossed back, "Catch me, if you dare!" Then she gave Buster his head and let him fly.

Rennin coaxed the mare, "Get up, Jewel." The horse would have gone into a high gallop had Rennin not been hampered by the pack mule.

Until dusk, Rennin did well to keep Rebekah in his sights. Finally, he came upon Buster tethered loosely in a small clearing with fresh green grass. Buster grazed contentedly. Rennin left Jewel and Jack by Buster's side and went in search of his wife. He followed a trail of clothes to a shallow area in the river, set off from the raging current by a ring of boulders. Rebekah swam there.

Rennin leaned against a tree, holding the garments he had gathered on his way. She called, "It took you long enough to get here. I thought we would begin our evening with a refreshing swim."

"Isn't the water a bit cold for swimming?" He smirked.

"It'll warm up quickly when you join me."

"But I don't want to freeze."

"Well, that's too bad. You made the rules for arguing. I won, and this is what I want to do. Now, start a fire, take off that splint because your arm has healed by now, and get in here."

Rennin grinned impishly. He started a fire, removed his splint, and tested his arm, which felt strong. He sat on the bank and removed his boots. Then, he started to wade into the water, which really was chilly.

Rebekah shouted, "Rennin Aidan O'Rourke! You leave those clothes on that river bank unless you want to go to California alone!"

"Come on, lady. Have you no mercy?"

"None!"

While he hung his clothes across a bough of a tree, he pretended to grumble. "You have no heart. You're a slave driver." Nonetheless, he swam to meet his wife.

"Rebekah! You *are* crazy! This water is freezing!"

She snuggled up against him because the water was only chest high. "How do you think I feel? It seems as if I've been waiting in here for you forever. I'm an icicle."

He pulled her close and whispered, "Then, let's get out of here. I'll warm you up." Oblivious to the world around them, Rennin and Rebekah locked in a deep passionate kiss.

The couple was shocked back to reality as a bullet whizzed past Rennin's head and a familiar voice laughed menacingly. "Well, O'Rourke, I see you decided da little Injun whore can give you some pleasure after all. What a hypocrite! You ain't got da guts to take whacha want, but I see she freely gives herself to you. Probly 'cause you're an Injun lover. I hear you was real tight wif Black Cloud. Maybe you was glad Pierre done 'im in."

Rennin put Rebekah behind him. "Bart! What the hell do you think you're doing? Put that gun away, and you can stop talking about Rebekah in that manner at once!"

"Whacha gonna do—shoot me? What wif—your fanger? I do believe your gun's hangin' here wif your clothes. Matter of fact, 'bout everthang you own is here on dese here horses an' mule." Bart began to rifle through the bags on Jack.

"Damn it, Bart!" Rennin started from the water. Bart shot into the water just at Rennin's feet. As Bart shot, Jewel reared, pulling her tether loose. She reared again and seemed to deliberately bring her front hooves down on Bart. As Jewel knocked him to the ground, his gun flew from his hand. Jewel stood over him and snorted repeatedly, daring him to move.

Taking advantage of the situation, Rennin sprinted from the water. He snatched his gun and hurriedly threw on his long johns. Training his gun on the man beneath Jewel's raised hoof, Rennin pulled his blanket from his bedroll and met Rebekah at the water's edge.

As she wrapped herself in the blanket, Bart attempted to scoot from beneath the mare. Jewel pawed the ground only inches from his head and snorted.

Rennin snarled, "I suggest you stay perfectly still, Bart."

"O'Rourke, what have you done to Pierre's horse?"

"Rebekah has loved her. You made the mistake of threatening Jewel's mistress. If my wife gives the command, her mare will crush your skull."

"Your wife? You married da..." Jewel snorted threateningly. "You married da woman?"

Rennin kept his gun pointed at Bart and talked to Jewel. "Easy, girl. Good, girl." He stroked the mare's neck. "Maybe you really are a jewel—an undiscovered treasure." Jewel nickered and nuzzled Rennin's hand. "That's a girl." Rennin soothed. "Back up, Jewel. Rebekah, get your horse."

Rebekah had dressed hastily. She took Jewel's reins and muttered, "I should let her kill you. You're a very bad man, Bart. Have you ever considered how displeased God is with you? That's why I won't kill you. I won't be responsible for sending your soul to Hell."

"I will!" snapped Rennin as he flung Bart's gun into the river. "Now, get up!" Rennin pulled the hammer back on his revolver.

"Rennin!" gasped Rebekah.

"Why are you worried about this vermin's soul, dear? He isn't. He obviously wants to join his old friend, Pierre."

"Come on, O'Rourke," said Bart, cowering. "I wudn't gonna kill eiver of you. I only meant to scare you a little."

"You took two shots at me!" growled Rennin.

"Yeah, butcha know if'n I meant to kill you, I wouldn't uh missed. You know I'm a crack shot. I ain't quite as good as you, but damn close."

Rennin grabbed Bart by the scruff of his collar and dragged him away from the horses. "You could've killed my wife and my child, you fool! Now, I suggest you pray for forgiveness before I send you to meet your Maker."

Rebekah stood there, wide-eyed with dismay. She had never seen Rennin so angry. "You-you're not really going to kill him, are you, Rennin?"

"Why should I spare him, Rebekah? So he can sneak up on us in California? By then we'll have a little one to consider, too. This dolt would probably just as soon kill a baby as a man. I'm tired of worrying about him."

Bart's tone turned to pleading. "O'Rourke, I'm sorry. Mrs. O'Rourke, I apologize for da thangs I said. Talk to your husband. Please?"

"Rennin," Rebekah said softly, "you thought it was terrible that I wanted to let the buzzards eat Pierre, but you want to kill Bart."

"I'll bury him. I won't leave him for the buzzards and the coyotes."

Rebekah's eyes filled with tears. "Rennin, are you really going to murder Bart? He's not even armed anymore."

"Neither were we. He would've shot us naked and left us for the vultures."

It had become dark and the only light illuminating the faces of the three people was the small flickering firelight. In the shadows, Rebekah could see that Rennin's cheeks glistened with moisture. For the first time, she realized he was serious about killing Bart. All this time, she had thought her husband was trying to frighten the other man. She became truly afraid that Rennin's anger would obscure his judgment. Rebekah laid a gentle hand on his shoulder and whispered, "Honey, you aren't a murderer."

Rennin slowly lowered the hammer on his gun. He gathered Rebekah in his arms and buried his face in her hair. As Rebekah held the man she loved, she could feel his silent sobs. Rennin said loudly enough for Bart to hear, "If he had hurt you, I would have killed him without a second thought. I love you so much."

Bart watched as Rebekah comforted her husband and thought all the while that it would be pleasant to be loved, but that he was too ornery to be loved by anyone, especially a woman of character.

Rebekah finally whispered, "Rennin, you're freezing. Get dressed." She looked at Bart, who had not moved. "You can gather some wood for the fire if either of you wants anything to eat."

Rennin paused in the middle of pulling on his boots. "Rebekah, did you just invite that vermin to eat with us?"

"I did. Don't argue. I'll only win again, and you haven't paid for today's argument yet. You'll be deeply in debt."

"Rebekah! This is no joking matter."

"Rennin, I believe Jesus ate with the sinners and tax collectors. Are we any better than He?"

Rennin was silent. Bart gathered wood and handed Rebekah a string of fish, freshly cleaned that afternoon. "To help wif supper, ma'am," he said with downcast eyes. "Mrs. O'Rourke, I'm truly sorry for all da bad thangs I done to you. I probly shoulda been shot, but thank you for sparin' my miserable life." He looked toward Rennin, who was feeding the horses, including Bart's nag. "O'Rourke."

"Don't talk to me, Bart. I'm not ready," Rennin said shortly.

Rebekah salted and mealed the fish and fried them in bear grease. She served them with corn fritters, sweetened dried apples, and coffee. The meal was eaten in silence.

Rennin gathered the dishes and took them to the river to wash. Rebekah prepared their bed. Bart went to his horse. "Mrs. O'Rourke, thank you for supper. It tasted mighty fine. I ain't eat nothin' that good since I left New Orleans. I best be goin'."

"Nonsense," said Rebekah. "You may sleep near our fire tonight." Rebekah and Bart heard Rennin slam a tin plate against a rock.

Bart chuckled wryly. "No, ma'am, I don't thank I'm welcome."

Rebekah looked toward the shadow at the river. "Don't worry about Rennin. He'll find it in his heart to forgive you, too. Give him some time."

Rennin came to the fire and grunted, "If you snore, I'll shoot you."

Rennin awoke to the smell of coffee, frying salt pork, and, if he believed his senses, eggs. Rebekah handed him a tin cup, filled with hot coffee. Sheepishly, Rennin asked, "Where did you get the eggs?"

"Bart."

"Where did Bart steal the eggs?"

"I didn't steal 'em, O'Rourke. There's a widow woman 'bout two miles upriver. She traded me some fresh salt pork and eggs for some rabbit skins and a side of venison. Real nice lady. 'Spectin' a young'un, too, but further along than your missus. Tree fell on her man. I helped bury 'im. Funny name though—Keturah. Never heard dat name afore."

Rebekah dropped her cup. "Keturah!" She looked at Rennin. "We have to go to her, Rennin. She's expecting. You know what has happened before."

"You know da lady?" Bart asked in surprise.

"Yes," said Rennin. "Her husband was the minister who married Rebekah and me."

"I can take you to her place. She took up residence in an ol' deserted soddie. She'd sure like to see a friendly face."

"Of course, we'll go to her," said Rennin.

"O'Rourke," said Bart, "can I talk to you today? Are you ready for my humble apology? I shoulda knowed you to be a good man from da first. You always talked like your missus and Keturah. Fine woman dat Keturah."

"Bart," Rennin said thoughtfully, "you were never as loathsome as Pierre. I always had a feeling that at one time you were an upstanding man. What happened to make you so angry?"

"Does dis mean you're willin' to forgive dis foolish man?" asked Bart, penitently.

"Yes, Bart, I can forgive you, but don't ever threaten my wife again."

"Wouldn't dream of it. She really is a good woman, O'Rourke. She was jest dealt a bad hand like me. Diff'rence is she made da best of hers. I folded.

"When I was your age I married a purty, sweet half-breed Choctaw and Creole mix back in New Orleans. Her momma had been Injun, an' she died in childbirth. Her father raised her to be a lady, but she was a fickle woman. Six months after we was wed, I come home early from a huntin' trip an' found her wif her daddy's young lawyer. In a rage, I shot 'em boff. I run away out west. I guess I sorta stopped trustin' folks, especially women. I figgered one had hurt me so bad, dey must all be rotten. After meetin' Mrs. O'Rourke and dat Keturah, I thank I was wrong. I jest got a bad one. Dare's some good ones."

"Yes, Bart, there are some very good ones; Rebekah and Keturah are prime examples. Let me ask you something. Are you smitten with Keturah Franklin?"

"Well, O'Rourke, I sure thank a lot of her, but I'm afraid she wouldn't cotton much to me if'n she knowed 'bout my past. I murdered two people; I've cheated an' swindled more'n I can count; an'"—Bart paused and looked at Rebekah—"you boff know what else I done. I really do regret hurtin' you, Mrs. O'Rourke. I don't know how you can be so kind to me."

Rebekah slipped her hand into Rennin's. "I forgive you, Bart. God turned something very bad into something wonderful. He brought me to the man I love more than my own life. Bart, why don't you ask God to forgive you, too? Keturah understands what it means to be forgiven."

"Maybe I will, Mrs. O'Rourke."

Rennin squeezed Rebekah's hand. "Bart, if we're going to be friends, maybe you should call us by our given names, Rennin and Rebekah. Some more advice: You might see if

Keturah Franklin is interested in having a new man in her life. After all, she's alone."

Like a schoolboy, Bart whispered, "Maybe Rebekah can ask her for me."

Two hours later, the trio arrived at Keturah Franklin's abode. At the sound of horses' hooves, she opened the door. Seeing Rebekah, an obviously pregnant Keturah greeted her with open arms. "Rebekah! Rennin! Bartholomew, I didn't expect you back."

Bart blushed. "I run into some ol' friends who happen to know you."

"I see. Please, come in. It's not much, but it's warm and dry." She ushered them in and said, "Have a seat. Coffee?"

"Yes, thanks," Rennin said and pulled a chair out for Rebekah. He took one next to her while Bart sat across from Rennin, leaving one chair for Keturah.

Rebekah said, "We're very sorry to hear about Jedediah, but why are you here? Why aren't you on your way to California with the Missionary Society or on your way back east?"

Keturah shrugged and said a little bitterly, "The Missionary Society didn't want to take an expectant mother without a husband. I have no family, so I stayed here. Where else am I to go?"

"California with us," said Rennin before he knew he had spoken.

"California with you and Rebekah?"

"And Bart." Rennin's mouth ran ahead of his brain. Rebekah kicked him under the table.

"Ouch!"

Keturah sat cups of coffee in front of her guests and started to laugh. At first she gave a little chuckle. Then, she laughed harder until she couldn't catch her breath. After several minutes, Keturah, through small gasps asked,

"Bartholomew, is Rennin playing matchmaker for you? Is there something you'd like to say to me?"

Bart stammered, "I um. Well, um."

Keturah began to laugh again. Bart fidgeted. Keturah turned to Rebekah. "I'm sorry. Rebekah, is there something I should know?"

"I'm not really sure, Keturah. Bart will have to answer that question." Rebekah turned to Bart with a smirk on her face. She was enjoying his discomfiture.

Bart began to sweat, but he took a deep breath. "Keturah Franklin, you're a fine woman, but I'm a crude and vile man. Rebekah O'Rourke has helped me to understand dat even a man as bad as me can be forgiven. Wif dat in mind, I'll tell you dat I thank highly of you. Matter of fact, I thank I love you. So, if'n you can see past my many faults, I'd like to ask you to marry me.

"You're alone an' 'bout to have a baby. You need a strong man to take care of you. I ain't real educated like you, an' I ain't been no saint. But I love you, an' I'd take care of you an' your little one. An' I'm trying to be a better man."

Keturah had stopped laughing and started crying. She sank into the last chair at the table. "Bartholomew Mercier, I knew there was a good man hiding beneath that gruff exterior, or I never would have allowed you to bunk in my barn all winter. I had hoped you would say those things to me before you left. I had no idea it would take a woman I'd misjudged and mistreated once to bring you to your senses. Yes, I'll marry you, you big oaf! I'll go to California or Timbuktu with you."

Keturah looked around at the three faces looking at her. "I'll confess something to the three of you. Then, I never want to hear it or talk about it again. Before I met Jedediah, I was a prostitute. I lived in a brothel in St. Louis. My mother had been a prostitute in the same brothel, and she died when I was born. The women reared me to be one of them. I was well educated because the madame wanted her girls to appear to be ladies.

"I met Jedediah on the streets one day. He literally stormed into the place and dragged me out. He took me away from all that. I became cold and judgmental against all forms of what I perceived as sexual impurity. It took Rebekah to show me what a bitch I was."

Keturah took Bart's hand. "Bart," she said tenderly, "your past sins cannot be any greater than mine."

Keturah turned to Rebekah. "Rebekah, do you remember how I told you I had lost four babies?"

Rebekah nodded.

"That was four I lost with Jedediah. Before that, I did away with three—no man pays for a pregnant whore." Keturah rubbed her protruding belly. "God has finally seen fit to let me have a baby. I have about two and a half months left. I didn't know when I saw you last that I was expecting. I had begun to think I would never be a mother because I had so callously murdered three gifts God had given me. Rebekah, your simple faith gave me stronger faith."

Keturah suddenly realized that Rebekah should be as pregnant as she. "Rebekah, what happened to your baby?"

"She died," Rebekah said simply without explanation.

"Who was the father? Was she your husband's child?" Keturah asked sympathetically.

Bart dropped his cup and caught his breath sharply.

Rebekah shook her head at Bart and answered. "Yes, she was Black Cloud's child. Rennin and I named her Firelight, and we buried her beside our Christmas tree. I have exciting news, too. Rennin and I are expecting a baby to born around our anniversary."

"That's wonderful!" Keturah exclaimed.

Nervously, Bart interjected, "I hate to interrupt all dis talk 'bout babies, but I believe dis lady said she would marry me. Did I hear correctly?

"You did," laughed Keturah.

"Den, when and how is dis event to take place—afore or after we git ta California, afore or after dat little tyke comes into da world?"

"I don't know. Maybe it will be on the way," declared Keturah. "No matter. When do we leave?"

"As soon as you can pack up," Bart said enthusiastically. "Dat is," he continued, turning toward Rennin, "if you really want us to go along wif y'all."

"We do," said Rennin. "Keturah, do you still have your wagon?"

"Of course, but it has been fitted with wheels."

"Good. Tell us what to pack."

"Almost everything is still boxed. I'll be taking my chickens and my cow. Both Rebekah and I need the milk and eggs."

"You'll get no argument from me," said Rennin.

Later that night while Rennin and Rebekah slept, Keturah joined Bart on the porch as he smoked his pipe. Quietly, Keturah said, "You were one of the men who raped Rebekah, weren't you?"

"How'd you know?"

"The way you reacted when you heard about her baby. For a split second, you thought it might have been yours. She and Rennin have forgiven you. I'm glad you've put the past behind you. That's why I had to tell you about my past. I'm no better than you, and you're no worse than I. Both of us are forgiven sinners. I'm happy God brought you into my life. I love you, too, Bart. Good night. Keturah kissed his cheek and went to bed.

Bart tapped out his pipe and stared toward the stars. "Thank you, Lord. Though I ain't worf it, thank you."

Forty-eight hours later, the two couples started once again toward the gold fields. Keturah drove her team hitched to the wagon. After several weeks, Rebekah once again rode Jewel.

Rennin and Bart took turns taking the lead. Bart was a different person than the one Rennin had known a year before, or even three days earlier. As Rennin pondered the power of God to change a heart and life so dramatically and instantly, he gazed at his wife. She glanced his way and smiled. It was as if they read each other's thoughts. Life could be good in the worst of times. Rennin turned his eyes west toward gold and adventure.

13

The Promised Land

Two months of hard traveling brought four weary prospectors into their first gold-rush town—several crudely constructed stores, a semblance of a hotel with a bath, a makeshift jail, an assayer's office, and numerous raucous saloons.

As Rennin surveyed the town, Bart longingly eyed each saloon. Simultaneously, three voices chorused, "Bart!" as three heads wagged.

"One whiskey?"

Keturah said simply, "Can you stop with one?"

"Yes, I can stop wif one," Bart said, shifting defensively in his saddle.

"Then, have one and enjoy it," said Keturah.

Bart entered the nearest saloon while Rennin and Rebekah went into the store for supplies and Keturah stayed with the wagon and horses. Within five minutes, Bart came into the store. "Well, pal, I won't be drinkin' whiskey in dis here town—two bucks for a single shot."

Rennin replied, "Everything here is so expensive it's highway robbery—ten dollars for a sack of sugar, seven for the flour, and five for the coffee. It's a good thing my family had money to begin with, or we would go without."

Bart confided, "I can't afford dem prices, Rennin."

"Don't worry about it. I got enough for both of us."

"I can't allow you to pay my way."

"Bart, you can pay me back when we strike it rich."

"What if'n we don't?"

"Then, we'll work something out. Bart, are we friends now—I mean truly friends?"

"I hope so. I know I consider you my friend. If'n you thank da same, den we are true friends."

"I do, Bart," assured Rennin. "Since I do, I was taught that true friends stand by each other. I have the money thanks to my ancestors. You'll have something that I'll need one day. It might not be money, but trust me—I *will* need you some day."

"Very well, Rennin. Thank you."

"You're welcome. I say let's head out of here." He jutted his chin toward the looming mountain range. "Let's head up into the mountains away from all the people. This area is saturated with panners."

"I'm wif you, but let's make camp soon. Keturah is due any day. I can tell she's miserable, though she won't complain."

"Neither would Rebekah."

A commotion broke out while Rennin and Bart loaded the supplies, when a young Chinese boy came flying out the door of the saloon and landed in the dirt at Jewel's feet. The horse neighed loudly, but did not rear in fear. Two larger and tougher-looking men followed the teenaged boy out the door. One bellowed at the boy as he crawled in fear under Keturah's wagon, "Come here, you little Chink! You spilled my whiskey. You're gonna pay." The man's dingy cambric shirt was soaked in whiskey.

The boy repeated over and over as he cowered under the wagon, "So sowwy. Was accident. So sowwy. Was accident."

While Rennin had a fifty-pound sack of flour on his shoulder, the gruff man yanked the terrified boy from beneath the wagon by his queue and threw him to the other man. The two began to toss the boy back and forth. Rennin made a triangle after depositing the flour in the wagon and Bart fired his gun into the ground. The men ignored the shot and tossed the boy to Rennin. "You want a little chunk of the Chink?" asked the man whose whiskey had been spilled.

Rennin caught the boy and held on to him tightly. He felt the child trembling with terror. He replied, "No, I want the whole boy."

He turned the boy's bruised face toward him. "Are you all right?" The boy, who appeared to be about thirteen, only blinked in expectation of a blow from the big man who held him.

As Rennin held the boy, the proprietor of the saloon came outside. "Chen Li, get back to work unless you want me to tan your hide, and the price of Samson's whiskey will come out of your wages." The boy started to pull away from Rennin, but Rennin held him firmly.

The boy looked at Rennin and begged, "Prease, mista. He will beat me."

"No he won't," said Rennin. "I won't let him."

The saloon owner growled toward Rennin. "Let the boy go. He belongs to me. His granddaddy died owing me some kinda money. The boy is my payment."

"How much do you want for him?" Rennin asked

Shocked by the question, the shrewd businessman began to calculate. "His granddaddy owed me a hundred and fifty. Chen Li has been working for me for three months, and he has broke more things and caused more trouble than I can count. We'll say that was at least another hundred and fifty. I have fed and clothed him. Let's call it an even five hundred, and you can have the little scamp."

"Three, fifty," said Rennin, feeling Chen Li's arm from elbow to shoulder. "I don't think he ate that much. He's too skinny."

"Four, fifty."

"Four hundred, cash. That's my final offer."

"Cash, not the promise of gold nuggets?"

"Cash. Right now, and if anybody comes after the boy or thinks he can rob me after I leave, I'll leave him dead in his tracks."

"I'll take it."

"Does the boy have any belongings?"

"A few clothes."

Rennin turned to the boy. "Chen Li, get your things and hurry. You're going with me."

While the boy ran into the saloon, Rennin paid the owner and Bart kept his gun, which he had fished out of the water, pointed at the two men who had followed the boy from the saloon. Chen Li returned, and Rennin lifted him to sit beside Keturah on the wagon seat. Rennin said, "You're safe now.

I'm Rennin O'Rourke." He nodded toward Rebekah. "My wife, Rebekah. You're sitting beside Keturah Franklin, and the other man is Bart Mercier.

Chen Li nodded, not knowing what to think. The group started out of town

As they passed the outskirts heading toward the mountains, a man in a black suit hailed them. "Mrs. Franklin!"

Keturah pulled the team to a halt. "Reverend Banks, how nice to see you again," she said half-heartedly.

"You're looking well, but I'm surprised to see you here with your husband deceased."

"I came with my friends and my fiancé. Let me introduce you. Rennin and Rebekah O'Rourke, meet Reverend Ichabod Banks, president of the Missionary Society, since Jedidiah died. And this is my fiancé, Bartholomew Mercier. You probably know the boy, Chen Li."

The reverend tipped his hat. "Ma'am, sirs. Yes, I know Chen Li. What's he doing with you?"

"He's staying with us now," said Rennin. "Reverend, are you up to performing a wedding?"

Both Bart and Keturah turned eyes toward Rennin. Neither of them would ever have had the audacity to ask the austere man to condescend to performing their wedding ceremony.

"Young man?" the severe-looking man questioned.

"Well, sir, we're headed to search for gold. It could be some time before we get back to a minister. I'm sure Bart and Keturah would like to erect one tent instead of two. What do you say? How would you like to do something civilized in this modern Sodom and Gomorrah?" Rennin leaned forward in his saddle, left forearm resting on the horn.

"I'd love to." The stern face grinned crookedly. "We wouldn't want anyone to have bad thoughts about Mrs. Franklin. If you all would like to come into my tent, you can leave in fifteen minutes as husband and wife."

"Can we do it dat easy?" asked Bart.

"There's not much to reciting a few vows."

Bart turned to Keturah. "Well?"

"Why not?" said Keturah, but she added, "Are you the only missionary in town?"

"I'm afraid so. Most of the others found the job just too difficult."

Keturah gave a little shudder as there was a perceptible drop in temperature. "Then, I guess you're the lucky man for the job."

"What about da baby?" asked Bart. "Keturah, do you still want the baby's last name to be Franklin?"

"That will not change. This is Jedediah's child and will have his name."

"Can we do dat, reverend?" Bart asked.

"Yes, Mr. Mercier, you can do that."

"Then, I'd like to marry dis lady."

Bart helped Keturah down. Inside the reverend's tent, Rennin and Rebekah stood as witnesses, while Chen Li watched this unusual assortment of people in amazed silence as Bart and Keturah exchanged vows.

Two more days of rugged terrain brought Rennin, Rebekah, Bart, Keturah, and Chen Li to a deserted clearing up the mountains with a stream flowing through it and several small caves in the mountainside. The two men looked at each other and nodded in agreement.

A voice behind them growled, "You don't wanna work here! We call this place Puma Pass. Six prospectors became puma dinner here. Nobody'll work it. They say it's cursed." The scraggly old prospector and his donkey moved on, delivering his warning without stopping.

Rennin surveyed his companions. "Are you afraid of pumas or curses?"

"No," said Bart. "I'm Cajun. I'll pull out my own voodoo curse." He laughed.

"I don't believe in curses," said Keturah

"Chen Li?" said Rennin.

"Mr. Wennin will take care of Chen Li. I be fine."

"Rebekah, honey, what do you think? I trust your intuition." He waited for an answer.

"Rennin, if a puma is killing men, it has a reason. Perhaps it's a female protecting her young. We should go out of our way not to disturb a den. The puma's spirit is strong. Rennin, your ancestors rode dragons and tamed tigers. Find that spirit within you. It's there."

"Then, it's settled. We stay," declared Rennin. "Let's set up camp."

The O'Rourkes and the Merciers, along with young Chen Li, set up camp. With the tents pitched, Rennin and Bart constructed a makeshift corral for the animals, and Chen Li chopped a supply of wood for the campfire. They left the food supplies stored in the wagon.

When the two men and Chen Li sat down for a break, they realized the women had disappeared. "Where are Rebekah and Keturah?" asked Rennin.

Bart shrugged. "Maybe dey're gatherin' some of da blackberries we seen."

"Maybe," said Rennin as he heard noise coming from the Mercier tent. "No, Bart. I think they're in your tent."

After a short rest the men started back to their work. The sounds coming from the tent did not sound pleasant, but distressful. As Rennin and Bart went to investigate, they heard crying and laughter. Bart flung the flap back.

"Come in, Daddy," greeted Rebekah.

"Bart." Keturah lifted her free hand. "It's a boy, Jedediah Bartholomew Franklin."

Rebekah carried the soiled linens to the stream and washed them. Rennin tagged along. "How are they?"

Rebekah smiled brightly. "They seem fine. Keturah had no trouble at all, and the baby has healthy lungs."

"Why didn't you come and get us?"

"What could you do other than watch?"

"Nothing, but I want to be with you when our baby comes, even if I can only watch."

"Very well," Rebekah laughed.

"What's so funny?"

"Maybe I'll bite your fingers rather than scream."

"We'll see about that!" Rennin pulled Rebekah to her feet and put his arms around her. "I say that we have supper, leave Bart and Keturah to their new baby, put Chen Li in the extra tent, hide in our tent, and do whatever we might like to do. How does that sound for an evening's plan?"

"Wonderful." She kissed him. "I say let's hide in our tent and do what's lurking in that mind of yours. Then, you can read to me about Rennin and Morgan since we haven't read in months. Then, if you read really well, no mistakes, no stumbling along, *maybe* we'll do what's lurking in that mind of yours some more. We probably will since I recall that you never paid your debt for our last argument." Rebekah playfully pinched Rennin's ribs.

She continued, "Now, excuse me so I can make supper and get these plans of yours underway."

After supper, Rennin and Rebekah did as they had planned. While they snuggled against propped bedrolls, Rennin lit a lantern and opened the neglected book that had come to symbolize their unity.

Rennin and Geoffrey shined lanterns around *The Rover*. She had run aground on a rocky shore and was stuck fast. In pelting rain and a stiff northeasterly wind, Rennin and Geoffrey descended the ladder to survey the damage. Surprisingly, the sloop had sustained minor harm, but it was wedged tightly between two boulders.

The two families stayed the night aboard *The Rover* and went ashore by the light of day. The boulder-strewn shoreline stretched steeply upward. On one side was a cliff with a hundred-foot drop into the churning ocean and jagged rocks. The white caps broke ferociously on the rocks. The other side was crystalline sand with sprigs of dried brown grass. Gulls screamed overhead. The brisk northeasterly wind bit through the cloaks they all wore.

Up the steep incline, the sand stretched back into a wooded area. Rennin and Geoffrey cleared an area in the woods and used the felled trees to make boards for two houses. Before the second house was finished, the first light snow fell. The date was October 1, 1623.

"Winter must come early here," remarked Rennin as he and Geoffrey continued to work on the second house. In two months' time they had erected two suitable structures with every available hand working long, tiring days—fulfilling the prophecy the old Chinese fortuneteller had made about Geoffrey, as young Ian helped as much as someone his age could.

Two days after they moved into homes where they sat on the floor, ate on the floor, and slept on the floor, a second much heavier snow fell. The children turned small pieces of leftover timber into sleds and zoomed recklessly down the slope toward the beach.

That winter was brutal. Many times they ate from the pickled herring and dried venison because fresh game was scarce. They learned to stretch rabbit stew for two days. An occasional wild turkey provided meat and broth for a huge pot of dumplings.

During the long winter, they had visitors, dark-skinned natives, who wore their hair with the sides shaved, but kept the center long. These men wore clothes made entirely of animal furs. Amazingly, they spoke halting French, so Rennin was able to communicate with them. *The Rover* had grounded on land claimed by the French. The Iroquois warriors showed Rennin and Geoffrey how to ice fish and promised to return in the spring to show the newcomers what crops to plant and which wild fruits were edible and which were poisonous.

Rennin and Geoffrey learned that winters were always harsh here and to be prepared with plenty of stored fruits and vegetables and preserved meat. During the cold winter the men made furniture for their homes, so that by winter's end they sat in chairs or on a divan covered with quilts, ate at a table, and slept in beds made of straw.

As the snow began to melt, Olewehah (Ol-le-way-ha) and Quantaleh (Kwan-ta-lay) returned as promised. They brought a few others with them, the hunters for the tribe, and a few farmers. The farmers provided seeds for a garden and gave instruction regarding the various fruit and nut bearing trees and vines. The hunters taught the families how to trap beaver and rabbits and how to tan furs and hides. They showed them that some of the animals Rennin and Geoffrey would never have considered edible were good to eat; for example, bear. They demonstrated how to prepare the meat and how to render the fat into grease for cooking just as if it were a hog.

Rennin had no idea how to repay the Iroquois for their kindness when, after two months of training, they took their leave. Olewehah told Rennin his payment would be a welcome spot by the O'Rourke fire. Thus, a lifelong friendship filled with honor and respect was born.

Summer brought a more relaxing time full of picnics and swimming. Lessons were put to the side to be resumed during the long cold winter months, although the two families preserved much meat and sun-dried many fruits and vegetables. They ate a new kind of bread made from corn that was milled like barley and ground into a powder. The texture was different, but the flavor was good. The corn itself was tasty eaten boiled on the cob or cut from the cob and fried with butter and salt. The goats Nancy had purchased to bring with them were invaluable for providing milk, cheese, and butter. The salt lick where the deer came supplied bounteous salt. Nancy had also insisted on bringing several chickens for eggs. Keeping the animals alive during the harsh winter had proven a chore, but they only lost three chickens.

A few years passed this way, with relative ease, comfort, and peace. The years brought Colin Aidan O'Rourke and Angela Maureen Montague into the world. Morgan joked that she was certainly glad Nancy had some girls so that she would not be totally outnumbered.

Near dawn on an unusually warm late November morning, Rennin and Geoffrey took the sloop and the three eldest boys out for a day of fishing. They had hardly been gone an hour when Olewehah burst through the O'Rourkes' door with his face painted strangely and in halting English demanded, "Where Rennin and Geoffrey?"

Morgan replied, "They took Donovan, Cameron, and Ian fishing on *The Rover*. What's wrong, Olewehah?"

"Gather children. Come." He waved her toward the door. "Much danger."

Alarmed, Morgan questioned, "What's happened?"

"Tell on way to safety. Come!" Olewehah commanded urgently. "Take to Clan Mothers."

Morgan and Nancy snatched a few belongings and prepared to leave with their Iroquois friend. Even as Olewehah reached for the latch of the door, the small party was greeted with a loud whoop as half a dozen Iroquois warriors burst through the door with tomahawks flailing and grotesquely painted faces.

Olewehah pushed the two women and children behind him. Loudly in his native tongue, he carried on a heated debate with his six tribesmen. In the end the six warriors reluctantly left, but one glared backward and said something that obviously angered Olewehah because he drew a wicked two-bladed weapon from his back and started for the man who then darted out the door.

Morgan laid a calming hand on the bare copper-colored shoulder. "Olewehah, what has happened to anger your tribesmen so? What has it to do with us?"

Olewehah turned sympathetic eyes toward the petite, gentle woman and answered, "You white. No time tell now. Must go. Lock door. Open only for husbands or Olewehah." Then he strode to the hooks above the fireplace and lifted both Rennin's musket and pistol. Handing the musket to Morgan and the pistol to Nancy, he commanded, "Load! Door open, not husbands or Olewehah, shoot! No talk. Shoot!"

Olewehah reached out and touched Morgan's cheek gently and spoke softly. "Olewehah much care for O'Rourke family.

Will keep from harm always." Then, he walked out the door but waited until he heard Morgan slide the bolt into place before he left the porch.

Through a small slit in the door, Morgan saw that the other warriors waited for Olewehah. They left together.

Morgan turned to her trembling friend. "Something terrible has happened, Nancy. Load that pistol." Morgan loaded the musket as Nancy loaded the pistol.

Nancy laughed nervously. "Morgan, if you shoot that thing, it will knock you down. Let me have it. You take the pistol. Now, watch my back. I'm runnin' next door to get Geoffrey's guns so we'll have extras. Emily Claire can shoot, and so can Duncan if he has to."

As quickly as Nancy's rotund body would move, she ran to her house and came back with the two guns and ammunition. She was winded by the time she returned.

For several hours, the two women stayed alert. When nothing occurred, they relaxed, but still jumped at every sound. As they made lunch, they heard a loud thud on the porch and then whooping that slowly decreased in volume.

Morgan stood beside the entrance with Rennin's pistol cocked while Nancy slowly cracked the door. Morgan held her breath as she peeked through the crack to see what had been thrown on her porch. Semiconscious, Olewehah lay there with a hole through his shoulder and blood seeping into the planks of the porch.

Morgan gasped, "Nancy, open the door." The two women and Emily Claire dragged the man who was almost as tall as Rennin through the door. Quickly, they washed his wound. Upon examination of Olewehah's injury, they determined a musket ball had gone clear through his shoulder. Squeamishly, Morgan cauterized the wound to stop the bleeding. Then they bandaged his shoulder and laid him on the bearskin rug near the fire, covering him with blankets. He slept soundly.

As it grew dark, Morgan and Nancy decided to light only one lantern so that they would have just enough light to see how to maneuver. They became anxious that the men had not yet returned from fishing.

Morgan knelt to check on their guest. Silently, Olewehah caught her hand, causing her to gasp. She whispered, "I thought you were asleep. How do you feel?"

Olewehah replied, "Will heal. Much thanks. Rennin no home yet?"

"Not yet. Will you, please, tell us what's going on now?"

Morgan sat on the floor near the Indian. He did not release her hand. Nancy sat beside her friend. Olewehah began. "Last night, drunk French trappers come to village. Shoot three braves. Molest women. Today, raiding parties try find guilty men to kill. Some braves want kill all white men. Molest white women for revenge. Olewehah no let hurt you." He squeezed Morgan's hand.

She whispered, "Thank you, my friend. You rest now. We'll make supper."

While the women prepared the evening meal, they could hear Olewehah's even breathing and knew he slept. Nancy whispered, "He's in love with you."

"What?" Morgan said in surprise.

Nancy nodded toward Olewehah. "He's in love with you."

"Nonsense!" said Morgan. "He's Rennin's friend."

"Yes," said Nancy. "And for that reason he will never act upon his feelings, but he is in love with you. He as much as told you so this mornin' because he thought he would most likely die today."

Morgan thought about how Olewehah had caressed her cheek and what he had said and how he had held her hand. "Nancy, what do I do?"

"Nothin'. Olewehah is as bloody bound by honor as either Rennin or Geoffrey would be. He will never betray his friend. And, for God's sake, say nothin' to Rennin. Olewehah is young. In a few years, he will have his own wife, and you'll only be a pleasant memory."

As they talked, the women heard stamping on the porch. Morgan suddenly realized that they had not slipped the bolt into place. As she started for the door, so did Emily Claire, who had said very little all day but had astutely observed everything. As the twelve-year-old girl's hand touched the latch, a big grizzled man with long, frazzled, black, curly hair and beard flung the door open, sending the child sprawling. When his eyes alighted on Olewehah, he drew his pistol and pulled the hammer back. Nancy quickly put herself between the intruder and their wounded friend, screaming, "No!"

The pistol discharged, and Nancy fell to the floor. Another blast came from the shadows, and the big man dropped with a thud. Morgan's shot had struck him in the temple.

Morgan fell to her knees beside Nancy, weeping. "Nancy, please don't die."

Still weak from his loss of blood, Olewehah sank to the floor beside Morgan. "Too late, Morgan," he said sadly.

Morgan blinked back her tears. Olewehah had never used her given name before. He had rarely spoken directly to her. In a strangled voice she said, "You lie back down. I don't want to lose you, too."

Leaning heavily on Morgan, Olewehah returned to the rug. Almost inaudibly he whispered, "Morgan."

She gently put her fingers to his lips and whispered as softly, "Don't say anything. It's enough that I know. You must never speak the words." He nodded and softly kissed her fingertips.

Morgan turned back to her dead friend. Emily Claire sat beside her mother, stroking her hair. Morgan put a loving arm around the child. "Aunt Morgan, is she truly dead?"

"Yes, honey, I'm afraid so."

Silent tears dripped down Emily Claire's cheeks. "But Angela is only a baby. Who will take care of her?"

"Don't worry, honey. God will take care of us even in hard times."

Olewehah asked, "Why God let bad men hurt innocent women?"

Morgan said, "God doesn't let bad men do things. He allows humans to make choices. Sometimes they're bad choices. Even then, He forgives us if we ask Him, and He always gives us strength to face hard times if we ask Him."

Olewehah lamented, "These very hard times. Dead friend. Dead trapper molest Olewehah's sister and betrothed. Would have hurt Olewehah's Morgan. Olewehah very angry. Wrong be angry, Morgan? Wrong want guilty men punished?"

Morgan shook her head. "No, my friend, you have every right to be angry and to want justice. Tell me about your fiancée. You will still marry her, yes? She's not to blame for any of this."

Olewehah heaved a great sigh. "Olewehah and Utoma (You-tome-ah) betrothed many years—since childhood. Utoma good woman. Olewehah no blame woman. Will marry her still. Make many sons like Morgan and Rennin. Olewehah more worry about sister. Her husband not so understanding. Chinowaya warrior who threaten Morgan. Thinks wife unclean now. Will try put her out of house. Chinowaya (Chin-oh-way-ah) know nothing of God who forgives and helps."

"What's your sister's name?"

"Anagua (Ah-nahg-wah)."

"I will pray that God will take care of her."

The conversation lulled. Silently, Morgan and Emily Claire covered Nancy. Morgan shot a glance toward the body of the trapper. "Emily Claire, help me drag this vermin from my house."

The two small women dragged the cumbersome load onto the porch, where they unceremoniously rolled the body off the porch. Morgan stood and looked toward the beach. Clouds obscured the moon. She could see nothing. She started as she heard a twig snap in the woods behind her. "Get me your father's pistol, Emily Claire, and reload Rennin's."

Morgan stood, poised to shoot whatever emerged from the thicket. From the woods sprang a four-point buck. Morgan laughed almost hysterically. "I don't need food tonight. You're lucky."

As Morgan turned to go inside, Chinowaya leapt up from beside the dead trapper with a horrifying scream. He shoved

Morgan through the door, causing her to fall and lose the pistol in the shadows. A shot pierced the darkness and a ball whizzed past the Indian's head. The only notice the man took of the missed shot was to laugh as he watched Emily Claire crawl on the floor, looking for the other pistol.

With a blood-curdling scream, Chinowaya jerked Morgan over by her arm and ripped her blouse. Morgan shrieked and clawed at the brave's face. Chinowaya slapped her, bringing blood to her lip and a welt to her cheek.

With a bellow of, "No!" Olewehah struggled to his feet. The weakened warrior was instantly felled to unconsciousness by his brother-in-law.

Chinowaya was besieged by a second combatant as Emily Claire jumped on his back. Viciously, he flung the child into the wall and mumbled harshly, "You next!"

With all the anger and protectiveness of a mother lioness, Morgan yanked the Indian's hair and screamed, "Leave her alone! She's only a child!"

Using brute force, Chinowaya lifted Morgan by the throat. He slammed her onto the rough-hewn dining table and began to rip her clothes. In that instant, a flash split the dimness, as a bullet grazed Chinowaya's shoulder. Duncan screamed as loudly as a five-year-old could, "Get off my mommy, or the next shot will *not* miss its target." Duncan stood in the shadows with Geoffrey's pistol, the hammer pulled back.

Chinowaya laughed coldly. "Brave little man." He, then, turned toward the small boy who stood staunchly, bluffing with the unloaded pistol.

Morgan grabbed the loaded musket. Chinowaya surveyed his dilemma and decisively wrenched the longrifle from Morgan's grasp. Duncan, knowing the pistol was empty, charged the Indian and hit him with the butt of the gun.

Angered by the child's persistence, Chinowaya threw Duncan into the wall. Emily Claire gathered the boy into her arms and murmured, "Don't watch. Let's try to get Colin and Angela and run."

Duncan whimpered, "But he'll kill my mommy, too."

Sounding like a full-grown woman, Emily Claire said, "No, Duncan, that's not what he has in mind."

During this time, Morgan continued to struggle with the crazed man, all the while begging him to stop.

On the beach as Rennin and Geoffrey tied *The Rover*, a gunshot penetrated the still night air. As if of one mind, the two men dropped everything and raced toward the sound, followed in close pursuit by two half-grown boys and one younger boy. Before they reached the houses, another shot resounded. They quickened their pace in panic.

Seeing the trapper's body by his porch, Rennin's mind was frenzied. He crashed through the door to see Nancy's covered body in one corner, the children trying to sneak out the door, his unconscious, bandaged friend near the fire, and Morgan's losing battle with a man twice her size. In one bound, Rennin seized Chinowaya and ripped him off Morgan. After a brief struggle, Chinowaya lay dead, his neck snapped from one quick twist Rennin had mastered in China.

Still feeling hands on her throat, Morgan gasped for air as she slid to the floor. Rennin fell to his knees and lifted her to him. "You're safe now. I'm home. Nobody will hurt you."

Rennin felt Morgan's arms tighten around his neck. She sobbed, "Don't let me go, Rennin. Don't let me go."

Tears streaming down his cheeks, Rennin smoothed Morgan's hair and kissed the top of her head. He whispered, "Never."

Across the room, with trembling hand, Geoffrey turned back the sheet that covered his wife. His husky body shook with grief. Holding Angela in her arms, Emily Claire snuggled up beside her father. "Papa!" she cried. Geoffrey pulled her to him and reached out his other arm for Ian.

Cameron took Colin from his little brother, and Donovan helped Olewehah sit when he began to stir. In terror, the Indian shouted, "Morgan!"

Surprised by the emotional use of his wife's name, Rennin turned to his Iroquois friend and spoke abruptly. "Olewehah, tell us what happened here."

Realizing the crisis was over, Olewehah sank back to the rug and sighed. "Rennin finally home. Morgan and children safe now."

Morgan recovered her composure. "Rennin, I can tell you what happened. Olewehah is weak from blood loss. Let him rest." Sitting up, she pointed at Chinowaya. "Dump that lowlife with the other trash outside."

Rennin summarily threw the body outside. When he came in, Donovan had made tea for everyone and was stirring the venison stew and making cornbread. Morgan explained the events of the last twenty-four hours. When she finished, everyone sat silently.

At last, Geoffrey broke the silence. "Olewehah, what about your sister and your girl? Where are they now?"

"Wait for Olewehah to return."

Geoffrey stood. "Let's get 'em. We will bring 'em 'ere to stay with us."

"Why you do that?" asked Olewehah.

Geoffrey said, "If you marry Utoma, will you be outcasts in your village?"

Olewehah lowered his eyes. "Depend on how Clan Mothers vote."

"Anagua would be an outcast, especially now that Chinowaya is dead, and 'er brother defended the white woman whose 'usband killed 'im. Correct?"

"You must think my people evil," said Olewehah.

"No," said Morgan hoarsely. "They just do not understand true forgiveness."

Olewehah said, "God who forgives and helps, but Anagua has papoose barely one year."

"Yes," said Geoffrey thoughtfully. "God always provides a way. Olewehah, I desperately need 'elp. Nancy is dead. I 'ave an almost newborn baby that I cannot feed. Anagua can 'elp me, and I can 'elp 'er. If she will nurse my child with 'ers, I will take 'er as my wife."

Olewehah's eyes widened. "You not know sister."

Geoffrey shrugged. "She's my friend's sister. She needs me, and I need 'er. That's all I need to know. Let us get the two ladies."

After a meal, Olewehah, Geoffrey, and Donovan left to bring the two Iroquois women home. Rennin buried the trapper while the other three men dragged Chinowaya to the village. They would bury Nancy when Geoffrey returned. Rennin would build her a coffin while the others were gone.

To everyone's surprise, Emily Claire bounded from the porch, but rather than snagging her father, she grabbed Donovan. "Donnie, be careful. Keep Papa safe. I love you, but I don't want to be all grown up just yet. Bring my father home."

The two young people embraced, and Donovan assured the girl, "I will, Emmy. I will."

On the trek to the Iroquois village, Geoffrey said to Donovan, "I thought you and Emily Claire 'ated each other. Is there somethin' I should know, Donnie?"

Donovan was thankful for the darkness because his face burned bright red. "Well, Mr. Montague..."

"Mr. Montague?" Geoffrey interrupted. "Not Uncle Geoffrey? Is it that bad, boy?"

"No, sir."

"What are your intentions toward my daughter?" Despite his grief, Geoffrey enjoyed making the young man squirm.

"Well, Uncle Geoffrey, some day we'll get married, with your permission, of course; but that's some day. Right now, we just like being together. We've not done anything wrong."

Gruffly, Geoffrey asked, "'Ave you kissed my daughter?"

"No, sir, not yet. We only held hands walking in the woods."

"'And 'olding? That's all?"

"Yes, sir. Honest!"

Geoffrey could keep up the farce no longer. He started to chuckle. Olewehah joined him as he realized what the older man was doing to the younger one.

"What's so funny?" Donovan demanded.

"Relax, Donnie," Geoffrey said affectionately as he put his arm around the boy's shoulders. "Come and talk to me in four or five years if you still want to marry Emily Claire. I'm sure we can come to an understanding at that time."

Donovan breathed a sigh of relief as he comprehended that through his sorrow, Geoffrey had had a bit of fun at his expense.

The three traveled in silence after that until they reached the Iroquois village just before dawn. They went directly to the longhouse and left Chinowaya's body. Geoffrey and Donovan waited while Olewehah roused the Clan Mothers.

In a brief statement, Olewehah told how Chinowaya had dishonored his people by attacking the families of white men known to be friends and how Morgan had actually killed one of the guilty trappers. Then, he made his request to marry Utoma forthwith and have Geoffrey marry Anagua so that they could leave the tribe and live among their white family. He also asked permission to take his baby sister, Holehah (Hoe-lay-ha) with him.

The rulers listened with stern, unbending countenance, but in the end they granted Olewehah's requests. Within the hour, the eldest Clan Mother performed the marriage ritual for both Olewehah and Utoma and Geoffrey and Anagua, who did all Olewehah requested of her, stoically, without a single question or dissention. Geoffrey gazed on the young woman who was at least fifteen years his junior, not much older than Emily Claire, with awe and admiration. Not only was she brave, but also beautiful. Without a living parent or a husband, the girl, for she was only a girl, looked to the Clan Mother, who permitted her brother's request, for guidance and trusted Olewehah implicitly. Olewehah was little more than a child himself and would have joined Utoma's clan upon marriage. Many of the women frowned on the removal of three women from their community.

Geoffrey whispered to Olewehah as they traveled. "Your society is matriarchal?"

"Know not that word."

"The women rule?"

The Indian tilted his head to the side and thought. "Equal, but Clan Mothers have final say. Yes."

The party arrived back at the cabins late in the afternoon. They had a simple burial service for Nancy, and Anagua took Angela to nurse along with her own daughter, Sintaya (Sin-tay-ya). Temporarily, Olewehah and Utoma lived with Geoffrey and the children until the men could build another house.

Within a week, the winds blew cold once more. The icy grayness descended upon the little band, changing the easy routine of life. Utoma, Anagua, and Holehah joined the children in their studies and learned to read and write and speak English. Morgan and Emily Claire dressed the Indian women as white women dressed.

Seeing the change, Olewehah approached Rennin and Geoffrey with an idea. He, too, wanted to dress and act as a white man. He also asked about changing their names. After much discussion, Olewehah became Oliver Montague, choosing Geoffrey's last name because they were brothers by marriage. Utoma chose the name Eula; Anagua changed her name to Anna, and named baby Sintaya, Cynthia. Cameron had already dubbed Holehah, Holly. Actually, he called her *his* beautiful Holly Berry.

During the winter months, there was a great deal of unrest between many of the French trappers and the Iroquois. Oliver suggested the families move further west in the spring, perhaps as far as the Ohio Valley. Rennin and Geoffrey agreed.

At Christmas dinner, Oliver announced that he and Eula were expecting a baby. Anna seemed uncomfortable after the announcement. In a while, she disappeared outside. Morgan followed her.

"Anna, what's wrong? You seem unhappy tonight."

Anna leaned against the porch post as a few snowflakes fell into her ebony hair. "Geoffrey not want wife. Want nursemaid. Geoffrey never touch Anna. Will never give him baby that way."

"Oh," said Morgan understandingly. She well remembered Ricardo and Danielle. "Anna, you must let Geoffrey know how you feel. Do you love him? I know you have only been married a short time, but have you fallen in love with Geoffrey?"

"Geoffrey good man. Good to Anna. Never beat Anna. Never force Anna. Not like Chinowaya. Anna approach Clan Mother about husband. Plan to put out of house, but then trappers come. Anna honored to be Geoffrey's wife."

"But do you love Geoffrey?"

"Anna not understand."

"Does he make your heart beat faster when he's near you? Do you think about him when he's not around? Would you feel as if your life were over if you lost him? Do you want him to take you in his arms and make you feel like a woman?" Morgan sounded like a lovesick adolescent as she thought of Rennin in her description of love.

Anna blushed. "Anna want Geoffrey's arms around her very much. Anna anxious when Geoffrey leave her. Worry he not come back. Anna enjoy Geoffrey. Geoffrey make Anna laugh when sad. Like Geoffrey's company very much. This love, Morgan?"

"Close," whispered Morgan. "Very close."

"Anna want Geoffrey feel same. It hurt Anna that Geoffrey not touch, not make love. This love?"

"I think so, Anna. You must tell Geoffrey how you feel."

"Iroquois have arranged marriage. Not love Chinowaya. Want leave. Very hard for Anna, this love. How to tell?"

"You talked to me," said Morgan. "Try to do the same with Geoffrey. I tell you what. Leave the children here tonight, and get Oliver and Eula to stay, too. That way you and Geoffrey will be alone. That will be easier." Morgan hugged Anna.

Unbeknownst to them, Geoffrey had heard every word they spoke because he had started to follow Anna himself and stood with the door slightly ajar. Nonetheless, Morgan and Anna set their plan into motion.

Geoffrey turned back into the house, feeling sheepish for having eavesdropped on the two women. He approached Rennin. "Rennin, I need to talk to you privately. Let us walk outside. I still 'ave the you-know-what 'idden in the smoke 'ouse. 'Elp me bring it in."

As Rennin and Geoffrey passed the women, Rennin winked at Morgan. She thought the men were headed to bring in the sled they had built for the children, which they ultimately were.

Away from the house, Rennin said, "What's bothering you, Geoffrey?"

Geoffrey related the conversation he had overheard. "What do I do, Rennin?"

"How do you feel about Anna?"

"She's delightful, but I 'ave never been with anyone but Nancy and Nancy 'as been gone such a short time." He closed his eyes and shook his head. "Besides, Anna is so young."

"Yes, she is, and it's unfair to her for you to keep yourself from her. You made her your wife. She's not your servant. Neither is she a child. Geoffrey, she wants to be your wife in every way. Let her. I feel sure you can love her if you give it a chance.

"Look at Oliver. I'm beyond doubt he loves Eula wholly, even though only a few weeks ago he was deeply infatuated with my wife. I was never jealous because I knew his love would evolve into the deep brotherly love he now feels. He was not even aware I knew.

"Just as Oliver's love for Morgan changed, even as my love for Morgan changed when I discovered who she was, or as my admiration for Kiandria changed to affection, your mere affection for Anna can deepen into an abiding love if you open your heart."

He put his hand on his friend's shoulder. "I know you loved Nancy, but you must stop mourning and live again. God has sent you another chance to love and to be loved. Seize it. Cherish it. Let it grow."

Geoffrey breathed deeply. "Then you will support Morgan in givin' us a night alone?"

"Of course. I'll give you several nights if you want them."

"Rennin, I'm as nervous as a boy about the 'ole thing."

Rennin laughed. "I'm sure she is, too."

Geoffrey laughed at the thought of a new wedding night, and he found himself relaxing, actually anticipating the night.

The two friends brought in the sled to the delight of a room full of children. After a hymn and a toast with warm cinnamon cranberry juice, Anna retreated to a corner to feed Angela since she had weaned Cynthia. Geoffrey followed her. As she laid the baby and the toddler on quilts and covered them with blankets to sleep the night, Geoffrey put his hands on her shoulders and caressed her arms. He kissed the back of her neck and whispered, "Let's go 'ome."

At Geoffrey's touch, Anna found her heart racing. She turned to speak, but only nodded her assent. Geoffrey helped her put on her coat, and they slipped into the gathering snow.

Rennin closed the book as he groaned, "Oh!" Then he laughed softly.

"What's so funny?" Rebekah wanted to know.

"Well, it seems that both their promised land and ours may not be so perfect after all."

Rebekah hugged Rennin more tightly. "Don't be silly. Anywhere is perfect so long as we're together."

"You're correct, Mrs. O'Rourke," he said, tipping her face to his.

14
Puma Pass

Rebekah and Keturah planted a garden soon after they arrived in Puma Pass. Rennin and Bart cordoned off an area five times the size allowed to an individual since there were five of them. They were careful to include much of the stream, as well as several of the caves. Of course, with the lore of the place, they felt they might be free to explore even more territory. It was decided that the two ladies could pan near the campsite while the men explored the caves and the mountains.

Rebekah and Keturah found gold first. It was only a few nuggets that had obviously washed from further up stream. Nonetheless, they enjoyed teasing their spouses that they were going to be rich without them. Rebekah joked around the campfire, "Yes, Rennin, if I become wealthy, what possible use could I have for you?"

Rennin smirked. Then, he threw Rebekah over his shoulder and said, "Bart, Keturah, Chen Li, excuse us. I need to show my wife what I'm good for." He carried her into their tent and closed the flap. The three remaining prospectors could hear Rebekah squealing and Rennin laughing for a while. Then, there was silence.

Chen Li excused himself. "I think this is a good time to go to sreep. Good night."

Bart sighed. "Mrs. Mercier, when do I get to show you what I'm good for?"

Bart saw Keturah blush in the firelight. Standing carefully so as not to wake the baby, Keturah replied, "Now if you would like."

Bart jumped to his feet. "I would like very much." With his arm around her shoulders, Bart and Keturah went to bed.

Several months passed. Baby Jed sat without help, and Rebekah began to look pregnant. The garden produced bountiful vegetables, the stream provided plenteous fish, and the woods gave ample game. Still, only a few nuggets came from the stream, and a small patch had been found in one boulder. Furthermore, there had been no sign of a puma.

One day, Rebekah mounted Jewel to take a few extra lanterns to Rennin, Bart, and Chen Li. They planned to explore one of the caves that day, and they had forgotten the lanterns when they left.

As horse and rider approached the cave, there were many loose rocks. Jewel stumbled several times and acted skittish. Rebekah dismounted. Stroking the mare's neck, she said, "You're having a hard time here, girl. I'll just get Rennin or Bart or Chen Li to come and get their own supplies. The foolish men should have remembered their stuff anyway." Rebekah rubbed the mare's nose. Jewel nickered and shook her head savagely.

As Rebekah turned to climb up the embankment to the cave, she came face to face with a mammoth puma. The cat snarled and swatted a paw at Rebekah. Slowly, Rebekah backed up, hoping not to alarm the fierce cat.

The puma snarled again and crouched on the ledge above her, preparing to pounce. Instantaneously, Jewel charged straight for the big cat. The horse neighed and reared and pawed while the startled cat snarled and swatted.

Hearing the commotion, the men darted from the cave. Rennin grabbed his shotgun on the way out the entrance. He raised his gun and took aim on the cat.

Rebekah screamed, "Rennin, don't shoot her! She's hurt."

Jewel stood still, but remained between the puma and Rebekah. The puma sat on her haunches and breathed deep rumbling breaths. Rennin kept the gun aimed.

Rebekah pleaded, "Rennin, be merciful. Look at her. There's a knife protruding from her hip. It looks as if it has been there a long time. She must be in agony."

Rennin lowered the gun and handed it to Bart. "Shoot her if you have to," he said as he walked slowly toward the wounded cat. With a silent prayer in his heart that he might possess a smidgen of the magic his namesake had displayed against a tiger so long before, Rennin held his hand in front of him as he walked and spoke soothingly. "Easy, girl. Let me take a look and see if I can help you."

Surprisingly, the puma sniffed Rennin's hand and rubbed her head against it as if she were a pet house cat. Rennin slowly ran his palm down the cat's side toward her hip. As his hand neared the puma's hip, she snarled and took a step back.

Rennin soothed again, "It's okay, girl. If you let me pull it out you'll get better." Once again, he ran his hand across the animal's side. Quickly he clutched the knife handle and jerked. The puma screamed and raised her paw. Bart raised the shotgun. Rennin put his arm over his face. The puma's paw came down, but without claws.

"Bart, don't shoot!" shouted Rennin.

The puma lay down and started licking her wound. Rennin rubbed her head as he cooed, "Let me look at your booboo, girl." The puma caught his hand like a kitten as he touched her hip.

He sat back in disbelief. "Good grief! This puma is tame. Some prospector must have tamed her when she was a baby and then left her. I'll bet she went into some other prospector's camp after that thinking her tamer was back. That prospector probably got scared and did this to her. She has been attacking out of pain and fear since she was wounded and abandoned."

The grateful puma laid her big head on Rennin's lap and purred like a kitten. Rebekah, Bart, and Chen Li made their way to the scene. Rennin sat there petting the beast.

Chen Li said, "Old Pete Sanford said he had a pet puma. Nobody berieved him. Then, he disappeared."

Rebekah ventured, "Rennin, what are we going to do with her?"

As he petted the cat's head, Rennin said, "I don't know. If she's to stay here she must learn to survive in the wild. I'm worried that with the smell of humans all over her she could fall victim to a stronger, wilder puma. I don't think she has any cubs. She seems too young. She probably has never had a mate.

"If she stays with us, other people could be a threat to her. And I really would hate to see her in a cage in a zoo somewhere like New York, but she would be safe."

Rebekah sat beside Rennin and rubbed the warm fur. "I think we should watch her and see how she does. If we see she's surviving, we leave her alone. Otherwise, we take care of her. Isn't she beautiful, Rennin?"

"Yes, she's beautiful, Rebekah, but remember she's a wild animal. She was never meant to be a pet."

"I know that," Rebekah said, struggling to get up. Rennin gave her his hand. She grinned. "I'm becoming rather awkward. Walk with me. You forgot your extra lanterns. I brought them to you."

Rennin walked with Rebekah, holding her arm for safety. Before he gathered the lanterns, he patted Jewel. "Good girl. It looks as if Rebekah was absolutely right about you. You have turned out to be a real jewel, a perfectly faceted diamond."

The horse nickered in reply. Rennin laughed.

Rebekah took the reins. As she put her foot in the stirrup, she said, "By the way, Rennin, did you know that Buster is going to be a father?"

"What?"

Rebekah shook her head jokingly. "Naughty boy. He didn't tell you about him and Jewel. Yes, they've mated. You miss a lot when you're up here. For example"—She took his hand and laid it on her abdomen. The baby kicked so hard that Rennin felt the form of his foot.

"Good grief!" he exclaimed.

"This baby is healthy, Rennin. I'm not worried about him."

Rennin kissed Rebekah and whispered, "I love both of you."

Bart called from the cavern entrance, "Hey! You can do dat later. We got work to do."

Rebekah laughed. "I have things to do, too. I'll see you later."

Rennin headed back to the cave with the extra lanterns. Rebekah called after him, "Rennin, you have company!" The puma padded closely at his heels. Rebekah rode away murmuring, "I'm not the one who has to worry about having her for a pet."

Rennin, Bart, and Chen Li lit the cavern brightly. Going deeper inside, they discovered a steep drop to another level. Rennin said, "Chen Li, I'll lower you. You're much lighter than either of us. It'll be easier to lower you. If you see anything of significance, I'll lower Bart."

Chen Li tied a rope under his arms, and Rennin used his body like a pulley to lower him to the next level. Once down, Chen Li lit two lanterns.

"Wennin!" he called. "Prease send Bart down."

Rennin leaned over the ledge. The boy pointed. "I think I found old Pete."

Rennin lowered Bart to be with Chen Li. Bart examined the decomposed body of the prospector. He lay at the bottom of the pit with a lantern and shovel on his back and a rope around his midsection. Bart said, "Well, Rennin da puma wudn't really deserted, an' da ol' feller didn't fall. The rope ain't frayed. I'd say his pardner let go deliberately. His neck is broke. I sure am glad I can trust you." Bart looked up. "Dat's a mighty long fall."

The puma looked over the ledge with Rennin and snarled. Rennin rubbed her back. "It's okay, girl. I'm sorry about your friend down there. You probably know who did it. He was most likely your first victim and the one who hurt you. You might even have been defending the fellow at the bottom."

"You're probly right. Please, make sure she knows it wudn't me," said Bart.

"She knows, Bart. I'll bet she remembers the other man's scent very well. What else do you see down there?"

Bart and Chen Li walked around, holding lanterns high and low. They examined the back wall carefully. Bart whooped. "Rennin, we definitely have sumpin' here! I don't know how deep or how long, but dare's a deposit on dis here wall. We hafta git down here wif more light and tools. Maybe Patty Puma can stand guard."

"Patty Puma!" Rennin laughed. "Why would you call her that?"

"I figger if'n she's gonna be your pet, she oughta have a name."

"Bart, she's not my pet."

"Maybe you're right. Maybe you're her pet."

Patty snarled, and then lay down and purred contentedly.

After giving Pete a proper burial, Rennin, Bart, and Chen Li mined the deposit they found. It was not extremely large, but it ran deep and was difficult to extract. The gold they removed was pure quality. Rennin made a trip to the assayer's office and filed a claim for all the territory they had staked. There was little question asked about the claimants with the promise of a high yield and a fee in the assayer's pocket. Rennin knew it was extortion, but he also knew that the women and Chen Li might be denied their stake without the payment.

As they worked, Patty was always nearby. She roamed between the cave and the camp, with occasional jaunts into the woods for food. None of the adults were afraid of her, and she guarded the crawling Jed as if he were her cub.

Rebekah and Keturah continued to pan the stream and to find nuggets here and there. With almost perfect weather—cool nights, but warm and usually sunny days, with a rain shower that watered the ground and passed over quickly every other day—the garden flourished. The ladies discussed more permanent structures in which to live, but they dared not ask Rennin and Bart to sacrifice time from mining.

"We could do it ourselves," said Rebekah.

Keturah laughed. The more she thought, the harder she laughed.

Finally, Rebekah shouted, "What is so funny?"

Still giggling, Keturah replied, "I was picturing us chopping down trees and dragging logs."

As Rebekah realized the absurdity of her comment, she laughed as hard as Keturah.

They continued to dwell in their tents, but the ladies did learn to hunt. It seemed as if Rennin and Bart lost track of days so intent were they on mining the gold deposit they had found. Occasionally, Chen Li stayed in camp to help the women with heavy or cumbersome chores.

Early one chilly morning, Rebekah, heavy with child, left camp on foot with a shotgun and a shovel. She announced, "Keturah, I'll be back later. There are two things I must find today. Rennin has completely lost track of his priorities. This evening I plan to jerk him back to his senses. While I'm gone, pop some popcorn and see if you if you can find any holly berries and some mistletoe." Rebekah led Jack and took some rope with her.

Keturah gasped, "Oh, my word! It's Christmas Eve. I had not thought about it being today either when I got up this morning, but Bart would have reminded me since he has been working on a rocking horse for weeks. I'll look for those things while you're gone, and I'll make some gingerbread men."

Several hours later, Rebekah returned exhausted, but she had found the things she sought. On Jack's back was a small spruce with roots and a turkey. She smiled wearily, but triumphantly at Keturah who had several strings of popcorn and some red berries and freshly baked gingerbread men.

"Would you like some lunch or a gingerbread man and some milk?" Keturah asked Rebekah.

"I'm not hungry," Rebekah replied. "I'd really like to lie down, but I want the tree staring Rennin in the face when he comes in. Will you help me? I also have a turkey for Christmas dinner. We can roast it in the stone oven we made."

Keturah helped Rebekah plant the little tree beside her and Rennin's tent. Then, they strung the popcorn and hung the berries on it. Rebekah waddled to her tent and unboxed the paper ornaments Rennin had so enthusiastically made the year before. As she carefully and lovingly placed them in the tree, she started to cry.

"Honey, what's wrong?" Keturah asked.

Rebekah sniffled, "Digging up this gold has changed Rennin. It's all he ever talks about anymore. He never reads to me, and I'm too awkward to make love. I ordered a Bible and a copy of Rennin's ancestor's book to be sent to Running Bear, although Rennin promised he would. I want *my* Rennin back."

She held up an angel. "Look at these. I want the Rennin who cuts out paper decorations and digs up trees and builds me a bathtub."

Keturah put her hands on her hips. "Tell him so."

"What?"

"Tell him how you feel. Bart and I have an agreement." She pointed toward her tent. "When that flap closes, there is no more talk about gold. We talk about our family and us. That is *our* time. We decided that a couple of months ago when I told Bart we were having a baby of our own. You just tell Rennin how you feel, or I will. You know I'm mean enough to do it, too."

Rebekah started to laugh as she put the last angel on the tree. "Yes, ma'am. Oh!" She caught her side.

Keturah saw the startled face. "Has your time come?"

"I don't know. That was the first pain I've had. Let's wait a while and see."

The two ladies plucked and dressed the turkey and set it to slow roast all night. They baked bread for stuffing and several pies. They snipped and soaked greens to cook, pulled yams, shelled pecans, boiled eggs, ground sage, and chopped onions and peppers.

Several times during the afternoon, Rebekah caught her side. Then, her water broke.

Keturah chuckled, "Looks as if Rennin's going to get a real gift for Christmas."

Wide-eyed and terrified, Rebekah said, "I want Rennin. He promised to be here. I want him now."

"You go lie down. I'll get Rennin."

Rebekah clutched Keturah's hand. "Don't leave me alone."

"I won't, silly girl. Now, lie down."

As she entered her tent, Rebekah heard Keturah calling loudly, "Patty! Patty, girl, come!"

From the ledge above the gold pit, Patty snarled and disappeared. "What's up wif your cat, Rennin?" Bart asked.

"I don't know, but she seemed disturbed." He shrugged and kept swinging the pick ax.

Forty-five minutes later, Patty returned. At the top of the pit she snarled and screamed repeatedly. Bart said, "Rennin, you better see what's wrong wif her. She ain't actin' right."

With some irritation, Rennin climbed the handmade ladder. "Come here, Patty. What has you so stirred up?"

Patty snarled in Rennin's face, and he saw that she wore a red ribbon with a note under it. Rennin unfolded the paper and read, "*Rennin, come home. Rebekah is in labor, and she wants you. Keturah.*"

Rennin turned to Bart and Chen Li. "Fellows, I'm having a baby. I have to go. Rebekah needs me. Damn! I've been neglecting her lately. What a fool I've been!"

Bart called, "Hold up. We'll go wif you. Dis here gold'll be here tamorra, but I ain't workin' 'cause it's Christmas. I made a rockin' horse for little Jed, an' I bought Keturah some new gingham for some new dresses. I ain't gonna miss 'em openin' their presents."

Flabbergasted, Rennin mumbled, "Tomorrow's Christmas? How could I get so wrapped up in this to miss the Savior's birthday?" He spread his hand toward the dig. "Bart, I've lost sight of what's really important. I have to get Rebekah a tree, but first I want to see how soon this baby will be here."

Breathlessly, Rennin charged into camp. Keturah waited outside his tent with her arms akimbo. "You get cleaned up before you go in there," she ordered. "You are *filthy*!" She handed him some clean clothes and glared at him.

Rennin bathed in the stream quickly and returned. Keturah stood there, arms folded, foot tapping, lips firmly set. "Did you take one minute to notice what this precious girl has been doing today?"

Rennin saw the tree. He groaned. "Oh, Rebekah, I'm sorry."

Keturah threw back the flap. "Say it so she can hear you. I'll give you ten minutes before I come back in."

Rennin walked in as Rebekah was in the middle of a hard contraction. He gulped, "I'm sorry, honey. I've been neglecting you."

She snapped, "Talk to me about that later! This is more important right now! Come over here so I can break you fingers!"

Rennin held Rebekah's hand. "Maybe you should break my neck for being such an idiot. I even forgot *Christmas*. Your tree is beautiful, and you already planted it."

Rebekah laughed softly as the contraction passed. "I thought I might be busy on New Year's. Someone else has other plans. This tree can be the baby's tree. We can carve the baby's name and birthdate on it. Then, I want a real house built beside it."

"That sounds like a wonderful idea," he agreed as he kissed her hand.

Keturah barged back through the tent flap. "Rennin, we have hours to go. Rebekah is nowhere nearly ready to deliver. Is there something you would like to do and somewhere you need to go?"

He shook his head. "I'm not moving an inch, Keturah. I'm here for the duration." Rennin turned to his wife, "Honey would you like for me to read to you about Rennin and Morgan's journey to Ohio?"

"If you stop while I break your fingers."

He laughed and picked up the neglected book. "Maybe I should read the Christmas story first with Bart, Keturah, Chen Li."

"Good idea. Do it before my labor gets harder. I would rather scream at Rennin and Morgan than at our Savior's birth."

Once Bart and Chen Li stepped inside the tent, Rennin read the Christmas story as he had the year before, and once again he sang "O, Holy Night." This time, Keturah sang with him in perfectly harmonic notes.

Then, Rennin sat beside Rebekah with her hand lying in his beneath the book. He read to her, but he stopped periodically as Rebekah squeezed his hand during contractions.

As soon as the first jonquil popped though the snow, the O'Rourke family and the two Montague families packed their belongings to move west. As if speaking of a child or a beloved pet, Morgan asked, "What about *The Rover*? We can't just leave her."

Rennin took her hand. "Le Boeuf at the trading post is going to take *The Rover*. He promised to take care of her until we come back. Tomorrow, you and I will sail her up the coast and spend the day alone. How does that sound?"

Morgan nodded. "I'd like that. We never get to be alone any more. With four boys, I'm always busy. Rennin, we're beginning to sound old."

"Uh-uh!" He pulled her into his arms. "We are *not* old. I will prove it to you tomorrow, but right now, I'm tired and want to go to sleep."

She pinched him. "I'd like to see you climb a trellis and sneak into my window."

Rennin sighed. "Alas, pretty lady, we don't have a trellis, which is very good for me."

Both laughed, for both were, indeed, weary from packing. They went to bed and slept in each other's arms with anticipation of a whole day alone.

The morning broke bright and fair with a steady southerly breeze, perfect for sailing. Rennin and Morgan left Donovan in charge for the day with a warning. "Don't let your authority go to your head. Mercy and compassion can be stronger weapons than punishment."

With light hearts, the couple sailed northward toward the trading post although parting with *The Rover*, which had always been a part of their lives, was like leaving an old and dear friend. As Rennin set the ship on course, Morgan slipped her hands under his arms and laid her head on his back. She said, "You know *The Rover* will sail northward now without you. Come and enjoy the ocean spray with me."

Rennin turned around to face Morgan. He pulled the pins from her hair and loosened it with his fingers. With a smile, he whispered, "You are still as beautiful as the first time I held you in my arms. Actually, I think you're more beautiful." He kissed her as he had not kissed her in a long time, and he said, "Heart of my heart, life of my life, you are my reason for breathing; and I will love you until the day I die."

He lifted her in his arms and carried her to their cabin. "What are you doing, Rennin?" Morgan teased innocently.

He gave a little laugh. "You know exactly what I'm doing, and it's exactly what you want me to do."

She raised her eyebrows. "How perceptive you are."

The day for departure arrived with a visit from Quantaleh. He came to tell Oliver good-bye. The two men had been friends since they were children. Quantaleh said in his native tongue,

"Look at you. White man's name; white man's hair; white man's clothes; white man's language. So do you have a white man's heart?"

Oliver squinted and folded his arms across his chest. "The color of skin does not affect the heart. Look at Chinowaya—he had a dark, cold, evil heart. Not so, with Rennin and Geoffrey. They are good men who do not look at skin color. They look at the man. Like God, they see the see the heart, not the skin."

Quantaleh questioned, "White man's God?"

Oliver responded, "No. True God. *My* God." He placed his hand on his chest.

Quantaleh grunted, "Humph! No matter. I came to say good-bye to my friend. I wish you much happiness." Oliver and Quantaleh grasped each other's shoulders.

Oliver said, "Good-bye, my friend." Quantaleh left.

Rennin put his arm around Oliver's shoulders. "Are you sure you want to go with us? We will understand if you stay."

Oliver looked at Rennin with soulful brown eyes. "Must go. This my family now. Go with family. You be family one day, too."

"What?" said Rennin.

"Cameron and Holly. I much approve. Anna will give Cameron permission to marry sister when day comes."

Rennin started laughing. "Good grief! Cameron is only eleven."

Oliver smiled knowingly and continued, "Not many moons, Cameron be grown. Donovan almost grown. Open eyes, Rennin. Boys no longer babies. Donovan"—He held up three fingers—"three years marry Emily Claire. Five years, Cameron marry Holly. You see."

As incredulous as the thought seemed, Rennin did remember he was only sixteen when he had married Morgan, and Donovan had just celebrated his thirteenth birthday. He sighed. "I'll take those few years, my friend. Let's go."

Having purchased four wagons for hauling household goods, supplies, and children, the three families started westward toward the Ohio Territory. Morgan, Anna, and Eula started out driving three of the wagons, while Donovan and

Cameron took turns at the reins of the fourth wagon, which carried the children. Emily Claire taught lessons to Ian, Duncan, and Holly as they traveled. Rennin, Geoffrey and Oliver rode horses that Rennin had also purchased.

Traveling was slow. Spring rains kept the group stranded at the Allegheny River. A few weeks into the trip, Morgan told Rennin they were going to have another baby. She was so sick that some days Emily Claire had to drive for her, but the sickness passed. Early June gave Oliver and Eula their first child, Rennin Chance Montague, whom they called Chance because he had come early and it was a great chance that he survived. Rennin was humbled and exalted at the same time that Oliver would name his son for him.

June also brought the families to a lush valley, which appeared uninhabited. Through the valley ran a wide lazy river. It was shallow for twenty feet out from the bank, but became navigable and deep near the center. Emptying into the stream was a smaller creek, which the children eventually dubbed Beaver Creek because of the abundance of beaver dams. The men agreed the place seemed perfect for a new home.

During the next few weeks, the men chopped trees and built homes of rough-hewn logs rather than planed boards for the sake of time. The women planted late gardens and prayed for a late frost. Donovan, Cameron, and Ian hunted for all the families. The families built their own smoke house and salted and cured meat from the domesticated farm animals they had bought over the years, as well as the wild game they hunted. Emily Claire, Duncan, and Holly caught trout, bass, and catfish in the river.

Work on the houses went on until the last ray of light so that by the middle of July, the families slept beneath roofs. During this time, many trappers came through the valley. Rennin, Geoffrey, and Oliver decided to set up a trading post as a means of income and of getting the supplies they needed without months of traveling. They called their little venture Montague, O'Rourke, and Montague Trading Post, or Mom's Trading Post as it came to be known, as did the entire settlement, eventually. Morgan suggested building a few rooms adjoining the trading post as well as a kitchen and dining room to offer lodging, baths, and meals to those who would be interested. Mom's Trading Post and Morgan's Inn came to be a regular stop for many trappers and the local Indian population who were quite different from the Iroquois.

Geoffrey and Anna were extremely happy, especially when Anna announced she was expecting a child. Anna radiated her joy and love for Geoffrey, although, at times, Geoffrey still had a hard time fathoming that his young, beautiful wife could possibly love him; but it was apparent Anna had stolen Geoffrey's heart.

The months passed in peace. The white men who ventured that deep into the untamed country were on good terms with the local Indian tribes. Many trappers were married to Indian women. Few white women risked going so far into the wild, although one missionary and his wife and sister lived in the valley.

The only medical treatment was provided by the Indian shaman. This shortage of medical attention proved to be the biggest challenge Rennin and Morgan faced during their first year in the valley and one of the biggest challenges of their life together.

Rennin stopped reading. "I don't think I should read this part to you right now. It might scare you."

"Why?" asked Rebekah as another contraction subsided.

"It's about Morgan and the baby. Things weren't quite as easy as the other four. It might worry you, but I'll tell you this: Morgan goes into labor for Christmas."

"Aren't we lucky?" snapped Rebekah as she crushed Rennin's fingers.

Keturah interrupted. "I'd love to hear more about your relative, Rennin. Perhaps, I can read the beginning, but right now we are almost ready to deliver a baby. Rebekah, you can push with the next contraction. I see a crown."

Rebekah screamed, "Rennin!"

He stroked her hair. "Push, honey. It'll be over soon. It's after midnight. We'll have a great Christmas gift."

Rebekah screamed and pushed and pushed and screamed. After fifteen minutes, Keturah announced, "It's a boy, a nice plump little rascal."

Rebekah grabbed Rennin's shirt, "If it's a boy, why do I still hurt?"

Keturah turned around from cleaning the baby while Rennin ran to see what Rebekah meant. Almost in a panic, he said, "Rebekah, push."

Rennin suddenly held a second chubby little boy.

Finally, Rebekah relaxed and held her two sons. Rennin rubbed the soft fuzzy little heads. "Well, Rebekah, we haven't chosen one name. Now, we need two. When we first talked we thought about our fathers' names. What do you think now?"

Rebekah laughed. "Number one son heralded Christmas. I'd like to name him Gabriel and Braden for my father—Gabriel Braden O'Rourke. Since our first son has an angel's name, our second son should also have an angel's name. How about Michael and Rowan for your father—Michael Rowan O'Rourke?"

Rennin nodded. "I love those names, and I love you. Next time we can have two little girls to name after our mothers."

"Next time!" Rebekah fairly shouted. "Let me recover from this time."

Rennin grinned. "Yes, ma'am." Then, he kissed his wife. "Merry Christmas, my love. Heart of my heart, life of my life, you are my reason for breathing; and I will love you until the day I die."

15
The Heart of a Villain

Keturah left Rebekah in Rennin's capable hands. After Rebekah nursed the babies, she slept. For a long time, Rennin watched his family before he succumbed to exhaustion.

Keturah allowed the new parents to sleep until she had prepared Christmas dinner. Of course, Rebekah had awakened several times to feed and diaper two babies, using clean torn flour sacks. She smiled to herself that the usually light sleeper, Rennin, had not heard the babies' cries. She laughed softly. "You would think he had given birth to twins."

Keturah and Bart entered the O'Rourke tent carrying two trays of food. Chen Li followed quietly, hoping to sneak a peek at the twins. Rebekah exclaimed, "Oh! You shouldn't have gone to all this trouble, Keturah."

"Nonsense!" snorted Keturah. "Consider it my Christmas gift to you."

Rennin started awake. Bart greeted jovially, "Merry Christmas, Papa!"

Keturah handed Rennin two envelopes as she grudgingly offered further news. "We have company. Reverend Banks rode out to deliver these, but I think he just wanted some decent cooking."

Rennin laughed. "Maybe he wanted some decent company. Invite him in, and let's all eat together."

When Bart went out to ask the preacher to come in, he was in a tree with Patty snarling at him. Jed sat pulling Patty's tail.

Bart could not refrain from snickering. "What's da matter, Rev'rend? Scairt of a little pussycat? Patty girl, come here. I gotcha sumpin'." Bart handed Patty one of the turkey legs and patted her head. "Merry Christmas, girl."

Bart glanced at the man in the tree. "You can come down. She ain't gonna eatcha. Come on in Rennin's tent. We's all gonna eat in dare 'cause Rebekah ain't up to comin' out jest yet. She only had twin boys early dis mornin'." Bart picked up Jed.

Cautiously, the reverend left the tree. Patty growled as he walked by, but he entered the safety of the tent with Bart.

Keturah served the meal and then passed out presents. She gave Rebekah a shawl that she had knitted at night. She said the gift was from Bart, Jed, and her. Then, she gave Rennin a new hat to replace the one Jed and Patty had turned into a toy and chewed. To Chen Li she gave boots, like "Mr. Wennin's."

Rennin blushed. "I haven't any gifts this year. My priorities were a little out of order, but no more." He lifted Rebekah's hand and kissed her fingertips.

"I do," said Rebekah. "In that box. Will you get it, Rennin?" She pointed to a box. Inside were three bandanas for Bart, three somewhat misshapen bun covers that Rebekah had just learned to knit for Keturah, a rattle made from a dried gourd for Jed, work pants and a shirt for Chen Li, and a new, leather-bound Bible for Rennin because the pages were loose in his old one.

Rebekah apologized, "Reverend, if I had known you were coming, I would have had something for you."

"The food and the company are enough," he replied with a stiff smile.

The conversation drifted from one topic to another until the reverend asked, "How are your diggings going?"

"Slowly," Rennin replied. "We've found a small rich vein, but it's difficult to extract."

"Might I offer my assistance?" the reverend asked. "The town is really not very receptive to the Gospel."

"In return for what?" asked Bart, skeptically.

The reverend shrugged. "Ten percent? A tithe, if you will?"

Bart and Rennin looked at each other. Bart tilted his head toward the entrance to the tent.

Rennin said, "Excuse Bart and me a minute. We need to talk outside."

Outside, Bart stated. "I don't trust 'im, Rennin. I didn't trust 'im when he married Keturah and me 'cause I thought he was snobby an' thought he was better'n me, but dat ain't it. Dare's sumpin' dark lurkin' under dat collar."

"Bart, could it be that you're afraid of him?"

"No. Patty don't like 'im neither. She was about ready to make 'im Christmas dinner."

"He's a stranger to her. That's all. She was being protective."

"Maybe," Bart conceded. "Maybe I'm still just selfish, but if'n he stays to help, I'm gonna keep a close eye on 'im. Rennin, you're too trustin'. Doncha remember Pierre?"

"You might be right, Bart, but we sure could use his help."

"All right, Rennin, but I'm gonna watch 'im real close."

"Agreed."

When the men told Banks he would be welcome to help, the reverend rode into town to pick up his belongings. He said he would be back at the end of the week. Bart, Keturah, and Chen Li went back to their tents, and Rebekah fed the twins. Afterward, she lay back with her eyes closed. Rennin softly kissed her head.

She smiled. "I'm not asleep, but I *am* tired. I have a feeling those two are going to keep me in that state for a while. Why don't you read to me about Morgan's Christmas baby? Surely, she gets a girl this time."

Rennin kissed his wife. "First, I'd like to read our letters. One is from my sister, Caitlin. The other is from Running Bear." Caitlin's letter congratulated Rennin and Rebekah on their marriage and impending parenthood. She included a longing to see them all. Running Bear's cryptic note acknowledged with appreciation his receipt of the book and the Bible and conveyed his mixed emotions about the loss of his niece, but joy for Rennin and Rebekah. He also confessed a newfound faith. His letter had come from the mission where he had gone to study more about God. Ashamed of himself, Rennin groaned, "I forgot my promise to Running Bear. Thank you for remembering, my love."

He picked up the book as he acknowledged, "Rebekah, this really has been a good Christmas. I promise never to lose track of what's important again. I love you. I'm the happiest man on Earth right now." He kissed her once more and opened the book.

Early on Christmas morning, Anna, Eula, and Emily Claire descended on Morgan's kitchen to prepare a Christmas feast. The turkey had been put into the oven the night before. So, Anna kneaded the dough for fresh bread while Morgan crimped crusts for pumpkin pies and Eula chopped the fixings for stuffing. Emily Claire peeled yams and sprinkled them with molasses and cinnamon and a clump of butter.

With all the food in its proper place to cook, Morgan went in search of Rennin who was pounding the children with fresh snowballs. He poised to pelt Morgan, but her look withered his enthusiasm. "What's wrong?" he wanted to know.

She took his hand and led him away from the children and the men who acted like children. "I'm in labor. 'Tis early, but by tonight we'll have another baby."

"Do you want to lie down?"

"Not yet. I want to open gifts before the contractions get bad. Then, I want to have dinner and send everyone home. I don't anticipate any problems, but I don't need an audience. You'll do just fine. I've done this four times before. If you need help, Anna, Eula, or Emily Claire can help."

They opened gifts and ate dinner. Then, Rennin explained the situation to Geoffrey and Oliver who promptly suggested a sledding adventure to the children. Emily Claire opted to be a child for the afternoon.

At dusk when all the children returned, Morgan still had not delivered. On the contrary, she was having more trouble than she had ever had before. Rennin sought the help of the two women in their company. When three more hours elapsed, Anna and Eula were concerned. Anna said, "Morgan have much trouble, Rennin. Baby breech."

Rennin tried to stay calm. "Can you get the baby to turn, Anna?"

"We try and try. Cannot get baby to move."

Morgan screamed, as she never had with any other delivery. "Rennin!"

With trembling hands, he grasped Morgan's small hand. He cried despite his efforts to control his fear.

In agony, Morgan grabbed Rennin's shirt collar. "Look at me, damn it! Remember Nana. She sent the herbs with me. Do it! Do it now!"

Rennin stammered, "I-I-I don't know how."

"Yes, you do!" snapped Morgan. "Look in your heart. Find the mystical part of you that you *know* exists. I'll say the words. You repeat them. Brush on the herbs and get my baby out! Don't you dare let my baby die, Rennin Drake O'Rourke! Now, do it!"

Rennin opened Morgan's chest of herbs and potions, which Elizabeth had insisted that she bring. Morgan groaned, "Use the black leaves and the clear vial. You only need a pinch and two drops."

Rennin removed the two items and a small bowl into which he crushed the leaves and dropped two drops from the vial. The mixture began to smoke. Anna and Eula clutched each other's arms as they watched Rennin's hands shake.

As he prepared the deadening herbs, the Indian shaman, Talulah, entered unannounced. Oliver had gone for him when Morgan showed great difficulty. The shaman stopped in his tracks as he watched Rennin in fascination.

When the concoction was ready, Morgan practically hissed, "Get the hyssop and the scalpel, Rennin. Hurry!"

Rennin turned with the items in his hands and shakily said, "Morgan, what if I do it wrong?"

Morgan pleaded, "Just do what I say. Please!"

Hearing the despair and distress in his love's voice, Rennin hesitated no longer. He threw back the sheet that covered her and dipped the hyssop in the mixture. With the hyssop, he painted a cross on her abdomen.

Morgan whispered weakly, "Elfringo et prodo spiritus." ("Open and bring forth life.")

Rennin repeated the words as he painted the cross. He, then, took the very sharp scalpel and cut along the lines he had painted. Within minutes, he handed Anna a baby girl that was not crying or moving. Anna stared at the baby and blinked back tears.

Morgan gasped, "Finish quickly, Rennin. See to the baby." Then, she said, "Sacrificum per amor, occludo et medicor." (Sacrifice of love, close and be healed.")

Rennin repeated the words as he ran his fingers across the incision he had made. The opening closed, leaving a rigid, ugly scar.

Morgan whispered, "The baby, Rennin."

He took the little girl who had begun to turn blue. "Morgan, 'tis your little girl that you wanted so much. Since you waited fourteen years for her, let's call her Rachel. Tell me what to do. She isn't breathing."

"I don't know what to do, Rennin. If you have to do what Nana did to your mother, do it."

Rennin gently rubbed the baby's chest and blew into her mouth for he remembered seeing his grandfather Fitzpatrick do that to a person who had dropped dead, and the person revived. As he worked he cried openly and without shame and talked to the baby and prayed. "Breathe; please, breathe. Live for Daidí. I already love you, my little darling. Oh, God, please let her live. We'll never have another chance to have a daughter. Please, give Morgan her spirit's desire." He held the baby to him.

Morgan said curtly, "Give me Rachel, Rennin. I shall do the incantation if you aren't able or willing."

He shot her a withering look that she ignored. Never had she said anything so calloused. In a controlled, but angry tone, Rennin responded, "You're too weak. You've lost too much of your own blood. I was hoping to avoid it, but I'll do it if all else fails."

Stubbornly, Morgan countered, "All else *has* failed, Rennin."

"Where is your mother's faith, Morgan?" Rennin flung. "Have you forgotten to pray?"

She growled, "Shut up and do what you must to save my baby or give her to me and get out!"

"She's my baby, too," whispered Rennin. He held Rachel close again. "Oh, God, I don't want to perform any more blood magic. I'm unsure I can, but I'll try for my baby. These are the things I learned as a child, but these are the same things people are burned alive for practicing in this world. Show me what to do. I don't want to dishonor You, but I want this baby to live."

Rennin laid the baby on the foot of the bed and knelt to cover her with his body. He had heard many times exactly what Elizabeth had done to bring his mother, Caitlin, back to life. He had witnessed her attempt to bring Aidan back from the dead when he was not actually dead. He whispered, "God, forgive me if I'm wrong, but I can't let her die." He spoke the words in the Gaelic, "Mach fuil augs annsachd beothaich anam. Nach deò." Then he stretched himself over the dead baby and said, "Blood of my blood; breath of my breath; restore sweet Rachel from the brink of death."

As he began to place his mouth on Rachel's, the little body jerked, and she began to wail with a force—the spell only half performed. Rennin gathered the little bundle and repeated through grateful tears, "Thank you, Lord."

Still angry, he reluctantly handed the baby to Morgan. "Here's my daughter for whom I was unwilling to sacrifice everything. Now, I'm stepping outside. I have to cool off." Rennin slammed the door as he went out.

Outside, Geoffrey gathered logs for his fire. The children were at his house. He watched as Rennin disappeared into the thicket. Geoffrey followed his friend into the woods and found him, his back against a tree and his eyes closed. Carefully, Geoffrey ventured, "Rennin?"

Quietly, Rennin replied, "She accused me of not being willing to do whatever I had to do to save my child. Her voice was icy. God! She sounded exactly like Quazel. Morgan has never been so cruel or cold in all the years I've known her. That was *not* my Morgan."

Geoffrey put his hand on Rennin's shoulder. "Rennin, mebbe the pain an' fear got the best o' 'er. No matter. She needs you, an' you need 'er. Sittin' in the snow an' feelin' sorry for yourself won't 'elp either o' you. Go back to your wife."

"I will, Geoffrey, when I've had time to cool off. I just need a little time alone."

Geoffrey patted Rennin's shoulder and headed back toward his home.

Rennin murmured, "Geoffrey, I began the blood ritual to revive the dead."

Geoffrey turned back. "Began?"

"God gave her breath before I could finish the act."

"And you feel this was wrong?"

"Magic, Geoffrey. I do have it within me, but I don't want it."

"Then this stays between us."

As he left the wooded area, Anna darted from the O'Rourke house. "Geoffrey, where Rennin?"

"'E is in there." Geoffrey indicated the thicket with his head.

"Morgan need him. Morgan sick."

"Go back to Morgan. I'll get Rennin."

Geoffrey went back into the woods. "Rennin, Anna came out lookin' for you. She said Morgan was sick."

Rennin sat up, alert. "Did she say what was wrong?"

"No, just that Morgan was sick."

Rennin sprang to his feet. "God, how could I be so selfish?" The tall man ran full speed back to the house. He dropped his coat on the floor as he came in. Breathlessly, he entered the bedroom.

"Morgan?"

The shaman restrained Morgan, trying to keep her in bed as she screamed, "Rennin, don't leave me! Come back! You promised you wouldn't leave me."

Rennin touched the shaman's shoulder. Talulah made way for him. Rennin held Morgan as she collapsed on his shoulder.

"'Tis all right now, my love. I'm here. You're safe. Rachel's safe. Nothing else matters. Shhh."

Morgan sobbed. Rennin continued to comfort her. "Don't cry. Shhh. I love you." As he spoke, Rennin soothed Morgan's matted, sweat-soaked hair from her face. He realized she was burning up with fever. He stood.

In a panic-stricken voice, Morgan cried, "Uncle Aidan, come back. Rennin ran away. Help me find him."

Rennin turned back to Morgan. "Love, I *am* Rennin. I'm not leaving. I'll be right back." He kissed her fevered brow.

In hushed tones, Rennin asked Eula to care for Rachel until Morgan's fever broke. She agreed, and Rennin sent everyone away. "I'll care for Morgan. When she's better, I'll explain everything you heard and saw today." Rennin asked the medicine man to stay in the settlement in case he needed his help, and Talulah agreed.

For three days Morgan's fever raged. Neither cold baths nor cinchona-bark tea brought relief. She trashed and tore at her covers. Repeatedly, she cried in her delirium for Rennin not to leave her, all the while mistaking Rennin for his father. Never did he leave her side, except to relieve himself. He hardly ate or drank, weakening himself.

Finally, Morgan was quiet, though her body burned within. From pure fatigue, Rennin slept beside her, his arm covering her lest she should move.

Early on the last day of the year, Rennin awoke as Morgan stirred and spoke, "Rennin?"

He softly touched her face. She was cool. He gathered her in his arms and allowed himself to release his fear and anxiety. For several minutes he sobbed without words.

Morgan felt her own weakness and simply lay in her husband's arms. At last she spoke. "Rennin, what happened? The last thing I remember is Geoffrey and Oliver taking all the children sledding. It was something terrible. I can see it in your eyes. Is it the baby? Did we lose the baby?"

Hoarsely, Rennin comforted, "No, she's fine. We have a daughter, and we call her Rachel. Eula is caring for her until you're able. She was born on Christmas Day, just before midnight."

"Then, what happened? How long have I been asleep?"

Rennin whispered, "Three days. I thought you were going to die."

"Well, I'm not; at least not yet. Now, tell me what happened, and if you lie, I'll know."

Hesitantly, Rennin told Morgan what had happened. She cried softly. "I'm so sorry, Rennin. I cannot believe I talked to you like that. I know you would give everything, do anything, for the children or me. Please, forgive me."

"Of course, I forgive you. You're the love of my life. I confess: I had bruised feelings temporarily. Then you decided to scare me out of my wits. Don't ever do that to me again."

Morgan laughed. "I must look a fright, but will you say our special thing to me?"

"Always. Heart of my heart, life of my life, you are my reason for breathing; and I will love you until the day I die."

"I love you, too, Rennin. Now, I need to ask you a favor."

"What?"

"Will you help me get a bath? I feel disgusting, but I also feel too weak to bathe alone. Then, I'd like to hold my baby."

Rennin heated water and carried Morgan to the tub. She asked, "Sit with me. Let me lean back on you."

He suddenly laughed. "Is that your subtle way of telling me I smell awful?"

"Well." She contorted her face.

Rennin slipped behind Morgan, and she relaxed on him. With honeysuckle-perfumed soap, he bathed her gently, as if she were a baby. He lathered her hair, and, then, she relaxed against the tub while Rennin washed himself.

Through half-closed eyes, Morgan surveyed her husband's scraggly appearance. "You need to shave," she commented.

Rennin chuckled. "You're definitely feeling better. You've never liked hair on my face."

"Your face is far too handsome to hide."

After bathing, Rennin put Morgan into a clean, warm nightgown. Then, he brushed her hair until it was almost dry, felt like silk, and shimmered like satin. He changed the linens and propped her in bed on several pillows. With a kiss and a tickle from his whiskers, he said, "I'm going to get Rachel for you."

Morgan laced her fingers around Rennin's neck. "You must know that if I had been in my right mind, I never would have said the things I said to you."

He kissed her nose. "It's over. I forbid you to say another word about it. I promise I shan't. Are we agreed?"

"Yes, my love. Now, bring me my baby. I need to start nursing her."

Rennin explained to Eula that Morgan was well enough to nurse Rachel. To Geoffrey, who had stopped by to see Oliver, he said, "She's still too weak to care for the other children, but in three or four days, I'll take everybody home."

Geoffrey assured Rennin that there was no hurry.

Back in his own home, Rennin laid Rachel in her mother's arms. Tears coursed down Morgan's cheeks as she choked, "She's so beautiful. Thank you, Rennin. Rachel's the most wonderful Christmas gift you could ever have given me. Are you upset that she'll most likely be our last child?"

"No, my love. You've given me a full quiver, and I still have you. I could not ask for more."

Morgan nursed her baby, and with Rachel nestled in her arms, she fell asleep. Relieved for the first time in almost a week, Rennin shaved, lay beside his wife, and slept soundly.

Rennin closed the book with a yawn. Rebekah reached up and caressed her husband's cheek. "Thank you for being so sensitive. I might've been afraid had I heard that while I was in labor."

The new father kissed Rebekah just as the twins began to wiggle and whine. He grinned. "My boys have impeccable timing. Let's get them fed and changed and get some sleep. I have work to do tomorrow. The first thing I have to do is to carve two names in a tree. Then, I might just have to build another cradle. Gabriel and Michael cannot sleep together long. They'll only be this small for a short time. I'm not going back to the mine, until Reverend Banks returns."

Rennin built a second cradle so that each baby had his own little bed. Both Rennin and Bart took off the week between Christmas and the New Year to spend with their families. Chen Li asked if they could have a small version of a Chinese New Year celebration, and his suggestion was met with enthusiasm and excitement although the date would be off a bit.

Near suppertime on New Year's Eve, Reverend Banks rode into camp. Patty came to life with a snarl.

The reverend said, "Your unusual pet does not like me, Rennin."

Jovially, Rennin responded, "When she gets to know you, she'll be fine. Welcome back, Reverend." Rennin shook the man's hand.

"Please call me Ike, short for Ichabod. I know I'm interrupting supper, but I brought something for tomorrow I hope will make up for my intrusion. Ladies, can you cook beefsteak? I have two for everyone. I thought we could celebrate the New Year."

"Thank you, Reverend. Yes, we can cook beefsteak, as rare a commodity as it is around here," said Rebekah.

The company sat down to plates of rabbit stew and cornbread and fresh milk from Belle the cow. That evening, Chen Li dressed Patty in a miniature, but brightly colored, dragon costume and got her to prance around for several minutes. He, then, displayed a small arsenal of fireworks. Jed squealed in delight, and the adults were well entertained.

The next day, the group dined on beefsteak covered with sautéed peppers, onions, and mushrooms; new potatoes in white sauce; and broccoli florets fresh from the garden, steamed and covered in cheese. The following day, the men went back to work in the pit in the cave. Patty lay near the fire until the horses disappeared; then, she stealthily followed them.

Many weeks passed uneventfully, except for the incident when Ike almost broke his neck. He had been mining with Rennin and the others. As he climbed the ladder to the ledge, he came face to face with Patty, who, as usual, snarled at him. He let go of the ladder, and if Rennin had not broken his fall, he probably would have shared the old prospector's fate.

Several weeks later, as the men swung their pick axes, the wall of the pit gave way, and they broke through into another room where the vein they had been mining seemed to continue. Chen Li crawled through the new opening into a large cavern even deeper underground. He shined his lantern around carefully. The walls on the north and west sparkled.

Chen Li crawled out. "Wennin, make hole bigger. You must see."

Rennin squeezed through the hole already in the wall and crawled out grinning from ear to ear. "Fellows, I think we might have hit the mother lode. We'll need a lot more light and maybe some of that black powder we bought. First, we need to shore up the ceiling. We don't need a cave-in."

Ike volunteered, "I'll go back to camp with Jack and Chen Li. We'll bring some lanterns and lumber so we can start bracing this place this afternoon. You two can get that hole big enough for all of us to be able to fit through."

Bart and Rennin agreed. Bart said, "Yep, while y'all are gone, me and Rennin can make dis here hole a mite bigger. Dat looks like a mighty tight squeeze for men as tall as da two of you. I don't relish da ideer of crawlin' through sech a little place. Rennin, did you feel like you was bein' born all over again?" Bart chuckled.

Rennin nodded with a grin.

"Fine," said Ike. "Chen Li, let's get going. Rennin, would you make sure Patty's not up there waiting for me. That's one reason I'm taking Chen Li with me—to protect me from her. I tell you, that creature hates me."

Rennin went up the ladder first. As Ike climbed out, Patty lay there, delivering her customary snarl. She lay still with a low rumbling growl in her throat, tail swishing, ears flattened.

Ike untethered his horse and Jack. He pulled Chen Li up behind him and they rode off. Rennin went back to work with Bart.

Ike rode into camp, whistling. "Ladies! We've discovered something in one of the caves that Bart and Rennin are bursting for you to see."

"Have you actually found a large vein?" asked Rebekah.

"I believe Rennin referred to it as 'the mother lode,'" Ike replied. "I have a few things to load on Jack. Then, I'll take you to the strike. I think you'll be greatly surprised."

"Is there some way to help you?" asked Keturah.

"Yes, of course. Keturah, you can help tie on a dozen or so lanterns. Rebekah, you pack up some sacks of food that won't spoil. We might be working in shifts, even at night. I'll strap on some lumber for bracing the ceiling and some black powder for blasting."

When everything was packed on Jack, Ike said, "Gather up the little tykes so we can see what their daddies have stumbled into. I'm so excited that I can hardly wait. Hop on that mare, and let's go!"

They rode toward the cave and then veered east. Rebekah said, "I thought you were working in the cave over there." She pointed west.

"We were until a couple of days ago. Didn't Rennin tell you that we moved?"

"No."

"Neither did Bart," said Keturah.

"Maybe they wanted to wait until they knew something for sure. They sure want you to know now!"

They pulled up outside a cave where they all had to duck through the entrance. Once inside, several lanterns lighted a spacious cavern. Ike showed Rebekah and Keturah a rope ladder, leading down into a pit about twenty feet deep. There were several lanterns lit, and light came from a tunnel.

Ike said, "Rennin, Bart, and Chen Li are in the tunnel. Go on down. I'll grab a few more lanterns and be there in a minute."

Keturah went down first. She carried Jed in a harness on her back. Likewise, Rebekah carried the twins in a dual harness with one on her back and the other on her chest— always alternating which baby was against her heart. Carefully, Rebekah went down the ladder. At the bottom, she called, "Rennin!"

At that moment, the ladder disappeared over the rim. Rebekah screamed, "Ike, what are you doing?"

"Ensuring my future, Rebekah." He dropped the sacks of food into the pit. "I would suggest blowing out all the lanterns but one. If it takes too long to get the gold, I'll bring you some more food. Before I leave here, I'm going to set gunpowder to ignite if your spouses get stupid. If your husbands try anything, you will be buried alive. Sorry. You really are nice ladies, but if there's one thing I've learned as part of old Jedediah's Missionary Society, it's to take care of oneself. By the way, Keturah, I figured you didn't recognize me. I've changed a great deal in thirteen years. I was only eighteen, but I wanted to tell you, 'Thank you for making me a man.' I truly enjoyed our night in St. Louis all those years ago."

Ike started to leave, but made one more comment. "Oh, if you check the tunnel, you'll see I didn't completely lie to you. Chen Li's in there. The little Chink's out cold, and he might have a few broken bones, but he's there. For such a little guy, he's a real scrapper," Ike concluded, sounding as if he admired the boy.

About half an hour later while tending to Chen Li's concussion, the ladies heard a gunshot and a snarl.

"Oh, God!" shouted Rebekah. "He's shot Patty."

In the other cave, Rennin and Bart heard the shot. Not long afterward, Ike showed up and lowered the lumber and lanterns into the pit.

"What was that shot, Ike?" asked Rennin.

"I eliminated a pest." Then Ike pulled the hammer back on his shotgun as he jerked up the ladder. "Gentlemen, I would greatly appreciate your mining the gold and passing it up. I'll gladly hoist."

Angrily, Rennin said, "Ike, what the hell is this?"

"I'm ensuring my future."

Rennin narrowed his eyes. "Patty! Patty, girl!"

"You needn't call her. That's the pest I eliminated. You see: We aren't strangers. The last time I tried to kill her, my knife obviously failed, but she left me with a lot to remember." Ike opened his shirt and showed the men three long scars, indicative of a puma's claws. "I owed her. I'm sure I got her this time. I found her bloody trail into the underbrush. She's gone off to die."

"Are you saying you're the one who killed old Pete?"

"Hell, Rennin! I worked with that old fool for months. He was too stupid to mine properly. I just had to wait for someone with a little more intellect. You're too trusting, but you aren't stupid."

Bart growled, "I tole you I didn't trust 'im. Are you even a preacher, Ike?"

"Yes, Bart I have a license. Your marriage is legal if you want to be married to the best little whore in St. Louis. Does she give you as much pleasure as she gave me? I'm devastated she didn't remember me. I remember her well. Of course, she was my first while I was just one of so many. I suppose I understand."

"I'll kill you!" ranted Bart.

Ike raised his gun. "Don't get stupid. Your families and Chen Li are not in camp. I have them safely stowed away, but they won't be safe if you get foolish. I planted gunpowder around the cave where I have them. It will go *'BOOM'* if you try anything."

"You bastard!" Rennin shouted. "You would harm innocent women and children?"

"In a flash. Believe me, the little brats are only innocent until they learn to walk and talk. I don't think those two women are as innocent as you'd like me to believe. I know Keturah isn't, as I've already said. On the other hand, Rebekah might be. Maybe I'll spare her and take her with me when I leave."

"I'll kill you when I get out of here, Ike!" declared Rennin.

Ike fired a shot into the wall behind Rennin and Bart, spraying them with dirt and debris. "I'll take my chances."

Bart stated, "An' you'll die, you fool. I know what Rennin O'Rourke's capable of, especially if you threaten Rebekah, an' now his chillun. Ike, be reasonable. We're willin' to share dis wif you."

"I found it! It's not yours to share." Ike shot the wall again. "Now, get to work! Don't even look for your guns. I have them. I won't tell you again. I'll start killing, and I'll start with the little useless Chink."

Rennin said, "Ike, you have the heart of a villain."

"Yes, I know, and I'm damn good at it, too."

16
Protector and Deliverer

With every blow of the hammer or every swing of the pick ax or every scoop of the shovel, Rennin thought of agonizing, torturous ways to kill Ike. So dark was his countenance that Bart cautioned him. "Rennin, you ain't no murderer. Remember how your forgiveness affected me. If it wudn't for you an' Rebekah, I might be standin' beside Ike, not you."

"Bart, don't tell me you aren't thinking of ways to do him in. You want to get to Keturah and Jed as much as I want to get to Rebekah and my boys."

"You're right, but I ain't gonna let 'im see how upset I am. We hafta keep our heads an' bide our time. We won't be no kinda use to Rebekah and Keturah dead. If'n we can git outta here wifout bloodshed, let's do. If'n we can't, then, Ike is responsible for his own soul burnin' in Hell. Know dis: I ain't plannin' to die, but if'n sumpin' happens to me, promise me you'll take Keturah back to da mission where your sisters are. She should be happy dare."

Rennin leaned on the pick ax. "Bart, how did you develop so much wisdom so quickly?"

Bart grinned. "I married a wise woman."

Rennin sighed. "We both did. I promise to see after Keturah if something happens. Will you do the same for me? Take Rebekah to my sisters and take Chen Li with her. He deserves to be loved."

"You can count on it."

Ike shouted, "Shut up and work! You have a lot of gold to mine for me. Hop to it!"

Back in the other cave, two angry women grumbled while they searched for a way to escape. Rebekah muttered, "If that lowlife thinks he's going to keep me in a pit, he has another thought coming."

The women plundered through the supplies that had been left in the unproductive mine. Keturah laughed while holding several large spikes in her hands. "He must think we're completely stupid. Rebekah, do we have a sledge hammer?"

"Yes."

"Come on, girl. We have a way up this wall."

Rebekah and Keturah hammered two spikes into the wall parallel to each other about two feet from the ground. They hammered two more spikes about two feet directly above those two. When the position of the spikes got above their heads, the endeavor became difficult.

In exasperation, Rebekah said, "Keturah, neither of us has the strength to swing the sledge over our heads, and Chen Li's arm is broken. The ledge is still too far to reach from the top spike."

Stubbornly, Keturah said, "Well, it was an idea. We'll think of something else."

Chen Li added, "God will pwovide a way out."

The two women looked at the usually quiet boy as he expressed his faith for the first time. At that very moment, they heard a rumbling growl above them.

"See," Chen Li murmured. "God heard our pwayers."

Rebekah looked up in surprise. "Patty! Patty, girl, are you up there?"

The puma stuck her head over the ledge and snarled.

"Patty," Rebekah coaxed, "push the ladder down. I can't take care of you or help Rennin down here."

Something that sounded like a whine came from the big cat and a drop of blood landed on Rebekah.

With a catch in her voice, Rebekah said, "Keturah! She *has* been shot."

Both women coaxed Patty to push the rope ladder down. As if she understood their desperation, the puma dragged the ladder to the edge and nudged it over with her nose.

"Good girl!" chorused the women.

Rebekah climbed up first. She examined Patty. "Oh, thank God! The shot wasn't bad. There's only a little buckshot in her shoulder, but I can get that out after we get Rennin and Bart."

Rebekah threw another section of rope she found at the top down for Keturah to tie around Chen Li. Then, Keturah came up, and the two women pulled the injured boy up.

Rebekah said, "Keturah, you take Chen Li and the babies back to camp." Rebekah picked up an abandoned shovel and lifted a small keg of gunpowder. She felt for the Lucifers she kept in her pocket. With a firmly set and determined jaw, she continued, "Patty and I are on a mission. Come on, girl."

Keturah detained her. "Rebekah, are you sure we can do this?"

"We have no choice. That vermin endangered the lives of my children. I may not actually be Pawnee, but I learned a lot from them. Go back to camp. Arm yourself. If Ike comes back, don't hesitate to shoot him."

The women started their separate ways. Keturah stopped. "Rebekah, you're the best friend I've ever had. Be careful."

"You, too," Rebekah said over her shoulder. "I love you, too. If anything happens to me, watch out for Rennin, Gabriel, and Michael."

Rebekah and Patty disappeared behind a boulder.

While Keturah and Chen Li anxiously waited in camp, Rebekah and Patty eased their way to the cave that was being mined. Cautiously peeking around the edge of the entrance, Rebekah saw Ike relaxed with his shotgun across his arm. She heard Rennin and Bart working in the pit as Ike gloated about finding such strong and capable miners that worked with only motivation rather than pay.

Stealthily as a cloud passing, Patty padded through the entrance as Rebekah tiptoed barefoot behind her. She shivered because the temperature in the cave was frigid. Rebekah raised the shovel and softly cleared her throat.

At the sound, Ike whirled around. "What the?"

Before he could finish his statement, Rebekah swung the shovel with all her might. "How dare you endanger my children!"

The blow knocked Ike off balance, and the gun discharged into the ceiling, showering everyone with debris, some of which was gold nuggets.

The shower of falling dirt and rocks took Rebekah off guard long enough for Ike to wrench the shovel from her grasp. He slapped her and flung her toward the edge of the pit. As he did so, Patty leapt onto his back, mauling him ferociously.

Ike shrieked, "You demon! I've killed you twice. Why won't you die? Rennin! Call her off! She's gonna kill me!"

Angrily, Rennin shouted back, "I hope she does! It'll save me the trouble!"

When Rebekah shoved the ladder into place, Rennin and Bart scurried to the top. "Patty, get off," commanded Rennin.

Patty paused in mid-bite and looked up at Rennin as if she were totally disappointed. Nonetheless, she obeyed.

Rennin grabbed Ike by the collar and dragged him out the entrance. Rennin jerked him to his feet and pummeled Ike across the face. Suddenly, Rennin slumped forward as Ike plunged his hunting knife into Rennin's upper right chest. Rebekah screamed and ran back into the cavern. Without warning, the shotgun blasted. Ike fell in his tracks.

Rennin, in Bart's strong grasp, and Bart turned to see Rebekah with the shotgun against her shoulder. Both were too stunned to speak. Neither could believe that this compassionate, forgiving woman had delivered a fatal shot to the villain in their midst. As she lowered the gun, Rebekah calmly said, "'*To everything there is a season, and a time to every purpose under the heavens: ...A time to kill and a time to heal.*' Bart, help me get Rennin to camp so we can start healing."

Later that day, Bart buried Ike; Chen Li rested after Bart set his arm; Keturah made supper for the tight-knit little group; and Rebekah watched Rennin and Patty sleep. Rebekah had stitched and bandaged Rennin's shoulder just below his collarbone. No vital organs had been hit,. Then, she had removed the buckshot from Patty's shoulder. As Rebekah watched Rennin sleep with Patty at his feet, her tears slowly trickled. Despite the necessity of shooting Ike, her heart was broken at the loss of life.

Unknown to her, Rennin watched her rock Gabriel and Michael to sleep, and he watched her tears fall. Feeling like a spy, he said, "Rebekah, you did the only thing you could've done. You saved my life—*again*. Come and hold me. I need to feel you close to me. I was terrified that maybe Ike had actually killed all of you, and we didn't know. I love you so much. I thank God for you."

Rebekah sat down softly beside Rennin. "I'm not sorry I killed Ike, Rennin." Her voice still quavered. "I'm just sad at the wasted life. I'd do it again. I have an idea. Let me read to you for a while."

"Okay, if it'll make you feel better."

She kissed him. "It always does."

The years flew by for the happy group in the valley. Business boomed because the demand for beaver pelts, bear skins, and rabbit furs was high in Europe.

During those prosperous years, Geoffrey and Anna had a son, Geoffrey Drake, and a daughter, Nancy Virginia; Oliver and Eula added a daughter, Catherine Ann; and Rennin watched Donovan and Cameron become men before his eyes and wished he could make time stand still. Each day as he watched Donovan and Emily Claire grow closer, he remembered his misspent youth. Rennin then turned his attention toward Cameron, who like his father, challenged every authority. True to Oliver's prediction, Cameron and Holly were inseparable.

Early one winter morning, Rennin proposed a hunting trip for only Donovan, Cameron, and him. "I've not spent enough time with the two of you lately. You're almost grown. Before I know it, you'll be spending time with my grandchildren."

"Daidí!" The boys shouted, but they enthusiastically packed for a weekend hunting trip while their younger brothers, Duncan and Colin, pouted that they were not included. Rennin promised to do something with the two of them when he came back.

The first night by the fire, Rennin sounded fatherly, all the while thinking of Aidan and missing him deeply. "Boys, I really want to talk to you about some things. First, girls."

Both boys hooted with laughter. "Da," Donovan interrupted.

Rennin held up his hand. "That's the other thing. Don't call me 'Da.' I like 'Daidí.' It makes me feel loved and special. I don't care if you're a hundred years old. I'm 'Daidí', not 'Da'. Is it a deal?"

Both boys agreed. "Fine, Daidí, but no matter what we call you, we love you," assured Cameron.

"Good," said Rennin. "Now, about the girls."

When the teens rolled their eyes, Rennin pointed a sharp finger at them. "Don't scoff at me. I married your mother when I was only sixteen. I loved her then; I love her now; and I'll love her forever. Nonetheless, she and I had to grow up too fast. We were children making adult decisions. We thought only with our hearts and bodies. Our minds, especially mine, took a voyage to oblivion. As a result, I'm the father of six children. One of them is in Heaven. My eldest son died before he ever saw the light of day. I never got to hug him and tell him how much I loved him. My heart was broken, but I never told your mother because she was hurting too much to deal with my pain.

"Boys, I've watched you with Emily Claire and Holly. Donovan, it's obvious you and Emily Claire are in love. That's great. She has grown into a fine young woman. In another year, I shall be proud to call her my daughter; but, Donovan, if you cannot control your urges, come and talk to me. If we have to let you wed sooner, we'll deal with that."

"Daidí," Donovan defended himself. "I'm not a fool. Uncle Geoffrey would kill me if I did anything more than give Emily Claire a goodnight kiss."

Rennin sipped his coffee deliberately before he said calmly, "But you have, haven't you, Donovan?"

Donovan's deep mahogany eyes grew wide. "We've not done what you're thinking. I swear." Donovan dropped his eyes and whispered, "Almost, but she got scared. I'm sorry, Daidí. It is hard."

Rennin pulled the boy's head onto his shoulder. "Donovan, I'm not so old that I don't remember. That's why I told you about your mother and me. She would be mortified that you know. I want you to remember that what happened with us was completely my fault. You've heard the stories of how she grew up. She was so innocent and naïve, actually ignorant of the consequences, that she didn't understand what we did. Her only thought was that she loved me, and she'd do whatever I asked her. I want you to know that no matter how much you love Emily Claire, actions have consequences—sometimes, very painful consequences."

Donovan sighed, "Daidí, do you think Uncle Geoffrey would really let us go ahead and wed? What difference will one year make?"

Rennin chuckled. "Well, let's see. You could build your own house. You'll not be living in mine once you're married."

"That shouldn't take a whole year, Daidí."

"What about furniture?"

"We can sleep on the floor."

Rennin arched his corrective eyebrow. "I think Emily Claire might have something to say about that."

Donovan grinned sheepishly. "Well, do you think I should formally ask Uncle Geoffrey for Emily Claire's hand? We could start building a house and furniture. Something to occupy us might keep us out of trouble."

Rennin rubbed his knuckles across Donovan's head. "I think you're making wise choices now, but I wouldn't add that last statement to Geoffrey. Leave it as you'd like to marry next summer. That'll be six months rather than a whole year."

Excitedly, Donovan asked, "Will you help me with the house and furnishings, Daidí?"

Rennin slapped Donovan's leg. "Yes, and so will Cameron."

Donovan snickered. "Cam needs to build his own house."

"Shut up, Donovan," said Cameron.

Rennin looked at Cameron. "Is there something you want to tell me?"

"No, Daidí. Donovan's full of bull," declared Cameron, defensively.

"Oh, am I?" said Donovan, a smirk playing on his lips. "Who was swimming bare-assed with Holly?"

"Shut up, Donovan!" Cameron pushed his brother.

Donovan pushed back. The two boys had always been best friends; but as much as they loved each other, they fought just as passionately.

"Stop it!" Rennin snapped. "Cameron?"

Cameron folded his arms across his chest and moved to the other side of the fire. "I've nothing to say. I'm not a sap like Donovan."

"You'd better start talking," said Rennin.

Donovan wagged his head. "Yep, Daidí, you've more to worry about with Cam than me. The problem there is that Holly's not nearly so proper or shy as Emily Claire."

"Damn it, Donovan! I told you to shut up!" shouted Cameron as he leapt across the fire and belted Donovan in the mouth. Astraddle his older, yet smaller, brother, Cameron held onto each side of Donovan's coat. "Don't say another word about Holly! She's perfect! She's absolutely perfect—beautiful, free, and untamed."

Rennin pulled Cameron off Donovan. "That's enough. Cameron, just how wild *is* Holly? Is Oliver going to hurt you—worse, Anna?"

"No, Daidí. Oliver and Anna already gave Holly and me their blessing. Yes, we were in the buff, but that's the extent of it. The only reason Donovan has anything to tell you is because he and Emily Claire were with us."

Rubbing his mouth, Donovan said, "I never said we weren't. Damn, Cam! I was jesting with you. The way you reacted, you'd think I gave away a deep, dark secret. Calm down. I'm sorry. I really like Holly. She's perfect for you, but I can see it now. You can sell tickets to the fights the two of you'll have. You'll be like Grandpa Aidan and Grandma Caitlin. You get more red streaks in your hair every day. With your Irish and Spanish temper and her hot Indian blood, you'll be obscenely rich if you charge admission."

The two boys began to laugh at the absurdity of the idea. Still giggling like a girl, Cameron said, "Sorry I punched you, Donnie. Holly has an adventurous spirit. She wants to experience life as much as I do, but she's also insecure about being accepted in a world where Indians are viewed as somehow inferior. I want to protect her from being hurt. I do love her. Daidí, other than swimming, we've done nothing to be ashamed of. I love Holly too much to hurt her."

Rennin smiled at his boys. "I believe both of you. I just want you to know that you can talk to me about any of this. I truly do understand. Now, let's get some sleep. We have turkeys to hunt tomorrow. You know Christmas is only a week away, and your mother wants turkey." Rennin sighed. "I'm beginning to feel old. Can you believe Rachel will be four next week? My baby is quickly growing into a young lady. I might scalp any rogues like the two of you or me."

They all laughed as they turned in for the night. Sleepily, Donovan said, "Daidí, we'll help you scalp any rogue that messes with Rachel."

"I'm with you," agreed Cameron.

The next morning the three O'Rourke men were up early. Donovan prepared his usual culinary delights. This time it was a breakfast of scrambled eggs, fried ham, and coffee.

Cameron woke up in a playful mood. He teased his brother. "Who's going to cook when you and Emily Claire marry?"

"Very funny, Cam."

"Is this what I have to look forward to all day?" asked Rennin as he stretched.

"Yes, sir!" quipped the adolesents in unison.

Rennin laughed as child-like as the two boys who were almost men. He scrutinized them with the loving eyes of a father. *Donovan's older, but smaller. Cameron's almost as tall as I am. Donovan resembles Morgan, dark hair and eyes. Not short at five feet eleven inches, he's small in comparison to the rest of us O'Rourke men. He also has inherited Morgan's gentle spirit, as has Rachel.* A smile spread across his face. Rennin thought about Duncan. *Looks like those two, but he's already tall for his age. So is Cameron for a boy of fifteen. Six-foot-two and brawny. His strawberry blond hair has many red streaks in it as Donovan observed last night. He has my emerald eyes and his grandma Caitlin's, or his grandfather Colin's, temper. Duncan has shown from infancy that he has the same temper. Then there's Colin, real mixture with my blond hair and apparent size and Morgan's soulful brown eyes and spirit.* Rennin sighed. *I see some of all those I left in my children.* He smiled at the thought, and then tore into the breakfast Donovan had prepared.

The turkeys were in great form for hiding that day. By lunchtime the men had not even heard a gobble, and the snow began to fall. As the flakes salted the ground, the carefree boys began to pelt each other and their father with snowballs. Carefully laying his gun on the ground, Rennin shouted, "This means war!" He returned snowball fire with alacrity.

The gaiety and laughter echoed through the woods until Rennin repeatedly pegged Cameron as he ran into a clearing and a crackling sound. Rennin shouted, "Cameron, don't move!"

Cameron froze. "Daidí, help! The ice is cracking. I didn't realize I was on the pond."

"Be still. Let me get you."

Donovan placed a restraining hand on Rennin's shoulder. "Let me go. I'm smaller than you."

Rennin shook his head, "I cannot risk both my boys. If you fall in, what am I to do? What do I tell Momma and Holly and Emily Claire?"

"Stop arguing," said Cameron. "Neither of you needs to come out here. Get a limb or something and slide it over here so I can grab it in case the ice breaks. I'll try to inch back onto solid ground."

"All right. Just be still," said Rennin. He tossed his small hatchet from his belt to Donovan. "Go get the longest limb you can. I'm not budging in case the ice *does* break."

As quickly as he could, Donovan chopped an eight-foot limb. When he got back, it appeared neither Rennin nor Cameron had batted an eye, but Rennin grabbed the limb and lay on the snow. He stretched as far as he could, pushing the limb in front of him. "Come on, Cam. You have a yard."

Hoping to distribute his weight more evenly, Cameron dropped to his hands and knees and crawled toward the limb. Just as he gripped the end, the ice snapped wickedly beneath him. Dangling at the end of the limb, Cameron's lower half plunged into the freezing water.

Over his shoulder Rennin shouted, "Donovan, hold the limb!" On his stomach, Rennin scooted toward the opening in the ice. Just as he reached the hole, the limb snapped under Cameron's weight.

"Cameron, give me your hand," commanded Rennin. Cameron grasped his father's hand, but the weight of the two large men was more than the thin ice could hold. Suddenly, both men floundered in the frigid waters.

Rennin fought to pull Cameron toward the bank of the pond. His eyes saw Donovan leaning over the ice just as he had. He scolded, "Donovan, get back before you're in here, too."

"Hush. Push Cameron toward me. He's already unable to move from the cold. You will be, too, in just a few more minutes. Daidí, you're our hero. You don't have to die to prove it."

With all his fading strength, Rennin pushed Cameron toward his brother. Donovan hoisted his brother onto the weak ice and dragged him to the bank.

Meanwhile, with stiffened muscles Rennin struggled to pull himself from the icy water. Donovan gripped Rennin's collar and yanked with all his might. He pulled Rennin partially onto the ice nearer the shore. "Come on, Daidí. Move. This ice is starting to crack, too." Rennin leaned on his eldest son and on shaky legs plodded to the bank as the ice gave way behind them.

With chattering teeth, Rennin said, "D-d-donovan, build a f-f-fire. We need b-b-blankets."

Donovan built a blazing fire and raced through the faster falling snow to camp to gather blankets and other supplies. In their frolicking, the men had wandered nearly a mile from their campsite. Donovan's lungs nearly burst from the frosty air as he gasped for breath at the tent.

Into a knapsack, he stuffed food, the coffee pot, coffee, and the change of clothes they had brought. He gathered all the blankets he could carry and started back to the pond.

The trip back to the pond took longer than the trip to the campsite because of Donovan's burden; however, he moved like a deer through the foliage. When he returned, Rennin sat almost in the fire, holding Cameron next to him. Both men shivered uncontrollably.

Donovan took control of the situation as he pulled Cameron from his father's arms. "Come on, Cam. We have to get off those wet clothes."

Cameron's teeth chattered and he could barely move on his own. "I'm s-s-sorry," he stammered.

"Shut up," said Donovan. "You enjoy making Daidí jump into the water to save you. This is the second time. Do you remember the Atlantic Ocean? Talk to me, Cam. Don't go to sleep. Keep moving."

"Y-y-you t-t-told m-m-me to sh-sh-shut up."

Rennin grinned, trembling. *At least Cameron's mind is working. He's bantering with Donovan.*

Donovan undressed Cameron and wrapped him in a dry blanket. The snow had slowed to an occasional flurry, so the covers would stay dry. Donovan massaged his brother's hands and feet and then put him close to the fire. He, then, turned his attention to his father. "Your turn."

Rennin tried to unfasten his own shirt, but his hands shook too hard. Donovan took his father's hands and rubbed some feeling back into them. "Let me take care of you right now." Rennin humbly nodded his assent.

Soon, Donovan had Rennin and Cameron wrapped tightly together under several blankets. "Hold on to each other. The body heat from each of you will warm the other." Donovan made hot coffee and gave each man a steaming cup. "Here. This will help warm you inside."

After he had drunk a cup of his own coffee, Donovan told the other two, "I'm going back to move camp over here under those pines." He pointed at a small stand with his coffee cup. "Will you be all right until I get back?"

"We'll be fine," replied Rennin, warming somewhat, "but your mother will be in a panic if we don't come home tonight."

"She'll understand when we get there. Besides, we still have to shoot her a couple of turkeys." Donovan grinned mischievously.

During the next hour, Rennin heard several blasts, and when Donovan lumbered up loaded with the rest of the camping supplies and two turkeys, Rennin commented, "Well, your mother won't be disappointed."

Donovan shrugged. "They were just sitting there, side-by-side."

Donovan set up the tent and built a smaller fire near the entrance. Cameron and Rennin moved inside as the snow picked up intensity. Donovan battled the cold and made a hot meal of venison steak, roasted yams, and apples. Hours after his unintended dip in the water, Cameron still shivered as he quietly ate. Rennin gave an occasional shudder.

After dinner, Rennin declared that he wanted to sleep, so he curled up under several blankets and dozed, though he heard the ensuing conversation.

Donovan asked, "Cameron, why are you so quiet?"

Tears dripped down the younger brother's cheeks. "You're right, Donovan. I've almost killed Daidí twice."

"Cam! I didn't me to upset you. I was only trying to get you to move and talk. Besides, neither of those incidents was your fault."

"Still, I'd rather die than lose him."

Donovan put a protective arm around his brother. "Both of you are fine. Be grateful for that. Daidí would be as mad as a hornet if he heard you talking this nonsense."

"I know," said Cameron wiping his cheeks. "I guess I'm still a little boy in many ways. I'm not ready to be a grown-up married man yet. Are you? I mean, really?"

Donovan shrugged. "Sometimes I think I am, but then I see just how much Daidí does have to deal with, and I get scared. Cam, I do love Emily Claire, and I'm going to marry her; but I think both she and I will have a lot of growing up to do together."

Donovan laughed. "You know, Cam, 'tis really funny. I couldn't stand Emily Claire when we first met. I even thought it was funny that she got sick with the pox before I knew how serious it was. I thought she was the most sanctimonious, self-righteous wench I'd ever met. The New World changed her. I realized I loved her not long before her mother died. I want to love Emily Claire the way Daidí loves Momma."

Cameron smirked. "You want to love the way Daidí and Momma love? What about the princess? You know what happened with the princess? Daidí won't tell us, but he told Momma."

"Sure, I know. That's exactly what I mean. I want a love that overcomes and surpasses even the wrong and bad things. Now, tell me when you first knew you loved Holly."

Cameron smiled. "The first time I saw her. She was angry and defiant and couldn't speak a word of English. Her eyes snapped, and her lips were firmly set. It was obvious that she didn't want to be with us. I decided to conquer her then and there. I remember I went up to her, and she glared at me as if she were thrusting a dagger into my heart. I stared right back. After about ten minutes she looked at the ground. I realized that she was absolutely terrified.

"Think about why she was with us, what the white trappers had done to her sister. Her brother almost died. She was ripped from her home to come to live with white people who did not even speak her language. I held my hand out to her, and she took it. I knew at that moment that I'd never let her go. She was my beautiful Holly Berry.

"I remember Daidí telling us about Uncle Kieran and Aunt Miranda and how they loved each other from the time they were five years old. In two or three years, I'll marry Holly; but I've decided I want to be a child a little longer. Our love can wait."

"Seriously," Donovan said, "what about the temptation Daidí was talking about last night?"

Cameron shook his head. "I've you and Daidí to come to if it gets unbearable. I'll cross that bridge when I get there, and..." He dangled his hand in the air.

Donovan's face crept crimson from his neck to his scalp at the implication. He looked over his shoulder at Rennin. "Daidí's terrific."

Cameron nodded. "He's the best father in the world." Cameron put his finger to his lips as he gathered Rennin's almost dry socks into a ball and threw them at his father's back. "Especially, when he's *pretending* to be asleep!"

Rennin rolled over and grinned. "You think that you're really smart, you little imp!" Then, he motioned for the two boys to come to him. Putting one arm around each of them, Rennin said, "I love both of you so much that I can never put it into words. You've heard what I say to your mother. Well, it's just as true for you. You are heart of my heart, life of my life, blood of my blood; and I will love you until the day I die." Rennin kissed both boys' cheeks as they returned his affection just as when they were five and seven years old, and Rennin had just returned from his long time away.

The next day, the three O'Rourke hunters trudged home. Morgan met them in the yard. "This is Sunday morning. Why are you so late?"

"'Tis a long story, Morgan," Rennin said as he put his arm around her. "Come inside and we'll tell you all about our grand adventure."

Rebekah closed the book when she saw that Rennin's eyes were shut.

"I'm not asleep," he said. "I was just praying for the kind of relationship with my sons that the Rennin of old had. My father was a good man, but he didn't show me much affection. He reserved his tenderness for the girls. Rebekah, boys need to feel loved, too. I want to do that. I want Gabriel and Michael and any others we might have to know I love them."

"You will," assured Rebekah as she lay down beside her wounded husband. "I love you, Rennin, and I will always tell you so and show you so." She kissed him softly on the lips. "Good night, my wonderful, loving husband."

17

Mother Lode

After several days of rest, Rennin once again returned to the mine with his arm in a sling. Bart had the first chamber lit with all the lanterns he could find. He greeted Rennin, "It's about time you came back to work. Me and Chen Li ain't gonna share if'n you don't get your butt movin'." Bart's grin nearly obscured the rest of his face. "We done struck the mother lode, but I guess actually, Rebekah struck it for us. Look up!"

Rennin looked at the area where the shotgun had blasted. Above their heads, the vein glimmered and sparkled.

"Ain't it beautiful, Rennin?" Bart asked, excitedly.

With reserve, Rennin said, "Is it going to drive you as mad as it did Ike?"

"Naw. I ain't gonna mind bein' rich, though. Rennin, you know I got sumpin' better'n gold in my heart and my life." He tapped his chest. "I got another surprise to tell you about. Me and Keturah are gonna have a baby. Imagine dat, Rennin. Me bein' a father. I love little Jed, but to have one of my very own. It's much better'n gold."

"They're more dangerous than gold," Rennin said wryly as he rubbed his shoulder. "You know, I didn't get this fighting to keep the gold. That monster threatened my family. I wanted to kill Ike myself. Bart, three times because of Rebekah and now my sons, I've wanted to kill. I did kill Pierre. I'm glad I didn't kill you, but I wish I'd been the one who killed Ike." Rennin sat down. "Bart, is a little gold worth all this?"

"Rennin, you ain't never been poor. You ain't never knowed need. In New Orleans, dare are chillun dat eat from garbage cans behind fancy restaurants. Dey will steal a man blind. Da little urchins wear rags. Back in town when we got here, I seen da same thang, orphans, deserted chillun, like Chen Li. Rennin, I know how dey feel. I was one of 'em 'til I was took in by an ol' widow woman. Course, she expected a lot from me, but da trade off was worf havin' food, clothes, an' a roof over my head.

"I been thankin'. We ain't gonna be miners forever. I'd like to use some of da gold to set up a home for da chillun. Whatcha thank? You and Rebekah wanna be a part of dat?"

"I think it's a wonderful idea. Let's do it with some of the first gold. Bart, let's put down roots. Let's build a huge home near the stream, one with living areas for our families as well as quarters for homeless children." He slapped his knee. "No, wait. Rebekah wants her own house. Let's settle down here and build houses for our families first. Then, let's build dormitories for both boys and girls. We'll hire a few men for a small percentage of the gold to help."

Rennin's excitement bubbled. "Keturah can teach them. She's very intelligent and well-educated. Rebekah can mother them to death. Oh, she'll love every one of them. Yes, Bart! Let's do it!"

Thus, it was decided how some of the gold would be used. Rennin posted letters home for Caitlin to secure contractors to come and build the homes and the orphanage. He also extended an invitation to his sister, Candace, and her husband, Thomas Goodman, who was a doctor, to come and be the resident physician.

The replies were swift. Not only were Candace and Thomas coming, but also Rennin's sister, Catherine, and her husband, Olaf Ishi, a giant of Swedish descent. He planned to come as the temporary headmaster of the school, and he and Catherine might stay on if they liked living in the area. Thomas already had another doctor who had come to work with him and could take his place.

Rennin and Bart had definitely hit a rich, deep vein of gold. They hired four reputable prospectors who had had no luck on their own, but were hard workers and men of character, in exchange for five percent of the yield to each man. Chen Li was set to receive ten percent of the yield, most of which would be kept in trust until he turned twenty-one or married. The men who came to work for O'Rourke and Mercier, Inc., the legal partnership Rennin and Bart formed, were content with their wages and treatment by their employers who were fair, impartial, and just.

Three months after inception, contractors, architects, and carpenters descended upon Puma Pass. Rennin and Bart took bids and awarded the job to MacMillan and Sons. Jacob MacMillan was a middle-aged man who had been a builder since his teens. The letters of recommendation he brought with him showed he had a respectable reputation and a successful business. His three sons, Joshua, Joseph, and John worked with him. Joshua was the architect while Joseph and John did the actual building. Jacob oversaw everything.

In no time at all, the MacMillans had elegant homes built on the banks of the stream in Puma Pass. They built a bridge across the stream and began to erect two more houses to be used by Dr. and Mrs. Goodman and Mr. and Mrs. Ishi when they arrived. About a mile upstream and around a bend, they also constructed four smaller, but nice houses for Rennin and Bart's employees.

The two main houses were ready in time for Keturah to give birth in her own bed. Bart beamed as he announced the birth of his son, Stephen Shane Mercier. He grinned and declared, "An' we gonna haf some more for sure!"

Rennin caught Bart's exuberance later at home alone. He asked Rebekah, "When are we going to have some more?"

Rebekah put her arms around Rennin's neck. "Gabriel and Michael are not even a year old yet. Give it a little more time."

"Jed is only seventeen months," Rennin surmised.

"I'm a little bit younger than Keturah, Rennin. There's no urgency. Besides, there's a problem."

"What's that?"

"I'm afraid I've forgotten exactly how to go about it since we've practiced so infrequently lately," she said with a twinkle in her eyes.

"Is it practice you want then, Mrs. O'Rourke?" Rennin said with a rakish gleam in his eyes.

Rebekah sighed. "They do say that practice makes perfect."

Enthusiastically, Rennin said, "That can be arranged." He scooped Rebekah up into his arms and raced up the stairs to their room.

"Rennin! It's the middle of the day. There are people everywhere outside, and the twins could wake up at any minute."

"We'll lock the door, and the boys can practice crying if they wake up."

"Rennin!"

"Not another word, lady. You wanted practice: You're getting practice." He kissed her ravenously.

Rebekah and Rennin lay snuggled under the sheets in their new store-bought bed. Rennin teased Rebekah, "Did we have an argument earlier?"

"Yes, and, darn it, I lost!" Rebekah added, not to be out done, "I guess that means you'll be teaching me to play poker tonight."

Rennin cleared his throat. "No, no, no. You were very rusty. I think you need extra practice."

She hit him with her pillow. As Rennin tackled her and she giggled, someone pounded on the door.

"Damn it!" said Rennin. "Let's pretend we're not home."

"Rennin, that's a insistent knock. It could be an emergency."

"Oh, all right. I'll peek out the window." He stuck his head out the window and shouted, "What do you want? I'm in the middle of something very important."

From beneath the porch roof, stepped Candace and Catherine. Rennin's tone changed dramatically to one of childish delight. "Candy! Cathy! We'll be right down."

The two sisters looked knowingly at each other.

Rebekah was mortified. "What will they think?"

Rennin chuckled as he pulled on his pants and boots. "They'll be wishing that their husbands were as crass." He laughed harder. "As I recall, Olaf and Cathy were crasser twelve years ago. I remember what Black Cloud and I saw down by the river. If they say a word, I'll remind them."

Rebekah fumbled with the pins as she tried to put her hair up. Rennin kissed her neck and whispered, "Leave it down. I like it down."

"Rennin, stop. It's not sophisticated."

"If I had wanted sophisticated, I would've married Allison Buckley."

"Who is Allison Buckley?" asked Rebekah with a spark of jealousy.

"An old flame. No, more like an old candle flicker, but she was sophisticated to the point of being snobby. I can't imagine her being willing to hug dirty little street urchins. I can't imagine her being willing to hug her own children."

Rennin took the pins from Rebekah and shook her hair loose. He turned her around. "You, my dear, are a flame; and just like a moth, I am drawn to you. You consume me, and in your presence I cease to exist."

Rebekah cupped Rennin's face in her hands. "Rennin, your sisters are waiting on our front porch."

"Let them wait a few more minutes. I've had them for twenty-four years. I've only had you for two." He kissed her deeply. "Uh! I promise we'll continue this later."

"I hope so," she murmured, and quickly ran her tortoise-shell brush through her hair.

Rennin and Rebekah opened the door hand in hand. Candace and Catherine smothered their little brother with hugs. Rebekah started to drift away, but Rennin held her hand tightly. After a few seconds, Rennin announced, "Candy, Cathy, this is my love, my Rebekah."

Candace and Catherine then showered Rebekah with hugs. Candace declared, "Rebekah, you are stunning, absolutely lovely."

Catherine put her finger under Rebekah's chin and surveyed her more severely. Rebekah locked eyes with Catherine, and her spirit refused to be subdued. Catherine appraised her sister-in-law. "I would say this little girl is tough as nails, yet soft as cotton. She runs over with love and compassion because she has suffered much. Oh, little brother, I don't think you yet know what a gem you've truly found. This woman will take you places you only dreamed of before. She is the magic that once was lost."

Rennin folded his arms across his chest. "Rebekah, Cathy is the family soothsayer."

"Yes," agreed Catherine, "and I predict that Rebekah will one day hit you with a cast iron skillet as Cammy did when you opened your big mouth when you were twelve. I'll tell you all about it some time, little sister. Welcome to the family." Catherine enveloped Rebekah in a hug.

Candace and Catherine were obviously related to Rennin. They had the same jade green eyes and sable brown hair as their brother. There were three years difference in their ages, but they could have passed for twins if Catherine had not had a few streaks of gray in her hair and walked with a limp as a result of a horseback riding accident when she was a child, Rennin told Rebekah later.

Thomas Goodman was a tall, thin man with hollow cheeks, and sandy blond hair. He had an infectious laugh, and his soft blue eyes twinkled most of the time. Olaf Ishi matched Rennin inch for inch and pound for pound. His deep-blue eyes were serious and compassionate. He confessed that he could have a temper to accompany his red hair and ruddy complexion, but his laugh was hearty and true.

Thomas and Candace had their two children, fourteen-year-old Mark and twelve-year-old Sarah with them; and Catherine and Olaf had their three children, ten-year old Magda, eight-year-old Rita, six-year-old Fritz, and one on the way.

As all the introductions were being made, Gabriel and Michael made their presence known. Rebekah excused herself, but the two aunts scurried behind her to meet their nephews.

When they were all back in the living room, the doorknob unexpectedly turned, and in walked a giant puma. There were screams of panic. Rennin hooted with laughter as he tapped his shoulder and Patty put her front paws on his shoulders and gave him a "kiss." Rennin said, "There's another member of the family you must meet. Everyone, this is Patty, Patty Puma O'Rourke.

The newcomers stood, mouths agape, staring at the animal while Rennin ruffled her neck. "Say, 'hello' to some more of my family, Patty." As if she understood, Patty fell back from Rennin's shoulders, turned toward the gathered group, and gave a snuffle. Rennin patted the puma's head. "Go to your rug." Patty ambled to an old folded quilt in the corner and lay down. Rennin continued, "She's harmless unless you threaten one of us. She's better than any guard dog I've ever seen."

The aunts noticed that both Gabriel and Michael had toddled to Patty and lay on either side of her.

Candace asked, "Rennin, are you sure she's safe?"

"Yes, killjoy, she's safe," replied Rennin mockingly. "But, Thomas, I'd like you to examine Patty. We know she was raised by an old prospector who was murdered. Then, she was left alone for a time. Patty's full grown, and we've had her for over a year. Tom, she has never been in heat. I think there could be something wrong with her.

Thomas tilted his head to the side. "Maybe that's a blessing, Rennin. Patty might be fine with all of you, but a wild male would be dangerous."

"True," agree Rennin, "but I'd like to know if I should expect one to start hanging around."

Thomas started toward Patty, but paused. "She won't bite me, right?"

"No, Tom, she won't bite."

Thomas sat down on the floor by Patty and rubbed her head. He talked to her as if she were a child. "Hello, pretty girl. My name is Thomas, and I'm Rennin's brother, sort of."

He took a breath. "Will you let me rub your tummy? I want to make sure everything is the way it's supposed to be."

"Uh," interjected Rebekah. "She's ticklish on her tummy."

Thomas nodded. "Most female cats are. I'm assuming her anatomy is the same as a house cat."

When Thomas rubbed Patty's stomach, she wrapped her front paws around his arm and scratched at it with her back paws, but she never popped out her claws.

In a soothing voice, Thomas said, "Easy, girl. Let me feel your tummy." Patty relaxed and purred while Thomas rubbed and squeezed gently. After a little, Thomas said, "Good kitty," and stood. Patty hopped up and rubbed around Thomas's legs. Amazed, he laughed. "Good grief! She acts just like a regular cat." After a few minutes of putting her scent on Thomas, Patty lay back in her corner.

Rennin laughed. "Well, she's claimed you now. I guess you're officially Uncle Thomas."

Thomas chuckled. "Well, Rennin, I have a diagnosis for my niece. You won't have to worry about any males panting after her. It appears that although she has the outward markings of a female, there's nothing inside to support that. I mean *nothing*. I felt no uterus, ovaries, nothing. I would venture to say her old prospector kept her alive. She's imperfect. Her mother probably left her to die. It's the nature of the wild. The strongest survive. So, love her as long as you have her. I bet she keeps away more vermin than just mice."

"Like Ike," muttered Rebekah.

"Ya," said Olaf. "You must tell us all about that incident."

"After supper tonight," said Rennin. "Right now, I think we should get all of you settled into your new homes."

Near midnight Rennin fell onto the bed beside Rebekah with a groan. She scooted close to him and ran her hand up his bare chest.

"What are you doing?" he asked, suddenly wide-awake.

"Practicing," she whispered.

He laughed softly. "You have the energy left for that?"

"Always. Don't you?" She kissed his neck, chin, and mouth.

He pulled her onto him. "If I don't, I'll borrow some of yours."

There had been few truly stormy days in Puma Pass, but the morning after Candace and Catherine arrived was one to be remembered. The rain fell so hard that Rennin and Rebekah could not see the two houses across the narrow river. They could hardly see Bart and Keturah's house. Patty stayed in, and the boys played happily near the hearth. Chen Li came to breakfast, but disappeared to study soon afterward. Rennin insisted that he continue his education. No building, mining, or visiting took place that day, although the gold practically lay in the open after the excavation by the workers.

Rebekah popped some popcorn and, snuggling up next to Rennin, laid the leather-bound book that was beginning to look worn on his lap. She ran her finger along his ear. "Today's a good day for reading."

"Lay your head on my shoulder and feed me popcorn while I read."

Almost magically, the book fell open before Rennin turned a page.

Six months seemed to fly by, and Rennin's eldest son was getting married. Donovan and Emily Claire had finished their house, and the day set for the wedding dawned bright and clear. Morgan shook Rennin from his slumber. "Honey, time to get up. We've a wedding today."

Rennin mumbled, "No. I cannot do it."

"What? Why?" Morgan said, irritably.

"He's too young. I'm too young. I just cannot do it." He turned his back to her and pulled the covers to his chin.

Morgan put her hands on her hips. "Rennin Drake O'Rourke, get your arse out of that bed."

He slowly slid to a sitting position. "Morgan, this time next year they might be calling me Seanathair. I cannot do it."

Morgan put her hand to her mouth and started laughing. "You sound just like Uncle Aidan. I remember it as if it were yesterday. He said, 'I'm too young to be a grandfather, but Colin's not.' Do you remember?"

Rennin opened the nightstand drawer and pulled out his father's watch that Caitlin had given Aidan the morning he sailed for Draconis. Rennin had not known Aidan had slipped it in his trunk until they had sailed for days. Suddenly overcome with emotion, he choked, "Yes, I remember."

Morgan sat on the bed next to him. He buried his face in her bosom and cried. "I want to go home, Morgan."

"Then, let's go."

"How can we? That would mean leaving Donovan and Cameron. This wild, untamed land is their home. They'll stay here. I'm not ready to leave them yet. Oh, Morgan, I miss my father, especially today. I know how he felt when you and I exchanged vows."

He stopped and rubbed the golden links from the watch chain that Aidan had made into two rings for him and Morgan. "I never realized how much love went into these little pieces of gold until now."

Morgan caressed the watch in Rennin's hand. "The chain is long. I don't think 'twill miss a few more links. Why not make two rings for Donovan and Emily Claire? It won't take long; and about twenty years from now, Donovan can remember how much love goes into a trinket."

"Lady, you're the best. I'll do that."

"I've another suggestion."

"What?"

"It's time for another butterfly. Throw on some clothes. We'll be back in time for the wedding and the rings. Come on."

Morgan pulled Rennin by the hand into a deeply wooded area. "We'll have privacy here. It's been a long time since I did this. Help me relax."

Rennin sat quietly with Morgan for what seemed like eons to him while she simply breathed and held her hands outspread. Finally, a sparrow landed on her hand. She whispered, "How appropriate. Uncle Aidan wouldn't want something ostentatious. You know what to do, Rennin."

The little sparrow flew away carrying years of news and oodles of love.

Meanwhile, Rennin made two little golden loops from the watch chain. And slipped them into the minister's hand, whose eyes became misty at the gesture.

Rennin returned home to dress for the big event. Morgan had just finished putting ribbons in Rachel's hair. Rachel said, "I'm going to the stream with Bubba."

"Yes, you are," said Cameron, scooping up the little girl. "But I shan't let you walk in case you trip and get that beautiful dress all dirty."

The wedding was to take place near the river, and Cameron was his brother's best man. Cameron looked at his parents. "Momma, Daidí, I'll take the children on. I think the two of you could use a few minutes alone."

"Go raibh maith agat," said Rennin.

Cameron grinned at his father's use of the Irish. "You're welcome."

"We'll be there in a little bit. Don't start without us."

Cameron laughed. "I promise to make Donovan wait." Then he left with his two younger bothers in tow and his little sister in his arms.

In a dither, Morgan started, "Oh, I have to change my clothes and fix my hair."

Rennin caught her hand. "Leave it down."

"What?"

"Weave some honeysuckle into your hair and leave it down. I want you to look like the girl I married eighteen and a half years ago. You grow more beautiful with each passing day, but I still like your hair long and over your shoulders. Do it for me. You once said you'd give me anything I wanted or needed. I want you to wear your hair down. Wear your kimono, too."

Morgan's eyes were wide. Rennin grinned. "You look beautiful in it. Contrary to popular belief, the most beautiful woman at this wedding won't be the bride. 'Twill be her mother-in-law."

"Rennin."

"Shhh. I'm not finished. The wedding's not set for another hour. I need to make love to you."

"Rennin, you'll make us late."

"They'll not start without us." He lifted her into his arms and took her to their bed.

"Rennin," whispered Morgan.

"Don't pretend you don't understand this time."

"Oh, I understand perfectly." She caressed his cheek. "I love you, Rennin Drake O'Rourke. I always have, and I always will."

He took her hand and kissed her palm. "Heart of my heart, life of my life, you are my reason for breathing; and I will love you until the day I die."

Breathlessly, Rennin and Morgan arrived at the wedding hand in hand. He wore the same suit of clothing he had worn when he met Pablo Morales. She wore her kimono and her hair down with honeysuckle entwined in it.

Cameron and Donovan looked at each other knowingly and grinned. They had to face the minister and bite their lips to keep from laughing. Geoffrey put his face in his hands and snickered. Emily Claire scolded her father. "Papa! Those two will always act like newlyweds. Don't laugh."

Geoffrey whispered, "Ain't love grand?"

"You and Anna should know. She's expecting again."

"What?"

"Oops. Don't let on that you know. She was planning to tell you after the wedding. That way you might forget about giving

245

your first baby away. Now, smile. Wipe that dumbfounded look off your face, and give me to Donovan."

"'E might not want you if you don't be quiet."

"He wants me, Papa, more than you realize."

"I was young once, little girl. I remember 'ow 'twas. I remember the first time your momma slapped me, as if she didn't want my attentions. I also remember our wedding night."

"Papa!" Emily Claire blushed.

The little tête-à-tête took place through plaster smiles as Geoffrey walked his daughter toward her bridegroom.

"Make Donovan's as memorable as mine," Geoffrey teased.

"Papa!"

"'Ush. 'Ere's your man. I love you, baby girl, always." He kissed Emily Claire's cheek and laid her hand in Donovan's.

The wedding ceremony went smoothly. The couple shed tears over Rennin's rings. Finally, Donovan and Emily Claire retreated to their house after a raucous celebration. They were surprised to find a bottle of French wine that Geoffrey had ordered many months before, and their bed sprinkled with rose petals, courtesy of Morgan, Anna, and Eula.

Emily Claire sat on the bed and whispered, "How sweet."

She jumped in fright as Donovan popped the cork from the bottle. She giggled at herself.

He poured two glasses and sat beside Emily Claire. "I wonder what this tastes like," he said, handing her a glass. Both shivered with their first sip, but they finished the glass.

He touched her cheek. "Don't be afraid."

"I'm not afraid."

Donovan sighed. "I am."

Emily Claire looked at her groom. "Me, too. I lied."

Donovan kissed his new wife. "I love you, Mrs. O'Rourke. In that dress and with that halo of baby's breath, you look like an angel."

Emily Claire put her arms around Donovan's neck and ran her fingers through his shoulder-length brown hair and gazed into his soft deer-like eyes. "Only for you, Donovan Alexander O'Rourke. Only for you."

He pulled her to him and kissed her timidly, knowing that this moment would end their childhood, no matter how much they might wish to reclaim it some day. With care and gentleness, Donovan slipped Emily Claire's dress from her shoulders. He stared at her with longing and breathed, "You're exquisite."

She unfastened Donovan's shirt. Her sky-blue eyes traveled with her fingertips over his rigid chest. He caught her hand and kissed her fingertips. He whispered, "With you as my prize, I'm the richest man in the world. I have struck the mother lode." Donovan covered Emily Claire's mouth with his. They lay down as one, and lost in each other, they became husband and wife.

Rebekah put her hand on Rennin's. "How would Rennin know what happened in his son's bedroom? Did Donovan tell him?"

"No," explained Rennin. "A note at the beginning of the book says that contributions were made by subsequent generations. I think Donovan and Cameron and the other children must have written parts of the story. The book was not published for nearly fifty years after Donovan married Emily Claire."

"I'm glad to know that. It makes more sense. I know I'd have a hard time describing our mostly nocturnal activities to my father." Rebekah giggled. "Do you see who's asleep?"

Rennin glanced toward the hearth. "Ah, yes." He softly closed the book. "I agree with Donovan. I struck a much greater mother lode than a vein of gold. You're my greatest reward."

18
Shaken, Rattled, and Displaced

A few weeks after his sisters' arrival, Rennin received a letter from Running Bear. It read:

Rennin O'Rourke,

I am a proud man, so writing this to you has taken a great deal of humility, yet courage. Your government is displacing my people. They insist that we live permanently on a tract of land, which they designate. They call it a reservation.

To be sure, I have great misgivings about such an arrangement, but my people are few and could not withstand a war with your army. Your government has noted that individuals with a sponsor can live apart from the reservation.

In light of this stipulation, I am requesting that you, my white brother, serve as my sponsor. I do not wish to live fenced in like cattle. If you serve as my sponsor, then my family and I can come and live near you and Rebekah. Sleeping Fawn is in agreement with my decision, although your government would not recognize her opinion. As a woman, she has even fewer rights than I do.

Rennin, though you are a good and much respected friend, know that my pride is severely wounded to ask such a favor; however, it is the lesser of two wrongs.

If you are willing to serve as my sponsor, please notify me, as well as the local Indian agent, Wilbur Ross, at the trading post.

I am at your mercy and in your debt and always

Your brother,
Running Bear

Rennin threw the letter on the table in disgust. "How can they, Rebekah? How can the government force these people from their homes and their way of life?"

"I don't know, Rennin, but you *are* going to help Running Bear and Sleeping Fawn, aren't you?"

"Of course, I am. Did you doubt it?"

"No, but you sound so angry."

"I *am* angry!" He struck the table with his fist. "I'm angry with our government, not Running Bear."

Rennin drafted three letters. One he sent to Congress to tell them how disgusted he was about the treatment of the Indians. Another he sent to the Indian agent, demanding that Running Bear and his family be allowed to leave for Puma Pass immediately. The last he sent to Running Bear, welcoming him to Puma Pass, but stating his sorrow at the circumstances.

Rennin, Bart, and Olaf rode into San Francisco to mail the letters. They returned with lumber, beds, and other furnishings for a house. Rennin was still so angry that he went to work building a house for Running Bear with his own hands, next door to his own, although the MacMillans came to help.

Rebekah took him some food one afternoon. "How large are you going to make it?" she asked.

"I don't know how many children Running Bear has now. When he left us he had two and Sleeping Fawn was expecting. I got beds for Running Bear and Sleeping Fawn and four children. I'm building a living area with an open dining room and kitchen, and three bedrooms, one for Running Bear and Sleeping Fawn and two for the children. I plan to make the children's rooms large so all the boys can be in one room and the girls in the other. Is it too much, Rebekah? This is a great deal different from what Running Bear is used to."

Rebekah shrugged. "I think Running Bear will be honored, but Sleeping Fawn might be overwhelmed."

Several weeks passed before Rennin received a letter from the Indian Agent telling him the date to meet Running Bear and his family in San Francisco. On the specified day, Rennin took Rebekah and a wagon to meet their friend.

As directed, Rennin entered the sheriff's office to find Agent Ross. Seeing a round, red-faced, bald, squatty man wearing a suit-coat and dozing in a chair, his spectctacles slipping down his nose with each rumbling snore, Rennin surmised he must be the man. "Agent Ross?"

The man started awake and answered, "Yes." He pushed his glasses back in place and smacked his lips.

Rennin extended his hand. "I'm Rennin O'Rourke. I've come to pick up Running Bear and his family."

Ross's handshake was weak and limp. "Why you want those savages is beyond me, but they're out back in the wagon. I'll be there shortly."

"Thank you," Rennin said curtly as he and Rebekah made their way to the back of the sheriff's office.

Out back, Rennin was moved to rage and indignation. He bellowed, "What the hell?" Locked in a prison wagon, sat Running Bear, dejected with bruises on his face; Sleeping Fawn, trembling and holding a tiny infant; two boys about eight and five; and a little girl about two.

As Rebekah reached through the bars and took Sleeping Fawn's hand, Rennin stormed back into the sheriff's office and dragged the slothful agent out the door, throwing him against the bars of the wagon. He growled, "Open those doors right now before I beat you within an inch of your miserable life. What did you do to my brother, you sorry, good-for-nothing lowlife?"

"He threatened me. He had to be subdued," whined Ross.

"No!" shouted Rennin, jabbing his index finger into the agent's chest. "Running Bear did *not* threaten you, but *I* am threatening you. If I find another bruise or scar beneath this man's clothing or so much as a scratch or scrape on his wife or his children, I will kill you, even if I have to hunt you down. Now, let them out!"

With a shaking hand, Ross opened the door of the wagon. Rennin helped Sleeping Fawn and the children to the ground. When Running Bear stood, shackles on his feet jingled. Rennin had not noticed them before. "Oh, for God's sake!"

The obese little man tried to run, but Rennin snagged his collar and slammed his bald head into the bars of the wagon three times.

"Stop it, Rennin!" screamed Rebekah. "You're going to kill him."

"That's right," hissed Rennin. "I am."

"He is not worth the effort," said Running Bear calmly. "Let him go, Rennin O'Rourke. Take my family and me home with you so that we never have to see this wretched creature again."

Ross moaned, "Mr. Running Bear, you know that I have to check on your progress."

Rennin held the little mole-like man off the ground by his collar and stared into his face. "If you set one foot on my property, I will shoot you dead. You had best be thanking God above that my wife and my *savage* brother have calmer heads than I do. You are only alive because of them."

While Rennin dangled the man in the air, Rebekah snagged the keys hanging in the lock of the cage and released Running Bear's shackles. Rennin tossed Ross into the dirt.

The sheriff came around the building. "Mr. Ross, what happened to you?"

"He tripped and fell into the bars of his wagon," said Rennin through clenched teeth.

Ross pointed at Rennin and shrieked, "That man is crazy, Sheriff. Arrest him. He did this to me."

Sheriff Roger Simpkins looked at the tall dark-haired man. "Rennin, did you hit Mr. Ross?"

"Yes, I hit the little weasel. The next time I *will* shoot him."

"Rennin," the sheriff said as he shook his head, "you know that is a public disturbance. You owe me a fifty-dollar fine."

Rennin reached into his pocket and tossed a nugget to the sheriff. "That ought to more than cover it. As a matter of fact, it might buy me a few free shots while we see if the rat can run."

The sheriff weighed the nugget in his hand. He pursed his lips. "I could go back inside and hear a strange noise. Then, I could discover a body in about an hour, plenty of time for you to be out of town."

Without locking the cage, Ross jumped onto his wagon and sped away. Running Bear looked from his friend to the sheriff in great confusion. "Do you want to go after him, Rennin?" asked Simpkins very matter-of-factly.

"No. Let the bastard go. He won't be back. Thanks, Roger."

Roger and Rennin shook hands. Then, Roger held out his hand to Running Bear who tentatively took it. "Welcome, Running Bear. There are more men than Rennin who don't judge a man by the color of his skin."

Running Bear nodded. The group migrated to the front of the jail. Running Bear started to climb into the back of the wagon Rennin indicated. "Running Bear, up here," said Rennin. He winked at Rebekah who understood perfectly. Rebekah sat in the back with Sleeping Fawn and the children.

Clucking to his team, Rennin asked, "Where are your belongings?"

With much shame in his voice, Running Bear replied, "We were allowed only to bring our clothes and a few blankets."

Rennin pulled up in front of the general store. "Come on, my friend. We need to get you some things."

Running Bear hesitated. "They will not allow me in there."

"Oh, yes, they will," said Rennin. "You're with me." Rennin reached under the wagon seat and handed one of the leather pouches that Running Bear had given him to the man beside him. It was filled with gold nuggets.

Proudly, Running Bear said, "I do not want your charity, Rennin."

"It's not charity. It's an advance on your wages. Did you think you would come here and not work? Oh, no." He shook his head. "The other men working for me get paid five percent of the yield from the mine, except Chen Li, a young Chinese boy that lives with Rebekah and me, who gets ten percent put into trust until he turns twenty-one because I've taken him under my wing as if he were a younger brother. You will get ten percent because you *are* my brother. I built those men houses. You and Sleeping Fawn have a house. Two of my sisters and their husbands have come here to help me start a home and a school for the orphans. They get paid, and I built them houses. Chen Li will be going to the school, and I expect your children to go to the school along with my children, my partner's children, and my nieces and nephews.

"There is one thing you should know. The man who was with Pierre Boudreaux is my partner. He's a new man, Running Bear. He has found faith and has been forgiven. Rebekah forgives him, as do I. Will you forgive the man?"

Quietly, Running Bear asked, "Did he kill Black Cloud?"

"No, but neither did he stop it."

A shadow passed over Running Bear's face. "Will he offer me his apology?"

"I'm sure he will."

"Then, I will forgive him." He gusted a breathe. "I am trying to have faith, too, but sometimes it is hard when those who profess to have faith treat my people so badly."

"I understand, Running Bear, but try to remember what *true* faith looks like. Remember what Jesus did."

Running Bear reluctantly took the bag, and together the two men entered the general store. The clerk looked up as the bell tinkled. In a surly tone he said, "You'll have to buy your goods somewhere else. We don't serve your kind."

"You do now," Rennin barked.

The chalky-skinned, platinum-haired boy looked up. His colorless, opaque eyest widened. "Mr. O'Rourke, is this Indian with you?"

"This *gentleman* is my good friend and blood brother, Running Bear. Alan Atkinson, you will treat him with the same respect you reserve for me. If I hear otherwise, you will be out one very important customer."

"Yes, sir, Mr. O'Rourke. How may I help you, Mr. Running Bear?"

Running Bear replied confidently, "I need to buy calico, gingham, linen, and denim for clothing. I should bring in my wife to figure how much."

Rennin peeked through the door and motioned for Rebekah to bring Sleeping Fawn and the children. Timidly, Sleeping Fawn entered the store with Rebekah.

Rennin explained to his wife what they needed, and Rebekah put her former sister-in-law at ease, helping her to choose material and thread and needles while jabbering in Sleeping Fawn's native tongue. Rennin and Running Bear gathered food supplies and tools. With the supplies loaded, the party headed to Puma Pass. Rennin sneakily purchased a sack of licorice twists and gave it to the children.

They traveled for two days. On the way Rennin told Running Bear about Patty and Ike. Running Bear reached inside his blankets. "I did salvage my books, Rennin. I started at the beginning, and I have read some from each of them to my family every night."

"What chapter are you on in Rennin's book?"

"Donovan and Emily Claire have just married."

Rennin laughed. "Imagine that. We are in exactly the same place. Why don't you read to us as we travel? We have about an hour before we finally come to Puma Pass."

Running Bear's eyes danced with delight. "I would love to do that."

In the midst the sloshing rain, Donovan burst through the door. Drenched from head to toe, he looked like a drowned rat; however, he bubbled with excitement. He engulfed Rennin and nearly soaked him to the bone. "Daidí! We're having a baby!"

Rennin slumped into his chair and mumbled, "Terrific. Congratulations."

"Daidí, what's wrong?"

Morgan chortled as she handed Donovan a towel. "Your daddy thinks he's too young to be a grandfather."

Donovan shrugged and grinned. "C'est la vie. Deal with it, Daidí, because 'Gramps' it is." Donovan laughed joyously. "Now, I get to tell Uncle Geoffrey. I wonder if he'll mope like you."

Rennin brightened. "I want to go with you. I want to see his face. Of course, he *is* six years older than I am."

Rennin felt truly silly when Geoffrey responded with enthusiasm. Back out in the rain, Rennin sheepishly hugged his son. "I'm happy for you, Donovan. I remember how excited I was when you were born. It was the second greatest moment of my life. Marrying your mother was the first."

Rennin started laughing. "Your mother thought you were the most beautiful thing in the world, but you were *so* ugly. You had a squished-up little prune-looking face"—He made mashing movements with his fingers and scrunched up his own face— "and you were so *pink*. Morgan counted all your fingers and toes. She was totally in love with you from the second she saw you. It took me about five seconds. Suddenly, you had the most beautiful little wrinkled face and perfect color. I would have punched anyone who said differently. You were my crowning achievement." He gave a little nod. "Still are."

Morgan watched the two men through the window as the deluge continued. She felt strong young arms around her as Cameron came down the stairs. "What's going on, Momma? Why are Daidí and Donovan standing in the rain like dullards?"

Morgan planted a kiss on her son's cheek. "You're going to be an uncle. Your daddy is coming to terms with being a grandfather."

"Can he not do it inside?"

Morgan laughed. "Rennin has never done anything the simple way. It would be too easy to talk about the baby inside a nice dry house over a relaxing cup of coffee or tea. Which would you like?"

"Coffee. I smell fresh olykoeks. Why didn't you wake me this morning?"

"What are you going to do on a day like this? All the others are still asleep. Your daddy and I had a little time alone until Donovan barged through the door."

Cameron teased his mother. "Alone? What did you two do with this time alone?"

Morgan popped him with the dishtowel. "You are rotten!"

"Well, Momma, you and Daidí act like newlyweds all the time. I hope Holly loves me as much as you love Daidí."

Morgan squeezed Cameron's hand. "You love her as much as Rennin loves me, and you'll receive the same in return."

"I do love her, Momma, but I want everyone to see it each day, the way no one has ever doubted that you and Daidí love each other. When I'm about to be a grandfather, I want to sneak off to our room and lock the door and make love as if it were the first time, just the way you and Daidí did before Donovan's wedding."

Morgan blushed. "How would you know what happened before your brother's wedding?"

"You looked like two youths who had been caught red-handed. Momma, when you came up, nobody looked at the bride because you were so pretty. Oh, I guess Donovan looked at her, but you glowed. You were radiant."

"Cameron, what do you want?"

"Nothing."

"Then, what have you done?"

"Momma, does there have to be something wrong for me to tell you that I love you?"

"Yes. Now, confess."

"Well"—He rolled his lips together—"what would you say if I told you I was going to be a father?"

Morgan shrieked as Rennin walked into the house. "Cameron David O'Rourke!"

"Twas jesting, Momma! I swear! You should see your face."

"What's the humor?" asked Rennin.

"Never mind," said Cameron, snatching a pastry, darting upstairs, and laughing loudly.

"I shall turn you into a newt!" Morgan shouted up the stairs.

Cameron, always the prankster, sent a lizard down the stairs. Morgan squealed, "Get down here, Cameron!"

Rennin hooted as Morgan put the lizard out the door. "What has that scoundrel done?"

"First, he told me he was going to be a father. Then, he sent the lizard down just to taunt me."

Cameron scampered down the stairs. "Come on, Momma. I was only teasing you."

Rennin folded his arms across his chest. "Fatherhood is *not* a laughing matter, Cameron."

With his eyes still twinkling mischievously, Cameron kissed his mother. "Sorry, but I just could not help myself, especially knowing that Daidí is about to be called 'Gramps', or is it 'Grumps'?" Cameron chortled and started messing with Rennin's hair.

"What are you doing?" asked Rennin, annoyed.

"Looking for gray hairs."

"That's it! Out of my house! Go live in a cave somewhere!" Rennin pushed Cameron out the door.

After they let the drenched rat back inside, the family spent an afternoon of parlor games, cards, and puzzles. The rain came so hard that Cameron did not even attempt to visit Holly.

Four days later, the rain still poured with only brief intermissions. The river swelled and crept slowly over its banks. Rennin watched anxiously. Finally, he voiced his concerns. "Morgan, if the rain doesn't stop very soon, we're going to need to move further up the mountain. I fear we're in for a flood. If it's still raining in the morning, I will insist that you and the children go up the mountain to Luc Favre's cabin. I'm sure Geoffrey, Oliver, and Donovan will feel the same."

"Rennin, do you think we're in that much danger?"

"Yes, I do, honey. I've never experienced a flood, but my intuition tells me to run away."

"When will you come?"

"As soon as we men get our belongings to the second floor. That's the best we can do to protect them."

Morgan slid into his arms. "Rennin, I'm frightened."

He held his wife tightly. "Try not to worry. I shall do everything I can to protect you. Let's have supper and see what the morning brings."

As Rennin and his family sat down to eat, lighting flashed and a loud crackle, followed by a shattering boom, startled Rachel into her father's lap. "Daidí! Make it stop!" she cried.

"Shhh, sweetie. It's only thunder and lightning."

Cameron peered through the window, and amid the continuous flashes of lightning observed, "That bolt split the maple, Daidí. This is a wicked storm."

Rennin said, "Thank you, Cameron, for helping me to calm your sister." He furrowed his eyebrows, and his son turned to face him.

Cameron grinned. "Oops. Sorry. It'll pass soon, wee bits."

Almost as Cameron spoke, the rain stopped. The air grew perfectly still, yet the lightning continued to flash fiercely and incessantly. The O'Rourke family looked from one to the other. A deafening roar met their ears. None of them had ever heard anything like it.

The house began to shake, and hail as large as a wagon wheel's bearing pelted the ground. "Cameron, get over here," shouted Rennin as he shoved the younger children under the table and grabbed Morgan's hand.

Before Cameron could move, the windows in the room exploded, showering jagged shards of glass all over him. He dropped to the floor and lay perfectly still.

The rumbling lasted only a few minutes. Rennin scurried on his hands and knees to Cameron. "Cam?"

"Dare I move, Daidí?" came a response.

"Yes, I think it's over. That must have been what Luc calls a tornado."

"I hope I never experience another one," said Cameron, struggling to sit up.

Rennin carefully began picking glass from Cameron's hands and face.

The consummate smart aleck, Cameron quipped, "There go my rugged good looks."

"Nonsense!" retorted Morgan. "Most of these are tiny knicks. You've cut yourself worse shaving."

"Thanks, Momma," Cameron said as he tried to smile. "Ouch!"

Rennin turned to Morgan, "Is anyone else harmed?"

"Only frightened."

"Good. Will you take care of Cameron? I need to check on our neighbors."

Rennin was unprepared for what he beheld when he opened the door. "Oh, my God!"

"What is it?" asked Morgan when she heard the distress in Rennin's voice. When he did not answer, Morgan told Cameron not to move and went to the door.

Across Geoffrey's house, lay the oak tree that had held the tree house and the swing. The horses in the barn whinnied in terror, and it was apparent that some of the hailstones had gone straight through the thatched roof. Oliver's roof was gone, but the most distressing sight was that Donovan's house lay as rubble, the planed boards little more than toothpicks and no evidence of furniture. All that met their eyes was a pile of sticks. Without a further thought, both Rennin and Morgan dashed across the way. Being his usual stubborn self, Cameron followed them.

Cameron was the first to see Donovan staggering around the rubble. Oblivious to his cuts and the blood that dripped down his face, Cameron ran straight to his brother, whose arm dangled, limp and mangled by his side.

"Donovan!"

Dazed, Donovan said, "Help me, Cam. I can't find her. Help me find her."

"What do you mean, Donnie?"

"Emily Claire. I can't find her. I had her hand, and then, she was gone."

Cameron called loudly, "Momma! Daidí!"

Rennin and Morgan came running as the other members of the small settlement trickled from the relative safety of their homes. Donovan collapsed into Rennin's arms. "Daidí, please help me find Emily Claire. I cannot find her."

"Of course we'll find her," comforted Rennin despite his dread. "Morgan, Cameron, take Donovan to the house. Get him warm. He's in shock."

Rennin saw his old friend's face. Geoffrey was as terror-stricken as Donovan. "We'll find her, Geoffrey. I swear it."

Rennin found Holly. "Are you all right?"

She nodded. "Good," he said. "Go to Cameron. He needs you now."

Without hesitation, the girl obeyed. The rain pelted the devastated people again. Frantically, Rennin, Geoffrey, and Oliver searched the rubble. Each dreaded what he would find.

After hours of clawing through the debris, Geoffrey threw a piece of wood across the yard and screamed in agony. "She's not 'ere! Where could she be, Rennin?"

"I don't know, Geoffrey. Donovan was holding her hand. His arm could be mangled beyond use." Rennin looked toward the sky. "Oh, God. What if? No, that's too awful."

"What, Rennin?"

"Geoffrey, what if the winds pulled her from Donovan? You see the havoc that has been caused by the storm—an oak tree with roots sunk deeply into the earth was uprooted. Emily Claire is much smaller than that."

Months passed, and Emily Claire was not found. Donovan lived as one who was dead. His arm healed, but it never returned to full usage. He hardly ate and rarely spoke. Most days he spent alone. He refused to believe that Emily Claire was dead. "No. She'll come back to me. She *will*," he raged when anyone tried to tell him otherwise.

After some time, Cameron approached his brother. "Donnie, I don't want to hurt you, but I'm still alive and so are you. I plan to marry Holly in less than a year. Tomorrow I'm traveling back east because there are some things I want to buy. I'll be gone about three or four months. I wish you'd come with me; but if not, then I'm going to beat the hell out of you because I need my brother and best friend."

Quietly, Donovan said, "I'll ride along."

Cameron breathed out a nauseous sigh. "Donnie, you need to let Emily Claire go and mourn."

"No, Cam. I can't give up hope. She *will* come back to me."

Gently, Cameron laid his hand on his brother's shoulder. "Donnie."

"No!" snapped Donovan, jerking away from Cameron's grasp. Taking a deep breath to control his emotions, he argued his point. "Do you remember hearing how Grandma Caitlin refused to believe that Grandpa Aidan had drowned? She was right. Do you remember how Momma refused to believe that Daidí would never come back and how she fought to clear his name and find him? She was right. I refuse to believe that Emily Claire is dead. I will be right, just like them."

"Donovan, even Geoffrey, her own father, has given up."

"Cam, please support me in this." He held his hands out as if begging for alms. "Would you give up on Holly?"

"I'm not sure after so long. You might be right. I'll make a deal with you: If you will show some signs of normality, I'll back you. For Pete's sake! At least eat. You look awful. Is this what you want Emily Claire to see when she returns?"

A slight smile flickered across Donovan's face. "Thank you, Cameron. I'll try."

The next morning, Rennin's two eldest sons headed east. After a couple of weeks, they arrived in New Amsterdam where Cameron bought several pieces of fine furniture for Holly's wedding gift. Then, they shopped for silk and satin for Holly to make her a "white woman's" wedding dress.

While Cameron examined the expensive material, Donovan stared at the back of a blonde woman, obviously pregnant. She felt the soft pink and blue flannel.

Cameron bounded up with his purchases in hand. "Are you ready, Donovan?"

"Wait. Cam, look at that woman. Of whom does she remind you?"

Cameron looked at the expectant mother. "From the back, she looks like Emily Claire. I'm sorry, Donnie. Let's go."

"I want to speak to her, Cameron."

"Don't be ridiculous! Her husband will be offended."

The woman rubbed her back with her left hand. Donovan clutched Cameron's arm. "Cam! Look at her hand! I have to talk to her."

Cameron blinked in disbelief. "It can't be. Go, Donnie. Talk to her." He gave his brother a gentle push.

With fluttering heart, Donovan approached the woman. He softly tapped her shoulder. "Excuse me."

The woman turned with a sweet smile. Donovan almost fainted. "Emily Claire!"

The woman asked shyly, "Do you know me?"

An older woman came to Emily Claire's side. "Young man, may I help you?"

"My wife," stammered Donovan. "This is my wife." He held out his hand. "See. We have matching rings that my father made for us."

The younger woman looked at the older woman. "Emily Claire. E. C. Those are the initials on my shawl." Emily Claire looked at Donovan. "Tell me who I am. I don't know who I am. Mr. and Mrs. Bufkin found me unconscious months ago. I didn't know I was married at first, and then I realized that I was expecting. I hoped this unconventional ring was a wedding band, but I didn't know what had happened to my husband."

Donovan was near tears. "The tornado ripped you from my hand." He lifted his arm with difficulty. "Everybody told me you were dead, but I knew you would come back, somehow, someday. I looked everywhere for you. The baby." He stared at her protruding abdomen. "You had only told me about the baby a few days before. How did you get here?"

Cameron stepped in. "Let's all go sit somewhere before you pass out, Donovan."

They all started outside. "Wait," said Donovan. "Did you want this flannel?"

"I don't have the money," Emily Claire whispered.

"Yes, you do. Tell me what you want."

Emily Claire looked questioningly at Mrs. Bufkin. The older woman nodded.

"Are you sure, Donovan? Is that your name?"

"Yes, to both questions." Donovan bought everything Emily Claire said she liked. Then they went to a tavern as Mrs. Bufkin summoned her husband to join them.

Cameron insisted on buying a meal for everyone and took over the introductions. He explained the the family relationships and went on, looking his sister-in-law in the eye, "For weeks we looked for you. Donovan was injured, too, but he searched for you high and low, Emily Claire. Moreover, he never believed you were dead."

Mr. Bufkin spoke for his party. "My wife and I were traveling inland when we encountered the same storm. It had rained for days, and when the wind hit, we thought we were going to die. In the morning light, we saw the body of a young girl at the edge of the river. We thought she was dead, and we were surprised to hear her moaning. She had a gash on her head and several broken ribs." He patted Emily Claire's hand. "How she made it to shore is beyond me."

"She's a strong swimmer," said Donovan.

"Obviously, but she was badly hurt. Maggie and I knew she needed medical attention, and we had no idea what we would find in the wilderness. So, we turned around.

"We brought this little lady with us. There was a shawl wrapped around her arm. It had the initials 'E. C. M.' embroidered on it. We have called her E. C. She has no memory of her past."

Tears coursed silently down Donovan's cheeks. "None?"

At the sight of Donovan's big brown eyes filling with tears, Emily Claire's heart skipped a beat. She timidly laid her hand on his. "No, but I would like to remember. How long have we been married?"

"Eight months, but we have loved each other for a very long time. I realized I loved you when I was thirteen."

"I'm sorry, Donovan. I'm sorry I don't remember."

He kissed her hand. "You'll remember in time."

Cameron had to lighten the moment. "Hey! Maybe if we give Emily Claire another whack on the head, she'll remember. Knock some sense into her."

Four pairs of eyes stared at him, incredulously. After a tense moment, Emily Claire laughed. "I think you've always been a troublemaker. Am I correct?"

"Daidí calls me a rake. Momma calls me a scoundrel. I won't repeat what you called me on one occasion."

"He deserved it." Donovan laughed. "I'll tell you about it, but I don't think the Bufkins want to hear it. Suffice it to say that you questioned his parentage. Now, I'm changing the subject. You *are* my wife. I'd like you to come home with me. Your whole family is there. Your father thinks you're dead. Mr. and Mrs. Bufkin, you said you had started inland." He turned his gaze to the older couple. "You're welcome to come to our little community, too."

William and Maggie Bufkin agreed, but left the final decision to Emily Claire. She looked into Donovan's eyes and felt as if those eyes drew her like a magnet draws iron. She could not resist the pull. Furthermore, she wanted to be pulled. "Yes, I'll go with you." She realized that Donovan had never released her hand. "Donovan, will you walk me to Mr. and Mrs. Bufkin's wagon? Cameron, will you bring Mr. and Mrs. Bufkin there in a little while? I need to talk to Donovan alone."

"Now that sounds like the Emily Claire I know," quipped Cameron. "Go on. We'll come later."

Donovan gave Emily Claire his arm, and they walked to the Bufkins' wagon on the outskirts of town. Away from prying eyes, Emily Claire demanded, "Kiss me."

"What?"

"I want to see if I feel anything. Kiss me."

Donovan pulled Emily Claire into his arms and kissed her passionately.

When he released her, she breathlessly declared, "I don't care if I ever remember. I'll start from this moment forth. Kiss me again."

As two wagons approached, curious families and friends came out of businesses and homes. Rennin commented to Geoffrey, "What on Earth did Cameron buy that would require two wagons?"

"'E is a little extravagant. 'E probably 'as mahogany furniture for the 'ole 'ouse," joked Geoffrey.

"He has extra people with him, too."

Geoffrey shrugged. "Our little community could stand to grow."

The wagons pulled to a stop. With her head covered by a scarf, Emily Claire sat between Donovan and Cameron. As Donovan helped her down, she whispered, "Which one is my father?"

Donovan brushed stray hairs from her face. "The one with red hair. The tall blond is my father."

"Where is my mother?"

"The very pretty Indian lady is your stepmother. Your mother died a long time ago."

"Do we get along?"

"Splendidly."

Emily Claire grimaced as she stood. "What's wrong?" asked Donovan.

She looked at him with saucer-like eyes. "I'm afraid my homecoming celebration might have to wait if that was a contraction."

"Mayhap 'twas just a cramp. We'll know soon," Donovan replied, trying to remain calm.

Oliver came out of the trading post after completing his barter with a trapper, and the three elder men of the village approached the travelers. "Welcome home!" shouted Rennin. "What all have you brought us?"

"A great big surprise for Uncle Geoffrey," called Cameron. "Donovan, give the man his surprise already," he whispered to his brother.

"Are you ready?" Donovan asked Emily Claire. She nodded. He took her arm, and they walked toward Geoffrey who stopped in his tracks.

Dismayed, Geoffrey first whispered, "Emily Claire." Then, he whooped and shouted joyously, "Emily Claire!" Running to meet the daughter he thought to be dead, he smothered her in hugs. "What 'appened? Where 'ave you been?"

"Slow down, Uncle Geoffrey," said Donovan protectively. "There's a lot to explain."

"Donovan, it'll have to wait." Emily Claire gripped his arm tightly. "My water broke."

Hours later, Donovan cooled Emily Claire's face with a cloth and spoke soothing words to a wife that did not remember how much he loved her.

Emily Claire responded, "Oh, shut up! I want to scream. I'm going to scream."

Morgan comforted and encouraged her daughter-in-law. "It won't be much longer. You're almost there."

Emily Claire grunted, "Will it be long enough for me to kill Donovan?"

"Why?" asked Donovan.

"You did this to me. It's your fault, you selfish prig."

Donovan smiled. "I'm glad your're blaming me. That tells me that some part of you loves me even if you don't remember everything."

"I hate you! I do remember! I remember everything! I don't hate you! I love you! Donovan, I remember everything."

"Well," said Morgan calmly, "do you think you can remember in a few minutes? I need you to push out this baby."

With a scream of sheer determination, Emily Claire pushed a little pink-faced wailing girl into the world.

"You have a daughter," said the proud grandmother. "She's beautiful."

Donovan held his daughter for a moment before he handed the baby to Emily Claire. "What do you want to name her? We never had a chance to discuss that."

"Memorie."

"'Tis a bit unusual. Are you sure?"

"She gave me back my memory. Yes, I'm sure. You choose her middle name."

Donovan squeezed his mother's hand. "Celeste, for my mother."

"That's perfect," said Emily Claire. "Memorie Celeste O'Rourke, welcome to the world."

Running Bear closed the book. "I am beginning to get hoarse. I would like to rest a while."

"That's perfect timing," joked Rennin. "Puma Pass is just over this next hill. Patty will probably come out to meet us. Don't be afraid of her. She's just a big pussy cat now that Ike is gone."

Just as Rennin predicted, Patty sprang into the back of the wagon before they reached the top of the hill. The children squealed at first, but soon realized she was harmless as Rebekah petted her.

Running Bear sat up very straight as they approached the booming town. "Rennin O'Rourke, you have started an entire town. Soon you will have your own general store, and you will have no need of the bigots in San Francisco."

Rennin pulled the team to a halt. "That's a terrific idea, Running Bear. You'll run it. You can read, cipher, do figures. You're a shrewd trader. You're perfect for the position. We'll begin construction immediately."

The inhabitants of Puma Pass turned out to meet Running Bear and Sleeping Fawn. Thomas instantly examined Running Bear for fractures to his cheek, but he was only badly bruised. After everyone else had met the new family, Bart cautiously made his way to the man who had once truly wanted to kill him.

"Running Bear, I'm Bart Mercier. I'm da man who was wif Pierre Boudreaux when he kilt your brother. I ain't got no right to ask it, but I'm here to beg your forgiveness. I'm truly sorry. I hope you can put away your hatred for me, though I deserve it. Maybe someday we can be friends."

Running Bear folded his arms across his chest. "Well, Rennin, you said he would offer me his apology, but I expected pride and arrogance to go with it. This man does not have the heart of a murderer."

"I once did," said Bart, "afore I found my faith."

"Ah, yes, faith. I, too, have faith. Yes, Bart Mercier, I forgive you as I have been forgiven." Running Bear extended his hand. "Perhaps, we can be friends."

Bart smiled happily and said, "Tincture of arnica will help dem bruises. Come into da house. I have some left over from my brawlin' days. Come on in an' I'll fix you up."

Rennin could have exploded with joy over seeing his two best friends mend their differences. He probably would have followed them had the ground not begun to tremble beneath his feet.

The vibration progressed rapidly to violent shaking and upheaval. The inhabitants of Puma Pass poured from their homes. Porch posts cracked, causing roofs to cave in; windows shattered; and there was a loud explosion from the area of the mine. Then, as quickly as the rumbling began, it subsided, but they experienced several lesser jarring episodes later in the day and for a number of days afterward.

Rebekah and the babies came to Rennin's side. He looked around at everyone. "Well, I guess that was our first earthquake. It seems everyone here is all right."

As pre-arranged as a long-distance signal if trouble existed, Rennin fired one shot into the ground with his revolver. One shot resounded from the mine. Two would have heralded bad news. "Everyone is safe up there, too. It's getting late. Let's appraise the damage before dark."

19
Another Beginning

After the earthquake Rennin and Bart, along with Running
Bear, Chen Li, and the other employees went back to work in
the mine. Many shoring timbers needed to be replaced
because they had given way under the stress of the
earthquake. The after shocks frequently showered them with
dirt and nuggets.

The construction crew halted building long enough to
repair the existing structures. Sleeping Fawn was quite
pleased with her "white woman" house, and the children
quickly blended with the ones who were already there.

Once all the houses were repaired, construction began
again on the school. Rennin, Bart, and Running Bear
requested that another building be added to the list, a separate
structure to serve as the general store.

Every Sunday, work of all kinds halted. With the lack of a
church, the families gathered for a time of Scripture reading
and picnicking. The time was spent as a day of rest and
relaxation.

Keturah suggested to Rennin and Bart, "If Puma Pass
continues to grow, perhaps the Missionary Society will send a
minister. It would be very beneficial for the children." Rennin
and Bart loved the idea, so once again, Rennin drafted a letter
stating the need for a minister.

Many nights both Rennin and Running Bear read from the
first Rennin's book, especially stormy nights. One particularly
rainy night as Rennin opened the book to read, Rebekah
commented, "I hope this is not the kind of storm they had in
the book."

"Me, too," said Rennin, "but tonight *is* very eerie. You
probably need to cuddle really close while I read about how
Donovan and Emily Claire, along with the rest of the group
recovered from their harrowing experience. That will take
your mind off the storm."

"Fine," agreed Rebekah, snuggling against Rennin.

With Emily Claire back and a new baby to care for, Donovan rebuilt his house. Before the winds blew from the north, Donovan, Emily Claire, and Memorie moved into their new home.

A quarter of a mile up the river, William and Maggie Bufkin also moved into a new dwelling. They found the inhabitants of Mom's Trading Post so delightful that they immediately felt as if they were home. The Bufkins were a childless couple in their late fifties. They became like grandparents to the children who were great in number by the time the Bufkins arrived. Other than Donovan and Cameron, who were grown, Rennin and Morgan had twelve-year old Duncan, ten-year old Colin, and five-year old Rachel. Geoffrey, of course, had Emily Claire, fourteen-year-old Ian and ten-year-old Angela, whose mother, Nancy, had died. With his second wife, Anna, he had six-year-old Drake, two-year old Virginia, and one-month old Nettie. Anna had eleven-year-old Cynthia from her first marriage. Oliver and Eula had Oliver's little sister, Holly who was to marry Cameron in the spring and three of their own children, seven-year-old Chance, three-year-old Catherine, and one-year-old Christian.

William and Maggie became known as Grandpa and Grandma Bufkin. They loved all the children, but they doted on baby Memorie because they had grown to love Emily Claire as a daughter during the months she had been with them.

As the Ohio Valley recovered from the devastating tornado that had hit several areas harder than it had hit Mom's Trading Post, more colonists streamed into the valley, although the homes remained scattered. Most folks moving into the valley were trappers, traders, or farmers. Because of this, business at Mom's Trading Post boomed. Life became stable.

The biggest excitement after the tornado, Emily Claire's homecoming, and Memorie's birth was the upcoming wedding of Cameron and Holly. Morgan helped Holly design a wedding dress fit for a princess. The young girl glowed as she smoothed the satin folds that Morgan had sewn. "Momma Morgan, I have never seen anything so beautiful."

Morgan ran her fingers through Holly's straight, ebony hair. "Your hair feels just like the satin of your gown. You will take Cameron's breath away. When he sees you, maybe for the first time since he he began to talk, he will be rendered speechless."

Holly giggled. "Cameron does like to talk, but I'll tell you a secret. I know how to keep him quiet."

Morgan teased her future daughter-in-law. "Do you do the same thing I do to Rennin?"

"What do you do to Daidí Rennin?"

"I put my mouth on his and kiss him for a long time. Then, we usually end up in bed where he tells me how much he loves me and how wonderful I am. Since I enjoy hearing those things, I let him talk all he wants."

"Yes, I kiss Cameron, and I am sure he would like to end up in bed. However, he will have to wait a little longer for that."

As Morgan helped Holly out of her wedding dress, she assured the girl, "Don't worry about it. Lovemaking seems to come naturally, and for Rennin and me, it only gets better as time goes by. When you love as deeply and passionately as we do, you just do what feels right—you seem to know what to do. Honey, just love Cameron and go with the flow until you get comfortable. Then, you tell Cameron what you like and don't like. Talk to each other."

She continued her sage advice as she hung the wedding dress on a wooden hanger wrapped in cloth. "Honey, sometimes there may be things you won't like. Tell Cameron, but don't completely give up on things that might be uncomfortable or awkward at first. Some of the very awkward things can become quite pleasurable, especially if you discover it's something Cameron likes. Making him feel good will make you feel good and vice-versa.

"Holly, remember that you can always ask my advice—you don't have to take it, but I'll listen and tell you what I know. I'm sure Emily Claire will be glad to talk to you, too."

"She probably needs more advice than I do, Momma Morgan. I'm Iroquois, and our tribe's customs were a lot different from white man's. I just want to fit into Cameron's world."

"Has Emily Claire said something to you?"

"A little. Remember how long Donovan and she were separated. She feels as if she's starting over."

"Of course she does. Bring her over one afternoon, along with Eula and Anna. We will have a good 'girl talk.' If it makes you feel any better, I happen to know that Oliver talked to Rennin when he and Eula were first married; and I would bet Cameron talks to his father. Boys need advice, too. Even Geoffrey and Anna talked to us, if that gives you reassurance."

Wedding plans and girl talk continued throughout the winter until the first Sunday in March. The missionary that had married Donovan and Emily Claire had made his way once again to Mom's Trading Post as prearranged by Cameron over a year before. The date was set although Rennin argued that Cameron should wait until August when he would be eighteen.

The day dawned clear but cold. The ground lay covered in pristine white. Morgan quietly tried to slip from the bed, but Rennin caught her hand. "Where do you think you're going?"

"I have decorating and baking to do."

"First you have a tradition to keep with me unless you want to be late for the wedding later."

"Rennin!"

"Come here."

She rolled into his arms. "Rennin Drake O'Rourke, you're still as naughty as when you were sixteen."

"Do you want me to change?"

"No, I love you just the way you are. You know if we do this thing this morning, we might still be late for the wedding. We will need to change clothes later."

"'Tis true. Mayhap our tradition is to be late for the wedding, but I'll take my chances."

Rennin slipped into Cameron's room where the groom paced before his window, hoping to catch a glimpse of his bride-to-be. "Forget it," said Rennin. "She's getting dressed at Donovan's, so you can't see her if she walks outside. She spent the night with Emily Claire. Holly is really taking the superstition that you mustn't see your bride on your wedding day very seriously. Relax, son. Your mother has given Holly all sorts of advice. I think it highly likely you'll be pleasantly surprised tonight."

"Daidí!"

"Cam, you seem to forget that I was sixteen when I married your mother."

"Daidí, you and Momma still act like you're sixteen. Neither Oliver and Eula nor Uncle Geoffrey and Anna act as badly as you two."

"Cameron David O'Rourke, your mother and I enjoy each other immensely. Frankly, I hope that lasts until we're old and gray and our bones creak when we make love."

Cameron hooted in laughter. "To think that Momma calls me a scoundrel. I get it from you naturally."

"Yes, you're a lot like me—pigheaded and with a will of your own, but I love you. That's why I made these for you." Rennin handed Cameron two rings made from Aidan's watch chain.

Cameron's eyes teared. "Daidí, if you keep this up, you won't have a watch chain."

"I'll still have the watch. Your grandfather would approve of the rings."

Cameron embraced his father. "Thank you, Daidí. Are you ready to give the groom away?"

"No, but I suppose I have no choice."

As the friends and family of the bride and groom waited in the candlelight in Morgan's living room, Oliver placed his baby sister's hand in Cameron's. The two Natives bore themselves regally as they walked down the aisle, and Holly was striking in the satin gown Morgan had made. They repeated tried and true vows, Holly with the most serious face anyone could remember seeing her have since the first day she left her tribe.

At the reception afterward, the joy was felt all around. William Bufkin played his fiddle in a lively fashion. As Rennin and Morgan danced, Morgan said, "This reminds me of the night after Uncle Aidan's and Ricardo's demons were exorcised. Do you remember how beautifully Ricardo played? Oh, I wish they could send messages to us. You said one day we would go back. You know our children will never leave this land. It's too wild and untamed. I think they'll actually be the ones to conquer this world, not us."

"You might be right, my love," said Rennin. "When they're grown and we're old, then we'll go home to spend our last days. Until then, let's live each one to its fullest. As soon as Cameron and Holly disappear, I'd like to disappear, too, with the most beautiful woman here."

"Rennin, you're incorrigible."

"Do you love me anyway?"

"You know I do."

"I have an idea."

"I'm afraid to ask," Morgan laughed.

"In June, we'll have been married twenty years. Do you remember the big gathering we gave our folks? Let's get married again and have a big reception like the one we were supposed to have and never did. Then, let's go back east, maybe to Boston, and have a real honeymoon."

"Are you serious?"

"Yes."

"Something like that is unheard of here, Rennin."

"I think I can convince this minister to do it."

"Can you remember the vows we spoke twenty years ago? Do you want to say them again?"

"I remember it as if it were yesterday. I want to repeat those words and then some. Will you marry me again, Morgan Celeste Fitzpatrick?"

"Does it mean that we can't sneak away as soon as the bride and groom disappear?"

"Not on your life!"

"In that case, yes, I'll marry you a thousand times."

It is hard to say which night was more magical—the one between the couple whose love had endured trial, trauma, and treachery or the one between the newlyweds who were only discovering what enduring love means. Rennin and Morgan disappeared, but no one was surprised. Inside their room behind a locked door, they made love as if it were the first time—with fire and passion and longing. They were one spirit with only the desire to be together.

Cameron and Holly disappeared into their new world as husband and wife. Before the door closed completely behind them, Cameron slipped Holly's dress from her shoulders. "I've waited for you since the day you walked into the yard of my house when you left your tribe. Amidst all the tragedy, you stood out like a brilliant ray of hope—my Holly Berry, so tempting and yet so dangerous. Are you going to be dangerous for me now?"

Holly wrapped her arms around Cameron's neck. "There is only one way to find out. Take me upstairs, Cameron. Play with the fire and see if I burn you. Make love to me."

Cameron scooped the hot-blooded Indian maiden into his arms and carried her to their bed, which had been sprinkled with dried rose petals by an understanding mother-in-law. The fragrance intensified the moment, and the honey they found in each other's lips sweetened both lives. Neither thought anything could be more wonderful as they physically became husband and wife.

Rennin dropped the book as a resounding thunderclap startled Rebekah closer to him. He teased, "You didn't have to knock the book out of my hand if all this talk about newlyweds gave you the same ideas it gave me."

"Rennin, don't tease. That really scared me."

"I don't believe you. You're braver than that. The thunder is a convenient excuse to get close to me."

"If you insist." Rebekah grinned.

Rennin blew out the lantern.

Part Three

Glory Days

20
A Time to Celebrate

As the MacMillans put the last coat of paint on the school, Rennin received a letter from the Missionary Society stating that Reverend Henry Lamar, a recent seminary graduate, his wife Evelyn, and their young daughter, Shasta, would be arriving in approximately two months to plant a church in Puma Pass. The MacMillans agreed to stay on and build another house and a church.

In addition to this news, Bart joined Rennin and Running Bear whistling gaily as they met to decide what supplies to order first for the general store. "Something has made you extremely jolly this morning," said Rennin. "Would you care to share it with us?"

Bart grinned. "I'm about to be a father again."

"That's not new. How many are you and Keturah planning to have in three years?"

"I mean today. Keturah started labor. I ain't staying here wif you two long today. I jest come to tell you to choose wisely. Now, I'm goin' home to see my baby bein' born. Rennin, when are you an' Rebekah gonna haf another?"

"It's not like we're not trying, Bart. God will give us another baby when He's ready."

"Well, when this un gits here, I'll be shoutin' out da door."

"We'll be listening for the announcement."

Rennin and Running Bear roared with laughter as Bart left. "Rennin, do all white men get so excited about the birth of a child?"

"No, but I think it's terrific. Running Bear, three years ago, Bart Mercier was worse than blight on mankind. Now, he's a wonderful man and a great friend."

"Yes. I like him, too. I think what you two are planning for the orphan children is admirable. I am proud to call you friends."

About six hours later while Rennin talked with the MacMillans about the preacher's house and the church building, he heard Bart whoop joyously from the porch. "It's a boy! Christopher Aidan Mercier!"

Rennin jogged to his friend's home. "Congratulations, Bart. Why Aidan?"

"Christopher is my middle name, an' you are my best friend. I hope you don't mind. You know you hafta be my son's godfather again."

"I'm honored, and I gladly accept again."

Thomas Goodman joined the two men on the porch. "Bart, let's talk a minute."

"Is sumpin' wrong with Keturah or Chris?"

"No, not now. They're both sleeping, but we need to talk."

"You can talk in front of Rennin. We ain't got no secrets."

"All right. Keturah is forty-three. This is her third child in three years. She lost a lot of blood with this delivery. I need to know a little about her medical history. It might be wise for her not to have any more children, at least not right away."

"What do you need to know?"

"Has she had a history of miscarriage?"

Bart glanced at Rennin, and Thomas caught the look that passed between them. "Bart, whatever you tell me will stay with me. It's part of the oath I took to become a doctor."

"Keturah wudn't always da upstandin' woman she is today. When she was young, she was a prostitute. She did away wif three babies. Den, she married Jedediah Franklin. She changed an' became da woman you know. She lost four more babies afore she had Jed. How bad is it?"

"I knew from the looks of things that there must have been previous loss. Her uterus is greatly stressed. At her age, she really must consider not having any more babies. Did she hemorrhage badly with Jed and Stephen?"

"She bled a lot with Stephen. I don't really know about Jed. Rebekah could tell ya."

Rennin spoke up. "I think she must have, Tom. Rebekah had a great deal of soiled linens to wash. I didn't think much about it at the time because both Keturah and Jed seemed fine."

"She's very strong, Bart. So, my concerns might just be my overprotective nature. Nonetheless, if you have another baby, I insist on delivering it, and that will be the last. I'll see to that. You're five years younger than Keturah. You must realize she's getting too old to have babies. If she were two years older, I'd insist on no more now; but I do understand her desire to be a mother and yours to be a father."

"Thanks for your candor, Tom. I'll talk to Keturah. We'll do all we can to be extry careful, but God might have other plans."

Tom smiled. "I can help Keturah understand her cycle so that you only have relations during her more infertile time. I don't expect you to abstain from making love to your wife. Lord knows, I couldn't do it either. As a matter of fact, Candy is expecting. She's forty. This will probably be our last.

"This little town is having its share of babies. Jeannie, Cathy's baby is only eleven months old and she's due any day now with another. Keturah just had one, and Candy is pregnant. Rennin, are you sure you and Rebekah are drinking the same water as your friends and sisters? Or, did she hit you with that cast iron skillet as Cathy predicted and kick you out of bed?" Thomas grinned at his brother-in-law and started home, but turned back. "By the way, Bart, women don't usually get pregnant while they're nursing."

"Keturah did—twice."

"I see. Come to think of it, so did Cathy. Well, I think you know what to do to help."

Bart nodded. Thomas waved as he crossed the bridge. Rennin put his arm around Bart's shoulders and Bart ran his fingers through his slightly thinning hair. "Well, Rennin, I'm still joyous over my second son, even if he's da last."

Rennin went home to share the news about Christopher Aidan Mercier and Candace. Cathy gave birth four days later to Wilhelm Randolph Ishi. Rennin seemed depressed. Rebekah slipped her arms around her husband's shoulders as he sat at the table and stared at his coffee.

"What's wrong?"

Rennin patted her hand. "Why do you think we aren't expecting a baby? The boys are almost two."

"I don't know. Would you like to sneak upstairs and try to make one while our two little nuggets are asleep?" She took his hand. "Come on. Even if we don't succeed in adding another little O'Rourke to the world, you'll feel better and be happier."

Rennin followed Rebekah like a little lost puppy. She ran her fingers through his hair as she backed toward the bed. "I love you, Rennin. If we never have another child, I'll always love you."

"Oh, Rebekah, I'm a silly man. I love you, lady."

"Say the words to me."

"Heart of my heart, life of my life, you are my reason for breathing; and I will love you until the day I die."

The new preacher arrived rather quietly. A messege came during breakfast for Rennin. It stated simply and honestly:

Dear Mr. O'Rourke,

My family and I arrived safely in San Francisco; however, the next morning when we were ready to continue our journey to Puma Pass, we discovered that our wagon had been stolen. All our belongings except for a few clothes and a small amount of cash were taken. I hate to say, we do not have enough money to purchase another wagon, or anything for that matter. We are staying in a room at the Half-Moon Boarding House.

Still, we are anxious to begin our work in Puma Pass. If you would be so gracious as to send someone to get us, your kindness would be greatly appreciated. I am looking forward to meeting you and starting a great work with you.

Sincerely,
Henry Lamar

Rennin grunted, as he grew more cynical with each passing day, yet his kindness was unshakeable. "Rebekah, can you believe this? This place *needs* a minister and the Word. Honey, do you want to ride into the city with me to gather our new minister?"

"Of course, I'll go. Mrs. Lamar might enjoy some feminine companionship. When do we leave?"

"As soon as we can pack a wagon for about a week's journey. It'll take at least two days in and two days back."

"Okay. You pack the supplies we'll need while I pack the food and take the boys to Aunt Candy. We should be ready in about an hour."

Rennin and Rebekah camped under the stars. She shivered in the cool night air. Standing behind her, Rennin wrapped his arms around her and kissed her neck. "It's been a long time since we were alone under the stars with no one anywhere around."

Rebekah reached her hand behind her head a pulled Rennin's face around to hers. "Yes, it has," she said as she brushed her lips against his.

He groaned, "Unless you plan on following through with what that kiss suggests, don't do it again."

She kissed him again. "Oh, I definitely plan on following through."

"I was hoping you would say that," he said as he turned her to face him. "I do love you, Mrs. O'Rourke."

"I'll never tire of hearing you say that. I love you, too, Mr. O'Rourke."

Rennin and Rebekah arrived at the Half-Moon Boarding House in the middle of the afternoon. As they entered the shabby parlor, a young pretty blonde woman chased a little dark curly-haired girl across the room. The child giggled and squealed as the woman scooped her up. "It's nap time whether you like it or not, little priss!"

Rebekah put her arm through Rennin's. "Remind you of something?"

He nodded. "Our two little scamps at home."

Rennin approached the reception counter. "Hello. I'm Rennin O'Rourke. I'm looking for Reverend and Mrs. Lamar."

The woman behind the counter yelled in a grating high-pitched voice, "Mrs. Lamar!"

The pretty blonde turned. "Yes?"

"This gentleman's lookin' for you and your husband."

Rebekah saw Rennin's eyes wander to the lady on the stairs, and she deliberately stepped on his foot.

"Rebekah!" Rennin said through clenched teeth.

Under her breath through a plastered-on smile, Rebekah whispered, "A preacher's wife can be beautiful. Just don't look at her with such wide eyes."

The lady came back down the stairs, carrying her daughter who fidgeted in her arms. "How may I help you? I'm Evelyn Lamar."

Rennin introduced himself. "Mrs. Lamar, I'm Rennin O'Rourke, and this is my wife, Rebekah. We've come to take you to Puma Pass."

Evelyn began to bubble. "Oh! I'm so glad you've come, but I'm surprised you came yourself. I expected you to send someone. And you're so young! I thought I'd be here with several older women and nobody to talk to, but, Rebekah, you're younger than I am!"

"I'm twenty," said Rebekah.

"I'm twenty-two. Henry will be so happy that he won't have to live up to the expectations of a lot of stuffy old men. Oh, that was indiscreet. Henry tells me that I must watch my tongue. He tells me my mouth gets ahead of my brain. Please, come upstairs to our room. Henry's studying, and I must get Shasta to take a nap or she'll be so cantankerous you can't stand her."

Rennin and Rebekah followed Evelyn up the stairs. Rennin slipped his arm around his wife's waist. He whispered, "She's pretty, but I couldn't stand the chatterbox. You have nothing to fear, my beautiful Rebekah with the eyes of a dove."

Evelyn burst through the door. "Henry, Mr. and Mrs. O'Rourke have come!"

Henry Lamar rose with his back to the group. He was as tall and as muscular as Rennin. His coal black hair was closely cropped. Slowly he removed his spectacles and laid them beside his Bible. He reached beside his chair and picked up a cane. Turning toward the group, he greeted them with a genuine smile encased in a clean-shaven baby face and highlighted by deep brown eyes. "Hello, Mr. and Mrs...Oh my! I'd expected someone much older."

Rennin extended his hand. "Reverend, I'm Rennin O'Rourke. This is my wife, Rebekah. Welcome."

Henry Lamar had a firm grip. "Mr. O'Rourke, please call me Henry, and my wife is Evelyn. At least in private, I'd like to be informal. Perhaps in the congregation I'll have to be Reverend Lamar. I really hate being so formal."

Rennin laughed. "Henry and Evelyn, welcome. We're Rennin and Rebekah. I think you'll find Puma Pass easygoing. If you want to be Henry and Evelyn, that's what we'll call you. Honestly, I expected someone single who is a recent graduate, seminary rules and all. I'd venture to say you're younger than I am. Are you as much a rule-bender as I am?"

"I'm twenty-three. I know I look very young. I suppose in twenty years, I'll be glad to keep my youthful appearance. I take I Timothy 4:12 very seriously. *"Let no man despise thy youth; but be thou an example of the believers in word, in conversation, in charity, in spirit, in faith, in purity."*

Rennin nodded. "Let that be your first sermon."

"Do you think?" Henry asked seriously.

"Absolutely. Now, about getting you to your pulpit. Rebekah and I are getting a room at the Green Gable Hotel tonight. We can leave in the morning. Why don't you join us at six for dinner, my treat? I'll buy you a beefsteak."

"Rennin, that really isn't necessary,"

"Get use to it, Henry. You'll have constant dinner invitations."

"Very well. Thank you. We'll meet you at six in the hotel dining room."

"I look forward to it."

Rennin and Rebekah walked arm in arm down the street to the hotel and talked as they went. "Rebekah, Henry looks like a baby. He probably only has to shave once a week, and he's a cripple. I wonder what happened to him. He has a lot to overcome."

"Rennin Aidan O'Rourke! Don't you dare judge that man by his appearance! Give him a chance."

"I will. And I'll help all I can."

"He doesn't need your help, Rennin. He needs your support. He has God's help."

"You sure have a way of putting me in my place. But you're right, as usual. He'll have my support."

"That's the Rennin I love. You know, I've never stayed in a hotel. This is a real adventure for me."

"I promise to give you something to remember. We've three hours until supper. I know just how to pass the time."

"Rennin, you're rotten!"

As he opened the door to their room, Rennin said, "Think of it as the honeymoon we never had. He lifted Rebekah into his arms and carried her over the threshold. He closed the door with his foot. "After Christmas, but before we open the school, I'm going to take you to New Orleans for a real honeymoon."

"Whatever you say, but right now, we have three hours to kill."

At dinner the men discussed the church building that would be complete by Christmas while the women talked about their children. "I have two boys that'll be two on Christmas Day, Gabriel and Michael," said Rebekah.

"Shasta will be two in February. Are your boys angels like their names indicate?"

"More like little dickenses sometimes." Rebekah laughed. "Oh, I've another baby both of you should know about. Actually, she's Rennin's baby. Her name's Patty." Henry and Evelyn waited for the hammer to fall, as they looked from Rebekah to Rennin.

"Rebekah! Don't tease me," said Rennin. "We have an unusual pet. Patty is a puma. She's as tame as any house cat, but as protective as a guard dog. She saved both our lives once from the last preacher we knew. Please, Henry, tell me you don't have murder lurking in your heart."

"The preacher?" said Henry, stunned. "You must tell me about it."

"Tomorrow on the trip. Right now I'm going to be audacious, as my wife tells me I am, and ask you what happened to your leg. Did it play any role in your deciding to go into the ministry?"

"I'll answer the last part first. Yes and no. I had felt the call to be a pastor for a number of years. My father laughed at me. He said, 'A big strappin' boy like you ought to do a real man's work. You'll have to take over the farm for me one day.'" Henry changed his voice to a growling sound to quote his father.

"I never really cared for farming. I liked books and people. Well, six years ago I was helping my father change a wagon wheel when the dam...darn thing slipped and landed on my leg. The bone popped clear through the skin. The doctor tried everything to save my leg, but gangrene set in and he had to take it off just below the knee. Now, I have a wooden leg." He tapped his leg with his cane. "Wooden legs don't go too well with farming. So, my brother-in-law took up farming with Pa, and I saved every penny I could scrounge and went to seminary.

"Professor Thompson, who taught Greek and Hebrew, took me home to dinner one night at the beginning of my last year, and never could get rid of me. I stole his daughter and married her three months later." He grinned toward Rennin. "You asked if I was a rule-bender earlier. I guess I am. But Evelyn's father helped us keep our marriage a secret. We had a baby. I finished my studies, and here we are after waiting quite some time for a call."

Rennin warmed quickly to the good-natured man. "I, for one, am glad you're here. I look forward to getting to know you. It appears that Rebekah and Evelyn have hit it off, and Shasta will have a number of playmates, although most of them are boys. My sister, Cathy, has a one-year old daughter, and my other sister, Candace, is expecting. Maybe it'll be a girl. Maybe Rebekah and I will have another baby soon. I'm going to take her on a real honeymoon after Christmas. We never had one. I want to show her some civilization."

"You sound a little sad, Rennin. Tell me your and Rebekah's story."

"It's a little complicated, and Rebekah might not want all of it told. I'm the youngest of seven children." He related most of the events of the last three years to much jaw dropping and eyes widening by Henry.

Rennin finished, "Black Cloud's brother, Running Bear, is also in Puma Pass. We have a Chinese boy living with us. Henry, your congregation truly is a mission field. In Puma Pass, the color of skin doesn't matter. I hope you can minister to a multiracial congregation. The only race we seem to be missing is a Negro. I'm an open abolitionist. There will be only free Negroes in Puma Pass. Is this more than you can handle?"

"No, Rennin. This is what I've dreamed of; yea, longed for. Look at me, Rennin. I'm a quarter Cherokee. I'm sure the reason the Missionary Society sent me, other than the fact that I bend rules, is either for me to fall on my face in failure or because I'd fit into your society better than a full-blooded white man. I prefer to believe the latter because with the help of God and men like you, I will *not* fail."

The inhabitants of Puma Pass welcomed Henry, Evelyn, and Shasta warmly although Olaf did comment, "You look as if you should be one of my students rather than their spiritual leader." Henry flashed his winsome smile and quoted his favorite passage in German and won Olaf immediately. Olaf never told Henry was Swedish, not German.

The church was indeed ready for the first service to be held on Christmas Day. As had become a tradition, Rennin's friends and family gathered at his house on Christmas Eve. He read the Christmas story and he and Keturah sang "O, Holy

Night." With the arrival of Candace and Catherine, the time expanded into a time of caroling after the first song by Rennin and Keturah.

The Christmas service was held at ten o'clock in order for the families to have time together in the morning. The new young minister once again read the Christmas story, but spoke about each person's need to, like the shepherds, come to the Christ Child.

Later, at Christmas dinner, Rennin told Rebekah how impressed he was with what Henry had said. Then, he said while Gabriel and Michael were napping, "I didn't give you all your gifts this morning. I have another surprise for you." Rennin produced two tickets for a steamer ship from San Francisco to New Orleans via Panama. "We leave January 5th. I'm going to give you the honeymoon you deserve."

"Rennin, we'll be gone for months. What about the boys?"

"With Candy, Cathy, and Keturah around, they'll be fine. We'll be back in time for the school's opening. Now, we have only a couple of hours before a birthday party. What would you like to do?"

"Let's read about Rennin and Morgan's plans to exchange their vows again. Weren't they supposed to take a *real* honeymoon, too? Is that what gave you the idea?"

Rennin shrugged. "Maybe. Grab the book so you can see what a great time they had after a few kinks. Maybe that'll make you anticipate our special time."

As the day of her twentieth wedding anniversary approached, Morgan unfolded her wedding dress from the cedar chest. Perched on her bed, Rachel, Emily Claire, Holly, Angela, and Cynthia watched as Morgan caressed the folds of cotton. They all breathed the deep fragrance of cedar. Morgan closed her eyes and was twenty years younger, walking on Colin's arm toward Rennin. Tears seeped from beneath her lashes as she remembered how much she loved those she had left behind.

Rachel touched her mother's hand. "Mommy, are you all right?"

Morgan wiped her eyes. "Yes, baby. I was just remembering and missing all the people Daidí and I left on Draconis." Morgan hugged the little girl close. "Girls, I need some time alone. I'm taking a walk. Don't worry about me. I'll be back in a bit."

Morgan wandered deep into the woods—farther than she had ever gone alone. She came to a clearing shrouded in shadows. Decaying leaves blanketed the ground, and golden-capped mushrooms grew densely in the dankness. No matter which direction Morgan walked, she brushed against the fungi and juice seeped into her skin. The mustiness filled Morgan's senses with cruel, evil memories. She thought aloud, "This is *not* where I meant to come. I've wandered too far from home."

Morgan shivered and turned to go back to a sunnier spot, but brambles blocked the way. Deep dread filled her as she realized she was lost. An intangible voice on the wind taunted her. "Morgan, it has been such a long time since we talked. It feels good to touch a familiar spirit."

Morgan gasped, "Who are you? Where are you?"

The haunting voice continued its sultry whisper. "Come, now. Surely you remember me. I'm right here with you as I have been all along. You simply would not acknowledge my presence."

Morgan replied. "I don't know you. I don't want to know you."

The voice laughed, deep and throaty. "Morgan, admit that you have missed me and all the power I can give you. You tasted it recently, and you liked it."

Morgan covered her ears with her hands. "Leave me alone. I've lost my way. I want to go home to Rennin and my children."

"Yes," hissed the voice. "Thank you for my girl. I've waited a long time for her. I should have known that Aidan's spawn would try to keep her from me. Morgan, do you think God gave her back to you? No. It was I."

Morgan shouted in terror, "Quazel! No! It can't be you. You're dead, and your spirit was banished to Hell."

"Oh, please! Some spirits were banished never to return. I thought that meant they couldn't go back to Draconis. But, my dear, this is not Draconis, and I was *never* banished. This world is large. I've followed you, waiting patiently. Morgan, what is it about the O'Rourke men? Why won't they die? Oh, of course. Rennin is part cat. He has nine lives. Let's see how many I've made him use. One, Colin didn't kill him for *defiling* you. Two, Ammar didn't kill him for *betraying* you. Three, he didn't drown in the Atlantic Ocean with that little green-eyed brat of yours. By the way, that was one for Cameron. Four, he survived smallpox, and that was two for Cameron. Five, Chinowaya failed miserably. Six for Rennin and three for Cameron—neither of them drowned or froze in the pond. Seven and four, the tornado didn't kill either of them, although Cameron took a good hit. That makes seven for Rennin. He only has two left. Cameron is catching up fast with four gone."

Through tears and screams, Morgan tried to find her way clear of the area. She cut her hands on the thorns and dripped blood onto the dead ground.

The voiced bounced from one direction to another. "Morgan. Morgan. Morgan. You can't escape me. Morgan. Morgan. Morgan. Oh, look. You've cut yourself. What a shame. It matters not to me. I don't want you. I want *Rachel*."

Morgan tore at the briars, gashing her flesh and ripping her clothing. The branches grew thicker and entangled her, choking the life from her. Her strangled voice cried, "Oh, God, not Rachel. God help me! Rachel! Cameron! Rennin! Rennin!"

"Morgan. Morgan. Morgan." Morgan awoke to Rennin's bathing her cuts with cool water and gently speaking her name and Talulah forcing her to breathe vapors from a cup.

Morgan flailed and punched toward the voice calling her name, albeit Rennin's voice. She tried to spring from the bed, but Rennin restrained her. She screamed in utter panic, "Rennin! Cameron! Rachel! Rachel!"

Rachel opened the door. "Mommy, I'm right here. What do you want?"

Morgan held her daughter and wept. "Rennin, what are we going to do? Quazel is here. She's back and after Rachel, and she's trying to kill you and Cameron because he has green eyes. He's the only one who got green eyes."

Rennin stroked Morgan's hair. "No, she's not, honey. You were hallucinating. You wandered into a part of the forest where mushrooms with tremendous powers grow. Talulah's people use them in many of their rituals. Breathe the vapors he has brewed for you. They counteract the effects of the mushrooms. Let Rachel go. You're crushing her."

Morgan released Rachel who planted a kiss on her mother's cheek. "It's all right, Daidí. I'll sit by Mommy until she feels better."

"'Tis a splendid idea," said Rennin as he tweaked his daughter's nose. Rachel giggled, but stopped when Rennin spoke very seriously. "You listen. Neither you nor your mommy, nor any of you, are to go into that part of the forest again. Do you understand?"

"Yes, sir."

Morgan breathed deeply of the fumes Talulah held. "Rennin, you didn't lie to me, did you? You didn't perform blood magic to revive Rachel, did you?"

"No, sweetheart. It was just as I told you. I began the ritual, but she cried before I could finish. If you need proof, ask Eula or Anna."

"I believe you. The odor in the woods smelled like Quazel's cave. Then, the voice I thought I heard, Quazel's voice, made me believe I had done some form of black magic. I just needed to be reassured. Oh, Rennin, I was terrified."

"Well, 'tis over now, and you must recuperate quickly. You only have four days before we get married all over again."

"Rennin, I went out to send a message to Daidí. I was missing everyone terribly. Somehow I got turned around because I wasn't paying attention. I meant to go to the clearing near the pond where you took your winter dip." Morgan grinned. "Will you take me there in the morning?"

"Yes, but, now, you rest. I love you, and all of us are safe. Quazel is *dead*. The demons were exorcised. They cannot hurt us anymore." Rennin softly kissed Morgan.

The shaman patted Morgan's hand. "So sorry you had bad experience. Stay away from golden mushrooms. Sleep. Tomorrow you feel better. Call if you need medicine man." He left, as did Rachel after giving Morgan another kiss.

Morgan held onto Rennin's hand as he started to leave. "Stay with me until I fall asleep. I'm still a little shaky."

He sat beside her. "What exactly is making you so shaky?"

"I need to tell you what the voice said. Please don't dismiss it as the effects of the mushrooms. Remember Uncle Aidan and Ricardo. Think about how I behaved when Rachel was born. Rennin, we've been through too much to ignore what I experienced today."

"Very well, darling. Tell me everything that happened."

Morgan trembled and cried and poured her story out to Rennin. He held her and whispered, "We won't ignore what happened. We'll keep our eyes wide open, just in case it was real." Then she related what she had heard during the battle with smallpox. Rennin was forced to tell her about his nightmares after his time of slavery. Both grew quiet.

After a time of silence, Morgan asked, "How did you know where to find me?"

"Rachel followed you. When she saw you fighting the air and the briar patch, she was frightened. She must have inherited my sense of direction. She came back and took me directly to you. She never panicked although she was terribly afraid. In that way she's like you, at least when you don't breathe mushroom mold or absorb mushroom juice through your skin."

"She's amazing," said Morgan groggily. Rennin laid her on her pillow.

The next morning, Rennin threw up the sash, and sunlight flooded the room. "Rise and shine, my sleeping beauty. The day is wasting, and I've a very special time planned for us."

Morgan stretched and slowly opened her eyes. "What time is it?"

"Mid-morning."

She sat up abruptly. "Rennin, why did you let me sleep so late?"

"After your ordeal yesterday, you needed the rest. Now, however, it's time to get up and get dressed, or you'll miss our picnic."

Morgan snuggled back under the covers. "If you want me, come and get me."

"Morgan Fitzpatrick O'Rourke, now is *not* the time."

Dismayed, she sat up straight. "Rennin Drake O'Rourke, I don't believe you said that. You're an imposter. My Rennin would never miss an opportunity to make love."

He stood still. "You're correct. I suppose we have a few minutes. Duncan is saddling my horse. It'll take him a little while." Rennin locked the door, and with a running leap, he jumped into the bed.

Morgan squealed, "You're going to break the bed, silly goose."

"Not doing that. Maybe doing this." Rennin pinned Morgan to the bed and kissed her ravenously. "Is this more like your Rennin? Grrr!" He growled and nibbled her neck.

"Not exactly!" she said, laughing out loud.

Before they could get any further, Duncan knocked on the door. "Daidí, the horse is ready. I put the basket on."

Rennin and Morgan laughed and Rennin called, "Many thanks. We're coming." Then, he pulled Morgan from the bed and playfully slapped her rump. "Get dressed and get down stairs."

Morgan came out the door wearing her yellow linen dress with the honeysuckle-print shawl. She left her hair long and flowing, the way Rennin liked it. He sat astride his steed and pulled her up in front of him. He whispered in her ear, "You're beautiful."

He turned his horse toward the clearing by the pond. Once there, he helped Morgan down and spread a blanket on the ground. He held his hand out to her. "Come on. Send your message to Uncle Colin."

Rennin lay on the blanket and watched her. This quiet, unintrusive feat of magic never ceased to amaze him. After nearly an hour, a bright-eyed scarlet male cardinal landed on Morgan's finger. She laughed. "I might've known Daidí's messenger would have the same color plumage as his."

Rennin whispered so as not to break the spell, "Morgan, ask Uncle Colin to get Aunt Lizzie or Ricardo to send us a message, if anyone there has this special ability."

A while later, the brilliantly colored bird fluttered away, carrying years of news and infinite love. Rennin unpacked his picnic of chicken, boiled eggs, sliced apples, biscuits, chocolate cake, and Rennin's homemade muscadine wine.

After several glasses of wine, Morgan was giddy and Rennin was completely relaxed. He slowly slid his hand up her leg as he kissed her sensuously. She returned his advances eagerly, pulled him closer to her, and unfastened his shirt. Morgan whispered coyly, "Rennin O'Rourke, are you trying to take advantage of my intoxicated state?"

"Yes, ma'am," he whispered as he slipped her dress from her shoulders.

"Try harder."

Finally, as the shadows grew long, Morgan slipped into her clothes and repacked the picnic basket. With his shirt in his hand, Rennin caught her in his arms from behind. "What's your hurry?"

She giggled. "Rennin, everyone will wonder what happened to us."

Shaking his head, he said, "Not so. They know exactly what has become of us, and they all wish they had thought of it."

She popped him playfully on the arm. "Rennin, you're still a rogue, but you're my rogue, and I love you."

He put on his shirt and took Morgan's hand. "Come sit down for a few minutes. I want to talk to you."

"Rennin, you seem so serious. What's wrong?"

"Nothing. I simply need to talk to you."

She sat down, anxious to hear what he had to say. On both knees beside her, he held her hands. "Morgan, my prize beyond value, though I've said I love you for more than twenty years, I can never put into words what's in my heart. You truly are my reason for breathing. Without you, I would cease to be. You married me twenty years ago while we were still children and had no real understanding what a lifetime commitment meant. You've stood by me through foreshadowings of Heaven and glimpses of Hell. Now, you've agreed to reaffirm publicly your faith in me, though I fall far short of what you deserve. Because I want the world to know how much I love you, I want you to wear this." Rennin opened a small black box, which held a full karat flawless diamond in an oval setting.

Morgan gasped. The only jewelry she had ever worn was her chain wedding ring and her jade dragon necklace. "Yes, Rennin, I'll wear the ring, but I'll never remove this little chain ring, for although it's plain and simple, it symbolizes the binding of our hearts and lives."

Rennin smiled at how unspoiled Morgan's spirit remained. "It's one of the stones Ricardo gave us. I've saved it to give to you at some point because it's as perfect as you are. If you feel so strongly about the ring Daidí made, I'll not ask you to overshadow it with this. Wear it on your other hand. You know I'll never take off my chain ring either. I wore it all the time we were apart. It served as assurance I'd hold you in my arms again. I do like the matching rings."

He placed the diamond on her right hand and sealed the gift with a kiss. "I love you, Morgan. I always have, and I always will."

Just as Rennin read the last line, there was a knock at the door. "It appears our first guests to celebrate two birthdays have arrived. I suppose we need to rouse the honorees. You get the boys, and I'll get the door."

21
Commitment

On New Year's Day, Rennin planted the little pine he and Rebekah had used as a Christmas tree at the beginning of the walkway to the school, with plans to plant next year's tree on the other side. Into the bark he carved, "Puma Pass Academy for Children, est. 1853."

Gabriel and Michael went with Rennin to plant the tree. Gabriel passively watched, but Michael wanted to help. Rennin allowed him to stomp the dirt around the roots and pour water from a bucket to water the newly planted tree.

Thoughtfully, Gabriel observed, "Papa, dat side needs a twee."

Rennin slipped his penknife into his pocket. "We'll put next year's tree there."

As Gabriel nodded, Michael screamed. Rennin turned around to see blood gushing from the child's hand. The penknife that Rennin thought he had put in his pocket lay open on the ground.

Rennin shouted, "Michael, what have you done?"

Through terrified screams, Michael answered, "I hepped put words on da twee."

Rennin calmed down a bit and removed his shirt, wrapping Michael's hand with it. "Let's get you to Uncle Thomas so we can see how bad it is. Uncle Thomas might have to stitch you up. Michael, you're too little to carve the words. You can't even read the words yet. Never bother Papa's knife until you're a big boy."

Rennin and the twins entered the house as Rebekah set the table for lunch. Without looking up she said, "It sure took a long time to plant the tree. What have you three really been doing—playing and leaving me with all the work to do?"

Gabriel informed her, "Mikedal had to visit Unkdal Thomas."

"Why?" asked Rebekah as she turned to see Rennin carrying Michael and holding Gabriel's hand.

Gabriel continued his explanation. "Mikedal cut himself wid Papa's knife."

"What?" Rebekah took Michael from Rennin. "Rennin, what happened?"

"I thought I put my penknife in my pocket, but I missed the pocket. Michael thought he could carve some letters in the tree, but he did a much better job carving himself. He has twelve stitches in his hand, but he'll be fine."

Rebekah threw up her hands. "That's it, Rennin. I am *not* leaving the boys for a long time no matter how much you want a honeymoon."

"Are we going to have an argument?"

"No. I simply won't go."

Rennin plopped into his chair. For a few minutes he pouted. Then, he grinned. "We'll take the boys with us. I'll ask Sarah to go along as a nanny, and I'll pay her to watch the boys so we can still have some time together. What do you say?"

"Rennin, why is this so important to you?"

"I don't know. My heart just says to do it." He stood and put his arms around her. "Draco whispered to me."

She pushed back and realized he was serious. "When did Draco speak to you?"

"It was a dream, but it felt real."

She splayed her hands on his chest. "Only if we can take Gabriel and Michael. Sarah will probably love to have her own money."

While Rebekah served lunch, Rennin secretly pulled the three tickets he had been hiding from the mahogany chest on the fireplace mantle. He smiled to himself. *I knew you'd do this, Rebekah. I know you well.*

After lunch, Rennin visited his niece to ask if she had packed her trunk as they had discussed. "Yes, Aunt Rebekah refused to leave the boys, especially now that Michael cut himself."

Candace came to Rebekah's defense. "Rennin, they're only two. It's not as if they're big boys who would understand their mommy's being gone for a while."

"Oh, I know. I guess deep down inside I didn't want to leave them either. Why else would I have made alternate arrangements before hand?"

"Because you learned a lot from your sisters," said Candace as she patted his cheek.

Rennin nodded. *Because a dragon spoke to me.*

With the bags packed to leave on the third, Rebekah snuggled up to Rennin that night, thinking she had upset his plans. "Forgive me?"

"For what?"

"Not wanting to leave the boys."

"Yes, I forgive you. I have a confession to make. I bought Sarah's and the boys' tickets the same day I bought ours."

"Rennin! You scoundrel! You don't want to leave them either."

"I suppose not."

She flung her arms around his neck. "I love you."

"I love you, too. Do you want to read about Rennin and Morgan's second wedding and honeymoon? They *do* leave their children for a little while."

"Of course. It might give me ideas for ours."

"Get our book." Rennin popped Rebekah's behind as she went for the book.

She turned and shook a finger at her husband. "I'll get you later."

"Do you promise?"

"I promise."

Rennin opened the book.

The night before their wedding anniversary, Morgan made Rennin spend the night with Donovan. "I want this to be just like a real wedding," she said. "So you can't see the bride until the ceremony."

On the morning of of the ceremony, Morgan slipped into her wedding dress from twenty years earlier. It still fit perfectly. She brushed her hair until it shone. Then, she placed a crown of honeysuckle and baby's breath in her hair. She gathered a matching bouquet, adding streamers of English ivy.

Morgan had a real wedding, with her eldest son giving her away and her second son standing by his father. This time, Morgan had three little attendants, Angela and Cynthia as bridesmaids, with Rachel as maid of honor. The girls wore soft yellow dresses and carried a single lily.

Once again, Morgan's beauty took Rennin's breath. From having read in London and without conscious effort, he quoted Shakespearean verse as she came toward him and William Bufkin played softly upon the violin.

> *Shall I compare thee to a summer's day?*
> *Thou art more lovely and more temperate:*
> *Rough winds do shake the darling buds of May,*
> *And summer's lease hath all too short a date:*
> *Sometimes too hot the eye of heaven shines,*
> *And often is his gold complexion dimm'd*
> *And every fair from fair sometimes declines,*
> *By chance or nature's changing course untrimm'd;*
> *But thy eternal summer shall not fade,*
> *Nor lose possession of that fair thou owest,*
> *When in eternal lines to time thou growest;*
> > *So long as men can breathe or eyes can see,*
> > *So long lives this, and this gives life to thee.*

Donovan whispered to his mother, "He's a hopeless sap, isn't he, Momma?"

"He's *my* hopeless sap. Take lessons. You can learn a lot."

Donovan laid his mother's hand in his father's hand.

The minister looked at the couple that had personified true love in his eyes. "Rennin and Morgan, I have watched you for many years, and I have seen your love endure joy and sorrow, sickness and health, good times and bad times. You have lived the vows you made to each other day in and day out. Now, I'm privileged and honored to be a part of your reaffirmation of commitment to each other. This is a new experience for me. I have never performed a reaffirmation ceremony. In all honesty, I've never heard of this ritual. I'm pleased to have this opportunity.

"Rennin, is it your wish to vow once again to be husband, protector, and provider for this woman?"

"It is."

"Then, repeat after me. 'I, Rennin, take thee, Morgan, to be my wife, to have and to hold from this day forward, for better for worse, for richer for poorer, in sickness and in health, to love and to cherish, until we are separated by death.'"

Rennin repeated the words as strongly as the first time, but his voice lacked the fear he had felt as a sixteen-year-old boy.

"Rennin, it's my understanding you have some special words to speak."

Rennin cupped Morgan's face in his hands. "Morgan, you blew into my life like a summer breeze and have filled my heart from that day forward. As God is my witness, I will be your protector, your provider, your lover, and your friend all the days of my life. As I grew up, I heard my father speak these words to my mother every day of my life, and since I could have had no better example, I made them my pledge to you twenty years ago and today I pledge them anew. 'Heart of my heart, life of my life, you are my reason for breathing; and I will love you until the day I die.'

"There have been times when I have failed you, times when my own needs and desires temporarily clouded my thoughts of you. Know this: Even during those dark hours, your love shined through, and I have never and will never stop loving you."

The minister turned to Morgan. "Morgan, is it your wish to vow once again to be wife and mate for this man?"

"It is."

"Then repeat after me, as requested, the same vows you made twenty years ago. 'I, Morgan, take thee, Rennin, to be my husband, to have and to hold from this day forward, for better for worse, for richer for poorer, in sickness and in health, to love and to cherish, until we are separated by death.'"

Morgan repeated the words, but she was no longer a scared and lonely child afraid of losing the only love she had ever known.

"Morgan, please share your special thoughts with Rennin," the minister said when she had finished.

"Rennin, for years you were my only joy, my only happiness, my only hope. I owe you all that I am and ever hope to be. Today, I pledge myself to you. I will be your joy, your happiness, your hope every day of my life.

"Those are the words I spoke to you twenty years ago. You are still my greatest joy, my greatest happiness, and my greatest hope. I pledge to be your abiding joy, your constant happiness, and your steadfast hope for now and all eternity."

Rennin stroked Morgan's cheek with the back of two fingers. "You are my butterfly, full of enduring grace and beauty. You are my strength when I am weak—my nourishment when I am faint—my laughter when I am broken—my courage when I am afraid. I love you."

Morgan shook her head and in a strangled voice whispered, "I have no other words, only my heart and my life. They are yours until the end of time."

The minister rescued Morgan. "Neither of you needs more words. You put us all to shame as it is. Rennin and Morgan, all of us have been blessed to witness the reaffirmation of your commitment to each other. Each of us can glean from your example. Go now and shine the light of love into a world shrouded in darkness. Rennin, kiss the woman so we can celebrate."

Rennin kissed Morgan soundly, and the ensemble at Mom's Trading Post celebrated in earnest. William played lively music, and often handed his fiddle to young Ian who was learning to play so that he could dance with Maggie. All those present danced and ate and laughed gaily, for this was truly a celebration of love that had touched everyone.

Cameron danced with his mother. "Momma, I've something to tell you. I want you to be the first to know, and I'm not jesting this time. I'm going to be a father. Holly told me at breakfast."

"'Tis wonderful, Cam. Mayhap you'll have twins. I'm amazed that I never had a set of twins, seeing as how both your father and I have twin brothers."

Cameron laughed. "I'll leave that to Rachel. You'll be back in time to deliver my baby, won't you, Momma? I trust Eula and Anna, but I want you there."

"We're only going to be away three or four months. As I recall, babies take a little longer than that to get here."

Rennin tapped Cameron's shoulder. "Stop hogging my wife. Dance with your own."

Cameron laid his mother's hand in Rennin's but held onto them together a few minutes. "Daidí, I'm proud to announce the arrival of another grandchild in February. Are you feeling older again?"

Rennin smirked at Cameron. "Not today. Today, I'm sixteen again. I just wish we had Draco to fly us to Boston."

Morgan squeezed Rennin's hand. "We'll make the most of our time under the stars. I promise."

"Are you going to wait until morning to leave, Daidí?"

"With a promise like that hanging over my head? No! The wagon is packed and ready to go as soon as this little sprite changes clothes." Rennin popped Morgan's bottom. "Move it!"

An hour later after Morgan had hugged her children over and over and reminded the younger ones to obey Geoffrey a dozen times, Rennin and Morgan drove toward Boston. As they crossed the river and topped the hill, they could still hear the laughter and revelry.

Rennin closed the book and said, "Rebekah, we leave tomorrow. You had better pack for the boys." He held up the book. "This is the last thing I have to put in my trunk except my toiletries. I'm with the other Rennin. Get moving so we can leave right after breakfast."

22
A Real Honeymoon

As the steamer ship in the Collins line treaded its way through the ocean waves, Rebekah turned green. Rennin cooled her face with a cloth and administered the powder Thomas had sent. "Thomas said to take this if any of us became seasick."

"Oh, Rennin, how long will this last? I have never felt so sick."

"You'll get used to the sea soon."

"Why am I the only one? You and Sarah are fine. The boys are fine. Rennin, maybe I'm with child."

"You weren't two weeks ago."

"No, this is worse than morning sickness."

"Relax and let the medicine work. I'll read to you for a while."

Rennin kissed Rebekah's head and retrieved the book from his trunk.

The trip to Boston was uneventful. Rennin and Morgan enjoyed their nights under the stars and even the nights in the rain. The fact they were alone together was all that mattered.

They arrived in Boston late in the afternoon and went immediately to an inn. There they refreshed themselves with a bath and tea with toast and jam. After their brief respite, Rennin and Morgan walked to the wharf and inhaled the salty breeze.

Morgan sighed. "Oh, Rennin, I do miss our years of sailing."

"We can build a small boat and sail on the pond or down the river."

"'Tis not the same, though it might be fun."

"No, 'tisn't. Do you want to leave Mom's Trading Post and move near the sea?"

Morgan shook her head. "I finally have some roots there. However, I do want to rent a boat and go out tomorrow. Let's sail out and spend the night at sea."

"If that is what the lady wants, that is what she'll get. Actually, we'll sail to Cape Cod and spend a couple of days before we come back and buy something from every shop in town. How does that sound?"

"Exciting!"

The next day, they sailed to Cape Cod. They spent several days enjoying the hospitality of an inn. They slept in a luxurious, oversized, soft, down bed. They dined on fresh clam chowder, broiled codfish, and stuffed flounder. They frolicked in the sea and lazed on the sand.

Rejuvenated from their time at the cape, Rennin and Morgan returned to Boston. There they spent days shopping. They bought gifts for everybody back home—fine leather shoes for everyone and store-bought dresses for the women and girls, as well as material for more clothes. Morgan chose elegant cloisonné combs for every female in the settlement while Rennin purchased shaving mugs for all the males, including those who were too young to shave. These items they decided would serve as Christmas gifts. They also bought sets of fine china and silver. For herself, Morgan picked out a china tea set decorated with yellow honeysuckle blooms.

Last, they visited Martin's Furniture Shoppe to get Rachel a cedar chest. As they were leaving, Morgan stopped near the entrance to admire an item that stood seven feet high and had a round plate with number on it at the top. It chimed gloriously as she stroked the glossy finish. Morgan's eyes traveled to the golden pendulum that kept rhythm, if a bit imperfect. Inlaid in the pendulum was a magnificent dragon of mother of pearl. *Take me home* met her inner thoughts. Involuntarily, Morgan whispered, "Draco."

Rennin turned. "What did you say, honey?"

"Rennin, I want this item."

"Why?"

"Someone has put Draco on the pendulum."

Rennin looked at the pendulum. The likeness was uncanny.

Morgan turned pleading eyes toward Rennin. "Please, Rennin? I never ask for things. I truly want it."

Rennin went back to the shopkeeper. "Tell me about this piece. What is it? My wife would like to purchase it."

The proprietor moved his glasses to the end of his long, thin nose. "It's quite old. It's a clock, used to tell time. About a hundred fifty years ago my great-great-great-grandfather returned from some ill-fated voyage. The ship was practically splinters. Many of the crew were missing, and the others were deathly ill. My great-great-great-grandfather ranted and raved about some place where he had ridden on the back of a dragon. He insisted that the missing crew members, including his brother, Mason, had stayed on this island. His rantings were harmless, but his stories were quite entertaining. Since he made exquisite furniture, the people left him alone even if they thought him to be a bit crazy.

Just Like Diggory, went through Rennin's mind.

Martin continued to speak. "However, he took the dragon as his mark. The clock is one of his first pieces. He said he learned to make them on an island, I believe he called it Draconis. As far as I know it is one of a kind. It is quite expensive."

Under her breath, Morgan whispered, "Danielle."

To the shop owner, Rennin said, "Your great-great-great-grandfather was Jason Martin."

"How did you know?"

"I've heard of him. His work is magnificent. What price for the clock?"

"I cannot let it go for less than a thousand."

"I can give you eight hundred—gold."

"Eight hundred? Perhaps. Would the lady be interested in any other dragon pieces? I have several original works in the back. Most folks find them bizarre, but your wife seems to appreciate the clock."

Rennin looked over his shoulder. "Morgan, would you like to see any other dragon pieces?"

"Yes, but I want this clock even if it is not actually Draco."

The proprietor asked, "Who is Draco?" as he led Rennin and Morgan to the back.

Realizing this man would never understand, Morgan replied, "An old friend who had a particular fondness for dragons. The dragon reminded me of him." *That was his voice I heard, but only Rennin will believe it.*

In the back under sheets were a settee, which perfectly matched the clock, and a dressing table and chair etched in detail with a dragon in flight. Rennin traced the pattern with his hand. *Take me home*, echoed through his mind. He looked at Morgan who gave a single nod realizing her husband had heard the voice, too.

"Mr. Martin, we'll take all of them. I will give you twenty-five hundred gold right now. I can't dicker with you because that's my highest offer."

"I'll take it, Mister—"

"O'Rourke. Rennin O'Rourke."

The two men shook hands. The deal was done. "It has been a pleasure doing business with you, Mr. O'Rourke."

Rennin and Morgan's wagon was crammed full as they started toward Mom's Trading Post. Morgan declared that she had never had so much fun.

"Why the clock?" asked Rennin as he drove the team.

"When I saw that dragon, I could hear it calling to me. It said, 'Take me home. You know I'm real. You can appreciate me. Take me away from here.' I know the dragon couldn't be Draco, but it could be one of his ancestors, and it was definitely Draco's voice."

Rennin nodded. "I heard it too. Jason Martin—the brother of Danielle's great-great-great-grandfather, Mason. He *did* stay on Draconis." He looked over his shoulder "And the workmanship on those pieces is incomparable. Someday they will be priceless."

"Thank you, Rennin. I've never wanted anything so much. I know it's only wood and glass, but it's like having a piece of home."

"You're very welcome," Rennin said as he kissed the delicate woman beside him. "You may repay me later beneath the starry sky."

She slipped her arms around her husband's arm. "I'll repay you right now if you find a nice secluded spot."

"Morgan! How brazen!"

"You like the idea. Admit it. The thrill of possibly being caught exhilarates you."

"Yes, it does. Get up, horses! This spot is too open. We have to find a more private place."

Rennin and Morgan made camp early in a thick, sheltered walnut grove. Almost before the fire was ablaze, Rennin engulfed Morgan in his muscular arms. "Time to pay up."

She teased him. "Ooo. What an eager beaver. Can't you wait for the sunset?"

"Nope."

"Well, if you insist," said Morgan as she started to unfasten her own blouse.

He leaned against a tree, propped one foot on it, and folded his arms. "Go ahead. I'm watching."

Slowly she unlaced her blouse and slipped if off, dropping it to the ground by her feet. Then, she let her skirt slide down.

Rennin remained like a statue and watched until Morgan stood before him wearing only her smile and enticing him with a come-hither finger.

"Oh!" He strode to her and pulled her to him. "You are the most beautiful thing I have ever seen." Kissing her passionately, he took her to the ground.

Some time later as they lay nestled under a blanket, a snapping twig near the wagon startled Rennin up. "Who's there?"

A raggedly dressed man stepped from the shadows. He looked over his shoulder. "Gee, Jared, I think we caught these folks indisposed. Get out here. She's something to look at."

Morgan pulled the blanket to her chin as Rennin reached for his pants. He heard the click of a pistol. "No need to move," came a voice that belonged to the man called Jared. "Well, Frank, looks like we found ourselves a rich couple from what I see on this wagon."

"What do you want?" asked Rennin. His pistol was under the wagon seat.

"Not much. Only small trinkets and gold. The big stuff might be valuable, but we can't carry that."

The man called Frank stomped toward Morgan, grabbed her hand, and snatched the diamond off her finger. "How much do you think we can get for this, Jared?"

Jared whistled. "What else does she have?"

Frank grabbed Morgan's other hand, but she jerked it back with some force. "No! You will have to kill me to get this one."

Rennin said sternly, "Give the man the ring. It's only gold. It's not worth dying for it."

"No, Rennin. This is my wedding ring. Your father made it. It will not leave my hand as long as I'm alive."

Frank laughed. "She's a feisty little lady, Jared. I wouldn't mind having *her*."

Morgan shot Frank a look that sent a chill over Rennin as he watched. Then, she spoke again, and her voice changed to a mesmerizing whisper. "You don't want me. As a matter of fact, you don't want anything that belongs to me. Give my ring back." Morgan held out her hand. When Frank did not respond, she reached into the fire and grabbed a handful of flames. She blew them toward Frank, catching his breeches on fire.

In his haste to put out the blaze, Frank dropped the diamond, which Morgan calmly returned to her finger. "If you so much as touch anything else that belongs to me, I'll do something much worse to you."

"Like what?" said Jared. "What are you—a witch?"

"A mage. There *is* a difference. Would you like another example of what I can do?" Morgan waved her hand and the horse near Jared reared, striking his hand and sending his gun sailing through the air and felling him to the ground. The gun landed beside Rennin who picked it up without a word, for he was as confounded by Morgan's behavior as were the bungling robbers.

Backing away, Frank helped his partner to his feet. "We're leaving. Just let us be on our way."

"Yes, leave," said Morgan, "but find a new line of work. If you try to rob anyone else, I'll send a disease upon you. Your flesh will slowly rot away, beginning with your groin. Now, go!"

The two men took off as if in a whirlwind. Rennin held the gun still. He cautiously asked, "Morgan, where are you? Give me my Morgan back. Now!"

With a shudder, Morgan turned blank eyes to him. "Are you afraid of me, darling? I do not wish to harm you. Rather, I protected you." She ran her hand over Rennin's cheek and pushed his hair back to caress his ear with an ever-so-slight point on it. "I was never able to have Duncan or Aidan, but you were so easy, like your grandfather, Alexander. I do rather enjoy you, my gorgeous, untamable golden boy."

In sheer panic, Rennin grabbed Morgan and held her to him. "Whatever spirit you are, I command you in the name of the Father and of the Son and of the Holy Ghost to leave Morgan. I bind you and send you to the pit of Hell never to return to this world or any other."

Frigid breath stung Rennin's chest. A muffled laugh came from Morgan. "After biding my time for all these years until I could be free, do you think I'll leave so easily? I wasn't so foolish as to manifest myself as the others did with that decrepit old priest around. I only had to wait for a time when Morgan's damned morality didn't matter so much. Rachel gave that to me. Besides, do you really think that a creature as sinful as you has the power to cast me out?"

"No, but my God does, and it is in His name that I command you to leave. Don't say another word. Leave my wife now!"

"Ha! Ha! Ha! Don't you think you at least need some holy water and oil?"

"No. I only need faith. It's not by my power or by anything I can say or do, but by the power of Christ alone that I compel you to leave. In the name of Jesus, go!"

Morgan shuddered violently, and a terrifying scream echoed through the trees. Morgan lay limp in Rennin's arms. Rennin heard a man bellow from the direction the robbers had run. *A willing vessel so close.* He swallowed the lump in his throat.

For what seemed an eternity, he held her. At last she stirred and looked at his ashen face. "Rennin! I told you the voice I heard was real. All of sudden, I couldn't speak. I heard and saw everything. It was *Quazel.* Strangely, she was actually protecting me. I don't know why, but I think she wanted me to do something evil."

"She's gone now." He glanced toward the direction where the scream had emanated. *But not banished, just expelled from my love.* "She probably wanted you to thrust a knife into my heart. Should we consider this life number eight?"

"'Tis not funny. Whatever spirit it was that inhabited me, however briefly, only wanted me to do harm. It was cold and completely selfish. It's scary to know that evil spirits might just wait, lurking, hoping for someone to invade. Let's pray for our children—that God will protect their hearts and minds." She, too, stared toward where Jared and Frank had run. *Just waiting. Will she ever be completely gone?*

"As you wish, honey." They prayed until late in the night. Finally, they fell asleep with a sense of peace.

Rennin looked at Rebekah who was grinning wryly. "What's on your mind?"

"Well, Morgan had her demon to try to spoil her honeymoon, and mine is this blasted seasickness."

"Hers passed. Yours will, too. Rest a while. Let the doctor's medicine work. I'll wake you later."

As his wife napped, Rennin played shuffleboard with Sarah and the twins.

Rebekah dreamed strange, unsettling dreams. She was deathly ill, having her flesh eaten away. She held rotting clumps of her skin and muscle in her hands. She could smell the putrid stench of decay.

She tossed fitfully.

Then she was soaring through the air on the back of a snow-white dragon. Her spirit had never felt so free.

The dream changed, and she was laughing, but sad because Rennin wanted a baby and she couldn't give it to him. Again, she reached inside her abdomen and held her womb, blood dripping, running down her arm. The next minute, she was surrounded by children, but she was exceedingly sorrowful, sobs eminating from her soul and great lament echoing around her.

Rebekah sprang from her berth. *I think I'd rather be sick if this medicine is going to cause me to have such disconcerting dreams.* She bathed her face in cool water, put on her shoes, and went in search of her husband.

She found Rennin laughing mirthfully as Gabriel and Michael tried to push the puck in shuffleboard. Seeing Rebekah, Rennin greeted her, "Hello, beautiful. Are you feeling better?"

"Some. I was having nightmares. Maybe the fresh air will clear my mind."

"I'm so glad you decided to join us."

"Actually, Uncle Rennin," said Sarah, "it's lunch time and, then, nap time. You and Aunt Rebekah can stroll around the deck or whatever else you might like." They made their way to the dining room.

After lunch, Sarah took Gabriel and Michael for a nap while Rennin and Rebekah strolled around the deck, holding hands. "Do you want to tell me the dreams you had?" Rennin asked.

"They were strange. I had the same feeling as when I dreamed you were shot with an arrow." She clutched his arm. "Maybe they're premonitions." She told Rennin her dreams.

"Oh, honey, I'm sure hearing that curse come from Morgan's lips planted those thoughts in your mind. Couple that with the medication, and you have the perfect recipe for nightmares."

"I'm fine, Rennin. Don't worry about me. And, I'm not sick any more. Let's go back to our room. I'm feeling rather energetic."

"Are you?"

"Huh-hum. After that, I understand dinner is a stately affair. I have several new fancy dresses to wear and take off."

"Yes, I think a trip to our room is definitely in order."

That night Rebekah danced with Rennin in the dining room that had been transformed into an elaborate ballroom with one long table covered in white linen tablecloths and an area near the end cleared for dancing. A string quartet provided music.

She was decked in an elegant black satin and taffeta dress. She wore an emerald choker at her throat and dangling emeralds on her ears and turned the heads of many men. As they danced, Rennin whispered, "If I were the jealous type, I'd shoot every man in this room. They're all looking at you. They can eat their hearts out because you're mine."

"Don't be silly. They aren't looking at me."

"Want to bet? Let's see how many ask you to dance."

"Rennin, what do I do if someone does ask me to dance?"

"Dance with him unless he steps out of line. Then, I'll kick him from here to eternity."

"Rennin, I've never danced with a stranger. I'm not even a good dancer. I would be so embarrassed."

"You're a wonderful dancer, and you're by far the most gorgeous woman on this ship."

By the end of the evening, seven different men had asked Rebekah to dance. Two of the older men asked her twice. Only once did she seek Rennin's eyes to be rescued. He promptly cut in on the young man and gave the youth a scathing look that sent him away like a dog just sprayed by a skunk.

On their way back to their cabin, Rebekah teased Rennin. "Marshall was a superb dance partner. He asked if he could throw you overboard."

"Which one was Marshall?"

"The little white-haired man. Are you a little jealous?"

"No, I'm a great deal jealous, but I trust you. You *did* get rid of the little pock-faced kid."

"You're so bad!" she said, punching his arm. "I wanted you to sweep me off my feet and tell me you would show me how much you love me."

"Oh, I see." Leaning on the rail and watching the waves churn, Rennin said, "How about this? Rebekah Sinclair O'Rourke, I love you. I can never show you how much, but I'd like to start with this." He held out a black velvet case.

Rebekah shakily took the case. "Open it," Rennin insisted.

She lifted the lid and gasped. "Rennin, what are these? Where did you get them?"

"They've been passed down for generations. They belonged to my great-times-nine grandparents. They were made by his father from a chain on a watch that belonged to his grandfather. Those people were Cameron and Holly O'Rourke. Rebekah, these are the rings that Rennin gave Cameron on his wedding day. My mother and father wore them. Candy brought them to me. You and I have never worn wedding bands. Will you wear these with me?"

"Oh, Rennin!" She put a hand to her chest. "Yes, but what about the diamond?"

"That's the diamond that Rennin gave Morgan. Will you wear it, too?"

"Of course, I will. Oh! I'm speechless."

"Have I swept you off your feet, Mrs. O'Rourke?"

She nodded. Rennin took the diamond out and placed it on Rebekah's right hand. He, then, took the smaller loop of golden chain and put it on Rebekah's left hand. "One on each hand because Morgan was right. I don't want to overshadow the chain that shows our souls are linked forever. Will you put the other one on me?"

Rebekah put the links over Rennin's finger. Still unable to speak, she sealed the placement with a kiss.

Rennin scooped Rebekah into his arms and carried her back to their cabin.

23
Romantic Interlude

The steamer ship U.S.S. *Majestic* dropped anchor in a small port in the Central American country of Panama. From there the passengers crossed the narrow, jungle-covered isthmus to board another steamer headed for New Orleans.

The two-day trek through the thick jungle was both fascinating and miserable. Rennin, Rebekah, and the children saw sights and heard sounds they would never see or hear again. The parrots thrilled Sarah with their florescent feathers and imitation of human voices. Michael and Gabriel squealed with delight as monkeys and other primates scampered through the trees and chattered and screamed.

Rebekah took in the wonders as she slapped the mosquitoes. Rennin apologized, "Honey, I'm sorry. I had no idea the mosquitoes would be so bad. I chose this way to cut off the travel time."

"Don't worry about it. The trip is only two days. Then, we'll be on another ship." Rebekah laughed blithely. "Rennin, please just tell me we'll travel by train or coach to get home."

"Yes, we'll be going overland to get home."

The second leg of the voyage in the warm, sunny Gulf of Mexico was relaxing and pleasant. Dolphins leapt in greeting, and flying fish sailed through the air in welcome. The blue-green water glimmered like stained glass.

Recovered from her seasickness, Rebekah stood on deck, absorbing the rays of the sun and breathing the ocean spray. Rennin quietly slipped his arms around her waist. She reached her hand above her head and ran her fingers through his hair. "I hope that's my husband behind me, or this could be scandalous."

"Pretty lady, why are you hugging a gentleman if you're unsure of his identity?"

"A gentleman would not be hugging me if I were not his. You smell like my husband, and you feel like my husband. Only one thing remains. If you look like my husband, you must be my husband."

"Well, turn around and see."

Rebekah slowly turned around. "Oh, my! You do bear a strong resemblance to the man I love. One further test will prove whether you are he."

"What is this test that I must pass?"

"Kiss me."

"Here? With all these people milling about?"

"That would *not* hinder my Rennin. You must be an imposter."

"No, my lady. I'm the real thing." He kissed Rebekah passionately. "Do I pass the test?"

They both laughed as Rebekah replied, "With a perfect score."

He took her hand, and they continued to watch the sun dance on the water. "Rennin, how much longer until we reach New Orleans?"

"Two days. We'll be arriving just in time for Mardi Gras. I saw a Mardi Gras celebration when I was eight, right after my *favorite* brother-in-law slapped me across the face for telling him not to talk to my sister so meanly. Father came to Natchez to meet a wealthy plantation owner about heading a boarding school for boys. He brought me with him. Father didn't take the position because he disagreed with the plantation owner's philosophy, but we took a riverboat on to New Orleans. The people of New Orleans take this celebration seriously—they put on a show with parades and floats and music and performing animals. You'll love it."

"When will it be?"

"About one week. After Mardi Gras, you can do some shopping. Then we'll travel by riverboat to Minnesota where we'll visit the mission and you can meet the rest of my family.

Then, we will head home. We should be home by September when the school opens."

"Rennin, I'm so excited I'm giddy."

"I guess I'd better not open a bottle of champagne at dinner. If you're already giddy, what will happen if you drink champagne?"

"Oh, I don't know." She dropped her arms over his shoulders and laced her fingers behind his neck. "Maybe, just maybe, you could have your way with me."

"This sounds promising."

"The sun is setting. It's time to dress for dinner and champagne." She wiggled her eyebrows.

Rebekah donned an emerald green velvet dress with a scalloped neckline. Her layers of petticoats rustled. She pulled her hair up and curled it into ringlets that hung to her shoulders.

As she removed the emerald choker from her jewelry box, "Wait a minute, Mrs. O'Rourke," whispered Rennin, running a finger across her collar bone. "I have another gift for you."

"You have to stop giving me things. I'm perfectly happy as it is."

"But giving you things makes me happy. I love to see the light in your eyes. Besides, this is another heirloom. I've had it for quite a while. I found it packed away in a trunk in our attic a long time ago. I've kept it until the right moment. Seeing you in that dress tells me this is the right moment. Close your eyes."

Rebekah closed her eyes. She felt cool metal on her neck. Rennin whispered, "Open your eyes." As perfect as the day it left China, around her neck, dangled Morgan's jade dragon. "It *is* lovely—even more so, on you."

"How did you get this, too? How did Cameron get *all* his mother's jewelry? Morgan did have other children."

"It's a long story. You'll hear most of it as we read some more. The diamond was obviously valuable, but the dragon sort of got lost. When I went searching in the attic, I found the book. The necklace was inside the book. Maybe someone used it as a bookmark. No matter. It's yours now. You can decide to whom you want to give it."

"Who has the clock, settee, and dressing table and chair?"

"Caitlin."

"How?"

"All I know is that several of Rennin's descendents were killed fighting for American independence. Rennin always wanted these things to belong to an O'Rourke. It fell to Cameron's lot by virtue of his descendents. Father had them because he was the only child who lived to adulthood. I'll get the things when we go to Minnesota because I'm the only one who can carry on the O'Rourke name. You've seen to that by giving me Gabriel and Michael."

Her hand splayed on his chest, Rebekah said, "Do you think Caitlin will just give you her things?"

"Caitlin would give me *anything*. She was seventeen when I was born. She seemed like my mother. She has always spoiled me rotten. All my sisters have. Camille, who is the closest in age to me, is five years older that I am. Caitlin's son was only about two years younger than I am. He died very young. She showered me with attention again. Then, she lost two babies. I told you she almost died." Rennin took a deep breath.

"You really love her, don't you?"

"Katie?" He nodded. "I suppose she's the most special to me. Honestly, I've never liked her husband, Maxwell. If I could steal her away from him, I would. He's cruel if you ask me." He put a hand to his cheek. "He sure slapped the stew out of me when I talked up to him. I can't figure why someone as loving as Caitlin married such an ogre." Rennin shook his head. "Oh, never mind. You'll meet them all, and you can draw your own conclusions. I just never understood why she married him so quickly."

"Maybe she sees something you don't."

"Well, she'll see why I married you. Are you ready for dinner, lovely lady?"

"Indeed. And dancing. And champagne." Rebekah winked at Rennin.

He offered her his arm. "Shall we?"

"We shall."

The U.S.S. *Faerie Queen* glided into New Orleans Harbor, a bustling commercial center. Longshoremen loaded and unloaded crates onto barges on the Mississippi River. Riverboats awaited passengers. The energy was contagious.

Two hansom cabs took Rennin, Rebekah, and the children to a hotel on the street called La Rue Bourbon. Their suite opened onto a balcony overlooking the hub of activity. Rennin said, "During the Mardi Gras festivities we'll watch from here. The revelers sometimes get rather raucous. There have even been instances of violence. We can watch the fun from here in relative safety, but tonight, my Rebekah, we're dining in one of the finest restaurants in the city."

Rebekah dressed that evening in a soft lavender, velvet and satin, off-the-shoulder dress. She and Rennin dined by candlelight on crawfish étouffée, Creole rice, and steamed vegetables smothered in butter, and drank a fine French wine.

After dinner, they strolled to the river's edge and viewed the rolling water. Then, they walked toward their hotel. They stopped to watch street performers—a pantomime and an organ grinder and his monkey. The monkey scampered up Rebekah's shoulder and stole her hatpin.

Rebekah's childlike laughter rippled through the square. The owner scolded the monkey. "Naughty, Samson, to steal the beautiful lady's hatpin." Rennin placed some coins in the organ grinder's hand and Samson handed Rebekah her pin.

As they walked on Rebekah said, "That was so cute."

"It's part of the act," explained Rennin. "Cute monkey steals some article. Owner scolds monkey and gives article back, fully expecting some kind of reward. That's how he makes his living."

"That's sad. What if the person doesn't reward him?"

"That's the chance he takes. Most tourists do reward him, so he gets by. The same is true for the pantomime and the string quartet on the corner. The coins in the bucket are their pay."

"I'm glad we don't live like that. I think you've rather spoiled me."

"As I intended. You may expect more." Rennin held Rebekah in his arms and kissed her in the moonlight.

The morning brought glorious sunshine. Rennin took everyone to a New Orleans coffee house for breakfast. "They serve something here that everyone must try. They're called beignets, little square pastries covered in confectioner's sugar," Rennin explained.

They finished a plate of beignets in short order. The adults drank New Orleans style coffee while the children drank chilled milk. Rennin allowed Sarah to try the coffee, but after a few sips, she asked if she could have warm cocoa instead.

After breakfast, the group walked around Jackson Square, formerly called *Place d' Armes,* but renamed after the victorious General Andrew Jackson. They watched various street performers, and Rennin gave each one a token he considered worthy. They stopped for the midday meal and ate deep-fried catfish and spicy fried potato wedges.

After lunch, each one had his caricature drawn by a street painter. They all laughed at the traits the artist emphasized. Rebekah giggled at the tiny spike the artist exaggerated in the center of Rennin's ears. Then, they went back to their rooms to rest before dinner. That evening, Rennin and Rebekah ate at a different restaurant before going to the theater.

As they entered the theater, the couple was handed a basket of peanuts and over-ripe fruit. "What is this for?" asked Rebekah.

"You throw it at the villain," Rennin explained.

In horror, Rebekah gasped, "We actually throw these things at the players?"

"Only the villain." Rennin chuckled. "It's part of the play."

Despite her dismay at the idea of throwing things at the actors, Rebekah threw peanuts with alacrity, but she refused to throw the squishy tomatoes. Rennin watched her laugh and fell deeper in love.

The next day, Rennin took the whole group across the river, and they spent a day and night on Biloxi Beach in a fine hotel established in the former capital of the French Colony. They returned to their hotel on Saturday, and on Sunday, although they were not Roman Catholic, they attended mass at St. Louis Cathedral. As they spent a leisurely afternoon relaxing, Rebekah remarked at the beauty and majesty of the church, but she was thoroughly confused by the service. She pursed her lips. "I couldn't understand a word the pastor said until he read the Scripture."

"Priest," Rennin said. "Much of the service was in Latin."

"And the kneeling and standing and sitting. I tried to keep up, but I got lost. I'm glad we sat on the back row."

"I took you there just so you could see the building. Its absolutely spectacular," Rennin said.

On Monday, Rennin and Rebekah visited the Cabildo, where the city council met; the Presbytere, which had once been the residence of the Capuchin monks, but was now the courthouse; and the U.S. Mint, where they viewed currency being printed.

Late in the afternoon, they walked slowly back to their hotel. They were delayed as a mournful funeral procession passed before them. The procession consisted mainly of Negroes singing deep forlorn melodies and horns that sounded as if they were crying. Trailing behind the horse-drawn hearse, the mourners wailed and lamented.

Rebekah shivered, and Rennin removed his coat and placed it around her shoulders. "I'm not cold. This is just plain spooky," whispered Rebekah. He put a protective arm around her waist.

Near the end of the procession, a dark woman, who wore a turban on her head, feathers in her ears, and a strangely designed cross around her neck, stopped and stared eerily at Rebekah. She approached Rebekah and shook her hand all around the young woman. Rebekah gripped Rennin's hand. He stepped between them. He touched the woman's shoulder. "Go away. Leave my wife alone."

The black woman's eyes widened. "You, sir, come from a long line of magic that has been lost. Behold!" She pointed at Rebekah. "The magic that once was lost has been restored. Beautiful lady, you worry that you have not born more children. All too soon, you will have *many* children, but only through sorrow." The strange woman put her hands around Rebekah's tiny waist. "Your womb has already known sadness. Your daughter, not his"—She pointed at Rennin— "was taken before she saw the light of day. Your womb will know tragedy. You will bear no more children, yet you will be mother to many."

Rennin jerked the woman away from Rebekah. "Get off her! We don't believe your witchcraft."

"But someday magic will relieve your agony," said the woman. "Before long, your temper will cause you great distress. You will beg for the magic to be restored."

Rennin threw coins at the woman. "Is this what you want? Leave us."

"You are a rash young man. I neither want nor need your gold. I do this for the magic in here." She touched Rebekah's temple and chest. "Yes, you love this woman, but that love will be challenged—stretched to a breaking point. Then, the magic will be the only thing to hold it together." The woman meandered after the funeral procession as the woeful sounds faded away.

Rebekah buried her face in Rennin's chest. "Rennin, what did she mean?"

"Ignore her. She's a superstitious old woman."

One of the onlookers asked, "Mister, do you have any idea who that woman was?"

"No, and I don't care," snapped Rennin.

"You should. She has some powerful magic. That was Marie LaVeau, the Queen of Voodoo."

"I don't care if she's Queen Victoria. Come on, honey. Let's go."

"But, Rennin, she knew about Firelight and about how I've worried about not getting pregnant."

"Don't fret about what she said, Rebekah. Have faith, my love. Come what may, God will provide"

That night Rebekah lay awake long after Rennin slept. She pondered the words of Marie LaVeau. She spoke aloud, "What magic?" She shook her husband awake. "Rennin, wake up."

"What's wrong, Rebekah?"

"That woman, Marie, said I was the magic that once was lost. Catherine said the same thing. What does that mean?"

"Rebekah," Rennin said irritably, "go to sleep. Stop thinking about that lunatic."

"Catherine isn't a lunatic. She said it too. Could it have something to do with the fact that I believe Draconis is real, and so many in your family have thought it to be a fairytale for so long?"

"I don't know. You really shouldn't give credence to what that woman said. That's the way of her religion. It's rooted in fear, not hope."

"Rennin, do you believe Draconis is real?"

He sighed. "I'd like to, but it's hard to think of a place that perfect without its being Heaven."

"But the other Rennin never said it was perfect, only mystical. Someday when we have no responsibilities, let's go look for it."

"What?"

"What can it hurt? If it's real, I'm positive we'll be able to see it because you, my love, are an exceptional man. If it's not real, then we'll be alone together on the open sea. We can do whatever we like. Remember that Catherine also said I'd take you places you'd only dreamed of going." Rebekah leaned her head on Rennin's chest and ran her fingers back and forth.

"We could do whatever we like right now," whispered Rennin who was suddenly fully awake. "That *is* magic."

Rebekah screamed as a loud commotion on the street woke her. Rennin jumped up, pulling her behind him. "Come on. The celebration has started."

All day long, there were parades and different forms of entertainment in the street below. Rebekah, Rennin, and the children watched from their balcony. They did not go out to dinner, but ordered hotel room service. At dark, there was a fireworks display over the river. One blast was louder than the rest, and the glass of the French door onto the balcony shattered.

Rennin grabbed Rebekah's hand. "Sarah, get the boys! Everybody get down." Several more blasts rang out before the police subdued a man who had drawn his firearms. Within an hour the hotel had replaced the windowpane.

The concierge apologized repeatedly. "I am so sorry. This is what happens when someone has far too much liquor."

"We're all fine," assured Rennin, but that night Rebekah watched him sneak into the boys' room. She listened at the door. He kissed each boy on the forehead as they slept. "If you're the only two I'll ever have, I must protect you better than today." Then, she heard him pray for God to send angels to watch over the boys and her.

When he came out, she was waiting. "Rennin O'Rourke, you think there's something to what Marie said too. How dare you pretend you didn't?"

He put his arms around her. "Okay. She spooked me, too. I just don't know what I would do if something happened to you or the boys. I love you so much."

"Hold on to that faith you talked about. I'm not going anywhere."

Ash Wednesday was more than dead. In addition to all activity being stopped, the day started out drizzly and progressed to a full downpour by noon. Rennin came to the davenport in the suite where Rebekah sat cuddled up doing needlepoint on domestic she intended to turn into pillowcases. He held up a seemingly forgotten book. "There's really nothing to do today. Do you want to continue the story?"

"Yes!" said Rebekah, tossing the embroidery to the side. "I really hate needlepoint. I'm glad I have boys."

After the incident in the walnut grove, Rennin traveled slowly. They slept late and camped early. "We need to get home, Rennin," said Morgan.

"We'll get there before the baby comes. I promise," he assured. "I just want as much time alone with you as possible."

As they rode along, thunder rumbled in the distance. "Well, Rennin, I think you had better find us some shelter to be alone in. A storm is brewing."

"I think I remember a rough cabin with a thrown-together barn around here. Didn't a couple named Riley say they lived somewhere around here?"

"Oh, yes. I remember them. They have a boy a little older than Rachel. Wasn't his name Ryan? They came to the trading post once, but that was almost a year ago."

They came to a trail off the dirt road. Morgan observed, "Rennin, the path looks as if nothing has traveled it in a while. Maybe they left. Will the wagon be able to go over all the vines?"

"I think we'll be fine." Rennin clucked his tongue and urged the horses forward as the thunder grew closer.

When they approached the house, there was no sign of life. Rennin pulled up and called out, but there was no answer. The barn was empty. Rennin drove the wagon into the barn and unhitched the horses for a rest. After he fed the animals, he and Morgan started to the house. Large drops of rain and insistent thunder hurried them along.

"The place looks deserted," commented Rennin as he opened the door.

"It's a mess for sure," Morgan said.

"At least it's dry," Rennin argued.

Inside, Morgan set down the basket of food she had brought in and found a broom. She swept and dusted and removed cobwebs. "Morgan," said Rennin, amused by her work. "We aren't moving in."

"Rennin, the place is dirty."

"Did you notice the bed is made, and the dishes are in the cupboard? The place is dusty, not dirty. The Rileys must have left in a hurry. It appears they took very little with them."

"You're right, but they've been gone a long time."

Morgan took the quilt from the bed and shook it out the door. She came back inside wondering where the child slept. Then she noticed a folded quilt near the hearth. A chill ran down her spine, and she swallowed a lump in her throat before she spoke. "The way the rain's coming down, I'd say we'll be here at least tonight. I'm glad we brought in some food and water." She replaced the quilt and turned the bed back. "Do you want salt pork, venison jerky or pickled herring tonight?"

"None of the above," said Rennin, slipping his arms around her. "I want you."

"Oh, really?" said Morgan coyly. "I suppose that could be arranged. The bed's clean and inviting."

"Yes, it does look inviting," He agreed as he pushed her gently backward. "Shall we test it?"

Sometime later, Rennin and Morgan lay snuggled beneath a delicately sewn patchwork quilt. Thunder continued to rumble, and rain pelted the roof. Without warning, the door flew open and in stepped a very unkempt little blond-haired, blue-eyed boy. He stood statue-like, staring at Morgan and Rennin. A single word escaped his lips in the form of a question. "Momma?"

Morgan vaguely remembered Mrs. Riley being about her size and having dark hair. Gently, she responded, "Ryan?"

In a fit of tears, the filthy, smelly little boy ran to her and fell into her arms. "Momma!"

Morgan looked toward Rennin who dressed quickly. She whispered, "Something's very wrong here. I felt it when I saw that." She cut her eyes toward the folded quilt.

Stomach roiling, Rennin tenderly pulled the boy from Morgan. "Ryan, look at me. I'm Mr. O'Rourke from Mom's Trading Post. Do you remember me?"

The boy stared blankly at him and looked back toward Morgan for reassurance. Timidly, he said, "You're not my momma."

"No, baby. I'm Mrs. O'Rourke. Do you remember eating teacakes with Rachel, Colin, and Duncan?"

"With milk," he replied.

"Yes, honey. Where are your momma and papa?"

He pointed toward the back of the cabin. "Out there."

"Out there?" Morgan said, confused. "Rennin?"

"I'll go see what he means. In the meantime, you clean him up." Rennin got his pistol from the basket they had brought in. Noticing a hat and seal-skin slicker on a hook by the door, he put them on. The slicker was a little snug, but it would keep him dry. He stepped into the deluge.

Morgan said, "Ryan, turn around so I can get dressed." The boy passively obeyed. Morgan set several buckets from the shelf near the door to catch water. They filled quickly and she set about heating some water for the washtub she had seen on the porch. She brought the tub in and mixed some hot and cold water.

She spoke softly, "Ryan, let's get you out of those dirty wet things and make you feel better." The child let her take off his clothes and lift him into the water. Morgan found some soap and washed him. As she bathed the child, she noticed numerous scars on his back.

Ryan said softly, "Momma and Papa can't talk to Mr. O'Rourke."

"Why, honey?"

"The man shot Papa. He lay on top of Momma, and she never got up."

Just as Morgan realized Rennin would be discovering two corpses, he walked back into the room. He was pale. "Morgan."

"I know. They're dead." She washed Ryan's hair before she spoke to him. "Ryan, did you know the man you saw hurt your momma and papa?"

He shook his head.

She asked, "Did he see you or know you were here?"

"No. He just took Momma's locket and the horse and left. I was hiding in the smokehouse because Papa told me to stay in the house since we had a visitor several nights earlier. But the man knew Momma. He called her Tabitha. That was her name."

"What did he say to her?"

"He asked her why she didn't wait for him. Then, he called her a horse. That's when he pushed her down on the ground."

Morgan and Rennin exchanged glances. Rennin asked, "Can you describe the man?"

"He had blue eyes and blond hair like mine. Oh, and whiskers."

"Ryan," said Rennin, "when did this happen?"

"The day after Christmas."

Morgan gasped. "You've been here alone all this time?"

"Yes, ma'am."

"What have you eaten?"

"Things in the root cellar. I stayed down there. I went in through the outside. I was scared the man would come back."

"Of course, you were."

Rather than try to comb the tangles from Ryan's hair, Morgan used her needlepoint scissors and cut the boy's hair short. Rennin found him some clean clothes in a trunk and threw the others outside. Morgan made some johnnycakes, opened the pickled herring and fed the little boy. He lay down on the bed and went to sleep.

"Rennin, are you thinking what I'm thinking?" Morgan asked thoughtfully.

He nodded. "Tabitha married Andrew Riley for convenience. The murderer is Ryan's father, but he doesn't know he has a son. It's better that way."

"No, Rennin. I figure it must be something like that, but that isn't what I was thinking. We have to take him with us. We have room in our home and our hearts for another little boy, don't we?"

Rennin pulled Morgan into his arms. "Yes, Momma, we do."

The next day, Rennin buried Andrew and Tabitha Riley while Morgan helped Ryan pack some things and explained that he was going to come and live with her and Rennin and Rachel, Colin, and Duncan.

"How sad," said Rebekah with tears on her cheeks after Rennin closed the book. "Poor child. I know how he felt."

Rennin held Rebekah. He had not considered how the story of Ryan would stir emotions in her. Rebekah whispered, "You're a lot like your ancestor. He took care of orphans, too."

The next two days Rebekah spent shopping. She helped Sarah buy grown-up clothes, and she chose souvenirs for all her friends and family in Puma Pass. Rennin shopped too. Rebekah knew he had bought her another surprise and could hardly stand it, for she knew he would keep her in suspense until they were well on their way up the Mississippi.

Saturday morning they boarded *The Mississippi Belle*, a riverboat, to go as far as they could toward Minneapolis. As

Rebekah watched the enchanted city move away, she caught sight of a familiar face on the dock. Marie LaVeau blew her a kiss and waved good-bye.

24
A Sense of Belonging

The trip up the Mississippi was long, but enjoyable. The riverboat made many stops along the way. When they stopped in Natchez, Rennin showed Rebekah a cotton plantation.

"All of the colored folks are slaves?" she asked.

"Most, if not all," answered Rennin. "A few might be free Negroes, but I doubt it."

"I wouldn't like to have no will of my own. Why doesn't the government do something?"

"That's a decision the federal government so far has left up to the state governments. Some states are free states where slavery is outlawed. Most of them are northern states. They're more industrialized rather than agrarian like the South. There's a lot of unrest over the issue." He took a deep breath. "I'm afraid of the final outcome."

"What do you think might happen?"

"I don't know, but it'll tear this country apart."

The riverboat traveled on to Memphis. There Rennin, Rebekah, and the children dined on barbequed pork, beef, and chicken. Sarah asked her uncle to build a pit barbeque when they returned to Puma Pass, and he promised he would.

Between Memphis and St. Louis, Rennin tried his hand at riverboat gambling, something at which he failed miserably. He lost enough to build another school on the Mississippi, and Rebekah taunted him mercilessly. "You simply are not a good liar. You don't know how to bluff."

Rennin scoffed, "Do you think you can do better?"

"Yes," she said confidently.

"This I have to see." He laughed heartily.

Rebekah changed into her green dress that showed her shoulders and donned her dragon pendant. She took the two hundred dollars Rennin offered her to prove her point and joined a table with several older men. There she giggled and flirted and batted her eyes coyly as she played. Not only did she win back the two hundred dollars Rennin had lost to the same group earlier, but three hundred dollars more.

Rennin was mortified. "I can't believe it! You didn't win. You merely distracted them so that they lost."

She waved her paper currency at him. "I have the money. That's what counts. Let's go to our room and celebrate."

Back in their room, Rennin gave Rebekah the gift he had bought in New Orleans, a carved, black-walnut music box designed to hold her jewelry.

They stopped in St. Louis where Rennin discovered the brothel where Keturah had worked had been shut down. Finally, they came to a place in the river that was too shallow for the riverboat. Rennin bought a wagon and two new horses. They traveled overland from Minneapolis for two days until they reached the mission.

Since Rennin had not sent word they were coming, the place suddenly bustled with life. Rennin discovered that he was not the only one who had withheld news. Cassandra and Constance had recently moved to Wisconsin, but Camille, and especially Caitlin, were in a dither.

Caitlin ran from her door, her arm in a sling. "Rennin! Why didn't you send me a letter? I have no rooms prepared."

"Katie!" Rennin engulfed his eldest sister and swung her around. Caitlin grimaced as Rennin squeezed her arm. "What happened to you this time?" he asked.

Caitlin waved her free hand as if nothing had happened. "Oh, that stupid cow kicked me."

She turned to Rebekah. "Oh, my goodness! Rennin said you were beautiful, but your're gorgeous. Welcome, Rebekah." She hugged her young sister-in-law. "I'm so glad to meet you. I'd thought I might never get to see you. And the babies aren't even babies any more, but they look just like Rennin at that age. Come in. Sarah, look at you. You've grown into a young woman."

Rennin tried to calm his sister. "Katie, relax. We plan to stay at Cathy's house. We'll gladly come and eat your cooking, but don't worry about rooms."

"Oh, fine. You unload that wagon then. I'm taking Rebekah and the boys on inside. I have to get to know my little sister." Caitlin put her arm around Rebekah's. "Come on, Gabriel and Michael. You, too, Sarah. I have warm snickerdoodles fresh from the oven." Caitlin tossed over her shoulder, "I'll save you some."

An hour later, Rennin dragged into Caitlin's kitchen where Caitlin and Rebekah were paring and slicing apples for pies, while the boys slept on a pallet, and Sarah had disappeared with her cousins. "Where are my snickerdoodles?" he asked in a surly tone.

"In the cookie jar where I always keep cookies," replied Caitlin. "What's wrong with you?"

"My back hurts. I had to unload four trunks by myself. Where's Max? Not that he'd be much help. He might get a blister on his hands." He grabbed two cookies and sank into a chair at the table.

"Rennin!" scolded Rebekah.

"Don't concern yourself, Beck. Rennin has always hated Max," Caitlin said indifferently.

"I'm sure I have a reason. Anyway, where is he?"

"He left for Minneapolis this morning. Surely, you saw him on the road. He'll be back at the end of the week."

"We didn't see anyone except Silas Barker on his way to the city; however, I did notice a dapple mare in the corral at Silas Barker's. Was it Max's?"

"Rennin Aidan O'Rourke, what *are* you suggesting?" asked Caitlin as she dropped her knife.

Rennin shrugged. "Well, if he's carrying on with Thelma Barker, you could divorce him and be rid of the ogre."

"Rennin!" Rebekah hissed.

"I swear, Rebekah, I think the horse was Max's dapple mare. Katie, I'm sorry."

"It's all right, baby. Max can be an ass sometimes." Caitlin rubbed her arm. "Peeling the apples has aggravated my arm. Beck, would you mind much finishing them? I have some liniment in my room to rub on it, but the stuff stinks to high heaven." Caitlin quietly left the room.

Rebekah plopped the bowl into Rennin's lap and handed him the knife. "Does the word 'tact' exist in your vocabulary? You finish the apples. I'm going to talk to Caitlin. Don't follow. If her husband *is* being unfaithful, her little brother might be the last person she wants to know." She stomped out of the room.

Rebekah knocked softly on the door. "Caitlin, may I come in?" Caitlin was quietly crying into her pillow. She had obviously rubbed some liniment on her arm because the odor was strong and she wore only her under garments.

Rebekah sat on the bed beside her newfound sister. Caitlin's shoulder, neck and forearm were black and blue. "Rebekah, you should've stayed with Rennin," she said as she wiped her eyes.

"Caitlin." Rebekah stroked the older woman's hair. "Did the cow grab your wrist and your neck?"

"What?" Caitlin said.

"Caitlin, from the second I met you outside, I felt as if I belonged to you and you to me. I loved you instantly." She touched Caitlin's neck. "A cow doesn't leave finger imprints. Would you like to talk about it? Was it Max?"

Caitlin nodded. She stood and pulled her dress back on. "Don't say anything to Rennin. He's so hotheaded that he'd probably kill Max."

"He'd deserve it," said Rebekah with an angry snort. "It's not the first time either, is it? Rennin said, 'What happened this time?' Max has hurt you before, hasn't he, Caitlin?"

"Yes, but please keep quiet. Max hates Rennin as much as Rennin hates him. He has always called Rennin a brat and a troublemaker. Once he even slapped Rennin for defending me. Rebekah, Max is as big as Rennin and twice as mean. Max might not be the one to get killed if confronted. I'd rather die than let anyone hurt Rennin." She touched her lips with her fingertips. "I changed his diapers. I fed him from a bottle with strained goat's milk. I taught him to walk and to talk and how to hold a spoon. I cared for him when he was ill. My son, Eric, died before he was a year old. I've never been able to have another child. Rennin's more than my baby brother. He's like my son. I love him with all my heart."

"So do I, Caitlin, but Rennin's not a child. Moreover, you're not a punching bag."

"Please, Rebekah, keep this between us."

"We'll be here two weeks. If you don't tell Rennin by the time we leave, I will. Katie, Max has to be stopped."

Both women sat holding hands without speaking for a while before Rebekah broke the silence. "Caitlin, haven't you confided in anyone about Max?"

"No, I dared not. He'd kill me."

"Was Rennin right? Was that your horse we saw?"

"Probably. It wouldn't be the first time."

"For Pete's sake, Caitlin! Why did you marry the man?"

She barely heard Caitlin's answer. "I was pregnant."

"You made love to him before you were married?" Her voice took on shrillness as she remembered Rennin's convictions before they wed.

"Not willingly, but Father didn't believe me. Yes, we went for a buggy ride alone, but I fought him. I lost the battle." She shook her head and closed her eyes. "Oh, before that, I thought he was handsome and very charming. Then, I found out what he was really like. If Mother had been alive, she would've believed me. I was only eighteen. What was I to do? Even with my family, I was alone."

Rebekah held Caitlin in her arms. "You're not alone any more. I'm here. Caitlin, I've been raped, too. I understand. If Max so much as touches you, tell me. Rennin has to know. Don't let this continue."

"That's not all, Rebekah. Max killed Eric. I'm sure of it. The baby was crying. Max got up and said angrily, 'I'll take care of him this time.' It surprised me, but I was so tired. I was thankful for the reprieve. Eric stopped crying. The next morning he was dead. Thomas had been here a couple of years. He was a young, brilliant doctor. He said that many infants die in their sleep. My heart couldn't believe his own father murdered him." She rolled her lips together and sighed. "Now, I do. The other two babies I've lost after Max beat me.

The first one I said I fell down the stairs. The second, I said the horse threw me. I think Thomas suspected, but he was bound not to say anything."

Caitlin laid her head on the younger woman's shoulder. "Oh, Rebekah! How I've needed you! I finally feel that I belong to somebody again." For the first time in more than twenty-five years, Caitlin sobbed out her fear, frustration, and fury.

An hour later, the two women came downstairs to the smell of fresh baked apple pie. Rennin grinned. "I made the pies for you, Katie. I'm really sorry for what I said earlier. It was thoughtless and insensitive. Will you forgive me?"

Caitlin held out her good arm, and Rennin hugged her. "You needn't even ask, Rennin. You know I do. I love you."

Rebekah and Caitlin set about making the rest of the supper. They baked sweet potatoes, snapped green beans, made fluffy biscuits, and sliced fresh hog souse. During the course of the meal, Max stomped through the door.

In true surprise, Caitlin said, "Max, I thought you would be gone until the end of the week."

He growled, "I caught up with Silas Barker. He told me Rennin was here. My business in the city will keep. I thought I'd better come home and entertain our guests."

"Don't worry, Max," said Rennin, "we're staying in Cathy's house. I *do* have another sister here who would like to visit with my family. Katie simply got first dibs."

"It's good to see you, too, Rennin. Are you going to introduce your wife and sons?" came the caustic reply through lips that had curled into a sneer.

The air in the room became cold, making Rebekah shiver. She introduced herself. "I'm Rebekah, and these are our boys, Gabriel and Michael. Please relax and let me make you a plate. Caitlin's arm is giving her a bit of trouble."

Max looked toward Caitlin, his mouth in a thin line, brow knit tight.

Rebekah served a plate for Max. As she worked in the kitchen, she mumbled, "Maybe you'll choke and die." In the dining room, she put the plate of food in front of Max with a plastered smile on her face. He took his first bite of souse and began to cough.

Rebekah put her hand to her mouth, her eyes wide. *Did I pronounce a curse on him?*

After his coughing spasm, Max, mumbled, "I got a piece of really hot pepper. Thought I was going to strangle to death." He shot Caitlin a dirty look. "You don't usually use hot peppers."

"Mine tastes fine," Rebekah chimed in. "It must have been a stray piece that was hotter than the rest."

Max just grunted and continued eating.

After dinner, Rennin prepared to leave quickly, saying that they were all tired after such a long trip. Rebekah hugged Caitlin and whispered, "If you need me, get me. I mean it." She looked sternly at Caitlin.

"I will," whispered Caitlin.

When Rebekah and Rennin were finally alone and all the children were asleep, Rennin said, "What was that last little bit of conversation with Katie?"

"She'll tell you soon. If she doesn't I will, but not yet."

"Max is cheating on her, and she knows. That's it. I should break his neck."

"Rennin, let Caitlin tell you what she needs to. Hold off on murdering Max just yet. You may have my permission to do so before our two weeks are up."

"Rebekah, what is it?"

"Rennin, I gave my word."

He stared at his wife, his brow in a deep furrow. She shook her head. "Don't start an argument. You'll only lose, and then you'll have to pay up. I'd like to relax a little. This has been a trying day. Read to me." She slapped the book into his hand with more force than necessary.

The rest of the journey back to Mom's Trading Post was long and arduous. Heavy rain fell often, and the rivers and creeks swelled to overflowing in many places. Several nights the three travelers huddled together in the seal-skin tent.

Ryan bonded easily with the two adults who found him to be a delightful child. Rennin tactfully picked the boy's brain about the man who had murdered Andrew and Tabitha, so that he could send a report to the closest authorities. From his description, Rennin drew a sketch, which the boy said resembled the man. Rennin asked, "Ryan, did you ever hear your parents discuss a man that you had never met?"

"Sometimes they argued about someone called Ranson. That's when Papa would punish her for being bad and she would sit on his lap and tell him she was sorry." Rennin and Morgan exchanged a solemn glance.

Finally, after much delay, Rennin brought the wagon into familiar territory. "We only have a couple of weeks left to travel," he pronounced. "Frankly, I'm looking forward to sleeping in my bed."

Ryan suddenly seemed uncomfortable as he fidgeted on the seat. "What's wrong, Ryan?" asked Morgan.

He turned his near-violet, eyes toward her. "I'm afraid."

"Why?"

"What if nobody else wants me to live with you? What if Rachel or Colin or Duncan hate me?"

Rennin pulled the horses to a stop and jumped down. He held his hand out to Ryan. "Come here, Ryan. I want to walk and talk."

He picked up the little boy into his arms and walked into the woods. Ryan said a little confused, "Mr. O'Rourke, I'm not walking."

"No, you're not. I want to carry you for a little while."

"Why?"

"Because I want to hug you. I want you to feel loved. Ryan, I'd like it very much if you'd consider living with us from now on, unless you have grandparents or uncles and aunts you would rather live with."

"I don't think I do. Momma never told me about any. If I'm your little boy, will I be Ryan O'Rourke?"

"If you want to be. If you want to stay Ryan Riley, 'tis fine, too. Your name isn't what makes me love you. You make me love you."

"Do you love me?" The little boy squinted through confused eyes.

"I do."

"I don't know if I want you to love me. That means you'll beat me."

"What? I will *not* beat you."

"Papa used to beat me. Momma said it was because he loved me and wanted me to do right. He would say, 'You're just like Ranson—no good.'"

Rennin puffed out his cheeks. "Ryan, I promise I will never beat you, and neither will Morgan."

"Oh, I know she wouldn't. She's too small and weak like Momma. Do you beat her when she's bad?"

"No!" Rennin ground his teeth to control his anger toward a dead man. "Ryan, did your papa beat your momma?"

"Only when she was bad."

"Ryan, I will not beat you—ever. I don't beat Morgan or any of my other children. That is not love."

"If I'm your little boy what will I call you?"

"What would you like to call me?"

"Not Papa. You're nice. What do your children call you?

"Daidí."

"Will you let me call you Daidí?"

"Of course, if that's what you want. Or you can call me Rennin or Uncle Rennin. Just don't call me Mr. O'Rourke."

Rennin sat down on a big rock in the woods. He left Ryan on his lap. "Well, what do you say?"

"Yes, and I'll call you 'Daidí Rennin.' I think I'll keep my name. It's too much to remember. Does this mean I can call Mrs. O'Rourke 'Momma Morgan'?"

"It does, indeed."

"Daidí Rennin, do you think Papa didn't like me much because he wasn't my real father?"

"Do you know he wasn't your father?"

The child nodded. "Yes, sir. Momma told me that my real father died."

"I don't know why your papa was so cruel to you, but, Ryan, I'm not your real father, and I like you very much. I tell you what: Let's try to put the unpleasant things behind us and look to a bright and happy future. But if you ever want to talk to me about your papa and momma, just let me know."

"Deal," said Ryan, sticking out his hand and beaming. Rennin shook his hand firmly. Then, the two went back to the wagon.

Ryan ran ahead and scampered to the seat, where he threw his arms around Morgan. "I get to call you 'Momma Morgan.' I belong to you now! I love you, Momma Morgan."

Morgan kissed the top of Ryan's head. "I love you, too, sweet boy."

Rebekah wiped tears from her cheeks. "It's important to feel as if you belong to someone. I'm so glad I belong to you, Rennin. And I'm glad Caitlin belongs to me. Rennin, we have to protect her."

"From what?"

She realized she had almost betrayed her promise. "Make her tell you tomorrow. I can't break my promise. She has two weeks to tell you, but that might be too long. Talk to her alone tomorrow."

25
Secrets Revealed

Rennin woke up just as the sun peeked over the horizon. Jauntily he headed out and stopped at Camille's house, where he asked if he could pack a picnic basket from her kitchen. "Well, of course," she replied. "Are you taking Rebekah to your favorite hiding place?"

"Not today. I'm taking Katie. I need to talk to her privately."

"Is something wrong?"

"No. Don't worry your pretty head. You know how I've always talked things over with Katie. Frankly, I just don't want Max around."

"I know what you mean. He has become a greater ass since you left."

"That seems impossible," said Rennin, his upper lip forming a sneer.

Camille paused in packing the basket. "Ren, may I tell you something without you flying off the handle?"

"I'll try." Rennin knew when Camille called him her baby name for him something was truly wrong.

"I don't think Daisy kicked Katie. I think Max did it, and it's not the first time. I can't prove it, but I'm suspicious." She held up her hand like a shield. "I mean—one day Herbert and I were running through the meadow. He grabbed my arm to pull me back with the intention of kissing me, but he accidentally jerked my shoulder out of place. So, I could just be all wet. But Herbert was devastated that he'd hurt me. Max doesn't seem to care that Katie is hurt."

"You think Max pulled Katie's arm out of place?" He shook his head hard. "That's preposterous. He's hateful and grouchy, but do you really think he'd hurt her?"

"Rennin, think of all the injuries she's had over the years. She's not clumsy. Do you really believe"—She began to count off on her fingers—"she fell down the stairs, her horse threw her, she ran into the door facing, the milk pail was so heavy it snapped her wrist, the cow kicked her, and on and on?"

"Cam, I'd kill him if it were true. I'd truly kill him."

"That's what I'm afraid of."

He ran his hand through his hair. "That's what Rebekah's afraid of. That's why she won't tell me what Katie said to her." Rennin kissed his sister's cheek. "Later, Cam. Say a prayer for me to control my temper."

As Rennin started to knock at Caitlin's door, he could hear Max growling at her. Rather than knock, he cracked the door and listened.

"Max, leave Rennin alone. He's the best man I know."

Max laughed. "The best! Seems you would reserve that title for your husband."

Caitlin seemed to have found some courage overnight. "Which husband, Max—the one who raped me so that I *had* to marry him or the one who's committing adultery with his neighbor's wife or maybe the one who likes to hit me when I disagree with him?"

"Shut up, you stupid tart," roared Max, "or I'll give you matching arms. Do you think I want to be tied down here to you, considering your *romantic interlude* before I met you?"

"Then, leave. I'll do nicely without you."

"Well, I won't do nicely without your money." Max's face took a sinister scowl. "Of course, you can't live forever. Maybe I'll see to that sooner than later, just like that little brat you birthed."

Caitlin dropped the plates she had in her hands. "You did! You killed my baby! I knew it!"

"Didn't really mean to, but the situation won't be the same for you. Watch your steps on those stairs, dear. One of your little falls might be fatal."

Rennin flung the door wide open. He flung the picnic basket into Max's face and grabbed him by his lapel, throwing his brother-in-law out the door. "You son-of-a-bitch! I will kill you! You've hurt my sister for the last time!"

Rennin belted Max in the gut and then uppercut him to the jaw. Max fought back viciously. A full-blown brawl ensued as those who lived at the mission poured into the streets.

Hearing the commotion, Rebekah sprang from the bed. Without looking, she knew what was happening. "Oh, God! Rennin!" She did not bother to dress, but flew out the door still in her nightgown.

Rennin's only advantage over Max was his youth, but Max was mean and angry. Soon it seemed that Max was getting the better of Rennin as a cut above Rennin's eye dripped blood and his eye swelled shut.

All at once, Caitlin stood on her porch with Max's pistol. "Max, stop it! Leave Rennin alone!"

Max stopped hitting Rennin who collapsed in the dirt. "You senseless whore!" shouted Max. "Do you want me to use that on you?"

"No, Max. I want you out of my life. I want a divorce. You can have Thelma Barker if Silas will let her go."

Max demanded, "Give me that gun, Caitlin."

"No. I'll give you the bullet. Now, pack your things and go," she reiterated.

Max stomped up the steps. As he passed Caitlin, he reached out, wrenched the gun from her hands and pushed her into the wall. "You and your *brother* have humiliated me. I will get even." He slapped Caitlin as hard as he could, causing her to stumble sideways.

The next thing Max felt was a milk bucket against his head. He dropped the gun, and Rebekah picked it up. "Max, I doubt Caitlin would've actually shot you, but you won't be the first lowlife vermin I've killed."

Max laughed loudly. "You're a perfect match for that little bastard out there on the ground. Or should I call him a perversion of nature?"

"Max, please be quiet," begged Caitlin.

"Why? You've disgraced me. Why should I keep your secret?"

"Max, please. I've kept yours."

Max laughed. "Guess again. Rennin!" He shouted. "You thought you killed your mother in childbirth. You were wrong." He pointed toward Caitlin. "Meet your dear, dear mommy."

Caitlin collapsed into a heap of tears. Rebekah pulled back the hammer. "Max, you really are a bastard." He grabbed her hands and tried to wrestle the gun from her, but she put up a fight. He twisted her arms down and squeezed her wrists. She tried to pull loose, jerking back and forth. The percussion from the shot reverberated. Max stood straight. The gun dropped to the wooden porch. Rebekah lay in a pool of blood.

Caitlin screamed, "Rebekah! No!"

Max ran like a rat with a cat on its heels. Before Rennin crawled to the porch, Max galloped away on the unsaddled dapple mare.

Caitlin shouted to the crowd, "Get Dr. Davies for heaven's sake!"

Camille raced down the road toward the doctor's office.

Rennin pulled Rebekah's head onto his lap. Caitlin touched his hair.

"Don't touch me, Katie. Don't ever touch me again. Lies. It's all been lies."

"Not all of it, baby," choked Caitlin. "I love you so much."

Rennin groaned, "It doesn't matter without Rebekah."

Rennin and Caitlin waited at the kitchen table without a word. It seemed the doctor would never exit Caitlin's room. Finally, Dr. Davies came downstairs, carrying a bucket and wearing a grave expression. Rennin sprang to his feet.

The doctor spoke kindly. "Sit down, Rennin. We have to talk."

Rennin sank into the chair. "Is she?"

"No. That young lady has a will to live, and barring infection, she will."

"Then, I don't understand," stammered Rennin.

Dr. Clayton Davies put the bucket outside the door, washed his hands with water from the pump, poured a cup of coffee, and sat beside Rennin. "Rennin, Rebekah was in the very early stage of pregnancy. The bullet tore through her womb. The only way to save Rebekah was to remove it. Otherwise, she would have bled to death. There will be no more children. I'm sorry. I'm going to check on her bleeding. If she's not bleeding, you may sit with her after I take care of you."

"I'm fine," protested Rennin.

"Bull!" snorted the doctor. "You got your butt kicked. You have a gaping gash across your eye, and you can't see through the swelling. You can hardly breathe because your ribs are either bruised or broken. Rennin, you look like hell and smell worse. Is that what you want Rebekah to see when she wakes up?"

"No. I'll let you stitch up my eye."

"I'll be down in a bit," said the doctor as he went back to Rebekah.

A single tear trickled down Rennin's cheek below his good eye.

Caitlin whispered, "Rennin, honey, you need a bath, too."

He shot her a look of contempt. Two tears slid down her cheeks. "Please, let me explain to you," she said with a catch in her voice.

"Explain what—that I'm a *bastard*?" Rennin said with coarse anger. "Please, do tell me. What should my last name be? Who's my father? I'd like to meet him."

"O'Rourke. Father," Caitlin said through clenched teeth.

"What?"

"You heard me."

"A perversion of nature, just like Max said." Rennin put his head on his hands. "Who else knows?"

"Thomas knows you're my son, but not who your father is."

"Of course. He was the doctor. Who else?"

"No one."

"Why did Max know?"

"I confided in him after Eric was murdered. I hoped it would remove his derision for me. It only made matters worse."

Softness spread across Rennin's face as he took Caitlin's hand. "You can tell me later. You've obviously endured years of hell, but I'm hurting right now. I need some time."

She kissed his fingers. "I love you so much, Rennin. I've always loved you."

He squeezed her hand. "I know. Would you get me some bath water? You're right. I do need a bath. After I see Rebekah, we can talk."

Washed, stitched, and bandaged, Rennin entered Caitlin's bedroom. Rebekah lay still and pale. He lifted her hand and choked a sob. "Darling, don't leave me."

He pulled the rocker beside the bed and held Rebekah's hand until he fell asleep. As he slept, he dreamed. In his dream, he heard a soothing voice and saw a glistening white dragon. The voice told him, "Rennin, now is the time to believe in magic. She is the magic that once was lost." He awoke when he heard a rustling.

"Rebekah!"

"No. It's just Caitlin. I brought you something to eat. Before you say that you aren't hungry, it's only broth, toast, and tea."

Caitlin put a tray in Rennin's lap and turned to leave. He stopped her. "Katie, wait. Talk to me. Tell me the truth—all of it."

She laughed nervously. "Do you need something stronger to drink? I do. I need it before I tell you. It's hard to talk about it."

"Get you a glass of brandy and come back. It's time, Katie. You can't protect me anymore."

She nodded and left the room. Caitlin returned with the bottle and two glasses. "You might change your mind before I'm finished." She sat on the floor beside his chair and poured a full glass. "Where do I begin?"

"At the beginning."

"As you wish," she said, taking a deep breath and finishing the glass of brandy. "Mother got very ill. Thomas said it was cancer. For a while she was so weak she couldn't get out of bed. For months she wasted away. Father was dejected. I often caught him drinking. He took to hugging me and crying. One night he was drunk. I tried to help him to bed. Before I knew what happened, he kissed me on the mouth. He called me 'Abby.' I know I'm the only one who looked like Mother. In his drunken state, he mistook me for her.

"I told him who I was. He said, 'I don't care. I need you, Abby.'

"I pushed him away and I remember saying, 'Father, it's Katie, not Mother.'

"He clutched my arm and glared at me. He snarled crossly, 'You've *never* refused me. You'll do as I say.'

"I was terrified. The look in his eyes was not Father at all. They were black, empty. The air around us was so cold. Rennin, I was sixteen. I didn't know what to do." Caitlin started to cry.

Rennin slid from the chair to the floor beside her. He put her head on his shoulder. "Shhh. Don't cry. I'll take care of you."

Caitlin heaved deeply and continued. "He pulled me into his and Mother's room. Mother was sleeping in the downstairs guestroom. She couldn't go up and down stairs. He was never rough, but gentle and loving. He continued to call me Abby.

"I lay awake all night feeling afraid and confused and dirty. When Father woke up the next morning, he sat up holding his head. When he turned around and saw me, he jumped from the bed, grabbed a quilt, and wrapped it around himself. In a daze, he said, 'Katie, what are you doing here?' I know I started to cry. Then, it was as if a lightning bolt hit him. He ran his fingers through his hair and started saying, 'Oh, God, no.' He crumpled to the floor in a heap. He repeated over and over, 'Katie, I'm sorry—so sorry.'

"After a while we talked. We promised each other that we would never tell anyone what had happened. Rennin, he never touched me again. Neither did he ever drink another drop of liquor, not even his usual after-dinner port.

"Time passed and Mother seemed to be better for a short time, but I wasn't. About six weeks later, I realized I was with child. I found Father in the barn and told him. I remember that he laid his head on old Dan, the mule, and cried. He whispered, 'My sin has found me.'

"I simply asked what I was supposed to do. He told me to let him think. A couple of weeks later, he informed me I was going to St. Louis to live with an older childless couple. I was to give the baby to them when it was born. He told everyone else I was going back East to a finishing school. He wanted me to receive some higher education because I would need to serve as hostess for the school after Mother passed on, which I did. I also had a tutor in St. Louis to teach me many things.

"Two months before I was due to deliver, an Indian rider came to the place I was staying with a note from Father. It said that Mother was dying and begging for me, but I was to come at night.

"I arrived about one o'clock in the morning. We had ridden hard and slept little to get here in a week—too hard for someone in my condition.

"I talked to Mother. Father had confessed everything to her. She told me not to give my baby away. She said that in most cases she would agree with Father, but her heart told her I would regret giving my baby away. I had barely stepped out Mother's door when I went into labor and my water broke. Father got Thomas for me. I stayed in the room with Mother, but Father forbade me to cry out in pain. He didn't want anyone else to know I was in the house. I was in labor until almost midnight the next night."

She took a deep breath and Rennin caressed her arm as she continued. "The cancer caused Mother's abdomen to swell. When you were born seven weeks early, Mother came up with a plan. She told Father to send me to Minneapolis for a few weeks until I had time to recover and to return to my normal size. She said to tell everyone that even through the cancer she had given Father a son. She died a few hours later. Father and I did exactly as we were told, and he sneaked me away before daybreak. Thomas went along as Mother's doctor. He really had no choice, considering the Hippocratic oath.

"I came home a month later. Father had found you a nursemaid for six months. Then, we started the strained goat's milk. I was never able to claim you openly as my own, but in my heart I have loved you as my son."

"I know you love me, Katie," said Rennin with a sympathetic stroke to her hair. "I'm sorry I was so angry before. Will you forgive me?"

"Me forgive you? Of course. Will you forgive me?"

"Yes. Katie, is that why Father was so harsh with me? I was a constant reminder to him."

"Maybe, but believe it or not, he did love you in his own strange way. He always tried to protect you. He became much harsher with me, too.

"Before a year was out, Father introduced me to Max. He had come as the new bookkeeper for the school. He was handsome and charming. I thought he loved me. One night we went for a buggy ride. Yes, I kissed Max in the moonlight and snuggled close to him, but he wanted more. He raped me, Rennin. I tried to stop seeing him, but Father thought we were a perfect match. Then, as fate would have it, I was pregnant again.

"When I told Father, he said, 'My sin against you has made you want a man.' I told him that I hadn't wanted Max, but that he had forced himself on me. Father said that it made little difference and that he would see to it that Max lived up to his responsibilities. So, Max married me. He hated me from day one. I now know for a certainty that he killed Eric and caused me to lose my other two babies. He stopped sleeping in my bed twenty years ago. Thelma Barker isn't his first indiscretion. On top of that, he has beaten me over and over. My broken wrist, my cracked collarbone, my torn hamstring—all his doing. I suppose I was being punished for my sin with Father. I deserved to be punished."

"Don't be ridiculous!" said Rennin. "It wasn't your sin. The only sin you've committed is the lying. Oh, Katie, why didn't you tell me the truth when I was old enough to understand? It would've hurt far less than this, and I would've taken care of Max long ago. You didn't have to endure all these years alone with your guilt and grief."

"Rebekah told me I wasn't alone any more. She's my daughter, Rennin. I've loved the thought of her forever."

"Tell me the truth, Katie. Did Rebekah know about me?"

"No, only about Max. She told me to tell you before the two-week visit was over, or she would. I was going to tell you about Max. She gave me the courage. No." She shook her head. "I probably would've taken the other secret to my grave, but I'm glad you know. I can only pray that you'll truly understand and forgive me. I just don't know how I'm going to face the others. They'll want to know who and why. I don't know what to say to them. I don't want to disparage Father to them. He's dead, Rennin. He can't defend himself."

He stroked Caitlin's hair again. "Tell them an upstanding, now deceased, older man took advantage of you, and you would just as soon keep his identity to yourself in order to protect his family. Tell them Mother and Father conspired to hide your shame, but you are, indeed, my mother and proud of it. That should put all of them in their place, Momma."

Caitlin turned a tear-stained face to Rennin. He smiled compassionately, but grimaced just as quickly, as the motion hurt his battered face. "I've always wanted to call somebody Momma, and you've always acted as if you were. I always thought it was because you had to take care of me. Now, I understand."

She hugged Rennin who squirmed and said, "Ouch! Watch the ribs."

Both laughed despite the injuries. Caitlin said, "I would've shot Max if you hadn't been in the way. I was afraid I'd miss and hit you."

"I swear if I ever see my"—He cleared his throat and growled through clenched teeth—"*Max* again, I'll kill him."

Caitlin shook her head. "He's gone. Leave it at that."

"I won't go looking for him, but if he comes here, he's dead—for you, for Rebekah, for my dead baby, and for my dead brother."

"Rennin, your anger frightens me."

"Momma, you sound like Rebekah."

"Listen to her. She's wise beyond her years."

Rennin eased back into the chair and took Rebekah's hand. "Momma, may I ask and tell you something?"

"Of course."

"Do you believe in magic—supernatural magic?"

"Have you ever wondered why your name is Rennin rather than Colin or some other name that begins with a C like all the rest of us?"

"I always thought I was named for Great-grandfather."

"Not exactly. Multi-great, yes." Caitlin picked up the worn leather-bound book entitled *Memoirs of Magic*. Rennin did not realize it had fallen from his coat pocket. "I read this book years ago against Father's wishes. He said it was 'poppycock and might put strange ideas into the head of the impressionable.' I never forgot how Rennin Drake O'Rourke's words stirred me. The red-haired Caitlin Fitzpatrick O'Rourke was Rennin's mother and Aidan was the love of her life. I insisted on giving you a magical name. You're named for two extraordinary men. Yes, Rennin, I believe in magic. You're living proof. Why do you ask?"

"When we were in New Orleans, this voodoo queen accosted Rebekah. She told her things the woman could not possibly know, yet she did. She also told Rebekah she would never bear another child. She was right, Momma. If she was right about this, she might be right about the other things she said. Some of them were terrifying."

"If bad things come your way, Rennin, deal with them head-on. Don't run away like I did. Stand together, and you can overcome anything. Rebekah believes in magic. Though she has never told me, I feel it. She *is* the magic that once was lost."

Rennin gasped. "Those are the exact words of the woman, and Cathy said them, too." He shivered.

"I've always heard confirmation comes in threes." She kissed him on the cheek. "Baby boy, I do love you. You've always been my magic. I'm going to bed. Try to rest. If you need me, come and get me."

"I love you, too, Katie—Momma. This will take some getting use to. Momma, one more thing: Do you believe that Draconis is real—that dragons are real?"

Caitlin nodded. "They've spoken to me many times. One in particular, Smoke, told me to fight back. I wish I had listened." She handed the book she had been holding to Rennin. "Why do you ask?"

"I was dreaming when you came in. A white dragon repeated that phrase."

"You get four affirmations. Perhaps, you *should* believe your wife is magic." She patted his shoulder and left silently.

For a long time, Rennin held Rebekah's hand with the book on his lap. He whispered, "The magic that once was lost." He looked down at the book on his lap. "Sweetheart, I'll read to you. If you can hear me, let me know when you wake up. If you don't remember what I read, I'll read it again later."

Rennin, Morgan, and Ryan traveled on, but they were delayed several times by inclement weather. Ryan worked like a Trojan to help Rennin get the wagon wheel unstuck from the mud one afternoon. That evening, he fell asleep from total exhaustion before supper. Rennin carried him into the tent and put him under his blanket.

By the fire as they ate, Rennin said to Morgan, "How could Andrew Riley be so cruel to that little boy? Morgan, he's a wonderful child. He's respectful, intelligent, creative, and mature for a six-year-old. I've a hard time believing he got all those traits from just his mother. That Ranson fellow couldn't have been all bad. Morgan, that man has to be Ryan's father. The sketch looks just like Ryan."

"Rennin, calm down," said Morgan. "When we get the information to the authorities, we'll see what we can discover."

"Oh, Morgan, what if we find some grandparents or other relatives who want the boy? They could be in England. Morgan, I simply won't let anyone take that little boy from us. He needs to be loved, and God knows that we can love him."

"Rennin, don't borrow trouble."

"I should've dug a third grave and let everyone think Ryan was killed, too."

"Daidí Rennin," said Ryan unexpectedly.

In surprise, Rennin said, "Ryan, we thought you were asleep."

"My stomach started growling."

"Come eat, baby," said Morgan

Ryan continued his question while he ate. "Daidí Rennin, do you think the man that killed Momma is my father? She said he was dead. Did she lie to me?"

"Ryan, you weren't supposed to hear what I said."

"I know. I didn't mean to listen. Are you angry?"

"No, I'm not angry."

"Then, tell me the truth." His lips turned down and he stared at the food on his plate.

Morgan took Ryan's hand. "Yes, baby, we do think the man you saw is your actual father. We think his name is Ranson—first or last, we don't know. We think that's how he knew your mother's name and that he was very angry she had married Andrew Riley."

"Ryan," continued Rennin, "we're going to try to discover the truth for sure, but we're afraid someone else might claim you and try to take you to live with them."

Ryan knitted his brows together. "I'm not a cat or a dog that someone can claim as a pet, or a cow or a horse that someone can claim as property. I'm a person and I can think and I have feelings." Ryan started to cry. "Daidí Rennin, Momma Morgan, don't let anyone take me away from you. I love you. Daidí Rennin, I want you to be my father."

Rennin pulled the little boy into his arms. "I will be, Ryan."

Morgan stroked Ryan's hair and he turned into her arms for a hug. "Sweetie," she said, "I promise no one will take you even if I have to turn them all into ugly toads."

Ryan laughed. "How could you do that?"

"Because I have magical powers."

"Don't tell anyone," said Ryan. "They might kill you."

"Then, we'll keep it a secret," said Morgan, and she touseled his hair.

The next day as they drove along, Ryan said, "Daidí Rennin, I have something to say to you."

"What is it?"

"I sort of lied to you."

"How?"

"When I said I didn't want to change my name because it was too much to remember, I lied."

"Do you want to change your name?"

"No. That wasn't the lie. The lie was the reason."

"You don't like the name O'Rourke?"

"'Tis not it either."

"Then, what is it?" Rennin arched his corrective eyebrow.

"When I came to the trading post last year, I ate cookies at your house."

"Uh-hum."

"Well, I saw Rachel. I decided I was going to marry her someday."

"You what?"

"Daidí Rennin, she's so pretty. Those big brown eyes could melt a heart of stone. I figured if I was an O'Rourke, I couldn't marry her, so I have to be a Riley or maybe it's a Ranson. Either way, I want to marry Rachel."

Rennin guffawed and Morgan bit her lip.

"What's so funny?" demanded Ryan.

"You're only six, and Rachel won't be six until Christmas Day."

"I didn't say I want to marry the minute we arrive. We have to be grown-ups. Daidí Rennin, I promise I'll never hit her. I'll treat her real special—the way you treat Momma Morgan." He dropped his head and his voice. "Oh, you probably don't want me to marry your daughter seeing as how I have a murderer's blood flowing through my veins. I understand."

"Ryan Riley!" said Rennin. "You're an outstanding young man. I'll make a deal with you. Come and ask me again in ten or twelve years. If you win Rachel's heart and she agrees, I'll give you my blessing; but you have to wait a minimum of ten years. Twelve would be better."

"It's a deal!" agreed Ryan, sticking his hand out. Rennin shook it.

Rennin looked at Morgan who held up her hand and laughed. "Don't look at me. Remember Cameron and Kieran. Cameron was eleven, Kieran but five. Speaking of Cameron, can't these horses go any faster? It's turning very cold, and I have a grandchild due in a couple of months."

"Three," said Rennin.

Rebekah groaned, "Did Ryan marry Rachel?"

"Honey!" Rennin clasped Rebekah's outstretched hand. "You're awake."

"Did you seriously think I'd leave you?"

"Well, now that my true identity's been revealed, I thought maybe you didn't want to be married to a perversion of nature."

"Rennin, you're still the best man I've ever known."

"You don't know everything."

"Yes, I do. I heard you and Caitlin talking. I just couldn't wake up. I know about the baby and that Marie LaVeau was right. I'm so sorry. I really wanted to give you more children."

"Shhh. I have you and the boys." He kissed her hand. "That's enough. Besides, Marie said we would have many children."

"Because of some form of sorrow."

"Maybe she was talking about the orphans. There would be sorrow associated with that."

"Not *personal* sorrow."

"Well, let's not worry about that now."

"All right. Rennin, I'm thirsty."

"I'll get you some cool water from the kitchen."

He lit a lantern from the one on the nightstand and left the bedroom. A minute or two later Rebekah heard him shout, "Oh, my God! Katie! Momma!"

26
Murderer in the Midst

Caitlin sailed into the kitchen. Rennin leaned over Max's body, his hand on a knife protruding from Max's chest. In horror she screamed and shouted, "Rennin! What have you done?"

"I didn't do it!" he shouted back. He turned around to see Caitlin. The front of her gown was covered in blood. "Momma, did you?" He pointed toward the body.

"What? No."

"Your gown."

She looked down. "Dear God! Not now! Rennin this is *not* what you think. It's my menstruation. I've started the change. I haven't bled in three months until now. Let me change clothes. Then, we'll decide what to do." She ran from the room.

Rennin put his hand in his hair and realized he had blood on him. Max was still warm. He had not been dead long. As Rennin sat on the floor, the door burst open. Doctor Davies, Herbert, and Sheriff Buckley all stood there. Caitlin walked back in on the scene.

For some time, nobody talked. Then, Ralph Buckley, the sheriff, said, "Rennin, what have you done?"

Rennin looked at their faces. "I didn't do it."

Dr. Davies examined the body. "He's still warm. The person who did this must be close by."

Ralph looked sternly at Rennin. "I'm afraid he's sitting here. Rennin, come along with me."

In shock, Rennin said, "What? No. I didn't do it. I came down to get Rebekah a glass of water, and he was lying there." He stood and backed away from the body.

The sheriff took Rennin's arm. Caitlin stepped in. "Ralph, you know Rennin doesn't lie. If he killed Max, he'd say he did."

"Caitlin, the man is dead in his own kitchen floor."

"It's not *his* kitchen. It's mine," Caitlin said, dipping her eyebrows and crossing her arms. "He was not welcome here."

"Yes, we know, Caitlin; and I don't blame you, but that doesn't matter." He held up one hand and pushed on the air. "He's dead. Rennin was sitting beside him, and he's covered in blood—not his own from what I can see. Now if Max was harming you and Rennin stepped in, that's another story."

"I told you what happened," said Rennin. "Momma was asleep. I was reading to Rebekah. She woke up and asked for water. I came to get it. I found Max right where you see him. Ralph, you've known me my whole life. I admitted to painting the clown's face on the school. I admitted deliberately mixing poison ivy in with the flowers I gave Frances Stephens. I admitted taking Mr. Stephens's horse so Black Cloud and I could break him. I own up to my wrong doing."

"Rennin, this is murder, not boyish mischief."

"But I didn't do it."

From upstairs, they heard Rebekah call Rennin. He started to her, but Ralph detained him. "No, boy. I have to arrest you."

Rennin protested, "Ralph, Rebekah needs me."

"Katie will care for her."

"Momma?"

Authoritatively, Caitlin said, "Ralph Buckley, don't you dare take Rennin out of this house."

"Caitlin, I'm the law."

"And I'm the killer."

All the men present echoed, "Katie?"

"That's right," she said. "Ralph, ask Rennin if I was covered in blood five minutes ago."

"It wasn't Max's blood. It was her own. Momma, be quiet."

"Shut up, Rennin." Caitlin stomped her foot. "Ralph, I came into the kitchen and found Max pilfering through the drawers. I told him to get out or I was going to get Rennin. He told me to go ahead so he could finish the job he started." Caitlin looked at Rennin with narrowed eyes and continued. "He started through the door to the dining room. I grabbed the knife from the butcher block and told him to stop. That's when he came toward me. I told him to stay back, but he just laughed and kept coming. I was really scared he was going to hurt me again and maybe Rennin and Rebekah. He reached out for me, and I plunged the knife into his heart. There." She raised her hands. "That's the long and short of it. You can take me to jail if you want, but I really thought he had come to keep his threat and kill me. I went to change clothes so I could drag him out of the house and get rid of him. I had no idea Rennin would come in before I could change clothes."

"Caitlin O'Rourke Schwartz, you're the worst liar I know," said Ralph. "How on Earth did you keep from telling everyone that Rennin was your son for twenty-five years?"

"I had to protect him."

"Just like now?"

"No, Ralph. Rennin didn't kill Max. I did."

"No, you didn't, Momma," said Rennin. "Neither did I. Ralph, if you think you have to take me to jail, I'll go; but do you think I'm going to run away? Don't you think I would have left by now? Do you think I would leave Rebekah lying upstairs in a bed? Even if I were guilty, do you believe that I would leave my wife and my two sons? Ralph, you know me. Have I ever run away from anything?"

"Besides my daughter?"

"Ralph, I didn't love her."

"I know, and for your information, she's very happy living in New York City. Very well, Rennin, I won't take you to jail at this moment. I'll investigate this homicide closely, but don't even consider leaving. Caitlin, tell the truth. Did you kill your husband?"

She looked at the ground. "No, Ralph, but neither did Rennin. I was asleep until Rennin started hollering for me. The blood on my gown is mine. I'm sure you understand, Doctor." Caitlin finished with a pleading look at Dr. Davies.

Gently he said, "Yes, Caitlin, I understand what it is."

"Ralph," said Rennin, "you might question the Barkers. After all, Max was having an affair with Thelma. Now, please excuse me. I have to take care of Rebekah." Rennin washed his face and hands and got a glass of water for his wife.

"Rennin," Dr. Davies called. "I'll go with you. I might as well check on Rebekah if she's awake."

As the two men climbed the stairs, Rennin asked, "Why were the three of you so quick to come running?"

"When I came out from examining Sally Whitfield, who has rheumatic fever, I saw Max's horse in the bushes. I figured he was up to no good, so I got Ralph and Herbert."

"I wish you had come ten minutes sooner. There would be no doubt that both Momma and I are telling the truth. How long do you figure Max has been dead?"

"He has probably been dead less than an hour, probably about half an hour would be a closer guess. He was still warm and rigormortis has not set in. Rennin, for what it's worth, I believe you. I'm sure Max had a number of enemies."

They entered the bedroom. Rebekah was in a panic. "Why didn't you come when I called? What's wrong?"

"Calm down, honey. Everything's fine," assured Rennin. "Max is dead."

Rebekah gasped. "What? Rennin, did you?"

Rennin cut her short. "No, honey. I found him lying in the middle of the kitchen floor, but Ralph was about to arrest me before Momma confessed."

"Caitlin killed Max?"

"No, she was trying to protect me."

"Ouch!"

"Sorry," said Dr. Davies as he pressed on her abdomen. "Rebekah, you're healing already, but don't plan to leave for at least four weeks."

"Four?"

"Yes, ma'am. Maybe six."

"That's fine," said Rennin. "It'll give me time to find out who killed Max."

"Well, Rennin," said the doctor, "I looked at the wound on Max. There's no way Caitlin could have inflicted it. The thrust broke Max's rib before the knife hit his heart. I don't know many women who would have the strength to do that.

Besides, Max could easily have overpowered her or most any woman. You're strong enough, and after this afternoon, you had motive. Moreover, you did threaten him. Of course, in your weakened condition, you wouldn't necessarily have been able to deliver the blow, but I would say someone who witnessed today's incident set up this whole scenario."

"That would be half the people who live around the mission."

"Count out the women. Who else had motive?"

"Silas Barker. Momma said that Thelma wasn't the first woman Max cheated with. I wonder if she knows who the other women were. Any jealous husband could be a suspect."

The doctor puckered his lips in thought. "A small man like me wouldn't have the strength either. Rennin, I don't know you, but you're Caitlin's son. Granted, you only discovered that today. I know it was a shock to you, but if Caitlin imparted any of the character traits I've seen in her over the last two years, you couldn't murder anyone in cold blood. Now, if for some reason it was self-defense or if you were protecting Caitlin, that's a different story."

"Dr. Davies," Rennin started.

The doctor held up his hand. "Please, call me Clayton."

"Clayton, I didn't kill him. That's not to say I couldn't or wouldn't under the right circumstances. I'm sorry to say I can't take credit for ridding the world of that vermin."

"All right, then, Rennin, I'll do what I can to help you. Ralph told you he would investigate carefully. We'll get to the bottom of it."

"Thank you, Clayton."

Rennin sat down in the rocking chair and took Rebekah's hand. "You're not to fret about this. I need you to get well and strong. Understood?"

She nodded as the grandfather clock with the dragon on its pendulum struck midnight. "I'm very tired."

"Go to sleep. I'll be right here when you wake up."

The doctor left to help transport the body to the undertaker.

Rennin started awake when Ralph Buckley cleared his throat. The very muscular sheriff said, "Rennin, I'm sorry, but I've been up all night questioning people. I started with Thelma Barker. Silas is, indeed, in Minneapolis. He stopped to get Ephraim Jones. They're together. Granny Morrison says she was on her porch watching to see if Max returned. She saw him enter and saw the shadow of two men fighting. Then, the light went out and all was quiet until you started hollering."

"Whoa!" said Rennin as he realized where this was headed. "Have you asked Caitlin if she knows any of the other women with whom Max had been involved?"

"Rosemary Jacobs and Pauline Simmons that she knows of. Paul Jacobs is an invalid and Moses Simmons is at most five-foot-eight. Caitlin is taller than he is. Doc says the person who killed Max had to be big and strong. Rennin, do you want to change your story? Did you have another fight with Max? Were you trying to protect Caitlin?"

"No, Ralph. I did *not* kill Max. I was reading to Rebekah until she woke up and asked for some water."

"He was here reading, Mr. Buckley." Rebekah vouched for Rennin.

With a crooked grin, Ralph said, "Forgive me, Rebekah, but you were asleep."

"Nonetheless, I heard him."

"There's no way you could have been able to discern the time you heard Rennin. It could've been before or after. The weapon is Caitlin's butcher knife. Rennin had Max's blood in his hair and on his face."

"Because I touched him and unconsciously ran my hand through my hair. Ralph, you can't seriously believe I killed Max." Rennin clenched his fist.

"Rennin, I'm sorry. Yes, I do. I'd like to hear you say it was self-defense or justifiable, but I think you killed your brother-in-law—stepfather—whatever you want to call him.

I've come to take you into custody. The judge will be here in a few weeks. Then, we'll have a trial. By then, maybe you can convince me that you had a good reason other than sheer hatred to kill Maxwell Schwartz. Now, come along peaceably. If you resist, Rennin, I'll shoot you." Ralph pulled his gun.

"Rennin," moaned Rebekah, trying to get out of bed,

Rennin took her hand. "Be still. Everything will be all right. Tell Katie to get me a lawyer—a good one because somebody really wants me to take the blame for this. You do what Dr. Davies tells you. I need you to get well. Gabriel and Michael need you to get well. I love you." He kissed her softly. "Be my magic, Rebekah. I need you to be my magic."

As Rennin and Ralph turned to leave, Caitlin blocked their way. "Ralph Buckley, how dare you? You know damned well Rennin is not a murderer."

"Caitlin, I have to go on the evidence, not my sentiment for the boy. But for your information, I *do* think Rennin killed Max. Maybe he was seeking some sense of justice for you or Rebekah. The fact remains that I believe he's guilty. Now, step aside unless you want to join him in a cell."

Rennin took Caitlin's face in his hands. "Momma, it's going to be all right. I need you to take care of Rebekah and hire me a good attorney."

Caitlin followed the men out the door and in a full run went to her sister's house. Rennin had not arrived at the jail before Herbert flew away on horseback. Caitlin returned to Rebekah's bedside. She stroked the young woman's hair. "Don't worry. I've sent Herbert to fetch Aksel Friedrich. He has never lost a case. He's the best lawyer I know. As a matter of fact, many times he has found the actual culprit while clearing his client."

"Caitlin, you sound so angry. Why?"

"Ralph Buckley actually believes Rennin's guilty. To think we were almost family once." She gusted a breath. "I wonder if he would have arrested Rennin if he were married to Allison."

"Rennin says Allison is a snob."

"He told you about her?"

"He said she was an old flame and if he had wanted to marry someone very sophisticated, he would have married her."

"He almost did. Good Heavens!" She put a hand to her cheek. "Allison had already made her wedding dress."

"What happened?"

"Well, as you know, we have a good many Indians who come here to learn to read, write, and speak English. We had a pretty young Indian girl come here. Her name was Misty Dawn. Rennin spent a lot of time with her. He taught her to ride with a saddle and to fish with a cane pole." Caitlin pulled the rocker closer to the bed and sat down.

"As you've probably surmised, Allison was jealous— perhaps, rightfully so. After all, Rennin was *her* fiancé. Allison began to butter up to Misty, sharing some of her older clothes and arranging her hair like a white girl. Rennin was surprised and pleased until Allison decided to help Misty curl her hair. Some time after they had been in the house, Misty burst out the door and down the street screaming at the top of her lungs. Allison had heated the irons so hot she had burned off almost all of Misty's hair. Allison stood in the doorway laughing and mocking, 'Oh, Misty, I'm so sorry. I didn't realize the irons were so hot.'"

Rebekah stared, wide-eyed, mesmerized by the story.

"Needless to say, Rennin was livid. After calming Misty from her hysterics and himself painstakingly cutting her hair so that the damaged hair was gone, he stormed to Allison's house. I could hear him all the way down the street."

She shook her head at the memory. "'Allison Buckley, you're a selfish, spoiled brat. You're cruel and mean, downright vicious. The wedding is off. I could never love a woman so cold and heartless and self-centered. I was hoping you'd develop some care and compassion for your fellow man. Obviously you're incapable of loving anyone but yourself.'" Caitlin squeezed her eyes closed with great regret and remorse written on her face.

"He came back into the house. I suppose I must have been staring at him. He said decisively, 'Katie, I will *not* marry her, not now—not ever. Frankly, she's a bitch!'

"I responded, 'Bravo! Baby, you can do better.' And, my sweet Rebekah, he did." She patted the younger woman's hand.

"How did Allison react to that rejection?" asked Rebekah.

"She cried and carried on for a few days. She came over here and apologized to Misty. Rennin refused to talk to her. She sat on the sofa and cried and cried on Max's shoulder. He comforted her. About six months later, she decided to go back East where the people were 'civilized.' She moved to New York and has been there since. I understand she married a wealthy industrialist."

"What happened to Misty Dawn?"

"We woke up one morning and she was gone. She left a note addressed to Rennin. The week between the incident and the day she left, the two of them were inseparable."

"Was he in love with her, Katie?"

"I think so," said Caitlin with a soft nod, "but he never said it. He tried to follow her, but came back alone. He was extremely melancholy for a while after she left. I never read his note. I don't even know what he did with it."

"It doesn't matter. I won't be jealous of something that happened almost ten years ago."

Caitlin took Rebekah's hand. "Rennin definitely did much better than Allison Buckley."

Rebekah closed her eyes for about ten minutes while Caitlin sat quietly. Suddenly her eyes popped open. "Caitlin!"

"What is it, honey?" said Caitlin, rising in alarm.

"Did Allison leave suddenly?"

"Yes, she just up and decided to leave. She announced her departure on Monday and left on Saturday."

"Just how much did Max comfort her?"

"Rebekah, what are you thinking?" She dropped the girl's hand.

"Help me sit up."

"Rebekah."

"Just in the bed, not a chair."

Caitlin helped Rebekah prop on several pillows. Rebekah grimaced and groaned. She took as deep a breath as she could. "Okay. Maybe we're looking the wrong way. Perhaps we should not be looking for a jealous husband, but an angry father."

"Go on."

"How did Ralph Buckley take the jilting?"

"He was furious. He threatened to kill Rennin for breaking Allison's heart. Rennin ignored it as posturing. Ralph calmed down until Allison left. Then, he was angry again for a while. But, like you said, that was almost ten years ago."

"How old was Rennin when Max slapped the stew out of him?"

"Eight," replied Caitlin in a huff.

"And you're still angry about someone mistreating your child almost twenty years later."

"Point made. Go on."

"Exactly how close did Max and Allison become after Rennin canceled the wedding?"

"I don't think they got *that* close." Caitlin shook her head. "Surely Max would've gloated about a pretty young girl finding him desirable."

"Unless he was afraid of the father." Rebekah arched her eyebrows. "For some reason I don't think Ralph would've approved."

"You're right. He watched Rennin like a hawk just in case he tried anything improper."

"I bet that nosy old Granny Morrison would remember if she ever saw them sneaking around together."

"Rebekah, don't be angry with Granny. She adores Rennin. If you're right, why did Ralph wait so long to kill Max?"

"He saw his opportunity to get even with Rennin at the same time. Caitlin, I bet Allison scurried away because she was pregnant."

"Oh, Rebekah, it's a reach, and how can we prove it?"

Rebekah threw her feet off the bed and yelped in pain.

"Rebekah, what are you doing?" scolded Caitlin as she tried to stop her daughter-in-law.

"I have to get out of this bed. I'm going to New York."

"What did you say?" growled Clayton Davies at the open door. "You get right back in that bed, young lady. Do you want to die and possibly leave two little boys as orphans? What if Rennin is convicted and hanged? Two little boys, who happen to be downstairs insisting to see their momma, would need you."

The doctor forced Rebekah back into bed. "Tomorrow you may walk around this room. In a week, maybe you will be able to go downstairs. We'll see. Now, why do you think you need to go to New York?"

"Clay," said Caitlin, "are you really serious about helping Rennin?"

Tenderly, Clayton replied, "You know I am, Katie." The doctor looked toward Rebekah, an expression of consternation on his face. "Oh, hell, Katie! I guess I can say my thoughts out loud now that Max is dead. I'd do anything for you or anybody you love. I love you, woman. I'm glad somebody killed that bastard you were married to. You deserve better. Maybe you don't think I'm better, but I love you. I would give you the sun, the moon, and the stars if they were mine to give."

Caitlin fell into the rocker and sobbed. Clayton fidgeted uncomfortably.

"For Pete's sake," said Rebekah, "take her in your arms, Clayton. Kiss her. It's obvious she feels the same for you."

"It is?" said Clayton. "She's crying."

"No, she's releasing her emotions."

Dr. Clayton Davies knelt beside the rocker and softly pushed Caitlin's hair from her face. "Is she right, Katie?"

Caitlin nodded. Clayton tipped Caitlin's chin up and gently kissed her. "I love you, Caitlin. I truly love you. I couldn't say anything as long as you were a married woman. It would've been wrong, but I've loved you from the moment I saw you. You brought those blueberry muffins to welcome me. It was barely daybreak, but you brought the light to my door. There you stood radiant as the sunrise. Your strawberry blond hair reflected every ray and your smile was genuine and from the heart.

"Then, just two days later, you were in my office with your jaw out of place. You said you didn't lean far enough out from the table when you bent down to get something you had dropped. I knew instantly you'd been punched. Three months later you had your fractured wrist and another ridiculous story. I've watched you live in hell for two years. I thought about killing Max myself just to make him stop hurting you." The man sighed.

"Caitlin, I'm a forty-five-year-old bachelor. I've never met a woman who so totally filled my heart and mind the way you do. I'm not much to look at, and I'm not a big muscular fellow. But, Caitlin, I'll love you. I'll never hurt you. I'll be good to you, if you'll give me the chance. I know you probably feel you have to wait now that you're a widow. I'll wait as long as you ask, if only I know I stand a chance."

"Oh, Clay," Caitlin choked through her tears. "I don't care about decorum. Max doesn't merit my honor. Clay nobody has ever loved me. I thought I didn't deserve to be loved. You don't know the whole story about Rennin. I've loved you for two years. I figured that feeling was something I'd hold on to and keep secreted in my heart. I never thought you'd love me or I'd have a chance to be loved."

"What about Rennin's father. Didn't *he* love you?"

"That's a long story. I'll tell you about it another time. Right now, I just want you to say it again. It's too good to be true."

"It's true. I love you, Caitlin. Now, how can I help your son?"

Rebekah told the good doctor her theory. Then she asked Caitlin a question. "Is there some way to get into the kitchen without Granny seeing?"

"The root cellar from the outside."

"Does Ralph know?"

"Of course."

Clayton got a gleam in his eyes. "You can't go anywhere, Rebekah, but a letter can. I'm going to write Allison with a story about her father needing her. I'll tell her to come see me first before she lets him know she's here. We'll get the truth out of her. Katie, how long 'til Rennin's lawyer arrives?

"At least two weeks."

"The judge is scheduled to come in five weeks. Maybe we can speed Allison home. Let me work on it. A telegraph might be better."

Further discussion was interrupted as two little boys barged into the room.

Dr. Davies left the Indian mission on horseback on his way to Prairie du Chien, Wisconsin, and the nearest telegraph. The message he sent Allison Buckley Newman made her pack a bag and leave the same day to return to the place where she had grown up. He returned harried and frazzled from the urgency of his trip and the deception he had perpetrated—something to which he was unaccustomed. He met Herbert Vance, Camille's husband, returning with the Honorable Aksel Friedrich, Attorney at Law.

The small man with thinning blond hair and wire-rimmed glasses was anything but small in reputation. His victory record was 51-0. He had never lost a case, even some in which he knew his client to be guilty. The three men rode directly to the one-cell jail, for there was little need for a jail in the community. The worst crimes the jail had seen were an occasional drunk or a brawl between teenage boys who were required to spend two or three nights together in jail as punishment for their behavior.

Gratefully, an exhausted Herbert went home to his wife when the doctor volunteered to escort Rennin's attorney. When they entered the jail, they found Ralph at his desk with his feet propped up and reading a newspaper. An unwashed, unshaven Rennin lay on his bunk reading his Bible that

Caitlin had brought him. Both were enjoying a plate of fried chicken, scalloped potatoes, glazed carrots, and blueberry cobbler.

The first words from Friedrich's mouth were, "Well, at least my falsely-accused client is not being fed bread and water. Who provided the food?"

"His sis...uh...mother," replied Ralph snidely as he stood. "And who are you?"

"Aksel Friedrich, Mr. O'Rourke's attorney. You will now leave us so that I may speak privately with my client."

Ralph laughed lightly and picked up his plate. "Come on, Doc. Let's wait outside."

Clayton responded, "Before I leave, I'd like to examine Rennin to be sure he hasn't contracted influenza in this draughty building. Please unlock the door, Ralph."

Ralph handed Clayton the key. "Lock it back when you're done. I'll be right outside."

Clayton opened the cell, and the two men joined Rennin, who shook the lawyer's hand. Then, he turned to Clayton. "Clayton, how is Rebekah?"

"When I left, she was fine. Katie is taking good care of her. I'll go directly to see her when I leave here and come back later with an update."

Rennin nodded. "Clayton, you know I'm not sick. What's afoot?"

"Rebekah came up with a hypothesis. She, Caitlin, and I decided not to say anything until your lawyer got here. I want to tell both of you at the same time what her theory is." Clayton told them the story. "The telegram I sent was to Allison. I concocted a story to get her back here, so we can question her. She sent a reply. She's on her way."

"Good," said Aksel. "Now, I want to hear your story, Rennin. Don't leave out a thing."

When Rennin finished his story, he saw that Clayton stared out the small barred window. "Rennin, you don't need me right now. Katie does." He turned from the window with damp cheeks. "I love your mother. She told me that nobody has ever loved her. I asked her what about your father, and

376

she said it was a long story she would tell me sometime. I hope you'll give me your approval. I want to make Katie forget all those horrible memories."

"Clayton, if my mother loves you, you have my approval. You seem to be a good man. She deserves to be loved."

He gave a deferential nod. "I'm going to Katie's now. I'll check on Rebekah. If she's up to it, I'll bring her to see you."

"That would be the greatest gift, Clayton. I miss her desperately."

"Let me go, too, Rennin," said Aksel. "I'm staying at your mother's as well. I'll be back. We have a defense to plan, but I need to unpack my books. Don't worry. I'll prove your innocence." Aksel and Rennin shook hands.

Rennin embraced Clayton. "Make her happy, Clayton. Treat her well. That's all I ask."

"That's my intention."

Three hours later, Clayton Davies returned pushing Rebekah in a bath wheelchair. He opened the door. "Rennin, surprise!"

Rennin flew to the bars as Clayton said, "She would've run over here if I'd let her. She's not quite ready for a foot race though. Open the door, Ralph."

"These are not visiting hours," said Ralph lazily.

Clayton grunted, "Ralph, do you want any of the roast beef, biscuits with gravy, corn, and rice Caitlin is preparing for dinner?"

"That sounds delicious."

"Then, open the damned door and go get your supper. We brought Rennin's."

Ralph looked perturbed. Clayton insisted. "Oh, lock her in with him. Let's go eat some of Caitlin's terrific cooking. I haven't had a decent meal in a week, and I'm looking forward to it."

Ralph reluctantly let Rebekah in and left with the doctor. Rennin fell to his knees beside the wheelchair and laid his head on Rebekah's chest. She stroked his unkempt hair and bearded face. She whispered, "Won't he let you bathe and shave?"

Rennin pulled back. "I'm sorry. I must smell dreadful. Aksel said he would see to it that I get a bath, but I still might not be allowed to have a razor. It could be a weapon, you know."

Rebekah snorted, "Ralph deserves to have his throat slit."

"Settle down. You haven't proven your theory yet."

"I know. Oh, Rennin, how can you be so calm?"

He held up a finger for Rebekah to wait. He opened his Bible and read Psalm 91:

> *1 He who dwells in the secret place of the Most High shall abide under the shadow of the Almighty.*
> *2 I will say of the Lord, "He is my refuge and my fortress; My God in Him will I trust."*
> *3 Surely He shall deliver you from the snare of the fowler and from the perilous pestilence.*
> *4 He shall cover you with His feathers, and under His wings you shall take refuge; His truth shall be your shield and buckler.*
> *5 You shall not be afraid of the terror by night nor of the arrow that flies by day,*
> *6 Nor of the pestilence that walks in darkness, nor of the destruction that lays waste at noonday.*
> *7 A thousand may fall at your side, and ten thousand at your right hand; but it shall not come near you.*
> *8 Only with your eyes shall you look and see the reward of the wicked.*
> *9 Because you have made the Lord who is my refuge, even the Most High, your dwelling place,*
> *10 No evil shall befall you, nor shall any plague come near your dwelling;*
> *11 For He shall give his angels charge over you to keep you in all your ways.*

12 In their hands, they shall bear you up lest you dash your foot against a stone.

13 You shall tread upon the lion and the cobra, the young lion and the serpent you shall trample under foot.

14 Because he has set his love upon Me, therefore, I will deliver him; I will set him high, because he has known My name.

15 He shall call upon me, and I will answer him; I will be with him in trouble; I will deliver him and honour him.

16 With long life I will satisfy him, and show him My salvation.

Rennin sighed and repeated, *"'For He shall give His angels charge over you...He shall call upon Me, and I will answer him; I will be with him in trouble; I will deliver him and honour him.'* Rebekah, I read that three or four times a day. I have to believe God's promise, or I would go insane. Plus, I have you and Momma and Cammy, Connie, and Cassie. Now I have Clayton and Aksel. Cassie has sent two letters from Milwaukee. She and Connie will be here next week. Faith, family, and friends—that's how I stay calm. Now, tell me about you and the boys."

"The boys are worried. They want to see their papa. I'm doing much better. Clay said I can start walking around the house, and by the time the judge gets here, I'll be able to move with ease. Rennin, I'm not worried about myself. I'll heal. Oh, but how I miss you! I don't care how badly you smell." She held her arms out to him. "I need to feel you close to me."

He lifted her from the chair and sat down on the bunk with her in his lap. After a moment, Rennin felt Rebekah's warm tears soaking into his shirt. He kissed her head. "Don't cry, my love. Everything will work out."

"I need to cry, Rennin. I need to scream. I need to mourn. My heart is breaking, and I can't even talk to you."

"Talk to me now while you're here. Let out whatever you need."

"I'm angry, Rennin. Max killed my baby, and he took away any chance of my ever having another. I'm glad he's dead, and I hope he's burning in Hell."

"I know. I'm angry, too; but I still have you, and we have Gabriel and Michael. I rejoice in the gifts I have."

"See why I need to talk to you? You make me think in a different way."

"As you do me. God knew what He was doing when He put us together."

"Yes, He did."

Rennin ran his hand along Rebekah's leg. "What is this?"

"Our book." She touched her neck. "I'm wearing my dragon. Caitlin said your father threw it away along with the book. He said it was tripe. She rescued them and sneaked into the attic to read the book. She used the necklace as a bookmark. She's glad we're reading this together. I thought we could read."

"It's a terrific idea." Rennin pulled the book from Rebekah's pocket. Pensively, he said, "When I was sixteen, I told Allison about this book and some of the stories about Draconis. She laughed at me and told me to put away my childish fantasy—to grow up and be a man."

"What about Misty Dawn?"

"What do you know about her?"

"That you were in love with her."

"Who told you that?"

"Caitlin told me what happened between her and Allison. I know you. I read between the lines."

Rennin opened to the very back of the book and slid his finger between the glued page and the binding. He removed a letter. "Yes, I was. Too much so."

He unfolded the letter and read:

My Dearest Rennin,

You are, perhaps, the single most wonderful person I have known or ever will know. I love you with all that is within me. Despite my love for you, I cannot and __will not__ live among your people. Too many of them are as cruel as Allison—a woman you thought to marry. For these reasons I am returning to my people—humiliated. Do not follow me. Let me go home where I belong. I am certain your God has a very special woman in your future. I wish you all the love and joy you deserve, and I shall forever treasure my memories of you.

Misty Dawn

"I followed her anyway and was summarily thrown out of her village. She died a year later from smallpox. She was exactly on the money. God had a very special woman in my future. Here you sit. Rebekah, I love you more than I ever dreamed I could love anyone—Misty Dawn included."

"I knew that, but I love to hear you say it."

He kissed his wife and looked at the letter unable to determine what to do with it. Rebekah caressed his hand and whispered, "Put it back where it was. It has been at home there quite a while."

He slid the note back into its hiding place and opened to the next chapter of Rennin and Morgan's life.

Rather than make camp with only half-a-day's journey left, Rennin drove the team forward. They were greeted by still, black quiet. He noiselessly put the horses in the stable, and without a sound, Morgan laid the sleeping Ryan in Cameron's old bed. "Welcome to your new home sweetheart," she whispered as she kissed his forehead.

Morgan met Rennin at the door to their room. Both fell onto the bed too weary even to undress. The next morning, they were rudely awakened as Rachel landed on their bed with a bounce and a squeal. She clapped her hands in delight. "You're home! You're home! What did you bring me?"

"Daidí doesn't even get a hug before he gives out presents?" Rennin asked, feigning a wounded look on his face.

Rachel sprang across the bed and into his waiting arms. "Daidí!"

"Hello, my sweet girl. I missed you."

Then, Rachel hugged Morgan. Rennin and Morgan looked toward their door to see two boys peeking around the door facing.

"Come on, you two," said Rennin, gesturing with his hand. Duncan and Colin piled onto the bed and gave hugs all around. Rennin smirked. "I suppose you two want presents, too."

"Do you have any, Daidí?" asked Colin.

"I might. Have you had breakfast?"

"No, sir. We saw your horses in the stable and came over here. We told Uncle Geoffrey though," Duncan assured.

"Well, take Momma downstairs and get breakfast started. I'll bring your first present when I come to breakfast."

"First," said Rachel joyously. "That means there's more than one."

The children pulled Morgan up, and she followed happily. She sent Rachel to gather some eggs, Duncan to get a slab of bacon from the smokehouse, and Colin to fetch some apples and butter from the root cellar. While they were out, she quickly mixed a batch of biscuits. Colin returned first and helped Morgan core a dozen apples and filled the center with honey, cinnamon, and butter. They placed them on the hearth to cook inside the Dutch oven. Morgan slid the biscuits into the recessed oven. She sliced the bacon that Duncan brought in and fried it to a golden crisp. Rachel returned with a dozen eggs, which Morgan fried over easy in the drippings from the bacon.

Just as Morgan took the biscuits and apples out, a washed and shaved Rennin peeked around the corner. "Is everyone ready for the first gift?"

The children chorused, "Yes!"

Rennin ducked back behind the door and knelt in front of Ryan. "'Tis going to be just fine. Don't be nervous. You in truth are a gift." He took Ryan's hand. "Let's go."

Rennin and Ryan walked into the dining room. Rennin announced, "Everyone, this is Ryan Riley. He has come to live with us."

Rachel put her hands on her hips. "Daidí, I've heard of bringing home stray dogs and cats, but not stray boys."

"Rachel Leanne O'Rourke!" Rennin scolded.

Two silent tears coursed down Ryan's cheeks. "It's all right, Daidí Rennin. I told you they wouldn't want me."

"What do you mean, 'they'?" asked Duncan. "I'm glad to have another brother. You can help me bring in firewood and feed the horses when it's my turn. We shall be great friends. Rachel is still just a selfish baby."

"I'm not selfish!" declared Rachel. "I didn't mean he couldn't stay. I just think it's strange that Daidí brought us a boy as a present. People are not presents."

"You're right, Rachel," said Rennin, "but children are gifts from God. Ryan's momma and papa are in Heaven. God led Ryan to Momma and me so we could have another gift. We want to share him with all of you. We will be his family now."

"Why didn't you say that in the first place?" said Rachel saucily. "Sure, he can be family, but he's not a present. Presents come in boxes or paper. If you put a person in a box, he's dead." Rachel clamped her hand over her mouth and spoke between her fingers. "Oops. I'm sorry. Ryan, I didn't mean to hurt your feelings. Momma tells me I need to be tackful. I don't know what little bitty nails have to do with not hurting people's feelings, but I'll try."

Ryan laughed. "Not tackful, *tactful*. It means saying even mean things in a nice way. I forgive you."

"I wasn't trying to be mean. I'm truly sorry about your momma and papa. I bet we can be friends yet."

"I hope so," said Ryan, and his violet-blue eyes twinkled.

"Welcome to the family," said Colin.

As they sat down to eat, Colin continued, "'Tis peculiar."

"What, son?" asked Rennin.

"Well, there's a fellow at the inn whose last name is Riley—Ranson Riley. He's a new trapper."

Rennin looked warily at Morgan. She asked, "What does he look like, Colin?"

"An awful lot like Ryan, only bigger. Blond hair and blue eyes. He's pretty young—a little older than Donnie."

"Does he have a beard?"

"No, ma'am. He said he did once, but it itched him; so, he cut it off."

"Have you talked much to him?" Morgan asked.

"Some. He comes in about once month. He usually stays two or three days and goes out again. He seems nice, but very sad. He said he once had a wife and a baby boy, but they died. He said his son died when he was a baby, and his wife died at Christmas."

Ryan jumped up and ran to Rennin. "Daidí Rennin, it's him! I know it's him! Don't let him hurt me!"

Rennin looked at Morgan as he enveloped Ryan in an embrace. "Do you think 'tis possible? I haven't even sent the sketch or Ryan's story to the authorities yet."

"'Tis possible, Rennin. If he came this direction, he could easily have found Mom's. Rennin, before you go off on a tangent, think. This man has a story, too. I'm beginning to feel there's more to this than we conjectured. Ryan, how long had your momma and Andrew been married?"

"Three years."

"I have a funny feeling, Rennin," said Morgan.

Accompanied by the doctor, Ralph opened the door. "Visiting hours are up. Rennin, I brought you a tub. You need a bath, but I won't give you a razor. Live with the beard."

Clayton took a reluctant Rebekah back to Caitlin's, and Rennin finally took a bath.

27

Justice

The judge arrived a week ahead of schedule, which infuriated Aksel Friedrich. "We have to stall the procedure until Allison gets here. Our whole case could depend on what she tells us."

The investigation by Aksel and Clayton Davies had revealed heavy boot prints in the root cellar, but Aksel felt the prosecution could argue that they belonged to Max himself. They also found a piece of flannel caught on the latch of the cellar door. It did not match any shirt of Max or Rennin, but they could not get into Ralph's house to find a corresponding garment.

The judge was inclined to go ahead with the trial. Aksel brought a motion before the judge to postpone the trial because a crucial witness for the defense had yet to arrive in town. In the spirit of fairness, the judge granted the defense another week for the witness to arrive, but no longer. The trial would begin in one week with or without the witness.

A week passed, and Allison still had not arrived. The trial began with the prosecution presenting its case first. Aksel did insist that Rennin be allowed to shave before the trial so that he would look presentable. The prosecutor opened by saying that he would prove Rennin O'Rourke had the motive, the means, and the opportunity to kill his stepfather, Maxwell Schwartz. He said that he would prove Mr. O'Rourke's hatred for the victim had grown so deep that he thrust a large, very sharp knife through the victim's rib and into his heart, ending his life abruptly.

First, the prosecutor called Ralph Buckley, who testified that Rennin and Max had had a terrible fight the morning before Max was killed. He testified that he had heard Rennin threaten to kill Max. He also said that the fact Max beat Rennin's mother and the fact that Max had revealed the truth that Caitlin was, indeed, Rennin's mother was something unknown to the defendant before the day Max was killed. He testified to the fact that Max had been the instrument by which Rennin's wife had been shot and rendered unable to have children and the death of Rennin's unborn child. He continued by describing the scene he had witnessed in Caitlin's kitchen with Rennin sitting beside Max's body and his hands and face covered in Max's blood. Throughout his testimony, Ralph changed position repeatedly, causing the chair to squeak over and over.

Aksel Friedrich asked Ralph, "Sheriff Buckley, did you see Rennin O'Rourke stab the victim?"

"No, but..."

Aksel cut his answer short. "That will be enough. Just out of curiosity, did anyone else in the house have blood on him?"

At the question Rennin almost came out of his chair, but Aksel shot him a look, settling him instantly.

"Yes, Caitlin Schwartz."

"Did Rennin confess to killing Maxwell Schwartz?"

"No."

"Did anyone?"

"Yes, Caitlin."

"Yet, you arrested Rennin." He scratched his head as if confused.

"Caitlin was lying. She later admitted it."

"Sheriff, how long have you known Rennin?"

"His whole life."

"Have you ever known him to be violent?"

"He has a temper."

"That was not the question."

"No, not without good reason."

"What kind of relationship has he had with Caitlin?"

"They've always been close, but..."

Aksel raised his hand. "They are close. Would you say he loves her?"

"Yes."

"Enough to protect her?"

"Yes."

Aksel pulled a handkerchief from his inside coat pocket and dabbed at sweat above his lip.

"Is it true that you tried to persuade Rennin to say he killed Max trying to protect his mother?"

"I asked if that is what happened. Then, the crime would have been justifiable."

Aksel paced in front of the witness stand a moment. "It's true, then, that the fight between Rennin and Max was a result of Rennin's trying to protect Caitlin."

"Yes."

"Did Rennin try to protect Caitlin for bearing the blame for this crime by taking the blame himself?"

"No." Ralph shifted position and grunted.

"So," Aksel rested his hands on the bar of the witness stand. "A young man bent on protecting his mother all day did *not* jump in and confess to murder to protect her."

"No." Ralph fidgeted.

Aksel turned to walk back to his table. "No more ques"—He turned back with his index finger raised—"Oh, one further thing. Did you investigate whether anyone besides Rennin, Caitlin, and Rebekah was in the house that night?"

"No one was seen entering the house."

"How many times have you pulled pranksters from Caitlin's root cellar?"

"Several."

"Is it possible that someone could have gone through the root cellar undetected?"

"It's possible."

"Your Honor, at this time, I'd like to introduce defense exhibit A." He handed the piece of flannel recovered from the latch to Ralph. "Do you know anyone who owns a shirt that matches this?"

Ralph shrugged. "Counselor, I do not know all the clothes owned in this town."

"Thank you. Nothing more. Reserve the right to recall."

Next, much against his will, Clayton Davies took the stand. The prosecutor asked the doctor to describe what the killer must have looked like.

"From the wound inflicted, the killer would have had to have been a large, or at least very muscular, man," Clayton replied.

"Does Mr. O'Rourke fit the profile?"

"He could, but..."

"It is a yes or no question, Doctor. Does he fit the profile?"

Aksel stood up. "Objection, Your Honor. The doctor has already answered the question."

The judge nodded. "Sustained. Move on, Mr. Page."

Todd Page continued. "Dr. Davies, it has been suggested that Caitlin Schwartz might have killed her husband. In your professional opinion, is that possible?"

"No, she would not have had the strength to break the ribs covering Max's heart, especially since her arm was in a sling—an injury I treated."

"What about the blood on her gown? Whose was it?"

"Her own—of a female nature."

"I see. Thank you. Your witness, counselor," Page said in a sugary tone.

Aksel did not stand at first, but questioned the doctor from his seat. "Dr. Davies, on the day of the murder, did you have the opportunity to examine Rennin?"

"Yes, I wrapped his bruised ribs and put seven stitches in his right eyebrow."

"Would these injuries have impaired Rennin in anyway?

"His vision would definitely have been impaired because his eye was swollen almost shut, and his bruised ribs would have made movement difficult and painful."

"Painful enough to reduce the amount of force he could have produced?"

"Most definitely."

"Dr. Davies, did you help me search the Schwartz home?"
"Yes."

"Will you please tell the court what we discovered?"

Clayton looked at the jury as he spoke. "The first thing we discovered was heavy boot prints in the root cellar. We followed the prints to the outside entrance. On the entrance latch was a piece of flannel."

"Was there anything unusual about the flannel?"

"There was dried blood on it."

Aksel stood and walked to the display area and picked up the material he had introduced earlier. "Is this the flannel?"

"Yes."

"Please continue to tell what we did next."

"We searched through Max's and Rennin's clothes and found no matching garments from which the flannel could have come."

"Thank you, Doctor. No further questions. Reserve the right to recall."

Todd Page interjected, "Redirect! Dr. Davies, was there any way of telling how long the flannel had been there?"

"Well," replied the doctor, "it wasn't dusty like the rest of the cellar. I would say it had not been there long."

"No more questions," Page said hastily and tugged on his own lapel. The prosecutor then called Caitlin to the stand. He introduced her as a hostile witness.

"Mrs. Schwartz, when you first entered your kitchen after your husband was killed, what did you see?"

"Rennin was kneeling beside Max."

"What was your first thought?"

Caitlin sat silently until the judge said, "Mrs. Schwartz, please answer the question."

"I thought Rennin had killed Max."

"Thank you. Counselor." Page smirked toward Aksel.

Aksel stood and walked to the rail that separated the witness chair from the rest of the courtroom. He leaned on the rail. "Caitlin, what did you ask Rennin?"

"I asked him what he had done."

"What was his response?"

"He said, 'I didn't do it.' Then, he asked me if I had done it when he saw the blood on my gown."

"Caitlin, is Rennin in the habit of lying to you?"

"No. He's more likely to be brutally honest."

"Thank you, Caitlin. That's all." Aksel patted her hand.

Last, the prosecution called Janelle "Granny" Morrison. She testified that she had seen Max go into the house and a light come on. Then, she saw two men fighting. The light went out and came back on a few minutes later.

Aksel approached the elderly woman with a smile. "Granny, why does everyone call you that?"

"I have played Grandma to all the children. They come to my house and eat cookies or pie. They do chores for me. In short, they keep me company."

"Even Rennin?"

"Especially Rennin. He's such a dear. He was the first one to call me Granny."

"That's sweet. Granny, you said you saw two men fighting. Could you tell who they were?"

"No, but one of them had to be Max."

"You saw the shadows through the curtains. Correct?"

"Yes."

"How did they appear? Were they fat or thin, tall or short?"

"Both were big men. One appeared to be taller, not much, but maybe three inches."

"You've known both Rennin and Max for a long time. Which one was taller?"

"They were right about the same."

"So, you saw two men, one of which was obviously taller that the other, fighting. Could you tell which was which?"

"Well, the taller one was Max. I saw him go in. When the light came on, I saw the shorter one was already there, as if he were waiting."

"You're sure the man was shorter than Max?"

"Oh, yes."

"Thank you, Granny."

The prosecution rested his case and glared at Aksel. The judge called an end to the proceedings for the day and told the defense to be ready the next morning.

Aksel went to speak to his opponent. "Are you sure you want to continue this charade? You're losing, Page. One—we have shown that some one else *was* in the house. Two—we have shown that Rennin himself thought his mother killed Max. Three—Dr. Davies has said that although Rennin is normally strong enough to have inflicted the fatal wound, that day, with all his bruising, he probably could not have done it. Last—Granny saw two men, who were not the same size, fighting. Get the point? Rennin's innocent. My witness still hasn't arrived, but I don't need her."

Page smirked. "One—that piece of flannel could have been there a long time. Two—Caitlin thought Rennin did it. He only questioned her *after* she questioned him in an attempt to throw her off track. Three—Rennin is young enough to overcome his wounds. Four—Rennin's ribs were bruised. Perhaps he was slightly stooped, giving the appearance of being shorter. Five—Rennin hated Max and threatened to kill him. Last—you have a semi-conscious wife who heard her husband's voice at some point. I think I'll play it out. Good night."

The next morning, Aksel was irritable. "It's a good thing Ralph isn't really dying. Allison would never get here to say good-bye."

Clayton joined Aksel, Caitlin, and Rebekah for breakfast. "I'll stay in my office today to wait for her. I have a feeling she'll be here."

Aksel took Rebekah's hand. "Are you ready?"

"I'll do anything for Rennin."

"Then, let's go. Clay, if Allison gets here, bring her immediately to me. Find out what you can as quickly as you can. If she will be no help, rudely keep your hat on for a while. If she can help, take it off before you enter the courtroom."

It appeared that every citizen within twenty miles of the mission turned out to watch the court proceedings. Even in the early morning, the smell from so many bodies packed together was stifling.

When they arrived, Rebekah and Rennin spent a moment holding on to each other's hands before the judge came into the room and announced court in session.

"Mr. Friedrich, are you ready?"

"I have my first witness here. As of this morning, my out-of-town witness still has not arrived. She had to come a great distance, Your Honor."

"Very well, call your first witness."

Aksel removed his suitcoat and hung it on the back of his chair. "I call Rebekah O'Rourke."

Rebekah wore the pink dress with the white pinafore she had worn for her wedding. Aksel suggested the frock to give her the appearance of innocence and vulnerability. "If Page attacks you, the jury will feel sorry for you," he had commented.

"Rebekah," Aksel started, "how long have you and Rennin been married?"

"Almost four years."

"In those four years, have you ever known Rennin to lie?"

"Objection!" shouted Page. "Whether Rennin O'Rourke lies to his wife has no bearing on this case."

"Goes to character, Your Honor," argued Aksel. "For the most part, Rebekah is a character witness. She did not even see the body."

"I'll allow it," said the judge. "Answer the question, Mrs. O'Rourke."

"No. Rennin is honest to a fault sometimes."

"There's something you and Rennin have been doing since before you got married that is very special to you. Tell us about it."

"One of Rennin's ancestors wrote his memoirs. Rennin often reads to me, especially when I need to relax."

"Did Rennin read to you the night Max was killed?"

"Yes. His voice reading to me is what brought me around."

"Rebekah, the prosecutor will try to make you say that you have no idea exactly when or how long Rennin read to you, but did it seem like a short time or a long time?"

"I'm not sure exactly how long, but I know I heard him and Caitlin talking. Then, her voice left. I felt Rennin hold my hand and talk to me. Then, he started reading. I awoke completely, and we talked a little. Then, I told him I was thirsty. He went to get me some water. He took a lantern with him. He barely had time to get downstairs before I heard him calling for Caitlin very loudly."

"Thank you, Rebekah."

Todd Page stood. "Mrs. O'Rourke, is your husband protective of you?"

"Of course."

"How protective is he?"

"I don't understand."

"Has he ever hit anyone or, God forbid, killed anyone because of you?"

"Objection!" shouted Aksel.

Page waved his hand. "I withdraw the question."

"Mrs. O'Rourke, what did you ask your husband when he told you Max was dead?"

"I asked if he had done it because I thought he might have had another fight."

"Thank you."

Aksel stood. "Redirect. Rebekah, what did Rennin tell you?"

"That he had not killed Max."

"Has Rennin ever lied to you?"

"No."

"No further questions."

The door to the courtroom opened. A bareheaded doctor and a stunning blonde woman entered.

Aksel said, "I call Allison Buckley Newman."

Ralph exclaimed, "What?"

Page objected. "This woman was not even in town at the time."

The judge said, "He can call his witness."

The scent of rose water wafted down the aisle as Allison walked forward. She took the stand and gave her father a cold, hard stare. She, then, looked at Rennin almost as hard, but a sad smile flickered across her lips.

Aksel approached Allison carefully. "Mrs. Newman, forgive us for getting you here under false pretenses, but we feared you wouldn't come if you knew the true reason we needed to speak to you. I'm trying to determine if there's any other man in town who is big enough and strong enough to have inflicted a fatal wound like the one Maxwell Schwartz received, a man who also had a motive to want Max dead. I realize this might be difficult for you because you might have to reveal details about your life you would've preferred to have kept secret."

"Just get it over, Mr. Friedrich, so I can return to New York where I belong. I never wanted to see this awful little town again, and I plan to leave as soon as possible."

"Very well. Mrs. Newman, were you at one time engaged to Rennin O'Rourke?"

"I was."

"Why did you not marry?"

"Rennin had no sense of humor. He sided with an Indian over me." She rubbed wrinkles from her skirt.

"Which one of you broke the engagement?"

"He did. He was terribly upset about my little prank."

"Were you distraught about the turn of events?"

"You could say that."

"Who comforted you in your time of distress?"

"Mostly, Maxwell Schwartz."

"Was this a short-term thing on the day Rennin broke the engagement or long-term?"

"Mr. Friedrich, cut to the heart of the matter. You want to know if I had a relationship with Max. Yes, I had a tryst with him. I lost my virginity with Max and tried desperately to become pregnant within in the first few weeks so I could blame Rennin."

Murmuring among the spectators about the brazenness with which the witness spoke brought gavel banging and the judge demanding order. "Quiet in my courtroom. Mr. Friedrich, get this over with fast. Mrs. Newman, do you think you could tone down your answers?"

"Why, Your Honor? I thought this was about truth." She looked at the man, petulance written on her face.

"Yes, well, so it is, but for the sensitive ears, please use less crude phrasing."

"Yes, sir."

"Now continue."

"The strategy did not succeed. However, I did become"—
She paused—"*with child* several months later. Max was
furious. He insisted I get rid of the baby. He came late one
night to take me to a woman that would take care of the
situation. My father discovered us. My father sent me away to
New York to have the same procedure done there. He told
Max that someday he would get what was coming to him.
Father blamed Rennin as much as he blamed Max because he
thought Rennin's rejection of me had disturbed my emotions
and judgment."

"So, your father was very angry, so angry that he
threatened Max?" asked Friedrich.

"Yes."

"Does your father hold grudges?"

"Normally, I don't know, but he said he would get even
with both Rennin and Max some day."

"Thank you, Allison. Again, I apologize for putting you
through this. I would not have called you at all if a man's life
were not at stake."

The prosecutor asked his questions. "Allison, do you think
Rennin O'Rourke capable of murder?"

"Absolutely not in cold blood. The man's sense of justice
is too great."

"Even if the victim had abused Rennin's mother and
rendered his wife unable to bear children?"

"Rennin's what?"

"Oh, yes, you didn't hear Max's announcement." He
bumped the heel of his hand against the witness stand.
"Caitlin is Rennin's mother. Now, do you think Rennin
capable of murder?"

She removed the hatpin from her hat and twisted the hat in
her hands for several minutes. The judge finally prompted her,
"Mrs. Newman, I understand the shock of the statement, but
please answer the question.

"If he had killed Max in a fight, yes, but still, I don't believe he would kill anyone in cold blood. I certainly do not believe Rennin would lie in wait for Max."

"Allison, Mr. Friedrich has tried to paint a very bleak picture of your father. Do you believe him capable of murder?"

"I don't know, Mr. Page. Do you consider sending your only child to a doctor in New York to abort your grandchild murder?"

Page clenched his jaw and fists simultaneously. "Your Honor, I request that Mrs. Newman's last four answers be stricken from the record."

"Can't do it, Mr. Page. Defense counsel did not object."

"Of course not—the answers played right into his hands."

"Get over it, Mr. Page. Mr. Friedrich, call your next witness."

Aksel said, "I recall Dr. Clayton Davies."

Clayton took the stand again. Aksel asked, "Dr. Davies, how tall was Max Schwartz?"

"Six-six, the same as Rennin."

"How tall is Ralph Buckley?"

"Six-three."

"The difference in inches is how much?"

"Three."

"Thank you."

Page sourly grunted, "No questions."

Aksel continued his crusade when he recalled Ralph Buckley to the stand. "Mr. Buckley, how much do you hate Rennin O'Rourke?"

"I don't hate Rennin."

"No?"

"No, I'm disappointed in Rennin."

"Why?"

"The arrogant little bastard should have married Allison. He broke her heart and drove her to do unforgivable things."

"With Maxwell Schwartz?"

"Yes."

"How much did you hate Max?"

"I loathed Max. Max was lower than a snake's belly. Not only did he ruin my little girl, but he also beat Caitlin and humiliated her by his philandering. He deserved to die for what he did to those two women and the others he used. I would gladly have married Caitlin after my wife died, and I would never have laid a hand on her. She is one of the finest women I know."

"Ralph, did you kill Max and set up Rennin to take the fall?"

"You can never prove that. Yes, I had as much motive as Rennin, but opportunity and means?"

"You know how to get into Caitlin's root cellar."

"Yes."

"Is this from your shirt?" Aksel held up the piece of flannel.

"Counselor, I do not own a shirt like that."

"Have you ever?"

"I do not recall owning a shirt like that."

Aksel realized he was getting nowhere. Ralph would not confess. "I have no further questions of this witness."

"No questions," said Page.

"The defense rests," said Aksel.

Rennin whispered, "You don't want me to tell my story?"

"No need," assured Aksel. "All we need is reasonable doubt. They have to acquit."

"But Max's killer is still loose."

"Is your heart broken?"

"No, but if Ralph tried to set me up…"

"Rennin, let it go. I can get him off as easily as you. All I have to do is bring you to the stand."

"You wouldn't!"

"I would. When they acquit you, you can confess if you like; but they can't touch you. It's called double jeopardy."

"Aksel, do you think I'm guilty?"

"It doesn't matter what I think."

"It does to me."

"In that case—no. I think Ralph did it, but we won't be able to prove it. You know he probably burned that shirt. Let it go."

The judge ordered a lunch recess. After lunch, the two attorneys presented their closing statements with Page going first.

"Gentlemen, the defense would have you believe that our sheriff, our *sheriff*, killed Maxwell Schwartz. Sirs, look at the evidence." Page loosened his tie. Even with the windows open, the air was oppressive. "The accused was found beside the body with the victim's blood on him. Even his wife and mother thought he killed Max. I can't blame him if he did it. Max was a lowlife. For years he beat and was unfaithful to the defendant's mother—a mother he thought was his sister until Max informed him that he was illegitimate on the same day he was killed. Then, Max caused the defendant's wife to sustain such an injury that she will never be able to give Mr. O'Rourke more children. For goodness sake, the woman he loves, the mother of his sons, almost died because of Max even as his unborn child did die. I understand Mr. O'Rourke's hatred and desire to see Max punished, but that does *not* give him the right to take matters into his own hands. As law-abiding citizens, you must find Rennin O'Rourke guilty."

"Hogwash!" said Aksel when his turn came. "Gentlemen, I don't know for certain that Ralph Buckley killed anyone, but I do believe in Rennin's innocence. Scripturally, our thoughts can be called murder, but not legally. Legally, if you have reasonable doubt, you must acquit Rennin. Do you have reasonable doubt? Let's look back at the evidence. We found a piece of bloodstained flannel, which belonged to neither Rennin nor Max, on the root cellar door: Obviously, someone else was in the house—*someone*, who could have killed Max. Granny Morrison saw two men fighting, one slightly taller than the other. Rennin and Max were the same height. Could it have been Ralph? He as much as admitted that it could. He fits the killer's profile as much as Rennin does. Reasonable doubt. Gentlemen, you have more than reasonable doubt; you have extreme doubt. You must acquit Rennin. Your acquittal doesn't condemn Ralph. It merely sets Rennin free. Please open your eyes. See the doubt. Set this young husband and father free. Acquit Rennin."

No one left the courtroom when the twelve men of the jury exited. The jury deliberated for about an hour before they came back with a verdict. Rennin stood, and for the first time he was nervous. He held his breath as the foreman read the verdict. "We find the defendant, Rennin O'Rourke, not guilty."

Rennin hugged Aksel. Then, he grabbed Rebekah and kissed her. Caitlin touched his arm. With one arm still around Rebekah, he pulled Caitlin in with the other and kissed her head. He clutched hands over Caitlin's head with his other sisters. "Ladies, take me home. I want to hug my boys, sleep in a warm comfortable bed, and make love to my wife. Sorry, Momma, but that's the way it is."

"It's all right, Rennin. Let's go. You and Rebekah can disappear while I make a very special dinner to celebrate."

The first thing Rennin did was to hug Gabriel and Michael. Then, Sarah took the boys to Caitlin's to help prepare the celebration dinner. Husband and wife found themselves alone.

Rennin sat on the bed with a heavy sigh. Rebekah sat beside him. "What's wrong? You should be happy."

Rennin pulled her close and buried his face in her loosened hair. She felt his body shake with silent sobs as he finally released his fears and worries. Rebekah comforted him. "Rennin, it's over. You're free, and you're here with me."

"Rebekah, I was so afraid of leaving you and the boys. I knew I was innocent, and I knew God would sustain me, but I was afraid of leaving you alone. The thought of not being here to be your husband and Gabriel and Michael's father broke my heart. Now, I have to ask how you can want to be with me. How can you want to be with someone born from incest? How?"

"Rennin, stop spouting such nonsense!" Rebekah shouted angrily. "God chose to create you. He does not make mistakes. You, yourself, told me that babies are always,

always, gifts from God. Do you want me to ask how you could possibly want to be with a woman who had already known the feel of three men—a woman who is now incomplete with a missing womb?"

"Rebekah, you know how much I love you. Please, don't say those things."

"And," she said, stroking his cheek and softening her tone, "I love you just as much. You are a terrific human being with a purpose that only God can show you. Now, accept who you are. Thank God for fearfully and wonderfully making you. Make love to me."

"What would I do without you?"

"Spout gibberish."

Rennin found himself laughing. He took Rebekah in his arms.

Rennin and Rebekah came to dinner with renewed spirits. Cassandra and Constance stayed another night. Camille and Herbert congratulated the freed man. Aksel and Clayton grinned from ear to ear. Aksel whispered to Rennin, "Page isn't going to arrest Ralph. He can't prove his case."

Rennin shrugged. "I'd just like to understand why he hated me so. Allison and I could never have been happy."

Even as Rennin spoke, he heard a soft knock at the door. "I'll get it."

He opened the door to find Allison. "Hello, Rennin. Caitlin invited me. I hope you don't mind. I really am happy for you. I knew you wouldn't have waited for Max."

"No, Allison, I don't mind. Thank you. I'm sorry about what you endured, and to have had your baby ripped from you. I am *so* sorry."

"Who said I aborted the baby? I said Father sent me away and expected me to do so. That's why our relationship has practically ceased. I only came back here because I thought the old goat was dying. No, Rennin, I have an eight-year-old daughter and a husband, who loves me despite my past. He and I have a five-year-old son together. I'm glad you and I didn't marry. Your Rebekah is gorgeous, and she seems to be loving and compassionate—just right for you. I just want you to know that I'm not the selfish, spoiled bitch you knew all those years ago. I'm still outspoken and headstrong, but I've learned what it's like to be truly hurt and to be truly loved and to truly love. I cannot apologize to Misty Dawn for the jealous, childish prank I pulled on her. I've done the only thing I could do to honor her—I named my daughter Misty Dawn Newman. However, I *can* apologize to you."

"Apology gladly accepted, Allison. I only wish you the best."

"Then, may I celebrate with you?"

"I would be honored." Rennin hugged Allison as Rebekah watched uncomfortably from across the room. He took her hand. "Let me introduce you to Rebekah. She knows about real pain, too. I think you'll like her."

Rennin led Allison across the room and formally introduced the two women. Allison noticed that she and Rebekah wore the same dress design only Rebekah's was emerald green and hers was royal blue. Rebekah said softly, "It's nice to meet you."

Allison kissed Rebekah on the cheek. "No, it's my pleasure." As she spoke, she glimpsed the jade dragon necklace and touched it reverently. "You share Rennin's fantasies. You *are* perfect for him."

The celebration lasted well into the night. Clayton cornered Rennin as many of the partygoers trickled out. "Rennin, I wanted to talk to you before you got ready to go back to California. Caitlin and I want to get married, and we want to do so right away. Moreover, we want to come to Puma Pass with you."

"Clayton, you have my blessing if I may be your best man, and I'd love for you to go with us. I need to get to know my mother rather than my sister."

"I'd be honored for you to be my best man."

Rennin began to laugh. "What will I call you?"

"Clayton or Clay. I want to be to be you friend, Rennin, not your father. Maybe Caitlin and I still have time, though, to give you one little brother."

"Or another sister." Rennin grinned.

"Whichever." Clayton laughed. "Rennin, I won't mind if Gabriel and Michael call me 'Grandpa,' especially if they call Caitlin 'Grandma.' You've decided to call her 'Mother.'"

"Nope—'Momma.' 'Mother' belongs to a dead lady I never knew. Nonetheless, I'd be glad for you to serve as a grandfather for my boys, very glad indeed."

Rebekah slid her hand into Rennin's. "What's the big conspiracy between the two of you?"

"No conspiracy—plans for the future," replied Rennin. "Clayton and Momma are getting married and coming with us."

"That's wonderful! When's the wedding, and when are we going home?"

"Tomorrow," said Clayton, "before Cassie and Connie leave and while the judge is still in town."

"We're leaving Monday morning," said Rennin. "There's one small catch. We'll have to go back by boat, or we'll be trapped in the mountains for the winter, thanks to our delay."

"I don't care," sighed Rebekah. "I just want to go home. I miss Keturah and Bart, Running Bear and Sleeping Fawn, Cathy and Olaf, Thomas and Candy, and Chen Li. Good grief! I miss Patty."

"Who's Patty?" asked Clayton.

"Rennin, you'd better warn them."

"I will. Hey, if Clay and Momma spend a week or so in New Orleans, it could be their honeymoon."

"Does that mean you approve?" Caitlin queried as she came to them. Rennin realized the party was finally over.

"Yes, Momma, I heartily approve. You deserve some happiness, and Clayton's a good man."

Clayton put his arm around Caitlin, and she laid her head on his shoulder. "You don't know how wonderful it feels to me to have someone truly love me, Rennin. I've waited a lifetime."

"Your wait is over," said Clayton. He kissed Caitlin. "Now, I'll say 'good night.' Tomorrow at three is the wedding."

Rennin and Rebekah slept late. Caitlin had insisted on keeping her grandchildren with her and giving Sarah a night to spend with her cousins. She asked only that Rennin and Rebekah come for lunch and help her get ready for her wedding to Clayton.

Rennin glanced at the clock on the nightstand when he awoke. It was already nine o'clock. Rebekah moaned as she snuggled closer to Rennin. "Good morning, handsome. What time is it?"

"A little after nine."

"We should get up and get ready for Caitlin's wedding."

"In a bit. We have plenty of time."

"What do you want to do?"

"Exactly what I'm doing."

"Is that all?"

"Actually, yes. I want to feel you beside me. It has been too long since I've had this comfort."

"Would you like to read to me? I'm dying to find out if Ranson is the one Rennin would like to have arrested."

"We can do that."

Being the impatient man he was, Rennin decided he had to confront Ranson Riley. Morgan insisted on going with him to help him maintain his self-control.

Ranson was having breakfast in the inn's dining room. Rennin and Morgan stared at him. Ryan was the spitting image of the man. Rennin clenched his fists. Morgan laid a calming hand on his arm. Clasping hands, they walked to the table where Anna had just served Ranson a plate of ham, eggs, and biscuits. Rennin sat down across from Ranson. "Ranson Riley?"

"Yes."

"I'm Rennin O'Rourke."

Ranson held out his hand. The scars around Ranson's wrists reminded Rennin of the shackles he himself had once worn. "Mr. O'Rourke, I'm so glad to meet you. I've heard much about you. You're practically legendary."

Rennin reluctantly shook the man's hand and continued as he sat across from him. "Mr. Riley, I need to talk to you about Andrew and Tabitha Riley."

Ranson almost choked on the bite of ham he had just taken. "What would you like to know?"

"Why did you murder them?"

"Murder? I don't understand. I didn't murder my cousin and *my* wife."

"There was a witness, a small boy named Ryan."

"Ryan!" Ranson practically shouted. "Andrew told me Ryan was dead. Where is he? Where's my son?"

Rennin shifted repeatedly in his seat. Morgan slipped her arms around him while she stood behind him. "Mr. Riley, I'm Morgan O'Rourke. My husband and I took refuge in the cabin owned by the Rileys on the way home from Boston. In the middle of a thunderstorm, we were surprised by a precious little boy who had been living alone for nine months. His name is Ryan. Mr. Riley, he told us a story about a man who came and killed his father and mother. He said the man shot his father, and he said something about the man lying on top of his mother. Were you that man? Would you like to tell us what happened?"

Ranson dropped his face into his hands. "Oh, God! That poor baby. He doesn't know how to interpret what he saw. Yes, I killed Andrew, but I would never have harmed Tabitha—never. I loved her too much."

Morgan sat between the two men. She continued to hold Rennin's hand because she knew he was ready to strangle Ranson. "Mr. Riley, tell us your version."

Rennin hissed, "If you didn't murder them, for God's sake, why didn't you at least bury them?"

"I couldn't. I wasn't able." Ranson looked at Morgan. "Dear, Lord! How you resemble Tabitha! Where would you like me to start?"

"The beginning would be nice," said Morgan.

Ranson glanced at Rennin who still held an icy stare. "I'm listening," said Rennin, barely moving his lips.

"Very well," said Ranson. "Eight years ago, both my cousin, Andrew, and I vied for the attention of one Tabitha McVeigh. Andrew was wealthy, while I was just a laborer. As a matter of fact, I worked *for* Andrew. Well, Andrew decided to come to Virginia and start his own tobacco plantation. He asked me to come as his foreman and gave Tabitha an ultimatum. She had to choose.

"Providentially, Tabitha chose me. We were married and sailed for America with Andrew. By the time we arrived Tabitha was expecting. We were very excited, but Andrew continued to sulk." He sat back a bit.

"I suppose I should interject here that during my youth, I came into some trouble with the law. That's when I went to work for Andrew. He promised the magistrate that he would put me to work and keep me out of trouble. All went well until we met Tabitha. Being five years older, very educated, and a successful entrepreneur, Andrew thought he had the better chance of winning her.

"Well, the outcome wasn't what Andrew had expected. We started the plantation. Andrew purchased some Africans as slaves. That way, he wouldn't have to pay them. I argued with Andrew about owning slaves. I told him to make them indentured servants, but he didn't want to pay the money for more workers.

"Tabitha gave birth to Ryan. Life seemed to be going well, but two weeks after Ryan's birth, three of Andrew's slaves came up missing. When they were caught, they said that I had helped them escape, which was totally untrue.

"Needless to say, Andrew was livid, and he wouldn't listen to me. He said I'd been trouble from the time he bailed me out of prison and that the time had come for me to pay for my transgressions. The next thing I knew, I was in shackles and headed for a British prison. I didn't even get to see Tabitha and Ryan."

Ranson rubbed his wrists at the memory. "It appears the shackles were too tight," said Rennin, feeling a small bit of kinship with Ranson.

"I almost lost my left arm, but that wasn't the worst thing. While I was in prison, I received a letter and a divorce decree from Tabitha. Andrew had told her I had received twenty-five years in prison when it was only five, although I didn't know that part until I talked to her. I received the letter only days before my release. I didn't realize it had been written two years earlier.

"The day I was released, I signed on as an indentured servant myself. I was hoping to get back in time to stop Tabitha from doing something she would regret. I confess I ran away from my obligation as a servant and went straight to Andrew's plantation. No one was there, not even the servants. The place was overgrown and deserted. Andrew must've known I'd come for my family.

"For months I searched for them until I found them at that cabin. Andrew wouldn't even let me inside. He told me Ryan had been puny and had died within his first year and that he and Tabitha were married. He told me she never wanted to see me again and had no desire to be associated with a criminal.

"I had to hear her say those words, so I hid until she came outside. It took two days before anyone came out except Andrew. I never saw a child. When Tabitha went to do her wash, I came out of hiding. It was the day after Christmas. She stared at me as if I were a ghost; but all of a sudden, she dropped her basket and flew into my arms. I asked her why she hadn't waited for me. That's when she told me about the twenty-five years. I couldn't help myself. I kissed her and held her." He pressed the heels of his hands to his eyes.

"When Andrew saw us, he flew into a rage. He started calling Tabitha all manner of names. He called her a whore. Before either of us could respond, Andrew shot her. She slumped into my arms, and I slid her to the ground. When I stood, Andrew had reloaded and shot me. That's when I shot back. Andrew's shot caught my shoulder. Mine was fatal.

"After that, I think I did lie over Tabitha. I remember begging her to get up, but she was dead. I didn't bury them because I was losing blood and it dawned on me I'd be blamed. Like a coward, I ran away. I went to an Indian village I'd been to before. They nursed me back to health. If I'd known Ryan was there, I would *not* have left him alone."

Rennin folded his arms across his chest. Ranson observed, "Mr. O'Rourke, you don't seem to believe me, but I suppose I didn't expect you to."

Morgan said softly, "Rennin, talk to Ryan again. Ask him specific questions. See if he has any memories similar to Mr. Riley's. Rennin, remember Kiandria. Mr. Riley deserves the benefit of a doubt. You haven't sent the information to the authorities yet. Let's be fair. Remember, too, Miranda and how confused a child's memories can be."

Ranson perked up. "Ryan's here in Mom's Trading Post? I want to see him."

"You will not go near him," said Rennin. "He's terrified you might hurt him." Rennin stood. "Don't leave, or I'll hunt you down myself." Rennin slammed the door, leaving Morgan there.

"I'm not going anywhere this time without my son," said Ranson. "I swear I told you the truth."

Morgan patted Ranson's shoulder as she started to leave. "For what it's worth, I believe you. Part of Rennin's problem is that he's very fond of Ryan. Ryan calls him Daidí Rennin. Do you understand?"

"Mrs. O'Rourke, I loved my son before he was born, and I loved his mother. If I thought the best thing for him would be to disappear and let your husband be his father, I'd do it; but I am *not* the monster he thinks I am."

"Mr. Riley, until Ryan overheard Rennin and me talking about the fact that the man he saw was probably his father, he thought you were dead, too. Don't do anything rash. Rennin's a fair man."

Rennin and Morgan found Ryan cowering beneath the bed where he had slept. "Ryan, come out," said Rennin. "We need to talk."

"Is he going to hurt me?"

"No, Ryan. I don't think he'd ever hurt you. I want to ask you some more questions about the day your folks were killed."

Still trembling, Ryan crawled from beneath the bed. Rennin sat on the bed with Ryan on his lap. "Ryan, when Ranson first saw your momma, did he seem angry with her?"

Ryan shook his head. "I thought maybe they were friends. When I sneaked into the smokehouse, they were hugging each other."

"What exactly did you hear him say?"

"He asked Momma why she didn't wait for him and she told him she would have been old and alone in twenty-five years. He said it was five, and she said Andrew had told her twenty-five. Then, he seemed angry. Next, he called her a horse."

"Are you sure that *Ranson* called your momma a 'horse'?"

"I think so, but it might have been Papa."

"Ryan, who shot your mother?"

Ryan's eyes grew big. "Papa. I think he was trying to shoot the man though, because he tried again and hit him."

"Is that when the man shot your papa?"

"Yes, sir. Then, he lay down on top of Momma for a long time. When he stood up, he pulled the locket from Momma's neck, took the horse from the barn, and left."

Rennin heaved a great sigh. "Ryan, do you understand the difference between murder and self-defense?"

The little boy looked perplexed. "I'll explain," said Rennin. "Murder is when you plan to kill someone or if you get very angry and kill someone. Self-defense is when you kill someone who is trying to kill you. You do it to protect yourself. Does that make sense?"

"I think so."

"All right. Think about what happened. Did Ranson commit murder, or was it self-defense?"

"I suppose it was self-defense. Papa did try to kill him first, but what about Momma?"

"Ryan, your momma was already dead when Ranson lay over her. He was trying to get her to not be dead. He didn't want her dead." He stroked the child's hair. "Ryan, your life has been turned topsy-turvy so many times in six years, and I'm afraid it's going to be turned upside-down again. Ranson Riley *is* your father. He loved your mother very much, and he loves you. He thought you were dead because that's what Andrew told him. Your mother told you he was dead because he was in prison for what she thought would be a very long time. She thought you and she would never see him again. He was only in prison because Andrew made up a story that sent him to jail so that Andrew could have your mother for himself."

Ryan laid his head on Rennin's chest. "Does this mean that you don't want me to live with you anymore?"

"No. I'll always want you, but your father wants you, too."

"But I don't know him." Big blue eyes blinked back tears.

Rennin caressed the boy's hair. "You didn't know me either a couple of months ago."

"Will you still let me marry Rachel someday?"

"Talk to me in ten or twelve years."

"If I do marry Rachel, may I call you 'Daidí Rennin'?"

"You may."

"What do I call you now?"

"How about 'Uncle Rennin' and 'Aunt Morgan'?"

"I suppose." He huffed a breath. "When do I have to leave?"

"Not right away. Let's start by meeting your father."

Ranson had not moved from the table where he had eaten breakfast. As a matter of fact, his half-eaten food still sat in front of him, congealed and dry. Rennin and Morgan came into the room, each holding one of Ryan's hands. Ranson stood. He did not know what to say or do. Unwanted tears escaped his eyes, and he blurted, "Ryan! You look just like me."

To her outer side, Morgan used her hand to motion for Ranson to come down to Ryan's level. Ranson walked slowly to where the trio stood and knelt in front of his son. "Hello, Ryan. I'm Ranson Riley. I'm your father." Inadvertently, Ranson reached out and traced a deep scar on Ryan's chin. "What happened here? Did you fall out of a tree like I did?" Ranson showed Ryan a scar on his chin.

"No, sir. I got that when Papa slapped me and I fell back and hit the woodpile."

"He did what?"

Rennin interrupted, "Ranson, apparently Andrew beat Ryan."

"Ranson?" said Riley. "Does that mean you believe me?"

"It does. Otherwise, I wouldn't have brought Ryan to meet you."

"Thank you, Rennin." He turned back to Ryan. "Did Daidí Rennin explain why I wasn't around?"

"Yes, sir. He said Papa lied about you and had you put in prison. Papa told me that I was like you—no good."

Ranson touched the boy's face again. "Oh, Ryan, you're *very* good. You're the greatest joy I've ever experienced. Do you understand what happened at your cabin?"

"Yes, sir. Uncle Rennin explained that, too. I can't call him 'Daidí Rennin' until I grow up and marry Rachel."

"So, you want to marry Rennin's little girl. She's very pretty."

"What should I call *you*?"

"Whatever you like."

"Pa, no, I think Daidí. That's what Uncle Rennin's children call him. He says it makes him feel special. I want my father to be special. Where are we going to live?"

"I don't know yet. We can figure it out together. Just being with you is very special."

"You're a trapper. You'll be gone a lot. Are you sure you want a little boy to worry about?"

Ranson looked at the floor. Ryan noticed the man was crying. He let go of Rennin's and Morgan's hands and put both hands on Ranson's cheeks. "You don't have to cry. Do you want a hug? Uncle Rennin says hugs make everything better."

Ranson looked at his little mirror image. "I'd love a hug." Ryan put his arms around Ranson's neck and the lost father squeezed the found son tightly. "Ryan, I've always wanted you. I've been lost without you. I'll tell you what. If Rennin will let me, I'll build us a cabin here. When I'm out trapping, you can stay with Uncle Rennin and Aunt Morgan. Having you back makes up for all the injustice I've been dealt. Rennin, will it be all right if I stay here—with Ryan, I mean?"

"Ranson, I think, for some reason, that we'll all be better for having you here." Rennin felt a kinship once more for the young man who was at least ten years his junior. "Ranson, within a week, it'll probably be too cold to trap. We're well stocked here for the winter. You and Ryan are welcome to stay with us—not in a room here at the inn, but in our house. Ryan already has a room. You can share it or use the one next to it. As we have breaks in the weather, we'll build you a place of your own."

"Are you sure?" Ranson asked.

"Daidí, please?" said Ryan.

"If that's what you want, Ryan. Which room do you want me to use?"

"Will you sleep with me for now? I'm kind of scared, and it'll make it easier to get to know you."

"All right. Rennin, I accept your offer."

Rennin offered Ranson his hand. Ranson took it eagerly.

Rennin closed the book. "It's getting late. Let's go. We have a wedding to attend. Rebekah, tomorrow after church, I have to make a visit. There is a little injustice that I need to settle."

"Rennin, maybe you should let it go."

"I can't. I have to ask him face to face. I have to understand why."

"I'll go with you."

"No. I have to go alone."

The wedding was a simple affair, but Caitlin was radiant. The years seemed to have melted from her face. Clayton bounced off the walls in his exuberance.

After a splendid early dinner, the guests left the bride and groom to themselves. Cassandra and Constance left for home. Rennin and Rebekah packed trunks to leave early Monday morning.

The next day after Sunday lunch with Camille, Rennin walked to the end of town to see Ralph. Gloomily, Ralph let him in. Allison sat on the sofa reading a book. Her bags sat by the door, packed to leave the next day. She came to the door and greeted Rennin warmly as the two old friends embraced. Ralph staggered back to the living room.

Ominously Rennin said, "Allison, I need to speak to your father—alone."

Allison eyed her father carefully and whispered, "Rennin, he's in an ill temper. Be careful. I think, perhaps, he has gone mad. Talk to me five minutes on the porch before you talk to him."

They stepped onto the porch. "Rennin, when Mother died, his mental state deteriorated. Then, he seemed better, but he talked about Caitlin all the time and how, if he could get Max out of the way, he could make Caitlin happy. Over time, he stopped that rhetoric; but when he said he would've married her on the witness stand, I knew the thoughts were still lurking in his mind.

"When you broke our engagement, Father sank deeper into his despair. He really went wild when he found out about Max and me.

"Now, Rennin, I'm truly frightened. I want to go home to Slade, Misty, and Isaac. Since yesterday when Caitlin married Dr. Davies, he has mumbled and grumbled to himself about how she could throw him over for 'that weakling, little doctor.'"

Rennin hugged Allison. "Do you think he would harm Momma or Clayton or himself?"

"I do. I know in my heart he killed Max and intended for you to die for it. What can I do?"

"Go see Aksel at the inn. He went over there last night after the wedding. Go now. The judge is still in town. He's at the inn, too. Perhaps, you can have your father committed to an asylum, maybe one in New York so you can visit him. Get Aksel and Judge Walker over here while I talk to Ralph. Everything will work out. Trust me."

Allison walked down the street as fast as decorum would allow. Rennin chuckled to himself despite the seriousness of the situation as he thought how Rebekah would have run without thought of proper etiquette. He went back inside and found Ralph nursing his fourth glass of scotch.

"Ralph, I'd like to talk to you before I leave."

"What do you want?" snapped Ralph. "Haven't you caused my family enough grief? I tried to take care of you, but you're a chronic ailment, like lumbago. You keep coming back."

"What do you mean that you tried to take care of me?"

"You're an arrogant little snot. You always have been. I gave Boudreaux five hundred dollars to make sure you never made it to California. I should've known the little weasel would fail. If you want something done right, do it yourself."

Rennin noticed that Ralph had his revolver in his lap. He tried to remain calm. "Ralph, would you like to explain that?"

"Oh, hell! It didn't work either, but it did get rid of that bastard, Max."

"Ralph, did you kill Max?"

"Of course, I did. Somebody had to watch out for Caitlin. Max hurt her a lot. He broke her arm and her wrist and her jaw. He killed her babies. He would have killed my ray of sunshine, too."

"Ralph, why didn't you just shoot him and say he was trying to resist arrest? You could have gotten away with that."

"Ah, but that wouldn't have taken care of you, boy."

Rennin sat down in the chair across from Ralph. Ralph pointed his gun at Rennin. "Look at you. How arrogant and narcissistic you are! You aren't even afraid of me now."

Rennin shook his head. "I'm concerned about you, Ralph. Talk to me a while. Exactly why do you hate me so much?"

"You hurt my baby. She allowed Max to ruin her because of you. Then, I made her kill her baby. Now, she hates me. Don't you understand? You're the cause of all our problems. I always knew. I saw Caitlin ride into town as big as a barrel. Then, there you were. She would never have had anything to do with that Max, if someone else hadn't already ruined her. You're living proof. I'd just like to know who it was, so I can take care of him too."

"He's been taken care of, Ralph. He's dead, but please go on."

"Good. I'm glad he got his just reward, but you. If you'd married Allison, she'd never have had anything to with Max. That man was despicable. Now, if that ninny wife of yours hadn't got in the way, Davies never would've poured out his heart to Caitlin. She was finally free to be mine."

"Ralph, how long have you been obsessed with Caitlin?"

"Am I obsessed?" He waved the gun in a circle near his temple. "Perhaps. Long before Donna died. Donna was very sick, and Caitlin was so kind and helpful. Even when she had bruises on her body, she would come and help with Donna and talk to me and comfort me. Donna was sick such a long time. She was in excruciating pain. Thomas said she might live another month, but the cancer would cause her tremendous suffering. I only did what she asked. I stopped her pain. I loved her enough to let her go."

"Ralph, are you saying you killed Donna?"

"No! I ended my wife's suffering. You don't know what it's like to see someone you love suffer like that. I did what she asked. I ended her suffering just like I ended Caitlin's suffering by removing that human parasite."

"What now, Ralph?"

"I don't know. Caitlin wasn't grateful. She and Clayton Davies. Ugh! I can't let that happen." Ralph looked at Rennin with soulless eyes. "I'll be gentle. She won't feel any pain, but I've decided that if I can't have her, no one will; and I'll go with her."

Allison came through the door with Aksel, Judge Walker, and Clayton. "Rennin, we heard most of what Father said."

"Ali, girl, my you have a houseful of suitors," Ralph acknowledged the roomful of men.

"Yes, Father." Allison knelt beside the chair where her father sat and cautiously took the gun from his hand. "There's one more I want you to meet. He's the best of all, but you'll have to come to New York with me to meet him."

Ralph looked confused. "Better than Rennin?"

"Yes, Father, better than even Rennin."

"It's not that Max Schwartz, is it? I don't like him."

"Ugh!" said Allison to placate her father. "Max is disgusting. No, his name is Slade Newman. He's wealthy and well-educated. You'll like him."

"Very well, I'll meet him."

"Good. You'll need to put on a jacket." Allison motioned for Clayton and Aksel who slipped a straight jacket onto Ralph. As soothingly as she could, Allison said in a strained voice, "Father, you need to rest a while before we leave."

While Clayton and Aksel took Ralph to his room to rest, Allison turned to Rennin, "I'm going to leave right away. Clayton has found a nurse and a very large colored man to travel with my driver and me. He also gave me some powders to sedate Father if I must. Judge Walker has signed an order to have Father committed to Blackwell's Island when we get home. I'll do it if he isn't any better by the time I get to New York. If he is, I'll bring him to live with me under supervision. I'm so sorry, Rennin. I wish I could make it up to you."

"Allison, I'm fine. Don't worry about me, but take care of your father. In some strange way, I suppose justice *has* been served today." He kissed Allison on the cheek. "Good-bye, Allison. Be happy." Rennin walked out the door.

28
Home Sweet Home

The trip down the Mississippi went much faster than the trip to Minnesota. Rennin made an overnight stop at the cotton plantation they had visited before in order to ask the owner if he had any slaves he would like to sell.

Howard Musgrave looked shocked. "Rennin, I thought yours was a family of abolitionists."

Rennin explained, "I want a housekeeper for my wife. After I compensate you, the woman will be free to go if she chooses; but since I'll pay her well, she'll probably want to stay."

"Will you take a trouble-making, pregnant fifteen-year-old off my hands? I won't charge extra for the one she has growing inside her. It'll probably be a rabble-rouser like its mother. I only suggest you not tell her she's free until you get home. She'll probably jump overboard to get away."

"Let me meet the girl."

Rennin was taken to Mabel Musgrave. "I want to talk to Miss Musgrave privately," he said. When they were alone, he explained his proposition to her.

Mabel bit her lip and scowled for a long time without comment, as if the idea just could not be true. Rennin began to think she would reject his offer when she finally said, "I git to leave Mazzer Musgrave?"

"Yes."

"Be free *and* git paid?"

"Yes."

"What about muh baby"

"Born free, but, Miss Musgrave, what about the baby's father?"

"Why you be acallin' me 'Miss Musgrave'? You's a white man."

"You haven't given me permission to call you Mabel."

"Lawdy mercy. You is strange. You has my permission, Mr. O'Rourke."

"You must call me Rennin."

"A darkie call a white man by his first name?"

"You have my permission. Now, should I buy the baby's father, so you can be together?"

Mabel laughed. "You really don't know what bein' a slave is like. Lawdy! Rennin, da mazzer is asellin' me ta git rid of da evidence. He's done come ta me, and he's right scairt I's gonna tell da missus. She'd have 'im castrated fo sho."

"Mabel, do you mean Musgrave is the father?"

"Yazzer."

"Does this kind of thing happen often?"

"More often'n you knows."

"Don't you want to do something about it?"

"Can't do nuthin'. Rennin, I's a slave—propty jest like a horse or hawgs. 'Sides, I is doin' sumpin'. I's goin' wit chu. Yazzer. I's gonna be free, and muh baby's gonna grow up free. I ain't gonna run off and not work fo you if you do's ya say. Yer missus is one lucky womern. You's fine ta look at, and got a good heart, too."

"Mabel, wait until you meet Rebekah, and she will insist that you call her Rebekah." He held up a hand like a shield. "You'll see I'm the lucky one."

Mabel was smitten with Rebekah and the boys immediately, and the moment they pulled into the Gulf of Mexico on their way home, Rennin handed Mabel the papers proving that she was free.

"Ain't you scairt I'll jump overboard?" asked Mabel.

"No," said Rennin. "You gave me your word. Mabel, I'll build you a nice house behind ours. You'll be free. All I ask is that you give me a month's notice if you decide to leave us, so I can find somebody to replace you."

"Yazzer, Rennin. I'll do dat, but I ain't plannin' to leave you and Bekah and dem boys neither."

Once again Rennin took his family through the jungle, but this time they were headed to the Pacific Ocean and relaxed into the voyage home once on the open sea. The weather was unusually stormy along the coast of Mexico. The captain said there was a hurricane, so the ship put in at Ensenda to wait.

While the rain pounded the roof of the dingy hotel, Rennin read to Rebekah.

Cameron and Donovan insisted on throwing a welcome-home party for Rennin and Morgan. They dug a pit and roasted a hog on a spindle over the fire. In the hot coals, they roasted potatoes and corn still in the shuck.

William Bufkin played lively music on his fiddle. The celebration was joyous and raucous. Ranson Riley laughed along with the crowd. Morgan grabbed Ranson's hand. "Come on! Dance with me."

"Morgan, I shouldn't."

"Why?"

"Rennin might not like it."

"He's dancing with Anna. I can dance with you."

"In that case." Ranson laughed, and he spun Morgan around the dance floor.

"You're an elegant dancer," Morgan said when the music stopped.

"Tabitha loved to dance. She was as light as a feather, and her laughter was intoxicating. You and she could have been sisters except for this." Ranson unintentionally touched the white strands of Morgan's hair. "How did you get this?"

Behind him, Ranson heard Rennin clear his throat. "Excuse me. I gave that to her."

"I'm sorry," said Ranson. "I didn't mean anything inappropriate. Excuse me." He walked to the outer edge of the crowd and watched as Rennin took Morgan in his arms.

"He's hurting deeply, Rennin," whispered Morgan. "He needs a friend."

"He's closer to Donovan's and Cameron's age than mine. Maybe one of them can talk to him."

"Rennin, you invited him into our home."

"I didn't take him to raise, Morgan, even if he's not much more than a baby."

"He doesn't need a father. He needs a friend."

"Maybe Geoffrey since he lost his wife. He can understand the boy's feelings."

"He might be young, but he's not a boy. He's a man, and a very handsome man at that."

"Don't look so closely. I'll get jealous."

"Rennin, don't tease. What he needs is a woman."

"Where do you plan to find him a woman? I refuse to share you even if you do resemble his Tabitha."

"That thought never crossed my mind. Mayhap one of the Indian maidens. Many trappers have Indian wives."

"Morgan, let him get to know his son. There's plenty of time for a wife."

"Yes, dear. Nevertheless, he needs a friend, and now he thinks he's offended you. Go talk to him."

"He *did* offend me. I don't mind his dancing with you, but no touching otherwise." He stopped dancing and folded his arms across his chest.

"Rennin, he only told me that Tabitha and I could have been sisters except for my white streak. He wasn't being offensive."

"All right, heart of my heart. I'll talk to him."

Morgan kissed Rennin. "Thank you."

He kissed her again, more passionately. "I'd do anything for you."

"I love you, too. Now, go. I'm going to bed. I'll keep your place warm."

Ranson leaned against a tree. Rennin nonchalantly leaned on the other side. "Ranson, walk with me."

Ranson jumped and caught his breath. "You startled me. I was lost in thought."

"Let's walk."

Nervously, Ranson walked with Rennin. "I was wondering how I'm supposed to rear a little boy alone."

"You won't be alone. You'll have your friends to help you. All you have to do is ask.

"Ranson, I want to tell you a story." They came to a fallen tree and Rennin motioned the younger man to sit. After the two became comfortable, he continued. "There was once a young man who angered a very wealthy, powerful man. The rich man conspired to spirit the young man away from his wife and two young sons. The young man was sold into slavery. Now, this young man was smart and cunning. Because he spoke several languages, he manipulated a beautiful Arabian princess into buying him before the actual auction began. He went to live in her father's palace and became her tutor and companion. The princess, being young and impressionable, fell in love with the man, and he allowed himself to care more for her than he should, clinging to her friendship in his loneliness.

"The princess was obligated to marry a selfish, cruel prince, which she did. However, the prince saw a way to inherit the kingdom." Rennin slid to the ground with his back against the fallen tree. He stretched his long legs in front of him.

"What happened?" asked Ranson.

"The prince accused the princess and the man of adultery, which was totally untrue. Nonetheless, they were found guilty by the High Council and sentenced to death."

Ranson stared, wide-eyed as a child. "They were executed?"

Rennin shook his head. "In an attempt to console his daughter, the king had the man brought to her chambers. Thinking they were going to die, the man and the princess did the thing of which they were accused. In a miraculous twist of fate, they didn't die. In actuality, the king helped them escape. Then, the man had to live with the fact that he had been unfaithful to his wife, a woman he had loved most of his life, a woman for whom he would gladly die.

"Well, after more than two years the man was reunited with his family. He was no longer the happy-go-lucky boy who had been ripped from his family, and his wife was no longer the shy, demure woman he had left behind. But, the love they shared stood the test of time, trials, and temptation. He confessed his infidelity, and she forgave him. Yea, she loved him all the more." He stopped talking for a long moment.

"Ranson, *I* am that man." He looked the younger man in the eye. "I'm telling you this because I know suffering. I want to be your friend. The feeling that you can't go on will pass. You're young, and, Morgan says, quite good-looking. God may send you someone else. He gave Geoffrey a second chance at love after his wife was killed. You must see that he and Anna are mad about each other. Don't give up hope. You have your son. Ranson, if you'll allow us to come into your life, this small band of people will be more than your friends—we'll be your family."

"I haven't had any family for a very long time, Rennin. My parents died when I was young—my mother when I was seven, and my father when I was twelve. That's when I went to live with Andrew, who was already a successful merchant. Of course, he didn't invite me to live with him until I was caught stealing from the baker because I was hungry. I've already told you the rest."

"Ranson, how old are you now?"

"Twenty-two."

"You're only two years older than Donovan. You really should get to know my two eldest sons. Donovan is serious, caring, and dependable. Cameron is silly, cocky, and devilish. They'll be your brothers just the way Colin and Duncan were prepared to be Ryan's brothers. You're settling here for Ryan. That's admirable, but be a little selfish and courageous. Open your heart to us. You might get your feelings hurt sometimes, but the love you'll have will more than make up for the little pains." Rennin stood, and Ranson rose beside him. Both blond, they could have been brothers, but Rennin stood a few inches taller.

Ranson exhaled a deep breath as if he had been holding it. "I'd like to try to make this a real home, Rennin—for Ryan and for me. I confess that I'm terrified. What if I'm not a good father? I've already been cheated out of six years of Ryan's life. Rennin, I helped him get dressed for your party. That was the first time I'd seen his little body since he was two weeks old." With a catch in his voice, Ranson went on. "Rennin, he had cane scars on his back. I have scars from being whipped in prison, but my baby should *not* have those scars. I feel as if it's my fault for not being here to protect him."

"Stop right there, Ranson Riley." Rennin pointed a decisive finger at the other man. "The evil inflicted on both Ryan and you was not your fault. All you can do is start from today. Fill your home with love, maybe someday a mother. You can do it, and I'll be here to give any advice you seek."

"Will you help me make a home for Ryan?"

"Both the building and the atmosphere."

Ranson heaved a great sigh. "A real home. It's almost too much to believe."

Rennin put a brotherly arm around Ranson's shoulders as they walked back to the party. "It'll be a sweet home—home sweet home."

Wind roared louder and rain sloshed harder. Suddenly, Gabriel and Michael crawled onto the bed with their parents, knocking the book from their father's hands. "I'm sorry, Uncle Rennin," said Sarah, following behind them. "They're afraid of the storm. Frankly, so am I."

Rennin motioned for his niece. "Come on, sweetie. There's room for you, too."

Sarah snuggled up on the outside of her uncle. Feeling safe in the strength of company, they all fell asleep.

Finally, after eight months away from home, Rennin and his family arrived safely in San Francisco. He was extremely grateful for the Divine Intervention on his family's part. After the trying time in Minnesota, they missed being afflicted with yellow fever as many residents of New Orleans had been. The hurricane played itself out, and they missed another earthquake farther south near Los Angeles.

Since Rebekah was anxious to get home, they did not spend the night in the city, but Rennin purchased two wagons and four horses so they could start home right away and transport all the household goods they had brought with them. Caitlin fretted about what to tell Candace and Catherine. Both Rennin and Clayton told her to tell them exactly what Rennin had already suggested. After all, that was the story the other three sisters had been told.

On the way from San Francisco to Puma Pass, Rennin told Caitlin, Clayton, and Mabel about Patty, which was a good thing. As Bart and Keturah sat on their front porch, Patty bounded away at a high lope. "Rennin's home," said Keturah.

"How do you know?" asked Bart.

"Patty has smelled him or heard him. She's headed down the road to meet him."

Half an hour later, the wagons topped the hill. Patty claimed Caitlin, Clayton, and Mabel before they could come to a stop, although Mabel was still wary of a wild animal for a pet.

Rennin pulled his wagon to a halt, and Clayton stopped behind him. The lush, verdant valley with its surrounding mountains lay before them. In their absence, Puma Pass had added several more homes for the MacMillans, all of whom had decided to stay. The school was immaculately landscaped with the exception of one missing pine that Rennin would plant next New Year's Day.

Rennin turned around and shouted toward Clayton's wagon, "Momma, where do you want your house?"

"Close to yours," she answered.

Rennin pointed. "Clayton, do you see that small pecan grove? The house about three hundred yards down is ours. How about putting yours in the clearing to the left?"

"Rennin, that spot is gorgeous. Katie?"

"I like it," Caitlin replied.

Rennin then addressed Mabel. "Mabel, you only have a couple of months left. After the baby comes, we'll get you situated in your own house. How about near that big boulder? It shouldn't take but five minutes to walk between our houses."

"Rennin, dat place is real purty, too. Da whole area is real purty. Dat'll be mighty fine."

Rennin rubbed Patty's head as she lay at his feet. "Patty, I think you took the surprise out of our homecoming." Patty snarled. "I forgive you," Rennin laughed. "Actually I missed you, too, girl. It's good to be home."

Everyone poured from their homes to greet the returning troupe. Candace and Catherine were frenzied at Caitlin's arrival with a strange new man that she introduced as her husband. Thomas had spent only a couple of weeks with Clayton before his family had left for California. Catherine said, "You have a lot of explaining to do."

Caitlin's lips formed a thin line. "You don't know the half of it."

A very pregnant Keturah raced to meet Rebekah. Rebekah scolded her, "Keturah! You're not supposed to have any more babies so soon."

Keturah laughed. "Rebekah, God has other plans. Bart and I stayed away from each other except on Valentine's Day. Even then, he did just what Thomas told him, but still here I am. Thomas will be on hand, and now, I understand I can have two doctors present. What can go wrong?"

"But four in four years?"

"They'll grow up close. They'll be tight. Now, what about you?"

Rebekah's face fell. "It's a long story. Help me unpack, and I'll tell all. I brought you some expensive French lace and a new French negligee, guaranteed to drive Bart wild, although obviously you don't need any help." They walked into the house arm in arm and giggling like schoolgirls.

As they unpacked, Rebekah told Keturah everything from the seasickness to the mosquitoes to Maria LaVeau to the incident with Max to the truth about Caitlin to the trial to the wedding. "Poor Rennin," consoled Keturah. "He must be devastated by all this. And how are you handling everything?"

"We're coping. Rennin adores Caitlin as sister or mother. He was angry with her for only a few hours. Once he heard the whole story, he embraced her openly. Caitlin doesn't want her sisters to know about her father. Rennin has agreed to keep the secret."

"I won't say a word."

"Now, tell me about this baby. You know what Thomas said."

"Rebekah, for several months we did nothing. Bart refused to take the chance. He said he would rather have me than a dozen children. Well, on Valentine's Day, Bart broke down; and as you can see, it only took once. At first, Bart was terribly upset, but he has come around to excited."

"Keturah, he's worried. So am I."

"Well, don't." Keturah patted her abdomen and laughed in a silly manner. "You know God has given this little one the best mother He could provide."

Rebekah suddenly broke into a cold sweat. After all these months, Marie LaVeau's words haunted her. She flung her arms around Keturah. "Keturah, I love you. I don't ever want you to leave me."

"Dear girl, I'm not leaving." Keturah took Rebekah's face in her hands. "I love you, too, my sweet Rebekah."

Caitlin knocked at the open door. "Am I interrupting? I finished unpacking Clayton's and my things."

"No, Caitlin, come in," replied Rebekah.

"Actually," continued Caitlin, "I'm going to talk to Cathy and Candy. I was hoping you'd come with me. I need your support."

"Of course. Keturah and I were just catching up on each other."

Caitlin scrutinized Keturah. "Rebekah told you."

"Don't worry, Caitlin," assured Keturah. "Your secret is safe with me."

"I'm sorry, Caitlin," began Rebekah.

"It's all right," said Caitlin. "Keturah's your best friend—more. She's the mother *and* sister you never had. I understand."

Keturah took Caitlin's hand. "Has Rebekah told you about me and what I used to be?"

"No."

"After you talk to your sisters, come have tea with me. I'll tell you, so you'll know we all have secrets." Keturah looked around. "Where are our men anyway?"

Caitlin said, "They're digging a pit barbecue because Rennin promised Sarah, and they want to use it tonight. They have a side of beef to roast. Rebekah, I'm afraid they left the furniture in your foyer."

"It'll keep," said Rebekah. Taking Caitlin's hand, she asked, "Are you ready?"

"No, but I have no choice."

Rather than tell her sisters individually, Caitlin got Candace and Catherine together. She sat them down and told them that she was actually Rennin's mother. Neither of them seemed surprised.

Candace said, "Katie, I was thirteen when Rennin was born. Thomas was Mother's doctor. I've always known that Mother was too ill to have conceived, or even have relations, and Father had sent you away. The thing that has confused me most is that I never knew you had a beau. Who was he?"

"Candace!" said Catherine sharply.

"It's a fair question," said Caitlin.

"No, it's not," said Catherine vehemently. "Some things are better left unsaid. She doesn't need to know everything."

"Who are you to say what I should know?" asked Candace, highly offended.

"The sister who's only eleven months younger than Katie and who shared a room with her."

Caitlin clutched Rebekah's hand. "Cathy, exactly what do you know?"

Catherine huffed toward Candace.

"I'm not leaving," defied Candace.

"She can stay," said Caitlin. "This is my story, not yours, Cathy."

Sufficiently chastised, Catherine said, "I saw what happened in the hall. I heard what he said. I was just too scared to stop it. I'm sorry Caitlin. I should've intervened. I was just too shocked and frightened."

Tears smarted Caitlin's eyes. "Oh, Cathy, how I wish that I had known you knew. I've borne this alone for so long."

Candace sat in stunned silence for several minutes before she blurted, "Caitlin! Oh, God! I'm sorry. I thought I had dreamt it. I thought I was having a nightmare. I was half asleep when I heard your voices. I didn't think it was real. I couldn't believe Father would've done that." Candace knelt at Caitlin's feet. "Please forgive me."

"Me, too," said Catherine. "Forgive me for not stopping it and for not coming to you and upholding you."

"The other three don't know. I'd like to keep it that way."

"Does Rennin know all of it?" asked Candace.

"Yes."

"Clayton?"

"Yes."

"What happened after that?"

"With Father?"

Candace nodded.

"Nothing. He never touched me again, and he never drank again."

"Well," said Catherine, "now, tell us about Max."

Caitlin finished her story, and Candace stated flatly, "I'm glad he's dead, and I hope he's burning in Hell. If Ralph hadn't tried to pin the murder on Rennin, I'd give him a medal."

Catherine grinned. "Well, now that we know all the bad stuff, tell us about Clayton."

"Clay is my dream come true," Caitlin said, her face aglow. "He's a wonderful, God-fearing man who loves me—truly loves me. Need I say more? You can get to know him for yourselves for we're staying here. I'm making a real home here near my son and his precious wife and my grandchildren. For the first time since I was sixteen, the word home sounds sweet—a place filled with love and trust, a warm, safe place."

That evening, the party in Puma Pass could be heard over the hilltop. Laughter was rich; music, full. Happy to be home, Rennin and Rebekah slept more soundly that night than they had in all the months they were away.

The very next morning, Rennin and Olaf went back to San Francisco to meet Roger Simpkins to get the first load of children for the school. The initial group had eight children: twelve-year-old Blake Combs whose father had brought him west with high hopes, but had been killed when his mine caved in; eleven-year-old Peter, who did not know his last name, so he called himself Jones; two ten-year-olds, Alex and Adam Sims, who had no idea what had become of their parents; eight-year-old Bethany Pace and her two-year-old brother, Carl; six-year-old Frances James whose mother worked in a saloon and left the child to wander the streets; and five-year-old Stanley Knox, who was reported to have never spoken a word and usually stared into space, so he was thought to be a deaf mute. Two older widowed women, who had been hired to serve as dormitory mothers, one for the boys and one for the girls, completed the group.

Some of the children, especially Blake and Peter, seemed angry to have had their independence taken away. The girls appeared relieved to have a roof over their heads and food every day. The younger children simply took the turn of events in stride, and Stanley sucked his thumb and went along for the ride.

The first night the children were at the school, Rebekah helped bathe and get them ready for bed. She decided to meet the challenge head-on and took Stanley as her charge for the evening. She said gently, "Come on, Stanley. Let's wash the grime off so you feel better and smell nice." Stanley did not respond, but sucked his thumb and stared into space. Rebekah gently shook him and held out her hand. Stanley took the proffered hand and followed stoically to Rebekah's house and the tub.

Rebekah removed his clothes and screamed in horror, "Rennin!"

Rennin came through the door. "Rebekah, what's wrong?"

She beckoned him with her hand. "Rennin, look." Stanley's entire body, arms, and legs were covered in deep scars, reportedly as a result of severe burns. "Rennin, what happened to him?"

"He was the only member of his family to survive a fire."

"No, Rennin. I've seen fire burns. This baby was scalded."

"I was told he survived a fire, Rebekah."

"Watch," Rebekah said. She lifted the kettle to pour water into the tub. Stanley ran as fast as he could and hid under the table. Rebekah set the kettle back on the stove. She put both hands to the sides of her head and said softly, "It wasn't an accident."

She crawled under the table, and held the naked little boy against her. "Rennin, please make Stanley's bath water while we wait under here."

Rennin made the water. Rebekah crawled from beneath the table. "Come on, Stanley. I won't hurt you."

Stanley sucked his thumb and remained still. Rebekah said, "Rennin, get in the tub."

"What?"

"If Stanley sees that the water won't hurt you, maybe he won't be afraid."

Rennin acquiesced and slid into the warm water. Rebekah gathered Stanley from beneath the table. She knelt beside the tub and put her hand in the water. "Look, Stanley. See. The water isn't hot. It won't burn you. Look at Mr. Rennin. The water isn't burning him. Will you go to him now?"

Rennin said tenderly, "Rebekah, he can't hear you."

"Yes, he can if he wants to." Rebekah smoothed the little boy's hair back. "Can't you, sweetheart?"

Rebekah handed the child to Rennin. At first, Stanley held tightly to Rennin's neck. He finally slid into the soothing water; and as Rennin gently bathed the small, scarred body, Gabriel and Michael zipped into the room with their grandmother in hot pursuit. Rennin laughed loudly. "Whoa! Stampeding buffalo! Look out, Stanley, they're headed our way."

Stanley jerked his head around to see Gabriel and Michael. Rebekah squealed, "Rennin, he heard you!"

"I believe he did," Rennin said.

The twins leaned over the edge of the tub. "Tan we get in?" asked Michael.

"I don't think there's room for everybody," discouraged Rennin, "and it's 'may we.'"

"Pwease," pleaded Gabriel.

Rennin said, "Well, Stanley, what do you say? This is your bath."

Stanley stared blankly at the boys. Rennin took his face in his hands. "Stanley, look at me. If it's all right with you for Gabriel and Michael to join us, come up here by me and make room."

Slowly, Stanley crawled onto Rennin's lap. Despite his self-made promise not to become attached to the children at the school since the ultimate goal was to find homes for them, Rennin hugged Stanley close and kissed his brown curls.

Gabriel and Michael quickly hopped into the tub, and water began to splash wildly. They squealed and dunked each other. A slight rumble escaped Stanley's throat. Rennin said, "Stanley, are you laughing at those two silly boys?" Stanley's response was to slap the water and cause his own splash.

After a while, Rebekah said it was time to get out. She dried the boys and put each of them in clean nightshirts. Then, she said, "Two cookies and a glass of milk. The last one to the kitchen has to wash the glasses. Gabriel and Michael sped away. "You, too, Stanley. Let's go."

Stanley hesitantly took his thumb from his mouth and reached up for Rebekah. She picked him up, and he laid his head on her shoulder. Rebekah looked at her husband. "Rennin, I won't make him sleep at the school."

"Rebekah, we had this talk. We can't allow ourselves to get attached to *every* child that comes to the school. Our goal is to find them good homes."

"But, Rennin, Stanley's special. Let's be his good home. Let's adopt him."

"Rebekah!"

Rebekah turned her two dove-gray eyes pleadingly toward Rennin. "Please."

Stanley lifted his head off Rebekah's shoulder and reached out for Rennin. Rennin took him and tousled his hair. He looked sympathetically at the child. "Stanley O'Rourke. How do you like that name?"

Stanley put his head on Rennin's shoulder and in Rennin's ear whispered, "Me home."

Rebekah slipped under Rennin's other arm and stroked Stanley's cheek. "Yes, darling. You're home."

29
Love in Bloom

School went into full swing in Puma Pass with Keturah teaching the younger girls and Caitlin teaching the younger boys while Olaf taught a mixed group of adolescents. Stanley walked across the bridge to school every day holding Grandma Caitlin's hand. Gabriel and Michael pouted that they were too young to go.

Rennin and Rebekah made a trip to San Francisco to file formal adoption papers for Stanley. With no parent stepping forward to claim the boy, he was ruled a ward of the state, and adoption papers were signed immediately. The whole affair took three days. Stanley Knox officially became Stanley Knox O'Rourke. Not knowing his exact date of birth, his birthdate was recorded legally the date of adoption minus five years—September 30, 1848.

Autumn came unnoticed until Thomas knocked on Rennin's door. Thomas entered wearing a disconcerted look. With some concern, Rennin asked, "Thomas, is something wrong?"

Thomas replied, "Yes. No. I don't know. I need to talk to you about Sarah, actually, Sarah and Chen Li."

"What about Sarah and Chen Li?"

"Rennin, I caught them necking."

Rennin snickered. "Thomas, Sarah is *not* a little girl any more. She has turned into a very pretty young woman. She's fifteen now."

"I realize that. Damn! I don't want to sound prejudiced, but Chen Li is Chinese. I'm just not sure about this mixing of the races. Rennin, I like Chen Li. He's a very well-mannered and polite young man. They were only kissing in the gazebo, but I'm afraid I reacted very strongly. Rennin, I'm truly worried. Hasn't Chen Li talked to you since I chewed him up and spat him out last night?"

"No, he came in and went to bed quietly with barely a 'good night.' Tom, does the color of Chen Li's skin bother you so much? Honestly, I'm shocked."

"I'm shocked at myself. I like the boy. If the sexes were reversed"—He shrugged—"I think I would feel differently. Rennin, what do I do? Sarah will not even speak to me this morning because I embarrassed her so." Thomas sank onto the sofa.

Rennin went to the stairs and shouted, "Chen Li, come down. I need to talk to you."

Solemnly, Chen Li descended the stairs. "Good morning, Rennin." He saw Thomas on the couch. "I thought Dr. Goodman might come today. Good morning, sir."

"Good morning, Chen Li."

Rennin said, "Sit down so we can talk."

Chen Li sat in a chair as far from Thomas as he could get. Rennin saw that he would have to act as arbitrator. "Thomas, is there something you'd like to say to Chen Li?"

Put on the spot, Thomas stared at his brother-in-law. Rennin cocked his eyebrow. "No? Okay. Chen Li, would you like to say anything to Thomas?"

Chen Li glowered at Rennin, but only for a moment before he responded, "Yes, there is. If there is one thing I have rearned from Rennin over these three years, it's to stand up for myself and speak my mind. Dr. Goodman, I am highly offended and deeply hurt by the things you said to me rast night. I have known you for almost three years, and I thought you were above bigotry and prejudice. Second, about Sarah, she and I have done nothing of which to be ashamed. I care for Sarah very much. As a matter of fact, I think I have fallen in rove with her. She's a wonderful, sensitive, compassionate young woman. I would never do anything to dishonor her. Finally, regarding my future, hopefully with Sarah, next year, I'll go to college. Rennin tells me I'll be gone three or four years. I plan to study engineering, for this country is growing by reaps and bounds. It will need roads and bridges, and, I think, railroads from east to west. When I return I will pray that Sarah has waited for me. Then, I'll seek your blessing and permission to marry her. I hope by then you will consider me worthy despite the fact that I am Chinese." Chen Li let out a great sigh of relief and loosened the grip on the arms of the chair where he sat.

Thomas was stunned by the passion and maturity with which Chen Li spoke. He struggled to compose his thoughts. "Chen Li, I apologize for the way I spoke to you last evening. I overreacted. I thought I was above bigotry and prejudice as well, but, in all honesty, the thought of my daughter marrying outside her race frightens me. I worry about how you would be received in society. I like you and admire you, Chen. You're a worthy young man."

"Does it matter at all how Sarah feels?"

"Of course, I care how Sarah feels."

"Do you judge the reverend? He's a quarter Cherokee and married to a white woman. They seem very happy. Am I so different?"

"No, you aren't. I'll not forbid you to court Sarah. You have my blessing. That does *not* mean I won't worry. I love Sarah more than you can understand until you have your own child. I don't want her to suffer any heartache."

"Mr. Thomas!" Chen Li sprang to his feet with a grin on his face. "I would do anything to make Sarah happy. I would protect her and care for her. Do you really mean it? May I court Sarah?"

"Yes, Chen Li." Thomas stood. "Let's start by your having breakfast with us. I'll tell Sarah. Maybe, then, she'll speak to me again." Thomas and Chen Li walked out the door with Thomas's arm around Chen Li's shoulders.

Rebekah called everyone to breakfast. Rennin went to the table laughing about the whole situation. He told Rebekah, Caitlin, and Clayton about his early morning adventure.

After breakfast, Rebekah asked Rennin to take a walk with her. As they walked, Rebekah said, "Rennin, the situation with Sarah and Chen Li is *not* funny. Thomas has legitimate concerns. I would never have been accepted into white society as Black Cloud's wife. There's a deep-seeded prejudice against all that is not white in our country. It will be difficult for Sarah no matter how much she might actually love Chen Li."

"Rebekah, do you disapprove of them as a couple?"

"Rennin, I love both of them. Marriage is hard enough without the added burden they would face. If they're determined to stay together, I'll support them. However, they must enter their courtship and possible marriage with their eyes open. They must know the opposition they'll face."

"You're right as usual. I'll talk to Chen Li. He says he loves Sarah and would protect her. He's thinking totally with his heart, not his head."

Later that day, Rennin took Chen Li riding. Perceptively, Chen Li asked, "Rennin, what do you have on your mind?"

"Honestly," replied Rennin, "I'm concerned about you and Sarah."

"Then, you disapprove?"

"No. I think Sarah could not have found a better man. Chen, I feel as if you're my little brother. I don't know if I've ever told you that I love you."

"I rove you too, Rennin. You're my hero. If you don't disapprove, then, what is it?"

"I want you to be aware of the obstacles you'll face because of your mixed-race relationship."

"I know it will be hard—harder than normal, but I rove her, Rennin."

"What if it's too hard for Sarah? Do you love her enough to let her go?"

"Rennin, you're asking me to tear out my heart." Chen Li looked east. "While I'm at college, Sarah will be free to see anyone she wishes. If she tells me marriage with me would be too hard, I'll ret her go. If she does that, Rennin, I will not return to Puma Pass. I could not bear to see her with another."

"Whether you marry Sarah or not, you'll always be welcome in my home. Chen Li, it's *your* home. Know this: Rebekah and I will support you and Sarah if you do wed."

"Thank you, Rennin," Chen Li said with a downcast countenance.

"Don't be sad. You have permission from the girl's father to court her. Enjoy this time. See where it leads." Rennin laughed. "You might find out how pigheaded Sarah can be; and I will warn you—she doesn't lose her temper often, but when she does, it's like a volcanic eruption."

"I'll take my chances." Chen Li grinned. "I'll race you home! I have a beautiful rady to court."

"Come to think of it, so do I," said Rennin. They spurred their horses and gave the beasts their heads.

That evening Caitlin and Clayton retired early. In the flickering firelight, Rennin held Rebekah close and whispered, "I know what they're doing."

Rebekah elbowed her husband. "Rennin O'Rourke, you are shameless."

"No," he said, settling into a snuggling position. "I'm happy for Momma. She looks ten years younger and acts even younger than that. Clayton is the best thing that ever happened to her."

"I disagree," argued Rebekah. "You are." She grinned mischievously. "We could do the same thing."

Rennin glanced at the clock against the wall. "Nope. Not yet. We have half an hour before Stanley comes downstairs for one more hug. I wonder if he'll ever fall asleep right away. Until then, let's read. I just happen to have the book beside me."

Ranson and Ryan became a real part of the O'Rourke family, living in Rennin's home for nearly two years. Ranson behaved like a brother to the O'Rourke boys on more than one occasion. Business boomed for the trading post, largely due to the exceptional pelts Ranson caught.

As fond as he was of both Ryan and Ranson, Rennin knew that it would be best for them to establish their own home, so the men of Mom's Trading Post worked tirelessly to finish Ranson's cabin before the first snow and the Riley men's second anniversary as residents of Mom's Trading Post. They were all thankful for the late fall onset. With all hands working, a small, cozy cabin was ready before the cold winds blew again.

Angela Montague, who seemed to have grown overnight, threw Ranson a housewarming. Ranson's friends showered him with gifts of furniture, linens, canned fruits and vegetables, and preserved meats. Overwhelmed by the love and acceptance he had found in this small community, Ranson slipped quietly into the night to ponder the feelings in his heart.

Standing in the brisk late October air and staring at the full, bright harvest moon, Ranson was unaware of the figure that sallied to his side. "The harvest moon is spectacular," Angela said, pulling her shawl more tightly about her shoulders as she shivered.

Startled from his reverie, Ranson jumped. "Yes, it is, Miss Montague," he repsonded politely. He chivalrously placed his coat around her shoulders.

"Thank you, Mr. Riley. Miss Montague? When did I become Miss Montague?"

"Since you are becoming a young lady."

"Yes, I suppose I am, but I would prefer *you* to call me Angela. All my friends do, and from now on, I shall call you Ranson."

"Very well, Angela. I understand this gala was your idea. Thank you."

"You're very welcome. I want you to feel comfortable here. I want you to have the home your spirit desires."

"I do. Everyone has made me feel as if I belong here."

"I think you were sent here for a reason."

"Something other than God's way of reuniting me with my son? What might that be?" He smiled teasingly at the young woman.

"Of course, Ryan was one very important reason. Walk with me, and I'll help you figure out the other reason."

Ranson offered Angela his arm as they walked through Morgan's dormant rose garden. "Look," said Ranson as he spotted a full-bloomed pink rose. He carefully picked the flower and placed it behind Angela's right ear. "A surprise for a beautiful and gracious lady."

Angela laughed blithely. "Papa and Uncle Rennin have traveled many places. I heard them talking once about flowers. It seems that someplace in Persia considers giving a single full-bloomed rose to a lady a declaration of love." Angela took the flower from her hair and smelled it. "I would like that."

Ranson blushed and asked, "Who's the lucky man?"

Angela touched the petals of the rose to his cheek. She stood on her tiptoes and kissed the unsuspecting man on his lips. "You. Good night, Ranson." Like a mirage, she vanished into the night.

Ranson tossed and turned through a sleepless night. Before sunrise, he sat alone at the small table and sipped strong tea. Dark circles lingered under his eyes. Disturbed by the movement in the strange, new house, Ryan tiptoed to his father's side. "Daidí, is something bothering you?"

Ranson set the boy on his lap. "Yes, something most peculiar occurred last night at our party."

"Do you want to talk about it?"

"I don't think you'd understand."

"Try me. You might be surprised."

Ranson told his son about Angela and waited for his response.

Ryan tapped his chin thoughtfully for a time. "Hmm," he said, "you do need a wife."

"Ryan, she's barely more than a child."

"She looks all grown up to me. Remember that I told you I want to marry Rachel O'Rourke. Uncle Rennin says I have to wait at least ten years. I only have eight left. Maybe it's just a matter of time before you can marry Angela. If you wait long enough, we could have a double wedding. Of course, then Angela would be old like you."

Ranson's jaw dropped. "Old? Never mind that. Ryan, I never said I wanted to marry Angela. I never even considered the possibility. She's the one with the idea."

"You don't like her or think she's pretty?"

"She's quite nice and a very pretty girl—I emphasize the word *girl*."

"She won't always be a girl, and like I already said, she looks mighty womanlike to me." Ryan rolled his eyes.

"She will always be ten years younger than I am."

"Aunt Anna is fifteen years younger than Uncle Geoffrey. I don't think he would be concerned about the age difference."

"Ryan, do you want me to court this girl?"

"I want you to be happy, Daidí. You need a wife. Angela would be fine with me."

"Ryan, I love you, but you're only eight. You can't possibly understand how confused I am."

"Aha! You do like her. Admit it."

Ranson stared confoundedly at his son, who seemed more adult than his father at the moment. "I admit it. I like her, but she's so young."

"Daidí, when did you turn twenty-four?"

"September first."

"Angela will be fifteen next week. I heard her and Cynthia talking. Cynthia turned sixteen two weeks ago. So, actually, Angela is only nine years younger than you. Of course, maybe you like Cynthia better."

"No. No. I like Angela, and Duncan likes Cynthia though he hasn't said so." He bumped the heel of his hand to his forehead.

"Good grief! What am I saying? Ryan, stop encouraging this folly. Get dressed. I want to talk to Uncle Rennin."

Ranson knocked at the O'Rourke family door before breakfast. Rennin opened the door wearing an impish grin. "What? You can't make your own breakfast?" he joked.

"I need to talk to you," Ranson said seriously.

Rennin sent Ryan to the kitchen. "Go tell Aunt Morgan to make a few more flapjacks. What's the matter?"

"It's woman trouble," Ryan said as he left the room.

Rennin looked curiously at Ranson and smirked. "Which woman could it be? Could she possibly be about five-foot-four with soft blue eyes and copper curls and goes by the name of Angela Montague? And to think Morgan was worried about your meeting a woman."

"For Pete's sake!" Ranson fairly shouted. "Am I the only one who didn't see this girl coming? *Girl*, Rennin, *girl*. She's only fourteen. Let me tell you what she did last night. She kissed me. *She* kissed *me*. I didn't kiss her. What am I to do? She's a sweet girl, but a girl nonetheless."

Rennin laughed loudly and pushed his golden lion's mane of hair back with both hands. "She appears to have been woman enough to have stirred you up considerably. Did you sleep at all last night? You look like hell. This *girl* has been eying you for years. I'm told she has talked about you since the first time you came to trade furs. Now that you've definitely settled here, she has come straight out with it. Angela has always gone after what she wants. You're what she wants."

"But, Rennin, she's a little girl."

"I don't remember little girls looking like that. She looks very grown up to me."

Exasperated, Ranson plopped into a chair. "You sound just like Ryan. She can't help how she looks. I would shoot a man my age for coming near my fourteen-year-old daughter. What must Geoffrey think?"

"Geoffrey is used to Angela's headstrong ways. Ranson, Angela stopped being a little girl a long time ago, almost before she was out of diapers."

Ranson buried his face in his hands. "Rennin, what scares me is that I liked her kiss. God help me! I like her, but I would never have thought about pursuing a relationship with her. She's too young."

"How much do you like her, Ranson?"

"Too much. I feel perverted to be honest. When I first met her, I thought she was at least sixteen. Still, at that time, I was hurting too much to even notice another woman, but notice her I did. It's hard *not* to notice Angela. Then, I got to know her. I like her. I really like her. Then, I found out she was only twelve. Two years hasn't made that much difference except that she has grown prettier by the minute. I can't Rennin." He shook his head hard. "It just seems wrong."

"Would it seem wrong in three years?"

"Then, she would be seventeen—truly a young woman."

"The age difference would still be the same."

"But it would feel different."

"Ranson, court the girl."

"What?" He shook his head as if to dislodge something from his ears.

"Tell her it will be a long courtship—at least three years. You'll be away a lot. When you're here, take her flowers. Go for picnics and walks. She might decide her infatuation is only that, not love; but if she doesn't, give yourself time to grow to love her."

"Then you don't think the age is that big a deal?"

"It's the normal thing."

"Maybe sixteen, but fourteen is just too young."

"Just take it slow and easy."

"What if I want to kiss her?"

"Then, kiss her, but leave it at that."

"Should I talk to Geoffrey?"

"Oh, yes, but not on an empty stomach." Rennin sniffed the air and smelled frying bacon. "Let's have breakfast."

Even with Rennin's reassurance, Ranson berated himself for what seemed inappropriate feelings for Angela. Several times he started to the Montague home, only to turn back. He talked to himself aloud about what to say.

As he made a new trail in the ground, Cameron approached him. Cameron sniggered. "Relax, Ranson. Daidí told me your dilemma. We all know Angela a lot better than you. She's very mature. Go and court the girl. Become my brother-in-law. Hell, I'll even be your best man. You helped me in my darkest hour. It's time I repaid that debt. Trust me. Angela's a gift that has been sent to you."

Taking heart from the young man who had become his best friend, Ranson finished his walk to Angela Montague's door. His hand shook as he knocked at Geoffrey's door. It took quite sometime for anyone to answer. He turned to leave as Geoffrey opened the door. Jovially, Geoffrey said, "Ranson, lad, come in. It's turnin' cold fast. We'll 'ave snow before the week's out."

Ranson heard the girls laughing inside. "I think it can wait, Geoffrey."

"Nonsense." Geoffrey closed the door behind him. "You've come to talk to me 'bout Angela, 'ave you? Let's walk."

"How did you know? Geoffrey, I suppose I've come to ask permission to court her."

"Thought you might come sooner or later. Scared you, did she?"

Ranson told Geoffrey about the night before. Geoffrey wagged his head. "Sounds just like 'er. Ranson, you don't 'ave to feel obligated to court Angela. If you ain't interested, tell 'er so."

"That's just it. I *am* interested. I just feel strangely about her age."

"You plannin' to marry 'er tomorrow?"

"No. I thought we should have a nice long courtship—at least three years."

"I like the sound o' that, but Angela might think it a bit long. She'll try to shoot you down to one, but *I* won't go for that. Compromise with 'er, an' let 'er think she got you to two."

"She'll have to be seventeen before I'll marry her."

"Agreed. That'll give you two years. You know she turns fifteen next week."

"I know. I think I'll approach her about courtship on her birthday when she won't be fourteen, if that meets with your approval."

"It does."

"Does it bother you that I'm making her wonder for a week?"

"No. It serves 'er right for bein' so forward and brash. I'll enjoy watching 'er squirm"—He clapped Ranson on the shoulder—"and it's our secret."

Ranson completely avoided Angela until her birthday. As a matter of fact, he spent time locked away working on a present for her, but made her think he didn't want to see her at all. Duncan paid Ranson a visit to let him know that he was courting Cynthia if he wanted to do some things together. It brought relief to Ranson to know he would have safety in numbers, for he had admitted to himself that he was sorely tempted by the tempestuous redhead.

As was true for each birthday for each child in Mom's Trading Post, they had a community celebration. This time they cleared the livery barn for a dance because the day chose to shower them with the first snow of the season. Ranson deliberately arrived late. Angela saw him enter. Geoffrey caught her arm as she started toward Ranson. "You will not seek out that young man. 'Tisn't ladylike. Let 'im come to you."

"What if he doesn't, Papa?"

"Then God has someone better for you. Be patient, little girl."

"Papa, was I too forward with him?"

"Yes. You may 'ave scared 'im away completely. No. Maybe you opened 'is eyes. I don't know."

After a while, Ranson made his way to Angela. "Did you save a dance for me?"

Haughtily she replied, "Maybe one."

As they danced, Ranson said, "Only one dance?"

"How many do you want?"

"All of them."

"Why?"

"Take a walk with me, and I'll tell you."

"Leave my celebration and go into the snow?"

"Yes."

"Alone with you?"

"Yes."

"Only if Papa says it's all right."

Ranson caught Geoffrey's eye and received a nod. Outside, Ranson and Angela walked as new flakes fell. Angela shivered. "Are you cold?" asked Ranson.

"No, nervous."

"Why?"

"I think I made a fool of myself the other night. I apologize. I shouldn't have been so forward."

"Apology not accepted. I liked your candor."

"All of it?"

"Especially that kiss. As a matter of fact, I'd like another, but first, I have a birthday gift for you. Close your eyes."

Angela closed her eyes. From his pocket, Ranson pulled a comb with a full-bloomed rose etched in it. He whispered, "A very pretty lady once told me that if a man gives a woman a full-bloomed rose, it's a declaration of love." Ranson carefully worked the comb into Angela's hair. "This rose says you're spoken for. I want to court you, but it has to be a long courtship. Let's say three years."

"Too long," said Angela. "One."

"Two."

"All right. Two. Two years from today."

"Two years from today, if you still think you want me, I'll ask your father for hand your in marriage."

Angela ran her fingers along the delicate etching. "Did you carve this?"

"Yes."

"I'll wear it every day. Thank you."

"You're welcome. Now, about that kiss." Ranson tipped Angela's face upward and kissed her softly.

"Again," she breathed.

He kissed her more firmly, and she slipped her arms around his neck. Then, she laid her head on his chest. Ranson held her in his arms. "You scare me, little girl, but I like what I'm feeling," he breathed.

As Rennin closed the book, he and Rebekah heard the pitter-patter of little feet.

"Hug!" shouted Stanley, and he received two great big hugs before he trotted off to bed.

"Well," said Rebekah, "it seems as if love is in bloom in the past and the present. Let's go fertilize our rose garden. Our love is growing healthily."

30
Bitterness Rooted Out

Reluctantly, Caitlin and Clayton moved into their own house. She actually complained to Clayton that she felt too tired to care for her new home. Unaccustomed to Caitlin's complaining about anything, he was instantly worried. "Honey, is anything else bothering you?"

"Clay, I urinate all the time, and today I just feel plain sick. I feel as if I'm going to vomit."

His eyes twinkled and a smiled played about his lips. "Katie, you're pregnant."

"I can't be. I'm too old. I'm going through the change. *You* told me that."

"That does not mean that you can't get pregnant."

Suddenly bursting with energy, Caitlin exclaimed, "Oh, Clay! Am I really? Be my doctor for a minute. Examine me so we can know for sure."

"I might not stop with an examination," Clayton teased.

"Then, we will have a celebration!" she replied, not to be outdone.

The doctor took over and Clayton examined Caitlin. He clapped his hands and grinned. "Yes, ma'am. We are having a baby."

She flung her arms around her husband. Then, she snatched her dress. Clayton caught her hand. "Hold on a minute. Where are you going?"

"I want to tell Rennin."

"Not yet. First, we have to have a private celebration."

An hour later as Clayton and Caitlin lay snuggled together, still bubbling with joy, some one knocked at the door. Clayton dressed hurriedly, but told Caitlin to take her time. Chen Li stood on the front porch as Clayton answered the summons good-naturedly.

"Dr. Davies," Chen Li began immediately, "Mabel is in rabor. She wants you rather than Mr. Thomas because she knows you. Will you come?"

"Of course, I'll come. Go back and tell Mabel to be calm. I'm gathering my bag, and I'll be there in fifteen minutes."

Chen Li jogged back down the hill as Caitlin came downstairs. Clayton turned around. "It's Mabel's time. She wants me. Why don't you come along and share our news?"

Caitlin gathered her shawl and Clayton got his bag. They walked hand in hand to Rennin's house. Clayton went straight to Mabel's room while Caitlin had tea with Rennin and Rebekah. Rennin said, "Momma, you have been grinning since you walked through the door, and if you don't stop stirring that tea, I'm going to take it away. Start talking."

"Clay and I are having a baby," she announced triumphantly.

"That's wonderful," said Rennin.

Rebekah smiled sadly and hugged Caitlin. She said softly, "That is wonderful news. I bet Clay is overjoyed."

"He's ecstatic. This is absolutely the perfect way to set up a new home."

Before anyone could say another word, Gabriel, Michael, and Stanley charged through the house on the stick horses that Grandpa Clay had made for them.

Caitlin laughed, "I might be too old for this part."

"No," argued Rennin. Then, to the boys he said, "Boys, ride the horses outside."

"But we're firsty," grumbled Michael.

Rebekah said, "Then, tie the horses to the porch rail and come into Momma's tea room. I'll give you some milk, and I believe it's lunchtime. How about some chicken, apples, and raisin bread to go with the milk?"

"Sounds good to me," said Rennin.

"I'll be back in a bit," said Caitlin. "I'm going to see if Clay needs a nurse to help him. I can't stand being away from him for so long."

Rebekah pulled the roasting chicken from the oven where she had started it some time before. Then, she opened the breadbox and retrieved a loaf of raisin bread.

"Would you like me to slice the apples?" asked Rennin.

"No!" snapped Rebekah. "I can do it! I'm not totally helpless!"

"Honey, what's wrong?" asked Rennin, perplexed lines etching his brow.

"Nothing. I'm fine."

"Then, why do you sound so angry?"

She turned around and threw the bread at him. "Because I *am* angry! Make your own damned lunch! Leave me alone!" Rebekah stormed out the back door, slamming it hard enough to rattle the glass window pane. Rennin opened the door to see her gallop away on an unsaddled Jewel. He turned back to see three little boys with wide wondering eyes.

Caitlin came into the kitchen. "Rennin, were you and Rebekah fighting?"

With a look of dismay on his face, Rennin replied, "I don't know what we were doing. She has never behaved like that."

"Go after her, Rennin. I think I know what's going on. She's hurting. Think about it." She pulled him out the door so the children could not hear. "I just told her I'm having a baby. Rennin, I'm forty-three, almost past childbearing years. She just turned twenty-one, yet she can't have any more children. It has hit her full in the face. Talk to her before bitterness can take root." She cut her eyes back toward the kitchen. "I'll take care of the boys."

Rennin found Rebekah after over an hour of searching. She was face down in the dirt in the cave where Ike had held her hostage. Rennin knelt beside her and softly rubbed her back.

She sat up abruptly and screamed. "Don't touch me! Don't ever touch me again! Why would you want to?"

Tenderly, Rennin said, "Now, who's spouting gibberish?"

Rebekah dissolved into tears and fell into Rennin's outstretched arms. After her tears were spent, she whispered, "I'm so ashamed. I'm angry. I'm jealous. I'm ungrateful. I'm selfish. When Caitlin announced her news, she needed me to rejoice with her. All I could think was, 'She's old. I'm young. God, this is unfair.' Rennin, she deserves this happiness, and I'm jealous of her."

"She understands. She told me exactly what you're feeling."

"That's not all. I resent Keturah's having another child when she was warned not to. I'm appalled that a fifteen-year-old slave would be blessed with a child she did not want. I'm ungrateful for my two precious gifts and another priceless child that was handed to me wrapped in beautiful bows in the form of scars. I'm not thankful for the greatest husband in the world. I'm angry. I'm hurt. It hurts so much." She pounded her chest with her fist. "And, I'm angry with you. You've acted as if it doesn't matter to you. I've not seen you shed one tear for our dead baby. Why, Rennin? Why?"

"I'm sorry, Rebekah. I've mourned alone. After what I made you endure in Minnesota, I thought I needed to stay strong. I was trying to be steady for you. Forgive me for making you feel alone. I suppose I've been seething inside, being eaten up with my own anger and bitterness. I didn't want you to know how devastated I was. It was too hard to admit. I had begun to think you were resigned to our fate."

"I am in that I know it can't change, but I'm still hurting, Rennin. I don't want you to be strong. I want you to weep with me."

"I will from now on."

For a long time, they sat silently, grieving together. After a while, Rebekah sighed. Then, she said, "I'm sorry I threw the bread at you."

He snickered. "At least I caught it."

"Let's go home. I need to apologize to Caitlin and see if my newest godchild has been born."

"Are you ready for that?"

"No, but I have to face life. I only ask that if I feel like screaming, you scream with me. If I cry, cry with me. Grieve with me, and heal with me."

When they arrived home, Rennin and Rebekah found Clayton grabbing a quick bite to eat. "Welcome back," he said around a mouthful. "Rebekah, I need you. Mabel is having a hard time. She's begging for you."

Rebekah looked at Rennin. "God really knows how to make us face our troubles."

"You don't have to go."

"Yes, I do. Clay, let me bathe quickly, and I'll meet you. Where is Caitlin?"

"With Mabel."

She nodded. Rebekah bathed hastily and changed into an old garment in case it was ruined. She entered Mabel's room before Clayton returned.

Mabel saw her and reached for her. "Bekah!" Rebekah took her hand. "Bekah, I's scairt. It hurts so bad. Is I goin' die?"

"No, Mabel. I know it hurts, but it'll be over soon. I'm going to stay with you until we have our baby. Remember you asked me to be the godmother."

Mabel screamed. "Where's Dr. Clay? I want Dr. Clay."

"I'm right here, Mabel. I told you I would only be gone a little while." Clayton examined Mabel and looked grave.

"Clay?" said Rebekah.

"Mabel, the baby is still breech. I thought he would turn on his own, but he hasn't. I have to turn him. It will hurt a lot."

"Jest git it out, Dr. Clay. I's goin' die."

"I won't let you die. If I have to, I'll take the baby."

Mabel screamed again. "How's you goin' do dat?"

"Let's worry about that if the time comes."

Rebekah held Mabel's hand while Clayton worked. Mabel screamed and almost broke Rebekah's fingers.

"Okay!" shouted Clayton. "We have the head down. Now, things will be smoother."

"I's still goin' die."

"No, you are *not*. Now, you can push."

After half an hour of pushing, Mabel delivered a healthy baby boy, and she did not die. She named him Adam Seth Musgrave. Despite her pain, Rebekah rejoiced with Mabel.

That night, Rebekah tucked in her three boys with a thankful heart. When she came downstairs, Caitlin was still there. Rebekah hugged her mother-in-law. "Caitlin, I'm…"

"Shh," said Caitlin. "You don't have to say a word. I understand."

When Rebekah went to bed, Rennin was waiting with their book open to the next chapter. "I thought you might need this tonight."

Rebekah nodded and laid her head on Rennin's shoulder.

Everyday Ranson spent with Ryan he grew angrier with a dead man for having treated his child mercilessly and a dead mother for not intervening on the child's behalf. He did everything he could to heal Ryan's wounded soul, but during the nights when he held the boy's sweat-soaked body and calmed his screams from the nightmares and memories of being tied and dropped in the well, he wanted to kill Andrew again. The one thing that steadied his heart was the time he spent with Angela.

Even in the dead of winter, Ranson checked his beaver and fox traps for he wanted to provide well for Ryan and, eventually, Angela. He would be gone three or four days at a stretch. At first, Ryan spent the nights that his father was away with Rennin and Morgan. After Ranson and Angela officially began courting, Angela asked Ryan if she could stay with him while Ranson was away. She told him she wanted to get to know him because she was going to be his stepmother in a few years. After discussing the proposal with Ranson, Ryan agreed, and Angela and Ryan began a new relationship.

Ryan talked to Angela about many things. She was a caring, compassionate woman. She told the boy, "Ryan, you know that my mother was murdered when I was only a baby. Anna is my stepmother, but I love her very much. I hope someday you will love me."

"Well, Angela, I like you. You know, I told Daidí he liked you, too. I was right. Actually, he more than likes you."

"Does he now? Tell me more." She smiled broadly.

"He might get mad. He has never been angry with me. I'm not sure how he would punish me."

"Ryan, Andrew was very cruel to you, wasn't he?"

The boy looked at the floor of the cabin. "Daidí says that he was a monster, and he is burning in Hell. Angela, sometimes when Daidí talks about Andrew, he looks as angry as Andrew used to look at me. It scares me."

"You know Ranson would never hurt you. He loves you so much. He blames himself for all the bad things Andrew did to you because he wasn't there to protect you."

"Daidí didn't hurt me. It wasn't his fault. Andrew hurt me."

"Let's make Ranson believe that."

"How?" The little boy chewed the inside of his lip. "May I tell you something else?"

"Of course."

"Sometimes I get upset when Daidí blames Momma for not protecting me. Andrew hurt Momma, too. She was afraid of him."

Angela lay down on the bed beside Ryan and put her arm over him. "When Ranson comes home, I'll talk to him. You get some sleep now."

After some time, Angela thought Ryan was asleep. She started to slip from his room. "Angela, don't leave," Ryan said. "I'm scared tonight. The wind is howling, and it's snowing hard. Daidí should have been home already. He said he would be back tonight."

"All right, sweetie, I'll stay."

"Angela, when you marry my daddy, what will I call you?"

"Whatever you like. I call Anna 'Momma', but I never knew my mother."

Groggily Ryan said, "I think I'll call you 'Angel' because you watch over me. Angel, I love you. Good night."

"Good night, Ryan."

When Angela awoke the next morning, Ryan was standing at the window crying. "Ryan, what's wrong?"

"It's a blizzard, Angel, and Daidí's not back yet. I'm really scared."

She climbed from the warm covers and wrapped Ryan and herself in the quilt. "Don't cry. Your daddy is smart and strong, and he loves us. He'll come through that door soon and laugh at us for being so silly."

"I can't lose my daddy. I just can't lose anybody else."

"We are *not* going to lose him. You listen to me. Ranson would not leave us," said Angela, who was deeply worried herself.

She went through the motions of the day. She stoked the fire and prepared meals, which neither of them ate. By suppertime, Angela was as frantic as Ryan, although she tried to hide it from him. Finally, she said, "Ryan, I'm going to talk to Papa."

"Angel, don't leave me!"

"I'm not leaving. I need to talk to Papa. My house is just across the way."

"You can't even see your house because it's snowing so hard. No, Angel." He stood in front of the door." You might get lost and die. I won't let you go."

"Ryan, I need to talk to my father."

"No!" He stamped his foot.

"Ryan!" Angela screamed as hot tears stung her eyes. Then, she pulled the frightened child close. "I'm scared, too, now.

Ranson is taking too long to get home. Papa and Uncle Rennin might go looking for him."

"They aren't stupid enough to go out in a blizzard. I just turned eight, and I'm smarter than that."

"All right. Let's sit by the fire and pray."

"Angel, I won't leave you. If Daidí doesn't come back, I'll take care of you."

"What about Rachel?" she asked, amused despite her fears. "I thought you wanted to marry her."

"I do, but I don't want you to be alone."

"I won't be alone. Ranson will come back."

In the wee hours of the morning a frigid gust startled both Angela and Ryan from their exhausted slumber in the chair by the fire. Thinking the wind had forced the door open, Angela dashed toward the Arctic blast. There, with icicles hanging from the ends of his hair, stood Ranson as stiff as a statue, his lips as deeply blue as his eyes.

It took only a moment to fly into action. "Ryan, stoke the fire!" Angela commanded as she slammed the door and slid the bolt into place. When she passed Ranson, he crumpled to the floor.

Within minutes, Ryan had a roaring fire in the fireplace. Angela said, "Ryan, help me move him closer to the fire. I can't move him alone. He is too heavy for me." The two dragged Ranson near the fire. Angela removed his wet clothes with trembling hands. Ryan massaged his father's feet.

Angela looked sharply at the child. "We have to get him warm. Papa says the best way to do that is body heat. I have to take off my clothes. Do you understand?"

"Yes. I'll help. You warm Daidí on that side, and I'll warm him on this side." Ryan took off his clothes and lay against Ranson's back with his arm over him. "I'll close my eyes, Angel. Go ahead."

She undressed and snuggled as close as she could to Ranson. She held Ryan's shaking hand in the process. After an hour, Ranson tried to speak. Through chattering teeth, he explained, "Sh-sh-shanty burned down. N-n-no sh-sh-shelter. C-c-came home t-t-to you."

"Shh," chided Angela. "Tell us later. Warm up now."

"B-b-beautiful Angela m-m-make me v-v-very warm. N-n-no clothes. G-g-geoffrey k-k-kill me."

Angela laughed with relief. "You must be better. You're worried about dying another way." She pulled away from Ranson.

He reached for her. "S-s-stay. F-f-feel your heart w-w-with mine."

She kissed his hand. "No, Ranson. Papa really would kill you. I love you, and I don't want to be a widow before I'm a wife. You scared me to death today as it is." She covered Ranson with a heavy quilt and saw that Ryan was sound asleep beside his father.

She pulled her clothes back on and sat beside Ranson. Stroking his hair, she whispered, "Rest. I'll be here when you wake up."

Ranson's still icy fingers found her hand. "L-l-lie b-b-beside me. I w-w-was s-s-scared, too. Th-th-thought I m-m-might n-n-never s-s-see you again. N-n-need you s-s-so m-m-much."

Angela lay beside the man she had chosen and held him tightly.

The sudden silence woke Angela. Ranson still lay beside her and breathed jagged, rumbling breaths. He was no longer cold. Rather, he was hot, burning with fever. She leapt to her feet and threw on her beaver-pelt cloak. Ryan followed her every move without a word. Angela caressed Ryan's hair. "Stay with Daidí. I'll be back as soon as I can."

"He's sick, now, Angel. Did he come home just to die?"

"No, Ryan, he won't die. He's young and strong, but I need Aunt Morgan. She'll know what to do, and she has all those medicinal herbs. The snow has stopped. All I need to do is get Aunt Morgan. I know he has pneumonia, but *she* can treat him."

Angela disappeared in a blanket of white. She returned with both Morgan and Rennin after a short time. Rennin carried Ranson to his bed. Morgan put Ryan to work boiling water to make willow and cinchona bark tea and Angela to work preparing a camphor poultice. Morgan bathed Ranson's face and torso with water from melting snow, trying to reduce his fever. She placed the poultice on his chest, and she and Angela forced a few sips of the tea between his lips.

For three days Ranson's body burned. He tossed and kicked his covers and mumbled in his delirium. All the while, Angela stayed by his bed and cared for him and listened to his incoherent ranting.

"No! No! Tabitha. Come back! Wait. Wait for me. Ryan! Daddy. Tabitha!"

Time and again Ranson called for Tabitha, and each time, Angela soothed his forehead. Finally, he was still and quiet though his fever raged. He drenched his bedding with perspiration, and Angela changed the sheets and quilts. Ryan sat with his father so Angela could wash the dirty linens and clothes. As she washed, she overheard Anna and Cynthia talking.

Anna said, "The Iroquois say a man's heart can be heard when his mind is not in control. You say Ranson has been calling for Tabitha? My poor, sweet Angela. Her heart must be breaking."

Cynthia chided her mother. "He's delirious, Momma. He's probably dreaming terrible dreams of his yesteryears."

"Still his heart should call for Angela."

"Momma, don't say anything to her. It would only make matters worse. You know she's crazy for him. Duncan could call for a harlot in his delirium, and I would still love him. I know Angela will feel the same."

Angela went back inside where Ryan waited patiently. He turned at the sound of the opening door. "He's tossing again, Angel."

"I'll stay with him, Ryan. You go see your Rachel." He started out the door, but Angela detained him. "Ryan, has Ranson ever told you that he loves me?"

"Not using those words, but he does."

"He's trying to convince himself to love me. I'm just a foolish girl. How could I ever have thought a man like Ranson could love a silly child like me?"

Ryan, put his hand on Angela's shoulder. "Angel, I love you."

She hugged the boy. "I love you, too, precious. You take a break now. Go play."

In the stillness, Angela sat with Ranson and talked softly as he jerked spasmodically in his sleep. "Your heart belongs to a dead woman. How do I compete with a ghost? Ranson, I love you so much. You said you *need* me, not *love* me. Maybe you were right all along. I'm only a child. You're a man. You've known love. You've been with a woman. I'm a naïve little girl to think that I could satisfy you. How I hate that ghost you love! Oh! But I love you. Do I stand and fight, or do I concede? God, please give me a sign. Show me what to do."

Ranson's body suddenly contorted in a seizure. Angela screamed, "What do I do? A spoon, a spoon." She managed to slide a wooden spoon into Ranson's mouth. After several minutes of violent writhing, he relaxed as if he were a rag doll. Angela sat on the bed and washed his face with a cool cloth.

Ranson started to mumble again as she put the washbasin on the table. "Angela! Where are you? Don't leave me. Angela! Angela! Please, answer me."

She stood still and listened to his frantic call until he tried to get out of bed. "Angela! Please, don't leave me."

She pushed him back onto the bed. "I'm right here, Ranson. I haven't left."

He lay back. "Angela...My Angela...Won't leave you...Coming home. Can't leave you. Angela. My beautiful angel." He relaxed temporarily before he mumbled Angela's name again.

"Angela...Won't fight anymore...Reason to live...Angela...I'll get home...I swear. Have to get home...Tell Angela...Love you...Need you...Want you, my perfect angel."

Angela stroked Ranson's hair. "You keep fighting. I need you, too. Don't you dare leave me. I love you. You said you would come home. Now, you get well and come back to me. I will *never* concede. I'll stand right here beside you and fight with all that is within me. I will not let nightmares about your past chase me away." She kissed his feverish brow. "I love you."

Sometime in the night, Ranson said calmly to the woman dozing in the chair by his bed, "Angela."

She woke instantly to the sound of his voice. "Ranson!" She touched a cool face.

He lifted a weak hand. "My Angela." he let his hand fall through the copper ringlets that draped over his fingers. "Angela, two years is so long. I don't know if I can wait two years. I love you more than I ever thought I could love again. The thought of saying those words to you kept me going through the snow. I love you. Every time I thought of you, I stopped hating. I don't think I even hate Andrew any more. I have so much to be thankful for. I have you and my son. You've made me want to live again. Marry me Angela. Let's convince your father that two years is a lifetime."

"Ranson, that would be almost impossible. Papa is more stubborn than I am. I love you, but we made an agreement."

"An agreement that might force us to sin. I know you want me, too."

"More than you know."

He breathed deeply and coughed hard. Angela gave him a sip of whiskey and peppermint oil mixed. "Aunt Morgan said to give you this if you cough."

Ranson took her hand. "I'll wait for you, my angel. Two years may seem like forever, but I'll wait."

She touched his fingers to her lips. "Just say it again. Tell me you love me."

"I love you. I love you."

Rennin closed the book as he realized Rebekah had dozed off. He lay back with her still in his arms. "I love you, *my* angel, my Rebekah. Love can only grow when bitterness is rooted out. The heart is, then, open to love all the more."

31
Heartbreak

Six weeks into Caitlin's pregnancy, she began to bleed. She was in a tizzy. Both Clayton and Thomas put her to bed. Mabel graciously took on both houses to clean. Catherine took Caitlin's class. Rebekah cared for Seth, as Mabel called her son, and sat with Caitlin to keep her company.

Caitlin confided her fear to Rebekah. "I don't think I can take the heartbreak of losing this child. This might be Clay's only chance and my last chance to have a child I really wanted from the beginning. Rebekah, I love Rennin more than I ever thought possible, but, in all honesty, I did not want him when I discovered I was expecting, considering the circumstances. The same was true for Eric. The next two I wanted desperately, but I lost them. I want this baby more than I wanted to be loved. I want the chance to be a real mother—in action and in name."

Rebekah held Caitlin's hand and reassured her. "Both Thomas and Clayton say if you stay in bed and take it easy, everything will be fine. You won't lose this baby, Caitlin. I know it in my heart. This time you will get your spirit's desire."

Caitlin took comfort from Rebekah's words and fell into the routine of being waited on hand and foot for the duration of her pregnancy.

Christmas came, and Rennin carried his mother to his house for the traditional Christmas Eve celebration, saying, "Momma, just because you can't be up and around does not mean you can't sing with us." So, Caitlin added her voice to the carols, and Mabel graced the group with a spine-tingling

Negro spiritual that made each spirit contemplate the sacrifice made for a freed soul.

Christmas Day was cool, but sunny, an experience Caitlin found odd, yet enjoyable. She had always had cold, and usually snowy, Christmases. After supper, Gabriel and Michael celebrated their third birthday at Grandma Caitlin's house with cake and ice cream made on the recently patented Johnson Patent Ice-Cream Freezer.

The next couple of days were uneventful. Rennin took an afternoon and insisted that Rebekah and he have a picnic. As they lounged in a meadow nestled in the mountains, Rennin read the continuing saga of his ancestors.

Rennin and Morgan had been back in Mom's Trading Post such a short time, and their home had changed, adding two new members, Ranson and Ryan Riley who would be there for quite a while to come. The February, after Rennin and Morgan had a real honeymoon and while Ranson and Ryan lived in the O'Rourke house, approached quickly, and before anyone realized the time had passed, Cameron banged on his mother's door in the middle of the night. Morgan dragged herself to the door only to be greeted by panic. "Momma, it's time. Holly needs you. I waited as long as I dare. Momma, she seems to be having a really hard time."

"I'm coming, honey. Just let me put on some clothes."

Morgan found Holly in dire distress. The terrified girl begged, "Momma Morgan, help me."

Morgan checked Holly and turned to Cameron. "Cam, get Anna."

"Momma, what's wrong?"

She grabbed Cameron's arm roughly and pulled him toward the door. Outside, she hissed, "You didn't say she was bleeding so heavily. She shouldn't be bleeding at all yet."

"She wasn't bleeding when I came to get you. Momma, how bad is it?"

"Bad. Cameron, she's losing blood—fast. The baby is not ready to come yet. It could be *hours*. She can't continue to bleed like this."

"Take the baby, Momma, the way Daidí took Rachel. I can't lose Holly."

Morgan rubbed Cameron's arm gently. "Get your father and bring the things I need. I'll do what I can, but, Cameron, you must prepare yourself. This is very bad."

With ashen face, he asked straightforwardly, "Is Holly going to die?"

"I don't know. Send Geoffrey after Talulah. I need all the help I can get."

Morgan went back to Holly and washed her face. Holly always faced difficulty head on. She confronted her mother-in-law. "Momma Morgan, am I going to die?"

Morgan choked on her words. "It's very possible. You've already lost too much blood."

"I see," said Holly, facing reality calmly. "What about the baby?"

Before Morgan could answer, Holly contracted and fresh blood gushed. She released only a whimper. "Momma Morgan, don't let my baby die. Whatever happens, save my baby. Make Cameron understand. The baby is more important than either of us."

Cameron came in with Rennin and Morgan's supplies. Rennin aked, "Morgan, is this necessary?"

"Absolutely," she answered.

Holly whimpered in pain again and called for Cameron. He clutched her hand. "Cameron, take care of our baby. The baby is proof of how much we love each other."

Cameron fought his tears. "Holly, don't leave me. I can't live without you. I don't want to."

"Yes, you can. You must for our baby."

"But, Holly, I don't care if we ever have a baby. *You* are my life."

"No!" growled Holly through clenched teeth. "Promise me. Give me your word. Cam, the baby is a part of me. Swear."

He relented. "I promise I'll take care of our baby. I'll do what is best for him or her."

She squeezed Cameron's hand. "I love you so much."

He rubbed her hand against his cheek. "My beautiful Holly Berry." Tears dripped onto her hand.

She whispered, "Don't cry for me, Cameron. I have burned brightly, if briefly. I'm not afraid. I know where I'm going."

The next sound Cameron heard was soft, weak crying. "My baby," gasped Holly. "Please, let me hold my baby."

"It's a boy," whispered Morgan. "He's perfect."

Holly held the baby and gently touched his fingers and toes. "Cameron, let's name him."

"What do you want to call him?"

"What we agreed, Rowan—Rowan Patrick O'Rourke."

Cameron sat beside Holly and Rowan. He stroked her hair and laid his head against hers. In the background Morgan whispered to Rennin. "There was hardly any blood, and what little there was came out bright orange. Rennin, she had lost so much already. I'm going to lose her." She swiped tears from her eyes. "I've failed Cameron."

Rennin rebuked her. "'Tis not your fault. 'Tis not anybody's fault."

Holly took a deep breath. "Cameron, hold my hand. I'm cold. I'm so cold. I love you."

"Holly, please," wept Cameron.

She breathed again, and her hand slipped from Cameron's.

"Momma!" Cameron cried through a sob. "Momma, please bring her back."

Morgan looked at Rennin, eyes stretched wide.

Rennin nodded. "Do what you have to. We're the only three here. No one else has to know."

For an hour Morgan performed the ritual and the incantation that Elizabeth had once performed on Caitlin, but to no avail. Finally, she looked Cameron forlornly in the eye. "I can't, baby. I don't have the gift."

Cameron turned pitiful eyes to his father. "Daidí?"

With a great sigh and a roiling stomach, Rennin attempted the spell half a dozen times. He shook his head and released his own tears.

Cameron nodded and walked into the snow.

During the morning Oliver and Anna prepared their little sister's body for burial. Cameron could not be found. Finally, in mid-afternoon, he returned with Geoffrey, Talulah, and Talulah's wife, Lahoma.

Barely glancing at baby Rowan, Cameron handed him to Lahoma and simply muttered, "Thank you."

Rowan, who had screamed all morning, wailed loudly as the woman took him. In broken English Lahoma whispered, "All right, little man child. Lahoma care you." She opened her blouse and nursed the baby.

Talulah offered an explanation as Cameron laid his head on Holly's chest and fell asleep. "Lahoma and Talulah have stillborn child two days past. Lahoma agreed nurse Cameron's son. Lahoma stay Mom's Trading Post one year. So sorry Holly pass. Cameron's heart broken. Will mend."

Over the next several weeks, Cameron talked to no one except Donovan, who, having thought his wife might be dead once, tried to console his brother. Late one evening, Donovan came to Rennin and Morgan. "Momma, Daidí, I'm afraid for Cameron. He's so distraught, I'm fearful he might do something stupid."

"Such as?" asked Rennin in alarm.

"Kill himself. All he talks about is being with Holly, and he hates the baby. He blames Rowan for Holly's death."

"Rennin," said Morgan, "if Donnie is this concerned, there is definitely cause for alarm. What do we do?"

"I'll talk to him in the morning whether or not he wants to talk to me. He can listen."

Immediately after breakfast, Rennin knocked on Cameron's door. Lahoma let him in. He asked her, "Lahoma, will you wake Cameron?"

"Cameron no here. Cameron leave last night."

"What?"

"Him say give note in morning." Lahoma handed Rennin a folded piece of paper. Rennin unfolded the note and read:

Dear Daidi and Momma,

Once you have read this, I'm sure you will no longer care what I do, for you will wish to disown me as your son. It matters not to me. I cannot stay. I cannot watch Rowan grow, knowing Holly sacrificed herself for him. Holly was my life. I am dead inside, yet I'm too cowardly to end my own suffering.

As for the baby, I'm keeping my promise to Holly. I'm doing what is best for him. The two of you are the best parents he could ever have. I'm leaving the rings you made for Holly and me, Daidi. When Rowan is grown, give them to him and tell him that I loved his mother with all my heart. I'm sorry that I cannot face him, but I grow angrier and colder each time I see him. My mind tells me I'm wrong, but I cannot get past it.

Please forgive me and understand.

Cameron

"Forgive him!" shouted Rennin. "Understand! I'll send him to Holly myself when I get my hands on him. The fool!"

Rennin stormed home. "Morgan! Read this crock of crap!"

Morgan read the note. "Rennin, how could he?"

"I don't know, but I'm going to find him. When I do, I'm going to treat him just the way he's acting—like a spoiled, selfish, inconsiderate brat. I'm going to kick his arse!"

"Rennin!" said Morgan.

"From here to sunrise!" he finished as he slammed the door behind him.

Rennin almost knocked over Ranson, who was preparing to check his traps, as he turned around. "Rennin, whoa! Where's the fire? What's wrong?"

"I'm going to find Cameron and murder him. He doesn't want to live? Well, he has just about ensured going to Holly when I find him." Rennin walked toward the barn as he talked.

"What do you mean, 'find him'?"

"He has run away like a selfish little boy. I'm going to find him and drag his worthless hide back. He has responsibilities. He was grown up enough to get married and make a baby. He's grown up enough to care for his own child. That is unless I do beat him to death. *Then*, I'll take Rowan and be his father. Damn that boy! What is he thinking?"

"He's not," said Ranson. "He's hurting. Rennin, let me go after Cameron. You're too angry. I can track him easily, and I can talk to him. I know his pain. Let me help this way. It's my turn to be your friend."

Rennin punched the barn door and brought blood to his own knuckles. "You're right, Ranson. I remember a fight I had with my father when I was young. He was angry and stubborn, and I thought I knew all the answers. The aftermath was disastrous although everything worked out in the end. Yes. Please, go after Cameron for me. When you find him, tell him"—He bit his lip—"tell him I love him. Tell him this is not the way to solve his problem. Bring him back even if you have to hog-tie him. Maybe you should take Donovan with you. He and Cameron have always been close."

"No, I'll go alone. Perhaps having some one who's not so close would be better for a change. I can be impartial, although I plan to make him see how foolish he is to give up his son. I know, having thought I had lost Ryan. I'll talk some sense into him, Rennin."

First, Ranson circled the community to discover which direction Cameron had gone. Then, he packed supplies and left. Morgan watched from the porch. She looked confused. "Rennin?" she asked. "What does Ranson have against his chest? It's moving."

"I don't know," said Rennin as he looked over Morgan. "Yes, I do. Oh, he's good. Smooth. Smart. Morgan, I think I love this lad. He's taking Rowan with him. He knows exactly what he's doing. I would have been too angry to consider it. Cameron is about to get a healthy dose of reality."

Cameron sat by his campfire and stirred the venison stew on his plate. Although he had warmed it over the fire, he had toyed with it so long that the gravy had congealed once again. A twig snapped behind him. He jumped to his feet and fumbled in his pack for his gun.

"I'm not here to kill you," a voice in the dark said, "but you had better be glad I'm not Rennin."

"Alackaday!" shouted Cameron. "You scared the hell out of me, Ranson. Are you checking your traps?"

"No. I came to bring you something you forgot."

"Did Momma send you?"

"No. I volunteered to keep Rennin from killing you. He sent this to you." Ranson handed Cameron a bundle.

"What is it?"

"The *trash* you left behind."

Rowan squirmed and whined at being disturbed.

"My God! It's the baby. Why did you bring him to me?"

"Nobody wants your discarded *refuse*. Rennin figures this is your responsibility. You have to deal with it."

"Then, take him to Oliver or Anna. He's their nephew. They'll take care of him."

"Nay." He shook his head with a deep scowl on his brow. "They don't want to look at the monster that killed their baby sister everyday. God! How could you expect that of them?"

"He's a baby for Pete's sake."

"Yea. Yours. Oh, and Holly's." Ranson pushed the blanket back from Rowan's face. He said thoughtfully, "Have you ever noticed how he puckers his lips just like Holly used to when she was thinking? Oh, never mind." He waved a dismissive hand. "It's simple, Cameron. If you don't want him, leave him in the morning. He will either freeze or some wild animal will have a meal. Either way, the little murderer is out of your life, and nobody else has to mess with him either."

"Ranson, you can't be serious."

"If he were mine..."

"What would you do? Drown him?"

"No. I'd desert him, and let him grow up knowing his father didn't love him and was too self-centered to see beyond his own momentary pain," was Ranson's blistering response. Cameron gasped, and Ranson continued. "It doesn't matter. You do what you want, but I'd love him—the way I love Ryan because Tabitha is a part of Ryan. Look at your son, Cameron. Take care of him for a few hours. If you still don't want him, leave him to die rather than to grow up knowing you blamed him for his mother's death and despised him. If he captures your heart in the middle of the night, go home; or at least take him with you. Get a goat. Strain his milk, or keep Lahoma around. He'll be eating food soon enough. Good-bye." Ranson laid the wine skins of strained goat's milk he had brought at Cameron's feet. "I'm sorely disappointed that you are *not* the man I thought you were." Ranson walked back toward Mom's Trading Post.

Rowan started to cry. Cameron called, "Ranson, wait. Don't leave me here alone with a baby. I don't know what to do."

"Feed him, change his diaper, and be sure to burp him." Ranson disappeared in the darkness, but he made a cold camp and kept watch over Cameron and Rowan.

Cameron stared helplessly at the bellowing baby he held. "Feed you? How?" Cameron looked in the bag at his feet and found the wine skins with animal skin nipples. "He brought you food. Of course, he did. He's a good father."

Cameron cradled Rowan and, even with so little practice, put a nipple to his lips. The baby sucked with force though he rooted at his father's shoulder at first. "I guess you were hungry. Leave you to die. Does he really think I'm that heartless? I left you with the greatest father in the world—your granddad. Granddad would move Heaven and Earth to take care of his children, possibly Hell, too." Cameron paused. "Granddad. My daddy."

Before Cameron realized what had happened, the bottle was empty. He thought aloud. "Burp. Rowan, you need to burp. Are you going to put half that milk back on me?" Cameron patted the baby's back. Rowan released a hearty burp and Cameron sat down. He laid Rowan back on his forearms with the baby's head in his hands.

Cameron stared at his son until the fire started to die. Holding the baby in one arm, he threw logs on the fire with the other. He sat back down with the baby. "Heaven help me! You look like your mother. You *do* pucker your lips like hers. What do I do, little one? I miss her so much."

Rowan made little squealing sounds and kicked his legs. "Is that your answer? I should scream and kick?" Cameron surprised himself as he laughed. "Ranson is crazy. It's too cold for you out here."

Cameron changed Rowan and bundled him warmly. "I guess you'll have to sleep with me." He went into the sealskin tent and snuggled under his blankets with Rowan nestled next to him. Rowan found his thumb, and both fell asleep.

Cameron woke early to little gurgling sounds. Rowan lay beside his father without crying. Cameron sat up and ran his fingers through his long strawberry-blond hair. Rowan kicked and cooed. Cameron's tears splashed onto the little face, and Rowan shook his head and frowned. Cameron lifted the little boy and pulled him into his chest. He held the baby close and sobbed for a long time before he spoke. "I'm sorry, Rowan. It's not your fault. I am so sorry. Oh, baby, your momma was so perfect. She was wild and free and never let the burdens of life crush her. Even you. Look at you. You're so like her. Let you freeze or be eaten, indeed! What do I do now? Do I go home and confess my folly and feel my father's fury?"

Rowan made his little squealing noise and kicked happily.

"Or do we leave?"

Rowan suddenly scowled and started to cry loudly.

"All right," said Cameron. "We'll go home, but first we'll eat and change clothes"

Cameron fed the baby and changed him. He hastily ate some dried fruit and venison jerky, and then packed his knapsack. "Now, how did Ranson have you strapped on? Let's figure this out." Cameron slipped on the harness Ranson had devised. Rowan burrowed against his father and slept. Cameron headed back to Mom's Trading Post.

As he started through the thicket, Ranson fell into step with him. "Want some company?"

Cameron jumped. "Stop that!"

"Stop what?"

"Sneaking up on me."

"Sorry."

"No concern of yours, huh?"

"So, I lied." He shrugged

"What if I had left him to freeze?"

"First, I would have kicked your ass. Then, I would have taken him back to Rennin."

"Did Daidí send him?"

"No, that was all my idea. I don't even know if Rennin knows I took him. However, Rennin was coming after you. I think your body would be in much greater agony had he come."

"Thank you."

"For saving your hide?" Ranson looked sidelong at his friend.

"For showing me that my heart doesn't have to be empty."

Ranson smiled. "You know, I know your heartbreak. It does get easier, and don't give up on love. I hope to find love again someday. Geoffrey sure did. Let's use him for our example."

"Are you suggesting I steal Duncan's girl? You know, he has his eyes set on Cynthia."

"Absolutely not. Duncan is as big as you. He might have something to say about it."

"True. That kid has always packed a powerful punch."

"No, Cameron. Get to know your son. There's plenty of time for a wife. Those are basically the same words Rennin said to me."

"My father is wise."

"When he's not irate."

"I think I'll go into my house and lock the doors.

"Won't do any good. He has an ax."

Cameron laughed with Ranson at the thought. Then, he asked, "Seriously, Ranson, how do I deal with the pain? Uncle Geoffrey married again the very next day—from necessity in the beginning, but look at him and Anna now. Does it take meeting someone to fill the void?"

"I don't know. I think you just live one day at a time. That's what I'm doing. And hold on to your precious memories and that." Ranson nodded toward the baby.

Cameron caressed Rowan's back and kissed his sleeping head. "I don't ever want him to know how foolish I was. How could I blame something so sweet and innocent for my heartache?"

"It's easy. I often blame Tabitha for what happened to Ryan until I consider how much she must have been hurting, too. The only truly guilty party was Andrew. He's dead. My goal now is to be a good father to Ryan and eventually a good husband to someone that God will send me."

"You've suffered as greatly as I, maybe worse. Do you think we'll ever be happy again?"

"I'm sure we will. For now, concentrate on being a good father. Make that baby proud to be your son. Bring honor to Holly by rearing her son to be a man like the one she loved, a man like his father and his grandfather."

"I thought you were disappointed in me." Cameron cocked his head to the side.

"Not really. I understand how much you've been hurting, and you've apparently come to your senses."

"Thanks to you. If you need a friend, you know where to find me."

"Sounds great. Rennin told me to get to know you and your brother."

"He was right, as usual. I hope we do become true friends," said Cameron.

"I anticipate it," affirmed Ranson.

They walked on with only the sound of snow crunching under their feet.

About suppertime, Cameron and Ranson came through the clearing into the village. Morgan kept a vigil from her window. She announced, "Rennin, they're back—both of them."

"Good."

"Rennin."

"Morgan, don't push. Who has the baby?"

"Cam."

"It's about damned time."

"Rennin, they're stopping and talking. I wish I could hear that conversation."

Ranson said, "Well, where are you going?"

"To see Daidí. He can kill me if he wants, but I think I'll keep Rowan between him and me. Thank you again, Ranson."

"Cameron, the one message Rennin wanted me to give to you was to tell you that he loves you. Remember that."

The two men shook hands, and Cameron started toward his parents' home while Ranson deliberately went to the barn.

Morgan warned, "Rennin, Cam is coming here."

Cameron knocked and opened the door. "Daidí!"

"What?" said Rennin, trying to stay angry. He remained standing to prove to himself that he was still slightly bigger than Cameron.

"Daidí," said Cameron. "I'm sorry. I...we"—He looked down—"need you. Help me, Daidí. I'm not sure how to go about this. My heart is still breaking, and I feel lost and alone."

Rennin took a breath and held his arms out to Cameron. Gently he said, "Never alone, Cameron."

Cameron fell into his father's open arms. Morgan asked, "Don't I count?"

"Yes, Grandma," answered Cameron as Morgan joined the group.

After a while Cameron went home so Lahoma could continue to feed Rowan, but he took over the rest of the baby's care. His broken heart found solace in the love of his son, and he developed a lifelong friendship with Ranson Riley, a man who truly understood Cameron's heartbreak.

Rennin closed the book with a sigh. Rebekah whispered, "So that was the first Rowan in your family." She lovingly caressed the little golden chain ring. "And I have Holly's ring. That story is heart-wrenching. Did Cameron ever remarry?"

"Many years later, but he and Rowan were a family for a long time. Katie still has an old family Bible that lists all the births and deaths and marriages. It goes all the way back to Alexander O'Rourke and Genevieve Brady, who were born in Willow Hollow, Ireland, sometime around 1530. It even lists the name Quazel Rodriguez Morales. It's very old and delicate. Katie is extremely protective of it."

"Rennin, we should get a new Bible and transfer all the information. I think there is a small change that needs to be made anyway."

"Rebekah, I'm not sure I want all my descendents to know that."

"I disagree. Caitlin has the right to have the tribute of being your mother."

"That's not the part I'm talking about, and you know it."

"Rennin, you're an O'Rourke, a true descendent of Alexander. That fact must be preserved for future generations who might want to seek Draconis."

"You really believe the place is real, don't you?

"Don't you?"

"In my spirit? Yes, I suppose I do."

Their visit to a magical time was interrupted as Chen Li galloped up. "Rebekah! It's Keturah. She's in rabor way too early, and she wants you. Both Thomas and Clayton are with her. Rebekah, I'm worried. When two doctors rook so dour, it is time to worry. Come quickly."

"Go," said Rennin. "Ride with Chen Li. I'll bring everything home, and I'll be there as fast as I can."

Rebekah arrived just as Keturah started to push. Bart looked at his wife's best friend with deep circles beneath his eyes. Rebekah raised her eyebrows in question. Bart closed his eyes to stifle the tears that would escape.

With a controlled scream, Keturah delivered a tiny baby girl and fell back, limp. Bart held his daughter, and Rebekah stood beside him with her hand on his shoulder as Rennin arrived. Keturah opened her eyes and held her hand up. Bart laid the very premature newborn in her mother's arms.

Keturah smiled weakly, "Bart, you take care of her."

"Don't talk like dat. You gonna take care of her."

"You know better. Rebekah, help Bart. Ask Mabel if she'll nurse my little girl."

Rebekah shook and nodded her head. "Keturah, don't talk nonsense."

"It's not nonsense. Ask Thomas. I knew the risk, and she's worth the sacrifice. Bart, her name is Keturah Rebekah Mercier."

Bart touched his lips to his wife's head. "Keturah, I ain't never knowed a woman like you. I don't know what kinda man I'll be wifout you."

"You'll be the man God has made you—a loving, compassionate servant of God and a wonderful father. Remember that I have loved you deeply."

Bart choked out his words, "I love you more'n I can ever say."

Keturah reached her hand to Bart's face. It fell with a thud.

Bart looked sharply at Thomas. "Thomas?"

"She's gone, Bart. I'm sorry. Clayton and I did everything we knew to do. I am so sorry."

Stoically, Bart lifted his daughter. "Will you be as precious as your momma?" He planted a kiss on the baby's head and heaved a great sigh. He turned to Rebekah, "Rebekah, I will need your help. Dis is too much for me to bear alone. Right now, will you take Keturah to Mabel and do as her momma asked? I sure 'nuff can't feed her. I ain't equipped for dat. Tell Mabel dat I'll pay her extry."

Rebekah took the baby. "I'll do it," said Rennin. "Stay with Bart. I'll be back shortly."

Then, Bart asked soberly, "Will da baby actually live, Thomas?"

Thomas said optimistically, "She's small, but healthy. Mabel will take good care of her. Just keep her extra warm and make sure she gets sunlight every day."

Rebekah put her arms around Bart, and he let her comfort him. The two cried together. When Rennin returned, Bart said pragmatically, "Rennin, we ain't considered a spot for a cemetery. Ike's buried up near da mine, but dat ain't a fit place for Keturah. We gonna need a cemetery."

"The land behind the church will be appropriate," thought Rennin aloud. "It's flat and, I suppose, sacred."

"Okay. Rebekah, I need help preparin' her."

Thomas said compassionately, "Bart, let Cathy and Candy do that."

"Thank you, Thomas, but it needs to be somebody who knowed her well."

As Bart and Rebekah dressed Keturah, Rennin made a simple coffin. Bart asked Rebekah, "Rebekah, what am I gonna do? I really need your help. I got four—*four*—babies. Promise me dat if sumpin' happens to me, you and Rennin will raise my chillun. Da school is great, but I want my babies to have a real momma and daddy."

"Bart! You aren't thinking of doing something drastic, are you?"

"Promise!" said Bart sharply.

"I promise. They will be my babies. I will have a houseful." Rebekah gasped. "Oh, God! Marie's prophecy! Bart, please don't die."

"I ain't plannin' to, but jest in case."

"I promise. If anything happens to you, Rennin and I will be mother and father to your children."

"Dat makes me feel better."

The family and friends of Keturah Franklin Mercier laid her to rest in the new cemetery. The day chose to be overcast to reflect the sentiment of the mourners. After the funeral, Bart asked Rennin to ride with him. "I got sumpin' to show you. I feel an urgency to git dis done."

The two men rode away in a light sprinkle to the last small cave in the area they had claimed. Bart explained, "I found dis day afore yesterdy, but I didn't git a chance the tell you."

They tethered the horses and walked over rocky terrain before Bart led Rennin through a small opening to the side of the cave. The slit in the rock was narrow and quite a squeeze for Rennin. Once inside, Bart swung his lantern around. "Rennin, we thought da other vein was rich. Look at dis."

"Oh, my word!" exclaimed Rennin.

"Our families won't want for nothin'—ever. Ten generations down da road'll be filthy rich."

"Bart, my family was already wealthy. This is obscene."

"Think of what we can do. Maybe a hospital. We got two doctors to start."

"Bart, you are the most generous man I've ever known. You put me to shame. I'm proud to call you my friend."

"Thank you, Rennin. Da feelin's mutual."

The earth trembled beneath their feet. "Earthquake!" shouted Rennin as the rumble grew louder. "Let's get out of here!"

Before they reached the entrance, they were showered with rocks and debris. In front of their eyes, gold chunks rained down with a sound like thunder. They fought their way toward the entrance. The small opening closed, and the vein of gold buried them.

32
Legacy

Rebekah waited dinner for over an hour. She was not particularly concerned about the earthquake in the afternoon because it was not severe and the ground tremored frequently. Finally, Chen Li spoke up. "This is not rike Rennin or Bart. Dr. Clay, I think we need to search for them."

"I think you're right," Clayton agreed.

Chen Li recalled Bart and Rennin riding toward the caves, so every man except Henry began a search in that direction.

Rebekah insisted that all the children be fed and bathed as usual. The school children had already had enough upheaval with Caitlin's being put to bed and Keturah's untimely death. Jed, Stephen, Chris, and baby Keturah were at Rebekah's house. Jed and Stephen seemed dazed, and Chris wandered around as if lost.

Caitlin decided to spend the night with Rebekah as well. She told her, "You don't need to be alone. Besides, I'm worried about Rennin, too."

Rebekah admitted, "Caitlin, I am so scared. I keep remembering what Marie LaVeau said—that I would be mother to many, but at great personal heartache. I've lost Keturah. What if something has happened to Bart? He made me promise that Rennin and I would take his children. It's as if he felt he would be gone soon."

"Rebekah, those are morbid thoughts."

"But what if?"

"Then, you'll be a mother to your best friend's children. You'll love and nurture them and teach them just as Keturah would have."

Rebekah curled up beside Caitlin. "Caitlin, I love you. Please, don't you leave me, too."

Caitlin put her arm around Rebekah. "I'll not leave you, my darling daughter. I love you, too."

"Daughter?"

"You *are* married to my son."

"Yes, I am. Your legacy of love and sacrifice are such an example. I see where Rennin gets his values."

"Rebekah, you're far stronger than I am. I can learn a lot from you."

"Well, right this minute, I think we both just want Rennin to walk through the front door."

As they spoke, the door opened. Rebekah bounded from the guest room. Clayton and Chen Li stood, faces drawn and tight. "No sign of them," said Chen Li. "We followed the horse tracks in the mud into the hills where we rost the tracks. Even Running Bear could not find them. It's too dark to search. We'll go again at first right."

In the small cave, Rennin regained consciousness. "Bart?" He sputtered and coughed from the dust. "Bart, where are you? Can you hear me?"

Rennin heard a slight groan and tried to follow the sound. Pain shot through his leg, causing him to cry out at its severity. He felt around in the dark and found the handle of the lantern. Amazingly, it was unbroken. Rennin fumbled in his pocket for the small box of Lucifers he carried. Finding them, he lit the lantern.

Rennin saw the bone protruding through the skin of his right leg and his ankle was pinned beneath several large pieces of gold. In utter determination, he leaned forward despite the pain and moved the chunks of gold. At the relief of the pressure against his ankle, Rennin fell back, sweating profusely.

After several minutes to regain his nerve, he dragged himself along on his side, looking for Bart. He found him almost completely buried by rubble. Frantically, he scooped and scraped and clawed the dirt and rocks away. "Bart! Can you hear me?"

Bart's eyes fluttered open. "Rennin, when you git outta here, take care of my little 'uns. Tell 'em how much I love 'em."

"Shut up!" growled Rennin. "We'll get out together."

"No, we won't. I'm hurt bad. I'm spittin' blood."

"Bart, you can't die. You can't leave your babies. They just lost their mother."

"You and Rebekah take 'em. She done promised. Now, you promise."

"You know I will. Bart, I don't want to lose you. You're the best friend I've ever had."

"I can't help it, Rennin. It ain't my choice. Maybe God knows I ain't much good wifout Keturah."

"Nonsense. What about our hospital?"

"Build it for me. Maybe I'll leave a legacy of goodness yet."

Bart coughed hard, and blood flowed from his mouth and nose. Rennin stripped off his shirt and wiped his friend's face. "Bart, hang on. By now, Rebekah has sent a posse to look for us. I'll start digging from this side. I need you, Bart. You make me more compassionate and thoughtful and merciful."

"No, Rennin. Your example has made me a better man. I love you like my brother."

"I love you, too, Bart. I don't want to lose you. We haven't had to become blood brothers. We're brothers in thought, in word, and in deed."

Bart coughed again. Rennin could hear the gurgling in his lungs, and he knew that Bart would not be with him much longer. Bart stopped speaking. He breathed raggedly a few more times and slipped quietly into eternity.

Rennin looked around him and let the hot tears flow unashamedly. Then, he declared loudly, "I will not die in here. I have too much to live for." With renewed vigor, Rennin scooted to where the opening should have been. Slowly and deliberately and through excruciating pain, he moved rocks. The pile seemed unending, and Rennin, too, had lost blood from the gash in his leg. He leaned against the cold granite and breathed. *Let me rest a little. I'll go on in a bit.* To conserve his coal-oil, he doused the lantern. Rennin closed his eyes and slept.

The rain fell harder. Late in the night, Rebekah was awakened from a nightmarish sleep by snorting, stomping, and whinnying. The ruckus woke Chen Li, too. He met Rebekah at the top of the stairs. Both carried a lantern. They clasped hands and hurried to the back door.

"It's Buster!" shouted Rebekah as she opened the door.

"And Buck," added Chen Li.

Rebekah called, "Rennin! Bart!"

"Don't waste your breath, Rebekah," said Chen Li. "Both horses' tethers have been snapped or chewed." He examined the reins. "I think chewed."

Rebekah rubbed Buster. "But you know where they are, don't you, boy? Even Patty can't find them in all this rain, but you remember where you left them."

She turned abruptly. "Feed Buster and Buck, Chen Li. Do it quickly. They are going to take us to Rennin and Bart."

Rebekah dressed hastily and woke Clayton. She told him her idea that Buster could lead them to Rennin. He woke the other men of the town.

When the men arrived at the stables, Rebekah had Jewel ready to ride. "Where do you think you're going?" asked Clayton.

"I said that Buster could lead us to Rennin. By 'us' I meant me. He'll do it for me. You'll need me along. And, Clay, only an act of God will keep me from going, so you needn't try."

"Yes, ma'am, but you know Buster would do it for me." Clayton patted Rebekah's cheek. "We'll find him, Rebekah."

"I know." She mounted Jewel and pulled Buster's reins. "Come on, Buster. Let's find Rennin."

The search party followed Buster to the small cave. Rebekah dismounted in a flash and raced into the cave. "Rennin!"

The men quickly followed. They called and searched to no avail. Rebekah leaned against the wall of the cave and shouted all the louder in desperation.

In the narrow passage that ran parallel to the wall, Rennin's foggy brain heard Rebekah's voice. He woke up and thought, *This is a pleasant dream. Rebekah's voice. I love Rebekah's voice.*

She called again. Chen Li joined her. Against the wall on the other side, it dawned on Rennin that he was awake. "Rebekah!" he called, but his voice was weak. For a moment he was unable to think. He knew Rebekah could not hear him. His hand slid onto a chunk of gold. He prayed, "God, please let this work." He picked up the chunk and banged with all his might against the wall.

Rebekah said to Chen Li, "Do you hear that noise?"

"Yes. Everyone, be quiet," called Chen Li.

When the hubbub continued, Rebekah screamed at the top of her lungs, "Shut up! Everyone, shut up!"

In the stillness, Rennin's steady pounding could be heard. Rebekah shouted, "Rennin, stop banging." The sound halted immediately.

She shouted again. "Rennin, if you hear me, tap three times." Three solid knocks resounded.

Rebekah shouted, "Again, three taps. Are you hurt?" Three solid taps came.

"What about Bart?" She called once more.

No taps followed. Rennin whispered, "He's dead."

Rebekah called, "Rennin, did you hear me?" He tapped thrice.

Her heart stopped in her throat and her stomach roiled as she called, "Rennin, is Bart dead?" Once again, the rescuers heard the three grating rasps.

"Oh, God, no," sobbed Chen Li, but he instantly pulled himself together and said, "Okay. We must figure how to get to Rennin." Shoulders squared, he strode toward the horses. Chen Li rubbed Buster's nose. "Okay, boy. Show me where Rennin went."

Buster nickered and went to the closed opening beside the cave entrance. There he pawed the ground. Chen Li pushed against the surface. Some of the rocks gave way. Chen Li called, "Rennin, can you hear me?"

Rennin's heart quickened. "Yes, Chen Li. There's a small entrance. The earthquake caused a cave in. I was trying to dig out, but I don't have the strength. The bone is sticking through my leg, and I've lost a great deal of blood. Bart is dead."

"Don't worry, Rennin. We'll have you out in no time."

Every lantern was lit, causing an eerie glow in the rain. Chen Li examined the entrance. He pulled a pick ax from his horse. Why he had brought it, he did not know, but he felt certain that it was Divine Intervention. After a dozen firm blows, more rocks gave way.

Chen Li held a lantern aloft. "Rennin, can you see any right?"

"A small beam," Rennin answered. "And I can breathe again. I think the air must have been running out in here."

"Stand by. We'll get you out."

Rebekah came up. Chen Li pointed at her. "Get out of the way. Wait in the cave. When we get Rennin out, we'll bring him to you."

"Who do you think you are?" asked Rebekah with a great deal of irritation and defiance.

In a commanding tone, Chen Li said, "The man, who knows what he's doing here. Every man here will move these rocks as I tell him. One false move could bring down more rocks. Some of these will be very heavy, more than you can move." Changing the tone of his voice to a compassionate one Chen Li continued, "Rebekah, Rennin needs a mathematical mind right now more than he needs you. He knows you're here. That is enough to strengthen his heart. Trust me. You know I rove that man."

"Okay." She released a long breath. "Just get him out." She returned to the shelter of the cave while the men began the rescue in the pouring rain.

Chen Li shouted orders. "Clayton, go back and tell Caitlin the news and bring back medical supplies so we can at reast stabilize Rennin's condition." He, then, gave orders to each man for cutting bracing logs and digging. The work was slow, but steady and sure.

The rain subsided, and just before dawn, Chen Li crawled through a secured entrance to Rennin, who breathed a sigh of relief. "I never thought I could be so happy to see your face."

At Chen Li's summons, Clayton and Thomas followed with medical supplies. They looked at Rennin, and then at each other. "I know it's bad," said Rennin, "but don't look as if my life is over. Moreover, I will *not* lose my leg. Don't even think about it."

Clayton said, "Rennin, at the very least, that leg will require surgery. We'll pray that no infection sets in, but these cases usually, not always, end in amputation."

"No," said Rennin decisively. "Do what you must, but save my leg."

Thomas said, "I hope you feel like getting good and drunk. You're going to need something to deaden the pain."

"I know. I can do it."

"Okay," said Thomas. "First, we have to immobilize your leg. It will hurt. Scream if you want. You don't have to be brave."

Rennin did scream and cuss. "Dear, God! If women hurt this much having a baby, how do they ever do it?"

"They are stronger than we are," said Clayton.

The sun broke through the clouds as Thomas, Clayton, and Chen Li dragged Rennin through the narrow entrance. Rennin grabbed Chen Li's forearm. "Don't leave Bart."

"I won't, Rennin. We'll bury him next to Keturah."

"Chen Li, start mining the gold in there."

"How can you think about that right now?" asked Chen Li.

"Bart wanted to use that gold to build a hospital. I could use a hospital right now. I want to fulfill Bart's dream. I'm not being greedy. The same deal goes as before, except, I want you to be my partner."

"Me?"

"Chen Li, you proved tonight that you've grown up. You're a man now. Yes, you."

"We'll talk about the details, Rennin. Now, you need medical treatment. Rebekah is waiting." He jutted his chin toward her.

Rebekah caught Rennin's hand. "Let's get you home so Thomas and Clay can take care of you. Caitlin is worried sick. Have you always been so much trouble?"

"Yes," said Rennin wryly.

Rebekah and Caitlin held onto each other as they heard Rennin's screams despite the huge quantity of whiskey he drank and a large dose of laudanum before Thomas and Clayton started to work on him. Suddenly, they heard Rennin screaming in anger, "No! Hell, no!"

Thomas came down the stairs with a cloth pressed to his nose. "Thomas, what happened?" asked Rebekah.

"It's what I get for trying to restrain Rennin when he's fighting mad. Talk to him, Rebekah. I don't think we can save his leg. He refuses to let us amputate, but he could die otherwise."

Rebekah went to the door and overheard Rennin and Clayton. "Clay, please do something. You were in the city just a few years ago. Surely they've developed some new techniques. Even if it's experimental, do it. Don't let Thomas take my leg. Please, Clay. I'm begging."

"All right, Rennin. There *is* something I can try. I'll make Thomas wait, but if gangrene sets in, we'll have no choice."

"I know, but, please, try everything else first."

Thomas returned with a broken nose. He pushed Rebekah before him. "Talk some sense into your husband."

She smiled. Rennin precluded her words. "Rebekah, don't. Support me in this. I need you to support me. I can't get drunk enough to lose this argument."

She kissed his cheek, whispered, "Magic," and put a finger to Rennin's lips. "Shh. Let me take care of this."

Rennin looked pleadingly at Rebekah as she spoke. "Thomas, we're going to try some of Clayton's newfangled ideas before we resort to drastic measures. Besides that, we'll pray. I believe in miracles. Please, abide by our wishes."

Thomas looked at Rennin. "God! Rennin, I pray it works. I don't want to take your leg. You must know that."

"I know. Let's try first."

"Fine. Just, please, don't punch me again. Your arms are perfectly strong. Well, Clay, are you ready?"

"Yes. Hold the top of his leg."

Thomas grasped the top of Rennin's leg firmly. "Damn!" Rennin exclaimed. "I think you enjoyed that."

"I did," said Thomas. "Rebekah, maybe he won't hit you. Hold his arms still."

Rennin clutched the bed sheets in his hands, and Rebekah lay across his arms and chest. Clayton swiftly yanked Rennin's ankle, snapping the tibia back into place.

Rennin screamed, "God Almighty!"

"Relax, Rennin," said Clayton. "That part is over. Breathe for a few minutes. Rebekah, boil me some water with salt in it."

"Salt?" grunted Rennin. "Are you trying to kill me?"

"No, Rennin. I'm trying to kill any bacteria that might be in the wound. You want to try my city doctoring. Deal with it."

"Give me some more whiskey."

Clayton handed Rennin the bottle. "Down it all. You're going to need it." Then, he stirred more laudanum into a glass of water.

Rennin chugged the rest of the bottle with a look of utter terror on his face, before he snatched the glass and finished the drug as if it were a glass of cool lemonade.

Rebekah brought the boiling salt water. Rennin was drunk and spoke gibberish. "Have to plant a tree tomorrow. Rebekah, how'm I gonna get the tree to the shhchool?"

"We'll get it there. Don't worry."

"Gotta carve it. 'In loving memory of Keturah Franklin Mershhier.' Didn't know I would need to add Bart'shh name."

"It'll be fine, honey."

Clayton washed the open injury with the saline solution. Rennin screamed despite the whiskey and dope. "Damn it! God, damn theshe men to Hell! Doctorsh are shadistsh. They enjoy inflicting pain."

Clayton continued to work, oblivious to Rennin's ranting. He stitched the wound and splinted the leg. By the time Clayton finished working, Rennin had passed out; whether from the pain or the amount of alcohol consumed, Clayton was unsure. Clayton talked to Rebekah. "We'll need to wash his leg every day with this solution. You go get some sleep with Caitlin now. I'll sit with Rennin. Thomas, go home for a while. Come back after suppertime. You can sit with this wonderful sleeping ass then. I'll stay now because I want to make sure he doesn't vomit in his sleep from the whiskey. If he starts running a high fever, and I mean high, or if gangrene sets in, we'll take his leg. I love him too much to let him die."

Rennin woke about three o'clock in the afternoon. He saw Clayton reading. "Clayton, do I still have a leg? I can't tell because my head hurts too much."

"It's called a hangover, Rennin. You drank a whole bottle of whiskey in addition to two doses of laudanum. Yes, you still have your leg. I promised you we would try it my way. I don't lie. If it comes to the other, I'll tell you."

"Thank you, Clay."

"You don't have to thank me."

Rebekah came in with a tray. "Am I interrupting a tender moment?"

Clayton said, "Rennin was just expressing gratitude."

"Clay, I'll sit with this stubborn wonderful man, who must enjoy scaring years off my life."

"You know better than that," said Rennin.

"I think I *will* rest a while," said Clayton. "Rennin, you eat. Rebekah, remember: lots of red meat and organ meats to build his blood and green vegetables. Rennin, I'll see you in the morning unless something goes wrong." Clayton left them.

Rebekah helped him slide up in the bed and prop on pillows before uncovering the tray. "Ugh!" he said. "Liver and onions." He looked at Rebekah with his nose turned up. "Isn't there something else?"

"Shut up and eat," she said. "Every bite."

"You are as sadistic as Clayton and Thomas."

"I'm worse," she argued. "You eat. I'll read."

"Oh, okay." Rennin took a bite and grimaced.

Rebekah laughed. "I have a pot roast cooking for later."

"Thank God!"

She opened the book they always read to each other.

Time passed, and Rennin watched Donovan and Cameron with their children. He lay in bed beside Morgan and whispered. "We did well, Morgan. When I see our children, I know that I've left a legacy of honor, of fortitude, and of love. Did we really teach those things to our children?"

"Yes, especially you because you learned them from Uncle Aidan. On the other hand, I learned them from you. Even as a child you had those attributes and more. I endured because I gathered, strength from you. I loved because you loved me. I learned because you taught me. I survived because you kept me alive with your faith, hope, and love. Rennin, the legacy you'll leave behind is greater and reaches further than you will ever know. Generations yet to come will sing your praises and honor you."

"Oh, Morgan, I'm only a man, who has tried to live a righteous life, albeit with many mistakes. You make me sound as if I am a king or something."

Their time to reflect was interrupted by pounding on the door. Ian stood there pale as powder. "Uncle Rennin, come quick. It's Papa. Something is terribly wrong. Anna is hysterical. She's so terrified she's speaking Iroquois."

Rennin did not change clothes, but ran to Geoffrey's house in his night shirt. Geoffrey lay in the floor clutching his chest. Rennin knelt beside his old friend. "Geoffrey, can you breathe?"

Geoffrey shook his head. "'Eart, Rennin. Third time. Last time I'm afraid."

"Why didn't you say something before, you stubborn goat?"

"Nothin' to do. Rennin, watch over Anna and the children. Make sure Angela waits another year. She promised."

"Come on, man. Breathe."

Geoffrey whispered, "I'm trying. Anna." He reached his hand out to her. "I love you."

Anna wept openly. "Geoffrey, please, fight harder. Don't leave me. I love you so much."

Geoffrey closed his eyes and breathed shallowly. Anna looked at Rennin. "Is he dead?"

"No. Ian, help me get him to bed."

Hours later, Geoffrey opened his eyes to see Anna sitting beside the bed and Rennin standing near the window with his arms folded across his chest. Geoffrey said, "There's one angel here, but this can't be Heaven. Rennin's here."

"Very funny," said Rennin. "You tried to send both Anna and me there before our time."

Anna held Geoffrey's hand. "I was so scared."

Rennin pulled a chair beside her. "Well, old chap, you will have to take it easy from now on."

"I don't want to be an invalid "

"Would you rather be dead?"

"No. I'd rather be with my family."

"Then, for God's sake let us all take care of you. You won't be an invalid. You just have to rest and slow down."

"Rennin, I don't want to be a burden to my family."

"You are talking nonsense," said Anna. "The burden would be not to have you at all. I love you, Geoffrey. You have been the best thing that ever happened to me. I would be lost without you. We have not had enough years together. I'm selfish. I want more."

"My Anna," said Geoffrey. "I'll do whatever you ask of me, you who makes my 'eart sing. I am still amazed that you love me."

"Then, listen to Rennin. Do not exert yourself. Do nothing that might hasten your death for I would not know what to do without you. You have been my bulwark for sixteen years. It's my turn to take care of you."

"All right, I won't work at the trading post or farm or trap. I can balance books sitting in a chair, so don't expect me to remain in bed. That would not be living, only existing. "

"Agreed."

"Rennin, my friend, does that meet with your approval?"

"Yes, but stay in bed for a few days to get stronger. Morgan probably has some herbs to build your strength back. I know she's mentioned hawthorn for heart trouble. I'll send them by your future son-in-law. I'm sure he would love to visit Cynthia."

"You mean Duncan. I 'ave two future sons-in-law."

"'Tis right. Ranson will be your son-in-law before Duncan. He and Cynthia have agreed to wait and court. Our families will be all intertwined."

Geoffrey laughed. "Rennin, I need to find my eldest son a wife. I'm beginning to worry about 'im. He acts like a monk."

"Well, we both know you and I are not monks. We are rather prolific," Rennin teased.

Geoffrey became thoughtful. "Rennin, what will we be remembered for? What 'ave we done that is worthwhile?"

"Well, for one, I have created five beautiful children. Yours are fairly nice, too."

"Yes, they are," agreed Geoffrey.

"Another thing is that we've started a town. Granted, most of the inhabitants are relatives, but there are William and Maggie and Ranson. You, my friend saved a damsel in distress."

"Nope!" objected Geoffrey. "Anna saved me."

"We saved each other," offered Anna.

"Geoffrey," said Rennin, "we've settled a wild untamed land. It will only grow and become stronger. I think that one day, this land will no longer belong to any nation. I think the people will unite and become one country free of tyranny. We will have helped to begin that. Our children's children will be servant to no one. Geoffrey, I find that to be a lasting legacy fit for a king."

Geoffrey laughed again. "You make our lives sound poetic."

"They have been."

"Rennin, you're good with words. You should write down all that we 'ave seen and done for our posterity. Let them remember us. Tell the bad with the good. Leave our legacy for those who follow."

"That's a very good idea. I'll do that, Geoffrey. I'll start tonight for I have much to tell. I'll go back to Draconis and tell her story as well. No one will believe it, but I'll tell it. We will be immortalized." Rennin grinned his mischievous boyish smirk. "You do have terrific ideas. Maybe I'll embellish our lives."

"No need," said Geoffrey. "Tell the truth. Our truth is already mighty unbelievable."

"All right. Only the truth. I'll tell the truth and love reliving most of the moments. Geoffrey, we *have* done well. We have a mighty, powerful legacy."

Rebekah closed the book. "He did leave a powerful legacy. *You* came out of that legacy. We're getting that new Bible as soon as possible. I want to record all the generations, including you. Don't argue. You will lose, and you're in no condition to pay your debt."

"I could let you extract the payment." Rennin grinned.

"You're feeling better. I would hurt you on purpose." She wrinkled her nose at him.

"Oh, be still my heart." He clasped his hands over his chest. "My love is cold and cruel."

She sat on the bed. "Ouch!" shouted Rennin.

"See. You're in no condition to pay."

"You win. You win. Let's talk about the tree we have to plant tomorrow."

"How are you going to do that?"

"I don't know, but it has to be planted with the inscription we discussed in my stupor."

"Chen Li can plant it for us. He loved Bart and Keturah as much as we did."

"God!" interjected Rennin. "How do we explain to the children?"

"I already told them. I also told them they are coming to live with us, and I asked Mr. MacMillan to start a new wing to the house. Rather than build Mabel a home, she will take Bart and Keturah's, and we'll have a bigger one."

"What would I do without you?"

"You've asked that question before. You would cease to exist."

"Yes, I would," he said seriously.

"Well, let's hope that is far into the future." Rebekah kissed her husband. "You rest a while. I have a roast to check. I love you."

"I love you."

Thomas came to sit the night with Rennin over Rennin's protests that he did not need a babysitter. Thomas argued that he was there to fill the first twenty-four hours just in case something went wrong. Rennin pouted for a while, but he knew Thomas was right. He finally slept after another dose of laudanum.

Following breakfast, Clayton arrived with his hot saline solution. Rennin grimaced as he saw his stepfather. Clayton smiled warmly. "Don't worry. It won't be as bad as yesterday. The wound is closed and has hopefully begun to heal. Grit your teeth and bear it."

The washing still burned, but not so nearly as badly as the day before. Clayton examined Rennin's leg closely. "There's no sign of infection," he informed. "That's very good. If you go three full days with no fever and no unusual swelling, for I expected some swelling, which should reduce over the next three days, I think you'll be in the clear. However, it'll take a good six to eight weeks for this leg to mend so that you can walk."

Rennin grinned. "I think your modern medicine will work. Don't misunderstand. I think Thomas is a fine doctor. He just hasn't had the benefit of learning modern techniques since he has practiced his entire career in a small out-of-the-way town. Your city experience coupled with Thomas's genuine love for his patients could be the pinnacle of medical practice.

"I want to talk to you about Bart's final request, his *legacy* as he called it. The little cave Bart took me to was filled with the purest vein of gold. He wanted to use as much of it as it took and build a hospital. Of course, he wanted you and Thomas to run the place."

Clayton laughed. "I think both Thomas and I would love to have a hospital, but I'll leave the business end to you. Thomas and I would practice medicine for free. We practically have—Thomas always and I over the last three years."

"I've meant to ask you why you left the big city hospital to come to the mission."

"Bureaucracy." He disposed of the blood-tinged water and sat in a chair near his patient. "My hospital, which my father founded as a matter of record, began to turn people away if they couldn't pay. You said Bart called the hospital his legacy. Well, I suppose I didn't want my legacy to be one of greed, but one of healing. Can you promise me that Bart's hospital will be that—a place of healing? I understand that the facility must make money, but please don't turn away those that can't afford care."

"I would never do that, and Bart would come back to haunt us if we did. The statement of purpose will include those very thoughts."

"Then, I'll happily work for Bart's legacy. Will you build it here in Puma Pass?"

"Of course. You and Thomas go as soon as you see that I'm on the mend and stake the area around the bend in the stream. We'll build the hospital in the valley there. Take Jacob MacMillan with you as part of the corporation. He deserves the recognition, too."

"Okay, anything else?"

"Yes, I need to talk to Jacob this afternoon about our plans."

"I'll send him around. Before that, Henry wants to visit you, but he's afraid he might upset you with his being an amputee."

"That's ridiculous. Tell him to come. I wish he'd had a doctor with some knowledge of modern medicine to give him a fighting chance to save his leg."

"From what he told me, his fate was inevitable. His leg was practically severed by the accident. It was far worse than a compound fracture. The muscles and ligaments were cut. He has dealt with his situation, and he's a fine minister. I'll send him around as well. Who else besides your mother, who is anxious to see for herself that you're all right?"

"Chen Li. First, I need to thank him for his valor and levelheaded actions." Rennin smiled. "That boy has turned out marvelously. I dearly love him. Then, I must ask another favor of him. I need him to plant the tree on the other side of the driveway to the school. We're going to carve a memoriam to Bart and Keturah in it. He loved them as much as Rebekah and I did. Since I can't plant the tree, it will be appropriate for him to do so with Rebekah."

"Bart's funeral is this morning. I'll send Chen Li immediately afterward. Mabel is going to stay with you and keep the two babies here. I know you might want to go, but, Rennin, you can't. You aren't able to move around yet."

"I understand. Send Momma in here first. Let me allay her fears."

Rennin had a day of visitors, all making sure he was actually recovering. The last visitor was Chen Li. Rennin stared in open admiration of the young man, who had repaid his debt of rescue in spades.

"Chen Li, sit down. I haven't thanked you yet for rescuing me yesterday."

"It's not necessary, Rennin. That is what family does."

"Nonetheless, I owe you my life. You were most impressive. It's time for you to go to college. You've proven to me that you're more than ready."

"I'll be going at the end of May. I'll celebrate my seventeenth birthday with my family and my girl."

"Of course, you will. Lord! How I'll miss you!"

"It will only be for a while. That is, if Sarah waits for me. Even if she doesn't, I could never *not* visit you and Rebekah. I would have to come for short visits anyway."

"At least Christmases."

"The very reast. But that is not what you wanted with me today."

"No. You're quite perceptive. Chen Li, I want you to plant the Christmas tree with Rebekah. Here's what I want inscribed on it." Rennin handed Chen Li a slip of paper that read. "*In loving memory of Bartholomew Christopher Mercier, who truly was a bearer of Christ, and his wife Keturah Franklin Mercier, who gave of herself to* all those around her. May their legacy of love for their fellow man endure for all eternity."

"That's too much to inscribe, Rennin."

"I know, but I couldn't shorten it."

"I have an idea. On the tree, 'In roving memory of Bart and Keturah Mercier, our dear friends.' Then, we can dedicate a wing of the school to them with all this inscribed on a plaque. That way, when the tree is tall, folks can still read about Bart and Keturah."

Rennin nodded. "That's an excellent suggestion. Do it. See to ordering the plaque. Let's put it in the dining hall. Every child or visitor will have to go to that room and eat. Although in Heaven it's already written that Bart and Keturah were truly servants of our Lord, I want the world to remember the legacy they left. God, Chen Li, I miss them."

"I do, too, Rennin."

"Go, now, and plant the tree with Rebekah."

Chen Li and Rebekah planted the tree that completed the landscaping of the school and wept together over the loss of their dear friends while Rennin mourned alone with only the comfort that comes from Above. Each remembered the legacy Bart and Keturah left on the hearts of those they loved.

33
Good-bye

The months passed too quickly in Puma Pass, and Chen Li celebrated his seventeenth birthday. The occasion served as both a birthday party and a going-away party. Chen Li was scheduled to leave two days later for Columbia College. Allison Newman had opened her home to him during the times that his dormitory would be closed.

The young man teased Caitlin that she was waiting too long to have Rennin's little brother, that she only wanted to cheat him of the pleasure of seeing the baby.

"I still have two days," Caitlin bantered.

Chen Li held out his hand. "May I?"

"Yes," she laughed.

Chen Li touched Caitlin's abdomen affectionately. "You had better hurry up in there. I want to see you before I reave."

Most of Chen Li's dances belonged to Sarah. After several hours, Rennin noticed that the couple lingered on the fringe of the crowd. He sneaked up behind them and whispered, "Take a stroll. When the guest of honor is ready to leave, the party's over."

Both Chen Li and Sarah blushed. "Are we so obvious?" asked Chen Li.

"Only to me. Go on. I'll close things down around here."

Chen Li and Sarah quietly disappeared and walked in the moonlight. They stopped on the bridge over the creek leading to Sarah's house. He touched her face. "What is this?" he asked as he felt her damp cheeks.

"I don't want you to leave."

"Oh, Sarah. Three years will fly by."

"They will drag for me. You'll have your studies and many new friends. Allison Newman will introduce you to New York society. I'll pine away here for you."

"I'll write you every day, and once I get to New York, I'll send you gifts every week. I rove you, Sarah."

"I love you, too. That's why my heart is breaking."

Chen Li lifted Sarah's chin and kissed her. She wrapped her arms around him and kissed him hungrily. She intimated, "Take me home. Momma and Papa will be helping Uncle Rennin clean up. We'll be alone. Make love to me. I want to be completely yours."

"Sarah?" Chen Li said, shaking his head.

"Please? I know you want to."

"Sarah, it would be wrong."

"Why? Because we haven't made vows before a lot of people?"

"No, because God says so. Sarah, Rennin has taught me to be a man of honor. To sneak off and make rove and have you possibly carrying my child would be dishonorable. I rove you far too much for that. I'll wait for you though my body aches. It's better than my heart aching or my soul's destruction. I'll think about you and imagine the day when I can take you and be with you as my wife."

Sarah cried. "I'm sorry. I'll be here when you return. I will be your wife."

He held her a long time before he walked her home and left her at her front door.

Chen Li met Rennin coming out his door. "Are you rooking for me?" he asked.

"No. Momma decided to grant your birthday wish. Her water broke five minutes after you left. I'm going to check on her. Do you want to come?"

"Yes. I'd rike to talk to you."

"What's the matter?" asked Rennin as they fell into step.

"Sarah."

"Did she turn on the water works?"

"She turned on more than that. She wanted to make rove. We didn't, although I wanted to very badly. Rennin, I'm afraid to reave her."

"What did we discuss months ago?"

"I know," said Chen Li defensively.

"Don't be insecure. You just have to rest in our Father's wise bestowment. He will give you what He deems best."

"Rennin, she is just so beautiful and sometimes wild and riberal in her thoughts. There are settlements popping up all over with many eligible young men—white men. What if she finds someone else? What if she decides a *Chinaman* is too much challenge?"

"Then, God will send you someone better."

"Rennin, she's your niece. How can you say there is someone better?"

"Chen Li, I love Sarah. *Better* doesn't mean she's not terrific. It only means maybe there is a better match for each of you." He shrugged. "Maybe not. Listen to your spirit's desire. Commune with the Holy Spirit, and your spirit will be in tune."

They arrived at Caitlin's house and simply walked in without knocking. Rennin called, "Clay!"

"In the bedroom," Clayton replied. "I'll be right out."

Clayton popped out. "I can't visit. Katie is wasting no time. This baby will be here before midnight."

"We'll share a birthday," laughed Chen Li.

Rennin asked, "Do you mind if we wait out here?"

"No, Katie will be happy to know you're here. It won't be long."

"Clayton!" Caitlin called from the other room.

"I have to go," declared the expectant father, grinning from ear to ear.

Rennin made a pot of coffee for the wait. He and Chen Li had hardly finished a cup, before they heard crying. Their ears perked up. Fifteen minutes later, Clayton brought out the baby. "Gentlemen, I'd like you to meet Roland Clayton Davies, III. Yes, my first name is Roland. That's what they called my father, so I was called Clayton to avoid confusion. This, however, is Roland."

"Let me see my little brother," said Rennin, holding out his arms. Clayton handed the baby to Rennin. "Chen Li, look. He's precious."

"Adorable. And obedient," joked Chen Li. "You ristened to me."

Clayton said, "Chen Li, Katie and I were thinking that since Roland *did* listen to you and you share a birthday, maybe you would be his godfather."

"Me?" He touched his chest and stretched his almond-shaped eyes wide. "You want me?"

"Yes. We'll go ahead and have Henry baptize him before you leave day after tomorrow."

"I'm honored. Yes, I would rove to. Rennin, I'm a godfather!"

Rennin and Chen Li spent a few minutes with Caitlin before they left her to rest. She took Rennin's hand before he left. "Tell Rebekah she was right. I got my spirit's desire."

Two days went by quickly. Roland was baptized, and Chen Li officially became his godfather. Then, Chen Li met the stagecoach, which now stopped in Puma Pass once a week. His body was about to head for the other side of the country, but his heart was staying in California.

Sarah sobbed and clung to Chen Li. He continued to remind her that he would only be gone three years. She buried her face in Thomas's chest and continued to weep as the stage pulled away. Chen Li stared out the opposite side of the coach in an attempt to check his own tears as the coach bounced away.

"She's lovely," said a soft, sympathetic voice with an aristocratic British accent.

For the first time, Chen Li took notice of his fellow traveler, a distinguished gray-haired lady. "Thank you."

"Parting is always difficult when you're in love. How long will you be gone?"

"Three years."

"A lifetime for one so young."

Chen Li warmed to the aged woman. "It does seem that way."

"You're a lucky young man. Apparently, her parents approve of you."

"I have known them for many years. Why would you observe that?"

The older lady smiled. "I was not so lucky. Let me introduce myself. I'm Moira Dahliwal. I observed such because your young lady is white, and you are obviously Chinese."

Chen Li nodded. "Dr. and Mrs. Goodman are not prejudiced although they did voice concerns about Sarah's and my marrying in that they are afraid that American society might not be so accepting."

"They're right." She gave a sad nod. "My husband and I overcame tremendous prejudice. You see, he was Indian. By that, I mean he was from India. We met there. My family was British aristocracy. His family was Indian aristocracy. Although our families socialized, it was taboo for their children to unite. We ran away together, and a kind, understanding missionary married us when we told him we had already consummated our relationship. We lied, but it served our purpose. We were married. After our parents rejected us, we came to America with the hope that society here would be more tolerant. A few people were. Most were not. You and Sarah have a head start. Her parents have accepted you. How do your parents feel? I did not see any Chinese people seeing you off."

"My parents died years ago. I came to America with my grandfather to search for gold. He died and reft me to a saloonkeeper. The saloonkeeper treated me cruelly. Sarah's uncle riterally took me away from him. He almost came to fisticuffs with the man, but paid him for me instead. Rennin O'Rourke has been my guardian for four years."

"Rennin O'Rourke? I've heard of him. He has a marvelous reputation. You love him very much."

"Yes, he and his wife, Rebekah. Rennin's mother had another baby two days ago. I'm his godfather."

"Congratulations! What is your name, dear?"

"I'm sorry. How rude of me. I am called Chen Li."

"Chen Li? Is it spelled L – I or L – E – E?"

"L – I."

"Have you ever considered changing it to the English spelling? It might help you to be accepted as an American rather than Chinese. And I do know that Chen is actually you last name, but here in this country, few think of such things."

"I have never thought about it. I'll discuss it with Rennin. Maybe I should change all of it."

"To what, dear?"

"John or Jim. Jim Lee sounds a rot rike my name." Chen Li laughed. "Maybe I should change it to something that doesn't begin with an L since I still have trouble with that English sound."

Moira laughed at the young man's sense of humor. "You could change it, but you must never lose your own identity. You are who God made you, and I think He has a very special plan for you. Chen Li, where are you going?"

"Columbia College."

"In New York? How delightful!" Moira took a card from her bag. "This is my address in New York. Come and visit me. I like you. Poojit and I were never blessed with children. I would enjoy your company very much, and, perhaps, one day I can meet your Sarah."

"I would rike that."

The stage traveled, and Mrs. Dahliwal slept. Chen Li pulled his pad from his satchel and wrote Sarah his first letter, telling her about the intriguing company he had. Moira awoke as he wrote. "What are you writing, dear?"

"A retter to Sarah. I promised to write her every day."

"That will be a difficult promise to keep, especially as your studies increase in difficulty. I suggest you write her and tell her to make it twice a week."

"I'll keep your suggestion in mind." Chen Li laughed. "I suppose it was a rather ambitious statement, but I'll do it as rong as I can. If it gets too difficult, I'll take your advice."

"How about some tutoring?"

"In what? My marks have always been excellent."

"Your L sound. I'll work with you all the way to New York."

"Yes. Thank you."

Moira was as good as her word, and she and Chen Li became close friends as they traveled. He continued to write Sarah at each night's supper stop and to mail the letters at each town with a post office. When they reached New York, Moira had her driver take Chen Li to the college before he took her home. She arranged to pick the young man up for dinner on Friday evening.

Meanwhile, Sarah moped around Puma Pass until her first letter arrived. She knew not to write back until she received a letter saying Chen Li had arrived at his destination. She refused to let anyone else read her letters and shared only the tidbits she deemed appropriate. Gabriel and Michael teased her by saying she wouldn't share her letters because Chen Li wrote smoochy stuff to her. They would pucker their lips and do little kisses toward her. At which time, she would become a child and chase them through the house or down the street.

Rebekah watched Sarah and was almost as sad as the girl. She told Rennin, "I think I miss Chen Li as much as Sarah."

Rennin comforted her. "Saying good-bye to your child is never easy. Chen Li has been like a son or at least a little brother to us. Of course, you miss him. So do I. I suppose it's time to read about your favorite couple in history. Bring me our book so I can comfort you."

He opened the book and began another story of good-bye.

Mom's Trading Post received so many orders from Boston for the pelts they carried that Rennin felt they needed a representative there. Discussion ensued regarding who would like to move to Boston. "I don't want anyone to leave," declared Rennin. "Peradventue, I can travel to Boston and hire someone as a representative, or mayhap one of our trappers would like to become more civilized."

After a great deal of haggling over the issue, Rennin decided he would first ask Marc Delacroix how he felt about going to Boston and settling down. He discussed the matter at the evening meal with Morgan and Donovan and Cameron, who had joined them that evening. After supper, Cameron approached his father. "Daidí, Marc is an excellent trapper, and he knows the best pelts. However, he has very little business sense. If we were not fair businessmen, he would be penniless. I've thought a lot about the prospect, and I think I'd like to go to Boston."

"What?" Rennin said, his mouth dropping open. "Why do you want to leave?"

"Daidí, I'm still a young man, and to be honest, I'm lonely. I know I have my family, but I've had a wife. I have a son. Daidí, you know I loved Holly more than life itself, but I've faced the fact that she's gone. Life goes on. I would like to someday find another woman and marry again. The likelihood of meeting someone here is slim. Ranson and Duncan have claimed the two available young ladies. Boston, on the other hand, is filled with young ladies."

Dipping his head from side to side, Cameron continued, "Daidí, Mom's needs someone with business sense to represent the company in the city. I have that sense. Moreover, I'm one of the heirs to the business. I'm an O'Rourke. I also think that, perhaps, I'll need an assistant. Ian needs to leave this place, too. Boston is not so far that we cannot visit from time to time."

Long sandy red hair touched the center of his back as Cameron shrugged. "Basically, you need me to go to Boston, and it's time I made my own way. If you need me to come home, send a courier with a message, and I'll leave immediately."

Rennin stared at his son in disbelief, yet he saw the logic of Cameron's plan. "How do I tell your mother you want to leave?"

"I'll tell her. Leave Momma to me. You know I've always been able to manipulate Momma." He grinned. "She can't resist my charm."

Rennin laughed uproariously. "You sound exactly like me with my mother. I miss her. When you go, come back to visit. I can't go see my mother. I will probably never see her again. Morgan's heart could not stand that. I'm not sure that mine could."

"I will, Daidí. Maybe soon I'll bring you a new daughter-in-law."

"Cameron, don't jump into a relationship because you're lonely. Wait for the right woman. You and Rowan deserve the best."

"I promise. Now, to suggest to Uncle Geoffrey that Ian should go with me."

"I think you'll be surprised. Geoffrey will encourage him to go. He wants Ian to find a wife. Talk to your mother first. Geoffrey won't be a problem. You know, Geoffrey would like to see a grandchild who can carry on his name. He still worries that his heart might not last until Drake is old enough to marry."

Cameron went into the kitchen and started drying the dishes. "What are you up to?" asked Morgan suspiciously.

"Why must you assume I'm up to something?"

Morgan grinned. "I know you. You're a little devil, and you're trying to soften some sort of blow. Have you decided to go to Boston?"

"Momma, are you practicing witchcraft right now? How did you know?"

"Mayhap, it was the way you stabbed at your beans, or kept wanting to say something at the table. Perchance, 'tis I think you *should* go. You need a life of your own. I love you, and I will miss you terribly, but I want you to be happy. Boston is not so far as Draconis. You had better come back to see me."

"I will, Momma. Daidí thought you would object."

"As much as I love your father, he has always underestimated me. I might be small in stature, but I'm strong and tough. I'm not easily broken although Rennin has always treated me like a porcelain doll. He thinks he has to protect me, so I let him protect me. If you divulge my secret, I'll strangle you."

"You could probably do it, too. My lips are sealed."

Cameron hugged his mother. "I'll write to you every week. I know you'll want to know what Rowan is doing, and I just might meet a woman in Boston. Of course, I'll have to hold her to the highest standard. She has to be strong and tough and not easily broken."

Geoffrey practically packed for Ian, so after Ranson's housewarming and Angela's fifteenth birthday party, Cameron and Ian made a trip to Boston to secure a building for the franchise there. Cameron left Rowan with his grandparents for the short trip. Rowan cried and held tightly to his father's neck. "Poppy, no go."

Cameron tried to comfort the little boy, who was less than two. "Poppy will be back very soon. Grandma and Granddad will take good care of you."

Rowan pouted. "Me go Poppy."

Cameron stroked the child's hair. "Not this trip. You'll go with me on the next trip, and I'll bring you a toy if you stop crying and behave while I'm away."

Rowan hugged Cameron again. "No cwy. Me good."

Cameron kissed Rowan's chubby cheek. "I know you'll be good. I love you."

The trip to Boston was uneventful for the two men. They rode into a city bustling with life, stabled their horses at the livery, and checked into the inn where Rennin and Morgan had stayed. Cameron spoke with the innkeeper. "I'm Cameron

O'Rourke. I need to know where I might find a merchant's shop to purchase."

"It's strange that you should come to town looking for a facility. Mr. Martin at Martin's Furniture Shoppe has become gravely ill and is no longer able to work. He has no children to take his business, only a daughter who has been reduced to working as a household servant for the Allgood family, so he wants to sell the place. I'm sure that if you were willing to purchase the existing pieces of furniture, you could sell those along with whatever goods you plan to provide."

"Where can I find Mr. Martin?"

The innkeeper wrote the address along with directions to Martin's house, and Cameron and Ian called upon the ailing gentleman. A stout nurse opened the door and allowed the two young men to enter.

Cameron observed the frailness of the sick man, but he recalled the name as the man who had sold the pieces of furniture to Rennin and Morgan. He spoke compassionately. "Mr. Martin, I'm Cameron O'Rourke and this is Ian Montague. I believe you met my father and mother several years ago. You sold them the dragon pieces."

"Yes, I remember them," replied Martin weakly. "How may I help you? Are you in the market for more furniture? I'm not able to show you any pieces, but you may take the key and look."

"I would like the key, but I'm interested in buying your building and all your merchandise. My father is expanding his business to Boston. Ian and I are to run the business here. Ian could sell a horse's skeleton and I know how to manage money. We will make a good team, just as our fathers have made an excellent partnership all these years. I have been given to understand that you would like to sell your place and your inventory."

"I have no choice, young man. The doctor gave me the long face. I can barely afford to keep the nurse. She has gone several weeks without pay because she is a kind and generous woman. My daughter has been forced to work for her keep as a menial servant. If I sell the business, I can at least set aside a small amount for Tammy and pay my nurse until I pass on."

"I'm very sorry for your misfortune. If I might examine the property and the inventory, I'm sure we can come to an agreeable price."

"Very well. The key is in the black valet on the bureau."

"Thank you, sir. If I do not make it back tonight due to the lateness of the hour already, I shall surely return early tomorrow."

"Take your time, young Mr. O'Rourke. Make a wise decision on your father's behalf."

Cameron retrieved the key. As they left he told Ian, "Snoop around and see if you can find out how much Martin would like to get for his place."

Ian walked the streets of Boston and talked to people while Cameron examined the store and its contents. They met at the tavern across from the inn for supper and ale. Cameron asked, "What did you discover?"

"He has asked for eight thousand. Is it worth it?"

"No wonder he doesn't have any money to support his daughter. He might be a gifted carpenter, but he is a dreadful businessman. I would give him three thousand for the building, but the pieces are exquisite. They alone are probably worth fifteen thousand. Of course, he would never sell them all at once, but three hundred here and five hundred there would add up nicely."

"You sound as if you are about to make a magnanimous offer. What do you have in mind? Are we going to go bankrupt?" asked Ian skeptically.

"No. Ian, we can afford to be generous. We have loads of money. Plus, he has a daughter to provide some legacy."

"She's probably a scraggly old maid who has always cared for her father." Ian gulped ale.

Cameron scowled and ate a bite of the roasted boar on his plate. "Does it matter? She's a human being with feelings."

"You O'Rourkes would give your right arm to help your fellow man. I tell you: Someday your kindheartedness will cost you your fortune."

"Do you view us with so much disdain, Ian?" Cameron laid his fork to the side, his stomach roiling at his future partner's implication.

"It's not that." Ian pushed his plate back. "I love every one of you. Lord knows, though, you are generous to a fault sometimes. How much do you plan to offer him?"

"Twenty thousand."

"That will be several years' income for him and us."

"I know, but you can market that furniture and make it back in no time."

"If you say so, Cameron."

"Have faith in your abilities, my friend."

Martin almost died of heart failure on the spot when Cameron handed him twenty thousand pounds. He did not argue with the young man, and Cameron left the day after he secured a house for him and Rowan for Mom's Trading Post, while Ian set up their business in Boston and found his own place to live.

Cameron returned to Mom's Trading Post triumphantly and with money to spare though he kept the actual amount he had taken with him from Ian. He liked Ian and was confident in his abilities, but Cameron had always had an underlying distrust of the childhood playmate. Perhaps, it all stemmed from the missing aggie on *The Rover*. Nonetheless, it was there. Cameron laughed at his silliness. Both Rennin and Geoffrey approved of the purchase and were enthusiastic to start the business in full. Rennin was also pleased with the purchase of the furniture. "There's no reason we can't sell more than pelts and skins. We might become a full-fledged mercantile."

Cameron packed his things to leave immediately after Christmas. He felt that lingering would only make his departure harder for everyone. He told Ranson to send his wedding invitation by courier. "You know I'll be here. After all, I'm supposed to be your best man. When you set the date, send the fastest rider you can, so I can get here before Angela drags you to the altar."

Before he left, Donovan told him that he and Emily Claire were expecting another baby. "Send me an announcement, brother," Cameron congratulated his sibling.

"You send me one if you meet a lady."

"Agreed."

Cameron spent his last night in Mom's Trading Post with his mother and father. He needed the time of quiet love to send him on his way.

The whole community turned out to say good-bye. He left in high spirits, but waited for Morgan to burst into tears. Rather, she threw him a kiss and waved until he was out of sight. Then, she collapsed into Rennin's arms and sobbed for hours.

"He'll be back, Morgan. He's not gone forever," comforted Rennin.

"I know, but 'tis still hard to say 'good-bye' to my baby," Morgan lamented.

Rennin held her tightly and suffered silently for he thought again how much Aidan had suffered when he had left for parts unknown.

Rennin held onto Rebekah tightly for a moment. "If it hurts this much to see Chen Li leave, what will we do when it is Michael or Gabriel or Stanley, or even Jed, Stephen, Chris, or Ketty?"

Rebekah sighed. "We will stoically hold our chins high even as Morgan did; and when they are out of sight, then, we will fall apart.

34
New Horizons

One gloomy morning when life had taken on a comfortable routine after Chen Li's departure, the stagecoach arrived in Puma Pass carrying Mitchell Stone, the bookkeeper Rennin had hired sight-unseen for the school and hospital, simply from the credentials he presented. Mitchell was a handsome man, tall with ebony hair and deep soulful brown eyes and perfect, pearly white teeth. With him he brought his younger brother, Dennis, who was his charge and looked exactly like Mitchell.

Mitchell proved to be an apt accountant and a likeable person. On the other hand, Dennis was a scoundrel, always playing practical jokes at school and causing a ruckus. Olaf dreaded the boy's presence in class for he hated to spank any of the children, but paddling Dennis became a weekly ritual.

Dennis's undoing was the day he put a snake in Sarah's lunch pail. When she opened her lunch and a snake slithered across her hand, all hell broke loose at the school. Sarah shrieked, "Dennis Stone! You sorry excuse for a human being, you are a dead man!"

Dennis roared with laughter until he felt Sarah's lunch pail against his head, not once, but three consecutive blows. Dennis wailed loudly, "You spoiled bitch!"

"Spoiled what?" she bellowed, just before she reared back and punched him in the nose, bringing blood and felling him to the ground. Then, she jumped astraddle the boy and proceeded to pummel him in the face.

Olaf pulled her off Dennis. "Sarah, stop it! I'm sure he deserved it, but you're a lady. What would Chen Li think if he saw you?"

"He would probably applaud me," retorted Sarah.

"Who is Chen Li?" moaned Dennis.

"My fiancé," gloated Sarah.

"That's a *Chinese* name," said Dennis derisively.

"What of it? Do you want another lick?" said Sarah, kicking his booted foot. "It's high time someone put you in your place. If it falls to me, so be it. With my brothers and cousins, you can bet that I can kick your butt. Want to put it to the test?"

"Sarah!" Olaf commanded.

"Uncle Olaf, don't shush me. You have beaten him black and blue, but it hasn't changed him. Maybe if a girl wallops him, he'll be shamed into reforming."

"Sarah, go to my office at once," ordered Olaf.

"But, Uncle Olaf."

Olaf turned a baleful stare upon Sarah. She obediently went to his office and waited. Meanwhile, Olaf washed Dennis's face and sent him home without further ado.

When Olaf entered his office, he found his niece reading her latest letter from Chen Li. She looked up at him with her big blue-green eyes and smiled a sly, mysterious smile. Olaf clapped his hands in rapid succession. "I applaud you. Well done. I would say you kicked his butt, even if it was rather unladylike."

The two laughed together. "Sarah, I want to have a serious talk with you. I've meant to do so before now. It has come to my attention that you're a mite too old to be in school here. I would like to suggest that you go back East to a wonderful finishing school I know. You would benefit greatly."

"Is it in New York?" she asked, sitting forward eagerly.

"No, Boston."

"Oh." She thudded back in her chair.

"It's closer to New York, though. Maybe during a holiday you can go to Allison Newman's and see Chen Li. Moreover, it would do you a world of good. It would help you become a real lady."

"Would it make me a better wife for Chen Li?"

Olaf chuckled. "Sarah, no doubt, he loves you just as you are, but it wouldn't hurt. I've already talked to Thomas and Candy. They are agreeable if you are."

"Yes, Uncle Olaf, I think I *would* like to go." Sarah laughed. "Perhaps, it will keep me from street brawls. How long will I be away?"

"Only one year, but you'll come back a new woman."

"What is the address? I have to write Chen Li and tell him where to send my letters. Uncle Olaf, I'm so excited!" She ran around the desk and hugged her uncle.

Olaf handed Sarah a slip of paper containing the address. "If you leave day after tomorrow and take the express stage and the train, you'll arrive in time for the beginning of the new year of school. I'll wire the school that you're coming. Write Chen Li tonight and pack. We will forward any mail you receive in the interim—unopened." He patted her on the back.

Chen Li received Sarah's first letter from here new address the day of his first planned outing at the Newman home. Allison had invited a few of her friends to meet the young man that she had liked the first time she visited him on campus.

The faculty was fond of and respected Chen Li for he was an exceptional student and a well-mannered young man; however, he had made few friends among the white student body. His letters from Sarah were his lifelines. Just a note that showed she understood his circumstances uplifted him. He re-read his latest before he left for the evening's engagement, noting that the letter telling of her plans had traveled more slowly than his girl, who was already settling in at her new finishing school. He had been surprised to get two letters so close together, only two days apart.

I'm sorry to hear you feel so alone in a big city. I think of you every day and pray for you every time you come to my mind. If it makes you feel better, this finishing school is not what I expected. I suppose that our love will need to sustain both of us. I hope my words encourage you as much as yours do me...

He did not finish, but got ready to leave.

Chen Li arrived at Allison's house wearing his best suit and feeling nervous. She greeted him amiably. Chen Li discovered that two of his classmates were in attendance. The fact that he was presented by the Newmans increased his worth in their estimation. From that day forward, they sought him to engage in many of their activities.

One of the men in attendance at Allison Newman's party was John Roebling. He talked extensively with Chen Li about engineering, specifically bridge building, and Chen Li expressed an interest in a transcontinental railroad. The conversation was overheard by another guest, Theodore Judah.

Jovially, Judah said, "Then, I am the one with whom you should be speaking. That concept is definitely in the near future." Judah and Chen Li talked for most of the rest of the evening. Chen Li left Rennin's address with Judah since the man had promised to get in touch with him if and when the railroad's plans came to fruition.

Chen Li also met Gregory Melohn, a local construction engineer and began working a couple of hours each afternoon in his office, gaining valuable on-the-job training and experience. However, the new position forced Chen Li to write the letter he had dreaded, telling Sarah he would be unable to write every day. Nonetheless, he wrote her faithfully twice a week no matter how tired he was after a day of classes and work.

Allison Newman agreed to allow Sarah to come for Christmas since neither Sarah nor Chen Li would be able to return to California for the holiday. Thus, he looked forward to seeing his beloved and mailed her the news.

Sarah acclimated herself to her new surroundings, but her spirit fought the restriction placed on her by Bostonian society. She hated she was expected to laugh only behind her hand and she was never to speak her mind in public and rarely in private. She loathed the idea that a woman was to be only an adornment on a man's arm and not much more. Only the poor and downtrodden women were expected to do anything worthwhile, and Sarah was as close to American aristocracy as one could get, coming from a very wealthy and influential family.

Sarah was of the mind that a woman could do and be anything she chose. Almost immediately upon hearing of it, she became a part of the women's suffrage movement, much to the consternation of her teachers.

The head mistress at L'Academie de Peau de Soie pour les Filles (Silk Skin Academy for Girls) was a woman who claimed to be a widow with a son that attended Harvard University. Beatrice Pryor was a stern, unhappy woman because in actuality, her husband had deserted her and their son, Baxter, when Baxter was only three. Beatrice had begun to teach and had risen in prominence as an educator and disciplinarian to her present position.

Every time a new group of girls came to the school, Beatrice called Baxter home to meet the eligible young ladies, but she camouflaged her intentions by having a cotillion for the girls and inviting many young men. Always, Baxter commented, "Mother, they're a bunch of snobbish, spoiled prudes, much like you." He would, then, kiss her on the cheek and be charming to the girls before he left.

In true form, Beatrice once again planned her "October Cotillion" for the new batch of girls. As Baxter danced with each girl in turn, he overheard the conversations.

"That Sarah Goodman is scandalous."

"Yes. I heard she joined the women's suffrage movement."

"I heard something worse. She's engaged to a Chinese boy."

"Sarah really does not belong here. She is too uncouth."

Baxter made his way to Beatrice. "Well, Mother, have I met everyone?"

"Almost," she sighed. "There is *one* more."

"Bring her on, Mother. How much worse than these can she be?"

"Much. Come on."

Beatrice led Baxter to a tall girl with light brown hair. She stared out the window, a silent tear trickling down her cheek. She whispered to herself, "You were wrong, Uncle Olaf. This place cannot benefit me."

"Sarah."

Sarah spun around at the sound of the harsh voice. Her blue-green eyes still glistened with moisture.

Beatrice shook her head in disapproval. "Sarah, let me introduce you to my son, Baxter. Baxter, this is Sarah Goodman."

Sarah appraised the young man. He was quite handsome, standing just over six feet tall and having a broad chest. His sandy hair was closely cropped and his hazel eyes, that varied color with every change of clothes, danced with mischief and independence.

Sarah spoke politely, "Mr. Pryor, it's a pleasure." She extended her hand.

Baxter took her hand and kissed it. "Miss Goodman, may I have this dance?"

"I would be delighted," Sarah replied graciously.

As they danced, Baxter ventured, "I've heard intriguing things about you."

"All bad, I'm sure," Sarah commented sardonically.

"That depends on your point of view. I found them fascinating."

"But I'm a hellion. Didn't your mother warn you?"

"Indirectly. She's too discreet to say anything profound. That's one thing that intrigued me."

For the first time in the five years that Beatrice had been head mistress, Baxter stayed for the whole event, saving most of his dances for Sarah. At the end of the evening, he found her.

"Sarah!"

"Mr. Pryor?"

"Please, call me Baxter."

"All right."

"Sarah, my I call on you again?"

"I don't know about that. I have a beau."

"Is he here?"

"No, he's at Columbia College. I'll see him at Christmas."

"I didn't ask you to marry me. I would just like to keep company with you. You are *not* boring."

"Very well," agreed Sarah, feeling extremely lonely. "As long as you understand that I'm spoken for, and you and I are only friends."

"Good. I'll be back Saturday. We can give Mother a nervous breakdown when she finds out it is you, her wild one, that I have decided to visit."

Both laughed at the prospect of shocking the overbearing, insufferable Beatrice Pryor.

Sarah studied etiquette, diction, and literature and spent her Saturdays in the company of Baxter Pryor. They picnicked in the park and attended the county fair. Baxter rowed Sarah across the lake and read poetry to her. He exposed her to the theater, the symphony, and croquet. They experienced five-star dining, and Sarah had her first French wine. On Sundays they attended the The Old North Church, an Episcopalian church, full of history, in Boston.

Sarah enjoyed her time with Baxter except the worship. She said the service was too formal and stilted and she did not feel the Holy Spirit. The pastor spoke well, but he did not have the feeling, the charisma, that Henry possessed.

"How quaint," laughed Baxter. "Do you believe you should feel some stirring in your spirit?"

"Yes!" Sarah exclaimed. "I've always felt the Holy Spirit move when Henry preaches."

"I should like to hear him sometime. I've always felt our preacher espoused good rules by which to live, but my spirit has never been moved. Church is merely a social formality."

"Then, someday you must come to Puma Pass and hear Henry," Sarah suggested innocently.

Baxter laughed again. "'The opium of the people."

"Pardon?"

"Karl Marx. That's what he calls religion. Have you read his *Communist Manifesto*?"

"Your mother would have a conniption."

"Not what I asked."

"Yes, Uncle Olaf ordered a copy. He allowed me to read it, but I disagree."

"Intriguing." The two talked at length about politics and religion. Baxter found a woman who could hold her own in debate irresistible.

For every hour Sarah spent with Baxter, Beatrice Pryor fumed. She considered the affair a personal affront. She could not understand why Baxter would make time with the one girl she deemed inappropriate. From the day she realized Baxter was seriously pursuing Sarah, Beatrice set out to make the girl's life miserable.

None of Sarah's writing assignments, though exceptional, were ever good enough. Sarah never stood erectly enough nor spoke softly enough nor enunciated clearly enough. Even the girls who had ridiculed Sarah in the beginning took notice, as did Baxter; and he confronted his mother.

"Mother, leave Sarah alone."

"Baxter, how could you fall for that girl?"

"She's beautiful and witty and compassionate and genuine and intelligent. How can you overlook that?"

"She's crude and unfit for Bostonian society."

"There are other cities besides Boston, Mother," Baxter said with a huff.

"Baxter! Surely, you wouldn't seriously entertain thoughts of going to California after that girl. I must assume you're simply making time with her because she amuses you."

"Gee, Mother, she's as rich as sin. Isn't that what you've been pushing on me for years?"

"Yes, I want you to marry a girl with money, but also breeding for God's sake! So, go ahead and have your fun; but, please, be discreet if you take that girl to bed."

"You are impossible!" Baxter shouted as he slammed the door to his mother's office. Outside he mused, *Take her to bed? Mother, that thought had not crossed my mind until you put it there. If I can get Sarah to make love to me, I can make her forget her little Chinese boy in New York. Thank you, Mother. You are actually good for something after all.*

Sarah took refuge in Baxter's company for he treated her like a princess. Nonetheless, she longed for the Christmas break. She dreamed of Chen Li's arms about her. She wrote him about her only friend, Baxter, and about how cruelly Beatrice treated her.

Chen Li was angered that anyone would treat Sarah so badly, but he found himself wishing Sarah had a female friend rather than a male friend. He talked to Moira with whom he dined every Friday evening. "Moira, I think I'm jealous. Am I wrong to feel so?"

"Do you trust Sarah?"

"Yes, but she's young and a bit tempestuous. Her need for comfort and friendship could be misunderstood. I'm afraid it could lead to something more."

"If it does, you'll have to deal with it at that time. You took that risk when you left her. All you can do for now is to write to her and assure her of your love, unless that has changed."

"No. I love Sarah. I haven't even met another woman besides Mai Ling."

"And what do you think of Mai Ling?"

"She's sweet and innocent. She needs someone to take care of her. Still, I love Sarah."

"Are you trying to convince yourself or me?" The wise older lady sipped her tea to wait for her implication to sink into her young friend's head.

"No one. It's a simple fact," Chen Li replied, rather unconvincingly.

"Then, write to her, and write Rennin. He gives you good advice."

Chen Li wrote both letters late Friday night, and on Saturday he shopped for Sarah. He found a sky-blue scarf intricately embroidered with butterflies. He mailed Sarah's letter with the package and a card that read, "*My heart flutters like the wings of a butterfly at the very thought of you. With all my heart, Chen Li.*"

Sarah wore the scarf on her next outing with Baxter, and she showed him the card. Behind her back, Baxter's countenance darkened as he realized he must lay his trap carefully and pull his net slowly so as not to scare away his fish. He was very afraid of losing this fish.

Rennin read Chen Li's letter with some concern and talked over the problem with Rebekah. "Thomas's letters from Sarah describe Baxter as a very nice person. Do you think he's *seriously* interested in Sarah?"

"I'm certain he's interested in Sarah," said Rebekah. "Why else would he spend every weekend at home with her? The more important question is whether Sarah is *seriously* interested in him."

"I'm almost tempted to go to Boston."

"Rennin, stay out of Sarah's business."

"What?"

"She didn't ask your advice. Chen Li did. If I were the one in Boston, what would you do?"

"Go to Boston."

"Christmas is only a few weeks away. Sarah and Chen Li will see each other. Send him a letter. Tell him to surprise Sarah with a visit in the spring. If he sees Sarah and Baxter together, he'll have a better understanding of the situation."

"That's what I'll do. You're a wise, wonderful woman."

"I know." Rebekah grinned and winked at Rennin. "Now, that you are so stressed, you relax while I read to you for a while."

Cameron wrote his family weekly to stay in touch and to keep Rennin abreast of the financial situation of the business. He and Ian were making a profit, and Ian had most assuredly taken advantage of the fact that there were many young women in Boston. Not a single Friday evening came that he did not dine in the home of some eligible young lady.

On one such evening, Ian insisted Cameron join him. "You have a governess to help with Rowan. Take one evening a week for yourself. You said you would like to meet a woman. How do you plan to do that staying at home? Lucia has a twin sister. Her name is Lucretia. She might be prettier than her sister. Come on. What do you have to lose?"

"Fine. I'll go. Maybe the girl will at least be a diversion; however, most of the ones I've met have not impressed me."

As Ian's friend, Cameron was welcomed warmly at the Allgood home. Lucia and Lucretia Allgood were attractive identical twins. They had long, straight, platinum-blonde hair; pale blue eyes, fringed with long blonde lashes; and a creamy complexion, totally unblemished by exposure to the sun. Both were statuesque, voluptuous women, and they were obviously pampered. Their hands were as smooth as silk. They bubbled with laughter and charm. With their mother dead, the girls carried on the social life of the family for their father, Nigel, a man who despised weakness and incompetence.

At dinner, Cameron was seated next to Lucretia and across from Lucia. A pretty, tall, slender, servant girl with a rosy glow on her cheeks and a slightly olive complexion served bread and wine. The girl stood out in sharp contrast to the pale twins with her dark sable hair, big doe-like brown eyes with long lacy lashes, and soft full lips. She returned with the soup tureen. As she reached the table, her toe caught on a wrinkle in the rug. She tripped, dumping the entire pot of soup onto Cameron's lap. Cameron caught her just before her face would have struck the sharp edge of the table.

While Nigel glared at the girl, Lucretia screamed vehemently at the already humiliated maid, "Tammy, you idiot! You clumsy buffoon!"

"'Tis all right," said Cameron compassionately as the color rose higher in the girl's cheeks. "It's only soup. I'm unharmed, and the clothes will wash." Cameron helped the girl up. "Are you all right?"

"Yes, sir. I'm so sorry. Are you burned?"

"No. The soup was not so very hot."

Lucretia snapped, "Tammy, clean up this mess. Mr. O'Rourke, perhaps father has something you can wear."

"That's unnecessary," said Cameron curtly. "Really, Miss Allgood, there's no need to berate Miss Tammy so. There's no harm done except a broken tureen."

"Yes, one that has been in the family for years," fumed Lucretia. "Tammy, the cost to replace it will come from your salary."

"No," said Cameron firmly. "I'll pay for it."

Lucia intervened with a soft smile toward Cameron. "Lucretia, calm down. Mr. O'Rourke is right. It's only soup and some broken porcelain. Tammy, please clean up the mess and send Clark to show Mr. O'Rourke where he can change clothes. I'm sure we have something suitable, although Father is not quite as tall as our guest. Tammy, don't worry about the tureen. It can be replaced. Clean up quickly and serve the rest of dinner." She stood. "I'm glad you were not burned, Mr. O'Rourke, but I need to speak to the cook about the proper temperature to serve soup."

Tammy wore a confused look, but did as she was told. Cameron changed into a pair of Mr. Allgood's breeches, and dinner went on smoothly.

After that engagement Cameron spent many evenings in the Allgood home, usually in the company of Ian and the two sisters. One evening, Cameron stepped into the garden after a round of cards with Nigel Allgood and Ian. Lucia joined him shortly.

"It's a beautiful night, Cameron. How much did you lose to Father this time? You must stop letting him win. You're a much better player than he. He's becoming suspicious."

"Only a pittance," he laughed. "Losing keeps me in his good graces so that I may continue to visit you, dear lady."

She smiled warmly. "Cameron, may I speak to you confidentially?"

"I suppose. How may I be of service to you?"

"It's about Ian." She bit her lip and drooped her eyelids. "Lucretia is quite smitten with him, though he is not particularly what I want in a man. How do I steer him toward my sister and away from me without hurting you?"

"It would be a relief to me," Cameron said under his breath.

"Pardon me?"

"Lucia, I'm not particularly fond of your sister. So, steering her to Ian will not bother me in the least. You, on the other hand, I like. I think you know that. Perhaps, we can work together. That is, if you would care to have me for a suitor."

"I should not play games with you, Cameron. You can see right through my scheme. That is actually what I was hoping."

"That's a relief. I'll talk to Ian."

Ian was more than agreeable because, in truth, he had been trying to figure a way of letting Lucia down easily. He much preferred Lucretia's forceful personality.

The evenings spent in the Allgood home were for the most part enjoyable; however, Cameron was bothered by the ill treatment Tammy frequently received, most often from Lucretia and Nigel.

One evening, Cameron returned home earlier than usual. Outside his door, he heard Rowan wailing and Mrs. Nash, the governess, screaming. Cameron peered through the window to see Mrs. Nash shaking the terrified child and then slapping him across the face. She screamed, "Shut up, you little devil. You made the mess. Clean it up." She threw a dishtowel at the baby. Cameron saw the overturned glass and the puddle of milk on the floor.

The father took a deep breath to calm his temper. He opened the door and walked in. "Mrs. Nash, you are dismissed. Pack your things and leave my house tonight."

"Mr. O'Rourke, you're home early!" She gasped and placed a hand on her ample bossom.

"'Tis a good thing, too." Cameron knelt beside the little boy who was wiping the milk. "Rowan, give me the rag."

Rowan handed Cameron the cloth, which Cameron laid to the side, and fell into his father's arms. "Me sowwy, Poppy. Me make mess."

"'Tis all right. I'm sure it was an accident."

"Mr. O'Rourke, I can explain."

"Mrs. Nash, are you still here? I told you to get out. *Now*. Before I lose my temper and slap you the way you did my son. He's barely three years old. Children make messes. He's too little to clean it by himself, and you're too big to treat him so cruelly. Please leave now before I toss you out the door. I'm much larger than you and quite capable of doing so. And I will make sure it hurts."

The woman fled from the room and left as soon as she packed her belongings.

In great need of a governess, Cameron discussed the opening with Lucia. She smiled. "Your dilemma solves my problem. Father has insisted I let Tammy go. She's not a good maid; however, I think she would be very good with children. She's a kind person, Cameron, and she needs an income."

"It would be unseemly for her to live in the house since I don't have a wife or a full staff at this time."

"What about the little cottage on your property? She could live there and come to the house to work. It would be proper, and she would have some sense of independence and privacy should she ever wish to entertain gentleman callers."

Cameron thought for a while. "It would suffice; however, she would have to entertain any suitors in the parlor of the house to protect her honor. I'll give her the opportunity, and I won't yell at her." Consequently, Tammy left with Cameron the next morning.

As he drove home he said, "Tammy, I don't even know your last name."

"Martin."

"Martin? Was your father the proprietor of the furniture shop?"

"Yes."

"Why are you working? I know your father died, but you should have had a nice annuity from the sale of the property. I'm the one who bought your father's store. I know how much I paid him."

"The money was missing from his account. I have nothing, Mr. O'Rourke."

"Damn! Someone stole it?"

"I suppose. I know nothing of my father's business affairs. What I do know is that I'm nineteen, penniless, and alone. Thank you for giving me a job. It would seem you have rescued me three times now. First, you bought my father's business for a tidy sum. Then, you kept me from injury when I fell. Now, this. I'll take care of your son, Mr. O'Rourke. That I promise; and if he spills his milk, I'll tell him how I spilled soup all over his father." She smiled.

Cameron laughed. "He would like that. Tammy, please call me 'Cameron.'"

"It would not be proper."

"I don't care. It's what I want."

"No. I would feel uncomfortable."

"Very well—at least for now. Eventually, you will call me by my given name."

Cameron introduced Rowan to his new governess. "Rowan, this is Miss Martin. She's your new governess. I promise she's nice, not at all like Mrs. Nash."

Tammy knelt to Rowan's level. "Hello, Rowan. Do you know what I see?"

Rowan shook his head. Tammy explained, "We have the same color eyes. Rowan, do you have any cookies and milk?"

He nodded.

"I'm starving. Let's have some." Tammy took the child's hand. "Come on. Show me where they are. Then, I'll tell you a story about two very mean sisters, a wicked witch, a damsel in distress, spilled soup and milk, a knight in shining armor, and a little prince."

Cameron stood watching Rowan show Tammy to the kitchen and thought aloud, "Two mean sisters?" He shrugged off an uneasy feeling and went about his business.

"I can't stand this," said Rebekah. "Just whom did Cameron marry?"

Rennin teased her. "My lips are sealed until we read that part."

"Where's that family Bible? I'll find out for myself," said Rebekah as she scampered from the room.

"No you won't. Come back here, Rebekah Sinclair O'Rourke!" called Rennin, giving chase. He caught her at the stairs. "I'll put an end to this nosiness right now," he said as he carried her to their bedroom.

35
Love Tested

The construction crew worked tirelessly to complete the new hospital. While they worked, Rennin received a letter from Sarah:

Dear Uncle Rennin,

You are the first person I'm telling about my decision. I've been reading about Lucy Stone. She has organized a number of conventions to fight for women's suffrage. This is something I strongly support. When I finish my studies here, I have decided to join the movement and I will be going to New York for a time. Miss Stone has already secured me a place to live so that I may aid in this cause. I am also going to nursing school. I'll be able to help at the new hospital.

I'm terrified to write Papa of my decision. I'm sending him a letter, but a week after yours. Please prepare him.

I love you all and miss you all very much. There's so much I wish I could discuss with Rebekah, but a letter is not appropriate for such a discussion. I'm anxious to see you, but I'll be a new woman when I return. Thank you, Uncle Rennin, for opening my eyes to a world beyond my own doorstep by taking me to New Orleans and through the jungle.

Give everyone hugs and kisses for me.

Sarah

Back East, Sarah told Baxter of her decision as he saw her to the train bound for New York. "I think it's a marvelous idea, although Mother will faint dead away. Will you be leaving in May?" He nodded with approval.

"That's the plan, but I shall miss you."

"I'll visit you there."

"Oh. I hadn't considered that possibility."

"Do you think I'll let you disappear from my life?"

"Baxter, I have a beau."

He smiled knowingly. "Many things can change in five months. Sarah, I..." Baxter forcefully pulled Sarah into his arms and kissed her firmly. She found herself responding eagerly. He released her. "Think about that while you're in New York," said Baxter. "See if Chen Li's kiss stirs your spirit like that. I'll see you when you get back, but your kiss will be on my lips until you replace it with another."

All the way to New York, Baxter's kiss tingled on Sarah's lips, and she felt guilty. As the train pulled into the depot, she spotted Chen Li with Allison Newman. Tears stung her eyes. *What have I done? Baxter, why did you do that? But I wanted you to do it. Chen Li, I'm sorry. I do love you, but how will you react to my decision? Will you support me as Baxter does, or will you disapprove?*

Sarah did not have time to think any longer. The train stopped, and she stepped onto the platform. "Sarah!" Chen Li called as he made his way through the crowd. He reached her and grabbed her hand. "Sarah!"

"Kiss me," she said impulsively.

"Here in front of all these people?"

"Yes, here and now."

Chen Li put a quick kiss on her lips.

"Not like that. Really kiss me."

He granted the lady's wish and kissed her soundly. As they kissed, they heard the exclamation, "Oh, my God! Did you see that? She's white, and he's a Chinaman. What is this world coming to?"

Chen Li pulled back. "Let's go, Sarah. Allison is waiting."

"Don't let that old bat's comment bother you," Sarah said defiantly.

During the holiday, Chen Li took Sarah to meet Moira. The older woman greeted her lovingly. After a time of visiting, Moira said, "Chen Li, I don't feel up to going out, but I would love some of Mr. Ling's cuisine. Take some money and run around there. Get some sweet and sour pork, egg rolls, stir fried vegetables, and fried rice. I bet Sarah has never had authentic Chinese food."

"No. It sounds wonderful. Shall I go with you, Chen Li?"

"No, no. You stay and visit with me," said Moira. "Chen Li knows where it is."

As soon as the man left, Moira said bluntly, "Let's discuss Baxter."

"Excuse me," replied Sarah in shock.

"Chen is greatly concerned about Baxter. Does he have reason to worry?"

"I don't know. I like Baxter…a lot."

"No, it's more. He stirs something in you that Chen never stirred. You're feeling guilty."

"How can you tell all that? Do you think Chen can tell? Oh, I'd never want to hurt him. I love him."

"Enough to let him go?"

"I don't understand."

"What if he met someone else?"

"Has he?"

Moira bit her lip. "Ask *him*. He tells me he loves *you*."
Moira moved from matters of the heart and asked Sarah about

nursing school and women's suffrage. Sarah had told Chen Li her plans. He had scowled slightly at first but said that he thought it would be an honorable pursuit if Sarah wished to work before they married and had a family. So, Moira and Sarah fell to discussing women working and the right to vote.

Meanwhile, Chen Li made his way along the crowded thoroughfare toward Ling's Authentic Chinese Restaurant. As he neared his destination, he saw the petite Mai Ling leave the restaurant carrying numerous boxes of food to the delivery wagon. The boxes were piled high enough to obscure her vision as she stepped into the street. At that very moment, Chen Li saw the milk wagon careening wildly down the street. People screamed and cleared the thoroughfare as the runaway cart headed for Mai Ling.

With no thought for his own safety, Chen Li dashed into the path of the oncoming wagon. He hit Mai Ling with a shoulder tackle that sent both of them sprawling onto the sidewalk. Boxes flew into the air and landed one after the other on top of the couple. Food covered them and the pavement. Several blocks down the street, the crazed horse was finally subdued. Apparently, the driver had succumbed to a heart attack while on his route.

Chen Li breathlessly asked, "Mai Ling, are you all right? You could have been killed."

She blinked in confusion before she answered. "Yes, I am fine thanks to you." She touched his lip that had been cut in the fall. "You are bleeding."

"I'm fine." He sat up.

Mai Ling lay still another moment. Then, she said, "We Chinese have a belief if you remember it. If you save someone's life, you are responsible for that life for the rest of your life."

Chen Li smiled despite his cracked lip and offered her his hand to get up. "I can think of worse fates." He held onto her hand as they entered the restaurant where Mr. Ling ranted in Chinese about, first, his daughter's safety and then about the ruined food that had been on the way to a party and the loss of money. Mai Ling quietly packed more food and loaded the wagon for her brother to deliver.

Chen Li talked calmingly to Mr. Ling and placed Moira's order. As he prepared to leave, Mai Ling said, "If you are responsible for me, what does that mean, Chen?" She looked at him with wondering eyes, and his heart skipped a beat.

"I don't know, Mai. I'll have to think about it."

On the way back to Moira's, Chen Li's spirit was disturbed. *What does it mean*, he asked himself, *not only for Mai Ling, but for Sarah also?*

He hardly ate anything, and when they left Moira's, Sarah suggested they walk for a while before they took a taxi to Allison's. It was obvious to Chen Li that she wanted to talk privately. His stomach churned and his heart beat so loudly Sarah must have heard it.

"Chen, what's wrong? Have you met another girl and are afraid to tell me?"

"I-I don't know, Sarah. I didn't think so until tonight." He told her about Mai Ling.

"Do you want to be responsible for her, Chen?"

"I'm not sure. I'm very confused. Until tonight, no one had stirred anything inside me but you. Sarah, is our love being tested, or have we grown apart? Was ours simply a childhood romance?"

"Maybe," she said honestly.

Chen Li took Sarah's hand. "Do you have feelings for Baxter? Be honest."

"I think I do, but I'm as confused as you are. I don't want to lose you, Chen. You were my first love and the best friend I've ever had." Tears started down Sarah's cheeks.

"Do we have to stop being friends even if we never marry?"

"I hope not. Let me meet your Mai Ling. You come to Boston and meet Baxter. We have always been honest with each other. We'll talk after that. Agreed?"

"Agreed."

The day after Christmas, Chen Li took Sarah to meet Mai Ling. He introduced the two women and watched carefully as he felt the tension in the air. Mai Ling greeted Sarah in a perfunctory manner. "Hello. Chen Li has told me a great deal about you."

Sarah smiled warmly and tried to put Mai Ling at ease. "He has not told me enough about you. The first thing he left out is that you are absolutely beautiful."

The color rose quickly to Mai Ling's cheeks. Sarah turned to Chen Li. "Chen, I would like to talk to Mai Ling alone. Why don't you go to that pastry shop we passed and bring us some of the delicacies to snack on in a bit?"

"Sarah?"

"Trust me, Chen."

He left the women. Mai Ling's voice shook as she asked Sarah to sit down. "Mai Ling," Sarah said gently, "don't be afraid of me. I think both you and I want what is best for Chen."

"Yes," answered Mai Ling softly.

Sarah came straight to the heart of the matter. "Mai Ling, do you love Chen?"

"Sarah, *you* are his fiancée. You are to marry him. What I feel or think makes no difference."

"Yes, it does. It could make all the difference in the world. Do you love him?"

Mai Ling looked into the cup of tea she had served her guest and herself. "More than my own life, but he is an honorable man. He has promised himself to you. My father is trying to find me a Chinese husband, but I do not want any he has suggested. He is considering sending me back to China. I have never been there. I was born her. I do not wish to go, but I have no choice."

"Yes, you do. You'll marry Chen Li."

"How can I do that?"

"Because I am giving him to you. We have come to realize the love we share is one of deep friendship, not the kind needed to establish a home. Besides, he is responsible for you now, isn't he?"

"He told you?" Mai Ling asked in disbelief, her almond-shaped eyes becoming almost round.

"Of course, he did. He's my best friend. I hope you'll be my friend, too."

"I should like that," said Mai Ling, releasing her breath as if she had been holding it.

Chen Li clumsily opened the door with his hands full of delicacies. "I hope I made wise choices," he said.

"You have made an excellent choice," said Sarah. "Only one question remains. Mai Ling, are you Buddhist or Christian?"

Mai Ling whispered, "I cannot disgrace my father. As long as I am in his house, I must remain openly Buddhist, but in my heart I have adopted Chen's faith."

Sarah stood and kissed Chen Li on the cheek. "You will always be my dearest friend, but I release you from any obligation to me. Marry this girl soon before she is spirited away back to China. Even if Baxter isn't the man for me, Mai Ling is the woman for you."

Chen Li took Mai Ling's hand. "Is that what you want?"

"Yes," she replied with downcast eyes.

"Then, I will speak to your father today. Thank you, Sarah. I still plan to meet Baxter and give you my advice."

"As agreed," said Sarah.

Rennin practically inhaled his breakfast and snatched his hat to take off to the hospital building site. "Rennin," Rebekah called. "Can't you stay home today? You have not spent a day with your family since you broke ground on the hospital except for Christmas and our anniversary. You promised not to lose sight of your priorities. Remember?"

He said sharply, "Rebekah, this is important. It was Bart's dying wish. Don't be so selfish."

She raised her eyebrows. "Rennin I think Bart would approve of your spending time with the children, all *seven* of them, and me."

"There'll be time after the hospital opens. 'Bye." He kissed her on the cheek routinely and left.

"Rennin, I'm not finished." Her words fell on deaf ears.

After Rebekah saw Stanley and Jed off to school, she told Mabel she had to go out. With a set jaw she saddled Jewel. Halfway to the building site, she saw Mitchell riding into town. He tipped his hat. "Good morning, Rebekah."

"Mitchell," she acknowledged his presence.

"Where are you headed?"

"To talk to Rennin."

"Don't bother. He rode up to the lumberyard."

"Ooo!" Rebekah grunted angrily.

"Trouble in paradise?" insinuated Mitchell.

"What?" said Rebekah, shortly.

"You seem upset with Rennin. Are you two having a problem?"

"Nothing that a cast iron skillet upside his head won't cure."

"You sound serious, Rebekah."

"I am." She turned Jewel around.

"Mind if I ride back into town with you?" asked Mitchell.

"Suit yourself, but I won't be good company."

"You're always good company," he argued.

"Tell that to Rennin. These days the only company he keeps is blueprints and contractors."

"Foolish man." Mitchell openly flirted with Rebekah.

She laughed lightly. "If you're trying to make me feel better, it's working."

"Good."

Rennin's daily routine changed only on Sundays. Rebekah grew more irritated with each passing day. She took the children on a picnic one Saturday by herself. She was determined that the children should have fun. The boys fished while she read *Memoirs of Magic* to herself.

Her half-reading and half-thinking of ways to get Rennin's attention was suddenly interrupted by a voice. "What are you reading?"

Mitchell sat astride his horse and looked down at Rebekah. She answered, "A book written by one of Rennin's ancestors. It's quite interesting. Have you eaten lunch today?"

"No."

"Please, join us. We have plenty."

"Are you sure?"

"Why not? I'd enjoy the company."

Mitchell dismounted and tied his horse loosely nearby. He sat beside Rebekah. "Please, read some of your book to me while I enjoy your cooking."

She laughed. "It's only partly mine. Mabel cooked some of it."

Around a mouthful, he said, "It's delicious no matter who cooked it. Now, read."

"You won't necessarily understand what's happening."

"I'd just like to hear your voice. You can read wanted posters if you'd like."

She laughed under her breath and shook her head. She read the next chapter aloud.

A strange new man rode into Mom's Trading Post. He stopped at the inn for the night and asked if he could post some bulletins outside the trading post's door. Without examining them, Rennin told him he could. As Rennin left for home he took his first notice of one of the bulletins.

Rennin read the writing beneath a crude sketch that was obviously Ranson Riley's face. "**Ranson Riley: Wanted for Failure to Pay Debts. Reward: Twenty British Pounds**."

Rennin saw the man who had placed the bulletin. "Mister, who and what are you? Are you the law?"

"No, I'm an operative for the British Labor Guild who wants all these people."

"*All* these people—what did they do?" He waved a hand across the wanted posters.

"They signed on as indentured servants and left town without fulfilling their agreements. The government considers it tantamount to robbery."

"What is their likely sentence if they're caught?"

"The original contract years plus two times the amount of time they have been missing served to their original master unless they can pay the money agreed upon in their contracts."

"Can someone else buy their contracts?"

"Sure. They just have to travel to the port of entry and settle with the customs official."

"Are they all the same?"

"No."

"How much say for this one?" Rennin pointed to Ranson's poster.

The bounty hunter pulled out a log and looked up the name. "Fifty gold sovereigns plus the bounty or he can serve, it looks like thirteen years. Of course, the magistrate could give him twenty years."

"That's pretty steep."

"He was a convict. They always cost more and usually get added time."

As Rennin discussed the price of others so as not to rouse suspicion, Ranson chose the worst time to return from checking his traps.

"Rennin!" he greeted his friend as he came through the clearing.

"Excuse me," said Rennin. He walked toward Ranson in an attempt to block the guild operative's line of sight. "Ryan, good to see you. Go to my house. I need to talk to you."

Ranson looked confused. "Now!" said Rennin with authority.

Ranson knew Rennin must have good reason to speak so sharply and to call him Ryan, so he started behind the trading post toward Rennin's house.

"Hold it!" shouted the bounty hunter, pulling his pistol.

"Put your gun away," commanded Rennin.

"And just who are you to give me orders?"

"I'm pretty much the law here in Mom's Trading Post."

"What is going on?" asked Ranson.

Rennin looked at Ranson."This is an operative for the British Labor Guild. He's looking for you."

"And I'm taking him back to Boston to collect my reward."

"Is that all you want?"asked Rennin. "I'll give you the twenty pounds. I'll double it."

"That means you would be harboring a fugitive, Mr. O'Rourke."

"Ask me if I care," snapped Rennin. "This man is my friend and undeserving to have ever been convicted of a crime."

"Tough luck," said the operative.

Rennin started to speak again, but Ranson cut him off. "Rennin, let it go. I might as well pay the piper. What's going to happen to me, Mister?"

"Toler. Bradford Toler. If you can pay your contract off, you can avoid going back to your master or to jail."

Ranson got closer and gaped at the flyer. "I don't have fifty gold sovereigns."

"Plus my bounty."

"How long?" asked Ranson.

"Thirteen years at least. Twenty years possibly."

"Twenty years!" He turned to his friend. "Rennin, I can't leave Angela and Ryan for twenty years."

"I'll buy your contract, Ranson. You can pay me back over time," said Rennin.

"So, Mr. O'Rourke, do you plan to come back to Boston with us?"

"If I must."

"Where can I keep the prisoner until morning?"

"He has a home here."

"He might run away again."

"No, he won't. Contrary to what you think, Ranson is a good man."

Toler stared at Ranson. As Toler sized him up, Ryan ran out to greet his father. "Daidí!" Angela followed him closely. Ranson embraced both of them at the same time.

He said loudly enough for Toler to hear. "I have to go away for a while. Let's go home, and I'll explain. Mr. Toler, you're welcome to come along. I won't run away. Neither will I kill you."

The next morning Angela was near hysterics. She was terrified Ranson would be taken away. He held her tightly. "Honey, nothing should go wrong, but if it does, take care of Ryan until I get back. I love you, and I'm going to marry you. Rennin is going with me. You know he'll do everything he can to bring me back."

"I love you so much, Ranson. What if they send you away? What are Ryan and I to do?"

"It won't happen. I promise."

Ryan, too, clung to his father. "Daidí, do you promise you're coming back? I don't want to lose you again."

"I'll be back, Ryan. I love you."

The trip to Boston was uneventful, and Bradford Toler grew to like both Ranson and Rennin. When they arrived, he acknowledged. "This seems very unfair, but you know this is my job."

"I know. I don't blame you, Mr. Toler," said Ranson.

Toler escorted Ranson and Rennin to the magistrate, who listened to the whole story and saw that Rennin was prepared to pay Ranson's contract. "Mr. O'Rourke, you may purchase Mr. Riley's contract. However, he will still have to serve two years in jail or forty lashes."

"Why?" asked Ranson in panic. His thoughts flew to Angela and Ryan. "Sir, please. I have a son. He's only ten. I've already been taken from him once, unjustly at that. I also have a fiancée. Are you willing to punish an innocent child again?"

"Mr. Riley, if you had not been a convict, you wouldn't have to serve the two years. It's the new law. I have no choice. I feel for your plight, but my hands are tied."

Ranson turned imploringly to Rennin. "Rennin, what do I do?"

"Your Honor," said Rennin, "if Mr. Riley could prove his original incarceration was fraudulent and unjust, would that make any difference?"

"It would to me. I'm inclined to believe him as it is. If you show me some proof, I'll grant him a pardon."

Rennin turned to Ranson. "Sit tight. I'm not leaving Boston. I'll be staying with Cameron. Ranson, I intend to find one of those slaves you supposedly helped to escape, and I'll get the truth from him."

Rennin sent Morgan news of his plan and traveled across town to Cameron's house. For three and a half months Rennin, with Brad Toler's assistance, searched for at least one of the slaves that Andrew had owned. During the time, Rennin enjoyed visiting with his son and grandson. He was thoroughly enchanted by Cameron's young governess. He also met Lucia and the rest of the Allgood family. Lucia was charming, but Rennin could not understand why he felt uncomfortable with her, other than the chill that gave him goosebumps every time they talked. He refused to say anything to Cameron about his misgivings, but prayed silently for God to guard Cameron's heart, mind, and spirit. He did, however, write to Morgan about his feelings and apprehensions.

Finally, after another three months, a total of six months of searching, Rennin found Terrance, a terribly disfigured slave, who had obviously been severely beaten many times. He admitted to Rennin that he had been one of the slaves Andrew had forced to pretend to run away. "Mizza Andrew promised to free us. He lied. I was too scairt to tell da truth. Mizza Andrew threatened to kill us."

"Andrew is dead. If you'll come forward and tell the truth now, I'll buy you and your wife and set you free," Rennin promised.

"Why?"

"I want my friend's name cleared, and I'm a fair man."

"Mizza Ranson was a kind man. Yes. I will tell da truth. Yous ain't got to buy me nor set me free."

"Nonetheless, I will."

"Well, only if'n I can come to live where you is."

"You will be welcome."

It took another two months for the magistrate to hear the slave's story and another month to file all the proper paper work. Ten and a half months after he left Mom's Trading Post, Ranson walked out of the jail free and pardoned, his record totally expunged. The six-week trip home seemed eternal. One year after he last held Angela, and nine months past the date they were to have been married, Ranson ran through the door and into the arms of the woman he loved and his son.

Rebekah closed the book when the boys came up with a string of fish. "This story is fascinating," said Mitchell. "I would love to read the whole thing."

"Maybe you can order a copy of the book."

"I'd rather hear you read it."

"Mitchell, it seems as if you're making advances toward me. I'm a married woman."

"One who is being neglected sorely."

"Mitchell, the love I have for Rennin can stand any test. Please respect that."

Mitchell nodded deferentially, but Rebekah missed the sad, longing look in his eyes.

36
Green-eyed Monster

Rebekah spent many days alone. Rennin was completely absorbed in the building of the hospital. After months of watching from a distance, Rennin invited her to go to San Francisco to pick up the woman he had hired to be the nursing administrator.

Rebekah had hoped to use the trip as a time to rekindle the spark of romance, but all Rennin could talk about was the different facets of hospital administration. "I never knew there was so much involved in running a hospital."

Rebekah shouted, "If you say another word about that damned hospital, I'll burn it down myself!"

Matters became worse when they met Monica Fulton's boat. Monica hailed from Liverpool and was an experienced nurse who had recently returned from a year in Crimea with Florence Nightingale. Rebekah had expected some gray-haired, grandmotherly type, but Monica was a thirty-year-old widowed beauty. Though she wore her sandy blond hair pulled tightly into a bun, ringlets constantly escaped and framed her cherub-like face. Her soft brown eyes radiated compassion, and her angelic voice soothed the wretched soul.

Rennin and Monica discussed plans for the nursing staff. Rennin told her about Sarah, and Monica wholeheartedly supported the cause of women's suffrage and Sarah's plans to enter the nursing field. "I do hope she takes a few administrative courses. A woman really needs some business sense. There are many who would attempt to take advantage of a woman, thinking she would not have any business accumen. And if women have the right to vote, they have power to protect themselves. Rebekah, what do you think?"

"I've never thought much about it, but, perhaps, I should in case Rennin is *unavailable* to take care of me. Someone would also need to manage the interest of our *seven* children. Of course, I'm sure Mitchell would *gladly* handle my affairs."

Rennin shot Rebekah a look, and she gave him a crooked smile.

Unaware of the tension, Monica exclaimed, "You have seven children!"

"Well," explained Rebekah, "Rennin and I have twin boys of our own, and we adopted another little boy. Then, when our good friends, Bart and Keturah Mercier died, we took their four children to live with us. Oh, I should have said eight. Rennin has another child, Patty." Rebekah hastened as Monica became wide-eyed, "His pet puma who has also forgotten how he smells."

"Oh, good. I thought you were awfully young to have had seven children. Still, it must keep you busy. How do you do it?"

"I have a housekeeper who helps a great deal, and Rennin's mother is nearby. Of course, both of them have young children of their own. Mitchell has been spending a good deal of time with the children lately."

"Rennin, how do you have time to be a father to so many?"

As Rennin started to speak, Rebekah said coldly, "He doesn't. He's a hospital administrator."

Rennin spoke sharply, "Rebekah!"

Rebekah stared defiantly at him with her jaw firmly set and her eyes flashing fire. She was ready for a fight. She preferred a fight over the neglect, but she realized this was not the time or place. So, she maintained her demeanor but kept quiet.

As the weeks progressed, Rennin stayed later and later at the site and worked closely with Monica reviewing applications. Many times, Rebekah sat alone in the rose garden and cried. On one such night far past midnight, she felt a gentle hand on her shoulder. Mitchell said softly, "Rebekah, let me help."

"You can't help, Mitchell. I'm afraid your idea for helping me would be wrong. I love Rennin, and I have no intention of being unfaithful to him."

"I would never ask you to be unfaithful even though I admit that I care for you. I have another idea, a way we can help each other."

"What do you have in mind?"

"Help me get to know Monica. I find her most intriguing, and I *am* a lonely man. Rebekah, I know you're jealous of the time she spends with Rennin. I'm certain the relationship is strictly business-related." He shook his head. "Rennin is obsessed with getting this hospital set up correctly. I can attest to that fact."

She let her tears fall without shame. "Oh, Mitchell, I feel so foolish. Yes, I'm jealous. It has been months since Rennin has been with me. You know what I mean. His kisses aren't even kisses any more. Have I lost my appeal?"

He let Rebekah lay her head on his shoulder and cry. He stroked her hair and kissed the top of her head. "No, you are a very beautiful woman. Rennin is a fool."

From out of nowhere, Mitchell found himself on the ground with Rennin astraddle him. "What are you doing with my wife?" Rennin belted Mitchell in the mouth.

"Stop it, Rennin!" shouted Rebekah. "It's not at all what you're thinking. Stop it!"

Rennin turned angrily toward Rebekah. "Rebekah, it's past midnight. You're in the rose garden wearing your nightgown in another man's arms. What am I supposed to think?"

She retorted just as hotly, "It's past midnight. You've been alone for hours with another woman, a very beautiful, unmarried woman. You've not made love to me in months. What am *I* supposed to think?"

"Mitchell?" Rennin questioned.

"I hugged Rebekah because she was crying. I let her cry and vent some of her frustrations with *you*. Yes, I think she's beautiful, and you're a fool for neglecting her. If I *weren't* a gentleman, I'd have pursued her. Rather, I've just asked her to help me pursue Monica. Do you object? Does Rebekah have reason to be jealous? The whole community is talking about it."

Rennin looked at Rebekah. "Do you think I've been unfaithful to you?"

"Yes," said Rebekah, nodding her head, "but not with Monica. You've given your affections to an idea, albeit noble. Rennin, you can build the hospital in Bart's memory *and* be my husband and a father to our children. Rennin, I need you more than I ever have. I've been trying to rear seven children under the age of six by myself. I *can't* do it alone."

"I hate to interrupt this moment of truth, but, Rennin, will you, please, get off me?" said Mitchell.

Rennin stood and apologized to Mitchell. "I'm sorry. I should have known better." He shuffled his feet. "I feel like an idiot."

"You *are*, but you're forgiven," Mitchell said.

"Mitchell, what is everyone saying?" Rennin asked with grave concern.

"The comments I've heard are that you're neglecting your family; and although most of the people hesitate to think you're in an adulterous relationship, it looks bad for you to spend so much time alone with Monica, not to mention putting her reputation in jeopardy."

Rennin sat down on the bench that Mitchell and Rebekah had been occupying. "I lost track of my priorities *again*, Rebekah. I broke my promise to you even after you pointed out my fault. How many times will you be willing to forgive me?"

"I believe Jesus said, 'Seventy times seven,' which Henry interprets to mean as often as asked."

"I promise from now on, I will only go to the site on Monday, Wednesday, and Friday; and you will go with me on Friday. I'll work at home on Tuesday and Thursday, and Saturday belongs completely to you and the children."

"I can live with that arrangement. Rennin, I love you so much. I would never betray you."

"I know that in my heart. I was jealous. Mitchell, I apologize again, and *I* will help you with Monica. It won't take much persuasion. She finds you attractive as well. Rebekah, let's go home. I'm staying home tomorrow. I need to be with you."

Rennin held Rebekah's hand as they walked. "How do you put up with me?"

"Sometimes it's a challenge."

"Am I an arrogant prig the way Ralph said, Rebekah?"

She laughed. "Sometimes. At other times, you're an angel in disguise."

"But this time I made you cry, and I drove you into the arms of another man. I'm glad Mitchell is *not* his brother."

"Yes, Dennis is rather a cad."

"Who cares? I'm back where I belong," Rennin said as they walked up the stairs hand in hand.

"So am I," said Rebekah, snuggling into her husband's embrace. "I'm in your arms."

"Yes, you are. I'm sorry." He held her face in his hands. "I love you, Rebekah." He kissed his wife passionately before he spoke the words he had the day they wed. "Heart of my heart, life of my life. You are my reason for breathing, and I will love you until the day I die."

Stanley and Jed quietly opened the door to where Rebekah slept. Walking to the bedside, Stanley gave Jed a strange look when they saw Rennin still asleep beside Rebekah. Stanley gently shook her. "Mommy, it's time to leave for school. Aren't you going to kiss us good-bye? Mabel told us to check on you."

Rebekah sat up quickly. "What time is it? I'm sorry. I overslept."

Rennin sat up beside her. "Honey, you stay in bed. I'll see the boys off to school."

"You?" asked Stanley. "You won't know what to do. Can you pack a lunch? Do you hold hands and give kisses?"

Rennin, indeed, felt ashamed that he had neglected the children for now he would have to earn their love and respect. "Yes, Stanley, I can pack a lunch, and I would love to hold your hand and give you a kiss. Meet me in the kitchen."

Jed and Stanley exchanged doubtful looks. "Scoot," said Rennin. "I'll be there in five minutes."

The boys obeyed, and Rennin dressed hurriedly. Once in the kitchen, he asked, "What would you like for lunch?"

"Mommy always has it planned," explained Stanley.

"Oh, I see. Well, let's see what Mommy has stored in here for today." Rennin went into the root cellar to see what Rebekah might have planned. He found a smoked ham hanging, obviously for supper that night. Then he saw two lunch pails; each held a chicken leg, bread wrapped in a moist cloth, and an apple. He returned triumphantly. "How does this work for you two?" He handed them the pails. "I think I'll add one thing more." He handed each boy an oatmeal-raisin cookie for desert and grinned.

"Looks pretty good," said Jed approvingly. "Did you do it, or did Momma Rebekah have it planned already?"

"I can't fool you. The pails were packed in the root cellar, but the cookie was my idea. You have to eat your lunch first, though."

Jed looked Rennin over. "Rennin, are you going to be staying home some now? Momma Rebekah has been very sad. You really should spend more time with her. She might die like Momma and Papa, and"—The child's voice choked on tears—"then, you'd be all alone with us children."

Rennin was taken off guard by the boy's candor. "Yes," he stammered. "Rebekah is not going to die any time soon, but I *am* going to spend more time with all of you. Why is she 'Momma' Rebekah, and I'm only Rennin?"

"She's earned it," said Jed frankly. "I'll give you a second chance, but you won't get a third. If you make Momma Rebekah cry again, I think I'll toss you out of the house. You promised Papa you'd take care of us, but you've spent more time taking care of his hospital dream. Rennin, I think Papa thought we were more important than a hospital. I might be only six years old, but I know how to show love. Papa taught me that. He spent *time* with us. He hugged us and told us he loved us. I miss Papa very much, and you're not doing a very good job of taking his place." The little boy's lip trembled and tears welled in his eyes.

Rennin was flabbergasted. "Well, I've been sufficiently chastised. I'll earn your respect, Jed. I apologize for neglecting you. Thank you for giving me another chance. Now, let's go to school."

Rennin took the boys' hands and walked them all the way to school. He knelt in front of them and hugged and kissed both of them. "I love both of you. I *am* sorry. I will *not* let you down again."

Stanley whispered, "I love you, too, Papa. I missed you."

Rennin returned to Rebekah, whom he found in the kitchen surrounded by screaming children, each demanding immediate attention. It suddenly dawned on him how much stress Rebekah must have been feeling. Rennin slammed his hand on the table. Every eye turned his way. He spoke softly, but firmly. "Be quiet. Sit in your chair. The next one of you who yells or demands anything will be soundly spanked. Your mother and Mabel are moving as fast as they can to take care of you. Wait your turn. What can I do to help, ladies?"

"Fill each glass with milk, please," said Rebekah.

Rennin poured the milk and helped serve the rest of breakfast. Rather than the bickering that usually took place at the table every child waited silently for Rennin to explode. When the meal was finished, Rennin said, "Gabriel and Michael, help Mabel with the dishes. Then, meet us outside. Stephen, wipe the table. Then, you meet us outside. Chris, come with me. I need you to help me gather some tools."

When the boys went outside, Rennin took them to a section of land near the creek. There they marked off an area with stakes and twine. Then, Rennin plowed the earth. He made six rows. Each boy was to have his own row of vegetables to grow and harvest.

Gabriel planted a row of cucumbers; Michael, a row of tomatoes. Stephen chose okra, and Chris was given bunch butterbeans. They saved peas and carrots for Jed and Stanley to plant when they got home. Rennin gave them strict instructions. "Every morning after breakfast, you're to tend your garden. Pull up the weeds and water the plants if it hasn't rained. When your plants produce food, you can help cook it and we'll all eat what you've grown. This is your own special vegetable row. If it dies, it will be *your* fault. Do not bother Mommy with it. This is yours. If you do well with the vegetables, next year I'll let you have a special farm animal to care for. We might just start our own ranch if you do well." He grinned and leaned on the plow attached to old Jack, the mule. "On top of the garden, each of you will have a chore to do daily from now own. Gabriel, you will help with the dishes. Michael, you will sweep and mop. Stephen, you will dust the tables. Chris, I will show you how to wash the dining table until you get bigger. Then, you can do some more. And your brothers will help you with your butterbeans."

"What about Stanley and Jed?" asked Michael, his face in a pout.

"You let me worry about what chores to give them, and you mind your own rat killing and your tongue. I will paddle your behind, boy."

"Yes, sir," replied Michael with renewed respect for his father's authority.

"Right now, you boys put the tools away and go fishing. Do *not* go swimming without an adult with you. I have to talk to your mother."

Rebekah had collapsed into a chair on the porch to watch the scene. Rennin sat at her feet. "Pack your bags. We're going to the city for a few days. You need a vacation."

"I can't leave the children."

"Don't even go there. We are *not* taking them with us. While we're in San Francisco, I'm hiring a nanny to help you."

"Rennin, don't put your responsibility on someone else." She brushed her stray hair from her face.

"That's not what I'm doing. I simply don't want you growing old before your time. I love you, Rebekah, and I want to make life easier for you. We can afford it, so why not give yourself a break and help someone who might need the income at the same time?"

"If you say so, Rennin. I won't argue. I'm too tired to argue."

"Damn! I thought I was actually going to win an argument, and you would have to pay the price for a change."

Rebekah laughed. "Let's say I lost. What do you want in payment?"

"Time alone with you. Hopefully nobody will be on the stage with us. I would prefer that."

Rennin got his wish. He and Rebekah had the stage to themselves. He took the opportunity to read again to his wife as they had done when love was fresh and new.

Cameron liked his young governess. He often insisted that she do things with him and Rowan. Needless to say, he was oblivious to the tension his special arrangement with Tammy caused with Lucia. Unknown to Cameron, Lucia saw to it that Tammy remained in her place. She took it upon herself to talk to the girl when Cameron was not around.

"Tammy, you must maintain the proper relationship with your employer. You're only a servant in his household. It would be unseemly for you to do certain things in his company. Now, sometimes, it will be fine for you to accompany him and Rowan. Other times, you must be discreet, or people will think you are a kept woman. I know you do not want your reputation tarnished."

Tammy kept a healthy distance between Cameron and herself, though she loved Rowan dearly. She doted on him, and if he asked her to do something, no matter how unseemly Lucia found it, Tammy gave in to Rowan's request. At those times, Lucia insinuated herself into being included.

One of these times was while Rennin was in Boston with Ranson. Lucia made sure Rennin knew which woman was the love interest in Cameron's life. She made it clear that she had her sights set on becoming an O'Rourke. Cameron only blushed and grinned, and Rennin caught his son's eye wander to the quiet, demure governess. Yet, Rennin kept his thoughts to himself.

Rennin was elated when it came time to go home. He wished Cameron the best, but encouraged him, "Don't close your heart to unexpected love. There's no need to rush into marriage. Give love time to grow."

"I will, Daidí. I'm not marrying Lucia any time soon. I plan to court a few years. I need that time for my heart to heal."

"Oh, Lucia, yes, well," was all the disapproval Rennin could allow himself to offer. "Just take things slowly. Keep your options open. I love you, Cam."

Rennin was anxious to get home for Morgan had written him a most disturbing letter. It seemed Duncan was experiencing some trouble in the affairs of the heart. Rennin tried to dismiss it as trivial, but he knew Morgan did not worry unnecessarily. When he left Ranson with Angela, he went home to care for his own family. After the proper greetings and a warm welcome home, Rennin took Morgan to the side. "How are things with Duncan and Cynthia?"

"Duncan is so jealous he could kill."

"Tell me the whole story."

"Well, a few months back, Talulah brought his nephew into the trading post. That's not unusual except that he's a very handsome young brave. His name is Hopam. Hopam has clearly set his sights on Cynthia. He made advances toward her in front of Duncan. It was all Oliver could do to hold Duncan back from starting a fight. Luckily, they only stayed a few days and they have not been back, but, Rennin, Duncan is still jealous. He watches Cynthia as if she encouraged the young man. I don't think that's the case. I think she was actually a bit frightened."

"I'll talk to Duncan. I'll find out his thoughts. Don't worry. I'm more worried about Cameron. I pray his loneliness doesn't bind him to a woman he will regret having committed to. Morgan, I don't trust Lucia. I don't know exactly why. She was pleasant, but there's something about her that I find disconcerting. I got a chill everytime I was near her."

"Did you tell Cameron?"

"No. I didn't want to seem judgmental. I just hope he keeps his heart open. I don't know if this woman is capable of true love. I think she wants Cameron as a token, something she has conquered."

Morgan shivered, thinking about how Quazel wanted to conquer the O'Rourke men.

Rennin's words brought her back to the moment. "Moreover, she doesn't seem to really have any genuine affection for Rowan."

Because he's not a girl. She laid a calming hand on his arm. "Rennin, now it's my turn to tell you not to worry. Cameron will put Rowan first. No woman is going to hurt his child." *If I have to, I'll see to it.*

"Of course, you're right, *if* he sees through her. I'll continue to pray toward that end. I hope I'm mistaken. I'm going to find Duncan. He took off immediately after I came in."

"If you find Cynthia, you'll find him."

As Rennin turned to leave, Duncan burst into the house. "He's back. He's fawning all over Cynthia, and she's terrified." Duncan marched to the gun rack over the fireplace.

"Whoa!" shouted Rennin. "What are you doing?"

"I am going to put the fear of God into that particular Indian. Daidí, he's hinting at joining their tribes. That means he wants to marry Cynthia. I will not have it. She is *my* fiancée."

"Give me that," Rennin said, wrenching the gun from Duncan's grip.

"Daidí!"

"Do you want to start a war? Let's talk this over. Is Talulah with this Hopam?"

"Yes, and he's as nervous as a turkey at Christmas. I've heard him trying to talk to his nephew. The arrogant fool pushed his uncle to the side, all because he knows that he is next in line to be chief, if I let him live that long."

"How is Cynthia reacting to his advances?"

"At first, she was polite and talked to him cordially. Now, she says she's afraid of him. Daidí, she's not encouraging him if that's what you were asking, but he doesn't seem to understand what 'no' means. Because of his status in the tribe, he's used to getting what he wants. He wants Cynthia, and he cannot have her."

"Stay calm, Duncan. I'll talk to him."

"Daidí, it's my battle. Let me fight it."

"All right, but I'll be your second. I have your back."

Duncan gave a sharp affirmative nod.

Rennin walked with his son to the trading post where Hopam had Cynthia cornered. In broken English he was proposing marriage.

"No, no, no," said Cynthia. "I am to marry Duncan. I love him. I do not even *like* you."

"But you most beautiful woman Hopam ever see. Hopam be chief one day. You be most important woman in village." Hopam put his hand out and touched Cynthia's face.

Duncan could stand no more. He flew across the room and jerked Hopam by his shoulders, flinging him to the ground. Duncan pinned the Indian with his forearm across the Hopam's throat. "You might be chief of your tribe someday, but neither Cynthia nor I am a member of your tribe. She is to be *my* wife. Leave her alone or I will kill you."

Duncan let Hopam up. The Indian was ready for a fight.

"No!" commanded Talulah. "You be chief one day, not today. Today you nephew. We go home. You no insult white friends and honorable allies. Rennin, Duncan, my humble apology." Talulah prodded Hopam.

"I will not apologize, Uncle," he said stubbornly and arrogantly.

Talulah shoved the younger man toward the door. Hopam looked over his shoulder. "We see whose she becomes."

Rennin dropped the book as the ruts in the road jostled him and Rebekah.

"Well, Duncan had good reason to be jealous," said Rebekah. "I don't trust that Hopam. I'm sure he's up to some mischief."

While Rennin and Rebekah enjoyed a few days alone, Chen Li escorted Sarah back to Boston. Baxter waited for Sarah on the train platform. When he saw Chen Li helping Sarah from the train, he seethed.

"There he is," said Sarah as she waved for Baxter.

Baxter wanted more than anything to turn and leave, but since he was taught to behave as a gentleman, at least publicly, he went toward Sarah.

"Baxter!" She greeted him with an affectionate hug.

"Sarah, it's good to have you back."

"I've brought someone to meet you."

"Chen Li, I presume." Baxter extended his hand coldly.

"Yes," Chen Li shook Baxter's hand. "Sarah has told me a great deal about you. I'm pleased to meet you."

"Likewise," Baxter said formally.

Sarah was oblivious to the tension because she was so excited about Chen Li's meeting Baxter. She wanted the two men to like each other.

Baxter helped Sarah into the coach. "Sarah, I only have time to drop you at the school. I have to get back to Harvard for a fraternity function. It's very important. Chen Li, where can I drop you?"

"I'm only here for the day. I'm leaving on the afternoon train. I'll spend the time I have here with Sarah."

"I see," said Baxter. He was quiet the rest of the way to the school. He dropped Sarah and Chen Li and promptly left. He had ridden in on horseback. He exchanged the carriage for his horse and galloped away without so much as saying good-bye.

Sarah gave Chen Li a whirlwind tour of the school and her favorite places, all of which Baxter had introduced to her. As Chen Li was leaving, she seemed melancholy. "What's wrong, Sarah?" he asked.

"Will you still write me even though we aren't engaged?"

"Yes. You're still my friend."

"I'll come up if you marry Mai Ling before you leave school."

"I would hope so."

"I'm disappointed you didn't get to know Baxter."

Chen Li laughed. "Sarah, the man left because he was jealous. He did *not* have a fraternity function. He simply didn't want to be around me. Tell him soon that we're no longer engaged."

"Are you sure?"

"Oh, absolutely."

Sarah went back to school happy Baxter was jealous, but she did not realize jealousy could be a green-eyed monster.

37
Doubts

Sarah began to write Rebekah consistently, seeking her advice regarding matters of the heart. She wrote about the change in her and Chen Li's relationship and about how she was drawn to Baxter no matter how hard she fought the feelings and in spite of Beatrice Pryor's objections. Rebekah read parts of the letters to Rennin; other parts she kept to herself for she knew they were personal and meant for her eyes only. One part went:

The woman truly hates me, Rebekah. I don't understand why. What worries me more is the distance Baxter has put between us since I returned from New York. Chen Li said Baxter was jealous. If that's true, why has he not pursued me harder? Rather than spending more time with me, he has distanced himself. Is he protecting his own heart? Is he afraid I have rejected him? I have not even had an opportunity to tell him of the change in the nature of my relationship with Chen Li. Should I corner him and talk candidly with him? Oh, Rebekah, write to me swiftly and give me your wise council.

Rebekah looked at Rennin. "What do I tell her?"

"Tell her to be honest with him. Write tonight. The letter will take a while to get there. A lot could have happened between the time she mailed her letter and the time your letter gets back to her."

Rebekah wrote her letter with love and sealed it with a prayer. It went off on the next day's stage.

Meanwhile in Boston, Sarah completed her time at the finishing school. She packed solemnly to leave for New York and nursing school. Beatrice took the opportunity to goad the girl one last time.

Knocking once on Sarah's door Beatrice entered, uninvited. "Sarah, Daniel will be driving you to your train. Baxter is unable to leave Harvard until tomorrow. He sends his apologies."

"It's just as well," said Sarah. "I have a life to live with or without Baxter."

Beatrice arched her eyebrows. "My dear, it will be without. I shall see to that. Good-bye."

Sarah left unobtrusively. On the train she cried softly and silently. *God, why did I let Chen Li go? Why does love hurt so much? Yes, I admit it. Oh, God, I love Baxter. I suppose I was only a diversion for him. Help me start over.*

As the train left the station, Baxter entered the school and went straight to Sarah's room. His mother met him in the hallway. "She's gone," Beatrice said authoritatively.

"Mother, she wasn't supposed to leave until tomorrow. That is what your letter said."

"I told you I would not let you become involved with that girl. She's out of your life. Be glad. You had your fun with her. Was she as good as some of your other conquests? Did she bed you well?"

Baxter glared at his mother. "Mother, if I never see you again it will be too soon. I've finished law school, and I'm moving to New York. I will find Sarah if it *kills* me. She was far more than a conquest. Don't you understand? She makes me alive. I *love* her."

"Baxter, don't be ridiculous! She is nothing more than a girl with loose morals. She played you for a fool and had her little Chinese boy, too. You have the cream of the crop to choose from here. What about Pamela? She adores you, and she is everything we ever dreamed of."

"No, Mother, she's everything *you* ever dreamed of."

"Baxter, if you go after Sarah, don't come back here."

Baxter grimaced slightly. "As you wish, Mother. Good-bye."

Unbeknownst to either of them, Pamela Scott, who desired to be Mrs. Baxter Pryor more than anything, had overheard the conversation. She smiled wickedly to herself for tomorrow she, too, would be leaving for New York. She had every intention of making sure Sarah knew that she had only been a conquest for Baxter. With Sarah completely removed from the scene, she had no doubt that she could win Baxter.

Chen Li and Mai Ling met Sarah at the train. The warm greeting from two friends cheered Sarah's heart temporarily. Chen Li began an immediate explanation of news yet unknown to Sarah. "Sarah, we have to tell you something."

"What?"

"Mai Ling and I were married last week."

"What?" Sarah said in shock.

"It was sort of an emergency."

Sarah looked back and forth from Chen Li to Mai Ling with big questioning eyes.

"No, not that," Chen Li defended their actions. "You know me better than that. Mai's father bought a ticket to send her back to China. We had to get married right away. We didn't have time to send for you. Do you understand? Will you forgive us?"

Sarah took a deep breath and nodded in a daze. "Does Uncle Rennin know?"

"I wrote him, but he has not received the letter yet. Many things have changed. Mr. Ling was not pleased, and I can't stay in the dormitory anymore. Temporarily, we are living with Moira. We have told no one at the college."

"Why aren't you living with Allison?"

"Mai is more comfortable in the more modest setting."

"Mai Ling, no, I suppose it is Mai Li now. Is that right?"

"Yes, since so many Americans do not understand that Chinese surname goes first, I am Mai Li now."

"I understand." Sarah scowled. "Why don't you go to Puma Pass and set up housekeeping? Chen can finish school more easily without the responsibility of a wife. And what if you should conceive? Everyone will welcome you in Puma Pass, and you can have a home waiting for Chen when he gets back."

"You disapprove?" asked Mai carefully.

"No. I just think Chen must finish his education. It's very important."

Mai looked at her new husband. "Is this your wish? Do you want me to go to Puma Pass?"

"Let's discuss it with Moira. I confess that I asked Rennin if I should send you home."

"If it is what you wish, I will do it."

"It would be easier for me to complete my studies. I have two more years."

"Yes, Sarah will have two years of nursing school at Academy of Mount Saint Vincent. She will be in the same city as you."

Sarah saw where the conversation was headed. "Mai, please don't be jealous of our friendship. I'm very happy for you. I think you're perfect for each other. You'll show your love for Chen more if you let him finish his education unhindered."

Chen Li put his arm around his young wife. She looked at him with eyes full of love. "All right, I will go to Puma Pass. I will make you a wonderful home. When you come home, I will give you many children."

"Thank you. I love you, Mai, only you." He looked at Sarah's serious expression. "How are things with Baxter?"

"Not good." She told her friends about Baxter's distance and his mother's sheer hatred.

"I'm sorry, Sarah. Perhaps I was wrong about Baxter, but I truly believe he loves you. Maybe he's afraid to tell you so."

"I have my doubts now, Chen. I think that I was only a diversion. Don't worry about me. I'll survive, and I have two very exciting years ahead of me."

Sarah settled herself into her new rooming house while Chen Li sent his young bride west. Sarah's roommate, Virginia Stanton, was a plain, quiet, introverted person who wrote most of her thoughts on the subject of women's suffrage. Sarah tried to carry on a conversation, but received only monosyllables in reply.

Two days after Sarah started classes, there came a knock at her door just after dinner. She opened the door and in utter confusion saw Pamela Scott. "Pamela, what are you doing here?"

"May I come in, Sarah? I know I've never been very friendly to you, but I feel it's my duty to inform you of a conversation I overheard. It's about Baxter."

"Please, come in. Is Baxter all right?"

"I don't know how to say this, so I'll simply be candid. The night you left I overheard Baxter arguing with his mother. He had apparently come to see you off. He was very angry he had missed you."

"Really?" said Sarah happily.

"Don't get so excited. He was angry that he had not been able to, he used the word, 'conquer,' you. His mother actually defended you. She told him she had opposed his relationship with you because she knew he was only out to bed you. She felt his behavior scandalous. Oh, Sarah, I'm so sorry to tell you this because I know you cared deeply for Baxter, but you were only a conquest to him. From the conversation I overheard, you were not the first innocent girl he pursued so, only to leave them used and ruined. It's even rumored that he has two illegitimate children. Mrs. Pryor called him an embarrassment."

Sarah was speechless. Finally, she said, "Thank you for coming, Pamela. Don't concern yourself for me. I come from hearty stock. I'll survive a small heartbreak."

Pamela hugged Sarah as if she truly cared that Sarah's heart was broken. Then, she walked slowly down the long corridor, but she skipped with delight to her carriage.

Sarah turned slowly. She shrugged. "I already felt that he didn't really love me. That only confirms my doubts."

Virginia looked sadly at her, but had no idea what to say.

Rebekah's letter arrived for Sarah, and Beatrice Pryor tossed it into the trash.

In Puma Pass, Rebekah fretted about Sarah. "Rennin, I have a terrible feeling. Something awful is happening in our dear Sarah's life. She's in pain. I feel it."

"Rebekah, you've done all you can. If Sarah is hurting and she asks for your help, all you can do is be supportive. Stop worrying. Let me read to you for a while."

Rebekah kissed Rennin's cheek. "You always try to make me feel better."

Life in Boston sailed smoothly for Cameron. Within six months, Ian and Lucretia were married. Cameron continued to court Lucia, but he let her know that he still needed time to heal from the loss of his wife and that he wanted to spend a great deal of time with his son. Lucia seemed to concur, but there were times he doubted she truly understood. Often he did not understand his hesitance.

Cameron spent his second Christmas in Boston at the Allgood home. The occasion was festive and lively with much brandy served. Rowan accompanied his father and laughed at the antics of those who had drunk too much. Near dark, Cameron had twinges of conscience. Tammy had been left alone, and this was the first Christmas after her father's death.

When Cameron expressed his concern about his governess to Lucia, she reluctantly suggested he and Rowan go and spend a few hours with the lonely girl. "Take some of this food with you so that she, too, can have a semblance of celebration."

"Are you sure?" Cameron asked. "I don't want to leave your company so soon."

"Yes, help her through this time. I can afford to be gracious, although I hate to let you go so soon as well."

Cameron held Lucia under the mistletoe in her foyer and kissed her soundly. "Good night, lovely lady. Merry Christmas."

Rowan turned his face upward. "Me, too."

A strange look spread across Lucia's face. "Well, all right." She gave Rowan a little peck.

As they walked home, Rowan commented honestly, "Cold fish."

"What did you say?"

"She's a cold fish, Poppy."

Cameron roared with laughter. "She's just not used to little boys."

"Well, if you plan to make her my mother, she had better get used to me."

When they arrived home, they found Tammy in the main house. She apologized. "I'm sorry. I just brought Rowan a gift. I wanted him to find it when he got home."

"Miss Martin...Tammy...please stay," said Cameron. "Let's have supper together. I have one more present for Rowan, too. I also have a gift for you."

"You shouldn't have."

"Don't be silly. It's only a small token of my esteem for you and something you need." Cameron handed her a large package that rested on one entry table.

Shyly Tammy opened the package, which contained a heavy fur cloak, gloves, muff, and bonnet.

"Your other cloak is falling apart," said Cameron.

"Thank you. I don't have a gift for you. I only have something small for Rowan. Is it all right if he opens it now?"

"Of course."

Rowan opened his gift, a delicately carved chess set. In way of explanation, Tammy said, "My father made it for me when I was a little girl. I can teach you to play."

"Poppy, too?"

Tammy looked bashfully at Cameron. "If he would like."

"I know how to play, but I would love the competition." Cameron felt his heart flutter. He laid it to the charge of the girl's innocence. He turned to his son. "Rowan, I have another gift for you. Stay here and set up the game while I get it."

Cameron was back in a flash. "Burrrr. It's really cold. This little guy wants to get warm." Cameron presented Rowan with a fuzzy white kitten.

The child squealed with delight. "Poppy! I'm going to name him Snowball."

"That's the perfect name," Tammy and Cameron said in unison. Both laughed.

After a relaxing dinner, Cameron and Tammy put Rowan to bed with Snowball in his arms. Tammy went down the stairs and slipped on her new cape that proved to be a perfect fit. Cameron touched her shoulder. She turned around reservedly. "Thank you for making this day enjoyable after all," she said sweetly.

"You're welcome." Cameron tipped her chin up and softly kissed her on the mouth.

She pulled back. "Why did you do that?"

"You're standing under the mistletoe." She followed his eyes up.

"Please, don't ever do that again, Mr. O'Rourke. It makes me very uncomfortable."

"I didn't mean to make you uncomfortable. Merry Christmas, Tammy, I mean, Miss Martin."

Cameron watched Tammy walk to the cottage through the gathering snowflakes. He went to bed feeling let down.

A few weeks after Christmas, just before Rennin and Ranson arrived in Boston, Cameron came home from work to see Tammy perched precariously on top of a wobbly ladder. "What are you doing?" he asked as the sight amused him.

"Snowball is stuck in the tree. He's afraid to come down. Rowan's very upset."

"You're going to fall. Climb down and let me go after him."

As Tammy started down the ladder, her foot slipped. Cameron caught her, and they both fell into the new-fallen snow. For a moment Cameron lay perfectly still holding on to Tammy's warm body. He pushed a stray hair from her face. "Are you going to make a habit of falling into my arms, Miss Martin? I find it rather pleasant."

Tammy gasped. "I certainly am not!" She sprang to her feet and ran toward the house, flushed to the roots of her hair.

Cameron sat in the snow and stared after her. *Whew! What has come over me? I would much rather feel Tammy in my arms than Lucia. Cameron, get a grip. She has made it plain that she has no interest in you.* He had seen her blushing face, and now watched watched her run. "Or has she?" Cameron turned to the tree. "Snowball, come down."

Rennin heard the sound of children returning from school. "Tomorrow, we go to the site, just the two of us. Pack something delicious for a picnic, and I'll let you fall into my arms."

"As you wish," said Rebekah, and she wiggled her eyebrows.

38
True Love Waits

Half an hour after Pamela left, the house mother knocked on Sarah's door. "You have a gentleman caller in the lobby."

"Is it Chen Li?"

"No. He says his name is Baxter Pryor."

"Really?" said Sarah, huffing a puff of air. "Tell Mr. Pryor I will be down shortly."

Sarah took her time dressing. She put on and took off four dresses before she pulled out the fifth, a seductive jade-green satin that fell from the shoulders in drapes. She smoothed the dress and let her hair fall naturally over her shoulders. Sarah put a touch of rouge on her cheeks and lips.

"What are you doing?" asked Virginia in the first complete sentence she had uttered.

"Putting the son-of-a-bitch in his place." Sarah turned toward her roommate, and her eyes snapped fire. "Do I look the part of a harlot?"

"Yes," answered Virginia with a disapproving sneer.

Sarah reached into her desk drawer and took her letter opener, placing it in her bag.

"Sarah, what are you going to do?" asked Virignia in horror.

"Cut his heart out if I have to. It will be good practice for surgery."

Sarah tied the sash of a matching hat with a long black and green plume, picked up the accentuating silk shawl and sashayed from the room. She entered the lobby where Baxter waited impatiently. When he saw her, his jaw dropped. He could not believe he was looking at his sweet, innocent Sarah.

"Sarah?" he said, eyes looking like full moons.

"Hello, Baxter," she said, smiling broadly and sliding her arm around his. "Let's get out of here and go somewhere private."

Baxter followed her lead without hesitation. "Where are we going?" he asked, still in awe of the sight he beheld.

"Somewhere quiet and special," she answered mysteriously.

They walked for quite a while until they came to a cemetery. "Who died?" asked Baxter.

Sarah bit her tongue to keep from answering, "You." Rather, she laughed. "Please, tell me you aren't afraid."

"No, it's just a strange place to visit at twilight."

"Baxter, it's quiet here, and we can be all alone." She led the way to a crypt with the name "Newman" inscribed in the stone. She felt for the key in a small cubbyhole.

Baxter took a step backward. "Isn't this desecrating a tomb?"

"No, Baxter, it's empty. No one has been buried here yet. A friend of mine recently purchased it. She knows her father will pass soon."

They heard a sound and saw a shadowy figure near a fresh grave. Both assumed it was the caretaker.

Sarah pulled Baxter inside and closed the door. She lit a lantern mounted on the wall beside the door. "It's not too spooky, is it?" she asked coyly. "Do you need me to protect you? Will you feel better if I slip my arms around you?" As she asked the question, she slid her arms around Baxter's neck and pulled his face to hers. She kissed him breathlessly.

Baxter pulled her to him and returned the passion he felt flowing from her eagerly. Then, he pushed her away and held her at arms' length. He panted, "Sarah, where is this coming from?"

"My heart," she whispered. "I want you, Baxter. Take me. Make me yours."

Baxter's heart pounded at the thought of making love to Sarah. "Sarah," he breathed in her ear. He kissed her neck. He ran his hands over her bare arms and his fingertips across the tops of her breasts.

Sarah slipped his waistcoat and shirt off his arms. Baxter found it hard to breathe. He took Sarah to the ground and unbuttoned the top of her dress and slid it off her shoulders.

At the sight of her perfectly formed breasts Baxter jumped to his feet. "No!" he shouted. "I will not do this to you. I will not do this. You're far too important for this."

Sarah found her voice. "Why, Baxter? Don't you want me?" she screamed viciously.

"More than anything," he replied honestly.

"Like you wanted all your other conquests?"

"What? What are you talking about?" He shook his head sharply.

"Oh, please, Baxter"—Her chest heaved with anger—"Don't deny that there have been others!"

"None like you."

She picked up a loose pebble and threw it at him. "I hate you!" Sarah stood with her bodice still unbuttoned. "Court me just to bed me, will you? I hate you, Baxter Pryor!"

"Sarah, what are you talking about? I have no intention of bedding you. Not until..."

"Until you 'conquer' me?"

"What has my mother said to you?" He spread his arms out to his sides, his palms facing her. "Don't believe anything she says. It's a lie."

"It wasn't your mother. It was Pamela. She overheard your conversation with your mother. Don't lie to me. Don't tell me you never considered taking me to bed."

"All right. Yes. I thought if I could get you to make love to me, I could make you forget Chen Li, but it was only a fleeting thought."

"Chen Li? I threw him away for you."

"What? He came to Boston with you."

"To meet you!" Her voice shrilled in the gloom. "I thought you...I loved you." Sarah fought back tears. "I gave Chen Li his freedom. He's married to someone else now." She pulled her letter opener from her bag. "I seriously considered cutting out your heart tonight, but that would be impossible. You can't take out something that doesn't exist."

Sarah pushed past Baxter and ran from the tomb, buttoning her top as she ran and throwing Baxter's shirt and vest into the dark. In the gathering dusk, she stumbled and fell; her letter opener clattered on a headstone, but she did not stop. Hot tears stung her cheeks.

Baxter ran after her. "Sarah, wait! I don't know what Pamela told you, but it was lies. I love you! Sarah!"

Baxter fumbled in the dark to find the shirt Sarah had tossed to the side. "Can I help you, mister?" asked a disdainful voice.

"She threw my shirt out here. Shine your lantern about. I have to go after her." Baxter found his shirt and buttoned it as he ran after Sarah, leaving the upper coat for any beggar who needed one.

The shadowy figure bent down and picked up the lost letter opener. He looked at the name inscribed on it and laughed wickedly. "Sarah Goodman. Miss Goody-two-shoes. Just wait until you get home to Puma Pass. I'll be waiting. I'll let you play the role of harlot for me." Then, he picked up Baxter's dropped wasitcoat, with the wallet still in the inner pocket.

Baxter arrived at the boarding house and met the broad, stern woman, who worked as the house mother. "Where do you think you're going?" she said with authority.

"I have to talk to Sarah!"

"Over my dead body."

"Please?" Baxter pled.

"When one of my girls comes back in tears and tattered clothes, the blackguard, who had his way with her, does *not* get past me."

"What? No. That's not what happened. Let me by."

The hefty woman pushed Baxter out the door and locked it behind him. He stood in the courtyard; not knowing which room was Sarah's, he screamed as loudly as he could, breaking all rules of decorum. "Sarah! Sarah! I love you, Sarah!"

In her room, Sarah threw her things in her trunk willy-nilly.

"Why are you packing?" asked Virginia.

"I'm going home," she replied, decidedly.

"What about the movement? Nursing training?"

"I'll start one in California and my father can teach me."

"What about the man, who's screaming your name in the courtyard?"

"He can drop dead for all I care."

"Sarah, you're making a mistake. That is the desperate cry of a man in love."

"True love waits, Virginia. You heard what Pamela said."

"Will you believe her, a woman who probably wants him for herself, or will you give him the benefit of a doubt? Hasn't he shown you that he loves you in any way? Do you truly love him?"

Sarah fell onto her bed and cried. "Yes, I love him."

"Did he take you tonight?"

"No. He said that he wouldn't do it. I was too important. He said not until something. I didn't let him finish."

"'True love waits.' That's what you said."

The girls realized that Baxter's cries had stopped. "Sarah," said Virginia, "what are you going to do? Are you going to let him slip away?"

Sarah opened the window and looked into the courtyard. Baxter was nowhere in sight. She did not see the policemen drag him into the paddy wagon and take him to jail.

"He's gone. He didn't wait very long. I'm going home, Virginia. I have to."

The next morning, Sarah took the first train to St. Louis where she would meet the stagecoach to go home.

About mid-morning, the police let Baxter out of jail, assuming that he had been drunk and slept off the effects. Baxter went directly to the boardinghouse where the same woman informed him, "Miss Goodman left this morning. She said she was going home."

Baxter hailed a taxi and realized his wallet was missing. He walked until he found the home of Allison Newman and a sympathetic ear. He poured out his story. "I can't go after her because I have no money. My wallet is missing. I will *not* go back to Boston. What do I do?"

"Baxter," said Allison, "you have someone who believes you. Go upstairs and bathe." She signaled the upstairs maid to prepare a bath for her guest. "I'll send my driver to your hotel for your things. Then, we'll make a plan for you to win Sarah's heart. Trust me."

While Baxter bathed, Allison sent for his things and Chen Li. After Baxter changed clothes, he found both Allison and Chen Li waiting in the parlor. At the sight of the Chinaman, Baxter almost turned tail and ran.

Chen Li put him at ease quickly. "She's stubborn, strong-willed, and hot-tempered. She's also innocent, naïve, and trusting. More importantly, you love her. Let's talk."

Sarah passively watched the trees move past her eyes. Suddenly, she was startled from her thoughts by a familiar voice. "Sarah? Sarah Goodman?"

Sarah glanced up. "Dennis? What are you doing here?"

"Our great-aunt died. Mitchell couldn't come back, so I came to take care of her will. Mitchell also thought it would be good for me to go back East for a while. May I say that you are looking lovely?"

"Why are you being nice?"

Dennis flashed a winsome smile. "Sarah, you aren't the only one who can grow up in a year. I'm sorry about the snake in your lunch pail. It was a foolish prank of a boy trying to get your attention."

"It wouldn't have been so bad if it hadn't been a *rattlesnake*. The thing could have bitten me."

"On that day *after* you hit me I wished it had. Now, I'm glad it didn't. May I join you?"

"Please."

The two old enemies chatted pleasantly until Sarah said she was tired. "Are you sleeping here, or do you have a berth?" asked Dennis.

"I have a berth."

"Then, I'll say 'good night.' Will you join me for breakfast?"

"Seven?"
"I'll see you then."

Sarah found it hard to sleep with the clickety-clack of the wheels and the constant jostling. Finally, she sat up and lit her lantern. *Maybe I should have gone by boat, all the way around the tip of South America,* she thought to herself. Rather than dwell on her discomfort, she unpacked her copy of *Memoirs of Magic* that Rebekah had given her and opened to the place she had stopped.

Ranson's homecoming was celebrated by the entire community, but Angela's enthusiasm outweighed all others. While every one greeted Ranson, Angela refused to let go of him. After much ado, the well-wishers went home, and even Ryan, tired, fell asleep.

Alone at last, Ranson pulled Angela into his arms and kissed her the way he had been dying to do all day. "Mr. Riley, that is a very suggestive kiss," said Angela when she caught her breath.

"Marry me, Angela. Tomorrow, let's ride out to the missionary's home. I don't want to wait another day to be with you."

"True love waits, Ranson."

"Angela, I have waited months longer than I agreed. How much longer do you want me to wait?"

"No longer, but we don't have to ride anywhere. While you were away, Donovan received his license as a justice of the peace. He can arrest wrongdoers or marry lovers. He will marry us tonight if we ask."

"I'm sorely tempted, but I suppose we should have our friends and family present. Besides, Cameron promised to be my best man. I'll have to send a courier to him to come immediately. It's winter. Travel will be difficult."

"Do you want to wait until spring?"

"No. True love might wait, but true lust might get the best of me."

"Send your courier. I'll have everything ready to become your wife as soon as Cameron arrives. I'd like Ian to be here, too."

Cameron packed to leave the day he received the communication. He packed Tammy, Rowan, and Snowball to go, too. Ian and Lucretia showed up to travel with them. Lucretia was excited to meet her in-laws. The unexpected guest was Lucia. She came with Ian and Lucretia, prepared to travel.

Cameron explained why he had not asked her. "I didn't think you would want to travel in the winter. Traveling will be harsh and difficult."

"Cameron, I want to meet *all* your family, not just your father. Is that asking too much?"

"No, dearest. I was only considering your well-being and comfort."

"Then, I'm going. I'm tougher than you think."

"I'm sure you are." *Doubtful.* He swallowed back unexplained bile.

Cameron and Ian left their business in the hands of a trusted employee, and the strange ensemble headed for Mom's Trading Post.

Lucia grumbled and complained about the cold and the travel conditions. She griped about the accommodations and the food. Finally, with every nerve frayed, Cameron spoke angrily to her. "Lucia, shut up. You asked to come. I warned you how it would be. Deal with it, and spare us the whining."

Ian bit his lip; Lucretia snickered; and Rowan squeezed Tammy's hand and grinned. Haughtily, Lucia said, "Cameron, is this the kind of treatment I can expect when we marry?"

"If the need arises," Cameron retorted stubbornly.

Lucia gasped and blinked back tears. "Don't cry," commanded Cameron. "The tears will freeze on your cheeks."

Lucretia laughed out loud. "Get tougher, sister. We have several weeks left to travel."

Cameron spoke to Lucretia as they traveled. "Lucretia, I apologize. I misjudged you. You're a strong woman."

"No, you didn't Cameron. I can be very demanding, and I was hard on Tammy. I'm glad to see she has found suitable employment. Rowan seems to adore her. I hope that if you marry my sister, she'll be able to garner the same affection. I have my doubts. She's not very good with children. Maybe she will learn a little with her niece or nephew."

"Are you?"

Lucretia nodded and smiled joyfully.

"Congratulations. Uncle Geoffrey will be thrilled."

The entourage arrived amidst fresh falling flakes of snow. They were greeted with hot cider, blankets, and food. The only thing Cameron took time to do before he headed to Ranson's cabin was to introduce everyone. Ian followed his example and took Lucretia to his father's home.

Cameron knocked loudly, and Ryan opened the door. "Cameron!"

Angela squealed and ran to the door to pull Cameron inside. "You're finally here!"

"I thought I'd let you know to make final preparations."

"Oh, I will." Angela grabbed her coat and started out the door. She turned back and pointed at Ranson. "Tomorrow, Mr. Riley, you are no longer free." She danced into the snow.

Cameron laughed. "And so the hammer falls."

Ranson grinned. "My heart has not been free for quite some time, Cam. Did you bring your luscious Lucia?" He hung Cameron's coat on a hook and offered him mulled cider and a seat near the fire.

"Yes, she came," Cameron answered indifferently, hovering over the flame to warm a chill all the way to his bones.

"Want to talk about it?" asked Ranson taking a seat in one rocking chair.

"Sometimes she really annoys me. She can be ill-tempered, demanding, rude, and extremely hard to please." Cameron plopped into the chair next to Ranson. "She complained all the way here."

"Cameron, do you love this woman?"

"Honestly, Ranson, sometimes I don't even like her."

"My friend, break it off now, before you both get hurt."

"Ranson, I've told her that I'm not ready for a commitment."

"Well, if you insist. Just take it slowly. True love waits. If she's meant to be your mate, she'll wait. *And* watch her with Rowan. How she treats your son is more important than any feeling you have for her."

Clutching both sides of his head and entangling his hands in his long strawberry blond hair, Cameron mumbled, "There's more."

"What?"

"Tammy."

"Tammy?"

"Rowan's governess. I really like her." He let his hands fall into his lap and heaved a distressed sigh. "She's beautiful and sweet and loving and innocent. And she loves Rowan. *But.* But she's made it clear any relationship with me beyond employer is inappropriate."

"What a dilemma! As I said, true love waits. Be patient. True love will show its face."

Cameron went home and heard Lucia's comment to Morgan as he entered the door. "Mrs. O'Rourke, there are so many Indians here. Do you feel safe?"

Cameron said sarcastically, "One of them might scalp you in your sleep. I hear they're unusually fond of pretty blonde hair. You had better watch out, especially for the youngest one."

"What?" said Lucia, her eyes wide with fear.

"That's right," said Rowan. "Poppy gave me a very sharp peasant knife for Christmas."

"What do you mean?" Lucia trilled in fear.

"Lucia," said Cameron more gently, but still irritated. "Where do you think Rowan got his coloring? Holly was Iroquois. Oliver and Anna are her brother and sister. This is *my* family."

"I-I didn't realize your wife had been Indian. They must be good Christian converts if you married one of them."

"Yes, they are. At least, the ones who live here in Mom's Trading Post are. Those around us are not, but they are not savages either."

"I'm sure we're quite safe," said Tammy.

"Why?" asked Lucia in a condescending tone.

Tammy replied humbly, "Because Cameron's family is greatly respected around here."

Cameron's heart fluttered at Tammy's use of his first name. Lucia jumped on the familiarity as well.

"Since when do you use Cameron's given name?"

Tammy showed a spark of life. "Since there are five men in this room who could be Mr. O'Rourke." Tammy turned to Rowan. "Rowan, are you as tired as I am?"

"I'm very tired."

"Let's take a short nap before supper."

After supper, Cameron found Lucia on the porch. "Aren't you afraid to be out here?" he said teasingly.

"Cameron, you were very mean to me today."

"Lucia, we were teasing you. Here, we aren't bound by societal restraints. You need to learn to relax." He hugged her. "You're very safe here with me. I'm sorry I hurt your feelings."

"If you hug me like this when we argue, you're forgiven."

Angela and Ranson's wedding took place in the dining room of the inn, which had been decorated to the hilt. Donovan performed his first wedding ceremony, and Lucia was once again taken aback by the unconventional vows, which Ranson and Angela had written specifically for each other.

Ranson held Angela's face in his hands. "Angela, my angel, you have taught me that hope is eternal. From this day forward I promise to give you hope even in our darkest times, though I pray they will be few. The Apostle Paul tells us that when all passes away, three things will remain: faith, hope, and charity, which is also called love. Today, I pledge to be faithful to you. I promise to give you hope, and I will love you with an undying love."

Angela responded with her own heartfelt words. "'*They that wait on the Lord shall mount up on the wings of an eagle. They shall run and not be weary; they shall walk and not faint.*' Ranson Riley, you have taught me that true love waits, but the wait is over. Now, I'm soaring. Because you have given my spirit wings, I promise to always lift you up far above myself. I promise to be patient and to wait with a love that bears all things."

Even Lucia had to admit the celebration, which followed the wedding, lifted her spirit and she had fun. Angela and Ranson disappeared as the festivities continued. Ranson lifted Angela into his arms. Stepping over the threshold of his cabin, he thought he must have gone to the wrong house. Angela laughed softly. "Momma, Aunt Eula, and Aunt Morgan have been busy." Throughout the house rose oil burned in small stone pots over candles, filling the room with an intoxicating perfume. Geoffrey had once again ordered a bottle of French wine and placed it beside the bed.

Ranson set Angela on the bed and opened the libation. He lifted his glass, "To true love and ending the wait."

Angela took a sip from her glass and then took both glasses and put them on the bedside table. "Ranson, I don't need liquor to relax me. I've waited far too long to become your wife." She lay back and held her hand out to him. He took it and melted into his angel's embrace.

Sarah closed the book and her eyes. Silent tears dripped onto the cover. *Lord, how long do I have to wait for true love? It wasn't Chen Li or Baxter.* She laughed bitterly. *Please don't tell me it could be Dennis. I don't believe he has changed that much. Oh, Baxter, was I wrong? If you follow me, I'll know.*

She finally fell asleep from fatigue. Baxter filled her dreams and heart.

39
I Will Fight for Your Honor

Chen Li escorted Baxter to the next train bound westward. "When you get to the end line, the stage will take you to Puma Pass. Remember that Patty won't hurt you. Deliver these letters." He handed the sandy-haired man a bundle held together with twine. "The one to Sarah vouches for you. Don't disappoint me. Baxter, make her listen. Bind and gag her if you must. Enlist Rennin and Rebekah's help. Rebekah is the most charismatic person I know. She has a way with people. She's magical." Chen Li gave Baxter another envelope. "This is some money for your journey. Don't be obstinate. I can afford it. Keep it on your person."

Baxter and Chen Li shook hands. "I wish I had not been a jealous fool when you came to Boston, Chen. All this could have been avoided. I count it a privilege to know you. I do love Sarah more than anything in this world. I *will* make her believe me."

"Godspeed and good luck, my new friend. I'll pray for you."

"I covet your prayers. Sarah has shown me that God is real."

The conductor called, "All aboard!"

The train pulled out, and Baxter waved from the window. "I'll see you in two years."

"Tell my wife I love her!"

With a tip of his hand from his head Baxter shouted over the engines and the tumult, "Consider it done."

In the hilly region of Ohio, Baxter was shaken from an uncertain slumber as he was thrown from his seat. In a daze he heard the panicked screams of pain and terror. He felt warm sticky ooze in his hair. It dawned slowly on him the train had derailed.

When Baxter came to his senses, he worked diligently to pull the wounded and dead from the wreckage. He held onto a gray-haired man that bled heavily. "Hang on, sir. The conductor is asking if there's a doctor on board."

"Too late," groaned the old man. "You remind me of someone I once knew."

"Who would that be?" Baxter figured he could at least keep the man talking, not leave him to die alone.

"Myself. What's your name, young man?"

"Baxter Pryor."

"It can't be." The man cough, and blood trickled from his mouth. "Beatrice raised you well."

"Sir?" Baxter knitted his eyebrows. "You know my mother? Who are you?"

"Melvin Pryor."

"What?"

"You were better off without me. Liquor."

"You can't be"—He shook his head—"You're dead."

"I will be soon. Forgive me. Forgive Beatrice." He coughed again and heaved a last breath.

Baxter sat back with the man's head on his legs. "She said you were dead. Why now?" He looked skyward. "God, I can't do this."

A voice echoed on the wind, "Yes, you can. You must," and a short vision of a white dragon drifted across his mind's eye. "You will ultimately affect the fate of Draconis."

He clutched the side of his head as the conductor approached him. "We've dispatched riders. Horses in the back cars." He looked down. "Is he..?"

"Dead," Baxter murmured. "Melvin Pryor."

"Are you all right, young man?"

Baxter shook his head, and then nodded. "I will be."

The conductor patted his shoulder and moved on to check on others.

Trying to process the last twenty-four hours, Baxter sat in the same spot until he heard the approach of several horses.

He rose to his feet. Once the work was done and railroad officials arrived, Baxter found his bag and without a word to anyone walked to the nearest farm. On the way to the farm, he took a diamond ring that he had purchased before he left Boston from the bag and placed it in his pocket for safer keeping.

The farmer, who was surprised to see a person from the train wreck, fed Baxter and let him clean up. His wife washed Baxter's grimy clothes and tended his injured head. Refreshed, Baxter was eager to be on his way. "Mr. and Mrs. Richardson, thank you for your hospitality," he said. "I have to get to California as soon as possible. I'm already days behind schedule. For how much will you sell me your horse? It's urgent I delay no longer."

"Mr. Pryor, my horse is only a nag. Ferrell, the next farm over, has several horses. He will most likely sell you one. I'll take you over first thing tomorrow." Mr. Richardson gave him a friendly pat on the shoulder.

Baxter agreed and slept one night in a comfortable bed. Ferrell sold Baxter a roan mare with white just above each hoof and an extra saddle he had. Baxter headed west once again. "Get up, Socks. That's your new name, girl—Socks."

Finally, in St. Louis, Baxter hopped a stage for San Francisco. He told the driver, "I want to bring my horse."

"Tie her to the back, mister. If she can keep up, she can come along. If we get filled up, you can ride her."

Socks tagged along tethered to the rear of the stage, and Baxter relaxed and bantered with several of the passengers. Days passed without event. Two days before the Rocky Mountains, Baxter dozed in the sweltering coach. He awoke to sounds of whooping and gunshots. "What now?" he shouted.

The older couple across from Baxter sat frozen with terror. He suddenly realized that the coach was running wild. He cautiously stuck his head out the window and saw several masked men chasing the coach and the driver slumped over, either dead or hurt too badly to drive. "Damn!" Baxter exclaimed. He took a deep breath. "Sarah, this is for you."

Baxter eased himself through the window and swung himself on top of the coach. As he reached the driver's box, he felt a searing pain in his shoulder. The next thing he knew, he hit the ground.

Baxter awoke to strange smells. As his eyes focused, he saw a man with long, straight, black hair wearing very few buckskin clothes and feathers in his hair. The man held a bowl from which smoke wafted upward. Baxter tried to rise. The man spoke to him in words he could not understand. Baxter sank back onto the animal skins that served as a bed as pain shot through his shoulder again and his head began to spin.

The man came to Baxter's side and spoke. "White man serious wound. Must rest. Bullet out. Much blood."

"How long have I been here?"

"Many sunrises."

"The other passengers? My horse?"

"Two white men, one white woman dead. No horses. You mostly dead. Strong will to live."

"I have to get to Sarah."

"Sarah your woman?"

"I hope so."

"Ah," said the medicine man with understanding.

Baxter tried to rise again. "No," said the Indian. "Must rest. No see wanted woman soon."

The wounded man did not argue for he was far too weak. For several weeks Baxter recovered under the watchful eye of White Owl, the Comanche medicine man. After a long delay, Baxter felt strong enough to travel.

White Owl grunted, "You not armed. You from great city in east. Out here, white man must be armed. Come." The medicine man led Baxter to a hole in the side of a rock covered by mesquite. He revealed a small arsenal. "Ask no question," he commanded. "Take shotgun and pistol and ammunition. Much need."

The next morning Baxter was awakened by a commotion. The natives chattered and laughed at the sight of a bedraggled horse with a saddle. Baxter looked through the teepee entrance. "Socks!" he shouted and ran to the weary creature. Removing the saddle, he saw massive blisters.

White Owl joined him. "Horse in much pain."

Baxter looked the mare over. "White Owl, this is my horse. Can you make her better?"

"Yes. Horse not take so long as man to heal. Two, three sunrises."

"It's a sign, White Owl. I must continue my journey to my wanted wife."

The Comanche touched Baxter's chest. "Heart aches without her. White Owl understand."

Three days later, Socks appeared to be the same energetic mare Baxter had purchased. Using the charred end of a twig, White Owl drew a crude map on a piece of deer hide. "Follow," he said handing the skin to Baxter. "Will take you to wanted wife."

Loaded with food, water, blankets, buckskin clothes, and weapons, Baxter mounted Socks. The only things remotely civilized that he still carried were a pack of letters and a diamond ring that he had somehow managed not to lose. He paused just outside the Comanche encampment, stroked Socks's neck, and held the box with the diamond ring in his hand. He sighed heavily. "Sarah Goodman, if you do not fall into my arms the minute you see me, I will kill myself exactly two minutes after I kill you." He sighed again, unable to comprehend a world without Sarah. He gently spurred Socks forward.

The first week after she arrived home, Sarah stared out the window hoping Baxter had followed her. After a week, she gave up and forlornly began life anew.

She apologized to her father. "Papa, I'm sorry about leaving like I did, but I had to come home. My heart needed my family."

"My dear girl, I'm glad to have you home. If you want to go back, I'll send you back."

"Right now, I want to be home, Papa."

"And so you are." Thomas Goodman held his daughter in his arms. "I'm so sorry you were hurt so badly. If I ever meet Baxter Pryor, he will feel my wrath."

Dennis Stone waited a couple of weeks before he knocked on the Goodman family's door with a bunch of wild flowers. "I'm calling for Sarah," he announced.

Sarah laughed when she saw Dennis. "You've changed."

"Sarah, will you step out with me? I refuse to let someone so full of life become a hermit. What do you say?"

She was speechless. "Come on, Sarah. I promise I have no snakes," Dennis coaxed.

"Okay, let's go," Sarah agreed.

He came every day from then on. Sometimes they stayed in and played parlor games. Other times, they went out horseback riding, picnicking, or simply strolling.

Rebekah commented at tea with Sarah, "I cannot believe the two of you are courting as much as you hated him."

"We aren't courting, Aunt Rebekah. Dennis is only a friend," Sarah said frankly.

Rebekah eyed Sarah carefully. "Perhaps you should make sure *Dennis* understands that."

Mitchell Stone, who was now officially engaged to Monica Fulton, and Thomas and Candace Goodman went to St. Louis on business for the hospital. After they had been gone a couple of weeks, Dennis came late one afternoon to ask Sarah out. "Sarah, take a ride with me. Wear something you would have worn in the city—maybe something green and shiny to bring out your eyes."

Sarah shivered at the memory of the last time she had worn green. She came out in a day dress of soft ivory linen trimmed in lace. Dennis cocked his head to the side and gave a crooked grin. "White? If you insist. You look beautiful."

Sarah blushed. As Dennis helped her into the buggy she asked, "Why did you say that about my white dress?"

"You might soil it in this old rig."

"I'm sure I'll be fine," she replied.

"I'm sure, too," Dennis said mysteriously.

He drove far past the settlement. "Dennis, aren't you going a bit far?" asked Sarah as the sun sank in the sky and apprehension rose in her mind when the temperature dropped drastically.

"I want to be completely alone with you."

She looked sideways at her escort. "Dennis, I think we should talk."

Pulling the buggy to a halt near a huge stand of redwoods, he helped Sarah down. Immediately, he pulled her to him. "Talking is not what I have in mind."

"Dennis, let go."

"Come, now, Sarah. Do you really expect me to believe your virtue is intact? Let's see if I can refresh your memory." In an mocking feminine voice, he said, "'I hate you, Baxter Pryor!'" Then he ran his hand across Sarah's breasts. "I was so hoping for green satin. It looked so well on you and even better off."

Sarah pushed back and caught her breath. "You were the one in the cemetery. I thought that visage looked vaguely familiar in the dusk."

Dennis pulled Sarah's face to his and kissed her roughly. She screamed and tried to push him away again. In a threatening tone Dennis said, "Don't scream. No one can hear you out here. Your brave knight will not come charging in on his gallant steed. Don't fight either. I don't want to hurt you. Think for a moment. How would 'Papa' feel if he knew about his little girl's rendezvous in the crypt?"

"He knows!"

"All of it? I doubt it. Don't worry. Your secret is safe with me so long as you share some of that affection with me. I just hate I'm not the one privileged to deflower you."

"Get your hands off me!" Sarah shouted furiously. She slapped Dennis across the face.

He growled, "We can do this the hard way if you want to." He grabbed her left wrist and twisted it behind her back and backhanded her across the face with his other hand.

Sarah wrenched her hand free and started to run. Dennis caught her shoulder and ripped her dress. Sarah lost her balance and fell. Dennis yanked her over and was on top of her in a flash. She felt the man's hand tearing at her under garments. In panic, her hand fell onto a large stone. Without a second thought, Sarah bashed Dennis against the head. He rolled off her with a groan. She hit him once more with all her might for good measure, and then climbed into the rig and headed for home, leaving Dennis lying in his own blood.

At the same time Dennis and Sarah drove out of Puma Pass toward the mountains, a lonely, weary rider came in from the other direction after having followed the Pacific Ocean shoreline for a great distance. He stopped a group of children. "Can you help me? I'm looking for Rennin O'Rourke."

"That's my father," bragged Michael. "We live right over there," he said, pointing.

"What about Sarah Goodman?"

"She lives in the big blue house across the bridge, but I think she's gone somewhere with Dennis." Without further conversation, Michael ran off to play.

"Dennis?" said the sandy-haired, unshaven traveler through clenched teeth. "Who the hell is Dennis?"

Undaunted even after his harrowing experiences and shocking revelations, the rider continued to Rennin's house. Rennin opened the door when the man knocked. "Yes?"

"Mr. O'Rourke, I'm Baxter Pryor. I've come after Sarah. Chen Li told me to come to you first."

Rennin surveyed the obviously exhausted man before him. "It took you long enough to get here."

"You would *not* believe what I've gone through to get here."

"Please, enlighten me." Rennin showed Baxter in and Rebekah served him something to eat and drink.

Baxter handed Rennin an envelope. "I have this for you from Chen Li." Rennin took the crumpled letter, and Baxter poured out his entire story from the moment he met Sarah. He finished by pulling a diamond ring from a pouch at his side. "I swear if that woman rejects me..." He shook his head, unable to put his thoughts into words.

Rebekah sat on the arm of Rennin's chair and put her arms around her husband's neck. "Rennin, it's as romantic as our beginning."

Baxter heaved a sigh of relief. At that very moment Sarah burst through the door in hysterics. "Uncle Rennin!"

Both Rennin and Baxter sprang to their feet. Sarah stood before them disheveled, her dress ripped from her shoulder, her hair partially undone, her face bruised, her lip bloody.

"Uncle Rennin," Sarah said again through a sob. Her eyes traveled to the other man. "Baxter?"

"Sarah!"

She ran to Baxter and fell into his arms and sobbed uncontrollably. Finally, she gasped, "I think I killed him."

"Who? Dennis?" asked Rennin.

"He...he."

"Did he rape you?" Baxter asked candidly.

Sarah shook her head. "He tried. I hit him with a big rock. I hit him again after I got him off me. I think I killed him."

"Where is he, Sarah?" asked Rennin.

She told them where she had left Dennis. Rennin started out the door. He took his gun from the hook by the entrance.

"I'm going with you," said Baxter.

"Baxter!" cried Sarah.

Baxter held Sarah at arms' length. "I'll be back. If he's not dead, I'll kill him. I will fight for your honor, Sarah. I love you."

"You don't know everything. He was in the cemetery. He thought we…"

"It doesn't matter. If we had, it would have been our business, not his. And he certainly had no right to touch you. I love you, lady. I will take care of you. Stay with Rebekah. I'll be back. I have a lifetime to spend with you."

When Rennin and Baxter rode away, Rebekah helped Sarah bathe and put her into a clean nightgown. She put Sarah in the guest bedroom. Rebekah stroked Sarah's hair. Silent tears dripped down the girl's cheeks. "I was so scared, Aunt Rebekah."

"I know," whispered Rebekah.

"How?" asked Sarah.

"When I was your age, I was raped. I'm so glad you were spared that horror. I'm proud of you. If the bastard's dead, he got what he deserved. If he's not, either your uncle or Baxter might kill him."

"What took Baxter so long to get here?"

"It's a long story, but he has gone through hell getting to you. He has been following you since you left New York. The man loves you, Sarah."

"I love him, too, Aunt Rebekah."

"Tell him. He needs to hear that you love him."

Rennin and Baxter found Dennis struggling to get to his feet. The two men dismounted.

"Need some help getting up?" yelled Baxter as he jerked Dennis to his feet.

"You!" said Dennis.

"Yes." Baxter smirked as he punched Dennis. "Oops. You fell down again. How dare you?" He pulled Dennis to his feet and punched him again. Deliberately and with each word punctuated by a blow Baxter said, "I! Am! Going! To! Kill! You!" Dennis fell to the ground again. He spat blood and a tooth.

"Rennin, help," whined Dennis.

"Why?" asked Rennin. "You tried to rape my niece."

Still defiant, Dennis said, "It's not as if she's an innocent little girl. This man already took her."

Baxter uttered a guttural growl as he threw Dennis against a tree. "You fool! You've no idea what you're talking about. Sarah *is* an innocent girl."

"Ha! I saw you!"

"You saw what you wanted to see. You've no idea what really occurred. Rennin, what will happen to me if I kill him? I think I can argue a case for justifiable homicide."

"I don't know. Let's see. Did you even touch him? I found the body. I assume he was thrown from his rig. The horses trampled him. You've been at my house all night wooing Sarah. Nobody will question my word, and nobody will miss Dennis, unless Mitchell misses him a little. Of course, Mitchell will probably be relieved to be rid of the burden. How does my story sound to you, Baxter?"

"Wonderful."

"Rennin, please?" begged Dennis.

"Most people have leave to call me 'Rennin.' You, however, will call me 'Mr. O'Rourke.' Baxter beat the hell out of him, and I'll send for Roger to lug him off to jail. Dennis, do you know what big hairy criminals do to little pansies who molest little girls?"

Baxter grinned. "It looks as if Sarah did a good job on him already."

"Second time," Rennin said.

Baxter snorted. "I'll gladly finish it."

Having been a pugilist in college, Baxter made sure Dennis begged for mercy before he stopped hitting him. Then, Rennin took the rope from his saddle and tied Dennis's hands. He looped the other end of the rope to the horn of his saddle."

"You're going to make me walk?" Dennis complained.

"Shut up, or I'll drag you."

Rennin locked Dennis in the smokehouse and wrote a note to go to Roger on the next day's stage. Baxter bathed, shaved, and changed into clothes purchased at the general store, at Rennin's insistence. Then, he went into the guest room where Sarah still lay like a little girl in Rebekah's arms.

"Mind if I come in?"

"I think that would be a good idea," said Rebekah. She handed Sarah a book they had been reading and kissed her on the forehead. "Remember what I said. I love you, sweetie."

Sarah held her arms out toward Baxter like a little child who was reaching for a beloved toy. Baxter sat on the bed beside her and put his arms around her. She laid her head on his chest. "I looked out the window when you were calling my name, and you were gone. Where did you go?" she asked.

"The police dragged me off to jail. They thought I was drunk."

"I'm sorry I wouldn't listen. I love you, Baxter."

"Still? After all these months?"

"Yes. What took you so long to come?"

Baxter laughed. "Settle back for a long story." Baxter told Sarah about his exciting trek to California. "Now, Miss Sarah Goodman, I'm here. I'm not going back to Boston. I figure Puma Pass has grown enough to need an attorney. I'll set up a law practice here. That is, if you'll marry me. I love you, Sarah. I want to spend my life with you. Will you marry me?"

"Yes. Oh, yes."

Baxter kissed Sarah gently. Then, he slipped the diamond that had miraculously stayed in his possession onto her finger. He looked down at the book on Sarah's lap. "Is this the same book you had in Boston?"

"Yes."

"Would you like me to read to you?"

"That would be nice. Uncle Rennin reads to Aunt Rebekah. I think it's extremely romantic."

Baxter chuckled. "Let the romance begin." He opened Sarah's book to where the ribbon lay.

Cameron prepared to go back to Boston. He disappeared the day before he was to leave, much to Lucia's irritation. Morgan went in search of her son and found him at Holly's grave. "I thought I'd find you here."

"Momma, how I miss her! Tell me what to do, Momma."

Morgan caressed Cameron's head as she had when he was a child. "Follow your heart, baby. The logical choice is not always the right one."

"You don't like her, do you, Momma?"

"Lucia or Tammy?"

"Momma, you know."

Morgan was very quiet for a time before she declared, "She's a bitch. That's all I'm going to say." *Maybe worse— demonic.* She shivered.

"Well, Momma, you've never lied to me." Cameron laughed. "Now, are you going to tell me what you think of the other one?"

"She's a scared little girl who needs someone to watch over her. I suppose the question is: Do you want strong and cold or weak and needy? One will grow. The other won't. Maybe it's neither. Time will tell."

As Cameron gave his mother his hand to help her up, they heard a noise in the thicket. Cynthia stumbled from among the brambles, her clothes ripped from her body, face bloodied and battered. Cameron scooped her into his arms. "Momma, run ahead. Get Uncle Geoffrey and Duncan."

Duncan met Cameron in the road. He took Cynthia from his brother. "What happened?" he asked gently.

Cynthia buried her face in Duncan's neck and whispered, "Hopam."

Reaching the Montague home, Duncan laid Cynthia in her own bed. Anna washed her wounds while Duncan held her hand. "I need to take off her clothes, Duncan," said Anna.

Cynthia turned her face from Duncan. "I'm sorry, Duncan. If you don't want me now, I understand."

Duncan took several sharp breaths and kissed Cynthia's hand. "I'll be back. I love you."

Anna and Cynthia heard the front door slam. Duncan strode to the barn and saddled his horse. Rennin caught up to him. "Where are you going?"

Duncan glared at his father. "Answer me, Duncan," demanded Rennin.

"To defend Cynthia's honor. Are you with me?" Cameron and Donovan, along with Ranson, Oliver, and Ian came to Rennin's side. "Are you *with* me?" Duncan repeated for all of them.

Within minutes, the seven men rode out of Mom's Trading Post. Knowing that both Duncan and Cameron had inherited their grandfather's temper, Morgan panicked. She saddled a horse to follow. Looking from her window, Cynthia observed the situation. She turned to her mother. "Momma Morgan is going after the men. I must go with her. Duncan is so angry he might do something impulsive."

Anna nodded her understanding. Cynthia sprinted to the barn and touched Morgan's arm, and without words, the two women knew each other's thoughts.

Taking all this in from the doorway of Morgan's house, Lucia refused to be outdone. She went to the barn. "I want to go, too."

"That is *not* a good idea, Lucia. This could turn out to be *very* uncivilized. They will not be dueling with pistols or swords," Morgan informed her.

"Is Cameron in danger?"

"Probably not, but the same is not true for Duncan. However, if something happens to Duncan, I can't assure you Cameron won't be his brother's second and do something on Duncan's behalf."

"Mrs. O'Rourke, I would like to go."

Morgan shrugged. "Suit yourself. Saddle up."

"I don't know how."

"I do," said Tammy quietly from the barn door. "I want to go, too. In case something should happen to Cameron, I need to know what to do about Rowan."

Lucia glowered at the woman she was beginning to perceive as her rival. Morgan looked from one to other. *At some point these two might be dueling over Cameron.* She said calmly, "Tammy, can you saddle two horses quickly?"

"Yes, ma'am."

"Please, do then. Lucia, you'll have to ride, and not sidesaddle. That would only slow us down."

The women left with Morgan praying, Cynthia worrying, Tammy feeling triumphant, and Lucia concocting a plot to get rid of Tammy.

The women arrived at the Indian village to hear a shouting match between the chief and Duncan. The chief said something that sounded ominous to the ladies from the east and went into his dwelling. He returned a moment later and announced, "Hopam challenge white man to fight for woman. Say he not know why white man want woman that already belong him."

"She does *not* belong to him," fumed Duncan. "He took her against her will and knowing she is *my* promised wife." He hit himself in the chest with his fist. "She is mine. I will fight him."

"Duncan," Talulah said in warning. "Is fight to the death. If you die, what happen to Cynthia then?"

"I won't die."

From out of the blue, Cameron spoke up. "I will marry her. As Duncan's brother I have that right. She will *not* marry Hopam under any circumstances. He's a criminal and should be punished."

Both Lucia and Tammy gasped. Morgan turned around and bluntly stated, "I told you Cameron might do something crazy."

The chief looked at both white challengers and nodded his assent.

Duncan took off his coat and handed it to his brother. "Thank you, Cameron. If something *does* happen to me, you'll learn to love Cynthia. She's much like Holly."

Cameron nodded and placed a hand on Duncan's shoulder. Cynthia suddenly flew to Duncan's side. "Please don't do this. I'm not worth this. Please."

Duncan caressed Cynthia's cheek. "You're worth far more. If I die, go with Cameron. He'll be good to you."

Tears streamed down Cynthia's cheeks. "But I love *you*, Duncan."

"And I love you. That's why I've provided for you, just in case."

The already frosty air turned colder when Duncan heard Hopam snort behind him. He turned around and saw the Indian armed with a large deer-skinning knife. Duncan nodded. He unsheathed his own knife from the scabbard on his waist.

The two men squared off, encircled by the crowd. "This is barbaric," whispered Lucia.

Morgan turned to her. "Any more so than two men meeting at dawn to shoot each other or dying at the tip a sword? And usually for no good reason other than one was *insulted*?"

The two men circled each other for several seconds before Hopam charged at Duncan. Duncan side stepped Hopam's first thrust and knocked him to the ground. Hopam agilely sprang back to his feet. Duncan gestured with his fingers for Hopam to come to him. "Come on. Try it again. I dare you."

More insulted by Duncan's taunting, Hopam lunged, stopped, and lunged again. His knife found flesh, but only the outside of Duncan's arm. Duncan winced, but was undaunted. He rubbed his wounded arm with his other hand and gestured again for Hopam with his blood-covered fingers.

Enraged at Duncan's arrogance, Hopam charged again in a blind rage. Duncan struck the Indian's face with his forearm, bringing blood from Hopam's nose.

The future Indian chief wiped his face and licked the blood from his fingers. He lunged again and deliberately rolled past Duncan. As he came up, Hopam threw ash into Duncan's eyes. Duncan blinked fiercely, trying to clear his vision. As Hopam thought he had the better of his adversary, he lunged, his hand raised high. Cynthia screamed, "Duncan, step left!"

Duncan listened to Cynthia's voice and stepped to his left. Once again, Hopam sprawled on the ground. This time, his knife was jarred loose and slid toward the feet of the crowd. Jumping to his feet, he turned, and in a bent-over run, caught Duncan in the midsection with his shoulder. Both men hit the ground hard. Duncan lost his knife as well.

Without weapons, the men punched and jabbed each other. Duncan's strength and size proved to be greater than his opponent's. After several minutes of vicious brawling, Duncan sat astraddle Hopam with his hands pressed in a vise-like grip around the Indian's throat. Hopam's face turned blue. Duncan released his hold. "No. I will *not* kill you. I want you to live with the fact you lost; but if you ever go near Cynthia again, I <u>will</u> *kill* you. A man like you will not make a good chief for these people. They know that now. You are disgraced."

Duncan stood and found his knife. As he was about to sheath it, he heard the chief shout, "No!"

The temperature plummeted.

Even as he heard the voice, he felt Hopam's blade in his back. As an act of sheer will, Duncan pulled himself free of the blade still held tightly in the Indian's grasp and spun around. As if with one motion, Duncan's knife moved across Hopam's throat. The Indian grabbed his throat, looked glassy-eyed at Duncan, and fell dead. Duncan, too, collapsed in a fit of coughing. He spat blood from his mouth.

Cynthia screamed, and ran to his side. Duncan looked at her with big, sad, brown eyes. "I'm sorry. I let you down." He looked for Cameron. "Cam?"

Cameron put a protective arm around Cynthia. "I have her, Duncan." Cameron motioned for his mother, who took Cynthia.

The chief gave Talulah a command in his native tongue. Talulah commanded in turn, "Rennin, bring Duncan."

Cameron and Donovan lifted their brother and carried him into Talulah's abode. Rennin followed. Inside, the medicine man said, "Put him back up."

The three stood to the side and let Talulah work. Outside, the others waited in fear. For once, Lucia had nothing to say. She was overwhelmed by the depth of devotion Duncan had for an Indian woman and realized that Cameron had felt the same about his dead wife. Her thoughts of Tammy changed to thoughts on how to fight a ghost or possibly make Cameron break a promise to his dying brother. She realized that if Duncan died, Cameron would, indeed, return to Boston with a new wife, and it would not be she—or Tammy.

Talulah worked steadily. He placed a long, thin, hollow reed into the wound in Duncan's back. He blew his breath into the reed. Each time he blew, blood spurted out. He blew until no more blood came. Duncan lost consciousness. When the blood stopped, Talulah replaced the reed with a piece of red-hot iron. Duncan twitched, but he did not open his eyes. Finally, Talulah packed the open wound with moss. He looked solemnly at Rennin. "Talulah do all Talulah can. Duncan must have will to live. Send in woman."

Cynthia came in full of apprehension. For days she did not leave Duncan's side. His fever came and went. After almost a week, he opened his eyes. They were met by the face of a haggard, but suddenly excited, Cynthia. She shouted, "Talulah!"

The shaman came to her call. He grinned triumphantly. "Strong O'Rourke blood flows in the veins of this man."

"Momma might say it's Fitzpatrick blood," Duncan said as he saw Rennin enter behind Talulah.

"A combination thereof," said Rennin. "Welcome back. Cameron has a request of you. As soon as you are strong enough, he would like you to marry this woman. He says to tell you that juggling thoughts of two is hard enough. He cannot handle three."

Duncan tried to laugh, but it still hurt too much. "Tell Momma and Aunt Anna to get everything ready. Give me one, maybe two weeks."

With eyes downcast, Cynthia took Duncan's hand. "You still want me?"

"I didn't fight for your honor to let you go. Will you marry me?"

Cynthia nodded and kissed Duncan's hand. "Your honor is my honor."

When Baxter noticed Sarah had fallen asleep, he softly closed the book, kissed her head, and slipped from the room.

Part Four

Going Home

40
A Wedding

Roger Simpkins came at the beginning of the next week and took Dennis Stone to jail. Baxter and Sarah made wedding plans, although Baxter cringed at the thought of meeting Thomas. Sarah laughed it off. "Don't worry about meeting Papa. He's just a big pussycat."

Baxter countered, "Yeah, I've met your idea of a big pussycat."

Sarah grinned. "That's right. Patty didn't eat you. She likes you. Patty is an excellent judge of character." She playfully patted his chest. "You won over Uncle Rennin. He's much tougher than Papa."

Baxter snorted a laugh. "I'm not sure I would be if I were a father."

While they waited for Sarah's family to return from their business in St. Louis, Baxter sent his mother a letter. In it he told her he would like her blessing, but he made it clear he would marry Sarah and stay in California with or without her approval.

When Mitchell Stone and the Goodmans retuned to Puma Pass, Mitchell was devastated about his brother's behavior, but everyone assured him that there was no reflection on his character. Thomas was tempted to shower his wrath upon Baxter, but after hearing his story and seeing the light in Sarah's eyes, he welcomed Baxter with open arms. The wedding plans progressed rapidly.

Sarah sent a letter to Chen Li and prayed he would be able to come. Baxter asked Rennin to be his best man if Chen Li was unable to get there. Rennin chuckled that he played second fiddle to his protégé. Sarah decided to ask Mai to stand as her matron of honor if Chen Li got back, but to stand only as a bride's maid if he did not. Then, Rebekah would stand beside her.

The date was set for December 1st. The day before the wedding, the stage arrived with surprises galore. First, Chen Li was there. He planned to stay until the day after Christmas. Second, Moira and Allison Newman with her family, except her father who had passed away just days after Sarah's escapde in the the new tomb, accompanied Chen Li. The biggest surprise of all was the last passenger to disembark— Beatrice Pryor.

Chen Li had paid the woman a visit and persuaded her to give Sarah a chance. The trip west proved to be a life-changing event for Beatrice. Chen Li introduced her to kindness and compassion and a living God.

Chen Li went immediately to the house Rennin had constructed for Mai and him. Allison and her family went to stay with Caitlin, and Candace insisted Beatrice should stay with them because she was about to become a part of the family. As Beatrice watched Sarah in her own element, she realized that Sarah was very much a poised and confident young woman who had learned to be assertive and self-reliant. She humbled herself and asked Sarah's forgiveness.

"Sarah, may I talk with you a moment?" Beatrice asked after dinner.

"Of course," Sarah replied graciously.

Baxter stood to join them. "Alone," said Beatrice with her mouth in a thin line.

Sarah nodded to Baxter. "Mrs. Pryor, let me show you Aunt Rebekah's garden on the way to the gazebo."

The two women walked in silence for a while. Finally, as they reached the gazebo, which stood in the middle of the settlement on the side of the creek away from the school, Beatrice said, "The garden is lovely. Will you be carrying some of your aunt's roses tomorrow?"

"Yes," said Sarah.

"Fine. Now, to the point," said Beatrice. "Sarah, I apologize. I judged you and treated you horribly. I wanted Baxter to marry, for my convenience, someone who could make my life better. I've had to work hard, and I suppose I had become bitter. I was wrong. I'm glad he was stubborn and followed you. I'll do my best to be a proper mother-in-law. There. That's the best I can do. I'm not a very affectionate or emotional person. For that I'm truly sorry. That's probably why my husband left me. He called me a cold, heartless bitch."

"I forgive you," said Sarah. "You're not completely cold. You obviously love Baxter. That's common ground for us."

"Yes, I do love him, though I've never shown it well."

"It's never too late to start."

"How do I start?"

"Be honest for one."

"Honest?" She gave a snort. "God had him meet his father as he was dying on the way here. I never told him the truth about that."

"He seems to have taken that in stride and holds no animosity toward you."

"I haven't yet told him I no longer have a position in Boston. I don't know what I shall do after the wedding."

"What happened?" The bride-to-be stretched her eyes wide.

"Do you really care?"

"Yes, I do."

"Pamela used her influence to see that I lost my position when she lost Baxter."

"Oh, no!" Sarah's fingertips flew to her lips. "I'm sorry. Uncle Olaf needs another teacher at the school. Perhaps, you can stay here."

"You wouldn't mind having me so close?"

"No. If you're close, we can learn to love each other. Let's start with a hug." Sarah held her arms open to the woman who had made her life miserable. Beatrice hesitantly put her arms around the girl. As they embraced, Baxter walked into the gazebo.

"I don't believe my eyes," he said.

Beatrice sniffled. "Believe it. I plan to do it more." Then, she hugged Baxter. "Believe it or not, I love you, you scoundrel; and I want you to be happy."

"I know, Mother."

"I have several things to tell you." She started across the creek.

He arched an eyebrow. "No more lies?"

Beatrice paused. "Never again."

The day dawned cool and clear. The Goodman home bustled with excitement. Sarah skipped down the stairs. "Good morning!" She kissed her mother and father and Beatrice. "This is the best day of my life! Today, I become Mrs. Baxter Pryor."

Sarah's excitement was contagious. Before long, the whole house was dancing to her tune. By ten o'clock, everything was set for a joyous occasion. The gentlemen escorted Baxter to the church while the ladies put the finishing touches on Sarah's hair and accessories. She inventoried her items. "I have something new, my dress. I have something borrowed, Rebekah's lace handkerchief. I have bluebonnets mixed with the roses. Oh, my goodness! I have nothing old."

"Yes, you do," said Beatrice, "if you will accept it." Beatrice handed Sarah a black velvet case. A French cameo was inside. "My mother gave it to me on my wedding day. Her mother gave it to her, and my grandfather gave it to my grandmother on their wedding day. I have no daughter to receive it. You will be my daughter. Will you take it?"

Sarah started to cry. "Oh, I'll mess up my face. Yes, Mother, I'll take it. Thank you."

"Mother!" Beatrice gasped.

"I-if it pleases you." Sarah held her breath

"Yes, I believe it does." Beatrice washed Sarah's face with a cool cloth. "Let this lie on your eyes for a few minutes to take away any swelling. You can pay me back. Have a granddaughter for me to carry on the tradition."

"I'll do my best," laughed Sarah, "but that is out of my hands."

Thomas knocked loudly over the commotion and entered when he received no answer. "Ladies," he shouted, "the groom is threatening to either go back to Boston or storm the gates of this fortress."

"He wouldn't," said Sarah.

Thomas laughed. "The former, probably not. On the other hand, the latter I would not put past him. Everybody, out! Attendants line up at the door of the church. Sarah and I will be there in a few minutes."

Everyone left, and Sarah asked, "Papa, is something wrong?"

"Yes. I'm giving my baby away," he replied misty-eyed.

"Papa," said Sarah, "I'm not your baby. Ruby is your baby. Just wait until you have to give her away."

Thomas grimaced at the thought, but said, "I have something for you and Baxter."

"What is it?"

Thomas handed Sarah a tube. She opened it to find blueprints. "It's your mother's and my wedding present, a house to be built. Baxter has an office adjoining it. If you want to make any changes, just speak to Mr. MacMillan."

"Papa, you're so sweet."

"That's not what you thought a few years ago when I was worried about you and Chen."

"You were still wrong about that."

"I know. I love you, baby. I want you to be happy."

"I love you, too, Papa."

When Sarah and Thomas arrived at the door of the church, Evelyn Lamar played "The Bridal Chorus." All eyes turned toward Sarah, but none danced livelier than Baxter's. The wedding itself was perfectly decorous. However, the reception proved to be another story.

No one had thought to tell Beatrice about Patty, who had wandered off for a few days as she frequently did. Smelling the food from the reception, Patty bounced into town ready to have her share. The first person she bumped into with a plate was Beatrice. Patty proceeded to take the drumstick right off the woman's plate. Beatrice went into a screaming fit.

Baxter saw his mother's terror. "Oh, my God!" he said. Then, he could not help but laugh. He started calling the late-arriving guest. "Patty! Patty!" Patty ran to Baxter and he bent down and petted her head. "Come with me and I'll give you your very own plate."

Beatrice shrieked, "Baxter, that's a wild animal!"

"No, it's not, Mother. This is Patty. Relax. She's tame. Actually, she's Rennin's pet."

Baxter led Patty to the fringe of the crowd and gave her some chicken, some deviled eggs, and a piece of wedding cake. He returned to find Beatrice in a fainted heap. "Oh, good grief!" he snapped.

Thomas waved some smelling salts under Beatrice's nose. Baxter gave her a chastising look. "Mother, why do you think this place is called Puma Pass? It's named for Patty. It was her home long before any of us came. She will *not* hurt you. Get used to her."

The rest of the day went smoothly. Baxter and Sarah caught the afternoon stage for a week at The Green Gable Hotel in San Francisco. Rennin whispered to Rebekah as they walked home, "There was nobody in that stagecoach with Baxter and Sarah. One hundred gold pieces says they don't wait until they get to the hotel."

"Rennin!" Rebekah chastised.

"I wouldn't wait," said Rennin. "You want to take the bet?"

"Not on your life," Rebekah laughed. "I bet they didn't wait until they were out of sight. That is going to be one hot and steamy relationship."

"It won't compare to ours." His eyes danced with mischief.

That night, Rennin sneaked up behind Rebekah and engulfed her in his arms. He pretended to growl, "Grrr," and nibbled her neck. "Yum. You taste better than Beatrice's chicken Patty stole." Rennin laughed heartily. "That was the funniest sight."

"Rennin O'Rourke, you are incorrigible. That poor woman was terrified." Rebekah started laughing. "But it was funny."

"I have an idea."

"What's that?"

"Let's pretend we're newlyweds. I'll race you upstairs."

"Okay. Just help me put these dishes on the shelf."

Rennin took the dishes and Rebekah took off out the kitchen door. "Cheater!" Rennin called after her, and he left the dishes on the table.

Later as they lay cuddled together, Rennin said, "Rebekah, do you realize that we have not read in quite a while. It has taken us years to finish one book. We're getting close to the end. Do you want to read some of it?"

"I really have enjoyed making our own magic tonight."

"Me, too. We'll make some more after we read." Rennin grinned roguishly. He laughed and retrieved the book from the nightstand.

Duncan recovered steadily from his injuries, and Cynthia quietly planned her wedding. She seemed distracted. No one knew of the conversation she had overheard between Lucia and Lucretia. The two women were still in Mom's Trading Post because both Cameron and Ian had decided to stay for the next wedding.

Cynthia methodically planned each detail so that there would be nothing missed. The affair was simple and without deviation from standard. The young bride quietly and honestly pledged her love, her fidelity, and her life to Duncan; and Duncan strongly and confidently pledged the same to her.

After the reception, Duncan lifted Cynthia into the rig and clicked the horses into a trot. "Where are we going?" she asked.

"'Tis a surprise," said Duncan with a twinkle in his eyes.

They crossed the river and rounded the bend. Nestled within a grove of cedar trees, stood a new cabin. Duncan grinned. "'Tis ours, removed enough so that we can be alone, yet close enough we can be home in twenty minutes."

"When did you do this?"

"Where do you think I disappeared to so often over the last year? Cameron put the finishing touches inside. I hope you like it."

"I'm sure I will." Cynthia's response lacked the enthusiasm Duncan had hoped.

The groom helped his bride down. "Don't go inside. I have to carry you over the threshold. I'll be back as soon as I settle the horses. We have a small barn, too."

Cynthia waited patiently for Duncan. He bounced around the corner of the cabin. "Ah, what is this vision I see before me? Could it be an angel or, perhaps, a magical creature?"

"No, silly."

Duncan scooped her into his arms. "No, something much better, my wife, the love of my life."

Cynthia laid her hand softly on Duncan's cheek. He pushed the door open with his shoulder and carried his bride into their home, which, as usual, the mothers and aunts had made romantically ready for newlyweds. Duncan kicked the door closed and carried Cynthia directly to their bedroom, which was decorated with the first crocuses of the year.

He set her on the bed and unpinned her flowing, charcoal tresses. He kissed her hungrily, and she returned his kiss with trembling lips rather than the fire that she had always showered upon him. Confused and not knowing what to do, Duncan continued what he thought was seduction appropriate for a wedding night.

As he slipped her dress from her shoulders, she screamed and jumped away from him. "No. No."

He suddenly realized Cynthia was remembering what Hopam had done to her. He stood and went to her. "No," she said again, putting her hands up to stop him.

Duncan said, "Shh." He slipped her dress back on her shoulders. "Shh. I can wait until you're ready. It's all right."

For the first time since she had been attacked, Cynthia allowed herself to cry. "Duncan," she said tearfully. Duncan pulled her into his arms and held her gently. He did not speak, but walked her slowly back to the bed. He sat back and leaned against the headboard and let her cry. "I'm sorry," she said after a while.

"Why? Nothing that has happened was your fault."

"Duncan, how can you still want me? I'm ruined. You will not be the first one or the only one. How can you live with that? Are you only feeling sorry for me because you know another man would consider me ruined?"

"Oh, darling, where did you get such ideas? I love you. I want to spend my life with you. Do you think I'm lying to you? Do you think I'm such a fool? Cynthia, I almost died for you. That is not an act of pity, but of love. Where did you get such foolish ideas?"

"I heard Lucretia talking to her sister."

"What did they say?"

Following a heavy sigh, she said, "Lucia said I was tainted and she could not believe you still wanted to marry me. Lucretia said you were honor bound to fulfill your commitment, and Lucia scoffed at that idea. She also said she couldn't understand how you, or Cameron for that matter, could want a savage for a wife."

"Oh, God! That woman! She is a snob and a bigot. I can only pray Cameron sees what she is and does *not* marry her." Duncan held Cynthia at arms' length and spoke firmly, yet gently, "You listen to me. I love you. It has nothing to do with *duty*. I have always loved you. That has not and will not change. Yes, I want you. I want you so badly it hurts. But I will *not* force you to do anything. When you're ready, you come to me. I'll be waiting."

Duncan got up and took his pillow and a blanket from the wardrobe. "Where are you going?" asked Cynthia.

"I'm going to sleep on the floor. I can't lie beside you without wanting you. You're my wife, but I'll wait. Go to sleep."

Duncan lay on the floor and pretended to sleep; however, he was so angry and depressed that he could not keep his eyes closed. Visions of Cynthia's battered body and ideas of how to rid his family of Lucia played on his mind. Silent, angry tears escaped, unwanted, from his eyes. He thought to himself: *Am I still such a child?*

Cynthia, too, could not sleep. She stared at Duncan's back. She longed to feel his arms around her, yet she was terrified. *I'm so selfish. I shouldn't make him wait. He would have died for me. He killed for me.* In a shaky voice she said, "Duncan, please don't sleep on the floor. I'm afraid. I *will* come to you, but, please, just hold me tonight. Don't shame me further by sleeping on the floor."

"Shame you? I'm trying to protect you from me. I'm a man, Cynthia. I won't shame you. Nobody has to know what happens in our bed. Go to sleep."

Cynthia turned her back to Duncan and tried again to fall asleep. After a few minutes, she felt his arm over her. He kissed the back of her head and whispered, "Go to sleep."

Three days later, Cameron and his group prepared to leave. Duncan rode down to wish him a good trip. Cynthia stayed home. When Duncan embraced his brother, Cameron looked closely at him. "What's wrong?" Cameron asked.

"Nothing," said Duncan.

"Bull." Cameron turned to the group. "I forgot something. Duncan, I need your help."

They walked to the stable. Cameron looked at his younger brother sternly. "What's wrong?"

Having inherited his grandfather Colin's temper, Duncan punched the wall of the stable with great force. "God! I think I broke my knuckles."

"No. They're only bruised. You've done that before." Cameron waved off Duncan's complaint. "Now, talk to me."

Duncan broke down and told Cameron everything and finished with, "Cam, don't marry that woman. She's not right for you. She has no soul. She's a selfish bigot. Have you told her one word about our family history—about Draconis? You need not answer for I know the reply. She would scoff and call you a fool. Now, Tammy? She's the one for you, trust me."

"Lucia will have to do a lot of changing before I marry her. Tammy has made it clear that she doesn't want me. That's beside the point. Let's fix your problem."

"How?"

"First, don't expect intercourse yet. Give it time. Until then, touch her. Do little things to arouse her. Make her want you. Trust me."

The two brothers walked out the door of the stable with their arms around each other and laughing.

"What did you forget?" asked Lucia.

"Brotherly advice," Cameron winked at Duncan. "And I'll take yours under consideration."

Duncan nodded. "'Bye, Cam. I love you."

"Love you, too, little brother."

All good-byes having been said, Cameron headed back to Boston.

Duncan's circumstances were slow to change, but he took Cameron's advice. He set out to woo his own wife. He started small with such things as bringing her flowers and preparing dinner for her. He would kiss the nape of her neck, and always tell her he loved her. He asked her to rub his tired shoulders and back, always being sure to be shirtless when she did, so that she would have to feel the touch of his skin. He gave her a puppy that one of the trappers was trying to find a home.

Several weeks after the wedding as they lay in bed in the usual fashion with Cynthia's back against Duncan's chest and his arm over her, he was overcome with desire. He had thoughts of taking Cynthia himself, but shook off the temptation with horror. Slowly, he began to caress her breasts through her nightgown. She took a sharp breath at Duncan's touch. He kissed the back of her neck and continued to touch her, moving his hand from her breasts to her thighs and back. He felt Cynthia's breaths become more rapid. He whispered in her ear, "I want you. I need you. I love you."

Cynthia turned over and pulled his face to hers. She kissed him ravenously. "Yes!" she panted. "Yes, now. Now."

The passion for which Duncan had longed sprang into bloom.

Rennin closed the book and eyed Rebekah with a wicked little grin on his face.

41
A House Divided

Michael and Gabriel raced into the house. "It's happened Papa," stated Gabriel as he dropped a newspaper into Rennin's lap.

"What's happened?" asked Rennin.

Michael rolled his eyes at his brother. "South Carolina has seceded from the Union. It's war, Papa, just like you said. You were right."

Rennin put his face in his hands. "Oh, God, help us."

In a concerned voice, Michael asked, "Papa will we have to fight in a war?"

Rennin mussed the twins' hair. "No. All of you are far too young to fight in a war."

"Well, what about you or Chen or Baxter or Mark or Running Bear?"

"No," said Rebekah vehemently. "There is no reason this war should touch us. We do not, nor have we *ever*, owned slaves. Your father purchased Mabel only to free her. We do not live in the North or the South. No. I will not allow my family to be affected by this."

Rennin looked gravely at his wife. "Honey, there is no way this war will not affect us. Whether directly or indirectly, we will all suffer from it."

"Rennin, are you considering fighting in this war?" Rebekah was near tears before the news had reached the rest of Puma Pass. Rennin's silence answered her question, and she fled the room.

Christmas of 1860 was a strained holiday in Puma Pass. There was any number of differing opinions regarding the involvement of California in the impending war. From the pulpit, Henry preached a sermon entitled *Higher Law*. It left most of the men in the community ready to leave for the East immediately when they considered the price paid for freedom.

One late February evening, a cavalry detachment rode into Puma Pass. The lieutenant left his men to meander near the creek, while he knocked on Rennin's door. Rennin opened with a confused expression. "I'm looking for Rennin O'Rourke," announced the young lieutenant.

"You've found him. Please come in."

"I have a letter for you, Sir. I'm to wait for a response."

Rennin read the letter carefully while Rebekah stood on the staircase and gripped the banister with white knuckles. "Lieutenant, what's your name?" Rennin asked when he had finished the letter.

"Lieutenant Wade Brooks, Sir."

"Lieutenant Brooks, have your men camp in the pecan grove. I'll have an answer for you tomorrow morning. I must pray and speak to my wife before I can render a decision of this magnitude."

"Of course, Sir. Yes, Sir."

Rennin closed the door behind the young officer and held the letter out to Rebekah. "Read it for yourself."

She read the letter and looked horrified. "Rennin, are you going to do this?"

He kept silent. Rebekah fumed. "Rennin O'Rourke! Damn your noble ideas! They want half—*half*—of our fortune to supplement the Army's resources. I don't care at all about the money. I will live in a hovel with you. That's what I'm worried about—your living." She shook the sheets of paper in the air. "Rennin, they want you to join the army with the rank of colonel. They say you'll be responsible for keeping the gold safe and flowing to the East, but you will *not* be out of danger. There will be those who will want to steal the gold. You'll be in harm's way. I've almost lost you three times already. Are you trying to make me old with worry?"

"Rebekah."

"No, Rennin, your charm and sweet talk will *not* work this time. Let someone else fight the battle. I cannot live without you."

"What about my conscience and sense of right and wrong? What about Higher Law—defending those who cannot defend themselves? The house, which is our country, is already divided. I cannot live with my personal house being divided. Rebekah, I *must* follow my conscience."

"Can your conscience not see what you're doing to your family? Rennin, you'll tear *us* apart. But, by all means, follow your damned conscience. Far be it from me to prick your heart." Rebekah stomped up the stairs and locked the door to their room behind her.

Rennin followed her. He grabbed the knob. "Rebekah, open the door," he said sternly.

"No. Go away. Go fight your battle."

"Rebekah, open the door."

"No. When they send your body home in a box, I'll explain to the children that you followed your conscience."

"Rebekah, open the damned door."

Rebekah did not answer.

"Rebekah Suzanne Sinclair O'Rourke, open the door!"

"Go to Hell, Rennin."

"Rebekah, open the damned door, or I will kick it in," Rennin threatened through clench teeth.

"Then, kick it in. *You* can explain that one to the children."

Before Rebekah realized what was happening, Rennin kicked the door in. He glowered at her, angrier than he had ever been. He slammed the door closed behind him. "Don't *ever* lock me out again."

She stood there wide-eyed with fear. "I-I won't."

Rennin grabbed Rebekah's hand and jerked her to him. He kissed her in his fury. She pushed him away, but he held her tightly and continued to kiss her. As if transformed, she melted into his arms. "Rennin," she breathed.

"Don't talk, Rebekah," he said. "I don't want to talk."

Hours later as Rennin held Rebekah, she whispered, "I'm sorry. I do understand your need to be a part of this war. I'm just so terrified of losing you. I love you so much."

"I love you, too, my darling. I promise I'll come back to you."

Rennin visited the soldiers' encampment early the next morning and informed Lieutenant Brooks that he would be going with them. "When do we leave?"

"As soon as possible, Sir," responded the young man. "If you answered affirmatively, I was to give you this." He presented a box with a uniform with epaulettes indicating Rennin's rank. "Once you put this on, Sir, you'll be my commanding officer. We'll leave as soon as you've made the necessary arrangements."

"Should I bring any one else with me?"

"If they wish to come, but they might not be a part of your regiment. They could be sent east to fight."

"I understand."

Rennin returned home and told Rebekah that he would be leaving by the end of the week. She shed no more tears and argued no more with his decision, but she clung to him in dread.

The night before he was scheduled to leave, Rennin held Rebekah, feeling his own dread and sorrow. She whispered to him, "Read to me, Rennin. I'll have to treasure the words tonight because it could be years before I hear your voice again."

"Okay, honey. Get the book."

She handed him the old copy they always used along with a new bound copy. "I had planned to keep this until your birthday, but now seems a good time. When you need me, read and know that I'll do the same. Somehow, Rennin, our spirits are magically bound through this book."

He caressed her cheek. "No, you're the magic that was lost. You've brought this book to life once again. I love you,

Rebekah. You *are*, as Rennin of old called Morgan, heart of my heart, life of my life. You are my reason for breathing, and I will love you until the day I die."

Rebekah cuddled into Rennin's strong embrace and he read aloud, struggling to control the emotion in his voice. Through trembling lips she mumbled, "Do *not* die. I cannot live without you."

Unable to make a promise he could not keep, Rennin simply fell to reading once more.

Many years passed and Cameron spent those years with Lucia, attempting to mellow her temperament. They argued frequently, but Cameron would come home to a happy child and gentle pleasant company.

One late evening, Cameron came home after a most unpleasant argument with Lucia. He entered the house and threw his valise across the room, knocking over the brandy decanter, breaking several snifters. After being awakened, Tammy, who had moved into the main house after Cameron hired a full staff of servants, rushed down the stairs to see what the noise was. The only concession she made to being treated differently than the other servants was to have her room next-door to Rowan's rather than in the servants' quarters.

"Mr. O'Rourke, what happened?"

"That damned woman!" snarled Cameron. "Now, rather than hiring good household help, she has purchased slaves. I will *not* have it. If she thinks I'll master a house that owns slaves, she'll be an old maid."

"Oh, I see," said Tammy with her usual disappointed voice when Lucia was mentioned. Seeing the broken glass, she began to clean up.

"Leave it alone, Miss Martin. I don't pay you to be a housekeeper. I pay you to be a governess," growled Cameron.

"This is Mrs. Ferguson's night to visit her daughter," Tammy reminded him as she continued to pick up the broken glass.

"Then, I'll clean up in few minutes. I don't care right now," Cameron snarled.

Calmly Tammy stood and spoke. "Mr. O'Rourke, may I say something to you?"

"Yes. What?"

"If Miss Allgood puts you in such a foul humor all the time, why are you courting her? Not only does she put you in an awful state, but she also puts Rowan in an abominable mood. He detests her. Have you never noticed?"

"Do you want an honest answer to your question, Miss Martin?"

"Of course."

"I'm courting Miss Allgood because the woman I would like to court won't give me the time of day. She has some antiquated notion that because she works for me, she can't have any other relationship with me. Although deep down inside, I think she wants me to take her in my arms and make love to her."

"That is preposterous," said Tammy, suddenly nervous.

"Truly? Let's see." Cameron took Tammy by the shoulders and pulled her to him. He kissed her fiercely. She pushed him away.

"Don't do that," she stammered.

Cameron smirked. "You haven't convinced me." He pulled her to him again and kissed her passionately once more.

Tammy pushed away again and raised her hand to slap Cameron, but he caught her hand. "Is that in truth what you want to do?" He let her hand go. "If it is, go ahead. Do what you deep in your soul want to do. Whatever it is, I won't stop you. Slap me. Hit me with the fire poker. Do what is utmost in your mind. I *dare* you."

She stood speechless. Cameron cocked his head to the side. "Well, I'm waiting."

Tammy felt short of breathe. She breathed hard and fast. Her head grew light. She looked like a lamb surrounded by wolves and trying to find a way of escape. Suddenly, with tears on her face, she flung her arms around Cameron and kissed him as passionately as he had kissed her.

He gathered her close and kissed her deeply. He panted, "Oh, God. Tammy. Tammy. How I have longed to hold you."

Cameron lifted her into his arms and carried her up the stairs. She whimpered like a child in his arms. "Cameron, I'm frightened."

"I won't hurt you. I swear I would never hurt you. I love you, Tammy." Cameron laid her gently on his bed and slipped her gown off. "God! You are so beautiful."

He slowly, softly kissed her, starting with her mouth. He kissed her neck, her breasts, her stomach, and her thighs and came back to her mouth. She trembled at his touch.

Tammy whispered shyly, "Cameron, I..."

He put his finger on her lips. "Shh. Please don't say no. Please." Cameron made love to Tammy as tenderly as possible, and she responded to his every touch. He held her in his arms with her head on is chest, and they slept.

Cameron awoke with a start to bright sunlight. He reached beside him. "Tammy? Tammy where are you?" His bed was empty. For a moment he thought he had dreamed the night before, but he could smell the lilac on the pillow beside him. Cameron dressed hastily and bounded down the stairs.

He rushed into the kitchen where Rowan sat alone at the table. "Where's Tammy?" he asked.

"She's gone," replied the little boy. "She said to give this to you." Rowan handed Cameron and envelope. "She was crying, Poppy. What did you do to her?"

Cameron's hand trembled. Deep worry lines etched his face. "I love her, Rowan. That's all I've done. I love her."

"Then, why was she crying? Why did she say she had to go away? I want her back, Poppy. I love her, too. She's the only mommy I've ever known. You make it right. You bring her back.

Whatever you did, you say you're sorry." Rowan left the table without asking to be excused.

Cameron opened the letter with trepidation and read the words he could not bear:

Cameron,

I suppose you have made me a woman, but I feel like a whore. I gave myself to you, a man who is not my husband, and socially never can be. I can no longer live under the same roof as you. I leave you shamed and ruined, although loved. Love is not enough. I have lost my honor and dignity. Please understand and leave me in peace. My heart will always belong to you even though I cannot. Do what is right for Rowan and know that I will always carry both of you in my heart.

Tammy

Cameron put his head on the table and sobbed. Unable to think clearly, he went to bed and stayed there for several days. During that time he wrote Morgan about what had happened asking, "Momma, what do I do?"

Morgan's reply came. "Do what is right."

He asked himself, "What *is* right? Do I leave Tammy alone? Do I go after her? Do I marry Lucia and give Rowan a home. What is *right*?"

Cameron lost his appetite and weight. Lucia nagged him to tell her what was wrong. "Nothing," he replied. "I have an important decision to make."

"Does it involve me?" she asked with her eyes alight.

"You're part of it."

"Oh, Cameron, just ask me. You know what I will say. Father approves. Just ask."

Jarred into reality, Cameron acquiesced. "Lucia, will you marry me?"

"Yes, Cameron. Oh, I have so much to plan. When will you talk to Father?"

"Tomorrow."

Lucia skipped gaily out Cameron's door. Behind him Cameron heard Rowan's indignant comment. "How could you? If you love Tammy, how could you ask that witch to marry you? Poppy, I hate her! If you marry her, I'll run away and go back to live with Grandma and Granddad."

"Rowan O'Rourke! You will do no such thing! I'm trying to give you a family. You need a mother."

"I need Tammy. You need Tammy. Forget convention. Go find her and bring her back."

"Rowan, you cannot always have what you want. Give Lucia a chance. She comes from a fine family. She'll make you a little gentleman."

"No, Poppy, she won't. You'll see."

Cameron and Rowan argued for weeks to come even as Lucia made her wedding plans, and Tammy found another position as a companion to an elderly widowed woman.

Rennin closed the book. "Honey," he said, "I don't want this night to end. I don't want to leave you."

Rebekah stroked Rennin's cheek. "You have to, but only for a while. I'll be waiting."

He kissed her hand. Finally, they slept fitfully. The next morning, Rennin, Chen Li, Baxter, Mitchell, and Mark left to fight a war that would change their lives forever.

42
Bigotry

Baxter and Mitchell left Rennin and went east to fight, Baxter back to Massachusetts and Mitchell to New York. Chen Li was sent to the engineering corps for his expertise. Mark Goodman was sent home because his vision was so severely impaired, much to the relief of Thomas and Candace. Rennin commanded the regiment in charge of gold shipments from California to the east. Lieutenant Wade Brooks served as his attaché, and the two bonded a lifelong friendship.

All the men wrote as frequently as they could. Usually their letters were disquieting. Actual shots were finally fired in April 1861, and from that point on, Rebekah did not rest at night. After reading a scripture passage in addition to Psalm 91, she read *Memoirs of Magic*. She finished the book, started over, and progressed rapidly, praying that she would be on the same page as Rennin in some attempt to bind their spirits.

On an unusually stormy night, Rebekah lay awake with an unexplained burden in her spirit. She whispered, "Oh, Rennin. I love you so much. Feel me, Rennin, and draw comfort from me." Visions of a pearly white dragon played on her mind and she felt comforted.

With a smile, Rebekah opened *Memoirs of Magic* and read again Cameron's revelation.

Rowan fought Cameron at every turn over his impending marriage to Lucia Allgood. He even made good on his threat and ran away. Cameron followed him and met Rennin returning the boy. The three O'Rourke generations spent one night together on the trail to Boston. Thinking Rowan was asleep, Rennin talked to Cameron openly and honestly. "Your mother let me read the letter. Cameron, didn't you learn anything the night before we almost drowned and froze?"

"I was a boy then, Daidí. I learned a lot. I'm full grown now. Maybe I was stupid. I was definitely lonely. Daidí, I would have married Tammy the next day. *She* left *me*. She has some lame-brained idea that she's not good enough for me." Using his hands like a scale weighing items, he went on. "I'm rich. She's poor. I'm the boss. She's a servant. Daidí, why doesn't she realize her ideas are as much bigotry as she thinks rich people feel toward poor people?"

"Do you still love her, Cameron?"

"It doesn't matter. She refuses to even talk to me. Oh, Daidí, I *am* thankful that God spared her the embarrassment of having an illegitimate child. No matter how much I would have wanted to claim our child she would have rejected me. She would have faced her shame alone. Why is she so stubborn?"

"Cam, you *cannot* marry Lucia Allgood if you love Tammy. It would be unfair to all of you."

"Daidí, she's a good woman. She'll make a good wife."

"What about mother?" asked Rowan from the tent's entrance. "Poppy, she's not mother material, at least not for me. Poppy, she doesn't think I'm as good as she is. She looks down on me because I'm half Iroquois."

"Don't be ridiculous, Rowan. She'll learn to be a mother. She has never had experience with it." Even as he countered Rowan's allegation, Cameron's thoughts wandered back to what Lucia had said about Cynthia and even Holly, and the fact that she had shown no real affection to her niece and nephew.

Cameron returned to the moment when Rowan snapped, "Fine, Poppy. Fine, but I'm disappointed in you."

"What?"

"Poppy! You have to marry *Tammy*. You made her your wife in the sight of God. You *lay* with her. How would Lucia feel if she knew? Poppy, if you don't give this more consideration, I'll tell her."

"Rowan Patrick O'Rourke! What happened between Tammy and me will stay between Tammy and me. Just because I sought advice from my parents, does *not* mean I betrayed that. You will never say anything to Lucia or anyone else. You will never threaten me with that kind of behavior again. Go to bed. When we get home, you will be punished for running away and for disrespecting me."

Rowan started to speak again. Cameron pointed at him. "Go to bed. Don't say another word."

When they arrived in Boston, Lucia was at the house waiting for them. "Oh, you're both safe," she said.

"I'm sure you're relieved," said ten-year-old Rowan, sarcastically.

"Rowan, go to your room," ordered Cameron. "I'll be up with my strap in a few minutes."

Rowan glared at Cameron and Lucia as he went up the stairs. He paused at the top of the stairs. "Lucia, did Poppy tell you why Tammy left so abruptly?"

Cameron and Rowan had a staring match. Without changing his line of vision, Cameron said, "Lucia, you need to go now. I have punishment to dole out. I'll talk to you tomorrow."

As soon as the door clicked closed behind her, Cameron marched up the stairs and pulled Rowan by the collar into his room. "Your pants off, Rowan."

"Poppy!"

"Now, and lean over the bed."

Rowan obeyed. Cameron spoke before he spanked his son. "Rowan, I've *never* liked spanking you, but your behavior lately has been reprehensible. I love you, and if I thought for one minute your arguments against Lucia had merit I'd break the engagement. Rowan, I'm lonely. I'm tired of being alone. I need a woman in my life. I want you to understand. I want your acceptance. I hope soon you can give it to me. I've always administered three lashes for an offense; however, today you're being punished for three offenses. How many licks is that?"

"Nine."

"Good. At least your studies haven't suffered."

"Unlike my heart, Poppy."

"Rowan, please be quiet."

"Why? Can you not stand the truth?"

"Rowan, would you like to go for twelve?"

"No, sir. Please, go ahead and get it over with."

Cameron administered nine licks deliberately and powerfully. He left Rowan in a heap upon his bed. Cameron closed the door to the bedroom and slid down the wall where he, too, wept. Within two minutes Rowan came out the door. "Poppy!" Rowan saw his father sitting by his door crying as hard as he had been crying. "Poppy!" The boy flung his arms around Cameron, who embraced him. "Poppy, I'm sorry. I won't run away again, and I'll try really hard to like Lucia. I love you, Poppy."

"I love you, too, my precious. I have an idea. Let's go to the tavern for dinner tonight—just the two of us. I might even let you taste my ale."

Cameron and Rowan slipped in unobserved by the other patrons of the tavern. They chose a table in the back against the dividing wall, where men sat on one side while women sat on the other. The serving wench arrived promptly. "Stew, mince pie, or ham?" she asked.

"Stew," Rowan said to his father.

Cameron nodded. "Two bowls of stew and a loaf of bread with butter and sides of sautéed onions and mushrooms. I'll have a pint and milk for my son," he ordered cheerfully.

As they waited for their food, they heard obviously feminine voices on the other side of the dividing wall. Cameron whispered, "That sounds like Lucia. Rowan, peek over the top and tell me who's over there."

Rowan got on his knees and peeked over the top. He plopped down in his chair, a deep frown on his lips. "It's Lucia and Aunt Lucretia. They're having dinner. Please, don't ask them to join us. You said just the two of us."

"I made you a promise," Cameron assured his son. "I meant what I said."

The serving wench brought their food. Cameron found himself listening to the conversation on the other side of the boards. He distinctly heard Lucia mention Rowan's name.

"Lucretia, I swear the day after Cameron and I are married I'm shipping that little half-breed monster off to school in England. I will *not* have that little savage with any children I might have. I cannot *believe* Cameron actually had an Indian wife. It's repulsive."

"Lucia, I'm sure she was a wonderful woman if Cameron loved her because he is an exceptional man. For Pete's sake, my mother-in-law is Indian. You're wrong about Rowan. He's a delightful child. I'm proud to have him as a nephew. You're also a fool. If you do *anything* to that child, you will lose that man. He loves his son more than anything or anyone else."

"We'll see. I'll not live under the same roof as him."

Before Cameron realized what had happened, he slammed his stein onto the table, sloshing beer over his hand. Rowan's eyes grew wide and his lip trembled. "Poppy, you won't let her do that, will you?"

"Hell, no!" he growled. At that moment, he chose to reveal his presence. He stood and peered over the dividing wall. "No! You will *not* live under the same roof as my son."

Lucia gasped. Cameron continued. "As of this minute, our engagement is off. I would not marry you if you were the *only* woman on Earth. You are a bigoted, selfish bitch. Good-bye." He turned to Rowan and took his hand. "Rowan, let's go home." He left serveral coins on the table.

Just outside the door, Cameron heard his name being called. "Cameron, wait!" Lucretia called after him.

He turned around. Angrily he said, "Lucretia, please don't try to defend Lucia's actions. I've found new respect for you. Don't lose it."

"I'm not going to defend her. She was wrong. You did the right thing." Lucretia stroked Rowan's hair and smiled at her relative. "No, Cam, I love this little boy. I've come to encourage you in another direction."

"What might that be?"

"Tammy. Cam, why did she leave you?"

"I don't wish to discuss it."

"I'm not as prudish as you think. Do you love her?"

He looked at the ground. "It doesn't matter. She has made herself perfectly clear."

"Go after her again and again until she relents. I think she already gave way to your charms. That's why she left. Am I right?"

Rowan tugged Cameron's hand. "Poppy, tell her. Aunt Lucretia isn't as mean as Lucia. She can help."

"Let me walk you home, Lucretia." Cameron gave her his arm. They talked on the way. "We made love. I love her very much, but she thinks she's not good enough for me. I was her employer. She thinks she has broken some kind of cardinal rule. How can I win her? Her ideas are as bigoted as Lucia's to the other extreme."

"God will provide a way. Have you forgotten to pray? Ask His forgiveness and Tammy's."

"Ask her to forgive me? I don't understand. I'm not ashamed of what we did. I would have married her the next day."

"Cameron, it was sin. She feels it deeply. Consider her innocence. Ask her to forgive you. Trust me. I *am* a woman, after all."

"Very well. What else?"

"Court her. Woo her. Make her feel guilty if you must for shunning you. If you want to stoop really low, send Rowan to her on your behalf."

"I'll go, Poppy," Rowan piped. "I'll beg her on my hands and knees to come back. Maybe that's what you should do."

"I'll do whatever it takes. I'll start by apologizing. It will have to be in a letter because she refuses to see me."

"It's a start," said Lucretia as they arrived at her house.

Ian stood in the doorway. "Hello, partner, what are you doing with my wife?"

"Bringing her home safely and listening to her wisdom. She can tell you about it. Thank you, Lucretia." Cameron kissed her on the cheek. "Come, Rowan. I have to get Tammy back even if I have to storm the walls of her domicile."

"Do it, Poppy. Go and get her. Drag her out and bring her home."

"I will if I have to, but let's not get that drastic at first."

Father and son rushed home with renewed determination.

Rebekah closed the book and wondered why people could treat those different from themselves so badly. The right to be equal for all men was part of why Rennin was fighting a war. Rennin believed strongly that all men were created equal, that they all were God's creation, no matter what the color of their skin. She had already seen the humiliation of the slaves and even Running Bear.

Her thoughts turned to Chen Li. She wondered how he was faring. Her curiosity did not last long when Mai came the next day with Aidan and Suzanne, her and Chen Li's two children named for the two greatest influences in Chen Li's life. Sarah showed up at the same time with Kristen and baby Keith.

The three women sat on the porch and the children played. Mai said honestly, "Rebekah, I am disturbed by Chen's latest letter."

"What does he say?"

Mai pulled the letter from her pocket and read a portion:

The Union army is fighting to free the slaves in the South, but I have seen colored soldiers treated much worse than most slaves. They are treated as if they are somehow innately inferior to the white soldiers. I, myself, have felt the same denigration. At first, I was relegated to digging trenches until my captain read my credentials. Captain Morris is a good and fair man. He saw my ability and has put me to good use. I am now in charge of all bridges, railroads, and a road maintenance crew. It is important to keep the troops moving.

Mai looked at Rebekah. "My husband has an engineering degree. He is extremely intelligent. Yet, because he is Chinese, they want him to dig ditches. Rebekah, there is something greatly wrong."

"I agree, Mai, but change will be wrought in one heart at a time. This war will legally free a group of people, but freedom from bigotry and prejudice will only come by the Grace of God, one person at a time."

Monica came up as they were sipping lemonade. "Mind if I join you?"

"Of course not," all the ladies agreed.

Rebekah asked, "Do you have a letter to share? It seems we all get together when one or more of us receives some news."

"Yes. Mitchell is coming home. His company has been disbanded."

"Does that mean the war is almost over?" Rebekah's voice held a hint of hope.

"Mitchell does not think so. He thinks this will be a long, bloody war."

The wives looked at one another. Without being prompted, they clasped hands and prayed.

43
Sacrifice

Mitchell's prediction proved true. The war raged on for four more years. During that time Chen Li came home on a visit for a month before returning to the engineering corps. However, Rennin and Baxter did not come home at all.

The ladies gathered to read Sarah's latest letter.

My dearest wife and love of my life,

Our Heavenly Father must have sent His guardian angels to watch over me today. Sarah, I have never seen so much blood. I do not think I can stand much more. I constantly hear screams of agony and see shattered limbs in the road. The only thing that keeps me sane is thinking of you and our children. How I long to hold you and to see our son! I fear he will be afraid of me for I will be a stranger to him, and Kristen will not remember me either. Tell them how much I love them and know how much I love and miss you. Remember me always before the Throne. I must go soon for the shelling is very near.

We have been fighting all day near Sharpsburg, Maryland. There are thousands dead, but neither side seems to be gaining any ground; moreover, McClellan does not seem disposed to send reinforcements.

Sarah, do not be frightened. I have been asked to take another commission, but I cannot write about it in a letter. It is something at which I will be quite good. I am not a soldier. If I take the commission, I might not be able to write you so frequently, but I feel it is something I must do. Pray for my wisdom in making this decision, though by the time you read this I will have made it.

I must go now for the battle is at hand.

Baxter

Sarah read the blood-spattered letter with tearful voice. It was the last communication she received from her husband. Even as they read the letter, a cavalry detachment rode into town. Upon seeing the ladies gathered as a group, this one larger than usual because most of the women were together in the rose garden, the young lieutenant rode up solemnly. He tipped his hat. "Ladies. Is one of you Mrs. Pryor, Mrs. Baxter Pryor?"

Sarah began to tremble and gasp, "No. No."

The lieutenant dismounted. Very compassionately he said, "Mrs. Pryor, I regret to inform you that your husband, who was serving his country as a spy, has been captured by the enemy and by now has been hanged. He died a hero, and I wish to bestow this medal to you in his honor."

Sarah screamed, "I don't want a medal! I want Baxter!" Candace caught her daughter as she collapsed. Beatrice walked calmly to the young lieutenant.

"I'm Beatrice Pryor, Baxter's mother. Thank you."

The young man looked at Beatrice. "I'm truly sorry for you loss. Ma'am, I have the worst job in the Army. I would much rather be taking the risk of dying than delivering the news of a family's sacrifice. Usually I only have to write the letters, and I've heard the Rebs don't even get that. They have to constantly check lists for names of their loved ones. Most people don't receive a personal delivery, but Mrs. Pryor is Colonel O'Rourke's niece. He asked me to do this." The lieutenant looked at Sarah. "Will she be all right?"

"Yes, in time. She's much stronger than she appears at this minute. She loves my son very much, but her heart will eventually mend."

The young man shook Beatrice's hand and then said, "I'm also looking for Mrs. O'Rourke."

Rebekah turned pale before she spoke. "Rennin too?"

"No, ma'am. Colonel O'Rourke asked me to deliver this to you." He handed Rebekah an envelope. "He said it would be faster than the mail."

Rebekah suddenly recognized the man. "You're the lieutenant who first came here, aren't you?"

"Yes, ma'am. I've been serving with the colonel ever since. He's a most revered man among his troops. You should be very proud of him."

"I am. I always have been. It's getting late. Will you and your men need lodging and food tonight?"

He looked at the soldiers who had accompanied him. "It's not necessary, but a home-cooked meal would be greatly appreciated."

"There are enough beds at the school for you to sleep tonight, and I'll see that you have a hearty meal in about three hours in the dining hall. I'll also reply to Rennin's letter tonight. Will you take it to him for me?"

"Of course, ma'am. Thank you. The colonel has sung your praises often. I see why. May I ask if there is any way for my men to bathe while we're here?"

"There are several tubs in the school. Use what you need."

"Thank you." Lieutenant Brooks tipped his hat to Rebekah and returned to his men with the news. It was obvious the news was well received from the whoops of delight that reached the women's ears.

Rebekah made the arrangements among the ladies to feed the band of soldiers in their midst. Then, she went home to read Rennin's letter.

My darling Rebekah,

Hello, my magic. How I miss your touch and how I wish I could have brought this tragic news myself and been there for Sarah. I know she must be devastated. She loves Baxter as much as you love me. Comfort her and give her my love.

How are my children? My boys are nearly men, and I am missing their growing up. And Ketty—is she still my angel? Damn my conscience! Sometimes I feel as if I have deserted you. Forgive me. I do love you so. Hug my children for me. Tell them that I love them.

I must give you some news that will most likely disturb you. I'm leaving this post. I've been called east to Pennsylvania. I'll be taking Wade (Lieutenant Brooks) with me.

Only, then, he will be Captain Brooks. I have his bars waiting for him when he returns from this terrible assignment. He has been my right arm, Rebekah. Meet his needs the best you can.

I know this news will worry you, especially now in the wake of losing Baxter. Read Psalm 91. It gives me comfort, as it will you.

I will give Wade time to reach you, and then I will read some more in *Memoirs of Magic*. I will be on the chapter regarding personal sacrifice. After you read this letter, read our special book. God willing, we will be on the same page at the same time. It will be as if we are together.

I love you, my darling. Pray for me. Hopefully, I'll see you soon. You are heart of my heart, life of my life. You are my reason for breathing, and I will love you until the day I die—which I pray will be a very long time.

All my love,
Rennin

Rebekah held the letter close to her heart. Then, she gathered ink and paper to write a response.

Rennin Aidan O'Rourke,

There is nothing to forgive. You are a man of honor and courage who is doing what is right. I love you all the more for it. I would ask that you be careful and take no unnecessary risks. You promised to come back to me. I know you to be a man of your word.

We are all well, and, yes, the children are growing like weeds—weeds with spectacular blooms. I would classify them as flowers. I'll deliver your messages and hugs first thing tomorrow morning.

Sarah took the news hard, but she'll survive. She has her family to support her. (And from the expression on your young lieutenant's face, perhaps, a suitor after the war if you bring him home with you.)

Your troops are bathing and sleeping in real beds at the school tonight, and we ladies are preparing a hearty feast for them. They will be refreshed for their journey back.

Pennsylvania is too far away, but I understand. I do fear that you will be in greater danger. Nonetheless, the Lord will sustain us. Hold on to your faith and my love.

Always your magic,
Rebekah

She sealed the letter with a kiss and opened the book to read the passage Rennin suggested.

The first thing Cameron did the night after his revelation about his fiancée was to compose a letter to Tammy.

My Darling Tammy,

How I have tried and tried to see you, but you refuse even to talk to me! I am a rake. I always have been, but I love you. I do not wish to have another woman in my life besides you. I've broken my engagement with Lucia. She is a cold, cruel woman who despises my son. I will not have it, for he is the light of my life.

Oh, my darling, I would never have you feel guilty about what transpired between us. It was all my doing. Please, forgive me. I have no excuse but that my love for you clouded my judgment. I would have you for my wife, Tammy, if you would see past your idea that we are not equal. I love you more than I ever thought I could love again. I have loved you since the day you spilled soup all over me. My heart and my home are desolate without you.

I ask your indulgence with the deception regarding this letter, but I knew you would throw it in the fire if you knew it was from me; however, you would never do that to Rowan. For your information, he was complicit in the deception. He knows everything, and he still loves you, perhaps, even more for he thinks of you as his mother. He misses you as much as I. I confess: I am not above pricking your conscience by using your love for him. He told me to do so. Yea, he told me to storm your residence and drag you home.

Please, come back to us. At the very least, see me and talk to me—in public if you would feel more comfortable.

Humbly yours,
Cameron

Rowan addressed the envelope in his child's penmanship and grinned. "This will get her attention, Poppy."

Cameron cocked his head to the side, "Rowan, do your friends mock you for calling me 'Poppy'?"

"Sometimes, but I don't care."

Cameron laughed. "I like it, but if you decide you want to change it to 'Papa', I'll understand."

The two bachelors waited patiently for Tammy's reply. Two days passed before Cameron received a cryptic note:

Saturday, noon, at the Tea Room. Bring Rowan. Miss Martin.

Both Cameron and Rowan grinned as if they had won the war rather than a small skirmish. They dressed in their finest clothes and arrived early at the Tea Room, a place that served tea and delicate finger food. Both knew that they would still be starved after eating there, but food was the furthest thing from their minds.

Tammy arrived promptly at noon. Before she sat down, Rowan threw decorum to the wind and engulfed her in an embrace. She could not refrain from returning the child's affection and hugged him tightly. She smoothed his hair. "At least your father is keeping you groomed nicely."

Cameron pulled out her chair for her.

"Thank you, Mr. O'Rourke."

Cameron sat down and looked at Tammy forlornly. "Must we be so formal?" He reached across the table to take her hand. She pulled it back.

"I came to tell you that I'm engaged. I'm marrying Paul Dodd when he gets back from England."

"Who is Paul Dodd?"

"A sailor I met at the wharf when I went to get fish for the Allgoods' dinner. He never felt comfortable coming to your house." Her voice was dry, without emotion.

"A sailor? He'll be gone half the time. Besides, you do *not* love him."

Tammy looked at Rowan. She was hesitant to speak openly in front of the child. Cameron sensed her distress. They ate their meal in relative quiet. Afterward, Cameron said to his son, "Rowan, the confectioner is just down the street." He handed the boy some coins. "Go and buy us something delicious for dessert. I need to speak to Tammy alone. We'll follow you in a few minutes."

Rowan obeyed, but before he left he kissed Tammy on the cheek. "Tammy, Poppy loves you and so do I. Don't marry somebody else."

Tammy was obviously flustered by the child's comment. When Rowan left, Cameron ordered two glasses of wine and began to plead his case. "Tammy, you know that you love me. Why are you going to marry Paul?"

"He's in my station, Cameron."

"Damn your ridiculous idea! Do you want me to kidnap you? I'll take you back to Mom's Trading Post. Maybe there you won't feel so proper."

"Cameron, this is the way it has to be. I have to be able to hold my head up. I allowed myself to be degraded when I came to your bed. Paul doesn't know. I pray that since it has been so long and we were only together once, he never will."

"I'll tell him. I'll tell him you're mine, and I will *not* let you go."

"You wouldn't!"

"I would."

"Cameron, leave me some dignity."

"Tammy, I would shout it to the world. I love you. I want you to be my wife, not some crude, smelly sailor's wife. You deserve better. Tammy, you're a lady. You'll be miserable married to him. Is that what you truly want?"

"No."

"Then, for God's sake, put your pride aside. Marry me. Let these bigots think what they may. You belong with me."

Tammy shook her head. "I knew I shouldn't have come. Cameron, you have me so confused that I can't think." She stood to leave.

He caught her hand. "Sit down." She did as he requested. "Answer one question for me. Do you love me?"

She finally looked him in the eye. "More than anything."

"Then, don't throw love away."

"I have to think. I'll send you a note."

Cameron and Tammy walked outside together and saw Rowan with a small crate of confections coming toward them. Tammy threw him a kiss as she turned on her way home. "Wait!" called Rowan as he started across the street without looking to see what was coming.

"Rowan, no!" screamed Tammy as she darted out just in time to push him from the path of an oncoming wagon. However, she was not fast enough to move out of the way herself. Her next scream was drowned out by neighing and hooves clomping onto to her body.

"Oh, God! No!" shouted Cameron. He knelt and lifted her into his arms. Seeing the proprietor of the confection shop, he commanded, "Bring the doctor to my house."

Cameron carried Tammy to his bed. George Mason, Cameron's butler, commented judgmentally, "Sir, should you put Miss Tammy in your bed? What will the doctor think?"

Cameron glared at him. "Damn what the doctor thinks! It's where she belongs, you old goat. If you don't like it, you can leave my employ. This woman will be your mistress as soon as I can make it so. Where the hell is the doctor?"

Dr. Gregory Cockrell arrived a few minutes later. He examined Tammy carefully and looked solemnly at Cameron. "It's not good. She was trampled by the horses." He indicated the imprint of a horseshoe across the left side of her face. "She has more on her body. If she survives the next forty-eight hours, there's a good chance she'll pull through. I've done all I can. All you can do is wait and pray."

Cameron sat quietly by the bed and held Tammy's hand, praying that her sacrifice of love would not end in death. Rowan knocked softly at the door. "Poppy, may I come in?"

Cameron held his hand out to Rowan. He pulled the little boy close as the child's tears flowed freely. "I'm sorry, Poppy. I was careless. I just wanted to hug Tammy again. Oh, Poppy, if Tammy dies, you won't go back and marry Lucia, will you?"

"Rowan, first, this was *not* your fault. It was an accident—pure and simple. Second, I would never marry Lucia. I never loved her. If we lose Tammy, it will be you and I always. My heart could not stand falling in love and losing another. I'm not sure it can stand losing Tammy."

"Poppy, talk to her. Make her fight to stay alive. I want Tammy to be my mommy. I love her so much. She's the only mother I've ever known. Surely, she won't leave me. She saved me. Poppy, if Tammy hadn't pushed me, I would be lying there. I owe her my life."

"Me, too, but in a different way. I owe her my emotional life. She resurrected me from an emotional death. Rowan, I want you to go to your room and pray. Pray that Tammy will be all right and pray that she will stay with us and love us as much as we love her."

Rebekah closed her book, fell asleep, and dreamed of Rennin. The next morning, Lieutenant Brooks and his troops ate a bigger breakfast than they would have if they totaled each breakfast for a week. Rebekah gave the lieutenant Rennin's letter. She asked causally, "Lieutenant, are you married?"

"Yes, ma'am. I suppose you asked that because you saw how I looked at Mrs. Pryor. She resembles my wife in coloring and size. I was thinking that could be Brenda. We have a son, Elijah, who is five now. I have not seen him since before he could walk. Mrs. O'Rourke, the colonel has asked me to bring my family here and work for him when the war is over. Please pray that it will be over soon."

"I will, lieutenant, and I'll pray for your safety."

The troops left, and Rebekah kept her word.

Wade Brooks rode into camp and went straight to Rennin's tent. He saluted. "Sir."

"Relax, Wade," Rennin said with a wave of his hand. "Nobody is in the tent but us."

"Yes, Sir. Your letter from Mrs. O'Rourke, Sir." He handed Rennin the envelope.

Rennin held the paper to his nose and inhaled. "Oh! It smells like her."

"May I say, Sir, that your wife is beautiful and quite wonderful?"

"Yes, she is," said Rennin. "Thank you, Wade. I also have something for you." Rennin handed Wade his captain's bars. "Congratulations. It's about time."

Wade beamed. "It means more pay to send home. I sure hope this war is over soon. When do we leave for Pennsylvania?"

"Tomorrow. Colonel Smith came yesterday. He's chomping at the bit to take over. Now, Wade," Rennin held up his letter. "I would like to read my letter in private."

Colonel Rennin O'Rourke and Captain Wade Brooks arrived in Pennsylvania to heavy fighting. "Come in, Colonel," greeted the general. "We've been fighting all day. It's good to have some fresh blood around here."

"I just hope it stays in my body," said Rennin.

"Amusing," the general said. "Colonel, we sent for you because there's a bit of mountain in Pennsylvania that we need to put some tracks through. Our engineers are quite busy elsewhere. Your friend, Chen Li, could do it easily, but he's in Virginia. Since the man is your partner, it's a given that you're rather familiar with blasting, having mined half the gold in California with him. We want you to blast us a tunnel through this area. Take as many men as you need to help."

"I need men who either know how to handle nitroglycerin or are crazy." He chuckled. "I've been told handling nitroglycerin *is* crazy. I want no more than half a dozen men as a blasting crew. After the blasting is done, then I'll need more to complete the tunnel."

The general handed Rennin a folder. "Here are dossiers on a number of men I thought might be helpful. Look them over and choose."

Rennin chose four men from the dossiers and, of course, Wade. They started the three-day trek to the site for the tunnel. On the way, they met numerous wounded soldiers. They were told that the fighting was fierce near Gettysburg and to avoid the area if they were on a special mission or they would most definitely be pulled into the fray.

They reached the Pocono Mountains and the designated spot on July 3, 1863, while the battle raged at Gettysburg. They immediately began to drill pilot holes for the nitroglycerin they had hauled carefully with them.

Once they had the holes drilled, they began the placement of the nitroglycerin. In an urgent whisper, Rennin called, "Wade, don't move. Your canister is leaking."

The men working with Rennin never ceased to marvel at the familiarity between the colonel and the captain. They watched as Wade froze in his tracks. He spoke carefully, "Rennin, what do I do?"

"Slowly put it back in the hay, and then, get the hell out of there."

Wade methodically leaned over the wagon to place the canister back into its protective padding of hay. As if in slow motion the men ran away as Rennin ordered them to get back.

A single drop of the volatile substance clung precariously to the bottom of the canister. Rennin ran with the agility and speed of a puma toward Wade. He snatched the canister and flung it with all his might into the side of the mountain. The single drop landed in the almost empty wagon as Rennin hit Wade with his shoulder and the two sailed through the air.

A loud *BOOM* was followed by a geyser of dirt and pebbles.

Rennin's screams were agonizing. "Rennin! You fool!" Wade yelled. He rolled the much heavier man off him "God! Help me!" he shouted at the other men. Oblivious that his own blood dripped from his hands and forearms and mingled with the blood gushing from Rennin's leg, Wade stripped his shirt and kerchief and tied off the shooting artery.

Rennin grabbed Wade's lapel. "Wade, don't let them take my leg. I already almost lost it once. This is battlefield medicine. They will *not* take the time to care for me the way my stepfather did. You do it."

"What do I do?"

"Wash it every day with saline solution. Please, Wade. I don't want to go home to Rebekah a cripple. Just don't let them take my leg."

Somehow the blasting crew managed to find a field hospital. The attendants washed Wade's arms and hands and bandaged them. He heard Rennin screaming from a nearby cot. "Captain Brooks!"

In horror Wade saw the amputation equipment. "No!" he bellowed and bounded from his cot. "No! I won't let you!"

Three attendants restrained him as he continued to protest. "No, don't. I promised the colonel. He says to wash his leg with saline solution. He knows what he's talking about."

"We don't have any!" snapped the doctor. "This is all I can do to save his life. Now shut up or I will punch you out."

"Please don't," begged Wade. "I'll take care of him."

Over his and Rennin's screams, Wade watched as the doctor cut Rennin's leg off just above the knee.

Rennin awoke to find Wade sleeping with his head buried on his bandaged hands and leaning on Rennin's cot. "Wade, wake up."

Wade jumped at the sound of Rennin's voice. "Oh, God, Rennin, I am so sorry. I tried. I tried so hard. They held me back or I would've taken the saw from that butcher. Can you ever forgive me?"

"It's already forgiven. The doctor did what he had to do. I'm alive. I must remember Henry. He survived losing his leg. I will, too. But how do I tell Rebekah?"

"Be honest. Just write and tell her you're coming home and what to expect. From what I saw, she would love you if you had no arms or legs." Wade held up his shattered hands. "I get to go home too. Is the offer to come and work for you still open?"

"You know it is. When do we get to leave this hell hole and return to the land shining with gold nuggets?"

The doctor walked up. "Well, Colonel O'Rourke, you seem in good spirits. How's the pain?"

"With just a little of that laudanum I can handle it," said Rennin.

"Good because I have very little."

"About the swings I took at you."

"Think nothing of it. I'm used to it. If we were equipped for better care, I would've tried it your way, but out here you would have died within days. At least I'm sending a real man back to his wife. In two or three weeks, barring any infection, I'll sign your release papers and you can go home. Captain Brooks, I have your papers in my hands. You are free to leave day after tomorrow."

"I'll wait for the colonel."

"Don't be silly, Wade." Rennin clucked his tongue. "Go home. I'll meet you in California. You know the way."

"Very well, Rennin. I'll get out there and set up a scrupulous bank for you. Then, I'll triple your money inside a year."

"I don't need the money. I want the smaller investors to be treated fairly. That's what I'm counting on with you. MacMillan will build you a nice house. You, Brenda, and Elijah can bunk at the school until the house is ready." Rennin turned to the doctor.

"Well, Doctor, will you supply me with ink and paper? I would like to prepare my wife for what will be coming home. Doc, don't worry about me. My Lord will sustain me. For the record, He gave me the best wife in the world. She'll deal with this little inconvenience with dignity. The only thing I'll miss is sweeping her up in my arms."

"You can still do that, Colonel. You have two reputable doctors in your neck of the woods from what I've heard. I attended medical school with Dr. Davies. Have them design you a prosthetic device."

"I will. Thank you for saving my life. Now, I just want to go home."

44
Together Again

When Rebekah received her letter from Pennsylvania, she fell, pale as death itself, into a chair. The gathered ladies of Puma Pass asked, "What is it?"

She handed the letter to Caitlin who scanned it quickly and then looked at Rebekah while drawing a sharp breath. She turned to their friends and smile directly at Evelyn. "It seems that Rennin and Henry are now two of a kind. Rennin lost his leg. He also says that nice lieutenant, who was promoted to captain, is coming to Puma Pass to start our very own bank. Rennin says Captain Brooks will probably get here before he does and that Mr. MacMillan should build him a house. Rennin is in good spirits and trusting in the Lord's sufficiency. That's it."

All the women knew that Caitlin had left out some parts, but no one asked about them for they were most likely private. All were broken over Rennin's misfortune, but refrained from making it sound as if his life were over. They all knew Rennin had the ability to rise above his trials and to become stronger because of them.

As Rennin's letter said, Wade Brooks and his family arrived without fanfare. Wade knocked on Rebekah's door. Gabriel answered and shouted, "Momma, it's Captain Brooks."

Rebekah hurried to the door. "Gabriel, invite our guests in next time. Please, come in."

Wade and his family entered reluctantly. "Mrs. O'Rourke, we don't wish to impose upon you. Colonel O'Rourke said we could sleep at the school until our house is ready. If you can show us where you want us, we'll be out of your way," Wade said politely.

"First things first," said Rebekah. "I'm Rebekah. The time for formality is over. Gabriel, take Elijah to the kitchen for some milk and cookies and then out to play with the other children. Now, come in and rest a bit. You'll have supper with me tonight. If I had more room, you would also stay here. Alas, with seven rambunctious children, room is scarce, and the one small extra room is now used by the nanny, Mrs. Gilmore."

"Thank you," said Brenda as she eased into a chair with a sigh. "Oh, my derriere is killing me. The seat on that wagon was so hard."

"Brenda!" Wade said in a chastising voice.

She furrowed her brow. "Wade, Rebekah invited us to rest a bit. I would like to rest a bit. You're being rude."

"Wade, please sit down," said Rebekah.

He sat on the edge of a chair and fidgeted. Rebekah summed up his mood quickly. "Okay, Wade. Why are you so uncomfortable around me? The last time we talked we had a very cordial conversation. Let's clear the air now so that our friendship can grow."

"Mrs. O'Rourke."

"Rebekah."

He nodded. "Rebekah, it's my fault Rennin was wounded. He tried to push me from harm's way. He saved my life. I only got my hands somewhat mutilated, but I did not lose the use of them completely. I'll never be able to do any heavy labor again, so I guess banking is a good profession for me. Rennin says he doesn't blame me, but I blame myself. Even after his heroic act, I wasn't able to keep the doctor from taking his leg, although I tried. I failed my commander and my friend."

"I see," said Rebekah thoughtfully. "You are a horrible person, Wade Brooks. How could you have *possibly* put yourself in harm's way during a war? It is *inconceivable*. Rennin should have let you die."

Wade stared at Rebekah with his mouth agape.

"Is that what you want me to say?" Rebekah asked. She knelt beside the chair where he sat. "Wade, you spent over two years with my husband. Do you ever remember his lying or not saying exactly what he thought?"

"No, ma'am."

"That's because Rennin is honest to a fault and brutally candid. If he says he doesn't blame you, he doesn't blame you. Neither do I. Put the past behind you. You have a beautiful family and a wonderful future ahead of you."

Wade smiled with relief as his confession cleared his conscience. "Yes, ma'am. Now, do you want to show us where you want us?"

"Fine, you can get situated and come back here for supper tonight. Leave Elijah to play. It will be much easier settling in without a little boy underfoot."

Wade was a mild-mannered, even-tempered man with light brown hair and dark brown eyes. He bore his six-foot frame with dignity, and he proved himself to be a proficient banker. Within months of his arrival, even before a bank was actually opened in Puma Pass, the community showed an increase in profits despite the war. Wade thought it wise to invest in the European market for the time being.

Rebekah took an active role in helping get the new bank off the ground. As she looked over the blueprints with Wade and Jacob MacMillan two days before Christmas, the stage came in as it always did on its ususal weekly schedule. Few people of note got off in Puma Pass. The driver delivered mail or packages to the general store, nothing more. However, this time Wade froze in mid-sentence as he looked up. Softly, he said, "Rebekah," and indicated with a nod of his head for her to look at the stage.

She turned to see what Wade wanted her to notice. Rennin, in full dress uniform, hopped from the stage on a pair of crutches. The driver called loudly, "Do you need some help, Colonel?"

"No," said Rennin. "I can manage one bag."

"I think you are going to need some help managing something else," joked the driver. "Look coming your way."

Rennin turned to see Rebekah charging up the street in a most unladylike fashion. Before he could speak, she engulfed him in an embrace and kissed him with joy and relief. "You're finally home!" she squealed.

He put both crutches under his right arm and held Rebekah with his free arm. He kissed her mouth and her face and her neck. He breathed deeply of the fragrance of lemon verbena that she wore that day. "I have missed you. Let's go home. Lock everyone out. I want to be alone with you." Then, he hesitated and looked at his missing limb. "That is if you can look beyond this."

"You still spout gibberish," Rebekah scolded as she picked up the bag, which weighed almost nothing, and they started home.

As they passed the schoolyard, they heard shouts of, "Papa!"

Rebekah laughed. "We won't be locking the door any time soon."

"I can wait a few more hours," said Rennin as seven children, ecstatic to see their father, surrounded him.

Several hours later, Rennin finally leaned back on his own bed. He laughed. "My own bed feels strange."

Rebekah crawled on top of him. "Would you like me to make it feel more familiar?"

He breathed deeply. "Please." He pulled Rebekah closer. "You will never know how much I've missed you. I love you."

"Show me," she whispered, and they spoke no more words.

Rennin and Rebekah slept late the next morning, and no one disturbed them until mid morning. About ten o'clock they heard a timid knock at the door. Rebekah whispered, "Rennin, we are totally undressed at ten o'clock. What will our visitor think?"

"That we are very much in love and making up for lost time."

She giggled. "You never change."

He grew solemn. "But I have changed, Rebekah—more than I can ever tell you." Rennin shook off his melancholy.

When the knock came again, Rennin said, "Put on your robe and toss me those longjohns." When they were covered, he called, "Who is it?"

Michael, the most vocal of the children answered, "Papa, it's us. We have a surprise for you. May we come in?"

Rennin smiled at the happy distraction. "Come in."

The seven children entered bearing a breakfast of flapjacks, sausages, strawberries, and coffee. Keturah brought a bouquet of fresh flowers.

"What a wonderful surprise!" Rennin exclaimed.

The children served their parents breakfast in bed and turned to leave. "Where are you going?" asked Rennin.

"It's Christmas Eve. We have to get ready for tonight," answered Michael.

"Have you had our normal celebration without me?"

"Yes, sir," said Jed, "but..."

"But what, Jed?"

"Well, Mrs. Pryor has a pretty voice, and she has sung my mother's part admirably, but nobody sings 'O, Holy Night' like you. It just hasn't been the same without you."

"And," chimed in Stanley, "although Grandpa did a good job reading the Christmas Story, he doesn't make it come alive like you do."

Ketty crawled onto the bed uninvited and snuggled up beside Rennin, and he placed his arm around her acceptingly. "Papa," she said, "we're going to do something special for Christmas this year."

All the other children chorused, "Shh, Ketty. It's a surprise."

"He won't know how we're going to do it, just that we are."

"Ketty," said Rennin, "if it's a surprise, I can wait."

"Okay. Reverend Henry planned it all. I'll just say that baby Patrick Stone is going to play Baby Jesus if he doesn't cry. If he does, then my dolly gets to do it."

Rennin chortled. "Okay. I can't wait to see the surprise."

The boys stared at Ketty with dagger-like eyes. Rennin furrowed his brow and shook his head at them. Then, he changed the subject. "Do we have a tree?"

"That's what we were going to do," explained Michael.

"Okay, then. Let Momma and me eat and dress. I'll meet you downstairs in an...two hours, and we'll go find a tree together."

Ketty cocked her head to the side. "Papa, can you dig up a tree without your leg?"

Gabriel scolded his younger sister. "Ketty! You are the most tactless person I've ever known."

"It's all right, Gabriel," said Rennin. "Ketty's right. I might have a little trouble. That's why I have six strong sons to help me."

"Yes, sir," said Gabriel, "but I think you can do it if you really want to."

"We'll see," said Rennin. "Now, scoot so I can put on some clothes."

The children scampered downstairs to gather the tools they would need and to wait for Rennin.

The returned war hero released a whispered laugh. "See. I have changed, Rebekah."

"Stop it," she chided. "Before you start wallowing in self-pity, you take a good look at Henry. He does almost everything any other man in this community does. You have more fortitude than anyone I've ever known. This is only a small inconvenience in your life. You'll go on and be an even greater man than you already are. You'll find a way to help those afflicted with an even worse disability. Do you understand me?"

Rennin looked at Rebekah with her firmly set jaw and snapping eyes. "Yes, ma'am," he said, putting the two breakfast trays on the floor. "I've been duly rebuked, and now

I think I should receive my punishment. I'm yours to command. How shall I pay for my shortcomings?"

She caught his drift. "I can think of a few ways. I'm so glad we're together again," she said as she straddled him.

"Rebekah?"

"Shut up. *I'm* in command here."

Rennin and the children went tree hunting as soon as the children gulped their lunch. Mabel and Mrs. Gilmore scolded them; they laughed at the women. Then, all of them including Mabel's son, Seth, and Rennin's little brother, Roland, left with Rennin while Rebekah and Mabel decorated with holly and spruce boughs before they prepared the food for the evening.

Weeks before, the children had already chosen a small cedar, so they took Rennin directly to the tree. The man commented, "This shouldn't be too hard. Ketty, hold these." He handed the little girl his crutches. "Chris and Stephen, hold the shovel steady for me. Seth and Roland, hold the burlap sack open. Michael, you will need to grab the tree when it's loosened. Jed, when I step on the left side of the shovel, you step on the right side. Gabriel and Stanley, help me keep my balance."

Three times they tried this arrangement, and three times they fell. After the third fall, Rennin lay on the ground laughing so hard his sides ached. "Papa," said Ketty impatiently, "we will never get the tree dug up like this. If you can't do it, move and let the boys do it. They've done it for two Christmases."

For the first time, Rennin glared disapprovingly at the little girl. "Ketty, you're being very ugly. I'll have you know that I can do this alone. I only asked the boys to help for fun. Adjust your attitude or go home and wait. Remember this— all of you. My hands are not missing. I can still spank you."

Ketty's lips pouted, and her eyes welled tears. Rennin pointed at her. "Drop one tear, and you go home."

She blinked hard to keep the tears back. "I'm sorry, Papa."

"You're forgiven. Come here and give me a hug." He hugged the little girl. "Okay. Now, everybody stand back. If I lose my balance, catch me."

Rennin methodically hopped from the ground to the shovel repeatedly until he had encircled the little tree and it popped loose from the ground. "Boys, put it in the sack."

Ketty beamed and put her arms around Rennin's waist. "You're still the same papa. You can do anything."

"I can't run," said Rennin with a wink.

"You can get a wooden leg like Reverend Henry," Ketty said with vigorous nodding. "He runs a little slow, but he can run."

"I'll do that. Then, he and I will have a race. Let's take our tree home."

The Christmas Eve celebration took on its old flavor with Rennin home. The Brooks family was thrilled to be included. The community seemed almost whole again, but Sarah was still in mourning, though she tried for Kristen and Keith to act normally.

Rennin never ceased to be impressed with Rebekah's capability to care for details. With his homecoming he had brought small trinkets for each person, which he happily translated into Christmas gifts, but Rebekah had furnished a lavish Christmastime in his absence. His pride in the gift God had given him swelled enormously.

Admitting that he was worn to a frazzle, Rennin and Rebekah played Santa and went to bed. The Christmas pageant the children put on the next morning was rather enjoyable even if "Baby Jesus" did cry at the end. Christmas Day passed peacefully, and Gabriel and Michael celebrated their thirteenth birthday without a hitch.

Rennin and Rebekah retired early that night, and he said to his wife. "I want to read to you. Where are you so we can get back to our routine? I need our stability."

She handed him the old copy of their book with a ribbon at her place. She did not tell him it was her second time through. She let him believe he was thrilling her for the first time.

Cameron refused to leave Tammy's bedside. Rowan took it upon himself to send a message to Rennin describing all that had transpired and his father's gloom. Upon receiving the letter, Rennin saddled a horse and packed lightly for fast riding. He well remembered Cameron's depression when Holly had died, and he knew his son needed him. What he did not expect was Morgan dressed in breeches and ready to ride with him.

Rennin said to her, "Morgan, I can ride faster alone."

"I'm going, and that's that. Cameron might need my magic."

"Morgan, you've not practiced magic in years."

"Draco told me to go. Now, are were going to argue, or are we going to ride?"

"I won't countermand Draco ever again. I well remember his ring of fire." He held up his hand. "We're going to ride, and to hell with what Bostonians will think when they see a woman dressed like a man ride into town."

"I have a couple of changes of clothes for the city."

Rennin saddled a second horse, and Morgan slung her pack onto its back.

They rode swiftly with little rest until they reached Cameron's side. A trip that normally took weeks pushing with a laden wagon, took them only eight days. When they arrived, they found Cameron by Tammy's bedside, and an untouched tray of food on the nightstand. Cameron had neglected his personal grooming. His hair was greasy, his beard was full, and he smelled horrible. Tammy still had not regained consciousness, though the doctor came every day to check her progress and force water and broth through her lips.

Cameron stood momentarily to greet them. "How did you know to come?"

"Rowan had the presence of mind to send a courier," said Rennin with a scowl.

Morgan spoke sharply to Cameron. "Cam, do you think you're helping Tammy by allowing yourself to go?"

"I don't want to leave her, Momma."

"Well, you *are* right this minute. You're going to bathe, shave, and change clothes. Good, Lord! I don't blame Tammy for staying asleep. She would probably vomit if she smelled you."

"Momma!"

"Shut up! Rennin, take care of this imbecile. I'll sit with Tammy until you get back. Then, you're going to eat. You must have lost twenty pounds. You look like a walking skeleton. If you argue with me, I will slap you silly—or should I say sillier? I am still your mother."

Cameron had learned many years earlier not to attempt to argue with Morgan if she was angry. He obediently went with his father and did as he was told. Rennin helped Cameron as if he were a child. Cameron choked out only a few words. "I'm so tired, Daidí, and I'm so scared. She's wasting away. A month, and I can't get any response from her. The doctor has given up hope. He says she's going to die, and he's surprised she has lasted this long. Paul, the man she planned to marry, came. He said he couldn't wait for her forever. Of that, I'm glad. He married the serving wench at the tavern. Tammy is completely free."

"I know, Cam," said Rennin soothingly. "We won't give up."

Cameron relaxed in the tub and let his father bathe him.

Meanwhile, Morgan sat beside Tammy. She took the girl's hand and stroked her brow. She let go abruptly and jumped away from the bedside. "Rennin! Cameron! Get in here!" she screamed.

The two men darted into the room with Cameron still half-groomed and with only a towel wrapped around him. He dripped water on the floor as he asked, "Momma, what's wrong?"

"I heard her thoughts when I held her hand."

"What?" asked Rennin.

"She's terrified. She's in a very dark, scary place. She's trying to wake up, but something evil is holding her back. She's just as afraid of the light she sees ahead of her. She knows if she steps through the light, she can never come back. And somewhere to the side she hears large flapping wings and a soft voice from a sparkling white creature telling her to hold on until the magic comes."

"Momma, how can I help her?"

"I don't know, Cam. I'm not sure you can. She has to fight this battle herself."

"Momma, if you heard her thoughts, maybe she can hear yours. Talk to her. Deliver messages for me—for Rowan."

Morgan nodded. "Finish cleaning up. Eat something and come back. We'll try to get through to her."

Cameron was back in less than an hour, looking and smelling much better. Rowan followed him. Morgan said, "Well, I suppose we're ready to try this."

Morgan started to take Tammy's hand again, but she was interrupted as George knocked. "Mr. Cameron, sir, there is a young woman downstairs. She came here from Salem and asked me to deliver this envelope to you."

In confusion, Cameron opened the sealed envelope to find a weird message.

Mr. O'Rourke,

It is not necessary for you to know who I am. You need only to know I have come to help. I have been outside your house for several days. Only when the petite one arrived did I know the time was right. She shares my gift—magic, and you believe in it for you have seen it first hand. I will not say a word. I would not endanger your life. If you will have my help, send all your servants to the church to pray when your butler tells me to come up.

The note was unsigned. Cameron handed the note to his mother. "It's your decision," said Morgan after she read the note. Rennin read over her shoulder.

"George, what does the girl look like?" asked Rennin, wary of the stranger.

"She's quite beautiful. She's very tall and buxom. She has jet-black hair and eyes just as dark. Her mouth is crimson, and she is wearing black. She is very...*alluring*."

Rennin and Morgan exchanged looks. Rennin said, "George, wait outside for a moment." When the butler had closed the door, Rennin said, "Tell her to go away, Cameron. Have your servants pray downstairs. Tell her *yourself* to go away." He reached into his pocket and pulled out an emerald on a chain. "This was my father's. He wore it to vanquish Quazel. I did not know he had slipped it in my trunk until we were far out to sea, and I don't know why I brought it today, except that I think I heard Draco tell me to. I think you should wear it when you go downstairs. Put it inside your shirt. Do *not* let her see it."

"Daidí, you can't seriously believe that is *Quazel* downstairs."

"Not Quazel herself, but something evil. Morgan said that something evil is holding Tammy back, and she's afraid. Cameron, don't sell your soul, or perhaps Tammy's soul, to the devil. If this woman looks normal when you go down—just like George said—bring her up."

Cameron took the amulet and dropped it around his neck and inside his shirt. He went out the door. "George, I'd like to speak to this woman alone."

"Yes, sir."

Cameron stopped on the stairs as the woman stood in the foyer with her back to him. A shiver ran down his spine and when he spoke, his breath formed a mist on the rapidly chilled air. "Miss?" The woman turned around. Cameron gripped the banister, but kept his composure. "Ma'am thank you for your offer, but Tammy would *not* approve. I must ask you to leave my home."

The face Cameron saw was anything but beautiful. It was contorted and disfigured. A wicked smirk spread across her face and a rasping voice said, "You *are* Aidan O'Rourke's grandson—prudent and distrusting just like him. What do you see, Cameron?"

"A hideous monster."

"You have your grandfather's talisman." She tilted her head to the side and sighed. "I did not know it had left Draconis." The woman opened the door to leave. "Tell Tammy to run toward the light. It's her only escape." The creature left the house.

Cameron shouted, "George!"

"Yes, sir?" the aging butler said from down the hall.

"Gather the household. I want you *all* to pray for a miracle and protection from evil. Please?"

The butler started down the stairs. Cameron said, "George, I'm sorry for speaking to you so sharply when I brought Tammy home. I love her, George. I want to marry her. I don't care about her station in life."

"I hope she accepts your proposal, sir," said George. "She's a lovely young woman." George went to gather the servants.

Cameron went back into the bedroom. "You were right, Daidí. I must be more vigilant. I'm so glad Rowan doesn't have green eyes. Momma, that thing said Tammy should run toward the light."

"Then, that's what she should do," said Morgan.

"Why? How can you trust her?"

"I don't, Cameron. Don't you understand? She expected you to do the opposite of what she said; therefore, she told you the truth. She tried to trick you."

Morgan took Tammy's hand. "Tammy, if you can hear me at all, squeeze my hand."

She felt a slight pressure on her hand. "She can hear me, Cameron. Tammy, don't be afraid. I'm here to get you out of that dark place. Cameron is here. He loves you so much, and he needs you to come back to him. Rowan is here, too. He wants you to be his mommy. I can feel your fear and confusion. Listen to my voice. Tune the others out. Go toward the light, but do not go *into* the light. Rebuke what ever is holding you back in the name of Jesus. That's it, honey. Go toward the light."

Tammy mumbled, "Cameron."

Morgan handed Tammy's hand to Cameron. "Talk to her now. She can hear you."

"Tammy," Cameron said softly. "Come on. Fight. Come back to me. I love you. I *will* marry you. Open your eyes. Tell me you'll be my wife."

Rowan took her other hand and chimed in, "Tammy, please. I love you too. I choose you to be my mother. Poppy needs you to keep him straight. We can't live without you."

Cameron kissed Tammy's fingertips and prayed aloud, "Oh, Lord, I know I don't deserve this woman, but I love her, Lord. I know You sent her to me. Please keep her safe and bring her back from wherever she is."

Again, Tammy murmured, "Cameron."

"I'm right here."

"Cameron," she said more loudly. All of a sudden, Tammy's eyes popped open. "Cameron!"

"I'm right here, darling. Welcome back."

She lifted a very weak hand to Cameron's face. "Yes, I'll marry you. Near the light I saw a glistening white dragon. Its voice told me to go home and marry Cameron. I dared not disobey it."

Cameron laughed tearfully. "That was Draco. I'm glad to hear you say that."

"Draco?"

"A dragon on Draconis. I'll tell you all about it."

"Draco said, 'The magic is here.'"

"That's because Momma has battled the darkness before and won. I'll tell you about it when you're healed. Now, let's get you strong enough to follow through with that promise."

"Cameron, I tried to wake up. I could hear you, but I couldn't wake up. I was so scared. Something dark had its hands on me and wouldn't let go. When your mother touched me, the dark thing got scared and loosened its grip. Ask me again. Ask me now that I'm awake."

"Tammy Patrice Martin, I love you. I love you more than I ever thought I could love again. You rescued me from an emotional void. You filled an emptiness in me. I want to spend the rest of my life with you. Will you marry me?"

"Yes. Yes. I love you, Cameron. I won't fight my feelings for you any longer. I'll throw caution to the wind for you. I'm so happy to be together again. Yes, I'll marry you. I'll spend the rest of my life making you happy."

"Well," said Rennin. "I suppose we can stay for a wedding."

Tammy looked at Cameron. "You'll have to pay for it. I don't have any money to pay for a big wedding, and I want this whole town to know I'm marrying you—especially Lucia Allgood."

Cameron chortled. "We'll be sure to invite her. I suppose we should thank her for throwing us together."

"Oh, Cameron. You don't know how mean she really is. She treated me much worse than Lucretia ever did. Lucretia never hit me."

"Lucia hit you?"

"Yes."

"The scars?"

"Not Papa. Lucia was very angry after you left that first night. I had embarrassed her. She beat me with a strap."

"Dear God! I swear no one will ever hurt you again. Why didn't you tell me? Why did she send you to work here?"

"Lucretia insisted. I thought you belonged in her social circle. I was ashamed that I allowed myself to fall in love with you."

"Tammy, you're beautiful and kind and loving and genuine. You're what I want and need—not social circles."

"I know that now. All I want is to be your wife." Tammy turned toward Rowan. "And your mother."

Rowan crawled onto the bed and put his arms around her. "I love you, Mommy. You saved my life."

"I would do it again. I love you, Rowan."

"I'm glad we're going to be a family."

"Me, too."

Cameron and Tammy's wedding left tongues and heads wagging for years to come. Almost the entire population of Mom's Trading Post came to Boston, except Donovan and Emily Claire because Emily Claire was due to deliver their third child any day. Duncan served as Cameron's best man because he had so unceremoniously warned Cameron against marrying Lucia years before.

As the wedding party celebrated, a note came for Cameron. He read it, and his face turned pale. He found Ian and showed him the note. Ian said, "I'll take care of it." He found Lucretia and they sneaked away from the reception with the note in hand.

Ian returned before Cameron left to take Tammy for a week at the inn on the cape. Ian caught Cameron's eye and shook his head sadly. Cameron excused himself and went to Ian. "What happened?"

"She really did it, Cameron. She jumped. She's dead. We didn't get there in time. Lucretia is devastated, but she doesn't blame you. She believes Lucia was crazy."

"Ian, what can I do to ease her pain?"

"Be happy. Cameron, I think I should tell you: Their mother committed suicide, too. They don't tell anyone for the shame of it. Lucretia is worried she'll lose her mind someday, too. I have to convince her otherwise."

"Tell her I said she should not fear. The Lord is with her, and she is well-loved."

The two men embraced each other. "Go to your wife," said Cameron. "Give her my love and condolences. I'm going on my honeymoon. I won't allow Lucia to ruin this for Tammy. Even in death she would try to hurt her. Don't say a word to Tammy. I'll tell her when we get back."

"Congratulations, partner. She's terrific. Cherish her always." Ian left unobserved.

The young ladies gathered around for Tammy to throw her bouquet. Rachel placed herself strategically in the line of fire and came away with the prize. At the sight, Ryan made his way to stand beside Rennin. "Uncle Rennin, it has been ten years."

Rennin turned slowly to look at the boy who grinned triumphantly. "So it has. What does my daughter say?"

"Why do you think she caught the bouquet?"

"Ryan, you must court her officially for at least one year."

"Yes, sir. In one year, I'll ask you again for her hand in marriage."

Morgan slipped under Rennin's arm. "Interesting conversation. They're all almost grown and on their own. When do we go home? You promised."

"Morgan, I don't know. What if Draconis is no longer visible to ordinary men and I'm not an exceptional man?"

"But you are, my love, as are your children."

"Are you ready to leave them, Morgan?"

"No. Not just yet. I'd like to see a few more grandchildren. I was just wishing and missing, especially since we both received some sort of message from Draco."

"Do you want to send a message home?"

"It's been so long. I'm not sure I can."

"You can. Let's find a quiet spot as soon as the bride and groom leave."

When Cameron and Tammy were on their way, Morgan and Rennin found a place to hide. Morgan sent a message on the wings of a dove telling all that she could remember and expressing the desire to be together again.

"As are Rennin's descendants," said Rebekah. "You, my love, are the most exceptional, extraordinary man I know. I love you. You have a promise to keep someday, too. We have to find Draconis."

"It might be harder now," said Rennin indicating his leg.

"We'll manage. We always have. But for now, let's sleep. Our children are not nearly on their own."

During the spring of 1864, Rennin received an unusual letter from Jean Henri Dunant telling him of an organization he was starting to aid victims in the battlefield. Part of the letter said:

As a casualty of war yourself, you have seen the need for better medicine on the battlefield. If you can help fund this organization, I would be deeply in your debt. Perhaps, something in your own country once it is reunited and healed can arise from my humble example.

Rennin thought and prayed about the situation for some time before he sent Monsieur Dunant a draft for fifty thousand dollars.

More time passed before Gabriel dropped a newspaper in Rennin's lap. The headline read: **LEE SURRENDERS! WAR ENDS!** Rennin dropped his face in his hands and wept.

The community in Puma Pass put life back on an even keel. Chen Li came home to a jubilant crowd. He received a hero's welcome with hugs from everyone. When he got to Sarah he held her longer. Before she could help herself, she sobbed in Chen Li's arms. After two years, she allowed herself to cry. "Oh, Chen, what am I to do without Baxter? He won't be coming home."

"You have two wonderful children to keep their father's memory alive. Maybe now is the time for you to begin a career. There are many things for you to consider. Your life isn't over."

Sarah pulled herself together and life went on. One morning as she hung her laundry out to dry, she saw a figure in the distance walking up the road on a day when the stage would not be coming. The figure was strangely familiar, but she shook off the eerie feeling and continued with the clothes.

Again, Sarah watched the figure as it came a little closer. It seemed to be limping. She went to the wash pot to get the load of white clothes. The figure appeared to be headed straight for her house. Sarah's heart pounded. She looked more closely at the figure that was still three quarters of a mile away. Sarah gasped and dropped the basket of clothes. As fast as her feet could carry her, she ran to meet the figure in total disbelief. Nonetheless, no power on Earth could have kept her from going.

When the figure saw that she had recognized him, he, too, ran. The whole way Sarah, called in amazement, "Baxter!" They met in the street with an embrace that Sarah would not release. She rubbed his face and his body. "You're real. You're not an apparition. They said you were dead. You had been hanged. Oh, my God. You're alive!"

Sarah wept tears of joy. Baxter consoled her. "Don't cry, darling. They tried to hang me. Don't laugh."

She shook her head.

"I saw a gray dragon. He told me I would not die. The noose broke. Can you believe it? They tried again, and the beam on the gallows cracked. Sarah, it was miraculous. After that, they refused to try again. I was a prisoner in the bayous of Louisiana. Down there they're superstitious enough to think I had some kind of voodoo power. They refused to kill me. If I had told them about the dragon, they would probably have worshipped me. I've been a prisoner of war all this time and treated with reverence, but they wouldn't let me write; and I couldn't escape though I tried several times. I'm home now, darling. I sent you a letter the minute I was released."

"I never got the letter. I thought you were dead."

Baxter held Sarah close. "I'm very much alive, and I will never leave you again—not for any cause. We're together again, and that's the way it will stay."

The commotion brought other people from their homes. Beatrice Pryor saw who it was and joined Sarah and Baxter in the street, oblivious to what decorum dictated for the first time in her life. Rebekah brought Kristen and Keith to their father. Baxter saw his son for the first time and held the daughter he had not seen in years.

The joy in Puma Pass was at last complete for they were all together again.

45
Progress

After the war, progress came swiftly to the West. Construction began in earnest on a transcontinental railroad. Chen Li contacted the proper authorities about working for the railroad in the engineering department. He was sorely distressed to hear that Theodore Judah had died while he was away in the war. After numerous letters, Chen Li was finally contacted to work out of San Francisco. He was told that there would be a large Chinese contingency working for the railroad and he would be in charge of them.

Some time later, Chen Li wrote to Rennin telling him of the mistreatment of the Chinese laborers. His comments disturbed Rennin greatly when he said, "*Their treatment is not much more than slave labor. Didn't we just fight a war to end slavery?*" He asked Rennin what to do to make life easier for his men as he had come to know them.

Rennin set about to bring change in many areas by running for the state legislature. As a congressman, he felt he could influence more change than as a private citizen. Rennin won a seat in the state legislature. One of his first proposals was for fair labor practices regarding Chinese immigrants.

Even after a small victory on paper, the actual practices changed very little. Chen Li stayed in constant contact with Rennin and informed him of the actuality of events. Rennin wrote his dear friend back:

Chen,

There is little I can do to change the hearts of evil men. Not only have I heard these things from you regarding cruel and inhumane labor practices, but also both Mitchell and Wade have written with concerns about the financial integrity of the men in charge of the railroad. I fear the two are connected. I have begun a covert investigation into the situation. Please keep your faith and support your subordinates in a Godly manner. Also, although I am not a supporter of labor unions, necessity sometimes requires drastic action. I cannot in good conscience advise you in this regard. You would be better served by discussing the legalities with Baxter. You know he's a good man and will do what is fair and just.

I keep you in my prayers as I hope you do me. I remain your constant and abiding friend.

Rennin

Chen Li knew Rennin was correct. Overtly he did what he could to make life easier for the men he oversaw, but he covertly wrote to Baxter and sought his advice.

Baxter returned Chen Li's letter:

Chen,

As of today, labor unions are illegal. You could go to jail for such a suggestion. You would most definitely be the target of retaliation by unscrupulous men. You could even be killed. Think of Mai and your children before you act rashly. Do nothing—and I mean _nothing_—without contacting me. I agree with your theory and your principles, and I will support you one hundred percent. However, I cannot help a dead man.

Chen, for all those who love you, be careful. You are respected among your employers, and some of them will listen to you. Seek the ones who are fair. Avoid the others. I believe that they might hesitate to harm you because of your connections, but evil works in darkness and secrecy. Send for me if you need me.

Sarah sends her love and knows all that has passed between us. I will keep no secrets from her. She is concerned for your safety. Take care, my friend.

Baxter

Through the years, Chen Li strove to provide safer working conditions and better wages for the Chinese who looked to him for leadership. During that time, the men in charge of the Union Pacific Railroad and the Central Pacific Railroad changed numerous times and scandal in the financial sector was uncovered.

The work was slow and hard, especially in the Sierra Nevada Mountains where Chen Li's men worked tirelessly, and he oversaw the technical aspect of blasting through the rock. Chen Li lost numerous men during this dangerous time. Finally, he went to Charles Crocker and demanded to be allowed to take the proper steps to ensure the men's safety. "Either let me do it, or my men walk."

A greedy grin spread across Crocker's face. "Chen, I can replace them with new workers for less money."

"Perhaps," replied Chen Li, "but they won't be trained, and the work will go more slowly. Moreover, you can't replace *my* expertise and me quite so easily. You'll lose this race you've started and your ten-thousand-dollar bet."

Fingers laced across his midsection, Crocker sat back and appraised the man before him. "You have more gumption than any of your fellow country men. Why is that?"

"Mr. Crocker, I'm an American. I'm a naturalized citizen. My children are American born. I've spent most of my life under the tutelage of Congressman Rennin O'Rourke. He has been my mentor and friend since I was thirteen. I fought for this country to preserve the Union. I left the engineering corps as a decorated captain. Most importantly, I'm a Christian. I have true faith. Mr. Crocker, I don't do this work because I need the money. I'm a partner in the mines at Puma Pass. I have more money than I can ever spend. No, I've dreamed of seeing a transcontinental railroad since I was a boy. This is a dream come true for me. Theodore Judah promised me a hand in this endeavor years ago when I was a student at Columbia College. But if it will better serve my fellow man to walk away, I'll do it."

"You really would. You would leave me in a lurch." Crocker sat forward. "Very well, Chen. Take more precautions for your men, but don't run me into the ground. I want to win this bet."

"I'll do my best. Thank you, sir." Chen Li felt as if a burden had been lifted from his soul. He knew accidents could still occur, but the casualty list would be smaller with safety measures.

The work continued at a steady, but safer pace; and with better management, productivity increased. Even the men on the graveyard shift made better time and laid more track with their minds at ease about their personal safety.

The race continued, and the controversy heated up over the financial practices of certain men in power. On April 28, 1869, Crocker won his bet when his crew laid more than ten miles of track in twelve hours. On May 10, 1869, the final golden spike was nailed into the laurel ties joining East and West at Promontory Point, Utah. Dignitaries for both railroads were present. Both Thomas Durant and Leland Stanford missed hitting the spike to drive it home with the sledgehammer. Neither possessed the physical ablity for repeated tries. Charles Crocker whispered something to Leland Stanford who called Chen Li over to him. "I understand that Crocker could not have gotten here first if it had not been for you." He handed Chen Li the sledgehammer. "Drive her home. Fulfill your spirit's desire."

Rennin did not spend all his time in Sacramento. He had learned how to order his priorities. He enjoyed watching his children grow and spent as much time as possible with them either by going home to Puma Pass or by bringing his family to the capital. The O'Rourke family maintained a home in both places.

Rennin's heart almost failed him the day the four oldest boys left for college in the east; however he was not surprised when Jed landed a job at a publishing company in New York and decided to stay there. Neither was Rennin surprised when Jed married Misty Newman though she was five years his senior.

Stanley pursued a career in medicine, specializing in the treatment of burns, a direct result of his childhood. He came home to Mercier Memorial Hospital to practice medicine, but he later became involved in the establishment of the first research hospital in the United States and the founding of the American Red Cross with Clara Barton. While in medical school, Stanley met and married a young nurse named Arlene Peele, who worked by her husband's side.

The most distressing event in the lives of Rennin's children was when both Gabriel and Michael returned to Puma Pass intent on marrying Shasta Lamar. The little girl, who had refused to take a nap, had grown into a ravishing dark-haired beauty. Both boys had always vied for her attention, but neither had ever seriously courted her. The anger, resentment, and jealousy between the two boys built an almost insurmountable wall between them. Rennin was heartbroken that the twins could live in the same house and not speak to each other.

Finally, at his wits' end concerning how to reconcile the two boys, he called a family meeting with Henry, Evelyn, and Shasta present. Rennin confronted the boys with their behavior and Shasta with hers for not putting an end to the feud. "You two are acting worse than Jacob and Esau, fighting over Shasta as if she were a prize. I'm sure she has an opinion. Speaking of that, Shasta, you can stop this ridiculous feud this minute. Make a choice."

"All right," said Shasta. "While you two idiots have been acting so absurdly, I made my choice." She held out her hand, which supported a wedding ring. "Stephen and I eloped last week, and none of you"—She surveyed the entire assembly— "knew the difference. Now that the cat is out of the bag, you two can grow up." Shasta stood haughtily. "I'm going to find my husband and start my home officially."

Henry put his face in his hands. "Thank God she's out of my house. I do feel sorry for Stephen."

"Henry!" said Evelyn.

"That woman is a handful, but she is no longer my handful." Henry grinned at his wife and then looked at Gabriel and Michael. "You two have a lot of making up to do. Your father was right. The two of you should never let a woman or anything else come between you. You're more than brothers. You were once one. Go off somewhere together and make progress in mending your broken relationship."

Gabriel and Michael sheepishly left the room together. Before they left the front porch, they embraced each other and started making plans for their future.

"Well," said Michael. "I'm joining the Navy. I always wanted to go to sea. Now, I have nothing holding me here."

"I'm staying here to take over the business for Papa," said Gabriel. "I have a feeling I need to stay close to Momma for a while."

"What's wrong with Momma?"

"I don't know. It's just a feeling I have."

"You'll send for me if you need me, right?"

"You know I will."

At the end of the week, Michael left to join the Navy, and Gabriel went to San Francisco to interview a new schoolteacher for his uncle, who asked him to take over as headmaster since his health was becoming poor. Olaf simply wanted to retire. Gabriel agreed.

Gabriel arrived in San Francisco early, so he visited some of the better shops to buy something for his mother. He continued to have a nagging feeling about her. As he browsed the window of a jewelry store, he turned around to leave and collided with a young woman, knocking her and all of her packages to the ground. He apologized profusely and received, "It's all right. Don't worry about it," as a reply. "Nothing is broken. I've survived worse." The young woman had a charming southern drawl. Her auburn hair reminded Gabriel of a fireworks display on the Fourth of July. Her brown eyes showed depth of character.

Gabriel helped the young woman pick up her strewn items. "May I help you take your things somewhere?"

"Oh, thank you, but I must hurry. I have a meeting in a few minutes. Thank you though." The fireworks display disappeared down the street.

"Gorgeous," Gabriel whispered.

"Sir?" said the proprietor of the store as he came out to see what the commotion was.

Gabriel asked, "Who is that young woman?"

The proprietor replied, "I don't know, sir. She's new in town."

"Never mind. I'd like to purchase the pearls in the window."

"Excellent choice, sir. Who's the lucky young lady?"

Gabriel laughed. "My mother."

Gabriel went to the Green Gable Hotel dining room for his business lunch. "Mr. O'Rourke, my word, you look like your father," said the maitre'd.

"I'll take that as a compliment," joked Gabriel. "Has Miss Deborah Fischer arrived yet? I'm supposed to have lunch with her."

"Yes, sir. Right this way."

The man led Gabriel to a table in the back. "Miss Fischer, Mr. O'Rourke has arrived."

The woman turned around, and Gabriel turned ten shades of red as he stammered, "Miss Fischer, so we meet again."

The woman held her composure. "Yes, only this time I have no packages. I hope the earlier incident will have no bearing on what you think of me."

"None whatsoever. How do you like California so far?"

"It's very pleasant."

"Miss Fischer, where are you from?"

"Natchez, Mississippi. My uncle, Howard Musgrave, suggested I contact Mr. Rennin O'Rourke about a teaching position at his school. I think you're a mite young to be my uncle's old acquaintance. Somehow, I don't think that they were actually friends. I think they disagreed very much in principle. I only went to live with my uncle because my father was killed in the war, and my mother was already dead."

As Gabriel took his seat across the table from the woman he explained, "Rennin is my father. He's a congressman now, and my uncle has retired as headmaster of the school. I'm the new headmaster." He touched his chest lightly. "We have enough students now to divide the courses. Just how would you teach history in light of the very recent war?"

"That's a fair question, considering I'm a Southerner, but my application was for algebra. Mr. O'Rourke, I'm about the same age as you. I wasn't much more than a child during the war. In principle, I agree with freeing the slaves; however, I've seen the destruction and devastation the Union army left on my home. Ten years ago, sir, I would not have been a teacher. I would have been spoiled and pampered. Perhaps, it was to the betterment of my character to have had the war."

"My father bought one of your uncle's slaves years ago, only to free her, of course."

"Yes, Mabel. I vaguely remember. Is she still with your family?"

"Yes. So is your cousin, her son, Seth." He dipped his head back and forth and toyed with his water glass as he made the declaration.

"Ah, yes." Deborah laughed a little bitterly. "My uncle was and is a scoundrel. He's an old reprobate. You see, he not only liked his slave girls, but he would have had his way with me also if I had not brained him with the fire poker. I'm exceedingly glad to be away from him. You see, Mr. O'Rourke, I do have a temper, and I will *not* have a man trifle with me." Deborah reached into her bag and handed Gabriel some papers. "Here are my credentials. If they meet with your satisfaction, I hope you'll hire me."

Gabriel reviewed the documents carefully. "You are highly qualified, Miss Fischer, and I like you. You're hired."

"Because you like me or because I'm qualified?"

Gabriel arched his right eyebrow. "I'm not trifling with you, but I do like you. Is there any reason I should *not* like my employees?"

"I suppose not."

They ate lunch and discussed important and trivial matters until Gabriel said, "We leave for Puma Pass in the morning. Ten years ago I would have warned you that we had a pet puma, but no longer. Patty died a couple of years ago."

"Mr. O'Rourke, you sound like a sad little boy."

"Patty was special. She was a member of the family. She's actually buried in the cemetery and has a grave marker."

"Please tell me about her."

Gabriel told Deborah the Patty saga and had her laughing and crying alternately. As they left the restaurant very late, Gabriel offered Deborah his arm. "You're not staying in this hotel?"

"I'm afraid I couldn't afford the prices here."

"I see. Where are you?"

"The bed and bath far up the street."

"No," said Gabriel. "That is no place for a lady. Let's get your things. I'll pay for your room here tonight."

"That would not be proper either."

"I didn't say you would be sharing my room." Gabriel smiled. "Although, that would be pleasant."

"Mr. O'Rourke!"

"Oh, be quiet," he said as he stopped between streetlamps. He took Deborah's face in his hands and kissed her. She responded with enthusiasm. "I have wanted to do that since this morning," he confessed after he released her.

"Mr. O'Rourke, do you believe in love at first sight?"

"I do now."

"Really?"

"Deborah, I would go to the justice of the peace tonight and take you home as my wife if you would agree."

"How scandalous! Where does he live?"

Gabriel laughed. "My mother would kill me."

"And hate me."

"Let's go." he grabbed her hand and crossed the street toward Judge Parker's home.

"Gabriel, are you serious?" Deborah asked as she caught his arm.

"Absolutely."

"But you hardly know me."

"Take a chance."

"What about my teaching?"

"You can teach. I won't mind."

"What about babies?"

"I hope you want some."

"I do, a whole passel."

"Then, why are you hesitating?" He paused long enough to look her in the eye.

"It seems so crazy. How can we be in love? We've known each other only a few hours."

"It seems right to me."

"Me too. All right. Yes. Let's get married."

Half an hour later, Gabriel and Deborah walked out the door of Judge Parker's home as husband and wife. She, indeed, shared his room at the Green Gable Hotel and gave herself to him without reservation. The next day, he bought a new rig and drove his bride home in style.

As they approached Puma Pass, Deborah became agitated. "I am so nervous."

"Leave everything to me," Gabriel said comfortingly.

He drove straight home and helped her from the buggy. She clung to his arm as they walked inside. Gabriel called, "Momma and Papa, come in here. I have someone for you to meet."

Rennin and Rebekah came in laughing. "Is this our new schoolmarm?" asked Rennin.

"Yes and no," replied Gabriel. "Let me introduce you. I proudly present Deborah Fischer O'Rourke."

Deborah tightened her grip on Gabriel's arm, Rebekah sat down on the couch, and Rennin said, "Repeat that."

"Deborah is my wife. Momma, don't get bent out of shape. I know we just met, but, well, it was love at first sight. There. That is the long and short of it."

"I'm not upset," said Rebekah. "Surprised that you would pull a stunt like this rather than Michael, but not upset." She looked up at her son with her dove gray eyes misty. "I know about love at first sight. I knew I would never leave your father the first day I met him. It's just that I'm being cheated out of all my weddings—Jed, Stanley, Stephen, and you."

Rebekah stood and went to Deborah. She held her arms out to the young woman. "You must be terrified. Come here. Welcome to the family." She embraced the girl. "I suppose I can throw a grand reception."

Deborah breathed a sigh of relief. "Thank you. I was scared."

Rennin hugged Deborah, too, and welcomed her. Although he silently fumed at Gabriel's action, he knew what was done, was done. This young woman was his daughter-in-law, and he would learn to love her.

Rebekah sat back on the couch. "I'll plan your reception tomorrow. Timothy MacMillan is coming for dinner. Rennin and I think he is going to ask for Ketty's hand. I'm too tired today to plan both events. I think I'll take a short nap before dinner. Excuse me."

Gabriel looked concerned. "Papa, is Momma all right?"

"I don't know, Gabriel. She has been tired a lot lately. I thought it was the conflict between you and Michael. Now, I just don't know. I'm going to take care of her for a while. Welcome again, Deborah. I guess you'll have to get MacMillan Construction busy on your house, Gabriel. I'll see you two at dinner."

Rennin went upstairs where Rebekah lay on the bed. He looked at the nightstand and picked up *Memoirs of Magic*. "This has been collecting dust. Let me read to you. I'm worried about you, Rebekah."

"I'm okay. I'm just tired. I would like to hear you read. That has always put me at ease."

Before they knew what had happened civilization found Mom's Trading Post. There was an actual road from Boston to Mom's, bridges included. Rennin began to have a strange, hemmed-in feeling. Morgan teased him that his spirit would never settle until they returned to Draconis. Rennin conceded that she was probably right.

A year to the date passed, and Ryan knocked on Rennin's door. Rennin opened with a knowing smile. "Persistence is definitely your strong suit."

Ryan's eyes danced merrily. "May I come in?"

"Of course. You're always welcome."

"I hope so," said Ryan, "because I have come to ask to officially become a member of your family. Uncle Rennin the time has come for me to call you 'Daidí Rennin' at last. We have a gentlemen's agreement. I've come to ask your official permission to marry Rachel. I love her. I've always loved her. I'll devote myself to her. Will you grant us your blessing?"

"He had better," said Rachel from the stairwell.

Rennin looked at his daughter, who had grown up to look just like her mother. "Does that mean you want to marry this imp?"

"Daidí, you know I do. I love Ryan. He won my heart when he was six and taught me what tactful means."

Rennin laughed. "You win. Yes, you have my blessing. When do you want this event to take place?"

"Three months," said Rachel and Ryan nodded his agreement. "I have to plan everything." Both young people smothered Rennin with hugs.

"That sounds like a plan. The first thing you need to do is to send your brother an invitation. Cameron has things to consider as well. Look what I received today."

Rennin handed Rachel a letter. "Your mother hasn't seen this yet, so keep quiet."

Rachel read:

Dear Momma and Daidí,

Well, Momma, it seems you have put the curse on me after all. Tammy, as you know, is well into her pregnancy. She swears she feels four feet kicking her. So, I guess you're going to get your twins before Rachel.

Speaking of Rachel: Daidí, do Donovan and I need to keep the promise we made all those years ago when you and I decided to take a winter swim? Should we teach Ryan a lesson? When is he going to marry my baby sister? You tell that scalawag I will break his arm if he touches her before.

How is Ranson's new baby? She was ill the last I heard. The winter wasn't only hard on her, but also on Rowan. First, he broke his leg sledding. Now, he's recovering from pneumonia. The doctor says he will be fine.

Well, send me news and give my love to all.

Cam

Rachel rippled laughter. "I'll write him today, Daidí. Isn't it nice to know Cam is so happy? Even in his letters you can feel his joy. He was sad far too long."

"Yes, it is. Donovan, Duncan, and Cameron are happily married. You're about to be. Now, if we can only get Colin married off."

"Don't worry about that, Daidí. If Theresa Beauvier comes down the river with her father again, she won't be going back."

"She has come the last ten times."

"Daidí, open your eyes. Haven't you noticed Colin and Theresa disappear when she's here? Maurice Beauvier almost had a stroke the last time. You were too busy helping Momma deliver Sharon Riley. Mr. Beauvier caught them smooching in the barn. At least, I think they were only smooching. Mr. Beauvier was livid. Donovan had his hands full calming that

French temper. He solved it by locking Colin up until Mr. Beauvier left."

"Nobody bothered to tell me? Maurice is a valued customer. I'll ring Colin's neck."

"That's why nobody told you. There has been a lot of progress around here, Daidí, but not with your temper. One angry father was more than enough."

Rennin smirked at his opinionated daughter, wondering if she had truly learned the meaning of tact. "You're right. I won't kill him. I'll just hurt him a little."

Ryan and Rachel laughed with Rennin, but he did not laugh when a few weeks later, Maurice Beauvier and his very pregnant daughter came into Mom's Trading Post. Rennin set his jaw firmly. "Don't say a word, Maurice. I only found out a few weeks ago the seriousness of my son's relationship with your daughter."

"What to do, Rennin?" Maurice asked in a heavy French accent.

"We have a wedding today," replied Rennin.

"J'espérais que vous diriez cela. Theresa est venu a préparé à rester." ("I was hoping you would say that. Theresa came prepared to stay.")

Rennin left the post and found Colin. He walked up and clapped Colin, who was grooming his brood mare, on the back. "Congratulations!"

"For what?" asked Colin, who did not know Theresa had arrived.

"You are going to be a father."

"I am?"

Disdainfully, Rennin said, "Theresa is lovely. I only wish you had followed the rules. It appears you put the cart before the horse."

Colin's face turned ashen. "She's here? She's...She's?"

"That's what happens when you play—you pay."

"Daidí, I was planning to marry her anyway when she came back."

"That doesn't make it right, Colin. What if you had been killed before she got back? How would she have dealt with an illegitimate child? What you did was selfish. I'm very disappointed."

"Is Mr. Beauvier ready to kill me?"

"No. He just wants you to marry his daughter."

"I will as soon as I can find Donovan. Tell her to get ready. I'll meet her at the house. I do love her, Daidí. I was foolish. I'm sorry."

Rennin nodded. "Make it right. I forgive you, and I love you."

An hour later, Colin and Theresa were married. There would be no honeymoon for them, but Colin began a house the next day.

For days, Theresa would not look Rennin in the eye. Finally, he pulled her into his office at the trading post. "Theresa, we should talk."

She spoke with a heavy French accent as she looked at the ground. "Zhou must zink moi a harlot. Ees what Père called me."

Rennin realized that for months Maurice had ridden the girl about her indiscretion. He spoke kindly. "Theresa, what you did was wrong, but it's over. You're my daughter-in-law, and I want to love you as such. I'll love my grandchild as much as any other."

"Zhou do not understand. Zhou blame Colin—I know. Zhou are wrong. I seduced heem. I wanted to make sure he married me. I had to leave Pere. He would not let me go otherwise."

"What do you mean, Theresa?"

"Père does not want to be alone. He always treated me like servant razzer zan daughter. He ees good trapper and customer for zhou, but he ees a cruel taskmaster. Look at my hands, Mr. O'Rourke." She held calloused and blistered palms up for Rennin to see. "Are zese zee kind of hands zhour wife or Rachel hase? Eef I were not so ashamed, I would show zhou zee scars on my back. Zey do not bozzer Colin because he loves me. I am surprised I still carry zis child as hard as Père beat me when he found out." Tears escaped her eyes.

Rennin asked candidly, "Theresa, did Maurice ever force you to act like his wife? Does this child belong to Colin?"

Theresa shook her head. "Non, Père never do zat. Oui, zee child ees Colin's. Colin ees zee only lovaire I ever have. He ees zee only lovaire I ever want."

Rennin hugged Theresa as a father should hug a distraught child. "Theresa, I don't think badly of you. I'll love you as much as I love my other daughters-in-law. Now, dry your tears. Let's start by your calling me 'Daidí.' That's what Colin calls me. You're part of my family now. I'll treat you as such." Rennin wiped the tears from her eyes with his thumbs.

"Answer one more question for me," he said. "Do you love Colin?"

"Oui, j'aime Colin beaucoup. Il m'accepte comme je suis. Je regretted seulement decvoir vous. S'il vous plait me pardonner. Ne pas blamer Colin." ("Yes, I love Colin very much. He accepts me as I am. I only regret disappointing you. Please forgive me. Do not blame Colin.") Theresa lapsed into her native French tongue in her excitement. She did not stop to think that Rennin might not understand a word she had said.

He took her face in his hands and surprised her by answering her in French. "Vous etes pardonne'. Je ne place pas de blame. Je souhaite seulement pour vous etre heureux. Si vous vie etait si avec Maurice, me permettre d'être votre père et vous aime en conséquence." (You are forgiven. I place no blame. I only wish for you to be happy. If your life was so miserable with Maurice, let me be your father and love you accordingly.")

Theresa threw her arms around Rennin. "Oui!"

Rennin said gently, "In English. Although Colin and I may understand you, others might not."

"Yes, Daidí. Zank you."

From that day forward Theresa held her head high and proudly introduced herself as Theresa O'Rourke.

Cameron, Tammy, and Rowan came for Rachel's wedding. They arrived several days before the scheduled event. Tammy told Morgan that Cameron had wanted her to deliver the babies anyway.

"Are you sure it's twins?" asked Morgan.

"It had better be. Look at the size of me." Tammy laughed. "It might even be triplets."

"Bite your tongue," said Cameron.

The two women laughed heartily. Theresa joined them, and she and Tammy compared abdomens. Both women were due about the same time. Tammy truly was triple the size of Theresa.

Cameron had his big brother talk with Colin. "Don't start," said Colin defensively. "You did the same thing. You just didn't get caught."

"Are you sorry?" asked Cameron.

"No. I love Theresa. I had planned to ask for her hand anyway, but she was afraid Maurice would not give his permission. It was her idea. She even said she hoped she conceived. That way he would have to give his permission. She was right."

"Is he really that much of an ogre?"

"Yes. You should see the scars on Theresa's back. A father should never treat a child like that."

"I agree. Ryan has them too, from his stepfather. Tammy has scars, but not from her father. He loved her. Then, take good care of Theresa and love her, brother. I wish you all the best."

Rachel's wedding day proved to be a truly eventful day. It was a perfect day in May. The morning was cool, and the afternoon was warm. The sun shone brightly with a few wispy clouds streaking across the sky in a hurry to be elsewhere. Morgan's rose garden provided the backdrop as Rennin gave his only daughter to be married to a young man that had always seemed like a son to him. In keeping with tradition, Rennin prepared Morgan breakfast in bed and suggested that they tempt fate and try to make another baby. Rennin, however, was not late to give his daughter away for he did not wish to incur the wrath of his baby.

Ryan and Rachel exchanged vows under God's canopy and celebrated with enthusiasm afterward. When the noon meal was finished, Ryan and Rachel left for a trip down the river to New Orleans. Theresa sighed and patted her abdomen. She looked forlornly at Colin and whispered, "I am sorry. I wish we could have gone on a trip togezer."

He put his arm around her. "I'll take you on a honeymoon when the baby is old enough to be left with his grandparents. I love you, Theresa. We don't have to be conventional."

"Do zhou truly love me?"

"Yes, I do."

"Will you love me eef I cause a commotion?"

"What do you mean?" Colin snickered.

"My water just broke."

Colin realized she was soaked. He picked her up, and she dug her nails into his shoulder as her first contraction hit. "It's all right," he whispered. "I'll be with you the whole time. Don't be afraid. I won't leave you." Theresa relaxed her head on Colin's shoulder while he got his mother's attention.

Because Colin's house was still unfinished, he took Theresa to their room in Rennin and Morgan's house. Morgan examined her newest daughter-in-law. She squeezed the girl's hand. "All right, Theresa, we're in for a long afternoon."

As Morgan stood, Cameron knocked at the door. He had a wry grin on his face. "Don't tell me," said Morgan.

"All right. I'll tell Theresa. Tammy's water broke, too. She's next door. You and she can scream together."

Theresa laughed despite the contraction that gripped her as Cameron spoke. Morgan went next door and sent Cameron for Anna and Eula. "I might need a little help."

Hours came and went. In the hallway between bedrooms, Morgan commented to Rennin, "Progress around here would be a physician. Magic is not always enough. I haven't learned to split myself in half."

Theresa progressed rapidly and without complications. By early evening, she had called Colin names in both English and French and had cursed her father to the lowest pits of Hell for making her subject herself to the "torture." Nonetheless, when all was said and done, Theresa gave birth to a healthy baby boy. Colin held the baby while Morgan cleaned up Theresa. Lying in a clean bed and wearing a fresh gown, Theresa held her arms out for both men in her life.

"Show me our son and seet by me," she said.

Colin put the baby in Theresa's arms and sat beside her with his arm around her. "You did a good job, Mère. He's perfect. What shall we name him?"

"After zhour grandfazers—Aidan Colin O'Rourke."

"Don't you want to honor your side of the family at all?"

"Zhou are my family. Rennin ees my fazzer. Maurice ees only zee man who sired me. Leave eet alone, Colin. I am Theresa Renée O'Rourke. Zis ees my son—Aidan Colin O'Rourke."

"If that is what you want, I'm pleased."

"Tres bon." Theresa laid her head on Colin's chest and fell asleep.

Next door, Tammy did not have such an easy time. Hours later, she had not dilated at all. Cameron looked his mother in the eye, and with unspoken words agreed. Morgan indicated her head toward the door. Cameron followed her.

Morgan did not hesitate. "Cam, she's having a lot of trouble. It could be a result of the internal injuries she suffered before. Her heart is racing, and her face is flushed. I'm worried about her having a stroke. You know what I can do. That's how Rowan got here. Talulah has done it several times since Rachel was born. Go in and talk to Tammy. Make a decision."

"What choice do we have, Momma? I will *not* lose Tammy."

"Explain the situation to her while I gather the things I need."

Morgan went to her room. Thinking Rennin was asleep, she tiptoed to her trunk. "Is it necessary?" he asked.

Morgan paused as his voice startled her. "I'm afraid so. I'm afraid she's going to have a stroke, Rennin. I've seen a number of Talulah's tribe have strokes during childbirth. I recognize the symptoms. Some have died. Many others have become debilitated. I can't let that happen to Tammy when I have the power to do something about it. I can't let Cameron lose another wife."

"Do they understand the consequences?"

"Cam does. He's talking to Tammy. Rennin, you know if I thought there was another way, I wouldn't do this."

"I trust your judgment, Morgan. 'Tis just that this world frowns upon practicing the hidden arts."

"We both know a physician can perform this procedure if he will. 'Tis not really magic. Someday it will be widely accepted and used without the present side affects. I'm simply ahead of my time."

Rennin grinned in the shadows. "No, my dear. You're timeless. Do you need my help?"

"No, Cam can do it."

"Fine. Tell me when my grandchildren get here."

"You have one new grandson—Aidan Colin. The whole family was asleep when I left the room."

"I'll see him in the morning then."

Morgan returned to Tammy. Anna still sat with her although Eula had left sometime earlier. Anna refused to leave Cameron, for in her mind he would always be her little brother.

Anna shook her head at Morgan. "Cameron explained to her. She agreed, but she is becoming delirious. Hurry."

Morgan prepared Tammy for the procedure. Cameron gently and tearfully lay across her and held her down. Within minutes Morgan said, "Anna, get Rennin quickly. I need more help."

"What's wrong?" asked Cameron.

"Nothing," said Morgan. "Tammy was right. 'Tis triplets."

"You're jesting, right, Momma?" said Cameron in disbelief.

"No. I am deadly serious."

Rennin returned with Anna. Morgan immediately handed a baby girl to Rennin and another to Anna. She pulled a third smaller baby out. "Two girls and a boy. Well, Cam, your family will not be small. The girls are identical—just like your father and your uncle Kieran. Then, there's your boy—like Declan and me. You got it all, Cam!"

Rennin and Anna took care of the wailing babies while Morgan took care of Tammy. Cameron felt her forehead. "She has a fever, Momma."

"I'm not surprised. Cool compresses and cinchona bark tea. You know how to make it. Go."

Cameron brought cool cloths and the tea. By morning's first light, Tammy opened her eyes and asked straightaway, "Where's my baby?"

"Babies," said Cameron wearily.

"Then, we have twins," she sighed.

"Triplets—two girls and a boy."

"Three? I was only jesting about three. How do I feed three?" Tammy was suddenly fully alert, and she tried to sit up. "Ouch! I forgot. Momma had to take the babies."

"Yes, so we have to stay here at least six weeks before you can travel. Daidí has already gone to the Indian village to find a nursemaid to help you. We'll take her with us and bring her back when the babies are weaned."

"Names. Have you named our children?"

"No. I thought we should do that together."

"Three names! This is going to be hard."

"Well, I thought I'd like to name our son for my uncle and for someone who encouraged me to pursue you. I'd like to call him Kieran—Kieran Duncan O'Rourke."

"That's a good name. How about our daughters? Maybe we should ask Rowan's help. After all, he *is* the big brother." Tammy cut her eyes toward the door. Cameron winked with understanding.

"I don't know," said Cameron. "He might come up with some hideous name like Prudence. Ugh! I will *not* have my daughter named Prudence."

"I will not," said Rowan.

"Oh!" Cameron faked a gasp. "I didn't know you were there."

"Yes, you did."

"You're getting too grown up. I can't fool you anymore. Come on in and meet your sisters and brother."

Rowan peered intently at the sleeping babies. "Why so many at once?"

Cameron snickered. "It wasn't my idea. Take it up with the Powers that be."

"I wouldn't question God's wisdom," said Rowan. "I have an idea for a name."

"We're listening," said Tammy.

"Holly."

"Rowan!" Cameron scolded.

"I think it's a wonderful idea," said Tammy. "What should we put with it?"

"Morgan."

Tammy said the name aloud. "Holly Morgan O'Rourke. It sounds nice. Which one?"

"The one that came out first."

"I'll have to ask your grandma," Tammy laughed.

"Nope," said Cameron. "She has a little ribbon tied around her ankle. Momma said it was so we wouldn't get them mixed up at first."

"So far, so good," said Tammy. "We have one left. My mother's name was Ruth. Lucretia put us together. Let's name the other one Lucretia Ruth and call her Ruth."

So the names were given, and Ryan and Rachel returned before Cameron and his much larger family left. Rachel announced that she was expecting a baby, and with that announcement Rennin packed his first bag to go back to Draconis though it sat in the closet for many years.

Rennin shut the book quickly as Rebekah's nose began to bleed. "How often has this happened?"

"A few times lately."

"Tomorrow, you go see Stanley. Rebekah, this is not just fatigue. I'm truly worried. Promise me you'll go."

She nodded solemnly.

46
A Reason to Go Home

Rebekah's prediction was correct. Timothy MacMillan did ask for Ketty's hand after dinner. Rebekah found the energy to laugh heartily at the young man's discomfiture as Rennin interrogated him about his intentions and future plans.

Timothy told Rennin that his grandfather had already offered him his part of the business after he worked for five years. Rennin kept his poker face stern and continued to ask him questions until the boy broke. "Mr. O'Rourke, I thought you liked me. I love Ketty, and she loves me. Please give us your blessing."

Ketty was not nearly so patient. "Papa! Stop it! You're only hassling Tim because you want to see him squirm. You've known for over a year this day would come. Now, treat Tim the way you would want to be treated."

Rennin stood and leaned on his cane. Although he had an artificial limb, he often used his cane to displace some of his weight. He glowered at the boy. "Timothy MacMillan, stand."

Timothy stood slowly as if he were terrified Rennin would belt him. "Timothy, I cannot think of a better man to marry my daughter. You have my blessing and my condolences," Rennin said looking at Ketty. "Do you really want to marry this girl? She's stubborn, opinionated, and hot-tempered. Can you handle that?"

"Yes, sir, I can."

"Then, welcome to the family." Rennin extended his hand to Timothy. The young man shook it with relief. "When would you like this event to occur? I'm sure Ketty will want something lavish. She'll try to spend all my money. So, tell me how I should plan."

"We haven't set a date, sir."

"Soon," piped Ketty. "I will *not* wait another year, Papa. Six months at the most."

"All right. Set a date. Timothy, I was only teasing you. I do like you, and I'm proud you've chosen my daughter." Rennin put his arm around the boy's shoulders and both laughed.

Rennin looked at Gabriel. "Gabriel, fetch us some champagne. We need to toast your marriage and Ketty's engagement. Deborah, I hope you can tolerate this family. We're a close-knit group." Rennin went to a large trunk under the bay window. "I feel a strong urge to give this to you." Rennin handed Deborah the copy of *Memoirs of Magic* that he had taken into battle. "Read it. You'll find out what kind of family we really are."

"Thank you," said Deborah as she read the name of the book and author. "Did you write this?"

"No. It was written some two hundred years ago by the first Rennin O'Rourke. I think you'll enjoy it."

Gabriel came back with a bottle of Bollinger champagne from the wine cellar. Rennin popped the cork and toasted the change of status of the two present children. Then, he insisted he was tired and took Rebekah to bed for she was obviously exhausted.

Rebekah kept her promise. She went to see Stanley at the hospital. Both Thomas and Clayton had all but retired and left the practice to Stanley and a few other younger doctors, although they still came for consultations and served on the board of directors for the hospital.

Stanley examined Rebekah carefully and drew some of her blood to put under a microscope. He came back into his office with a grave countenance. "Momma, you're very sick."

"I know," said Rebekah. "What can you do to make me better?"

"Nothing. Momma, you have a kind of cancer in your blood. It's called leukemia. There's nothing to be done."

"Cancer? Does that mean I'm going to die?"

"Yes, Momma. I can give you tonics to strengthen you and salicin for pain, but you'll have to take the medicine with milk or sodium bicarbonate, or it'll hurt your stomach."

Rebekah sat for sometime without speaking. "Stanley, how do I tell Rennin? He can't handle this. He isn't as strong as everyone thinks. He needs me so much."

Stanley realized for the first time since he had come to live with Rennin and Rebekah how right his mother was. He saw, too, her love for the man he called Papa. Her thoughts were not for herself, but for the man she loved more than her own life.

"Do you want me to tell him, Momma?"

"No. I have to do it. How long?"

"I don't know. Six months, maybe a year."

She nodded. "Okay. Ketty has to get married right away."

Rebekah rode home slowly. She stroked the neck of the buttermilk-colored mare. "Girl, your grandmother was my first horse. She saved my life. I've made a decision. Ketty has to get married next month. Then, I want Rennin to take me to look for Draconis. Yes, I believe it's real. He promised he would take me someday. Well, it has to be now. You'll go to live with Ketty. She's always wanted you anyway."

Rebekah lay on the couch to wait for Rennin to come home. The door opened. She called, "Rennin?"

"No, Momma. It's Ketty."

"Come in here."

Ketty went into the living room. "Momma, Tim and I set a date. Papa will have a fit."

"When?"

Ketty closed her eyes for fear of hearing screaming. "Two weeks."

"Leave Rennin to me. Two weeks is good."

"Momma, you didn't even ask why."

"I know why."

"Aren't you angry?"

"Disappointed, but what's done is done. Ketty, *I* need you to get married right away. Leave everything to me. Nobody else needs to know, not even Rennin."

"Why do you need me to get married so soon?"

"Stanley told me I'm very sick." Rebekah sat up weakly. "I may only live six more months. I'm sorry I won't get to hold your baby."

Ketty blinked in disbelief. Rebekah continued. "Now I have to tell Rennin. He could *not* deal with both pieces of news at the same time."

"Whatever you say, Momma." Ketty meandered up the stairs, too shocked to react, but tears began to trickle down her cheeks.

Rennin bopped in the door in a very good mood and saw Ketty walking up the stairs in a daze. "What's wrong with Ketty?"

"I told her she has to get married in two weeks."

"Why?" demanded Rennin.

"Sit down."

"No. Should I go and find Timothy?"

"No. You should sit down and listen to me."

Rennin sat beside Rebekah. She took a deep breath. "You have a promise to keep to me. We must go in search of Draconis. Rennin, we have to do it *now*. Stanley told me that I have leukemia. Do you know what that is?"

Rennin nodded. "He has to be wrong. Get another opinion."

"He's not wrong. Stanley is a very good doctor. That's why Ketty has to get married as soon as possible. I want you to write to Jed, Michael, and Stephen. Get them home so I can say good-bye. Tell Chris to marry Molly Brye so I can leave everyone settled."

"Rebekah, I can't live without you."

"You'll have to. Hopefully, we'll be on Draconis. We'll find our spirits' desire. You'll have something to look forward to. I will *not* stay here and have my children watch me die. Are you a man of your word, or not?"

"You know I am. I'll make the arrangements. I'll buy us a boat. I'll take some bullion for the dragons. Right after Ketty's wedding, I'll go to the capital and resign my position. I'll do anything for you."

"All right. Read the last chapter of the book to me. I need to rest. Let's go upstairs."

They walked up the stairs hand in hand. Rebekah reclined in bed on many propped pillows. Rennin opened the book. "Do you really want me to read this? It's rather depressing."

"I think it's ultimately uplifting. I have a confession. I've already read it once while you were at war."

Rennin acquiesced and finished the story.

Year after year, Morgan asked Rennin to take her home. Always there seemed to be some reason to wait until one morning Morgan got up and started packing her trunks. From the bed, Rennin asked, "What are you doing, honey?"

"I'm going home, Rennin. The time has come. You can go, or you can stay. Either way, I'm going home."

He sat upright. "You would go without me?"

She sat on the bed. "Rennin, I can't explain it. All night it was as if voices in my head were calling me home. I have to go—now."

"Today? Voices?"

"Don't worry. They were friendly voices. It'll take a few days to pack. Donovan, Duncan, and Colin understand. After I get packed, I'm going to visit Rachel in Salem for a few days and then Cameron in Boston. If you don't go, I'll hire a ship in Boston to take me home. Those are your plans, Rennin. That's how you laid it out."

He got up and opened the closet. He pulled out the bag he had packed years before and set it in the corner. "All right. Let's get packing."

She flung her arms around him. "It can wait another hour."

Chuckling, he said, "I once told Cameron I hoped we made wild passionate love even when our bones creaked. My bones creak sometimes these days. Are we about to make wild passionate love?"

"You better believe it!"

A week later, Rennin visited Geoffrey's well-kept grave. Geoffrey's heart had finally given up two years before. "Well, Geoffrey, I'm going home. I suppose I've felt the pull as much as Morgan, but I've fought it. I dread the thought of never seeing my children and grandchildren again. Lord, Geoffrey! We have our first great-grandchild now. Memorie married a boy from Virginia. They're living there, and they have a baby boy. Another thing that bothers me is that I'm too old to sail Morgan and me home. I have to hire a ship and crew. Why did I wait so long, Geoffrey? Why didn't I take you with me? None of that matters now. I just came to say good-bye. Donovan will do a good job as a leader in Mom's Trading Post, and Oliver will still be here. Geoffrey, my grandfather told me that Morgan and I would conquer strange new worlds. Did we?"

"Yes, we did, Rennin," said Morgan behind him. "Think about it. I brought Victor Jordan to the Throne of God and righted grave injustices. You won the hearts of a princess and a king. We came together to a wild new land. We established a thriving community based on love, tolerance, and acceptance. Our children are spreading those values to other places. Yes, Rennin, we conquered a great deal, and we have experienced so much. We did what Granddaddy Duncan said we would do."

He stood and held her close. "And now 'tis time to go home. I'm ready."

Surprisingly, the good-byes in Mom's Trading Post were cheerful rather than tearful. Rennin and Morgan's three sons, who still lived there, knew their parents had dreamed of this always. Therefore, they supported and encouraged them.

The trip to Salem, Massachusetts, where Ryan and Rachel had moved to expand the furrier business, was peaceful and relaxing. Rennin and Morgan treated the few weeks on the road like another honeymoon. They arrived invigorated at their daughter's home.

Rachel stared at her parents, mouth agape. "You're really going? All these years I thought the two of you were jesting. Sometimes I wish I could go with you. I always loved your stories of dragons and magic."

With a little concern, Morgan asked, "Rachel, what do you know of magic?"

"More than you think."

"Rachel, what have you done?" asked Rennin, rising alarm in his voice.

"Yes, Rachel," said Ryan with his arms folded across his chest. "Tell your parents what you've been doing."

"Ryan, you act as if I've done something wrong. All I've done since we've been here is save lives."

"Rachel," said Rennin, "what Ryan is saying is that this is *not* a tolerant community. One mistake and they will accuse you of unspeakable things."

"Then, maybe you picked the wrong time to visit because I made my first mistake last night. I performed the procedure you used to deliver me. The baby was stillborn even after the procedure. The woman is still alive though now she is burning up with fever. Mr. Beecham will not allow me to give his wife the cinchona bark tea. Momma, the smell when I opened her up was pungent."

"Then the baby had been dead a long time," said Morgan. "Your patient was festering before you got to her. She *will* die, Rachel. When she does, these people will come for you. They'll at the very least accuse you of practicing witchcraft—a crime here. They could accuse you of murder."

"I've successfully done this procedure and many other things in the last seven years. Doesn't the fact that I've helped so many people count for anything?"

"No," said Rennin bluntly and with a head shake. "Gratitude is not as strong as fear. Rachel, how long have you practiced this secret art?"

"Ever since I was a child and followed Momma to the mushrooms. It came naturally."

"How could we not know?"

"I've been discreet. Daidí, I have powers far stronger than Momma's—maybe because you have powers you don't know about."

"I *know* about them, Rachel. I've chosen not to use them with good reason. They are not conventional powers. I have the power to control the will of some, but why would I want to force another person to do my bidding? I know I can cast out demons. I've done it. I could probably cast any spell Seanathair Alexander ever heard, but I've seen too much evil associated with the power I could wield. I never even let Seanathair know how strong my abilities were. I preferred to leave that to Ricardo. When I left Draconis, I left my birthright by choice. This world does not accept our kind, Rachel." He placed a hand on his daughter's head and gently touched the tiny protrusion on her ear. He sighed. "You must be prudent if you choose to use your power. You could endanger the lives of all those you love. Your gift is not a toy. It's a responsibility. I pray that if you all stay in this world that the O'Rourke curse eventually becomes diluted to the point of being parlor tricks. It cannot survive if it is not controlled."

"Daidí, I meant no harm. I only wanted to help."

"Rachel, this world is not yet ready for a female physician either. Ryan, I suggest you and your family up and go home. I feel we're all in grave danger."

"Daidí Rennin, do you think it's imminent?"

"Yes."

Ryan turned commandingly. "Rachel, pack up now."

Rachel did not argue, but began packing to move. Morgan quietly helped her daughter.

"Momma, did you know?"

"About your daddy?"

The daughter nodded.

"Yes, but I thought he didn't know. Rennin never ceases to amaze me."

As night fell, there arose a ruckus outside the Riley home, complete with loud angry voices and pounding on the door.

Rennin reached into his valise and pulled out his loaded pistol. "Answer the door, Ryan, carefully."

Mr. Beecham stood in the doorway. His face scarlet, he snarled, "I want that witch you have in there. She killed my wife and baby."

"Rachel has not harmed anyone," said Ryan softly. "Mr. Beecham, your baby had been dead for many days. If you had sent for Rachel sooner, Mrs. Beecham would be alive."

Beecham screamed, "Are you saying this is my fault?"

"No," replied Ryan. "It's an unfortunate tragedy. I'm truly sorry for your loss."

"Mr. Riley, in the seven years you've lived here, your wife has rendered four of our women barren. She, herself, said the procedure would render them unable to bear more children. Those who agreed to have it done did so in fear. They have repented, but they must suffer the consequences of their sin."

"Sin?" Ryan stretched his blue eyes wide. "They and their children are alive. All would have perished if it had not been for Rachel."

"Alive? At what cost—the damnation of their eternal souls?"

"Mr. Beecham, get off my property and take your friends with you. Rachel did what any good midwife would do. She tried to save mother and child. I'm sad she failed this time. If it will make you feel better, we're leaving Salem in the morning. Good-bye." Ryan closed the door in the bereaved man's face.

Rennin looked at Rachel, his green eyes glistening with unshed tears. "Do you see, baby?"

"Yes, Daidí."

All of a sudden, a flaming torch flew through the windowpane. "Riley! Send her out or die with her! She's a murderess!" Beecham's angry voice shouted, and it was joined by cheers.

Ryan grabbed his musket, but Rennin steadied his son-in-law's hand. "Take it with you. We cannot fight an angry mob. Get everyone out through the root cellar. The wagons are loaded and ready to go down by the river. Trust me, Ryan."

As another torch caught the linen curtains on fire, Ryan escorted, Rachel, their two children, Zoë and Drake, and Morgan to the root cellar door. He pushed to open it, but someone had barred the door. "Daidí Rennin," he called. "I can't open this alone. I need your help."

Rennin pushed the doors. "My God! These people are crazy. Together, Rennin and Ryan burst the doors open after repeated tries.

Drake whined and pulled Morgan's hand. "Come on, Grandma."

The small group cut through the woods to the wagons until Morgan stopped in her tracks. "My ring," she gasped. She turned back toward the house.

"Morgan, where are you going?" shouted Rennin after her.

She called over her shoulder, "I lost my wedding ring. I know where it is. I'll be right back."

"No!" screamed Rennin. "Let it go, Morgan. It's only a piece of gold."

"It's my wedding ring. You know I'll die before I leave that ring," Morgan argued.

"God, no," Rennin thought aloud. He had put Drake on his shoulders. He quickly handed the boy to Ryan and muttered, "Stubborn woman." He ran after Morgan. She disappeared though the root cellar door.

"Morgan!" he called again.

As she entered the root cellar, flames shot though the roof and timbers crackled.

"No!" bellowed Rennin, visions of the inferno that claimed his grandmother Fitzpatrick and Seamus O'Donnell flashing across his mind. He jerked the root cellar door open. Flames and smoke billowed out. "Morgan! Morgan!" His frantic screams blared over the roar of the blaze.

At the wagon Rachel shrieked as she saw the flames shoot skyward. "Ryan!"

"Take the children and go, Rachel! Now!"

Twice in one evening she did not argue, but obeyed without hesitation. "Ryan, be careful. I love you."

"Go!"

Ryan ran back to the house and saw Rennin battling the flames. "Daidí Rennin! Stop! You can't go in there."

"I have to. Morgan's in there."

"Daidí Rennin, it's too late. Come away. Momma Morgan would not want you going after her. Daidí Rennin, she has gone *Home*." Ryan physically dragged his father-in-law from the door.

Lip trembling, Rennin looked solemnly at Ryan. "But she went without me."

Ryan's heart broke for he had never heard words so sad. Rennin sat in the grass and sobbed.

Rachel drove the wagon across the river. The water was not so deep at the ford that she could not cross on foot. Leaving the children with orders to stay under the seat, she came back to the house. Taking in the sight, she knew what had happened. She cried, "Momma!"

Ryan caught his drenched wife in his arms. Suddenly, the three mourning adults froze as a brilliant florescent-green luna moth flew unscathed from the flames and landed on Rennin's shoulder. A soft, gentle voice, Morgan's voice, whispered for all three to hear, "Rennin, stop crying. Don't mourn for me. If you can only remember me with your tears, then, put me from your mind. Rennin Drake O'Rourke, you have a promise to keep. Take me home. Spread my ashes in our meadow. You are heart of my heart and life of my life. I have loved you until the day I died, and I will love you for all eternity."

The moth fluttered against Rennin's cheek and drifted away on the wind.

"My God," said Ryan after a long, poignant pause. "Go back to the wagon, Rachel," he said gently, having become aware of voices coming their way. Rachel did as he asked. "Come on, Daidí Rennin."

"No," said Rennin stubbornly. "I want to speak to these people. They will help me extract Morgan's remains. I want them to see what they've done."

Beecham and the men with him rounded the corner of the house. Rennin looked up from the ground and glowered at the crowd. He spoke with a tenor Ryan had never heard him use—an ethereal, haunting tone. "I hope you're satisfied. You've managed to murder the most beautiful woman who ever lived. My father once called her his guardian angel. All her life she has done nothing but care for others—even some who did not deserve it. She passed those characteristics on to her daughter—love, compassion, willingness to help."

Rising, Rennin stood, regal, and an aura of gold surrounded him. "I tell you this moment, this town is cursed." He moved his arm in a sweeping arc. "Your ignorance, prejudice, and lack of compassion will be your undoing. Beecham, you, *yourself*, will fall victim to the rabid hatred that will arise. You will go down in infamy. I hope that you all feel the flames of Hell leaping around you even as my wife, a Godly woman, felt flames engulf her body. Years from now, you will remember the names Morgan O'Rourke and Rachel Riley for they will come back to haunt you."

Feeling some remorse and shame, Beecham dropped his head and turned to leave. Rennin sprang forward to block his exit. "Don't you walk away from here! When these flames die and all that is left is dust, you will help me find my wife's remains, though they be only ashes. I will take her home where she belongs. I will not even bury her in a place so cruel and cold. I will not bury her at all for she never liked the dark. She will be free in the meadow of our home to create beauty for all those around her to see."

Beecham called a young boy to him and whispered in his ear. "Yes, Father," the boy responded.

"Bring it," said Beecham mysteriously. Beecham turned to the crowd. "Go home. We have acted foolishly and caused too much harm."

Beecham sat on the grass with Rennin and Ryan. They waited all night. Near morning, it began to rain, but the rain cooled the smoldering coals. In the dreariness, Rennin searched for some sign of Morgan. In the ashes he found three things: a perfect diamond whose setting had melted in the heat; surprisingly intact, a jade dragon on a gold chain; and a gold chain loop. "Why didn't these melt?" he asked himself in wonder. Rennin slipped the diamond and the necklace into his pocket. The small loop he pushed half way onto his little finger. "Her hands were so tiny," he said to Ryan who stood beside him.

"Daidí Rennin, I've measured off around where you found these items. I figure these will be Momma Morgan's remains." He got closer to Rennin. "The area glowed too. I think she made it so we could see her."

Rennin nodded and glared at Beecham without words. As the rain stopped and the sun broke through the clouds, Beecham's son ran up. "Father, here is what you asked for."

"Thank you." The boy gave his father an exquisite brass urn and a shovel. "Mr. O'Rourke, if you will hold the urn, I'll do the other."

"Give Ryan the shovel. I don't want you to touch my wife."

Rennin examined the urn. It was covered with etched butterflies and honeysuckle and in the smooth space provided, the boy had engraved Morgan's name with artistic precision. Rennin looked at the boy. "Your work is beautiful. The urn is quite appropriate. Thank you."

Ryan gingerly scooped the ashes he had measured off and placed them in the urn. As Rennin walked away, Beecham said, "Mr. O'Rourke, I'm..."

With his back still to the man Rennin said, "Don't say it. Live it." Ryan and Rennin walked on to the wagons where Rachel waited anxiously.

Rennin bade his daughter farewell. "Comfort those in Mom's Trading Post. You might want to change the name. Put an R in it to make a funny word. Tell Donovan I said to make Ryan a partner immediately." Rennin removed Morgan's clothes, trinkets, and herbs from his wagon. "These are yours now, Rachel. Use them wisely."

With that said, he drove toward Boston.

Rennin arrived in Boston unobtrusively. He knocked quietly at Cameron's door. Rowan, who was still exuberant at twenty, though he was engaged to marry Ellen Brent, a girl whose pigtails he had pulled the first time he met her, opened the door. "Granddad!"

Rennin came in carrying the urn and a small valise. Cameron greeted his father. "Daidí! Where's Momma?"

"Cameron, get everyone to sit down," Rennin commanded quietly. "Ellen, too."

When everyone was seated, Rennin told them calmly all that had transpired. Cameron caught sharp breath after sharp breath. "I can't breathe right now," he choked. "Not like that. Just not like that."

"Cameron," Rennin said sternly. "Did you listen to anything I said? Your mother told me not to cry, and now I'm telling you. Cameron, you're the only son I have who truly inherited his mother's magic *and* the O'Rourke spirit. I have all the dragon pieces for you because you will appreciate them and pass that appreciation on to your children. I want these pieces to *always* go to someone with the last name of O'Rourke. May a devastating curse fall on the man who takes control of them if he is not a true O'Rourke."

Rennin turned to his eldest grandson. "Rowan, have you given Ellen an engagement ring yet?"

"No, sir. I want something perfect."

Rennin reached into his pocket. "You won't find a more perfect diamond. Have it remounted and pass it down so that your firstborn son will give it to his fiancée."

"Granddad, this is Grandma's diamond."

"She doesn't need it anymore. You don't get the wedding ring. It's mine. Besides, you have the ones I made your father and mother." Rennin fingered the small loop affectionately. "However, you do get the necklace." Rennin handed the pendant directly to Ellen. "Wear it as something old on your wedding day. Then, pass it down to your first son's bride on her wedding day. These two things should always be worn by O'Rourke brides." Rennin kissed the girl on the cheek and looked into her eyes, golden as a cat's. "Your eyes remind me of my grandmother."

"Granddad, are you leaving right away?" Ellen asked without questioning Rennin's story, but accepting it as wholly true.

"As soon as I can make the arrangements."

Ellen looked at Rowan. "Then, maybe Rowan and I can wed before you leave. My father will agree."

Rowan looked like a trapped animal. Despite their grief, both Rennin and Cameron smirked behind their hands.

Rowan mellowed quickly to the idea. "That's an excellent suggestion. Will you give us two weeks to throw a wedding together, Granddad?"

Rennin nodded. "I can give you two weeks."

It took Rennin longer than two weeks to hire a crew that pleased him. He looked for good, reliable men, but not necessarily exceptional men just in case Draconis had become hidden to ordinary eyes, which he felt was sure.

The grandfather celebrated Rowan's nuptials with him. After several months, Rennin finally went to the docks to board *The Typhoon*. He packed strangely with only a few clothes, Morgan's urn, and several bags of gold and gems. "For the dragons," he had explained.

Rennin embraced Cameron one last time and felt the amulet under his shirt. He touched Cameron's chest. "Pass that to Rowan, too. He has inherited more than you know. It will not manifest itself for quite sometime—generations perhaps—but one of his descendants will have green eyes. He will probably need this amulet. I have one more thing for you."

Rennin handed his son a thick volume of pages bound together with string. The pages were written in Rennin's hand. The top page read, "*Memoirs of Magic* by Rennin Drake O'Rourke."

"Add what you think should be added, but see that it is published. Most people will think it's a fantasy, but know that it's true—every word of it. Cameron, be careful. I won't be around to pull you from the waters again. I love you, Cameron, but I have to go home. My reason lies here." He caressed the urn. "And on Draconis. I have promises to keep."

Cameron handed Rennin something, too. "This was to be your Christmas gift this year. Take it now. Rowan drew it from memory. I think it looks great."

Rennin threw back the oilskin around the package. It was a portrait of every one of Rennin's descendents with him and Morgan at the center. "The boy is talented," Rennin said with a catch in his voice. "Encourage him to use his talent. I'll treasure this forever."

Rennin walked up the gangplank. Cameron called behind him, "Daidí!" Tears streamed down the grown man's face.

"You'll be fine," Rennin said in a strained voice.

"I love you, Daidí."

Rennin threw his son a kiss and the ship pulled from the harbor. Cameron watched until it sank over the horizon.

Rennin turned to Rebekah without speaking. She finally asked, "How did Cameron die?"

"Believe it or not, he drowned rescuing one of his grandchildren." He became silent. A sigh gave way to, "Do you know how hard that parting must have been for Cameron and his siblings, as well as Rennin?"

"Rennin," Rebekah said calmly. "I know it will be hard for us, but in a few months my children will see me no more anyway. If you don't wish to stay on Draconis, you can come home, but please take me there."

"We're going to go, Rebekah, and I would never leave you."

She asked honestly, "Rennin, where is the amulet? You have everything else."

He hopped to the settee and tapped the underside of one of the drawers. A small compartment, from which he drew the emerald charm opened. "I've never worn it."

"Maybe you should have. Maybe you would've seen Pierre, Ike, and Max for what they really were."

"I don't think it works like that, Rebekah."

"No, they were only evil humans, not spirits. Or maybe they *were* inhabited by evil spirits."

"The spirits have not manifested themselves in a long, long time. Not since Tammy almost died."

"They haven't given up, Rennin. They're waiting for the right moment."

"Who gets all this stuff—Gabriel or Michael?"

"You'll know by how they react to the things." Rebekah took off the jade dragon. "Give this to Deborah to wear at the reception tomorrow night. I think she has the right spirit."

"Then, she needs the diamond and the wedding ring. Are you willing to give those up?"

Rebekah laughed softly and handed both things to Rennin. "How about you? Are you willing to give Gabriel your ring?"

Rebekah drew on her inner strength and threw a jubilant celebration for Gabriel and Deborah. Just before the bride and groom were to come down, Rennin presented them with the rings and the necklace.

All night Deborah fingered the jade dragon. Rebekah made her way to her daughter-in-law. "Do you like it?" she asked.

"It's beautiful. Wearing it, I almost feel as if dragons are real."

"They are," Rebekah whispered. "You just have to know where to look."

She motioned for Deborah to follow her. In the library, which had been added to the house, Rebekah pulled a worn volume of *Memoirs of Magic* from the shelf. "Read this."

Deborah caressed the leather cover and smelled the scent of the leather. "Thank you. I will. Papa Rennin already told me to read this. He gave me a newer copy."

Rebekah nodded and hugged the ood copy to her chest. "Then this one goes with us."

Two weeks later, Ketty's wedding occurred without incident, except that Michael arrived late. He brought a woman with him. At the reception, Michael introduced the woman as his wife—Maria Diaz O'Rourke. With the unrest in the Caribbean, Michael had been stationed in Cuba where he met Maria. He had only just married her and brought her home when he received Rennin's urgent telegram.

Jed and Stephen arrived two days later. With all the children present, Rennin and Rebekah held a family meeting at which Rennin described Rebekah's condition and revealed their plans.

"Papa, you can't be serious," said Michael. "We have ships all over, and no one has ever seen this magnificent place. It's a fantasy."

"Shut up, Michael," said Gabriel. "This is Momma's dying wish. Have you no spirit? Leave them alone."

"Gabriel, the place is *not* real. What are they going to do: Go out and die on the ocean?"

"Michael," Rennin said. "You sound like your grandfather. Open your heart, son. You might be surprised. We've made a decision. You don't have to agree with it, but I do expect you to respect our decision. All of you will be well provided for. We have more money than we can ever spend. I already bought a yacht. We'll be using it. Tomorrow, I'm resigning my position in the House of Representatives. I'll do this or die trying. Am I clearly understood?"

No one voiced dissention, and Rennin followed his plan to the letter, encouraged to follow his spirit's desire by his mother who would have given anything to go with him, but knew someone needed to stay behind.

Rennin had a private meeting with Gabriel. "Son, you've shown that you believe in the unbelievable. Michael has received some very nice things for his home he plans to make in Florida, but I want you to have all the dragon pieces. I've told you the history and the stories, which I believe are true. There's one more thing I want to give you. Within the next century, I think one of your grandchildren will need it." Rennin gave Gabriel the emerald amulet.

Gabriel's hand shook as he took the enchanted piece. "It's magic, Papa. I'll guard it well." He slipped it around his neck and shivered.

"I'm as sentimental as the first Rennin O'Rourke," laughed Rennin. He also handed Gabriel several leather journals. "I've kept these over the years. They are by no means as poetically written as the first Rennin wrote, but they're your mother's and my history. They're my thoughts and feelings. I don't care if they're ever published. You can try if want. I mainly want my family to read them."

"I'll read them, Papa, and I'll have them printed so others can read them. You always said your penmanship was chicken scratch."

Rennin laughed. "So I have. It is. Maybe you can decipher it."

"Papa, I believe, but if you get out there and don't find it, I'll be right here in Puma Pass in your house."

"It's yours now."

"I hope you find Draconis for Momma, but I'll miss you desperately."

"We all go away at some point. Think of it like that."

"But you aren't even taking a crew to help you."

"I don't need them. Rebekah and I go alone."

A few weeks later, loaded with provisions and several concealed cases of gold nuggets for the dragons they hoped to find, Rennin and Rebekah O'Rourke waved good-bye to all those they loved.

Epilogue
(Nearly one hundred years later)

The woman with the slightly graying dark hair and light brown eyes grabbed the sides of her head in anguish. The screaming and the moaning would not stop. She looked down at the charred remains of her son and husband, yet she could hear the agonizing wails of a child. Her mother's heart followed the sound until she came upon a boy about the same age as her own child. He sat beside the badly burned bodies of a man and a woman.

The toddler cried as if his heart would break. The little boy was adorable. He had obviously never had his first hair cut for his chestnut ringlets fell over his ears. His eyes were such a vivid green that he could have been identified solely on them, just like his father's that stared in glassy emptiness. The grieving woman touched the little boy's hand. "Would you like to come with me? I'll take care of you."

In need of comfort, the child reached up for the woman. With the boy in her arms, she saw the medical alert bracelet that he wore. Looking back at the body of her own son, she stroked the brown curls. "Everything will be fine."

She slipped the bracelet off the child's arm. "Sit right here for just a minute." Putting the boy back on the ground, the woman dropped the bracelet into the fire. She cautiously removed the hot bracelet and put it on the arm of the charred boy's body. Then, she carefully and lovingly carried the body of the boy and placed him beside the man and woman. "I'm sorry," she whispered.

She went back to the other boy, who had stopped crying and watched her curiously. She lifted him into her arms as two policemen and a fireman came around the smoldering train car. "Ma'am," called one of the policemen.

"Yes?" She turned tearfully toward the officer.

"Ma'am, are you all right?"

"I think so. My husband is dead. I think my son is all right. Those people aren't though." She pointed toward the couple and the baby.

The fireman knelt beside the couple, and he searched the pockets of the the man for identification. "Michael O'Rourke," he said, holding up a driver's license. "From Puma Pass, California."

"See to collecting the bodies," the policeman said, and then escorted the woman and the boy to the portable triage unit where they were pronounced fit to be released. An Ameri-Rail official approached the woman. "Ma'am, where were you headed? We're trying to reroute the survivors."

"Miami. I live in Miami."

"I understand your husband is dead. I'm so sorry. I need you to come with me to identify him, so we can send his body with you."

The woman nodded in a zombie-like fashion. After a while, she and the boy were on their way to Miami.

The O'Rourke Family Line
(Ancestors of Rennin Aidan O'Rourke)

Generation 1
Alexander O'Rourke: Born, c. 1530, Willow Hollow, Ireland (*Wizard, Island of Draconis.*)
  Married, Genevieve Brady
  -Elizabeth Gilhooley (Mother—Quazel Rodriguez-Morales)
  -Duncan Sean O'Rourke*

Generation 2
Duncan Sean O'Rourke: Born c. 1550, Stonebridge, Ireland (*Also known as King Satin, Ruler of Draconis.*)
  Married, Priscilla Cecelia Callahan
  -Anna O'Rourke (Died in infancy)
  -Aidan Duncan O'Rourke*

Generation 3
Aidan Duncan O'Rourke: Born   1576,   Stonebridge, Ireland (*Liberator of Draconis.*)
  Married, Caitlin Leanne Fitzpatrick
  -Kieran Sean O'Rourke
  -Rennin Drake O'Rourke*
  -Genevieve Marie O'Rourke
  -Shannon Michael O'Rourke

Generation 4
Rennin Drake O'Rourke: Born 1596, Draconian Waters
  Married, Morgan Celeste Fitzpatrick
  -Donovan Alexander O'Rourke
  -Cameron David O'Rourke*
  -Matthew Oded (Mother—Princess Kiandria Oded)
  -Duncan Paul O'Rourke
  -Colin Aidan O'Rourke
  -Rachel Leanne O'Rourke

Generation 5
Cameron David O'Rourke: Born, 1615, Draconis

Married, Holly Montague, 1632 (*Also known as Holehah of the Iroquois Nation,* Died, 1633 in childbirth)
Married, Tammy Patrice Martin, 1643
-Rowan Patrick O'Rourke* (Mother—Holly Montague)
-Holly Morgan O'Rourke
-Lucretia Ruth O'Rourke
-Kieran Duncan O'Rourke

Generation 6

Rowan Patrick O'Rourke: Born, 1643, Ohio Territory
Married, Ellen Brent, 1653
-Cameron Rennin O'Rourke*
-Patrick Oliver O'Rourke
-Geoffrey Ian O'Rourke

Generation 7

Cameron Rennin O'Rourke: Born, 1654, Boston, Massachusetts
Married, Nancy Shay Montague
-Ian Sean O'Rourke
-Devlin Daniel O'Rourke*
-Sylvia Suzanne O'Rourke
-Colleen Diane O'Rourke

Generation 8

Devlin Daniel O'Rourke: Born, 1675, Boston, Massachusetts
Married, Melissa Beecham (*Last surviving member of the Beecham family of Salem, Massachusetts. Parents tried and hanged as witches, 1685.*)
-Barbara Anne O'Rourke
-Melanie Louise O'Rourke
-Josephine Christine O'Rourke
-Rennin Patrick O'Rourke*

Generation 9

Rennin Patrick O'Rourke: Born, 1695, Lexington, Massachusetts
Married, Catherine Churchill, 1712 (*Died, 1713 in childbirth*)

-Aidan Cameron O'Rourke*
Generation 10
Aidan Cameron O'Rourke: Born, 1713, Concord, Massachusetts
    Married, Frances Haughton, 1720
    -Gayle Ann O'Rourke
    -Janice Leigh O'Rourke
    -Duncan Shane O'Rourke
    -Donovan Michael O'Rourke
    -Jeannie Ruth O'Rourke
    -Colin Sean O'Rourke*
    -Seamus Ian O'Rourke
    -Timothy Daniel O'Rourke
Generation 11
Colin Sean O'Rourke: Born, 1732, Boston, Massachusetts (*Died, 1777, Battle of Saratoga.*)
    Married, Patricia Simmons, 1752
    -Rowan John O'Rourke*
    -Roland Thomas O'Rourke
Generation 12
Rowan John O'Rourke: Born,   1753,   Boston, Massachusetts (*Died, 1781, Fort Griswold.*)
    Married, Liza Danaher
    -Rennin Duncan O'Rourke*
Generation 13
Rennin Duncan O'Rourke: Born, 1771, Boston, Massachusetts
    Married, Michelle Riley, 1790
    -Rowan David O'Rourke*
    -Leslie Renee O'Rourke
Generation 14
Rowan David O'Rourke: Born,   1791,   Pittsburg, Pennsylvania
    Married, Abigail Johnson, 1810 (Died, 1828)
    -Caitlin Danielle O'Rourke
    -Catherine Mary O'Rourke
    -Candace Elizabeth O'Rourke
    -Cassandra Leann O'Rourke

-Constance Celeste O'Rourke
-Camille Patrice O'Rourke
-Rennin Aidan O'Rourke* (Mother—Caitlin Danielle O'Rourke)

Generation 15

Rennin Aidan O'Rourke   Born   1828,   Minnesota Territory (*Also known as Friend of Dragons; Colonel Union Army, wounded, Pennsylvania; California State Representative; Founder Puma Pass, California, Puma Pass Academy, Mercier Memorial Hospital, and O'Rourke Enterprises*)

Married, Rebekah Suzanne Sinclair (*Also known as Eyes of a Dove of the Pawnee Tribe.*) 1850
-Firelight O'Rourke (Daughter of Rebekah and Black Cloud, honored brave of the Pawnee Tribe– stillborn)
-Gabriel Braden O'Rourke*
-Michael Rowan O'Rourke
-Stanley Knox O'Rourke (Adopted)
-Jedediah Bartholomew Franklin (Guardian)
-Stephen Shane Mercier (Guardian)
-Christopher Aidan Mercier (Guardian)
-Keturah Suzanne Mercier (Guardian)

May 5, 2001—original completion date

Janet Taylor-Perry, B.S., M.A.T.
Author; Editor; Educator; Owner-Operator, Dragon Breath Press, LLC

Like many of her characters, Janet is a history buff and loves anything of historical significance from old cars to old cemeteries. Get to know Janet and you'll see why she's been critically acclaimed at the Faulkner Wisdom Competition and why her writing continues to receive 4 and 5-star reviews—It could be that readers see so much of her in her characters: mother, educator, author, editor, entrepreneur, and a person who has overcome great obstacles and still holds on to her faith.

janettaylorperry.com —For a reading experience EXTRAORDINAIRE!

The Legend of Draconis

Book III

Last of an Exceptional Breed

Draconis Closes Its Doors

Five-year-old Troy Tomerson meets would-be fairy Renée Peyton who promises to show him magic. They drift apart and are drawn back together, even as they are pulled to a place that must be myth.

As a real "bad boy" playing quarterback for the Oakland Raiders, Troy discovers faith, true love, and that he is not who he thought he was.

Troy and Renée endure a ping-pong life as they are catapulted to a place they thought only a fairytale and become involved in the final restoration of a land where only exceptional people may go.